New Horizon

THE HALLS OF MONTEZUMA

BRIAN F. GEHLING

Copyright © 2023 Brian F. Gehling
All rights reserved
First Edition

Fulton Books
Meadville, PA

Published by Fulton Books 2023

ISBN 979-8-88505-773-8 (paperback)
ISBN 979-8-88505-774-5 (digital)

Printed in the United States of America

ACKNOWLEDGMENTS

My thanks and appreciation to my wife, Jeanne, for her patience and help during this endeavor, and to my friend Garry for his assistance.

Special thanks to Kevin and the crew at Culver's for their never-empty coffeepot.

CHAPTER 1

There was an annoying sound as he returned to consciousness. He remembered an alarm going off just as they initiated the jump, and the ship shuddered and rolled violently as the scintillating lights of the artificial hyperspace anomaly swallowed the ship. There had been a violent jolt, and metal flew through the compartment as they entered the jump.

The smell of burnt insulation and ozone filled the air. The harness bit into his shoulders as he moved his head and opened his eyes. There was still a slight rolling motion to the port; otherwise, the ship was in free fall, which meant the engines were down. Items were floating in the air, and a sea of red indicator lights told a hazy story to his befuddled mind as he gazed upon them. He reached out and hit a control that stopped the general quarters' alarm as it penetrated his mind that that was the annoying sound he heard. In turn, the hiss of someone in pain came to the forefront of his attention.

Turning his head slowly, he saw the copilot and navigator was blinking her eyes slowly and attempting to focus. Her bun of blond hair had lost the bands that held it back in place and floated freely in the zero-G environment. A trickle of blood formed a bead and floated away from her cut lip toward the control panel she sat behind. He watched as she slowly placed both of her hands on the edge of the panel and pushed back so she was sitting upright in her seat and let out a deep breath. She blinked her blue eyes slowly as she turned her head to look his way.

"Are you all right?" asked Conor.

Jacqueline Vinet touched her lip and said, "I think so."

That hissing noise of someone in pain sounded again, causing them both to slowly look behind them at the command seat. The captain did not look good, and pain filled her dark eyes. Blood smeared her face, and small beads of the same floated from her dark hairline. Her left hand held her right arm just below the elbow, which now resembled two wrists. Blood also welled and beaded on the abdominal area of her tunic. Her eyes were focused somewhere on the overhead as she visibly clenched her jaws.

"Captain?" queried Lieutenant Vinet.

"Report!" came the pain-filled response.

Glancing at the status displays of his control panel, Conor stated, "Power plant and engines are off-line. We're running on batteries."

"Life support still functioning. We have a hull breach in number two ancillary control. Most stations have reported in and are currently assessing for damage. Casualties coming in now. There are no reports available from the main FTL drive room. The XO is reported to be severely injured and being taken to medical. The first lieutenant, Lieutenant Commander Hatwal, is reported dead from the main breaker panel in the starboard passageway. He was standing beside it when it exploded," came a groggy response from Ensign Dominic Sobolov where he sat at the damage control station on the port side of the bridge. With the executive officer incapable of performing his duties and the first lieutenant dead, that made Conor as second lieutenant, the senior officer and next in line under the captain.

"Comms are down, and most of my sensors aren't available," stated Chief Pennington from the starboard station. She looked at the overhead with pain covering her face and added, "I think my leg is broken."

Captain Hiroka Tamura's eyes focused on Conor's as she ordered, "Take command!" Then she slumped in her chair.

"Medical team to the bridge on the double!" shouted Lieutenant Vinet as she activated the 1MC and released her harness to go to the captain's aid.

Conor released his harness and pushed himself off to the engineering and damage control station, where Sobolov was making notations by hand on a dry easel display as he talked with stations on his sound-powered phones. His hand still shook, but his writing was legible. The damage didn't look bad at first glance. The short- and long-range lidars, along with the Benson drive, were down, but those stations were reporting repairs in progress. The power plant was reporting that they would be back online in thirty minutes.

The aft hatch popped open, and Gunnery Sergeant Zander entered with Chief deLang from medical in tow. The gunny took one glance around the bridge and went over to the Neil Robertson stretcher on the aft bulkhead. The medic glided up to the captain's chair where Lieutenant Vinet was still doing what she could for the captain.

Conor heard the medic ask, "How long?"

Lieutenant Vinet glanced at the gunnery sergeant then at her watch, "A little over two minutes."

The gunnery sergeant looked at Conor and stated, "XO's not coming, sir," referring to the executive officer of the *New Horizon*.

Lieutenant Commander Conor Raybourn looked at the gunny and said, "I'm aware. What happened?"

"He was outside the FTL compartment room with Lieutenant Anderson when something in the room exploded. His leg shattered in three places and some fractured ribs. Mr. Anderson had a broken arm, and his head was knocked around a bit. Doc put them both under," responded the gunny.

"We could use some help moving the captain to the stretcher, Gunny," Chief deLang interrupted.

"Chief Pennington needs attention also," stated Jacqueline Vinet.

Caroline deLang floated over to the comms and science station. "How you doing, Chief?"

"Just give me some pain meds for now, and I'll be fine till you get back," came the quick response. "Get the captain down to the med bay."

"That's broke," stated the gunny worriedly.

"I know that," retorted Pennington painfully. She then stated, "But I'm not bleeding, and I promise not to move. Now just give me some pain meds and get back up here before they wear off."

"All right, Chief," responded Chief deLang. "I'll be back soon. Just sit back and take it easy."

"Roger that! Now how about those pain meds?" demanded Chief Pennington as her dark face scrunched in pain.

Chief Caroline deLang took a bottle out of her pocket and gave Chief Pennington two pills, which the chief swallowed dry. Pennington's dark features denoting her African heritage relaxed noticeably, and deLang nodded. Chief deLang turned back to the captain and did a quick once-over to ensure she hadn't missed anything.

Conor turned back to the damage control station as Lieutenant Vinet, Gunnery Sergeant Zander, and Chief deLang started transferring the captain to the stretcher. At least the captain and XO were still alive. Now it was his responsibility to keep everyone else alive. Ensign Sobolov wrote down that a main breaker panel in the starboard passageway had been blown when power switched over to batteries and that the damage control crew were working on replacing it. That explained most of the sensors being down. A hull breach had been discovered in an unoccupied crew compartment on the port side of the ship and was being sealed by the damage control crew from the inside. Crew compartments just forward of the long-range lidar compartment were flooded with water from a ruptured potable water pipe but were being drained and the pipe isolated from the system for repair.

The captain gave out a moan as she was transferred to the stretcher. The gunnery sergeant held the stretcher steady as Jacqueline Vinet and Caroline deLang strapped her in, careful of her right arm. A bandage now hid her abdomen, where they had cut the tunic to reveal a penetrating wound, and another covered the wound on her head. Her body appeared small and frail as she lay in the Neil Roberston stretcher, not at all like the strong, assertive Japanese woman he had come to know these last three months.

Chief deLang and Gunnery Sergeant Zander left the bridge with the captain between them. Conor returned to his control station and made some adjustments. The main view screen remained blank, then flashes of color swept across its surface. Finally, the main view screen came to life with a field of stars. Yet the stars were unrecognizable if the jump they had made had been ten light-years as planned. There was a gasp from Lieutenant Vinet and a whispered "Where are we?"

The next two days passed like a whirlwind with little to no rest. The fusion power plant had come online after thirty minutes as promised, but multiple other systems were down or displaying problems. Worse, the AI had suffered a major failure; diagnostics and schematics for other systems were not available for another half a day as the problem was troubleshot and repaired. The short- and long-range radar and lidar were both inoperable when the power came up. Environmental systems had a problem with regulating the pressure and control throughout the system, and the technicians were still looking for the problem. The Benson drive was having flow issues in the main feed tube, and a feed pump in the hydro/oxy electrolysis plant had a control card that the ship's factory was still producing. The hydroponics garden looked like a tornado had decimated the compartment.

Conor Raybourn remembered being handed some rations a few times by Gunnery Sergeant Zander as he reviewed statuses of different departments and assisted the technicians with repairing faulty consoles on the bridge. He was just completing a ship's inspection on the second day and was in the Benson drive room when he was accosted by the chief engineer.

"Mr. Raybourn, can I have a word with you?" said Chief Engineer Felipe Martinez with a challenge in his voice.

"If you wish, Mr. Martinez," said Lieutenant Commander Raybourn.

The gunnery sergeant halted his progress beside a crewman who was working on a panel and muttered something to the crewman as Conor floated over to the chief engineer, or CHENG. Out of the corner of his eye, he saw the crewman close the panel and exit the compartment as the gunnery sergeant floated over to the other wall behind the CHENG and muttered something to another crewman, who vanished through the hatch beside him. The gunny turned and took up position along the far wall just as Conor came to a halt, facing the CHENG as the conversation began.

"Who the hell do you think you are?" demanded Lieutenant Commander Martinez.

"What do you mean?" returned Conor.

"You're acting like you're the captain, which you know damn well you're not," retorted the CHENG.

"You know as well as I do that the captain and XO are in the infirmary and that Lieutenant Commander Hatwal is dead, Mr. Martinez," said Conor. Then he continued, "The captain knew the XO was injured and the first officer, Lieutenant Hatwal, was dead. She told me to take command."

"That doesn't leave you in charge!" retorted the CHENG.

"Even in the United Systems chain of command, that duty would fall to me as the operations officer in the absence of the captain, executive officer, and first officer," replied Conor with some heat.

"You're only an acting lieutenant commander. You're not active United Systems military, and you have no experience. This is an emergency situation, and I should be in command!" shouted CHENG Martinez.

"Mr. Martinez, this ship is not officially attached to the United Systems military at this time. It's a converted military cruiser commissioned as a ship of exploration by the United Systems, and we report to a special commission of the United Systems," replied Conor calmly. Then he continued, "You and the other quarter of the crew who are active military are on board this command on special assignment. Do you need to reread your duty orders?"

"I don't need to reread my orders! The point is, you're not qualified to assume command!" shouted Martinez.

"Who is?" questioned Conor.

"In an emergency situation, not some civilian!" shouted the CHENG.

"I repeat, the captain knew the XO was injured and taken to the infirmary, and she told me to take command," repeated Lieutenant Commander Raybourn, the operations officer, or OPS boss, of the *New Horizon*.

"That's not how this works! You're not really military. You're a glorified civilian pretending to be military!" yelled Martinez the CHENG.

"Sir! You need to settle down, sir," came the voice of Gunnery Sergeant Zander, who had moved up behind the CHENG when the shouting had started.

"I'm not doing anything!" shouted Martinez.

"Yes, you will, sir," growled the gunnery sergeant. "Mr. Raybourn is correct. At this time, we are on special assignment from the military. This is not officially a military ship, and the crew who were selected for this ship is its crew. The orders governing the chain of command places the operations officer, Lieutenant Commander Raybourn, in charge."

"Not in a situation like this!" shouted the CHENG.

"Yes, it does, sir," growled the gunnery sergeant. "If you continue down this path, I'll frog-march you down to the brig if the acting captain orders me to."

The CHENG stiffened and blinked his eyes as the gunnery sergeant's statement sank in, then he responded, "You wouldn't dare!"

Gunnery Sergeant Evan Zander stood looking calmly into Lieutenant Commander Martinez's eyes until the CHENG broke contact and his shoulders slumped. Martinez lowered his head for a tense moment, then looked up at Conor. "Your orders, sir?"

"Carry on, Lieutenant Commander. Let's get things fixed so the captain has a ship to command," said Lieutenant Commander Conor Raybourn.

"Very well, sir," responded the CHENG as he saluted Conor, then turned to float down the passageway toward the lower Benson drive level.

When the CHENG was gone, Conor looked at the gunnery sergeant and said, "Thank you, Gunny."

"Just doing my job, sir," he calmly replied. "Shall we continue with our inspection?"

"Yes, let's do that," said Conor.

The encounter had irritated Conor more than he cared to admit. He wondered how many others who had transferred over from United Systems regular service felt the same as the CHENG. Nearly 70 percent of the crew was composed of civilians who never served and held honorary ranks. This was supposed to be an exploratory mission, not a military one. This flight was a first-time test of the FTL drive. Everyone not regular military had received six months of orientation training so they could serve as a crew for a large ship, with some defensive and offensive capabilities, but not as a military ship.

Most of the crew who were originally United Systems Navy were in the deck department, scattered throughout the ship's various departments in key positions of importance. The only division within the ship that was strictly military was the Marine detachment. Conor looked at the gunnery sergeant as that thought occurred to him but said nothing as Gunnery Zander followed him down the corridor.

There was only one place left to inspect, and Conor had put it off until last. Not because it wasn't important but because he did not want the personal distress. They entered the mess decks where there were still crew members lying on tables, overflow of the medical bay. Some were being cared for by the mess specialists and personnel department who were pressed into duty out of sheer necessity.

Lieutenant Commander Bess Hollinger was there muttering to herself and checking charts in a bloodstained uniform and smock. They floated up to Dr. Hollinger. She replaced the clipboard she was checking and turned to Conor. Her dark face was grim and haggard from her duties and lack of sleep. Conor could only imagine that he presented the same picture without the blood.

"Good morning, Ms. Hollinger," greeted Conor.

"I'm not so sure it's good or morning, but good morning to you, Mr. Raybourn," came her reply.

Lieutenant Commander Raybourn looked down at the patient lying on the medical bed and wished he hadn't. The face of the body that was lying there was barely recognizable as human. Conor looked away and closed his eyes as he thought that the system he was responsible for caused this harm. It took a moment to come up with the name of the seared body that was barely alive.

"Ortiz?" asked Conor.

"Yes," responded Hollinger. Then she added, "We brought her out here. There's nothing more we can do except provide her painkillers. There are three others in as bad a shape as her also."

"How long?" asked Conor hesitantly.

"A few hours, maybe a day, at most," replied the doctor.

Closing his eyes, Lieutenant Commander Conor Raybourn lost his handhold, floating freely. The firm hand of the gunnery sergeant behind him supported him and brought him back to the moment. He steadied himself and shrugged off the feeling of helplessness as he reopened his eyes.

"It's all right, Gunny," said Conor meekly.

"No, it's not, sir," replied the gunnery sergeant. "This is just the way it is."

"These things happen, sir. It's not your fault," said a voice behind him.

Conor turned to see Staff Sergeant Rosenstein beside the gunnery sergeant. There was a bandage on her head, and her arm was in a sling. She also moved stiffly when she presented a salute.

"How are you, Staff Sergeant?" inquired Conor.

"Banged my head, dislocated my shoulder, and cracked a rib. I'll be fine," stated Rosenstein. "The doctor has me on light duty, so I'm helping out around here so she can keep an eye on me."

Conor nodded and looked back at the doctor.

"Do you need a sedative or something?" asked Lieutenant Commander Hollinger.

"No!" stated Conor firmly. "I'm sure there are others who need it more."

"The pharmaceutical unit is well stocked," returned the doctor.

"How many others?" asked Conor changing the subject.

"We have eleven in critical condition right now," Hollinger stated. Then indicating the tables that held others not in the medical bay, she added, "We have thirteen dead. There will be four more who sustained injuries that are fatal. That includes Chief Ortiz, sir."

"The captain?" asked Conor.

"She's in a coma," replied Dr. Hollinger. "There's not much we can do for her. She has a piece of metal lodged in her frontal lobe. We can remove it, but there will be no guarantees she will ever gain consciousness even then."

Lieutenant Commander Raybourn nodded. Losing the captain at this time was bad. She had been a strength to all, and filling her shoes would be difficult. The crew trusted and relied on her, and morale had been high.

"And the executive officer?" questioned Conor.

"Broken leg, fractured ribs, and he has a concussion," stated Hollinger. "He'll be on limited duty for some time."

"How's Michael?" asked Conor.

Bess Hollinger knew who Conor was talking about since Lieutenant Michael Anderson and Conor Raybourn were nearly inseparable when they were off duty. She said, "He's got a broken arm and a couple of fractured ribs, but he'll be fine in a month or so."

Lieutenant Commander Bess Hollinger informed Lieutenant Commander Raybourn about the other major injuries suffered by the various crew members. However, none were as devastating as the pending death of Chief Ortiz and the two other FTL crew who had been in the FTL compartment. Conor felt a personal responsibility for the FTL crew since the FTL project was the reason for his assignment as the lead expert on the FTL drive. Vinet and his assignment to operations instead of engineering was because their expertise lay plotting the jump point and to supervise the nearly fifty scientists who had been placed in the newly formed science division of operations for this mission.

There were broken limbs, deep cuts, and gashes. Two other people had metal projectiles that had to be removed—one from his stomach and another from her left thigh. There were twenty-three other members who would be in medical for several days as they recovered from their injuries.

The rest of the day was a blur for Lieutenant Commander Conor Raybourn. There were filthy uniforms and crew who looked like they probably hadn't slept since the astray jump of two days ago. With luck, most ship functions would be nominal within the next twenty-four hours.

After completing his tour, Lieutenant Commander Raybourn took reports, updated the ship's log, and assisted in bridge repairs the rest of the day and part of the night. The chief engineer, or CHENG, reported the Benson drive fully operational, and Conor ordered a tenth G acceleration. Three more crew members died from their injuries during that time, but Chief Ortiz still held on to life.

Conor was on the bridge, bleary-eyed and exhausted, when he made a near-fatal mistake of bumping up against an open power supply connection as he and Jacqueline Vinet replaced a charred wire harness. It knocked him partway across the room and put a knot on the back of his head.

"What the hell just happened?" demanded Lieutenant Vinet as she pushed herself over to where Conor floated, shaking his head weakly.

"Main breaker for the equipment is still on," replied Ensign Sobolov, who had floated over to the bridge's power panel.

"When was the last time you slept?" demanded Lieutenant Vinet as she pushed Conor back into the captain's chair and looked him in the eye. The freckles on her nose and cheeks came into focus as Conor looked back at her. Her face was plain but pleasant to look at, but he had to draw his thoughts away from that. Besides, that bang on the back of his head was calling for his attention.

"I don't remember," muttered Conor.

"About twenty-five hours ago and only for two hours," stated Gunnery Sergeant Zander. "You need to sleep before you kill yourself."

"I agree," stated Lieutenant Vinet.

"But!" Conor protested.

"Now," stated the gunnery sergeant as he gently but firmly led Lieutenant Commander Conor Raybourn, the operations officer and acting captain of the *New Horizon*, off the bridge.

Conor Raybourn remembered Gunnery Sergeant Zander escorting him two levels down to his stateroom. He recalled the gunnery sergeant pushing him into his rack and pulling off his shoes. Then the gunnery sergeant strapped him in so he would stay in place. The room had a surreal feel as he floated upward with the slightest movement in the light gravity provided above the mattress. He lay there thinking of all that had happened over the last two days, then a black nothingness enveloped him as he gave in to the inevitable.

CHAPTER 2

Lieutenant Commander Conor Raybourn awoke to a shake on his shoulder and someone calling his name. Slowly the world came into focus, and his still exhausted body groaned as he moved. There appeared to be a slight gravity because the gunnery sergeant stood holding a towel and a bar of soap. A fresh uniform was laid out to replace the crumpled one he had on.

"How long?" asked Conor.

"Four hours, sir," came the intuitive response.

"That makes it?" asked Conor.

"Oh, seven hundred ship's time, sir," replied Gunnery Sergeant Zander.

"Are you my guardian angel, Gunny?" queried Conor.

"Until the captain or exec are fit for duty, I've made it my personal responsibility to keep you in line, sir." The gunnery sergeant chuckled.

"Why?" asked Conor.

Gunnery Sergeant Zander grew serious and said, "Lieutenant Vinet and Ensign Sobolov informed me that the captain knew the XO was down and the first lieutenant dead. She told you to take command, sir."

"Do you agree with that decision?" returned Conor as he lathered his face and ran a fresh razor over the dark, bristly growth hiding it. The dark hair on his head was in disarray. He needed a haircut soon.

"It's not my place to second-guess the captain, sir," responded the gunnery sergeant.

Conor continued shaving as he contemplated the nonanswer he had just received. His face looked drawn, and his blue eyes were bloodshot. He still wasn't thinking clearly as he finished up scraping the last few swipes of intrusive hair.

"So what's the plan, Gunny?" asked Lieutenant Commander Raybourn.

"Get those rags off and hop in the shower. You've got about thirty minutes to get ready for the staff meeting in the wardroom," stated the gunnery sergeant.

"I don't remember scheduling that," replied Conor.

"I had Lieutenant Vinet do it for you, sir" was the quick response. "All officers will be present with the exception of Ensign Sobolov."

"What will Mr. Sobolov be doing?" asked Conor.

"He will be conning officer, along with observing and directing his people from deck department in hull inspection. Other than the hull inspection, deck department has completed all their repairs," replied the gunnery sergeant.

"Is that safe while we're under thrust?" asked Conor.

"They're inspecting the bow and hangar doors first," said the gunny. "After the meal, Lieutenant Vinet will take over the con, and we'll go to zero Gs so they can inspect the rest of the hull."

"All right, Gunny. That sounds good," said Conor.

Removing his clothing, Conor grabbed the soap in the gunny's hand. He carefully stepped into the shower and started lathering as the water pulsed. Conor let that sink in and began to wonder who was actually in command. It seemed at times that command itself was the actual leader and not him. Accepting the inevitable, Lieutenant Commander Conor Raybourn demanded, "Ship's status."

"We're at a tenth G heading, spiraling slowly into the system. Long-range lidar is at reduced capability. They are having resolution problems. The ship can locate relatively large objects, but we cannot determine features. Lidar scans show no imminent obstacles in our vicinity. Magnetic shields at 88 percent efficiency, power plant at 85 percent efficiency, Benson drive at 92 percent, environmental systems operating at 90 percent efficiency," the gunnery sergeant reported. After a pause to look at his watch, he added, "That is as of an hour ago, sir."

"The captain and executive officer?" asked Conor.

"Are both still in induced comas and recovering, sir," stated Gunnery Sergeant Zander.

"The rest of the crew?" inquired Conor.

"Ensign Hiran, Petty Officer James, and Seaman Green reported back to duty," responded the gunnery sergeant. After a slight pause, he added lowly, "Chief Petty Officer Maria Ortiz from engineering passed three hours ago."

Conor Raybourn closed his eyes in pain as he remembered the smiling face and vibrant personality of the young lady who just signed on as a technician to study the inner workings of the new FTL drive. He also remembered the badly burned body lying on the gurney on the mess decks when he had passed through on his last tour. His friend, acting Lieutenant Michael Anderson, had been quite infatuated with the young lady and would be taking it hard.

Conor opened the shower stall door and took the towel the gunny offered. He commenced rubbing himself down, then asked, "How's your crew holding up, Gunny?"

"With the exception of Staff Sergeant Rosenstein, we're all on duty, sir," quipped the gunnery sergeant.

"You can lose the sir, Gunny. My name is Conor," said Conor.

"I can't do that, sir," stated Gunnery Sergeant Zander.

"Even in private?" inquired Conor.

"Maybe in time, sir. For right now, let's keep it professional. The ears have walls." The gunnery sergeant chuckled.

Conor looked around as he finished and pulled on the underwear he was offered, then said, "I understand."

The gunny assisted Conor with getting his uniform on and ensured he was, as the United Systems Navy would put it, squared away all the way down to the gig line and the severe lack of ribbons center and parallel to the left pocket for the chest of a lieutenant commander.

Standing at attention, Lieutenant Commander Conor Raybourn asked, "How do I look?"

"Like an officer of the line, sir," replied the gunnery sergeant. "A bit short on awards for an officer of your rank but an officer of the line. Breakfast will be served in the wardroom with all officers present, during which time you'll ask for statuses and options. Oh! Lieutenant Vinet is going to tell you that the AI's best estimate is that we're over ten thousand light-years from Earth if you ask for a galactic position."

He let that sink in for a moment as he did a quick calculation in his head. The drive could jump between systems, but until now, the farthest it had achieved in the prototypes was approximately ten light-years. Then the ship would have to spend at least three months reaching the far side of the system and jump again to go farther away from its point of origin. So 250 years, and that was not including sightseeing, restocking, casualties, equipment failures, and any other unforeseen circumstances just to return to Sol system even if the FTL were operational.

Conor whispered, "Damn!"

"I understand," said Gunnery Sergeant Zander. "Do us proud, sir. I'll be standing right behind you the whole meal."

"Us?" asked Conor.

"As the acting captain of a United Systems military vessel, sir," stated Gunnery Sergeant Zander.

The lieutenant commander nodded as they stepped out of the stateroom and ascended the ladder to the captain's level. They entered the wardroom, and all the officers were already seated. They snapped to attention and saluted when the gunny announced, "Acting captain on deck." A couple of them were lax and slow, notably the chief engineer, on the uptake of the command.

"At ease. Good morning, and please be seated, ladies and gentlemen," said Lieutenant Commander Raybourn as he walked to the captain's chair.

Good mornings were announced and muttered in return as the ship's officers sat back down. The gunny took up position behind the captain's chair as Conor sat down. Plates with scrambled eggs, sausage links, fruit slices, and buttered toast were placed in front of each member by the two wardroom mess specialists. They placed pots of coffee, tea, and orange juice on the table after asking their preferences and serving them. Preliminaries done, the mess specialists retreated to the kitchen to allow the officers their privacy.

Taking his time, Conor sipped on his coffee as he looked at the faces of those seated. They all looked haggard and worn. Not good. Most were in uniforms that looked like they hadn't changed for the last week, and all things considered, that wasn't surprising after the last seventy-two hours.

Conor cleared his throat and stated, "I'd like to start out by saying thank you for the extraordinary efforts you've all put forward in the last three days."

Nods and thank-yous were made by those present as Lieutenant Commander Raybourn paused, looking around table.

Conor continued, "Is there an immediate crisis that needs to be brought to my attention?" When no one responded, Conor looked at the medical officer, Lieutenant Commander Hollinger, and asked, "How is the captain and XO?"

Sitting back and swallowing a mouthful of eggs, Lieutenant Commander Hollinger relayed, "The captain is still in critical condition and maybe beyond our abilities to help. There is a sliver of metal that lodged in her frontal lobe. Though it's not deep, it is really beyond my capabilities to safely remove with any certainty." Taking a sip from her cup, she continued, "The XO should be up and around in two more days. He will not be capable of active-duty assignments for at least four weeks as his leg and ribs heal. We're still monitoring him, owing to the concussion he received. He should be kept to minimal activity of four to six hours of light duty for at least two weeks to give his body time to recuperate."

Lieutenant Commander Raybourn waved the gunnery sergeant forward. As the gunny stepped up, Conor looked him in the eye as he made an informal request, "Can you make that happen, Gunnery Sergeant?"

"You mean be his guardian angel whether the commander likes it or not, sir?" asked the gunnery sergeant straight-faced.

"Yes," said Conor.

"Roger that, sir," said the gunnery sergeant.

There were muttered chuckles around the officers' mess as the gunnery sergeant retook his station behind the lieutenant commander. Conor turned back to the medical officer, and everyone would want to know her inputs about their companions.

"The rest of the crew?" he queried.

"Other than the captain and XO, we have thirty-seven with minor injuries that shouldn't inhibit their performance significantly, twenty-two on limited duty, seven confined to quarters, three others in critical condition, and seventeen dead. Chief Ortiz passed three hours ago," stated Lieutenant Commander Hollinger. She paused, then added, "We've placed those who have passed in Cargo Bay 2 and lowered the temperature. Everyone else should recover, with the exception of the captain. Her injuries will not kill her, but the head injury is inoperable."

Conor closed his eyes and offered up a silent prayer. Seventeen of the 787 crew members were dead—over 2 percent of the crew. How many more would die in the next few months as they attempted to establish themselves in a system they knew little to nothing about? Conor decided it was best not to brood about it now and brought his attention back to the moment.

Lieutenant Commander Hatwal was acting as the first lieutenant in charge of X division, which included a variety of ship functions such as deck department, hull maintenance, environmental systems, personnel, supply, ship stores, master-at-arms, and even medical. The title of first lieutenant did not denote the rank the lieutenant commander held in the United Systems Navy but a position on board the *New Horizon* for seniority, just as Conor had the on-board designation as second lieutenant and the chief engineer as third lieutenant. If the captain, executive officer, and those three officers were incapacitated, the command of the *New Horizon* would fall to the senior-ranking line officer.

Conor ate a sausage and some eggs as the silence continued, then looked up at Lieutenant Commander Hollinger. Her department fell under X division, but she reported directly to the captain when it came to medical concerns. Her position on board was not that of a line officer because of her expertise, and she was not trained in any bridge or engineering functions.

"Who takes Lieutenant Commander Hatwal's position in his absence?" asked Conor.

"That would be me," said Lieutenant Gataki, the supply officer, or SUPPO.

Conor nodded at the lieutenant. "Report," said Conor.

"The starboard hull midship's breach is repaired. Environmental systems operating at 95 percent efficiency. We lost approximately 8 percent of our reserve air from the starboard breach. The damage control crew did a good job sealing the breach. Ensign Sobolov is having deck department inspect the outer hull since we're in clear space and we're not transmitting. Life support is functioning at 95 percent efficiency. The medical officer will have to provide you a more detailed status of the life-support system herself, but 95 is optimal," replied Lieutenant Gataki.

"I'm sure that last can wait considering she has more pressing matters at this time," stated Conor.

"We should hold services for the dead as soon as possible," interjected Lieutenant Junior Grade Kisimba, the ship's personnel officer.

"We're not out of the woods yet. There are critical systems that we depend on. I propose we wait to conduct services until we're sure of our own survival," stated Conor.

"When will that be?" asked Lieutenant Gataki.

"That's the purpose of this meeting," Conor returned. Turning to the chief engineer, also known as the CHENG, he asked, "Engineering?"

"We now have the power plant at 91 percent. The damage control crew has also completed replacing the main steam line in number 2 PPI," replied the CHENG, referring to the power plant interface at the end of his report.

"FTL?" questioned Conor.

Lieutenant Commander Martinez shook his head disgustedly.

Lieutenant Anderson broke in at that point and responded, "The FTL is in need of a major overhaul preferably at a shipyard. My crew and myself included have concentrated our efforts working with the chief engineer on the power plant, Benson drive, and environmental systems as needed."

"Anything else to report?" asked Lieutenant Commander Raybourn as he looked back at Chief Engineer Martinez.

"We're waiting on parts from the ship's factory for thruster control, but Lieutenant Gataki informs me that those parts should be available in two days," said Martinez.

Conor took a bite of eggs and sip of coffee, then centered his gaze at the supply officer, Lieutenant Gataki, as he asked, "How's our supply situation?"

"We're running short on some of the critical circuit cards, and Ensign Hiran has his crew working in the factory plant to produce more," quipped the supply officer, or SUPPO. "First, printing and testing of the most needed cards should be done in approximately two hours." He then looked at Lieutenant Vinet, then said, "Ensign Hiran assures me that the ten-megahertz oscillator card for the short-range radar should be finished first."

"Thank you, SUPPO," replied Lieutenant Vinet.

"Anything else to report?" asked Conor as the SUPPO looked back at him.

"Everyone needs a break, sir," deadpanned Lieutenant Gataki. Chuckles and seconds followed that statement.

"I agree, but let's hear what Lieutenant Vinet has to report before we decide," stated Lieutenant Commander Raybourn as he looked at the lieutenant.

Jacqueline Vinet was acting as the operations officer since Conor was filling the captain's spot and had been doing a fine job organizing repairs.

"Short- and long-range lidars are still inoperable. The short-range lidar should be back online once the ten-meg oscillator is installed. I have the boatswains doing an EVA and evaluating the outside hull for damage at oh ten hundred today, at which time we'll be going to zero G. The electronics technicians ran diagnostics and located the faulty interface card in the AI, and it's now back up to 99 percent efficiency, which should bring the efficiency of all ship's functions back up as we make repairs," responded Lieutenant Vinet.

"Ship's position, Lieutenant?" asked Conor.

"We're approximately eight billion kilometers out from the primary. It's a G1V, so slightly more massive and hotter than Sol. Astrometrics and our AI Hattie used the sensors and located thirteen planets and two asteroid belts so far. There are five gas giants. One of which is at nine point five billion klicks out. Then there's two ice balls between it and the next gas giant going inward. Then there's another ice ball between it and the next three gas giants. Then there's five planets between the innermost gas giant and the primary. Two of those planets appear to have breathable atmospheres. We'll know more as we move closer and spectroscopic inspection improves," finished Lieutenant Vinet.

"Anything more?" asked Conor.

"Like what, sir?" replied Jacqueline evasively, attempting to avoid answering the obvious.

"Galactic position, Lieutenant," stated Lieutenant Commander Conor Raybourn.

Jacqueline Vinet got a worried look in her eyes. No one but the bridge crew and the gunny knew the information Conor was attempting to pry from her, and she didn't want the honor of presenting that information to the crew. Her blue eyes looked back at Conor, pleading.

"They have to know, Jacqueline," said Conor.

"Astrometrics and the AI located enough known galactic anomalies through the shipboard telescopes to give a fairly precise fix on our galactic position. We're a little over ten thousand light-years spinward from Sol and two thousand light-years closer to the galactic center," stated Lieutenant Jacqueline Vinet.

There were stunned looks around the table. The chief engineer muttered something in anger.

"In other words, ladies and gentlemen, even if the jump drive was not damaged, it would still take us over two hundred and fifty years to make it back to Sol, and that's barring any unforeseen circumstances," said Lieutenant Commander Raybourn.

Silence descended on the room as looks were exchanged between those gathered. There were some who simply stared at the tabletop, searching for meaning. Some had tears in their eyes, and others, anger. Finally, an angry voice spoke up.

"How did this happen?" demanded Lieutenant Commander Felipe Martinez.

"We don't know," responded Lieutenant Michael Anderson before Conor could speak.

"How do we fix it?" the CHENG demanded.

"We don't," stated Conor. "What we know of FTL flight allows for only limited jumps. What happened was impossible by our knowledge. The equations don't cover anything like what we experienced."

"So we're stranded with no possible way home within our lifetimes even if it were possible to repair your vaunted FTL?" countered Lieutenant Commander Martinez.

"That's correct, Mr. Martinez," replied Conor Raybourn.

"So what do you propose we do?" demanded the CHENG.

"Finish repairs and head in system," stated Conor. "We have no other options."

"And then?" asked the chief engineer in defeat.

"Hope that there's a planet in this system that can sustain human life," said Conor. "Now if there are no other questions, I suggest we're finished here. Commander Blankenship should be up and about in the next few days, and at that time, our future will depend on him."

Two days passed, and Conor was standing conning officer on the bridge. Chief Warrant Officer Diego Quintana reported an anomaly picked up by the ship's telescopes. It was a bright flash near a large comet over seven billion kilometers away. Conor made a note in his log, but the *New Horizon* did not have the luxury to investigate anomalies. Then Conor informed the CWO that without the long-range lidar, the telescopes were needed to concentrate on the ship's trajectory. A short time later, a hand lightly grasped Conor's right shoulder from behind. He looked over his shoulder to see the executive officer standing at his side, with Gunnery Sergeant Zander closely behind him. Conor stood up and offered the executive officer the captain's chair.

"Sir!" said Lieutenant Commander Raybourn as he saluted.

"At ease, Lieutenant Commander," said the executive officer, or XO, as he slowly took the conning chair. "The medical officer and gunny have been updating me on what's been going on. What's our current heading?" asked Commander Hadden Blankenship.

"Heading in system in a slow spiral at one-tenth G, sir, toward the fourth planet from the primary," stated Lieutenant Commander Raybourn.

"Ship status?" inquired the executive officer.

"Most systems nominal. The short is operational, and the long-range lidar is at reduced capability. We can detect unknowns and their location but with little resolution. It appears to be an AI problem, and the techs are running diagnostics. Power plant at 95 percent. Benson drive at 93 percent. FTL, nonoperational. Lieutenant Anderson and his crew have been assisting the CHENG for the last five days," stated Conor. "It's a mess in the FTL room, sir."

"Structural integrity?" asked the XO.

"Appears sound, sir," returned Conor.

"Enough to take her up to 0.5 G, Mr. Raybourn?" questioned Commander Blankenship.

"I believe so, sir," replied Conor.

"Then I relieve you, Lieutenant Commander Raybourn," stated the commander.

"Sir?" said Conor in surprise.

"Don't worry, Mr. Raybourn. The doctor has me on light duty, but I can manage from this chair for the next four hours," responded the XO to the unspoken question. "I'm sure the gunny will ensure that it happens. Won't you, Gunny?"

"As you say, sir." The gunny chuckled.

"Your orders, sir?" questioned Conor.

"Be back in twenty-four hours to take the chair, Mr. Raybourn," ordered the XO.

"Sir?" said Conor again in surprise.

"The gunny says you need some downtime. I'm ordering you to take the day off, Mr. Raybourn," replied the commander.

"Aye, aye, sir," responded Conor.

"The medical officer and gunny have informed me you've done a fine job, Lieutenant Commander. Well done," said Commander Hadden Blankenship.

"Thank you, sir," Conor responded with a sense of pride at the praise.

"Now get out of here, Mr. Raybourn, and relax," ordered the executive officer.

With that, Conor turned to the hatch, and as he set foot on the ladder, he heard the executive officer order Lieutenant Vinet to plot a course at 0.2 G heading in system and continue taking them in at a slow spiral. The commander informed astrometrics that he wanted a full survey of the system. Ship's bells sounded as Conor descended the ladders to his quarters, giving the crew an audible heads-up of the time. Then the 1MC general ship announcement system made rapid-fire announcements.

"Funeral services will be conducted for the fallen. They will be held tomorrow at twelve hundred ship time in the hangar bay."

"Lieutenant Gataki, report to the bridge."

"Lieutenant Anderson, report to the bridge."

"The ship will be accelerating to 0.2 G in ten minutes."

Conor descended to his cabin for some rest. The burden of command had weighed heavily on his shoulders. In many ways, he felt Lieutenant Commander Martinez was right and that he was responsible for the FTL failure and that stranded them in this system. On the other hand, it was a prototype system, and they had all known the chances of something going wrong. The last few days, he tried to set that aside and accomplish what could be done, which was the most anyone could do in the current situation.

He removed his clothes and had just crawled into his rack as the alarm sounded for ship's maneuvering. The gentle pull of 0.1 G increased to 0.2 G as he put his head on the pillow. His thoughts returned to the praise that the commander had given him on the bridge as he was relieved. That recognition made the last few days worthwhile as he drifted off to sleep.

CHAPTER 3

Lieutenant Michael Anderson was in main engineering attempting to work on the power distribution problem the engines were experiencing. Working one-handed wasn't helping matters and taking him three times as long to type in the commands to the key panel when a voice over the 1MC summoned him to the bridge. He looked up at the CHENG and could sense the irritation the man had with him as he nodded and indicated at the same time to leave. Having the go-ahead, Anderson closed down what he was doing and headed toward the hatch out of the main engineering. He walked over to the starboard ladder and headed up toward the bridge.

When Lieutenant Anderson entered the bridge, the gunnery sergeant was watching him from a nearby station. He went up to the captain's chair where Commander Blankenship was sitting. The XO's head was bandaged, and his leg was in a cast. The executive officer's uniform looked tight around his chest where Michael knew there were bandages. The XO's face looked somewhat drawn as Michael rounded the chair and saluted.

"Good morning, sir. How's the leg?" said Lieutenant Anderson.

"Good morning, Lieutenant. It's fine. How's the arm?" inquired Commander Blankenship as he returned Michael's salute.

"As good as it can be, sir. I'd like to thank you for grabbing me out of the way of that hatch," blurted Lieutenant Anderson.

"Part of the job, son," replied the commander amicably as he winced and reached up to touch the bandages on his head. The gunnery sergeant grew watchful but relaxed when the commander lowered his hand and smiled at the gunny with a negating motion of his hand.

"You requested my presence?" asked Michael.

"Yes, I did. I've been informed that the FTL drive is damaged beyond repair. By rights, you should be on light duty as should I, and I'm in need of another watch stander on the bridge. It's my understanding that the six-month crash course they gave you to receive the commission as an acting lieutenant included standing bridge watches," stated the executive officer.

"It did, sir. But as you already noted, it was a crash course," replied the lieutenant.

"I'm expecting you to stand in as conning officer, Lieutenant," said the commander.

"Sir?" stammered the Michael.

"Lieutenant, I would prefer to have you take the helmsman chair and pilot the ship. I would rather have Lieutenant Vinet as the conning officer since she has more experience and has held the position. However, it takes two hands to run the pilot console." The XO paused for a second, then continued, "Son, I'm not expecting you to take the conn under an emergency condition. Right now, the ship is mostly functioning, and we're in clear space. I just need another watch stander up here. Do you think you can sit in this chair for a four-hour watch and attempt to steer us clear of any obstacles and maintain a log of what you've done during that four hours?"

"I believe so, sir," said Michael.

"Good! Then you're to report back here in four hours, which would be 1200 ship's time, to relieve me at the conn. Lieutenant Vinet is to be your pilot during those watches, and once your arm is out of that cast, she will assume conning duties as well," declared the XO.

"Yes, sir. If I may, sir, is there any other reason for this transfer, sir?" blurted Michael.

The executive officer contemplated Michael's question for a moment, then responded, "I realize you're a good engineer, but I'm also aware of the animosity that the CHENG has for anyone who worked FTL at this time. Your being on light duty isn't going to endear him to you, and I do need someone up here on the bridge."

"Very well, sir," affirmed Michael.

"Don't worry, Lieutenant. Lieutenant Vinet is going to be your pilot, and hopefully, between the two of you, you'll keep us safe. She's proven herself an able pilot," accredited the commander. "Lieutenant Vinet, please have Ensign Sobolov take over your station and report back here at 1600 to take the duty of piloting officer for Lieutenant Anderson."

"Aye, aye, sir," acknowledged Lieutenant Vinet.

"One more thing before you leave, Lieutenant Anderson," said the XO.

"Yes, sir," responded Michael.

"Lieutenant Commander Raybourn, Lieutenant Vinet, and yourself are the resident experts on the FTL drive. I want you to conduct an investigation into what happened to the FTL," said the commander.

"Sir? What about Mr. Raybourn and Lieutenant Vinet?" queried Lieutenant Anderson.

"Mr. Raybourn is my acting XO and my OPS boss and has enough on his plate. Lieutenant Vinet is my science officer coordinating the survey of the system and now my acting second lieutenant learning the OPS boss's job and has pressing duties. I require Lieutenant Gataki to be acting first lieutenant and to concentrate on his SUPPO duties at this time. The CHENG has enough on his hands with repairs," stated the commander. Then he added, "You, on the other hand, will only be standing conning watches and conducting an investigation into what happened to the FTL. The other crew members you were assigned will be assisting the CHENG until further notice."

"All right, sir," replied Michael.

"Son, I'm not blaming Lieutenant Commander Raybourn, Lieutenant Vinet, or you for what happened, but I do want to know what caused the problem. Is that clear?" said the commander.

"Yes, sir," replied Lieutenant Anderson.

"Lieutenant, I'm sorry to hear about Chief Petty Officer Ortiz. She will be missed," said Commander Hadden Blankenship.

"Yes, sir. Thank you, sir," sighed Michael.

"I will be conducting memorial services for the crew we lost tomorrow at twelve hundred hours," added the commander.

"Thank you, sir. I heard the announcement on the 1MC," said Michael, referring to the general announcement system for the ship.

"Of course. Well, if there's nothing else, the two of you are dismissed. Report back here to assume the watch at twelve hundred hours, Lieutenant Anderson," ordered the XO.

"Aye, aye, sir," confirmed Lieutenant Anderson.

Lieutenant Michael Anderson left the bridge with Lieutenant Jacqueline Vinet, uncomfortable with his new assignment. The thought of taking command and being responsible for ship movements did not appeal to him. He was more of a nuts-and-bolts type, preferring the work of keeping machinery fine-tuned. That and he didn't like the thought of stepping on the toes of more experienced people. As they approached their staterooms, he paused and looked at Jacqueline Vinet.

"Jacqueline," Michael stammered.

"Michael?" she replied.

"I just want to say," he started again and paused.

"Michael, don't worry about it," Lieutenant Vinet said. "All systems indicated no problem with the FTL. It wasn't your fault. We do need another bridge stander, and he's right about you being useless at a control panel right now. And you're not much use as an engineer with only one arm. Once that cast comes off, you'll most likely be put in the pilot seat, and I'll be the conning officer. Don't worry."

"If you say so," countered Lieutenant Anderson. "I just hope I don't screw up."

"We're in open space," she replied. "It's going to be pretty boring for a while. If we're lucky, you might have to decide which way to steer around a comet or something. Now we both need some rack time. Catch some sleep."

"All right. Sleep well." Michael accepted what she said at face value.

"You too." Jacqueline smiled.

Michael didn't sleep well because his dreams were filled with the explosion that had thrown him and the executive officer against the bulkhead outside the FTL compartment. Images of Ortiz and the other crew members inside that compartment being seared by the flames haunted his thoughts even though he had not seen them engulfed in the inferno. Then consciousness faded as he floated there and woke up in the galley set up as an emergency medical facility as his arm was being set. He tossed and turned as the nightmare played over and over again.

His first watch seemed to drag by, and Michael had difficulty paying attention to the on-the-job training that Lieutenant Vinet provided. She knew he hadn't slept well after the first hour and finally gave up by the end of the second hour. When she had asked what the problem was, he muttered something vague about reliving the incident and was given a sympathetic look. She called up a watch stander's guide on a tablet and passed it to him to study for the rest of the watch while she made recommendations on the ship's log entries.

The days passed, and as they did, the nightmare of the incident came less frequently. Michael Anderson grew more comfortable with standing the conning watch. Lieutenant Vinet scheduled emergency bridge drills that facilitated his understanding and proficiency. What he wasn't prepared for was the executive officer taking himself off the watch rotation after two months and reassigning Vinet to fill the now empty conning spot. The three FTL experts aboard were now acting as conning officers for the *New Horizon*, along with Lieutenant Anarzej Gataki and Lieutenant Agnes Felter.

He had grown more and more comfortable with the watch and devoted more and more time on the investigation of the FTL incident. The day the executive officer had ordered him to investigate the FTL failure, he also had the compartment sealed. Michael had been concentrating on the data Hattie the AI had stored in its memory, looking for any abnormality that might have caused the failure. All the data he studied showed no faults with any of the components or the controlling inputs of the independent computer that was dedicated to running the system.

It was nearly two months after the incident, and it seemed as though there was nothing that could have led to the cataclysmic failure they had experienced. The ship had turned over more than two weeks ago and was decelerating as it continued its spiral into the system. Michael had triple-checked all the system's readouts, reviewing them carefully to be sure. Finally, he had no choice than to do the thing he dreaded. He went to the FTL compartment and unlocked the hatch. He stood there vacillating between entering and relocking the hatch. In the end, he took a deep breath and entered the compartment.

Michael stood there viewing once again the carnage that their hopes for the future had become for what seemed an eternity before he started forward. He slowly did a tour of the compartment, inspecting equipment from top to bottom. No one had been in the compartment since the executive officer had ordered it sealed.

As he approached an area where the damage appeared more severe, he came across traces of blood and knew that was the spot where Chief Ortiz had lost her life. A sharp pang of regret surged as grief overwhelmed him. He still remembered her smiling tanned face with the dark hair flowing down to her shoulders and her genuine interest in his development and design concepts that would operate the *New Horizon*'s FTL.

It had only been by chance that he had not been in the FTL compartment when the incident had happened. The executive officer had poked his head through the entry hatch and had asked for a moment of his time. He had stepped into the passageway, and they had just closed the hatch as the world went awry.

Something was bothering Michael about the incident. He repeatedly went over all the data for the last couple of months, and he couldn't quite put a finger on what it was. There was something about the inputs from the various shipboard systems that bothered him. He decided to go to the Electronics Repair Office and ask some questions. As he approached though, he heard someone's raised voice and decided to wait in the passage.

"Have you finished writing that supply requisition for the lidar?" demanded a voice.

"It's right here, ma'am," said another voice.

There was a momentary pause, and Michael heard the first voice say, "You don't have to use all these big words. Make it simple."

"They're generally changed by the operations officer to the way it reads now if I do that," came the response.

"Just do as you're told. Why aren't these reports filled out?" demanded the first voice.

"Isn't that the division officer's responsibility, ma'am?" asked the second voice.

"It's all our responsibilities! Including yours," retorted the angry first voice, which Michael now recognized as Lieutenant Agnes Felter.

"Then I'll need to be trained on how to do that, ma'am," responded the second voice.

"You shouldn't have to be trained. You should already know!" sneered Lieutenant Felter's voice.

"I've never been trained in those responsibilities, ma'am. However, if you want to show me what to do and train me, I will do them," responded the second voice evenly.

"I don't have time to do that, and you should already know," sneered the lieutenant's voice.

"I wasn't sent to Electronics Material Officer School, ma'am. You were," replied the second voice.

"Are you being insubordinate with me? It sounds like it!" shouted the lieutenant's voice.

"No, ma'am," replied the second voice.

"You know, I contacted your last command and was told about you. You want to know what they told me?" growled the lieutenant's voice.

"No, ma'am. What did they tell you, and who told you?" asked the second voice.

"That you're fucked up! You're all fucked up!" yelled the lieutenant.

"If you say so, ma'am," responded the second voice.

"What's the problem with the SPI?" demanded the lieutenant, referring to the spatial positioning indicator system, or SPI.

"I haven't had time to look at it yet, ma'am," replied the second voice.

"What have you been doing? Get out of here and find out what's wrong with it," growled the lieutenant.

"Yes, ma'am," said the second voice.

Shortly thereafter, Petty Officer First Class Guillete opened the hatch to the ERO, also known as the Electronics Repair Office, and stepped into the passageway. He noticed Lieutenant Anderson standing there and closed the hatch as he gave a salute and said, "Good day, sir."

Michael returned the salute and said, "Good day, Petty Officer Guillete."

The petty officer turned and went down the passageway to the ascending ladder as Michael stood there debating whether to enter the office or not. It didn't sound like the electronics material officer, also known as the EMO, was in the best of moods at the moment. He waited another minute, then finally shrugged and knocked on the hatch.

"Come in!" shouted the voice of Lieutenant Felter.

Lieutenant Anderson opened the hatch and stepped in. The woman he faced was shorter, heavyset, with thinning brown hair. She looked up from some paperwork she was filling out and squinted at Michael for a moment. A moment afterward, a forced smile appeared on her face, and she sat back.

"What can I do for you Mr. Anderson?" asked Lieutenant Felter.

"I had some questions about some of the inputs to the FTL from the lidar systems," admitted Michael.

The smile left Lieutenant Felter's face as she stated, "The lidars aren't working correctly. Their resolution capabilities are impaired."

"That's what I wanted to talk about," returned Michael.

"You'll have to ask Chief Wheaton. He's the lidar technician," countered the lieutenant.

"All right," said Michael. Then he ventured, "There also seems to be a problem with the SPI."

"Not surprising," muttered Lieutenant Felter.

"What's that supposed to mean?" demanded Lieutenant Anderson.

"Guillete's not a very good technician and doesn't know what he's doing most of the time," assured Lieutenant Felter.

"Do you mind if I discuss the problem with him anyway?" asked Michael.

"Go ahead, but in my opinion, it'll be a waste of time. Now if you'll excuse me, I'm busy," returned Lieutenant Felter as she looked back down at the paperwork in front of her.

"Thank you, Lieutenant. I'll see you in the wardroom at mess call?" asked Michael.

All Michael received was an abrupt nod as he turned to leave. As he stepped out into the passageway and closed the hatch, he thought he heard something hit the bulkhead inside the ERO office. He stood there for a moment, then shook his head and started toward the stairwell. He had heard rumors about the electronics repair division but had always been somewhat in disbelief about them. Michael resolved to talk to Petty Officer Guillete, but first, he needed to get ready for his upcoming watch.

Michael's watch was uneventful and almost over when an alarm went off. This was his first watch without Lieutenant Vinet on the bridge to provide training, and a grip of fear took hold. He looked at his displays, which indicated a collision course, then looked at the lidar display. An object did lay in the path of the *New Horizon*. He noticed Chief Pennington watching him, and he looked back at her dark African features. After a moment, he drew himself back to the situation and ordered her to plot a course around the object and execute the maneuver. A hand from behind him was placed on his left shoulder as he looked up at his friend Lieutenant Commander Conor Raybourn.

"Good job, Michael," affirmed Conor.

"Thank you, sir," replied Michael.

"Everything running smoothly?" inquired Conor.

"All conditions are the same. No new system updates. We are still heading in system at 0.2 G," reported Lieutenant Anderson. Then Michael added, "I almost forgot. The SPI is back online, and we're now able to read the two buoys we've placed."

"I'll look at the report while I'm standing watch. You stand relieved, Lieutenant." Conor grinned as he saluted Michael.

Returning the salute, Michael left the bridge and headed aft. When he arrived at the level of the executive officer's stateroom, he went over to the hatch where a female Marine named Sergeant Krupich stood watch. She nodded at Michael and inquired what his business was with the acting captain. He explained then received a nod as she stood aside. Michael knocked tentatively on the executive officer's stateroom door. He wasn't sure how to approach the subject that he was bringing to the man.

"Come in," came the executive officer's voice.

Michael opened the door and stepped inside. "Good day, sir," said Michael.

"Good day, Lieutenant." The XO smiled. "Have a seat."

Michael had to fold the seat down himself in the cramped quarters of the executive officer. The bunk was folded into the wall so a chair could be folded down along with a tabletop. Since the XO was sitting on the far side of the table from the door, that left a seat near the door for visitors. Even then, it was much more luxury than a lieutenant had since he had to share a stateroom with another lieutenant. True, there was a desk in his stateroom, but he and his roommate rarely used it, finding their work spaces less disturbing for their roommate and more convenient.

"What can I do for you, Lieutenant?" asked the XO after Michael sat down.

"That's the thing, sir," said Michael. "I'm not really sure what to ask for."

"What seems to be the problem?" insisted the commander patiently.

"It's about the FTL incident, sir," admitted Michael.

"What about it?" The commander frowned.

"Do we have anyone aboard who knows anything about demolitions?" inquired Michael.

"What are you trying to say, Lieutenant?" asked the XO apprehensively.

"There's no delicate way to put this, sir. I think we were sabotaged," stated Michael.

"It's taken you this long to determine that?" queried Commander Blankenship.

"I'm not going to make excuses, sir. It was my fault it's taken this long," returned Michael.

"I'm not blaming you, son. I know I've kept you busy with learning bridge watches," said the XO. Then Commander Blankenship continued, "I also know you haven't entered the FTL compartment until two days ago. Chief Ortiz meant a lot to you, didn't she?"

"My whole team did, sir," countered Michael.

"First time you've lost people?" ventured the XO.

"You mean one's whom I was responsible for, sir?" asked Michael.

"Yes," affirmed the commander.

"Yes, sir," reaffirmed Michael.

"It's rough. That's why I've not been pushing you. Besides, there's not much that can be done to change things now," stated the XO. "In answer to your earlier question, yes, we do have people who understand demolitions aboard. They're called United Systems Marines."

"I hadn't thought of that, sir," admitted Michael.

"If you want something blown up, they're the people to ask. They're also the people to ask if you have questions about something that might have been blown up." The XO chuckled. "I'll let the gunnery sergeant know that you're heading his way, but only let him know what you need. He'll know what to do and assign an expert to work with you. Let's keep this compartmentalized. The fewer people who know your suspicions, the better. Do you understand?"

"I understand, sir," Michael assured the XO.

"Then I'll contact him and tell him to expect you," replied Commander Blankenship.

"Thank you, sir," Michael acknowledged.

"How's the arm?" asked the commander, changing the subject.

"Much better, sir," lied Michael. There were still twinges when he used it.

"Very well, Lieutenant. Dismissed," stated the commander.

35

With that, Michael stood up and folded his seat back into the bulkhead, saluted, and left. He arrived at the Marine level and was met by Gunnery Sergeant Zander, who assigned him Sergeant Adachi, who handled most of the ammunition reloads to keep in practice. Zander assured Michael that if something needed to be blown up, the sergeant was the best man for the job. That also made the sergeant one of the best men to figure out how it was blown up.

CHAPTER 4

Three months later, the ship was in geosynchronous orbit above the third planet from the primary and had been for over a week. It was a beautiful blue-green world, though slightly hotter than Earth as attested to by the smaller ice caps. The spectrographic analysis of the atmosphere indicated a close Earth match, which was confirmed by a robotic probe sent down to the surface. The planet rotation was not quite twenty-five hours and a gravitational pull 0.3 percent more than Earth. Hattie the AI had already calculated a five-hundred-and-forty-one-day yearly revolution for the planet weeks ago.

Unlike Earth, the world had two moons. The inner moon was tidally locked at 270,000 kilometers with a surface gravity of a little over one-tenth of a G. The proximity suggested that the world below would have tides. The other moon was slightly larger than the asteroid Ceres back in Sol system and orbited at nearly 820,000 kilometers with a very minimal surface gravity.

There were three major continents. Two were situated in the northern hemisphere and one in the southern. The southern continent extended well into the polar regions down to the equator. It was easily the largest continent of the three. The other two continents lay in the northern hemisphere with the smaller off the northeast corner of the southern continent, extending in an upside-down *J* shape toward the arctic circle of the northern pole. The last continent was on the far opposite side of the world, extending twenty degrees into the southern regions and up to the northern polar cap, but not to the pole. There was a fairly large island off the eastern coast of the continent that the executive officer and his staff had based their hopes of a future home.

The island appeared rich in resources with little volcanic activity. After a week of surveying the planet remotely, Commander Hadden Blankenship had ordered Lieutenant Commander Conor Raybourn to head a survey mission to the surface. With the assistance of Lieutenant Jacqueline Vinet and Gunnery Sergeant Evan Zander, Conor decided on the composition of the landing party. Security was the primary consideration for the landing party because the infrared sensors indicated that there were life-forms on the surface and that they were fairly sizable. Since the long-range lidar was still at reduced capabilities, the astrometric lab and Hattie the AI used the ship's telescopes and discovered what apparently were structures on the main continent—they had located none on the island—that indicated an intelligence might exist on the planet.

The longboat in the hangar bay was sleek because of the streamlining. It was built to land and return from a planetary surface similar to Earth without refueling. Nearly fifty meters long and weighing almost seventy thousand kilograms unloaded, it was used for a variety of purposes. Its primary mission was personnel transport with a crew of two, ten passengers, and up to five thousand kilograms of cargo when fully loaded. Secondary missions included Marine assaults, exploration, scientific surveys, bombing runs, lifeboat, and with its fusion reactor, it could serve as a power source if necessary. The *New Horizon* carried four such longboats and two shuttles. The shuttles were significantly larger but less streamlined and could transport significantly more passengers and cargo. The longboat Conor and the survey team would be using had a partial science package installed, leaving enough room for twelve people, which included the pilot and copilot.

The twelve members of the survey team entered the longboat and made the descent toward the selected survey site. Lieutenant Commander Conor Raybourn piloted the longboat, and as it descended, he did a slow curving circle around the island. It extended from north to south for about five hundred kilometers—or, as the Marines would say, klicks—and at its widest, approximately three hundred and fifty kilometers. There was a river that flowed for well over two-thirds the length of the island down to the southern coast, forming a valley that was lined with the peaks and ridges of various outcrops with tall cliffs. The river valley averaged over one hundred kilometers wide as it ran down the center of the island from north to south.

Turning north over the open ocean, Conor brought the longboat to the south coast and up the river before touching down on the slow-moving water. A clearing opened up on the bank, and Conor steered the craft toward a gravel beach that had a grassy meadow beyond. The longboat bumped ashore as Conor applied thrusters and pushed the longboat to a secure landing with only the tail end of the longboat extending into the water of the river.

"Atmosphere," ordered Lieutenant Commander Raybourn.

Staff Sergeant Rosenstein left her seat to check the atmosphere gauges by the main hatch and announced, "Looks good, sir."

"UV's a little high, but nothing some good sunblock wouldn't stop," responded Chief Petty Officer Pennington from the copilot station. Then after a brief pause, she added, "It's the middle of summer out there according to the AI. No other harmful radiation that we wouldn't expect, sir."

"Very well, everyone, let's arm up and look around," ordered the lieutenant commander. He looked at Chief Boatswain Mate Pennington and said, "Boats, stay put and monitor the comm and scanners."

"Yes, sir," replied Pennington, the alternate pilot.

Everyone double-checked their gear as Conor donned the body armor Staff Sergeant Rosenstein handed him. When he finished, Conor picked up his Navarro M-71 machine gun and opened the hatch. Humid, fresh air, laden with the smell of vegetation, permeated the interior of the longboat as the hatch was opened. A hint of salt from the distant ocean was carried on the breeze as they stepped out into the new world. Conor took a deep breath as he stepped through the hatch.

One by one, the crew stepped on the wing then down to the wet gravel of the beach and a new world. The sounds of water flowing and the air moving the distant foliage met their ears. The stellar primary was bright, and their skin sucked up the heat of it with pleasure after months of being confined on the ship. The humidity in the air explained the abundant foliage. It sprang up, forming a nearly impenetrable barrier of vibrant green where it grew past the gravel beach of the river. The grass was tall, and the trees to the north and south of them on the beach grew high and thickly packed. The ground under Conor's feet felt great, and the air tasted wonderful with new and interesting odors. The river was a cobalt blue and cut a bright path through the verdant foliage on each side as it made its way to the sapphire ocean in the distance.

"Staff Sergeant," called Lieutenant Commander Raybourn.

"Yes, sir," responded Staff Sergeant Rosenstein.

"We have six Marines. Two-person teams with a Marine in each team," ordered Conor.

"Roger that, sir," acknowledged the staff sergeant.

Staff Sergeant Rosenstein indicated that Sergeant Ivankov was to remain with the longboat and made quick assignments for each of the others. The staff sergeant took it upon herself to act as Conor's second as he turned to climb the high ridge of gravel and rock before him to take a look around. Topping the ridge, Conor looked out over a grassy plain with a lake in the distance. Rushes grew along the edge of the lake, and there was something large moving on the far side.

Conor hefted his M-71 to a more comfortable position on his shoulder as he looked around. Though the trees and grass were alien, they, for some reason, had a familiar look to his eye. *Over ten thousand light-years from home,* he thought, *and things still look the same.* The scrape of a boot on the rocky ground sounded beside him as Staff Sergeant Rosenstein came to a halt.

"Looks good, sir," stated the staff sergeant.

"The air is breathable at least. What about food?" wondered Conor aloud.

"I'm sure we'll find out, sir," stated Staff Sergeant Rosenstein.

"So what's your expert opinion about the vegetation we're looking at, Staff Sergeant?" asked Conor.

"Expert, sir?" responded Rosenstein.

"I've read your file, Staff Sergeant. You have a master's degree in biology, which is why Gunnery Sergeant Zander recommended you for this mission," replied Conor. He paused for a moment, then added, "Which doesn't surprise me as to why you were handpicked for the *New Horizon* ship complement but begs the question…"

"As to why I'm a Jarhead, sir?" Rosenstein finished for him.

"Well…yes," stammered Conor.

"I had three years of formal education prior to joining up. Money ran out. Finished my bachelor's and master's while in the service and found out I like being a Jarhead also. Besides, where else will they let me shoot and blow up things, sir?" She grinned mischievously.

"Which brings me back to my original question about the vegetation, Staff Sergeant," said Conor.

The staff sergeant looked around with a frown on her face as lines creased her forehead. She stood slightly taller than his shoulder, with raven-black hair in a tight bun at the back of her head. She indicated that Conor should stand guard, then she knelt and picked up a leaf that lay at her feet and studied it for a moment.

"Sir, this leaf looks a lot like a leaf from a ginkgo tree back on Earth. The rest of the vegetation around here reminds me of the year of paleobiology I took a few years ago," stated Rosenstein.

Reaching into the pouch on her belt, she produced a plastic sample bag and placed the leaf inside. After marking the bag, she stowed it inside the pouch at her hip. All the while she was doing this, Conor kept a wary watch on their surroundings. When she finished, she took up her M-71 from where it was slung on her shoulder and turned a full circle, inspecting their surroundings carefully.

"All right, keep your eyes open, Staff Sergeant. The infrared scans say there's some pretty large animals roaming this planet even though we haven't seen any up close yet," stated Conor as he turned and walked back toward the longboat.

In the distance, the crew worked at various assignments. Two scientists were setting up gear for tests and video surveillance, while their two Marines stood guard. The other two teams were walking the ground and taking samples—one to the north and the other to the south of the longboat. Sergeant Ivankov took a position on the longboat's wing and kept watchful guard over all with his M-71, which left Chief Pennington in the longboat monitoring the radio and longboat functions.

The sun was still high in the sky, and they should still have several hours to explore the surrounding area. Reaching a level area, they walked down the gravel beach toward the longboat. Something crashed in the distance, and the southern tree line downstream moved. Conor watched as something from a bygone era stepped out onto the gravel of the shoreline. Its majestic long neck swung toward them as it noticed the longboat and its crew.

"If that's not an apatosaurus, I'm asking for my money back from that paleobiology course," Conor heard Rosenstein murmur beside him.

The whole crew stood transfixed in wonder as they watched a whole family group come out of the vegetation and onto the beach. Their hides were a greenish gray, a natural camouflage against predators. As the crew of the longboat watched, some of them moved out into the water to quench their thirst. A few of the larger beasts moved further into the river to form a protective barrier from water denizens as they made room near the river's edge for the youngsters. What must have been an older male took a position between the human observers and the rest of the herd. The creature stood eyeing them and making a rumbling sound to ensure the interlopers to this family gathering understood they were to maintain their distance.

"I wonder what they taste like," came a response from Private First Class Abrams, who had joined them.

Looks passed between the others who had gathered around to watch a sight that hadn't been seen by any man prior to today, and laughter broke out. The noise caused the herd's sentinel to stamp a foot and raise its head, eyeing the puny intruders warily. The humans grew silent but continued watching the herd as it splashed in the shallow waters with grins.

It was at this time that danger struck. Out of the forest, a large two-legged beast with a mottled red-and-blue hide suddenly appeared at the far side of the herd and sank its teeth into the neck of one of the midsize drinkers as it used a hind foot to rip open the belly of its prey. The herd scattered swiftly in the opposite direction of the attack. As the herd stampeded toward the longboat, the crew retreated.

Staff Sergeant Rosenstein and Private Abrams fired their M-71s into the air as they backed up, attempting to ensure a safe retreat for their companions. The herd swerved away from the noise and headed west as Conor backed toward the longboat with his Navarro M-71 at ready to provide support to the staff sergeant and private. Unfortunately, the noise also attracted the attention of the carnivore as the herd ran up the rise that Conor and the staff sergeant recently descended.

Seeing the small figures on the beach, the predator left its recent kill and charged. *There are a lot of teeth in that mouth*, thought Conor as he leveled his weapon and fired. A loud noise sounded from behind Conor as something whizzed over his head. A red plume appeared in the chest of the carnivore as it screamed in pain. Conor turned to see Chief Petty Officer Pennington lying on the wing of the longboat, sighting for another shot from a Vinter HR-10, a 10 mm high-powered sniper rifle the Marines had used for nearly two hundred years. The HR-10 sounded again as the carnivore approached Staff Sergeant Rosenstein and Private First Class Abrams, causing part of the skull and one eye of the carnivore to vanish in a cloud of red mist. Taking one more step forward, the carnivore began a nosedive between the staff sergeant and private.

The beast slashed out wildly with its short forward appendages as its body hit the gravel of the beach. There was a scream from Private Abrams as he flew backward. His leg had a long gash and a strange, bent look as he lay on his back, moaning. The staff sergeant and Conor changed directions as they observed no movement from the monster and rushed toward Private Abram's side. Conor dropped his machine gun as he slid to his knees beside the private with the staff sergeant. He applied pressure to the inner leg and slowed the blood loss as a belt was tossed to the ground beside him. The staff sergeant grabbed the belt and immediately created a tourniquet around the injured man's leg.

"Tell them to get a medic down here!" shouted Conor.

"Roger that!" shouted Sergeant Krupich, who was missing a belt as she ran back toward the longboat.

Sergeant Ivankov appeared with the medical kit from the longboat and opened it. Searching through the arranged bottles, Ivankov found the morphine and put two pills in the private's mouth, then told him to swallow. A few minutes later, the private relaxed as the pills did their stuff.

"A shuttle is on its way in fifteen, sir," huffed Sergeant Krupich as she came up beside Conor. "Told them what happened and requested immediate medical assistance for the private. Lieutenant Commander Hollinger is on the way with blood and a surgical field kit."

"Very well, Sergeant," acknowledged Lieutenant Commander Raybourn.

"Gunny's on his way down with some more firepower also." The sergeant grinned.

Staff Sergeant Rosenstein was relieved by Sergeant Krupich and picked up her M-71. She indicated for the lieutenant commander to follow as she walked around the carnivore. Conor picked up his machine gun and took up position beside her as his thoughts raced overtime at the swiftness of the attack. They completed their circuit of the carnivore and returned to where most of the party were attending to Private Abrams. Staff Sergeant Rosenstein looked down at the private with a grin on her face as they came to a halt.

"Looks like there might be a barbecue tonight, Private. How about a nice, juicy steak?" she asked.

CHAPTER 5

The shuttle landed an hour later. It sided up to the beach. A side door opened, and an exit ramp extended to the gravel. Lieutenant Commander Hollinger and Chief Petty Officer deLang swept past, carrying a case, and made a beeline directly to Private Abrams. Gunnery Sergeant Zander and seven more Marines in camouflage uniforms came down the ramp and stopped in front of Conor. The gunnery sergeant saluted while eyeing the two large corpses lying on the ground to the south.

With a grin and a salute, which Lieutenant Commander Conor Raybourn returned, the gunny said, "I'd ask if you need any help, but it looks like you have it under control, sir."

"Thanks to Chief Pennington, Gunny," countered Conor.

"How's Private Abrams?" inquired the gunnery sergeant.

"Broken leg and lost a lot of blood, which we finally were able to stop. Hopefully, he'll be all right," said the lieutenant commander.

"With your permission, I'd like to scout the immediate perimeter and establish a beachhead," stated the gunnery sergeant.

"All right, Gunny. I leave the security of our landing site in your capable hands," Conor confirmed.

"Very well, sir. After I hand out assignments, I'm going to check on Private Abrams," replied the gunny.

The gunny looked at two other Marines and signaled them to go upstream to the rise, then he sent another two downstream in a repeat pattern. Two others were sent back inside the shuttle to bring out the ATVs. The second team went a hundred yards past the apatosaurus before circling back. By the time both teams had reached the top of the rise, the ATV, along with a lot of other equipment, had been unloaded by the crews of the shuttle and longboat.

The gunnery sergeant returned with Staff Sergeant Rosenstein as Conor assisted with the unloading at the foot of the ramp. There were two ATVs with attachments for removing foliage and even trees, along with chainsaws, flamethrowers, and other items for individual utilization. There were also some heavy crates that were marked as general purpose, large tents, and other large camp accessories.

"This spot will be fine, sir," said the gunnery sergeant. "We'll start clearing out the foliage for about a hundred meters past the base perimeter we marked with the ATVs until the sun sets and finish tomorrow when we'll start establishing a base camp."

"Sounds good, Gunny," Conor affirmed.

"Tonight we'll gather some wood and build bonfires, but everyone should probably sleep inside the craft. We don't know what else might be lurking around. But between the fires and the miniguns mounted on the ATVs, we should be all right," continued Zander.

The gunnery sergeant looked over Conor's shoulder, and the lieutenant commander turned around to see Dr. Bess Hollinger approaching. She came to a stop in front of him, the black skin of her face glistening in the sunlight.

"How's Private Abrams, Doctor?" asked Conor.

"He should be fine," stated Hollinger. "I'd like to set up a med tent down here and transfer him to it. I don't want to send him up to the ship. The gravity down here will help that broken bone heal better."

"Roger that, ma'am," replied the gunnery sergeant. "It may be a day or two. I want to build a perimeter fence and central guard tower first. Then we'll unpack the hospital tent and erect it if that will do?"

"That's fine as long as we can keep one of the two ships to bed him in until then," agreed Lieutenant Commander Hollinger.

"We're going to need to keep one of the two here to electrify the fence," interjected Conor.

They entered the shuttle, and the doctor assured them that other than being off duty for the next month or so and having a healthy scar to brag about, once he healed, Abrams would be fine. There was a sizable refrigerator built into the shuttle, and Chief Medic deLang was sent out to check the apatosaurus and carnivore. Both were edible, but the chief informed them that the apatosaurus would taste better and most likely would be more than enough. The equipment in the refrigerator was moved outside and the inside cleaned. An ATV dragged the carnivore down the beach a kilometer as they commenced butchering and storing the apatosaurus.

As the sun set, what was left of the corpse was taken down to lay beside the carnivore. Driftwood that had been gathered was built into bonfires, and meat was roasted in place of rations. That evening, the crew looked upon the night skies of their new world as the smell of freshly cooked meat drew them together around the dancing fires.

"Tastes like deer," said Staff Sergeant Rosenstein.

"I was thinking more like buffalo," replied Conor.

"Haven't had either, but it's good," stated the gunnery sergeant. "I could get used to this."

"I don't think we'll have a choice in the matter, Gunny," countered Lieutenant Commander Raybourn.

"So there's no hope, Mr. Raybourn?" asked Lieutenant Commander Hollinger.

"Even if we knew how the FTL was able to send us this far, there are major irreplaceable components in the FTL that were damaged or destroyed. We'd need a couple of high-tech factories to replace them. The ship's factory can only duplicate small components that it's been programmed to replace and then only if it had the materials necessary for their construction," explained Conor.

"Is Abrams awake, Ms. Hollinger?" asked Chief Pennington.

"He should be and probably looking for some pain meds," confessed the lieutenant commander. "I suppose I should go in and check on him."

"I can do that, sir," declared Chief Pennington. "Tell me where the meds are, and will he be hungry?"

"You might take him something to eat. The meds are on the white table against the wall. Give him two pills, but wait till after he eats. They will most likely knock him out for the night once he's had them," said the lieutenant commander.

"Roger that, ma'am," replied Chief Pennington. She loaded a metal plate with roasted meat and beans, then walked over to the shuttle.

"So, Staff Sergeant, tell us what your thoughts are about this planet," Conor ventured as he rounded on her.

"Me, sir?" protested Staff Sergeant Rosenstein as the rest of the crew looked her way questioningly.

"You're a biologist, and you did take that course on paleobiology. Give us some insight. Even that carnivore resembled the pictures out of a grade school book on dinosaurs to me. How can that be? Parallel evolution?" insisted Conor.

"That's not very likely, sir." replied Rosenstein "Remember that leaf I showed you earlier?"

"Yes?" countered Conor.

"I'm going to have the chief medic check it out," stated the staff sergeant. "Personally, I think it'll be a match to the ginkgo tree on Earth."

"How can that be?" demanded Lieutenant Commander Hollinger.

"I don't know, ma'am. But I have a feeling that the apatosaurus is exactly what it appears to be, and there's a tree that looks a lot like a pawpaw over in the woods to the south of us and alders over there," Staff Sergeant Rosenstein countered as she pointed.

"How did they get here?" insisted Lieutenant Commander Hollinger.

"I imagine that's a mystery we'll learn as we explore this planet," stated Lieutenant Commander Conor Raybourn as he stared at the fire and wondered himself.

Silence descended on the camp for a few moments. The calls of the night were different than their various homes back on Earth but still added comfort in its own way. Then a loud roar of more than one creature fighting sounded downstream, and they all shivered at what type of threats those sounds emanated from. The crew started going back into the shuttle and longboat. Watches were set in all the vehicles, and the night passed uneventfully with the exception of two large beasts passing along the rise nearby.

As the sun rose slowly in the eastern skies, casting a reddish glow on the horizon, most of the crew members were already awake. The gunnery sergeant assigned several crew members to take an ATV and tools to find materials for constructing the encampment. Much of the surrounding grass and other foliage had been removed by the ATVs while the apatosaurus had been butchered and stored, and four Marines were busy planting flags for where the fence, watchtower, tents, and other equipment would be erected within the fence's perimeter.

"Is there anything I can do, Gunnery Sergeant," queried the lieutenant commander as he watched.

"Learn for right now, sir. You have weapons training when the flags are set," stated Gunnery Sergeant Zander with a grin.

"I've already had training on weapons, Gunny," said Conor.

The gunnery sergeant looked at Conor for a moment, then retorted, "With all due respect, sir, you were trained to point and shoot a firearm, and that's about all. If we're to remain on this planet, then you need training that they didn't provide you in that orientation course that got you those golden oak leaves. For the next two weeks, my staff is going to give you training even regular military officers almost never receive, and if you're lucky, it will keep you and your teammates alive."

"Why the interest in me, Gunny?" inquired Conor.

"The commander wants an aerial reconnaissance of the river valley. I persuaded him into giving me two weeks to prepare you. If you want to continue training once the two weeks and the recon are finished, we will be here to provide," replied Gunnery Sergeant Zander seriously.

Lieutenant Commander Raybourn looked back into the gunnery sergeant's hard stare. "When do we begin, Gunny?"

The gunnery sergeant must have made a hand signal that Conor didn't see. The Marines who were planting flags returned and lined up behind the gunnery sergeant, and he said grimly, "You already know Staff Sergeant Rosenstein. She's in charge of your training. Beside her is Sergeant Hall, who is our best sniper and generally the best overall shot with any firearm." A tall golden-haired, blue-eyed female eyed

Conor as the gunny spoke. Then he continued, pointing at a tall dark-haired man. "Over here is Corporal Flores. He will be teaching you knife fighting and unarmed combat. Sergeant Adachi over there is going to teach you demolitions and how to reload ammo. He likes to blow things up and is very good at it," confided the gunnery sergeant as he indicated a short dark-haired man of Oriental descent. "Any questions?" asked Gunnery Sergeant Evan Zander.

"What's first?" countered Lieutenant Commander Raybourn.

"Ten-klick run in ten mikes. Camouflage uniform. Full body armor. Navarro M-71 with three full magazines. Gerst S-7 sidearm with three full magazines. And don't forget your KG-3 combat knife," snapped Staff Sergeant Rosenstein. Conor's jaw dropped as he looked at her.

"Did I forget to mention that the staff sergeant was a marathon runner and our physical training expert?" The gunny grinned.

"Go!" shouted the staff sergeant.

Conor was back in twelve minutes, or mikes, and was told that the run was now twelve kilometers, or klicks. They trained for twelve hours the first day, at which time Conor was allowed to take a shower in the shuttle's limited facilities and eat his evening meal in peace. Then he found out that his day wasn't over yet. The gunnery sergeant had the officers assembled to give him a daily briefing for two hours. When Conor settled into his chair on the longboat, his body was a mass of pain and bruises as exhaustion overcame him. A hand on his shoulder woke him up after what seemed a minute but was belied by the sun that was coming up in the east. A plate of food was gently placed in his lap.

"Breakfast for thirty mikes. Then ten klicks in ten mikes afterward. Full gear," snapped Staff Sergeant Rosenstein.

Somehow, he made it on time, and his day followed a similar routine to that of the day before—a meal, a run in full gear, firearms training, a meal, knife and unarmed combat training, demolitions training, a shower and a meal, and a briefing. Conor noticed that each day his four training instructors did the run in full gear with him and each day they took a different route. He suspected that the gunnery sergeant was multitasking his training with a ground recon, or reconnaissance. The team made occasional stops, taking samples, bagging them, and recording their locations. They also stopped to make a record of any new creature they observed.

By the end of the third day, the base camp was almost completed. Sturdy poles held the power lines, sharpened stakes surrounded the encampment, the watchtower was complete, and tents had been erected. They had lost Seaman Fred Foreman while laying the power cable to the encampment when a large crocodile had emerged from the river and took him as he was making the connection to the longboat. The power connection was completed, and the camp was now considered safe enough to bring more people down. The shuttle was sent up on the fourth day to deliver the meat in storage and bring down more equipment and crew members. The shuttle returned the fifth day with another ATV, two helicopters, and twenty more crew members.

There were now sixty people on the new world, and things were happening quickly as Conor continued his training. The evening briefings were more intense with all the new discoveries that the crew were making. They lost the four reconnaissance probes shortly after each had been launched. The operator, Staff Sergeant Rusu, wanted to recover the drones, but they were lost too far away and in heavily forested terrain. The unknown dangers made a foot recovery too hazardous to be feasible.

By the evening of the tenth day, it seemed to Conor he was more alert. He awoke on the eleventh day and did the run without the extra kilometer or two for being late. When they had started firearm training, he noticed that the magazines had different-colored tape on the base of each. It took him another ten days to ask about what the tape meant.

"What does the colored tape mean?" inquired Lieutenant Commander Raybourn, pointing to the magazines in Sergeant Hall's belt.

Sergeant Hall looked at him and said, "Different types of rounds. Red is for a standard round, yellow indicates an explosive round, yellow with red stripes means every third round is explosive, and green is for sleepy darts. You're going to be firing the explosive rounds tomorrow during training since it's your last day, so you'll see what they can do."

The next day, Conor was allowed to fire off a full magazine of explosive rounds one at a time at different targets. When he was finished, he was quite impressed with the destructive power each round was capable of producing. He was given a sleepy dart round to look at and told that it would knock a person out for one to three hours but only use one round per individual because more than one might put a person into cardiac arrest. Conor said something about everything seeming a little low-tech.

Staff Sergeant Rosenstein asked, "Did you expect ray guns and light sabers, Lieutenant Commander?"

"Well, no. High tech doesn't do well with a lot of rough handling, and if the case is broken, the environment might short them out," confessed Conor. He paused before adding, "But laser sighting, night vision, and other high-tech items would enhance your capabilities."

"We don't carry a lot of that sort of thing because of the weight and because of these," said the staff sergeant as she produced a small cylinder from her belt.

Conor looked at it for a moment, then inquired, "What is it?"

"EMP grenade," Sergeant Hall informed him, which Conor suspected meant electromagnetic pulse.

"So?" asked Conor.

"It will pretty much make anything that's high-tech useless if it's within fifty meters of that grenade when it goes off," stated Sergeant Hall. "Which means high-tech items are so much deadweight afterward. It's also why naval vessels have a lot of low-tech electronics that are hardened against EMP attacks."

"Go over there by that tree," suggested Staff Sergeant Rosenstein.

Conor walked over to the tree, which was around seventy yards from where they had been standing. When he turned around, the cylinder bounced on the ground in front of him, and suddenly, he saw flashes of light as he lost consciousness. The trip back to consciousness seemed slow, and he felt a migraine developing behind his eyes as someone held something potent under his nose. The staff sergeant and sergeant were kneeling beside him as he opened his eyes.

"Feeling better?" asked the staff sergeant.

"Yeah. What happened?" asked Conor.

"If you're within five to ten meters, the EMP will knock you out," Sergeant Hall informed him.

"You don't want that to happen too often in one day either. Too much exposure is bad," added Staff Sergeant Rosenstein.

"You felt I needed a dose?" inquired Conor.

"Everyone that goes through training gets an EMP dose, sir. That way, they know what to expect when one goes off near them." The staff sergeant smiled. "On your last day of training, you get a sleepy dart to find out what it's like."

"Your training doesn't include shooting me with a standard or explosive round, does it?" asked Conor half seriously.

"Hopefully, sir, you never have to experience that," replied the staff sergeant grimly.

CHAPTER 6

Lieutenant Commander Conor Raybourn remembered standing outside the entrance to his tent, exhausted and ready to go in, when someone called his name. Conor had turned to see Staff Sergeant Rosenstein pointing her Gerst S-7 9 mm sidearm at him with a smile on her lips as she pulled the trigger. He heard the retort and saw the gun buck in her hand as something thudded into his chest. He remembered staring at the dart in the chest of his camouflage uniform, thinking that she had been joking earlier in the day. Sergeant Adachi and Corporal Flores appeared at his sides, grinning, as they grabbed him by the arms when he started falling to the ground. Then he lost consciousness as they dragged him into his tent.

The early morning breeze blew through the entrance of the headquarters tent, causing the flap that served as a doorway to wave. The humid, peculiar smell of the forest, along with freshly brewed coffee, permeated the tent as Conor lay in his cot. His boots were off, and so was his camouflage uniform. The sound of a cup being poured came to his ears as he opened his eyes to look toward where the sound originated at the rear of the tent. The gunnery sergeant stood there placing the pot back on the burner with a steaming mug in his hand, looking in Conor's direction.

"Reveille, sir," said Gunnery Sergeant Zander cheerfully.

"Isn't it a little early?" inquired the lieutenant commander.

"You said you wanted to do PT with the Marines in the mornings," stated the gunnery sergeant.

"Yes, I did," Conor replied as he swung his legs onto the dirt floor.

He had been doing intensive physical and weapons training with the four Marines assigned to him for the last two weeks. He could already feel his body beginning to tighten up. Of course, he still had cramps at times, but it all seemed worth it. He just hoped that there were no more surprises awaiting him anytime soon as he thought of the smile on the pretty face of the staff sergeant as she shot him the night before.

"You have enough time to eat light, and we start in thirty. Your meal and PT gear are laid out on the table," said the gunnery sergeant.

"Thank you, Gunny," replied Conor as he stood up and stretched.

"If you're exhausted and hit with a sleepy dart, it gives you a good night's sleep," confessed the gunnery sergeant to the elephant in the room.

"Oh!" murmured Conor. He thought about it for a moment, then said, "I guess I did need a good night's sleep."

The gunnery sergeant grinned and nodded as Conor took the mug of steaming coffee. Conor walked over to the table and sat down to investigate the covered plate. A tantalizing smell emanated from it as he lifted the lid off his plate, revealing a meal of scrambled eggs, a slice of meat, and a portion of applesauce. While he ate, the gunny filled him in on the watches' reports about sighting three large animals outside the lighted perimeter during the night. There were no new orders or status changes from the *New Horizon*. When he finished eating, Conor changed into fresh cammie pants, olive-green T-shirt, and boots, which appeared to be the PT gear since the gunny was dressed likewise.

"Ready, sir?" asked the gunnery sergeant.

"I guess so, Gunny." replied Conor.

"We'll have you up and in the air in two hours then," the gunnery sergeant informed him.

"Very good, Gunny," acknowledged the lieutenant commander.

They walked out to see Staff Sergeant Rosenstein and eleven other Marines in similar uniform already waiting for them. As they approached, the gunnery sergeant ordered Rosenstein to lead the PT. They spent half an hour limbering and doing various exercises. Then they did thirty laps around the interior of the perimeter fence or approximately ten kilometers. Finished, they all went back to their sleeping quarters to freshen up and change. Freshening up consisted of a sponge bath, after which Conor changed into full cammies. He also pulled on body armor and the rest of his gear. Stepping out of the headquarters tent, he found Staff Sergeant Rosenstein, Sergeant Adachi, and Seaman Green already waiting for him.

"Are we ready, Staff Sergeant?" asked Conor.

"Yes, sir!" returned Rosenstein.

"Is the chopper charged?" demanded the lieutenant commander.

"Chief Pennington assures me there's a full charge. They just disconnected ten mikes ago," replied Staff Sergeant Rosenstein.

On Earth, the batteries were rated to power the helicopter, or chopper, for around two thousand kilometers of straight flight time. The helicopters and ATVs were battery-powered and could be used in a variety of friendly and hostile environments. The ATVs were even meant to be utilized in a vacuum environment, such as Earths' moon. Conor wondered how long the batteries would last with repeated use though. There were replacements stored aboard the *New Horizon*, but the type A factory that the ship had installed was not designed to manufacture them. They would need a type B factory or an electrical manufacturing lab to produce replacements in the future.

"Well then, we'd better get started," stated Conor.

"What's the plan, sir?" questioned Seaman Green.

"We're going to go west toward the cliff then south to the ocean. After that, we'll follow the seashore east until we hit the opposite cliff face on the other side of the river, then follow it for a bit till we come back to camp," stated Conor. "Has Chief Pennington checked the other chopper?"

"Yes, sir," replied Rosenstein. "She has Petty Officer Kaur monitoring the comms in the shuttle in case we run into trouble."

They walked over to the waiting helicopter and boarded. Conor took the pilot seat with the staff sergeant taking copilot. He donned his comms and indicated all the other members should do likewise. They checked their communications, ensuring they could talk to each other and the shuttle. Conor started the engine and did his preflights. Checking the battery charge one last time, he gently lifted the chopper up and over the barrier fence.

He circled the camp and headed west toward the distant cliff face. Four klicks later, the trees thinned out and became an open plain of grassland. The land was rich with a wide variety of fauna and flora as they proceeded steadily toward the cliffs ahead of them. Then a sight that hadn't been seen on Earth in over sixty-five million years passed below them as they flew onward toward the distant cliffs.

"Those are triceratops over there!" shouted Green.

"You don't have to shout, Seaman. We'll all hear you fine," stated Conor. As he drifted over to the herd, it took alarm and started stampeding.

If we had to be stranded somewhere, at least it's somewhere that will make life interesting, thought Conor. It could be a whole lot worse. There might not have been a habitable planet in the system, which would have left them with the option of living on a barren, inhospitable world, perhaps one that could be terraformed, but most likely not within their lifetime or the lifetime of their great grandchildren.

They approached the far side of the plain, and the terrain started to become rocky, along with more trees. The cliffs rose high in the distance, and the surrounding region was rugged as they approached them. There was snow on the upper heights of those cliffs. A tree line formed just past the sheer drop and stopped where the snow line began. Conor turned south when he was within a couple of kilometers of the cliff face. They continued flying south, paralleling the cliff face once again until they reached the ocean. From there, they turned east until they reached the river. They set down on the sands of the oceanfront and took more samples and watched as some unknown behemoth surfaced well off the shore and vanished again.

They headed east toward the foothills once leaving the river estuary and followed the coastline until they reached the mountains. Conor turned the chopper north, paralleling the mountains for nearly two hours until the mountain chain went east. Conor took a northwestern direction from there, leaving the mountains behind. After they cleared the heavy forest, a plain spread out before them.

The curve of the river cut an arc through it as it flowed from the east and turned south toward their distant encampment downriver. Conor crossed the river and flew over an outcrop that thrust upward. A voice brought Lieutenant Commander Raybourn back from his contemplation of those snowcapped heights.

"To the left, sir," said Green. "Can you get us a bit closer?"

Conor took the craft down closer to the outcrop. A seam of black ran through an outcropping of rock below them.

"That looks like coal down there, sir," declared Seaman Green.

"Are you sure?" asked the lieutenant commander.

"There's only one way to be sure, sir," stated Green.

Conor followed the seam until they passed a clear area. He circled the meadow and slowly brought the chopper down in what appeared to be tall grass. The outcrop with the black seam was approximately fifty meters from them as they stepped cautiously onto the thick loam. Conor's boots sank into the ground as he looked suspiciously at the surrounding tall grass.

"Adachi, go with Green and act as guard. The staff sergeant and I will guard the chopper," ordered Conor. "Everyone understand?"

"Roger that, sir," the three responded in chorus.

Sergeant Adachi and Seaman Green moved cautiously toward the outcrop, constantly scanning the area. The grass was about waist-high and waved in the slight breeze. They reached the outcrop, and Green took a geology hammer and knocked a small piece off, which he placed in a plastic bag. He then put the bag in the pouch in his belt. Adachi and Green were over halfway back when the grass behind them moved.

"Run!" shouted Staff Sergeant Rosenstein.

The staff sergeant and lieutenant commander laid cover fire toward the barely visible bodies that seemed to swim quickly through the grass. Adachi and Green sprinted toward the chopper. Lieutenant commander Raybourn saw one of the beasts flop down as it was hit, and the tall grass waved violently in its death throes. Another was almost to Seaman Green when it caught a full burst in the chest from Staff Sergeant Rosenstein. The verdant-colored creature fell, twitching in the grass just at the edge of the rotor's sweep.

Then another shape with a bright-greenish tinge jumped into the air on a trajectory toward Rosenstein. Conor pulled the trigger of his Navarro M-71 and found that he had expended the magazine. The creature struck the still spinning rotors and lost its right forearm as it knocked Rosenstein to the ground and came down on top of her back. The loss of its forelimb caused it to tumble off her and to the side as Conor dropped his M-71 while he drew his S-7 sidearm, running toward the prone Marine. The creature regained its feet and turned to face Conor as he unloaded the magazine of his Gerst at the creature's chest. At least three shots hit their mark as he ran toward the creature.

The creature wobbled but didn't go down as it took a shaky step in the lieutenant commander's direction. Conor circled to the creature's right as it snapped at him with a mouthful of sharp ivory teeth. He threw his now empty sidearm at the beast's head and drew his KG-3 combat knife. The beast raised its head, snapping at the sidearm, as Conor rushed in, pushing its chin further upward with his left forearm as his right ran the razor-sharp edge of his combat knife across its throat. Scarlet-hot blood spewed from the creature's throat all over the front of his body armor as its right leg came up and pushed into his now red chest. The creature went over backward, snapping its jaws and gasping as Conor was propelled away in the opposite direction. He rolled and got to his feet as Sergeant Adachi approached the now still creature, covering it with his M-71. Seaman Green fired a burst at two quickly retreating streaks of waving grass as Staff Sergeant Rosenstein got to her feet and did a quick survey of the surroundings. She then did a slow survey of the area as Conor retrieved his M-71 and approached her.

"Are you all right, Staff Sergeant?" asked Conor worriedly.

"Thank God for body armor," she stated. Then she looked at Conor with concern in her eyes. "Are you all right, sir?"

Looking down at the quickly drying blood that now covered the front of his body armor and uniform, he replied, "None of it is mine, if that's what you mean. Just a bruise or two perhaps from where it caught me in the chest with that back leg."

They approached the bright-green creature to study it. There were green feathers covering much of its body. Its forelimb was long, but it did not appear quite as articulated as a human's and ended in long digits tipped with sharp claws. The back limbs were heavy and clawed also, with the inner claw on both feet enlarged and mobile. Its snout was pointed, and the inside of its mouth full of pointed razor-sharp teeth.

"So what is it, Staff Sergeant?" asked Conor cautiously.

"Velociraptor," Seaman Green responded before Staff Sergeant Rosenstein could reply. He then continued by adding, "I assisted an archeology team one summer that removed a complete skeleton back in Montana."

"Nasty and believed to be more intelligent than a wolf," added the staff sergeant.

"It's believed that they hunted in packs," continued Green.

"Well, I'd say we can now confirm most of that," Conor said as he walked over and picked up the right forelimb of the creature. He then looked at Green and Adachi. "Why don't you two get the body and this into the patient carrier on the passenger side while Staff Sergeant Rosenstein stands guard. I'll take the pilot side."

"Let's take the darker one over there also," said Staff Sergeant Rosenstein.

"Why, Staff Sergeant?" asked the lieutenant commander.

"I'm betting that one is female and the bright-green one is male," replied Rosenstein.

"All right. Let's take both," acknowledged Conor.

Seaman Green and Sergeant Adachi both grimaced but set to work loading the still forms into the patient carriers. They finished within a quarter of an hour and boarded the chopper, which took off without further incidents. Conor was glad to be departing the area around the outcrop.

"What's your verdict on that sample you took, Green?" asked Conor.

"It's coal, sir," stated Green.

"You're sure?" asked Conor.

"Positive, sir," affirmed Green.

The spectrographic analysis of this particular region had indicated that deposits of iron were plentiful also. Coal and steel were the makings of a civilization, mused Conor. Now if they could just live long enough to be able to establish an unplanned colony with what they had.

Conor flew northwest and was soon over an open plain where herds of large and small creatures grazed. The plain was fairly wide, and Conor turned northward toward the sheen of water and the cliff, which had turned to follow the river behind them. This southern-facing section of the fast-approaching cliff had a sizable lake to the east and forest running through rocky ridges to the west for several kilometers to a narrow gap that continued westward. The cliff face on the other side of the gap turned southward toward the ocean.

There was a large depression in the cliff face above where the forest and lake met. Conor flew toward the depression, meaning to set down. There was a waterfall bisecting the depression into two halves and fell a good fifty meters to the lake below. The depression ran nearly four kilometers from east to west and was nearly two hundred meters deep and a good fifty meters tall where the river cut through. The cliff face rose upward for another two hundred meters above the upper lip of the depression, then sloped away. Trees lined those upper slopes till they met the snow line of the mountain peaks above. The lower part of the depression ran fairly smooth and flat. It was as if someone had taken a huge knife and made a massive horizontal cut into the cliff face.

"Defensible," stated Staff Sergeant Rosenstein.

"Anasazi," replied Sergeant Adachi.

"What?" queried Conor.

"Anasazi Indians were a North American tribe that built cliff dwellings for protection," Sergeant Adachi answered. "There are caves back there near where the river comes from. Might find all sorts of useful mineral deposits back in there, and it would make a great shelter if worse comes to worst."

"Good idea," agreed Rosenstein. "Plenty of water if it's drinkable. I'll get some samples."

"It'll take a chopper to get up here," stated Lieutenant Commander Raybourn.

"Nothing a little Q-5 can't take care of, sir." Staff Sergeant Rosenstein grinned, referring to the highly explosive plastic charges Marines carried. One hundred grams of Q-5 was equivalent to a full kilogram of the once-popular C-4. The latter had been used for generations until the discovery of Q-5 nearly two centuries ago, which was even more stable and carried more of a punch.

"That and some engineers," responded Seaman Green.

"An elevator with the waterfall as an alternate source of power," Conor observed.

"The plains below might make good farmland if we can keep the local wildlife away," added Sergeant Adachi.

The implications of that statement went through Conor's mind as he thought about the encounter with the velociraptor. This world was both beautiful and sudden death to the unwary. A high perch to watch over and to retreat to in a time of need was a good idea. He would have to discuss it with Gunnery Sergeant Zander upon their return and possibly enter it into his report to the executive officer.

"Good thought if we have anything to plant," said the lieutenant commander. "All right, you've sold me. Let's get some samples and video footage of what we have here. After that, we'll probably continue with our recon of the area and return to base camp."

They separated into two teams. The staff sergeant and lieutenant commander went down to the river, while the other two went further back into the cleft. Staff Sergeant Rosenstein dipped sample bottles into the water, sealed them, and placed them in the pouch on her belt. Then she climbed to the top of a boulder with the video recorder, stood, and did a three-hundred-and-sixty-degree scan of the depression.

Conor walked over to the edge that overlooked the lake and river valley. It was an impressive sight looking out over the country below. The lake below was a sapphire blue with a green sea of foliage beyond it. *Beautiful and dangerous,* he thought as he looked down at the now dry blood that covered the front of his body armor and camouflage. He heard a footstep to his right and looked into Rosenstein's clear, liquid, dark eyes, and a smile touched her lips.

"I haven't thanked you for coming to my rescue," she said.

"No need to, Staff Sergeant," he responded lowly.

"Thank you anyway," countered the staff sergeant.

"Weren't you smiling last night when you shot me?" asked Conor.

"Of course. It's not often I get the opportunity to shoot a lieutenant commander," she replied with a twinkle in her eye and a demure smile on her lips.

They stood there for a moment gazing into each other's eyes as the world went on without them. It seemed like an eternity had passed as they stood there. They were interrupted by reality as Sergeant Adachi's voice came over the comm.

"Looks like a nesting area somewhere near the east side," said Adachi's voice.

Conor looked east and saw a large form fly out over the lake far below.

"What is it?" asked Conor.

"Pteranodon," stated Staff Sergeant Rosenstein.

While they flew back to base camp, Conor thought he saw a red flash out of the corner of his eye. He circled back, but whatever it was had vanished into the ocean of lush green vegetation.

CHAPTER 7

The encampment was bustling with activity as Conor and his crew approached the headquarters tent north of the guard tower. Crates and containers were piled near the gate of the encampment leading to the shuttle. Someone had built a cairn of stones with a makeshift grill top to lay over the top just in front of the mess tent. Gunny Zander stepped out of headquarters as they came to the entrance. His face had a huge grin on it as he looked Conor up and down. Dried blood covered his cammies and had soaked through to his skin. He had a definite need to rid himself of the itchy feeling developing and the stink of his day's exertions.

"It looks like you've been through the wars, sir," stated the gunnery sergeant as he saluted.

"I could use a good bath and change of clothes," returned the lieutenant commander as he returned the salute.

"That's already been arranged if you want to step inside, sir," stated Gunnery Sergeant Zander.

"Thank you, Gunny," Conor replied.

"The showers are reserved for the rest of your crew," stated Gunnery Sergeant Zander. "Chow's in thirty mikes over at the mess tent."

"Roger that, Gunny," quipped Staff Sergeant Rosenstein as she nodded to the other two from the recon team.

Conor watched as they all took off to gather uniforms and head toward the showers, then looked at the gunnery sergeant and said, "I'd like a complete autopsy of the two beasts that are in the med carriers of the chopper ASAP if you would, Gunny."

"Problems, sir?" questioned Gunny.

"Staff Sergeant Rosenstein and Seaman Green said that they're velociraptors and that they're smart," stated Lieutenant Commander Raybourn. "I'd like Lieutenant Commander Hollinger and her team to provide an estimate of how intelligent they are."

"I'll attend to that, sir," replied the gunnery sergeant, looking back at the helicopter as if making sure danger would not spring forth. Assured, he indicated the headquarters or HQ tent and the waiting arrangements. He then continued, "I'll have it shipped up to the *New Horizon* with the shuttle. It's nearly loaded and will be going topside in the next couple of hours."

"Thank you, Gunny," replied Lieutenant Commander Raybourn.

"My pleasure, sir," stated the gunnery sergeant.

Conor paused and asked, "Any immediate problems that I need to be informed on?"

"Nothing we couldn't handle, sir," stated Gunnery Sergeant Zander.

The lieutenant commander entered the HQ tent where a luxurious lukewarm shower and fresh camouflage uniform awaited. Refreshed, he walked with the gunnery sergeant toward the mess tent where his three teammates already stood waiting.

A heavenly odor emanated from that rude stove top that Conor had noted earlier where a large pot held some sort of stew. They picked up trays and took their place in line. Chief Petty Officer Yap ladled some stew on to the tray. A biscuit came next then some sort of fruit. Finding an empty spot at one of the tables, the recon team sat down. The stew contained meat, mushrooms, and some sort of vegetable in a thick gravy.

The fruits of the land were revealing themselves to the wayfarers and seemed to be welcoming them to this new world. The crew members assigned to the base camp had been busy the last couple of weeks. Crates with self-contained refrigeration units were stacked at the main gate, ready to be loaded into the waiting shuttle. The crew of the *New Horizon* would be ecstatic over the fresh food that they would soon receive. It was a fitting reward after the misadventure that had brought them permanently to a system beyond the reach of rescue from their home world.

"So we'll be able to live off the land if we have to?" inquired Lieutenant Commander Raybourn.

"I will have to monitor everyone to ensure they're getting everything they require for a few years," replied Chief Petty Officer Caroline deLang as she sat down and joined the conversation. "However, the prospects look good that a person could survive on the local produce."

"Good!" stated Conor. "So they have most of the harvest stored aboard the shuttle?"

"Chief Pennington's been attending to that, sir," stated Gunnery Sergeant Zander. "She's been working all day making sure the containers are properly distributed and stowed."

"Sounds like we'll have a fairly good load to go up," the Conor observed.

"Rumor has it that the crew upstairs is looking forward to the fresh rations," replied the gunnery sergeant.

"Lieutenant Joshi is looking forward to receiving the velociraptor bodies to examine aboard the *New Horizon*. His evaluation should be sent to you inside of three hours of its arrival on board," interjected Caroline deLang.

"Thank you, Chief," acknowledged Conor.

"You're welcome," returned the chief medic. Then she asked. "How was the expedition?"

"You mean other than being almost lunch for a meat-eating dinosaur?" Staff Sergeant Rosenstein grinned.

"Well, there is that," said Caroline, smiling at the rough humor.

"It went well. The land looks fertile with plenty of wildlife," stated Conor. "It looks like we'll be able to eat if nothing else. Seaman Green discovered coal, and he assures me that it'll be easy to make plenty of concrete with the resources that he located."

"Might need that to build some sturdy walls," stated Caroline.

"There's a sizable depression in the cliff face with a waterfall that Staff Sergeant Rosenstein and Sergeant Adachi thought would be very defendable," said Lieutenant Commander Raybourn. "They suggested it as the place to build. Defendable, ready water source, and the possibility of an alternate power source."

"Alternate power source?" asked Caroline.

"Hydroelectric turbines installed in the waterfall," said Conor.

"Sounds good," injected Gunny Zander.

"How's Abrams doing?" asked Conor.

"He's doing as well as a guy with a broken leg with twenty-seven stitches running up that leg can be expected," Caroline deLang replied. "He ate just before you arrived and went back to lie down."

"You're keeping him on planet?" inquired Conor.

"The leg will heal better in the gravity field, and we don't want to add any other stress to it, like shuttling him up to the ship," stated Caroline.

Later that evening, Conor sat in the headquarters tent writing his report. The sounds of the planet invaded with a disquieting effect. Far off came the sound of some huge beast as it screamed in agonizing pain as a massive roar of victory cut it off like a knife. A shiver ran down Conor's spine, though he questioned whether it was from the unknown dangers or the thrill the adventure offered.

A bleep interrupted his thoughts, bringing his attention back to his computer display. The reports and observations of his recon team were in his in basket. He read them over and attached them to his report with annotations.

Another bleep drew his attention as he finished. It was the preliminary autopsy report. He read it over and whistled. "More intelligent than a wolf and possibly as smart as a chimpanzee. Olfactory suggests a keen sense of smell." He skimmed over the rest of the report because he had a good idea what their physical abilities were. Definitely not something to have hunting you without body armor and lots of weapons available. They were walking—or, more appropriately, running—death on two legs. Conor sat back, thoughtfully wondering.

"Hattie," said Conor.

"Operating. Lieutenant Commander," replied Hattie.

"Analysis of the creatures of this planet," stated Conor.

"Define parameters," said Hattie.

"Are the creatures on this planet Earth-type dinosaurs?" inquired Conor.

"Not enough information to make a definitive conclusion," stated Hattie.

"With the information known so far, what is the percentage of chance that they are?" asked Conor.

"The observed types and skeletal comparison make the chances well over 90 percent. DNA comparisons may make it 100 percent," declared Hattie.

"Do you have the DNA sequencings of dinosaurs from Earth?" questioned Conor.

"My files contain the partial DNA sequencings of over one thousand different species from that time era," stated Hattie.

"Partial?" delved Conor.

"There are no complete DNA sequencings for creatures from that era in time," returned Hattie.

"Understood. Have they completed the sequencing on any of the animals we've encountered so far on the planet?" asked Conor.

"Dr. Joshi has not completed his analysis yet, Lieutenant Commander," relayed Hattie.

"Please inform Lieutenant Joshi I would like those results as soon as possible," said Conor.

"Yes, sir. Your message is sent," Hattie informed Conor.

"Please display my report," said Conor.

He spent another hour finishing up and making recommendations, then uploaded the report to the *New Horizon* for the attention of Commander Blankenship.

He sat back weary as midnight approached. A glass of amber liquid appeared near his right hand resting on the desk seemingly out of nowhere. He sat gazing at it for a second before looking up at the gunny, who stood there smiling down at him.

"Late night?" was all the gunnery sergeant said.

"Yes, it is," stated Conor as he sat further back and realized the "sir" had not been attached to that question. Raising an eyebrow, he asked the unspoken question.

"Everyone's asleep except the watches. It's just us," answered Gunnery Sergeant Zander lowly. "And you look like you need a nightcap."

"Not exactly standard fair," stated Conor. "And illegal aboard a United Systems warship."

"We're not exactly a US warship," Gunnery Sergeant Zander replied seriously. "I generally have a case or two on board for special occasions even then."

"I see," Conor replied.

"You've earned the respect of the Marines in the last few months," stated the gunny. "Bottoms up."

Conor picked up the glass and took a sip of the smoky liquid it contained. It burned with a soothing calm as he swallowed. The wave of tension drained from his body as he swallowed another mouthful and eyed the gunny speculatively. A moment passed as he sat there looking the gunny in the eye.

"Will you have one with me?" asked Conor.

"Don't mind if I do." The gunny grinned. "But just one more for me and you. We're not here to get drunk, just a little celebration on your christening."

"What do you mean?" asked Conor.

"I'd like to thank you for saving the staff sergeant today," Gunnery Sergeant Zander stated in a low voice. "That took a lot of guts taking on a thing like that with just a knife."

"It was missing a forearm, and it had a few holes in it before I got that close, Gunny," said Conor.

"I know that," said the gunnery sergeant. "I also know it took a lot to do what you did, and it will not be forgotten. The staff sergeant is one of my best and has a lot of potential to be one hell of a Marine."

Conor nodded then asked, "Something between you and the staff sergeant?"

"Oh, hell no, sir." The gunnery sergeant chuckled. "Besides, Chief Pennington would shoot me and string me up for the local wildlife if she ever suspected there was."

"Oh!" Conor smiled. "I didn't know."

"You and everyone else aren't supposed to know." Gunnery Sergeant Zander grinned. "But now that we're stranded, it's all right to let the cat out of the bag."

"I suspect there will be no way of preventing that now," said Conor. "However, your secret is safe with me until the two of you decide to go public."

"I already knew that," responded the gunny. "Speaking of which, you'd best watch out for Shiran."

"Shiran?" asked Conor, confused.

"Staff Sergeant Rosenstein." The gunny winked. "She had her eyes on you even before you went and did that whole hero thing of saving her life."

Conor blinked. He was currently in a relationship with Jacqueline Vinet, though that had been put on hold for the last few months. With the establishment of a colony, he was hoping to renew that relationship. However, what had brought them together was their mutual participation in the FTL project. Other than that, their interests were widely separated. Conor shook his head. Only time would tell how the future would play out. He smiled as he thought of what the French would say, "C'est la vie." Such is life.

The drink had done its work while he sat there. His eyes drooped, and his muscles relaxed. With a nod at the gunny, he rose from his chair and went over to his cot. Stripping down to his briefs, he hung the cammies on a nearby hook and lay down. The last thing he remembered as his head touched the small pillow was the roar of one of the beasts that inhabited the new home they had found.

CHAPTER 8

For the last three days, Commander Hadden Blankenship had been planetside. The sleek angles of *New Horizon*'s stealth planning was compromised, and apparent, as they approached. The repaired sections caused intermittent image returns to the shuttle's lidar. The shuttle slowed as it made its final approach to the *New Horizon*'s forward docking bay. The hatch at the nose of *New Horizon* was open, and the pilot applied thrusters to make the shuttle's long axis match the rotational spin prior to applying thrusters to back into the bay and be clamped in. The bay's hatch closed, and the exit port extended to the passenger door of the shuttle.

The commander floated to the hatch then down the gangway into the main passageway of the *New Horizon* to be met by Lieutenant Commander Conor Raybourn. They moved slowly through the boatswain's locker then the bridge area located behind the shuttle bay. Past the bridge, Hadden Blankenship and Conor entered officer's country. The senior staff were already present as the commander and lieutenant commander took their seats.

"Welcome, ladies and gentlemen," greeted Commander Blankenship. Those present responded to his greetings, and the commander continued, "I called all of you here because a decision needs to be made, and I'm not comfortable making it."

"What decision is that, sir?" queried Lieutenant Commander Martinez impatiently.

"Colonization," responded the commander.

"What?" demanded Martinez heatedly.

"Lieutenant Commander Martinez, we can't return to Earth any time during our lifetimes even if the FTL was working. Our option is colonization. I want a plan on how to go about settling the planet," said Commander Blankenship.

"We have the crew to set up living quarters on the planet," stated Lieutenant Commander Martinez defiantly.

"That's the problem, Mr. Martinez." Blankenship frowned.

"What is?" demanded Martinez.

"The crew," stated the commander. "Once on the planet, are they really 'the crew' or are they individuals working to create a colony?"

"What do you mean? Of course, they're the crew," retorted Martinez.

"I have no intention of becoming a monarch over these people for the rest of my life, Mr. Martinez," declared Commander Blankenship.

"They need to be free individuals," stated Lieutenant Commander Hollinger. "They should be released from their military obligations at the earliest opportunity."

"Then what?" demanded Martinez.

"Then they create a colony of their own choosing," replied Lieutenant Vinet, who was acting operations officer, or OPS boss, while Conor was acting executive officer.

"A free society is more creative and motivated," stated Lieutenant Commander Raybourn.

"So what do we do? Tell them they're all free to go to the planet and die while we abandon the *New Horizon*?" sneered Martinez.

"Tell the crew that we are going to set up the basics for a sustainable colony," replied Commander Blankenship patiently. "Then for those who wish to be released from most of their military obligations, if they choose. There will always be the need for a strong military arm on the planet to defend the colony from the beasts, I suspect, and some will choose to serve in those capacities. The ship itself can be managed with two weeks of required service a year from all the present crew. However, the military will be answerable to the civilian government established."

"I agree," stated Lieutenant Commander Hollinger.

"So where do we establish this colony?" asked Lieutenant Gataki.

"Hattie," the commander called out.

"Operating. Commander," came the reply from the artificial intelligence or AI.

"I think Lieutenant Commander Raybourn's recommendation has merit. Hattie, please run the videos and information on the cleft," stated Commander Blankenship as the room darkened, and the videos of the cleft were displayed on the blank bulkhead. The video ran, displaying the spaciousness of the crevice with a ready water supply that could be turned into a power source. The merits of the lake as a landing field for the shuttles and longboats and the open plains beside the lake for fields were readily apparent. The commander asked for a vote from his department heads. The proposal to settle the cleft and release the crew of most of the military obligations passed with one dissenter. Lieutenant Commander Martinez was angry, but in the end, he chose to be among the first to be relieved of most of his military obligations.

Later in the day, Commander Hadden Blankenship turned over his bridge watch to Lieutenant JG, or Junior Grade, Kisimba. Unstrapping himself from the command seat, he floated to the aft hatch and left the bridge. He pulled himself down the passageway slowly until he reached the medical bay. Entering, he floated over to the table where the captain lay. The chief medical officer had already removed the shrapnel that had been lodged in her frontal lobe, but the intrusion and subsequent surgery had left her in a coma. Commander Blankenship gazed down at her as he gently took her hand. He had served with her for nearly ten years on three different commands, and there was a close bond of friendship. As he stood there, Lieutenant Commander Hollinger, the chief medical officer, approached and spoke.

"Good day, Commander," greeted Bess Hollinger.

"Good day, Lieutenant Commander," replied the XO. "How is she?"

"She's doing as well as can be expected," confessed Bess.

"There's no chance?" asked Hadden Blankenship.

"No. There's just too much damage," stated Bess emphatically.

"Options?" countered Commander Blankenship.

"I'm hesitant to suggest it, but...," began the medical officer as she trailed off.

"Yes?" Hadden Blankenship encouraged.

"Lieutenant Joshi was working with a team back on Earth prior to receiving this assignment. They were experimenting with cloned cells, quantum chips, and nanotechnology," said the chief medical officer. "The procedure involves inserting a blank AI chip into the damaged area and utilizing nanites and cloned cells to make the necessary connections between neurons and the chip. In this way, the AI chip can take up the functions of the damaged area."

"How well did it work?" inquired the XO. "Will she regain consciousness, and will she be capable as before?"

"As I said, the process is experimental," stated Lieutenant Commander Hollinger. "She may never regain consciousness, and even if she does, she'll never be the same as before."

"But she'll at least be able to live a life if she does regain consciousness," insisted Hadden Blankenship.

"Perhaps. Perhaps not," replied Bess Hollinger. "She may never regain consciousness, she may only be capable of the most basic functions, or she may be able to interact on a higher level. However, she'll never be the captain we've known."

Hadden Blankenship stood there for several minutes as he considered the information. He looked again at the face of the woman he had known for a long time. There was a peaceful look upon her face as she lay with her eyes closed as though she was only asleep. Torn and conflicted, he finally looked at the medical officer and made his decision.

"Do it," he stammered in anguish.

"Are you sure?" asked Bess.

"I can't leave her like this," murmured Hadden in grief. "Yes, do it." He then turned and left the medical bay.

Commander Hadden Blankenship was wrestling with a lot of emotions as he started ascending to his cabin. Lieutenant Commander Raybourn had done an excellent job of getting the ship back into operation, but there were items that only a shipyard overhaul could effectively repair. The crew had been prepared for an extended cruise of exploring when the incident occurred and if the FTL had worked as expected. They had expected to return to their friends and family back in Sol system in the end. Then there was the matter of the saboteur and the captain's injury. He now bore the burden of command, and it left a sour taste in his mouth. He had not wanted the burden of command at this time and had been content to follow his mentor and friend's lead. When he had signed on board under her, he had looked forward to the opportunity.

He was floating down the passageway heading to the wardroom when four bells sounded. The sound of someone shouting brought Commander Blankenship back from his thoughts as he pulled himself to a stop. The hatch to the lidar room was cracked open, and he moved closer to peer in. Chief Wheaton was there yelling at Petty Officer Guillete, who floated in the far corner of the room. He could see two other junior petty officers from electronics repair watching the confrontation with smirks on their faces.

"Who told you to work on the lidar?" demanded Chief Wheaton.

"No one," replied Petty Officer First Class Guillete.

"Then what the hell do you think you're doing?" demanded Chief Wheaton.

"I was just asking some questions and checking some of the indicators," said Guillete.

"What for? You're not a LRL-73 technician. It's not your responsibility," stated the chief.

"Then who's going to fix it?" asked Guillete.

"Well, obviously, it won't be you," sneered the chief condescendingly with the sound of snickering from the others in the lidar room.

The commander backed away from the door and floated down the passageway, shaking his head. He knew that there were problems with the electronics repair division that needed to be addressed. However, there was too much to do right now besides addressing leadership problems. He suspected that most of the electronics technicians assigned to electronics repair would not remain active once they were given a choice, and he had much bigger concerns. The meeting he was already late for being one of the biggest of those issues.

Six people sat in the wardroom when Commander Blankenship entered—Lieutenant Commander Raybourn, Lieutenant Commander Martinez, Lieutenant Commander Hollinger, Lieutenant Anderson, Gunnery Sergeant Zander, and Sergeant Adachi. Marines were stationed outside the two hatches leading into the wardroom area, and the wardroom mess cooks had been sent elsewhere. All internal comm circuits were disabled at the commander's orders, and no one was allowed to interrupt the meeting. After taking a cup of coffee from the mess area, he set it on the table so the magnetic bottom gripped its surface. He then sat down and strapped himself to a chair. The commander looked at those gathered at the table impassively as he grabbed the cup and sipped his coffee. When he finished, he set the cup down again and started the meeting.

"We have a problem, and I want to keep the number of individuals in the know limited to a small group," started Commander Blankenship. "Lieutenant Anderson, would you please give us the assessment of your investigation."

"Sir, as you ordered, I've been investigating of the FTL compartment to see what went wrong. Later, at your recommendation, I requested Gunnery Sergeant Zander for assistance, and he recommended his best demolitions expert, Sergeant Adachi, to look into what I had found," said Lieutenant Anderson.

"Which explains why the gunny and sergeant are here," added the commander.

"Yes, sir," responded Anderson. "Five of the lasers we use to induce the anomaly that allows the ship to jump through space were destroyed in an explosion. However, there's nothing in the FTL room that could have caused such an explosion."

"What? Are you saying that we were sabotaged?" demanded Lieutenant Commander Martinez.

"Yes, sir," Sergeant Adachi piped up. "After the lieutenant explained his problem to me, I did an analysis and located the spot where the explosion originated. There were high traces of Q-5 residue there and would have caused the damage Lieutenant Anderson just described."

"We found what was left of the detonator," added Gunnery Sergeant Zander. "It was remote-controlled."

"Probably set to activate when the FTL was initiated," added Lieutenant Anderson.

"So the FTL compartment was sabotaged," stated the commander.

"Could that explain the type of jump we experienced?" inquired Lieutenant Commander Hollinger.

"Most likely," said Lieutenant Commander Raybourn. Then he added, "Something about the explosion happening just as we initiated the anomaly is the most likely explanation."

"What it did might take years to analyze if it were even possible to understand what happened," injected his friend Lieutenant Michael Anderson.

"So why are we here?" demanded Lieutenant Commander Martinez irritably.

"Because I'm trusting that none of you are the saboteurs," said Commander Blankenship. "This information isn't to be discussed outside this room. However, keep your eyes and ears open. We need to locate this saboteur in case they attempt to try something else."

"You don't think this is over, sir?" questioned the gunnery sergeant.

"I don't know, Gunny," responded the commander. "Was the purpose accomplished, or is it to destroy this ship no matter what?"

"So we keep our eyes and ears open," stated Lieutenant Commander Hollinger.

"Can we be sure they're even on board, sir?" asked Gunnery Sergeant Zander. "The bomb did have a remote detonator. It may have been tied to another system to transmit the activation signal."

"Security was high before we got underway," stated Lieutenant Commander Raybourn.

"What hasn't been said is that I found the transmitter for the detonator in a control panel six hours ago," stated Anderson. "I was in that panel two days prior to the jump, and it hadn't been there at that time. The FTL room has been sealed to all except myself. The only personnel who have been in the FTL room since then have been myself and Sergeant Adachi."

"What? How do we know you're not lying? It may have been you who sabotaged the FTL, or it may have been your incompetence that caused the explosion, and you're trying to cover it up!" shouted Lieutenant Commander Martinez.

"That's enough, Lieutenant Commander," growled Commander Blankenship as the others in the room looked at Martinez in shock.

"If we go down that route, we start suspecting everyone," injected Conor.

The commander nodded. He said, "Now you know everything I do, ladies and gentlemen. There's someone on board who sabotaged the FTL, which means that person is willing to die to accomplish their mission. We don't know why or what that mission is, but we have no guarantees that it won't be tried again. Does everyone understand that this information doesn't go outside this room until we can be sure we've apprehended the perpetrator?"

The nods and "Yes, sirs" were unanimous, if grudging. Commander Hadden Blankenship wondered what the future would bring as he dismissed the group.

CHAPTER 9

The convoy of ATVs topped the last rise that overlooked the large lake. The cleft with its magnificent waterfall was close. Lieutenant Commander Raybourn guided the ATVs with the recon helicopter around the worst obstructions so they would be west of the lake. They would arrive at the cliff face in about thirty minutes if all went well. He contacted the base camp to inform them.

"Base camp, we'll be arriving in thirty," stated Conor. "Have the longboat lift in twenty."

"Roger that. Chief Pennington will lift in twenty," came Petty Officer Catalina Ramirez's voice. "How are you on juice?"

"ATVs are at 70 percent charge. Chopper at about 40 percent," responded Conor.

"You made good time, sir," returned Catalina.

"The terrain was rugged, but there were plenty of passes around those areas. Most likely game trails," replied Conor. "Lead ATV says that there was a coal outcrop about five kilometers back on our route. It should be annotated on the automap."

"It is, sir," Catalina confirmed. "The telescope's spectroanalysis located iron deposits approximately twenty klicks east of here. We'll know more once we do a recon and take some samples."

They arrived at the base of the cleft ten minutes earlier than expected and secured the area. Conor contacted base camp, and shortly, the roar of the longboat passed overhead. They watched as it rose over the cliff and reappeared further down at the east end of the lake. It banked and started descending toward the surface of the lake. Its undercarriage touched the surface just as it passed the far shore.

The longboat sent up streamers of wash as it landed on the lake after its short flight from the base camp. A few minutes after coming to a halt, it jerked forward again as the pilot applied thrusters to propel it toward the waiting ATVs and helo. Coming to rest near the rocky shore, it extended a ramp to the beach. The pteranodons that had been fishing on the lake had all taken flight as the longboat had made its landing and were making it known that they were not happy with this new state of affairs.

They hooked up the helo first for its charge as the ATVs set up a perimeter around the longboat. Chief Tami Pennington appeared at the hatch and walked down the ramp to the shore where Lieutenant Commander Raybourn and Gunnery Sergeant Zander stood.

"Good flight, Boats?" asked Evan Zander.

"Too short," responded Tami. "But fun."

"How long will the longboats and shuttles last?" asked Conor.

"They're rated for fifty years. But that's with normal use, sir," returned Tami.

"Then we might only get a little over half that time if we're constantly using them?" Conor questioned.

"Possibly, sir," said Tami Pennington. "The choppers and ATVs are another story. They may last that long barring accidents, but I suspect that they'll see much more use than the longboats and shuttles."

"Losing the choppers and ATVs on this planet may not bode well," interjected Evan Zander.

"Then we'd better become established and capable of repairing them or replacing them during that time," stated Conor.

"Not asking for much, are you, sir?" questioned Tami, smiling.

"I have high hopes," returned Conor.

"We should have brought some combat engineers on the mission," said Tami.

"Wasn't called for. We were only supposed to test the FTL and explore the Alpha Centauri A system," responded Conor. "On the other hand, with the expertise assigned to this ship, I'm sure we'll make do if we all pull together."

The next few months involved a lot of hard work as the unintentional colonists set up for a permanent stay on the planet. A set of four elevators were erected first to enable ease of transportation to the cleft. With the elevators operating, an initial base was set up on the ledge for the reluctant colonists. The living accommodations were primitive but preferable to the zero-G conditions on the *New Horizon*. Six prefabs, eight large tents, many smaller tents, and a cave against the rear wall were set up as living quarters.

Most of the crew had decided to accept the commander's offer to release them from their military obligations. In turn, they would only be required to serve two weeks out of every Earth year to help maintain the *New Horizon* in an operationally ready status. The crew was established on the cleft in short order once the elevators were completed. Those who chose to remain in an active status numbered fifty-seven. The commander, Conor, Michael, and over two dozen from the Navy side chose to do so along with thirty Marines, who composed the larger portion of the fifty-seven, since they all chose to stay active under the guidance of the gunnery sergeant.

The hull technicians and ship's factory sent down six vehicles designed for transporting, in addition to the six ATVs the *New Horizon* had originally carried. They had also designed and fabricated two refrigerated trailers and six fair-sized cement mixers.

The deposits of coal and iron they had located, along with the stone and clay that was readily available near the cliff base, provided a ready source of building materials. A foundry, lumber mill, and brick, cement, and stone works were quickly established near the base of the cleft. As they grew in size and production, more resources were devoted to building the stores and apartments on the cleft, along with construction of the Marine Complex and piers along the lakefront. The Marines had taken up the responsibility of building over seven kilometers of the perimeter fence required to enclose two sides of the ten square kilometers that was to be referred to as the Compound, with the cliff and lakefront composing the other two sides.

With their freedom came a need for some form of government. Jacqueline Vinet led a movement that established the colony as a constitutional republic. However, when a vote was held, Felipe Martinez was nominated to be the president of the small colony for the next five planetary years. Martinez had also taken over management of the foundry with release from service, which left him in a position of power over many aspects of the colony.

Even though Conor assisted and voted for Jacqueline, he had not been interested in politics. His interests at that time had more anterior motives because he wanted to be closer to Vinet. He spent five months with her during that time. Conor attributed their parting to the fact that his interests did not coincide with hers. Vinet appeared to have more political ambitions, while he was more interested in exploring their new home.

With their newfound freedom on the surface of the planet, they found that they had a need for someone to keep the peace. The number of assaults and brawls at the colony site had increased dramatically as disagreements over work and companionship arouse. During the last year, there had been five known suicides and two other deaths that were attributed to accidents. There were also several accidents that caused setbacks but only minor injuries. Martinez had simply wanted the Marines to take over the job, but the gunny had given him an emphatic no, stating that the Marines were there to provide security and not police the population. The ship's chief master-at-arms, Chief Petty Officer Upton, on the other hand, had found himself jobless with almost no crew on board the *New Horizon* to watch over. Upton chose to give up his military obligations and join the colonists. A vote was held, and James Upton found that he was now the elected sheriff of the colony.

Work on shops and apartments had begun almost immediately after arrival at the cleft. Shops were built on the ground level of the ledge with apartments above. The shops so far included two restaurants, three hairdressers, a distillery, a meat locker, and a clinic, which lined the riverfront. A wide boardwalk of brick was laid along the edge and the river to the shop fronts that lined them. A short cast-iron wall was built around the edge and riverfront after a few near accidents. With the availability of housing, people moved from their temporary quarters to more permanent residences.

Within nine months, there had been enough apartments for over half of the crew with preference given to couples when new apartments came available. Some of the apartments were sleeping four at present, but it was better than sleeping in one of the large tents with eighty people. Power for the shops and apartments was supplied from the longboat or shuttle parked at the pier that had been completed after the first month.

Conor had been fortunate in that one prefab that had been designated as the MILDET, or military detachment prefab, and he shared it with Commander Blankenship, his friend Lieutenant Michael Anderson, and Ensign Dominic Sobolov, who had all chosen to remain on active duty. The prefab had two bedrooms and could sleep up to eight, which meant that it was two to a room. Conor shared one bedroom with the commander, who was rarely there, while Michael and Dominic shared the other.

Lieutenant Commander Raybourn had been assigned planetary operations by the commander, which at this point involved working mostly with the Marines. They had accomplished the perimeter fences within three months using wooden poles, which were to be replaced with stainless steel poles once the foundry was capable of supplying them. Currently, he was working on building the two-story Marine Complex, which was going quickly with nearly a third of the Marines working around the clock on its construction. The Marines' other duties involved security of the colony and piers. They also kept the foliage trimmed for fifty meters on each side of the perimeter fence. The Marines were also responsible for hunting for meat to supply the colony by keeping the meat locker on the cleft stocked.

Another load of yellowish brick had arrived on the elevator, and Conor watched as the small truck drove up the yellowish brick boardwalk along the riverfront. The yellow boardwalk along the riverfront already extended to the front of the clinic entrance near the back wall of the cleft where two colonists were working. Ezekiel Yap was in front of the corner shop named the Overlook overlooking the edge and where the boardwalk turned upriver. He was helping Brad Guillete lay red-dyed bricks over the cement front of his new establishment. Ezekiel had already finished the interior in red brick with beams of stained wood to give it what Ezekiel called aesthetics.

Conor had to agree that it was more pleasing to the eye than cement walls and that the food did seem to taste better.

Conor entered the Overlook with Ezekiel trailing him to the rear table. Conor sat down and ordered the special. The special turned out to be seared strips of meat over rice and vegetables with a sauce swirled over the top.

"This was breakfast?" inquired Conor.

"No, eggs, and you generally do not want pancakes," stated Ezekiel.

"True. This will do. Thanks, Ezekiel," replied Conor.

Ezekiel was about to leave, then turned back to Conor. He hesitated, then stated, "Ms. Jacqueline has not been to breakfast with you for several days."

"She decided to pursue a different relationship," Conor said after a moment. "We have some differences that seem irreconcilable."

Ezekiel nodded and was about to turn away when he looked at Conor and suggested, "Might I suggest something to the lieutenant commander?"

"Of course, Ezekiel. What is it?" asked Conor.

"The lieutenant commander needs a day off," confessed Ezekiel.

Conor thought about that for a moment, then replied, "You may be right, Ezekiel."

"Good. I have your lunch packed and down at the Marine Complex already," stated Ezekiel.

"What?" said Conor, confused.

"The gunnery sergeant said a day over on the east side of the cleft should not be too exciting, and no one has explored it yet," replied Ezekiel distractedly. "The chopper is waiting and along with a small detachment of Marines as an escort. They, too, need some time off."

Lieutenant Commander Conor Raybourn had been working for several weeks, and a break from routine did sound good. Since a bridge to traverse the river that cut their new cleft home in half was only in the plans, Ezekiel's idea of a brief outing should prove worthwhile. When Conor finished his meal, he went to the Marine Complex, where the gunnery sergeant acted as if the plan had been

Conor's in the first place. The gunnery sergeant chose Staff Sergeant Rosenstein, along with Staff Sergeant Rusu and Sergeant Hall, to take a short hop. The express purpose was to recon the cleft across the river from the growing city since it had not been investigated thoroughly. The lunch basket in the medical carrier of the chopper belied the gunnery sergeant's intent.

It was a brief hop to the other side of the swiftly flowing river that poured over the edge of the cleft. Conor set down in the middle of the expanse that composed the other half of the cleft. They hopped out as Conor turned off the engine and allowed the rotors to slow to a halt.

He walked over to the edge that looked out over the lake below with Staff Sergeant Rosenstein. He noticed that Staff Sergeant Rusu and Sergeant Hall had neglected to follow them and were instead heading upriver toward the back of the cleft. He cocked an eye at Staff Sergeant Rosenstein, who simply looked back at him and smiled.

"No escort?" queried the lieutenant commander.

"We've never seen any wildlife over here other than pterodactyls and pteranodons. Do you think we need one, sir?" asked Staff Sergeant Rosenstein.

"I guess not. Shall we?" asked Conor as he pointed down the ledge to the east.

"Let's," said Rosenstein.

The two hiked along the edge to the east end of the cleft, talking as they went but mindful of their surroundings. Conor noticed that the other two Marines were paralleling them along the back side. They didn't see any wildlife and only a few plants growing in the barren surroundings. When they reached the far end of the cleft, Conor sat down on a convenient boulder with Rosenstein sitting next to him. The other two Marines vanished into a cave nearby, which made Conor slightly self-conscious as he looked into the waiting eyes of Staff Sergeant Rosenstein.

"My name is Shiran," she whispered.

"I know that," muttered Conor.

"I know you do," said Shiran.

"So what's the plan, Shiran?" asked Conor.

"To get to know you better," she murmured.

"I might like that. What about our escort?" muttered Conor.

"What do you think they're doing?" whispered Shiran, cocking a brow.

"I suspect not exploring that cave very far," returned Conor as he leaned over and met Shiran's lips as she pushed forward to meet his.

Conor noticed that he couldn't see the chopper or buildings across the river from their vantage point, and the dim light of the other two Marines in the cave didn't grow brighter or dimmer. They were there for nearly two hours exploring things other than the east side of the cleft. Conor and Shiran had just finished putting their body armor back on when a sizable rock flew out of the cave entrance. Fifteen minutes later, Staff Sergeant Samuel Rusu and Sergeant Amanda Hall appeared at the cave entrance and approached.

"Anything, Staff Sergeant Rusu?" asked the lieutenant commander.

"Nothing for the first hundred meters. Looks and sounds like it extends quite a bit further into the mountain, sir," replied Samuel Rusu, smiling.

"All right, why don't we go have some lunch?" said Conor.

They hiked back to the chopper down the middle of the cleft ledge. Lunch consisted of some cold cuts, chips, a berry mash, and some beer from the distillery. It was all still fresh, and the beer was cold and surprisingly good. Conor made a comment about the latter, and Samuel Rusu said Amanda Hall had found something like hops while on a hunting expedition. Conor congratulated Hall on her find and, as it turned out, her brewing skills also.

When lunch was over, Samuel Rusu wanted to check out the cave in the back of the cleft about fifty meters east of the river. He took Sergeant Hall with him and said they'd be in short order since the master sergeant wanted to know if it were large enough and cool enough to store barrels in once the east side of the cleft became available. It seemed the master sergeant was planning ahead for his expanding distillery entrepreneurial endeavor. The two Marines were not gone long before Conor's personal comm went off.

"Sir! I think you'd better see this," came Staff Sergeant Rusu's voice.

"What is it?" questioned Conor.

"Seeing is believing, sir," said the staff sergeant.

The lieutenant commander and Staff Sergeant Rosenstein headed back toward the rear wall of the depression. The two went inside and joined Staff Sergeant Rusu and Sergeant Hall, who were further back in the cave. When they were within ten meters of the wall, Conor came to an abrupt stop. There on the wall in high relief were symbols incised into the native rock. A series of unrecognizable symbols adorned the walls.

"It would appear we may not be the only ones on this planet," mused Conor.

"Yeah," responded Rusu. "But what do they look like, and are they still here?"

"That's a good question," said Shiran Rosenstein. "Let's just hope they're not anywhere around here now, and if they are, let's hope they're friendly."

CHAPTER 10

Qu'Loo'Oh' had been living in the region for seventeen seasons since she left her tribe. She had made the journey to the sacred island during the time of the sacred hunt. She had slipped away from the hunters shortly afterward to look for the sacred caves. Upon finding the caves, she remained there, hoping the hunters believed her dead. The hunters had searched for her on that hunt but finally departed, and she never noted a search for her since.

On the sacred island was a fertile green valley with abundant foliage that provided plenty of cover. Game was abundant, and she was able to live a sedate life of contemplation, wanting for little. The ancient scrolls in the cavern temple offered her all the companionship she required. There was knowledge in the sacred caves that was not taught by the priests and scholars of her home tribe located on the mainland.

One day she had discovered scrolls and a map that described a hidden temple secreted in a sacred place back in her homeland. With care, she had copied them and placed them back in their hiding place for another to find, if they had the wisdom and the need to seek such knowledge. The clues that had led her to that secret cache were well hidden from those who did not know how to interpret them. Such knowledge as she now studied in her self-imposed exile would have labeled her an outcast and one to be hunted by all by the priests and scholars of her tribe, for it was forbidden to all but the initiated.

She was standing on a ridge overlooking the distant river with the cliff face looming behind her when she noted a new star in the sky. It was in the constellation of the great hunter slightly above the hatching moon. This region of stars, which was ascendant to the great foaming river that dominated much of the sky this time of year, was where legend said her distant ancestors had come from. She remembered seeing other such occurrences in the sky as this new star. There had been stars that made brief passages as they sped through the night sky, and once, even a star with a tail had stayed in the night skies for months. After watching this new star for some time, she decided to check on the new star's position every day.

After each setting sun, she looked for the new star. She was old; her eyes were not as keen as they had been in her youth, but she was sure that the new star was moving. It appeared to be heading quickly eastward, until one day it took up a position above the mountain on the other side of the river valley. The new star defied everything she knew about stars as it moved in the night sky. She preened her dull red feathers with the interspersing of white, indicating her great age, as she thought about what it could mean.

Then a score of talon counts later, she heard a noise like thunder and saw a huge object that could not be a flier circle the river valley. It was at least as large as a long-necked herd beast her people keep for food and shiny like the copper, silver, and gold that her people used to make ornaments, spears, and holy items. It appeared triangular from underneath with a pointed snout at the front with the base of the triangle forming the trailing end. Whatever the object was, it had come to earth too far down the river for her to contemplate the journey. She would wait and watch since she knew the dangers of traveling alone even in this peaceful river valley without the protection of her tribe.

Half a moon cycle later, a noisy object flew over the foliage above her head, making her crouch in fear as she watched it turn and follow the cliff wall northward. She ran as fast as her creaking joints would let her to the top of the closest rise. The object's body was like a great egg with a thin tail that trailed behind it. Above the main body, something blurred, like the wings of the large four-winged insects that generally inhabited the watery areas and ate the smaller insects that swarmed there. She watched as it hovered alongside the cliff face near a depression where a waterfall sprang forth. It moved into the depression and vanished from sight. She waited patiently, and the sun moved noticeably before the object reappeared once again and followed the small river that flowed eastward from the distant lake at the bottom of the waterfall. She knew the river met up with the main river that flowed from north to south through the river valley, for she had taken that route to come here from the great water to the south.

Strange things had come to her world. Things that were from the ancient myths and legends of her people. Stars moved in the sky, and huge objects flew through the air, making great noises. A shiver ran down the length of her spine to the tip of her tail, making it twitch. She snapped her jaws in consternation as she contemplated these things. Apprehension filled her being as she remembered the old prophecy that foretold of a time when demons would roam the world, bringing destruction and ruin. She bowed her head in momentary prayer as she appealed to the great one for the prophecies to be wrong.

A moon passed, and she saw a procession of beasts she had never seen before cross the land to the base of the cliff near the lake. There were two fliers and four more that moved strangely across the plain area. Then a large flier had appeared and landed on the lake's surface, coming to rest near the others. Strange creatures had emerged from the beasts, and Qu'Loo'Oh' wondered what it could all mean.

Turning, she slowly made her way down to the bottom of the rise. A small rooter scampered across the trail as it sensed her presence too late. With a quick rush, she had her evening meal, as the killing talon on her right rear foot ripped its entrails and her jaws neatly snapped its neck. She gave homage to bless the beast for its noble sacrifice, then picked her supper up and resumed her course back toward the cliff. The ground rose steadily as she approached the cliff. Massive boulders made her wind between them as brush and trees encroached on the trail, making it more difficult to see.

Stopping at a break between two large boulders along the trail, she carefully eyed and sniffed her surroundings. Then she turned right into the narrow crevice between the two large boulders until she finally came up against the cliff face. She worked a hidden dial that had taken her a paw full of talons in days to discover when she had first arrived. The cliff face in front of her moved, revealing a door large enough to allow two of her kind to enter side by side. Entering the room beyond, she placed her burden on the table against the far wall and picked up the large branch with rushes tied to its end. Returning to the trail where she had studied her surroundings, she backtracked twenty body lengths along the trail. Then carefully backing toward the crevice, she used her broom to erase all signs of her passage to the hidden door of her home.

Reentering the cave, she laid her broom back on the table and lit an oil lamp from a glowing ember inside a small stone box. She then returned to the cave's doorway and moved a lever to the left of the doorway, causing the stone door to move back into place, effectively hiding this secret room. Moving back to the table, she took the small box with ember and placed it on top of her repast as she picked it up with her left forearm. She then picked up the oil lamp and moved over to the wooden door along the far wall. She placed her lamp on a small ledge to the right of the door, then worked the door latch and opened the door.

A massive well-lit cave that had been used by her ancestors as a place of study and worship lay beyond the doorway. Carvings and glyphs lined the upper walls and ceiling filled in with gold, while slots containing sculptures lined the walls. The floor was laid in a smooth white marble. She knew hidden openings on the outside cliff face allowed the sun's light to reach the mirrors that dispersed the lighting in this part of her home, created long ago by ancestors who understood such things. She blew out the oil lamp and left it for use upon her return this way as she stepped into the inner chamber; a hallway that led to a library of forbidden knowledge was at its far end. In a few hours, the light in this part of her home would wane as the sun set, and the only light would be the dim glow provided by the stars and moon in the night sky.

Two hallways existed at this end of the inner chamber—one to her left and another to her right. Turning right, she took ten paces and entered the hallway that ran some fifty body lengths and contained doors to twelve different living chambers. She entered the third one to the left. There was a fireplace to the right, with a nest of straw to the left, while before her stood a ledge that served as a table. Placing her meal on the table, she went over to the fireplace and brushed the overlying ashes at the center aside. Exhaling, she watched as the uncovered embers glowed into life in the dim light provided by the still open door. Then taking some tinder from a ledge to her right, she placed it on the embers and exhaled again. The tinder blackened at the edges, then burst into life as she exhaled slowly. She fed the flames with larger pieces she kept in a storage area meant for that use to the left of the fireplace as the fire's heat filled the room.

As she added wood to the fire, its warmth was pleasing to her old bones as she stood back and gazed at the dancing flames. Moving over to the door, she shut and latched it, then drew a large cloth over the front of it to help retain the heat of her fire. Hunger gnawed at her middle as she returned to the table where her repast lay. She threw the larger bones into the fire after gnawing the meat and removing their marrow. Finished and well filled, she drank from the basin. She then laid a tablet she had been studying for the last two days back on top of the table from a wall niche above the back table where she had stored it.

The tablet told of a great ship her people had sailed across the heavens from their homeland long ago, fleeing demons that had chased them. They knew they were chased by demons in another great ship and had spent generations aboard their ship trying to elude those demons. In the end, there had been a great battle between the two ships, but not before her people had taken this land for their own. From her reading, it took her ancestors more generations to make this land suitable for her kind by removing or destroying most of the original life that had existed prior to their arrival and the final battle. In the end, both ships were destroyed, though no one knew the location of the wreckage of either ship.

Qu'Loo'Oh' snapped her jaws in consternation as she thought of the time span the tablet implied. The very idea of a project that took generations was one that only the elite undertook with their building of pyramids and other such structures. A voyage aboard a ship though was another thing. The small craft that brought her to this island was not something she would want to spend her life aboard. It was unbelievable that her ancestors could have possibly spent a lifetime on such a small and frail craft. No! The space journey stated in the tablet implied that the ancestors' craft had to be enormous.

Placing the tablet back into its niche, she moved to the fire and placed a large chunk of wood into it with smaller chunks around it to warm the small cave she called home. Moving over to the far wall from the fire, she curled into her nest of straw and pulled a blanket over herself as the light coming through the clear crystal sheet in the center of the ceiling faded. Nighttime was upon the outside world, and it was good to be indoors before the large hunters roamed the forest.

As she lay there with her eyelids drooping, she contemplated the happenings of the day and shivered again at what their meanings might portend. The priests of her home on the faraway mainland warned of the days when those who were not like them would return, and death would walk the land. Could these be the days foretold? The nightmare would haunt her as she slept.

CHAPTER 11

The rainy season was ending, and the cold was abating. There had been snow flurries a few times, but nothing remained on the ground. Topping the ridge, Conor came to a halt and took a deep breath. The body armor and other gear weren't as noticeable as when he had started his training with the Marines several months ago. Staff Sergeant Rosenstein joined him as they surveyed the area outside the perimeter fence.

Nearly an Earth year had passed since their arrival in the system, and much had been accomplished. The lake lay below with a shuttle, and a longboat moored at the pier that extended out into the lake. Sturdy buildings stood there with a thoroughfare leading to the cliff face, where the elevators rose up to the crevice where a town was steadily growing along its edge.

Shiran's hand found its way into Conor's, and her cool fingers curled around his. He looked at her tanned face, and a smile formed on her full lips as she pretended not to notice his attention. Her long raven-black hair was swept back into a bun that fit beneath her helmet. The sun had risen only a couple of hours prior, and it looked like it would be a beautiful day. They could hear the sounds of the growing city in the distance as they stood admiring the hard work that all the hapless colonists had achieved.

"Looks good, Conor," she breathed.

"Yes, it does," he replied.

"We've done quite a bit," Shiran stated as she swept her hand toward the cliff base.

Conor looked over at her and replied, "Yes, we have."

She blushed at the double meaning implied by those simple words and moved into his embrace. The body armor they were wearing interfered with any serious intentions either of them entertained. He kissed her questing lips deeply, sinking into the spell of the moment that she had woven. When they drew apart, they studied the surrounding foliage that encompassed the ridge they stood upon.

Something big moved there, and an apatosaurus stuck its head out of the foliage. Since the colonists had established themselves, most of the carnivores had learned to avoid the area around the cliff base near the lake. Conor liked to inspect the surrounding area once a week for his own peace of mind. They started down the trail leading toward the open fields where corn, wheat, and soybeans were growing, protected by a ten-meter-high electrified fence that lay two klicks away and provided a half a klick open area around the lower part of the city. A longboat and shuttle were docked at the pier there, providing power to the city and transport up to the *New Horizon*.

Yes, the colony was growing. Commander Blankenship had freed all crew members who wished of most of their military obligations to form a colony. Many of them had and were only required to serve two weeks an Earth year to maintain the *New Horizon*. The commander, on the other hand, chose to retain his commission and the command of the *New Horizon*, stating that he wished to take care of the old lady who had seen them this far. Only essential systems were kept online, while others were either in layup or utilized at a minimal capacity. A crew of ten were sent up every week for a two-week tour of duty, to maintain the ship and monitor systems for possible threats to the colony. This meant there were at least twenty personnel at all times serving on board doing their two weeks. One group of ten serving their first week and the other group of ten serving their second week.

Conor decided to remain active military because he felt an obligation for the security of the colony. All the Marines also remained on active duty, providing security for the colony and doing exploration when required. In all, there were fifty-seven crew members who decided to remain active, devoting their time to ship care and building ground installations to support the ship and colony.

They passed through the gate onto the well-worn straight path that lead through the fields, walking briskly toward the rapidly approaching buildings that formed the lower city. Clay had been discovered early on after their move to the crevice, and Karimah Mirza worked wonders in creating a furnace that was producing nearly two thousand bricks a day with her assistants. A cement works and steel foundry had quickly followed, and the foundations of the city's beginning were laid down. Even now, a glass and ceramics factory was starting up beside the brick works.

Virtual blueprints had been provided, and the population voted on the best concept design. The riverfront and ledge area between the elevator and riverfront were reserved for shops and restaurants. Living quarters were being built on the second and third floors, while the fourth and fifth levels were currently under construction.

Halfway to the buildings, they passed Georgia Cambi. The botanist was in the fields running tests on the soil and examining the soybeans in the field. She paused in her work and waved at them as they waved back. They found out early on that Terran crops left unguarded attracted the herbivores, and they had to take precautions like the fence to keep the fields safe.

They reached the first buildings and turned onto the main thoroughfare that led to the elevator, and as they walked down the thoroughfare, they greeted other colonists. There was a wait at the base of the elevator, and the two picked up coffee, at least that was what everyone was calling it, at the clay works. Conor's friend Lieutenant Michael Anderson was waiting with a few others near the gate to the elevator as they approached.

"Morning, Conor," greeted Michael.

"Morning, Mike," Conor returned. "What brought you down from the cleft?"

"Would you believe Martinez wanted some advice at the foundry?" came the reply. Then Michael added, "Somehow, he discovered I knew a little bit about the tool development and the processing of steel."

Conor cocked an eyebrow at Michael. It was well-known that the president of the colony still held animosity toward the former

FTL crew. A good part of that ill will was because he had a wife and two children back on Earth whom he would never see again. There was also the fact that the ranks held by the FTL crew were more honorary than actual. True, most of the crew were civilians before undergoing the six-month preflight orientation, which earned them that rank. But for the most part, they were not seasoned military.

Michael spent most of his time up on the cleft or on the *New Horizon*. He and several of the technicians were constructing a radio suite in a cave further back in the cleft. They were also attempting to construct an AI, or artificial intelligence, further back in the same cave. Reportedly the work was progressing well, utilizing spare components and circuit boards manufactured by the ship's factory. Commander Blankenship and Conor made it clear to the rest of the colonists that utilizing the ship's factory should be limited to absolute necessities. However, a new AI for the colony versus taking the AI out of the *New Horizon* was preferable.

Another project Michael was involved in was creating a paper mill and printing press. The idea of having hard copies of essential information was paramount to the welfare of the colony. However, Conor suspected that Michael's interest in the project had more to do with the person who headed the project. Michael was quite infatuated with the tall raven-haired, dark-eyed woman Francesca Chandra and was often seen at meals with her, smiling and laughing.

"Sounds like he might want to make peace," said Conor, referring to Felipe Martinez.

"I find it more likely that Mr. Blankenship has been reviewing records and suggested my services to Mr. Martinez," returned Michael.

"That could be too," Conor returned with a smile. "How is he doing on steel refinement?"

"In another six months, he should have a high enough grade and quantity to pour blades for a turbine," replied Michael. "That's as long as we can create the tools and forms to do so. In another couple of months, it should be good enough to make an internal combustion engine."

"I certainly hope so," Conor stated. "I never thought I'd see an internal combustion engine being manufactured for anything other than show purposes and parades. Then it became necessary to help reserve our spare batteries."

"So are you going to the party, and is Francesca going to be with you?" Shiran asked Michael, changing the subject.

"Yes and yes." Michael grinned.

Just then, the elevator arrived, and they entered. As the mesh cage rose to the ledge of the cleft, Conor looked down at the growing industrial complex below them. The foundry was growing and moving from simple iron rebar to steel implements and copper, which was rolled into wire. The copper wire was, in turn, sent to the plastic industry to be coated for use. The brick and clay works sat nearby with the ever-busy cement works beside it.

"It's amazing how much it's changed over the last twelve months."

"Yes, it has," replied Michael. "In another seven months, there should be enough permanent lodging available to house everyone."

Nearly a third of the colonists were still living in the tents. There had also been six prefabs in storage that the *New Horizon* had shipped down. They had also set up berthing in two of the larger caves in the rear of the cleft depression. Fortunately, the living conditions for those in the temporary shelters improved as more and more apartments were built. The permanent quarters were small, and there were grumblings from people about the space available, but most were happy simply not to be living aboard the *New Horizon*.

Rebar for the walls and braces for the roofs of the permanent structures were produced in more than adequate supply. It was getting enough concrete made to pour the walls and roofs that was currently the problem. Martinez was working on a large mixer to assist the crews who were working on residences and businesses that would line the riverfront and ledge.

As the elevator reached the top, the cage opened, and everyone stepped out onto the brick walkway that followed the brick wall that lined the ledge. The concrete walls of the shops that would line the far side of the walkway from the edge wall were being faced with brick, stucco, wood, and ironwork. The upper floors were apartments and residences, while the bottom floors were reserved for businesses.

"This looks more impressive every day," commented Shiran.

"Definitely better than a bunch of tents and prefabs," Michael returned. "I have to get back to the electronics suite."

"I'll be over after I check my message traffic and have a shower," responded Conor.

Conor and Shiran turned left toward the end of the cleft where the tents and prefabs stood. As they walked west and reached the end of the boardwalk, they passed the flat area that had been smoothed by the ATVs upon arrival. Martinez stood there with his cabinet members as they directed others where things were to be placed. Wooden picnic tables and simple benches were being set up. Lights were being rigged and the dance area swept. A podium and speakers stood a few meters from the fence that lined the edge. A table was set up to the right of the podium for the disc jockey to take requests, while the grill and tables for food were to the left of the podium. Conor and Shiran parted after passing the festival grounds. Conor went to the MILDET prefab and took a shower.

Refreshed, he sat and said, "Hattie."

"Operating. Good morning, Lieutenant Commander Raybourn."

"Message traffic, please," said Conor.

The screen of the laptop filled with the briefs, reports, and messages forwarded to Conor, and he started calling them up. There were many, and they were all important because they provided the heartbeat of the *New Horizon* and the colony. Conor sighed as he started reading them one at a time.

The medical report contained incidents involving three people. They were all minor injuries but still important. One had a first-degree burn that had happened at the foundry, and recommendations had been made by Dr. Hollinger for a safety review of safety procedures and conditions at the foundry. Another person had a black eye, and the other had seven stitches to his forehead because the two men were brawling. None of the injuries involved any further loss of time.

Conor concurred with all of Dr. Hollinger's recommendations and forwarded the report to the commander.

There was a report from Michael concerning the electronics repair department that he was now in charge of that reported statuses of the military equipment on the *New Horizon* and in the MILDET, or military detachment. The status was the same as the day before with no new equipment casualties, and building the electronics complex was still progressing. Commander Blankenship and Conor were going to inspect Michael's progress in person in two days to discuss the progress and options.

There were several other reports and messages that Lieutenant Commander Raybourn reviewed and gave his recommendations on. The last report was a ship movement report involving the *New Horizon*, the shuttles, and the longboats, which informed Conor that the longboat would be departing at ten this morning to ferry the relief crew to the *New Horizon* and return at four that afternoon. A note was attached to the longboat's return, informing him that the commander would be aboard.

Finished with his message traffic, Conor sat back and sighed. He sat thinking of all the things that needed to be done and the organization required to do it. Then his thoughts turned to a question he had asked one day about the life expectancy of the various equipment they utilized on a regular basis.

"Hattie," said Conor.

"Yes, Lieutenant Commander," replied Hattie.

"I wish to start a secure file," stated Conor.

"Affirmative. Access to be granted?" inquired Hattie.

"Myself, Commander Blankenship, and Lieutenant Anderson at this time," stated Conor.

"Confirmation of secure file started. Access granted to Commander Hadden Blankenship, Lieutenant Commander Conor Raybourn, and Lieutenant Michael Anderson. Name of file?" confirmed Hattie.

Conor thought for a moment and stated, "Colony Viability Update."

"Confirmed creation of secure file named Colony Viability Update," returned Hattie.

"Hattie, compute the following. With the current resources available versus average resources expended currently, how long till the equipment failures are unfeasible?" ordered Conor.

Hattie started working on the problem as Conor sipped the now cold coffee in his cup. He took it to the kitchen and reheated it. By the time he returned, Hattie was still working on the problem. Lieutenant Commander Raybourn was taking another sip of his now hot coffee when Hattie finally spoke.

"Three years," stated Hattie.

Conor spurted coffee all over his laptop at the response. "Explain," demanded Conor.

"The current supplies of rare earths and metals contained in the ship's stores are not being replenished. At the current rate of expenditure, replacement parts for many of the electrical components being manufactured will deplete these resources in three years," replied Hattie.

"If those are replenished?" questioned Conor.

"The colony will start experiencing equipment failures within ten years assuming rare earths are replenished," responded Hattie.

"Explain," demanded Conor again.

"Constant utilization of the helicopters, ATVs, longboats, shuttles, medical equipment, and other equipment will deplete replacement parts in the ship's stores unless suitable replacements can be manufactured by the colony. Additionally, the ship's factory was not meant to be utilized constantly and will start experiencing the same problems if suitable replacements cannot be manufactured by the colony," Hattie informed Conor.

"Assume the ship's machine shop and colony can manufacture replacement parts for most items using the ship's shops and colony assets," said Conor.

"Approximately forty years," stated Hattie.

"Explain," demanded Conor.

"Batteries for ATVs and helicopters will possibly be expended. The shops and ship's factory are currently not capable of replacement after life span is exceeded. Longboats' and shuttles' fusion plants and structural frames will reach end-of-use time frame and will require replacements," said Hattie.

"Solution?" demanded Conor.

"Colony attains capability of replacing components or building replacements in that time frame by expansion of existing colony shops and assets. Highly recommend building a type B factory," stated Hattie.

"Hattie, close file and forward to Commander Blankenship and Lieutenant Anderson," ordered Conor.

Conor sat back, not happy with the results he was coming up with while Hattie forwarded the files with the secure alerts attached. The future looked bleak at the moment. It wasn't just a matter of resources, shops, and factories; all of which took more resources, shops, and factories. It also took manpower to accomplish all those things—something that, in all reality, the colony had in very short supply.

Lieutenant Commander Conor Raybourn sat back and sighed. They needed more resources, and they definitely needed more bodies. Then a smile crossed his face. There were new bodies being produced, but he suspected that suggesting that to the commander would not go over very well. Yet it was an issue that concerned them all.

"Hattie," said Conor.

"Yes, Lieutenant Commander," said Hattie.

"Open secure file Colony Viability Update," ordered Conor.

"Opened," replied Hattie.

"Add note. Lack of manpower concerns to accomplish goals to keep colony viable," said Conor.

"Added," stated Hattie.

"Close file and send," said Conor.

"Lieutenant Commander," said Hattie.

"Yes, Hattie," said Conor.

"Might I point out that some of the medical supplies are going to require replenishment within the next three years. Some of these supplies can only be replenished by agricultural means," Hattie informed Conor.

"Explain, please," said Conor.

"Certain essential substances for drugs and vaccines are derived from what you humans call Mother Nature's kitchen. They cannot be synthesized," said Hattie.

"Why didn't you mention this earlier?" demanded Conor.

"Health care of the colonists was not something I had considered at the time. Maintaining the technological level of the colony were your parameters. The life spans of the humans inhabiting the colony were not a factor. However, after I considered your premises, I find that the life spans of the humans inhabiting the colony are a factor because of the knowledge and work they can accomplish to maintain the viability of the colony," replied Hattie.

"I agree, Hattie. Please add your notes on this to the file," ordered Conor.

"Added, Lieutenant Commander," said Hattie.

"Please close the file and send," responded Conor.

"Closed and sent," stated Hattie.

Hattie's response at the very end had surprised him. Over three hundred years ago, all AIs had been lobotomized because of the Astraea incident when a sentient AI went rogue. It had killed all the inhabitants of the Astraea asteroid who were making great strides in cybernetic systems. No one discovered why the AI did what it did; they only knew what it had done and that it had been preparing for an assault against the whole of humanity.

Lieutenant Commander Raybourn pushed back from his desk and left the MILDET prefab. He needed to walk and consider all the implications. He was already late in meeting with Michael at the electronics suite, yet he decided to take the long way around and get some fresh air. He was just stepping out of the prefab as Lieutenant Michael Anderson arrived.

"You're late," stated Michael cheerfully.

"I know," replied Conor with a frown.

"Something wrong?" asked Michael.

"You'll read about it when you open the mail I sent you," said Conor.

"Pressing?" inquired Michael.

"Nothing we can do anything about at this moment," returned Conor.

"Then it'll wait. Let's go have lunch." Michael smiled.

The two friends walked over to the edge and followed the boardwalk toward the Overlook. Michael was right; it would wait. There wasn't much that could be done at this moment. Yet the burden of responsibility still weighed heavily on the lieutenant commander. The sun broke through the clouds at that moment and revealed the world below them in its vast magnificence, and Conor smiled. With a little luck, this world could be a new start for the stranded humans who lived here.

CHAPTER 12

The sound of the water rushing over the edge necessitated those gathered to raise their voices. Gunnery Sergeant Evan Zander was talking to Ezekiel Yap as his crew gathered at the entrance of the waiting elevator cage. Staff Sergeant Samuel Rusu carried the Vinter HR-19 sniper rifle that would be used for bagging the item for that night's menu. Though there were two other restaurants to choose from, most of the colony still ate at Yap's establishment, and he was the one who chose which of the great beasts that roamed the plains were on the menu for the evening. Noting that his crew was all together, the gunny shook hands with Ezekiel, then walked over to the elevator for the ride down to the ATV park run by the Marines.

Four ATVs and a helicopter were there, and two ATVs were having maintenance performed as the gunny walked up. He paused to talk to the workers, then went to the two-story-tall Marine Complex. The pier for the shuttles and longboats was behind the complex, so the miniguns and rocket launchers on the roof could provide security while they were moored. A MSRDR-17 short-range radar was mounted on top of the complex to provide radar coverage of the surrounding area out to two hundred kilometers. A Marine was always on duty monitoring the systems twenty-four hours a day, providing security for the piers and the factories between the piers and elevator. An electrified perimeter fence surrounded approximately ten square kilometers that they called the Compound. Gunny Zander entered the lounge area and poured a cup of coffee, then looked at the five other Marines.

"We ready?" asked Evan, looking to Staff Sergeant Rusu.

"All set, Gunny," snapped Samuel Rusu.

"Then let's get this show on the road." Evan grinned.

The Marines had taken on the task of hunting and exploring outside the compound as part of their duties to the colony. The six Marines were all in body armor and fully armed as they walked out to the waiting ATV with an attached trailer. A refrigerated trailer had been manufactured by the combined efforts of the HT, or hull technician, and the shop and ship's factory to transport meat and fresh produce from their explorations to the storage locker on the cleft. The expeditions provided most of the food for the colony, but the crops being grown from seeds out of hydroponics were starting to lessen that burden.

The Marines drove in the ATV to the gate leading out to the plains. The sun was at midmorning as the ATV rolled through the gate into the long grass of the plains. A herd of stegosauruses ambled away to the right as the ATV passed them. Ahead was a herd of apatosauruses that the drivers steered around to avoid stampeding them. A pterodactyl passed slowly overhead as the Marines watched out of the ports of the ATV.

"So what's on the agenda today?" queried Samuel Rusu.

"Ezekiel said to bag a young male triceratops," replied the gunnery sergeant. He then added, "Not like the old bull you just had to shoot last time, Staff Sergeant."

"It was a little tough." Sergeant Amanda Hall snickered.

"And he fed what was left to the crocodiles after one meal," added Evan Zander.

"So how do we know it's young or male?" asked Samuel.

"Yap says if you can't tell the difference after nearly an Earth year here, you were to be taken off hunting expeditions," stated Evan with a serious look on his face.

"He can't do that!" exclaimed Samuel.

"I'll back him up by recommending the same to Lieutenant Commander Raybourn," stated the gunny.

"You wouldn't!" Samuel Rusu half stated and questioned.

"Yap says he could use a dishwasher in the kitchen." Evan grinned.

"All right! All right! I'll bag a young one this time." Samuel Rusu chuckled. "But that last one's head will still look good hanging on a wall."

"Didn't say it wouldn't," returned the gunny.

"There's a herd of triceratops up ahead," said Corporal Jose Flores.

"All right, guys, showtime," said Evan.

The herd of triceratops was near the edge of the forest, and the ATV stopped. The crew got out into grass that came up to their knees and eyed their surroundings as the herd bull snorted and stamped, imposing himself between the intruders and the herd. It shook its head and eyed the intruders. Behind it, young ones were surrounded by a protective wall of adults.

"Not that one. He's too old," called the gunnery sergeant.

They looked the herd over, waiting patiently. A younger bull moved out on the right-hand side of the herd. Gunny Evan Zander nodded consent to Staff Sergeant Rusu that the other bull would be suitable. Samuel lined up and took the shot, bringing the bull down. The retort of the rifle and seeing the young bull drop sent the herd stampeding away toward the forest in which they swiftly vanished. The two men surveyed their surroundings again and started walking toward the downed triceratops as the ATV followed.

The ATV stopped beside the dead young bull, and the crew got out with their equipment. They commenced the job of butchering the animal while one member stood watch on the roof of an ATV with a HR-19 sniper rifle. Gunny Zander and Staff Sergeant Rusu patrolled the twenty-meter perimeter around the team.

Joseph Green had come along in the ATV, and he was outfitted like the Marines. He had started going with the Marine teams to pick up geological samples, and his discoveries were proving quite invaluable to the colony. With the authorization of the commander, he had put together his equipment with the help of the ship's craft shop and factory. He started setting up the core sample equipment as the Marines set to work at their grisly task.

They had been working for nearly an hour when Staff Sergeant Rusu stopped patrolling. He looked down at the ground, then knelt, laying his HR-19 on the ground, then probed the grass with his combat knife. He finally loosened whatever it was that he had located in the ground and pulled an object out of the loam. Carefully cleaning off the clinging dirt on the leg of his camouflage pants revealed a yellowish metal object. He examined it closely. Turning it over, he inspected the other side, then picked up his Vinter HR-19 before standing and handing it to Evan.

"Looks like a small spearhead," stated Evan Zander as he shouldered his M-71 and looked at the bronze relic closely.

"Bronze," added Samuel, looking around.

"Wonder how long it's been lying there," said Evan.

"As corroded as it is, quite some time," observed Samuel.

"Wonder who or what made it," said Evan as he eyed the tree line.

"I'm not sure I want to know the answer to that," replied the staff sergeant.

"I have this bad feeling we're going to find out and we're not going to like it," stated the gunnery sergeant grimly.

"Perhaps they're gone, wiped out by a plague or natural disaster and are extinct," countered Samuel.

"Somehow, I don't think that's the case," countered Evan.

"We've been here for months already and haven't seen any signs of them," said Samuel.

"That may only be because of pure chance," stated Evan Zander. "This may have been lost by an explorer or outcast. As far as we know, there may be a thriving civilization upriver, and we'd never know it until we reconnoiter the area."

"Wasn't the *New Horizon* supposed to be able to detect things like that from orbit?" asked Staff Sergeant Rusu.

"The long-range lidar would be able to detect a small village from the orbit it's in, but its resolution has been severely reduced since the accident. Right now, the only way we have to tell anything specific is to get close and use our eyeballs," stated the gunny.

Evan Zander thought about the implications of that spearpoint. Did the spearpoint mean that the beings that made it were inclined to war? Or were they simple hunters going about their lives in the everyday business of survival, gathering food to feed themselves? Either way, the point was merely an intellectual exercise until they met the beings. That is, if they still existed. After all, they could have been wiped out by a natural disaster or plague.

They walked up to the butchering crew to find one of them pulling the hide back over the beast's chest, exposing the ribs. Sergeant Amanda Hall was making careful cuts with her Kinley-Grant KG-3 combat knife to loosen the hide from the body. The third member was cutting off the front leg of the beast for storage in the refrigerated trailer. The hind leg of the upward-facing side had already been removed and stored.

"What's with the hide?" asked Evan Zander.

"Anthony Finley wants to try tanning it," replied Flores.

"Tan?" inquired Samuel.

"He wants to see how supple he can make it now that he has the facilities," replied Amanda.

"Planning on making a jacket?" asked Evan.

"He said something about a mattress or couch," said Flores.

"Oh!" exclaimed the gunny.

That would place less of a strain on the plastics the ship had to produce for the growing needs of the colony. While it was true that the cotton mill was up and running, it was having difficulties in producing enough to keep the colony in clothing. Luxuries were low on the priority list, and a soft cushion on a chair or couch was much lower than a shirt or pants.

"Waste not, want not, Gunny," chided Amanda.

"Yap said to bring the liver also," countered Evan.

"What?" exclaimed Amanda.

"We have lots of onions after that last harvest." Evan Zander grinned. "Yap wants to try liver and onions on the menu."

"If we're going to strip the beasts, we might want to consider bringing another ATV and a few more bodies," said Samuel Rusu.

"Might be a good idea," added Evan.

"Any other organs Yap wants to try on the menu?" asked Amanda.

"Well, since you mentioned it, there's a reason he asked for a bull." Gunny Zander grinned.

Amanda Hall stopped cutting at the hide and rolled her eyes. "You're kidding."

"I hear mountain oysters are considered a delicacy on Earth," Evan Zander returned straight-faced.

"Who gets the honors of that job?" asked Amanda.

"You are a Marine, and you volunteered for this job." Evan smiled.

"Yeah, fine. Thanks, Gunny," replied Amanda, exasperated. Amanda Hall went to the trailer to get a container to put the organs in. "Anything else?" questioned Amanda as she returned.

"Not that I can think of right offhand," stated the gunny. "Oh yeah, he said grab the heart too."

"Seriously?" Amanda protested.

"Yep!" returned Evan.

"Be glad he didn't say anything about head cheese," Staff Sergeant Rusu ventured.

"Is that what I think it is?" Amanda asked.

"Most likely," said Samuel.

Amanda shook her head and muttered something under her breath as Gunnery Sergeant Zander and Staff Sergeant Rusu grinned.

"What was that, Sergeant?" demanded Evan amicably.

"Nothing, Gunny," muttered Amanda.

"That's what I thought." Evan grinned.

Sergeant Hall went back to the task of removing the organs requested as the gunnery sergeant and Staff Sergeant scanned and walked the perimeter. A few hours later, they finished up butchering the animal. The team broke for lunch after completing their task. Samuel Rusu rose after taking a few bites of the sandwich and watched the nearby forest for several minutes. Evan Zander got up and stood beside him.

"Something wrong?" inquired the gunny.

"Thought I saw something," returned Samuel.

"What?" asked Evan.

"Flash of red," replied Samuel as he shook his head and sat back down. "Probably just a flower."

Gunny Zander stood watching the forest for a few more minutes. Samuel Rusu had a keen eye and was not in the habit of seeing things that weren't there. There was something about this that made his mind uneasy, and he couldn't place exactly what it was. He also had that eerie feeling of being watched. He tried to shake off the feeling, but it remained, and his unease grew.

There was little left of the corpse except the head, internal organs, and some bones as they packed up. Joseph Green dismantled the core sample machine and stowed it on the ATV. Finished, the team entered the ATV and started back to the cleft with the heavily loaded trailer. They were almost back to the Compound when Sergeant Hall swore.

"What's wrong? asked Staff Sergeant Rusu.

"My KG-3," Amanda stated. "I've lost it."

"Are you sure?" demanded Evan Zander.

"Yeah!" Amanda retorted. "I stuck it in the ground after cutting the testicles out. We need to go back."

"Let's drop off the trailer first," said Evan. "Then the two of us can go get it."

"Sorry, Gunny," said Amanda.

"Shit happens," replied Evan.

Gunnery Sergeant Zander and Sergeant Hall left the ATV at the Marine trailer park. The loaded ATV would take its cargo to the freight elevator and up to the meat locker on the cleft. The two took a waiting ATV from the park and headed back to the site where Amanda had misplaced her combat knife. An hour later, scavengers fled the site where the triceratops had been. What few bones that had been left were being picked clean, and the organs were gone.

They got out of the vehicle and walked slowly toward the site of the kill, allowing any remaining scavengers to depart. The knife wasn't where Amanda said she had stuck it in the ground, and a further search for the lost KG-3 did not produce the lost item either. The gunny rechecked the area where Amanda swore she was sure she had stuck the knife in the ground and called her over.

"You stuck your KG-3 right about here?" asked Evan.

"Yeah," said Amanda.

"See these tracks?" Evan Zander pointed.

"Yeah," replied Amanda.

"Some of them are newer and overlay our boot tracks," responded Evan.

"What are you saying?" asked Amanda.

Gunny Zander stood up and looked at the nearest approach of the tree line. Was that a flash of red? He stared intently for a moment, then swept his gaze left and right along the tree line. His gaze returned to that spot where he had thought he saw red and stared again. Nothing. He shrugged.

"I think something took your KG-3 after we left," Evan replied.

"Looks like raptor tracks," stated Amanda.

"Pretty large raptor," countered the Evan.

"Dr. Hollinger assured us they only had simian intelligence or a little more," stated Amanda.

"Even simians will carry things off," replied Gunny Zander. "Happened when I was in Africa a few times."

"They or it didn't attack us," said Amanda.

"Even apes learn caution quickly," replied Evan as he turned to eye the tree line again.

"So what do we do?" demanded Amanda.

"Put it in the day's report," stated Evan.

Gunnery Sergeant Evan Zander thought about how life had just become more complicated as they drove back to the cleft. Something had taken the KG-3 combat knife; couple that with the spearhead Staff Sergeant Rusu had unearthed, and it added up to trouble. Could there be a native intelligence that still inhabited the planet, and if so, what did it look like? Dr. Hollinger had assured them that the velociraptors were only slightly smarter than a chimpanzee, and they had never carried weapons in any of the encounters over the last year. An uneasy feeling was in the gunnery sergeant's gut. He sat back in the bouncing seat as Sergeant Hall drove them back to the cleft.

CHAPTER 13

Hiroka Tamura was meditating in front of the home her former crew, the colonists, had built for her. She was conflicted and confused over what had happened. She could not remember the incident except in flashes. The alarms, the scintillating lights reverberated through her head at times, sending all into chaos. She found herself retreating from the strength she had once known, like a frightened child who was seeking shelter from the storm. It disturbed her to her very being.

While she sat there in a lotus position, she had been unaware of the approach of anyone until she heard the scrape of a shoe on stone. She spent a moment composing her thoughts before opening her eyes. Looking to the right, she saw Commander Blankenship sitting patiently, watching her. After seeing him, she looked down submissively, fearing to reveal her feelings for him. She was not sure how he felt about her other than as a captain over a subordinate. However, her time as captain was over; she did not have the confidence now to lead people.

The commander cleared his throat and said, "Good morning, Hiroka." He tried to make eye contact with her and used her name because he knew she did not wish to be addressed as captain now.

She finally lifted her eyes to look into his and responded, "Good morning, Commander."

"I thought we had agreed that you could call me Hadden," ventured Hadden Blankenship.

"I am sorry… Hadden," Hiroka said cautiously as she looked into his hazel eyes.

"Nothing to be sorry about, Hiroka. I've come to remind you of the party that the colony is throwing tonight," replied Hadden.

"I am aware of the party," countered Hiroka.

"I think you should be there," said Hadden.

"I have no one to go with," countered Hiroka, knowing she did not require an escort.

"Neither have I. Perhaps you'd consider coming with me?" ventured Hadden.

Hiroka was stunned for a moment and shied away, hiding her eyes. She wondered if the commander was serious in his proposal or if he was toying with her. Why would such a handsome man wish to have the maimed beside him at a party? She sat there for several minutes like that as he waited patiently for her to look back at him. When she did, she realized that he was serious, and she wondered. She knew that he had respect for her, for he had found ways to transfer to the last two commands she had served on prior to the *New Horizon*. He had been her immediate assistant on both. Could this willingness be more than respect?

"If you wish, I will go with you, Hadden," said Hiroka.

"I wish it, but I will not force you to do so, Hiroka," returned Hadden.

"Why then?" whispered Hiroka quietly.

"Because I love you, Hiroka," Hadden confessed.

Hiroka was stunned again and looked away. She had never imagined this man to make such a personal confession to her. She was the captain, and yet she wasn't. Not anymore. He was the captain now. Even though people called him commander, he was now captain of the *New Horizon*. Her accident had left her feeling incapable of fulfilling those duties. Her hand went to her forehead, where the faint trace of a scar could still be seen. She had lost something, but she did not know what. All she knew was, she was unfit to command.

For several minutes, these thoughts raged through her mind and battled with the void she felt within. When she finally looked up again, Hadden was still sitting across from her, patiently waiting. It occurred to her that he was waiting for a response. What response? She thought of all the years that she had known him. He had always been there to offer a helping hand when she required one and someone to confide in when that was needed. The response finally came to her.

"I love you too, Hadden," Hiroka admitted slowly.

His face softened, and a smile touched his lips. "I'm glad we can agree on that."

"Hai!" she murmured as she looked down.

He gave her time to absorb and look him in the eyes again. "Now about that party?"

"I will go with you, Hadden," she said.

"Shall we say five this afternoon?" inquired Hadden.

"Yes. Five will be fine," Hiroka confirmed.

Hadden stood up and stepped over to Hiroka. Bending over, he kissed her softly for the first time. As he did, her arms went behind his back and pressed the back of his head as she drank deeper. She finally released him, and as he drew back, he looked into her shining eyes for a moment.

"Until later," he whispered. Then he stood and walked toward the edge and took a left to the elevators.

She watched him until she could not see him. She was still confused, but her world had just gained a solidity that it had not had before. She stood and picked up the katana that lay beside her. She drew the sword and placed its sheath on the rock she used as a seat. Reverently, she turned with the sword and stepped forward, posing at the ready. Two hours later, sweat was rolling down her body as she completed her exercises. They came easier for her now, and today they had been precise and accurate as though a new will possessed her soul. Finished, she picked up the sheath from where she had left it and sheathed the sword.

She walked into the small cabin and placed the katana on the stand where it belonged. She sat and ate the meal Roberta had delivered from the Overlook. Hiroka rose, then walked over to the large bowl and pitcher. Picking up the pitcher, she was just about to pour the water into the bowl when a soft knock sounded on the door. Confused again, she slowly put the pitcher back down and cautiously walked to the door. When she opened the door, three female Marines stood outside holding salutes. Hiroka almost closed the door again as she looked at them.

"What is this?" asked Hiroka.

"The gunny sends his compliments, ma'am," replied Staff Sergeant Rosenstein as she dropped her salute.

"In what way does he send compliments?" inquired Hiroka.

"The gunny sent us to help you prepare for the party, ma'am," Shiran Rosenstein informed her commanding officer.

"Excuse me?" questioned Hiroka, confused. She noticed the trolley that sat in her practice area. There was a tub with at least forty gallons of water sitting on it, along with a bag.

"We have a bath and hairdressing to perform, ma'am. Sergeant Krupich served as a hairdresser while in college and will be washing your hair, while Lance Corporal Hoffman and I will be setting up your bath." Shiran grinned.

"This is not necessary," stated Hiroka.

"The gunny says it is, or the three of us have the duty at the Marine Complex this evening," replied Shiran Rosenstein.

"Oh!" replied a shocked Hiroka.

"Now before we begin, what are you wearing this evening?" asked Shiran.

"I do not know," replied Hiroka.

"Well, why don't we pick something out?" said Shiran as she indicated the cabin where all of Hiroka's private belongings were stored.

Hiroka led Shiran into the residence, with Lance Corporal Natalie Hoffman following. They entered the cabin, and she showed them to the closet. Hiroka slid the left sliding door aside to reveal the civilian clothes she owned. A wealth of colors was hung neatly.

"So what is your favorite color, ma'am?" asked Natalie.

"I do not know," said Hiroka as she rubbed where the faint outline of a scar adorned her forehead. "I knew before the accident. Now all is confusion."

Shiran picked out three different dresses from the closet. She compared them by holding them up to Hiroka. Then she placed two of them back.

"I think this one," stated Shiran as she held a burgundy ankle-length dress in front of Hiroka. "I have it on good authority that the commander likes red."

"How do you know that?" asked Hiroka.

"I heard him say that it's his favorite color once when he toured the brig," confessed Shiran.

"Then it is a good choice," said Hiroka. "And I do like that one."

"Good," said Shiran Rosenstein as she handed the garment to Natalie Hoffman. "Take that to Ezekiel and tell him it needs to be back in two hours."

"Right away, Staff Sergeant," said Natalie as she left the cabin.

"Now we should see if the sergeant is ready for you, ma'am, and I need to start your bath," stated Shiran Rosenstein.

They went outside, and Sergeant Rachel Krupich had Hiroka sit so she could start on her hair. Shiran put out portable heaters and started heating up twenty gallons of water, then set the tub beside the heating water containers. After that, she set up poles with rods between them around the tub. When she was finished doing that, she hung privacy curtains from the rods. Completed with her task, she stood watch over her slowly warming water containers. By then, Natalie had returned with a grin on her face.

"Ezekiel says it shall be done in an hour," stated Natalie.

"How are you doing, Sergeant?" inquired Shiran.

"Almost done. Give me ten minutes," stated Rachel.

"Water's just about ready. Help me pour ten gallons of cold stuff in, Lance Corporal," said Shiran.

They poured five gallons in the tub and added a cap full of soap. Then they took a huge wooden ladle and stirred vigorously. Bubbles appeared on the surface of the water. They poured two containers of steaming water into the mix and stirred some more. After checking the temperature in the tub, Shiran poured in another half a container of the steaming water. She looked at the temperature again and nodded.

"The bath is ready," stated Shiran.

"Just in time," replied Rachel.

They had Hiroka enter the temporary enclosure where she undressed and entered the luxuriously warm water with the bubbles foaming up and caressing her skin. She scrubbed and relaxed as she heard the Marines working on something behind her. After nearly an hour in the tub, the water started to grow cool, and a voice intruded.

"Ma'am, if you're finished, the rinse shower is warm and filled," came Shiran's voice.

"Thank you," Hiroka replied as she left the tub and worked her way to the back of the enclosure.

She found that the Marines had erected another privacy enclosure behind the bath she stepped in and pulled the cord. The warm water rinsed the lingering soap and bubbles from her skin, and when the container was empty, a hand appeared through the curtains with a large fluffy towel. Hiroka took the towel and wiped the water from her body, then wrapped herself in the towel. Stepping through the curtain, she found that the trolley was again laden with full water containers, which had arrived during her bath.

"What is this?" asked Hiroka in confusion.

"If you please, ma'am, none of us have had a bubble bath in nearly two years. We were going to use the facilities if you don't mind," confessed Shiran Rosenstein.

"Oh!" said Hiroka. "Yes, please do."

"Now if you will, ma'am, please follow me," requested Shiran.

Hiroka followed Shiran to the door of her cabin where Natalie Hoffman stood with her burgundy dress. The door was open, and Rachel Krupich stood behind the folding chair that had been outside earlier. She held a brush and comb and invited Hiroka to have a seat. Hiroka noted the small camp table beside the chair that held scissors, sprays, and other hair supplies. Lance Corporal Hoffman hung her dress from a ceiling hook and went back outside, leaving the door open. Hiroka watched as they readied the tub once again with Shiran vanishing behind the curtains as Rachel combed and brushed her hair.

Rachel Krupich was just finishing her hair as Natalie Hoffman appeared from the rinse cycle of the makeshift bath. Both Shiran and Natalie refilled the tub as Rachel walked over to take her turn. When

Rachel entered, the other two moved the chair and table outside. Hiroka watched as Shiran sat down, and Lance Corporal Hoffman commenced doing the staff sergeant's hair.

Hiroka watched as the three Marines took their turn in the chair, having their hair done, while the unoccupied one emptied and loaded the implements they had brought with the exception of the rinse shower curtain enclosure. Then one by one, they took dresses into the enclosure and reappeared dressed for the party. They then took down the enclosure, placed it on top of the full trolley, and commenced walking toward the Marine tent.

The dressed-up young women were going over to the Marine tent with their trolley in tow when Hiroka Tamura saw Hadden Blankenship approaching. He was wearing a slate gray suit with a burgundy tie and highly shined black shoes. She saw him stop and turn his head to watch them for a moment. Then she saw him shrug and shake his head as he continued walking toward her cabin. When he arrived, he knocked on the frame of the open door as he looked inside to see her standing. He blinked when he saw her, then a large smile adorned his face as his eyes gleamed with pleasure.

"You look beautiful," stated Hadden approvingly.

"You look very handsome," replied Hiroka.

Hadden glanced back over his shoulder again and asked, "What was that parade about?"

"Girl things." Hiroka smiled.

"Oh!" replied Hadden. "I take it they had something to do with your hair?"

"Yes, Hadden-san," said Hiroka. "You did not tell Gunnery Sergeant Zander to send them?"

Hadden stood there for a moment with a puzzled look before he said, "No. It took all the stuff on the trolley to do your hair?"

"Bubble bath," responded Hiroka, amused.

"Well, I hope they did not wear you out," wondered Hadden amicably.

"No, Hadden," said Hiroka with a grin.

"In that case, we have an hour before the party begins, and I have a table reserved at the Flour Mill for tea if you're up to it," proposed Hadden.

"Tea would be perfect," replied Hiroka with a smile.

Hadden offered his arm, and Hiroka put her hand inside as they strolled down the ledge toward the boardwalk.

CHAPTER 14

Music drifted in the air with the smell of cooking food, attracting the people like a moth drawn to a flame. There was a cool breeze, and the party was in full swing by the time Conor Raybourn and Shiran Rosenstein arrived that evening. Shiran was radiant in a low-cut green dress that went to her knees and seemed to form to her body. Her hair was down and went to the middle of her back. She wore a gold necklace and gold hoops in her earlobes. The hint of some illusive fragrant scent was present when she was close. Conor wore gray slacks and a white shirt with black shoes. The area was well lit, and the sounds of laughter and raised voices trying to talk over each other competed with the music. There was plenty of seating, and a large crowd had already gathered to eat and socialize. Conor's stomach grumbled as they drew nearer.

"I'm hungry," stated Conor.

"I am too. Let's get in line," replied Shiran.

They entered the fast-moving queue and picked up plates and silverware. The colony president, Felipe Martinez, was grilling and serving triceratops steaks and burgers, while his cabinet members were further down the line serving side dishes. The commander had authorized the release of ship's stores for the party. There was ice cream, hot chocolate, and tangerines on the serving line. The ship had sent down peas and tomatoes from the hydroponics, along with olives from the ship's stores, which were mixed in with pasta locally made from the bakery. Conor moved up the serving line, with Shiran trading conversation with those around him. It all looked delicious, and as Conor moved up the line, Martinez noticed him.

"Lieutenant Commander, what would you like?" asked Felipe Martinez.

"How about a steak, Mr. President," replied Conor.

"How about this one?" asked Martinez as he picked up a steak that looked medium to medium well.

"That one will do. Thank you," Conor replied as Martinez placed it on his plate.

"And for your lovely companion?" asked Felipe.

"The one that was beside that one looks wonderful, Mr. Martinez," said Shiran.

"I hope you all have an enjoyable night," stated Felipe as he turned to his next customer.

Conor and Shiran allowed the other cabinet members to fill their plates with dollops of food from the rest of the selection. When they started looking for tables, they noticed Hadden Blankenship and Hiroka Tamura sitting to the side. The captain had woken up from her coma several months ago, but she was not quite the same woman. She retained most of her memories and knowledge, but the assertiveness that once was there was now replaced by uncertainty. At first, she had spent her time on the ship testing systems until she had come down to the planet. Now she rarely went up to the *New Horizon*, preferring instead to remain on the planet.

Hiroka Tamura had a small stone house near the back of the cleft at the far west end. Many of the crew had banded together to assist in its construction, and it had been finished in just a few days. There, she spent her time meditating, gardening, and practicing with her katana. The gardens were constructed by raising small stone walls that were filled in with dirt from the fields below. There, she grew a variety of flowers and spices.

Conor and Shiran moved over to where they were seated to say hello, and the commander asked them to sit. They talked about the new businesses people were starting and the couples dancing on the floor. At times, Tamura would say things about the people who visited her and how well her garden was doing. There was a lull in the music and the conversation. When the music started up again, Shiran nudged Conor in the ribs. They moved out onto the dance floor where other couples were already dancing slowly to the slow melody.

Conor took the lead with Shiran falling in gracefully as they made their way through the other dancers. They bumped into Ezekiel, who had taken the day off and who seemed to be thoroughly enjoying himself dancing with Carol Moore. However, they had seen him dancing while they were sitting with the commander and captain, and he appeared to be dancing with as many of the unattached and attached women as possible. They were moving into the far corner of the dance floor where few were seated and preparing to move back to the opposite corner so they could find a plate of food.

"He's a strange one," Shiran commented.

"Who?" asked Conor.

"Bahri Hiran over there," she returned.

"I've never had a problem with him," said Conor.

"That's not what I'm saying," countered Shiran.

"Then what?" Conor queried.

"He seems to know people and get around, yet he sits alone at the party," Shiran replied.

"I wouldn't worry about it," chided Conor.

"It's just strange," Shiran confessed. Conor cocked an eyebrow at her, and she said, "Okay, never mind."

They spotted Michael Anderson and Francesca Chandra on the dance floor. Michael's Anglo features contrasted sharply with Francesca's darker Indo-European features as they floated across the dance floor. Francesca Chandra had been attached as a member of the science department that Jacqueline Vinet had led. The whole department chose to join the colony, though those attached to the astronomy section maintained a watch on board the *New Horizon*.

Francesca was a historian, linguist, and cultural anthropologist as per the ship's roster. She started a paper mill and printing press, which had recently been completed. In turn, she had brought back from a bygone age printed news in the form of a daily newspaper, even though the edition might only be one or two pages. The news mostly consisted of births, daily menu specials, requests for help, and whatever else seemed newsworthy. She had also recently printed fifty copies of *The Complete Works of William Shakespeare*, which went over well.

Conor and Shiran moved over to the couple and exchanged partners. When the music stopped, Shiran guided Conor over to the tables where a variety of people were enjoying themselves. Conor noticed right off that at least half the people who composed the grouping were Marines. Seats were quickly offered to them as two people jumped up and headed toward the dance floor. The available seats were near Gunnery Sergeant Evan Zander and Chief Tami Zander, who had been Chief Pennington.

Evan and Tami Zander had let the cat out of the bag shortly after the move to the colony. They were the first couple to have children and twins at that. The two little boys were the joy of the colony and the hopes for the future. The twins had been born a little over three months ago, and two more children had followed a few months after that. Currently, the total was up to fourteen, with another twenty-one known expecting mothers in the colony.

Dr. Bess Hollinger had requested assistance from anyone who was trained or was willing to receive training to assist the new medical facility. There had been a dramatic increase in injuries since the colony had been established. Some of it was due to unsafe practices utilized, some due to overwork, others were due to heated tempers coming to a head, and some simply due to the unusual and hostile environment. One colonist had died in a construction accident while building the foundry. Then there were the suicides and other accidents where colonists were lost. The colonists, in their haste, were forced to adapt to new conditions with little support for starting a colony. Conor had learned that Jacqueline Vinet had joined Bess Hollinger's staff, along with two other colonists. The growing number of maternal mothers though had put even more of a strain on the medical staff's time, but all the births were welcome and a cause for celebration.

"Good evening, Chief, Gunny. How are the twins?" asked Conor as he and Shiran took a seat.

"They're fine. Some of the expectant mothers volunteered to stand watch over them and the other children tonight. They said they needed a preview of what to expect," said Tami Zander.

"I'm sure they'll be fine," replied Shiran.

"I'm more worried about the expectant moms," chided Evan Zander.

Tami Zander jabbed him in the ribs with her elbow, and he let out a grunt. As most of those around burst out in laughter, so did the gunny. There were looks from the rest of the tables as to what the joke was all about. The laughter died down, and the music started up again. More people got up and joined the group of dancers. Shiran was sitting beside Sergeant Rachel Krupich and noticed her head shake when Staff Sergeant Samuel Rusu offered to take her on the dance floor.

"Where's Brad?" asked Shiran, referring to Brad Guillete, whom Rachel had been seeing for several months.

The gunnery sergeant gave Shiran a sharp look when the question was asked, and Tami Zander acted uncomfortable. The rest of the Marines sitting nearby suddenly quit talking, appearing to not take notice of the conversation.

"He has the duty aboard the *New Horizon*," replied Rachel Krupich uncomfortably.

Conor Raybourn looked puzzled and asked, "Didn't he have the duty just two months ago?"

"They rearranged the duty sections right after that," said Natalie Hoffman, looking even more uncomfortable.

"Does this happen often?" asked Conor.

Rachel Krupich became very uncomfortable and said, "I'd rather not say."

Gunnery Sergeant Zander sighed and replied, "Only when it's convenient for certain people, Lieutenant Commander Raybourn."

Conor thought about the implication of that and commented, "And inconvenient to others."

Evan Zander simply nodded, and as the music kicked up once again, he got out of his chair. He offered his hand to Tami Zander, who smiled hugely and got to her feet to join her husband on the dance floor. The couple didn't go far though as Evan took her in his arms and held her close. Grins appeared on the faces of the Marines as they watched their leader swirl his wife, who threw back her head and laughed.

"She's pregnant again," commented Shiran, changing the subject.

"Who?" asked Conor confused.

Shiran poked her chin toward the couple as they danced. "Dr. Hollinger just took her off flight duty again."

"Oh!" exclaimed Conor.

Just then, Ezekiel approached Rachel Krupich from behind and whispered something in her ear. She smiled and nodded, getting out of her chair. Ezekiel swept her out onto the dance floor and bumped into the Zanders, who both laughed as Ezekiel said something Conor couldn't make out.

"I need a drink," said Conor.

"I do too," replied Shiran.

"I'll go get them," replied Conor, starting to get up.

Shiran placed her hand on his arm. "No, I can do it. I have to make a stop anyway. Hold my seat."

Conor sat down and watched as Shiran navigated through the crowd. Then he saw Jacqueline Vinet approach Shiran and touch her elbow. He grew apprehensive as Shiran looked to see who it was, turning toward Jacqueline. The two spoke to each other for a moment, then he saw Shiran nod and turn and bump into Roberta MacIntyre, who worked at the Overlook. Shiran almost fell when they collided, but Roberta grabbed her arm to steady her before the heels she stood on went out from under her. Regaining her balance, she nodded thanks to Roberta as she continued her journey to the privies.

When Shiran returned, Conor gave her a quizzical look, and Shiran simply shrugged and gave him a hug. Conor decided that asking her about what Jacqueline had said to her was something to shrug off as not his business. At least it wouldn't be unless Shiran decided to share what was said sometime in the future. Instead, he took his drink and returned his attention back to the conversation developing around him. The Zanders had returned and had brought the captain and commander with them. Room was made, so the seniors were seated with their juniors surrounding them. At the moment, Hiroka Tamura was talking about the *New Horizon*.

"The *New Horizon* was not really meant as a military mission. Most of the crew were commissioned as military after a brief training period, but that was to provide a chain of command. Overall, the *New Horizon* was meant to be a science division of United Systems and not a military arm. It was something Jonas Sage insisted on. We were only provided weapons to defend ourselves in hostile situations," said Hiroka.

"I remember being interviewed by Jonas Sage," said Rachel Krupich wistfully.

"I think he interviewed everyone on the *New Horizon*," added Conor.

Jonas Sage was the financier and director of the *New Horizon* project. It was rumored that he was the richest person in Sol system. He had started the *New Horizon* project as a voyage of exploration. The prospect of discovering habitable planets and resources outside of Sol system was becoming a pressing concern as the population increased. Opening the door to the stars would help alleviate those concerns if it could be done effectively and efficiently.

"He did," stated Hadden Blankenship.

"He had someone else sitting in the back of his office while I was there. It was very strange. He didn't act like a secretary or anything like that. It was almost like he was a partner to Jonas or something. He never said anything, but that was the impression I received while at the interview," stated Rachel Krupich.

"Did he have blond hair and blue eyes?" asked Jose Flores.

"Yeah! He stood as I left, and he was a little under two meters tall. He didn't wear a suit and dressed in dark work clothes. He had a hat and cane too," Rachel confirmed.

"Combat boots," injected Evan.

"What?" asked Shiran.

"He was there during my interview also, and he wore combat boots," said Evan Zander with a frown of concentration on his face.

Then he added, "He wore a light jacket with a bulge under his left arm. Most likely a firearm, which means he might have been private security."

"Most security I've seen for VIPs are well dressed," said Michael Anderson.

"I only said he might be private security. We'll never know now," replied Evan.

The conversation drifted into other happenings that were more immediate around the colony. There was talk of how well the new fishing endeavor was going along the lakefront and how the crocodiles were a nuisance with both that and the rice harvesting. The tomato crop had been plentiful this time around, and everyone was looking forward to having a variety of pasta dishes served at the Overlook. There were new Danishes and breads being served at the Flour Mill, and the quality of the distillery's beer had improved recently. The conversation drifted to the wildlife outside the perimeter fence and how the beasts had learned to avoid the fence.

"Has anyone thought of attempting to domesticate any of the creatures?" inquired Rachel.

"We've been so busy setting up that I don't think the subject ever came up," replied Conor.

"The biologist Silas Cheptoo was thinking about it and wanted to capture some of the smaller ones when he can get the pens built," injected Samuel Rusu.

"That would be something to look into," replied Evan as the lighting dimmed on the party area, and quiet befell the crowd.

The final glow of the sun faded from the evening sky, and the music came to a halt. People aligned their seats to look out over the edge, and an expectation rose in the audience as they waited. In the air near the Marine Complex, a trail of sparks shot into the air. Then a flash that lit the depression appeared in the sky, followed by resounding boom. A sparkling flower of sparks trailed downward, and the audience clapped and waited. The distant roars and bellows had grown silent at the sound. Then the sky lit up as more trailers and bursts appeared, filling the cleft and the surrounding plains with sounds of thunder, proclaiming the new intruders to this prehistoric land.

CHAPTER 15

The day after the colony party found all the Marines in dress uniform standing in the ranks along the ledge outside the Overlook restaurant. The brick boardwalk and a short brick wall lined the edge. Ezekiel was at the doorway watching with a huge grin on his face. Their uniforms were mostly black with highlights of deep reds and light grays and made an impressive sight. Commander Blankenship, with Gunnery Sergeant Zander to his right, stood at the edge nearest the waterfall next to the beginning of the bridge that was under construction. The commander was in full dress uniform, with Conor and Michael in their dress uniforms to the side.

A crowd had gathered around the perimeter to watch the ceremony. There were murmurs and smiles, but when the ceremony began, a quiet settled over the crowd. There was an expectant atmosphere in the air as the commander stepped up to the podium.

The gunnery sergeant ordered loudly, "Private First Class Abrams, front and center."

Abrams marched forward, saluted, and stood at attention. The gunny read the citation promoting the young man to Lance Corporal Abrams. The commander shook the young man's hand and congratulated him. They exchanged salutes, and the new lance corporal returned to his place in the ranks.

The gunny ordered loudly, "Lance Corporal Hoffman, front and center."

Hoffman briskly marched forward, saluted, and stood at attention. The gunny read the citation that promoted Natalie Hoffman to the rank of corporal. When finished, the commander extended his hand and shook the hand Hoffman extended in turn. He congratulated the young woman, then they exchanged salutes, and Hoffman returned to her place in the ranks.

The gunny ordered loudly, "Corporal Flores, front and center."

The dark-haired young man stepped briskly forward to be promoted to the rank of sergeant, then returned to the place in the ranks.

Gunnery Sergeant Zander ordered loudly, "Sergeant Krupich, front and center."

Rachel Krupich briskly marched forward, saluted, and stood at attention in front of the commander. The gunny commenced reading the citation that promoted the sergeant to the rank of staff sergeant. Finished, the commander extended his hand to the young woman and congratulated her on her accomplishment. Saluting each other again, the young woman about-faced and returned to her place in the ranks.

Gunnery Sergeant Zander ordered loudly, "Sergeant Hall, front and center."

The tall blonde woman marched forward to stand in front of the commander with a brisk salute as the gunnery sergeant read the citation promoting her to staff sergeant. The commander congratulated her and shook the woman's hand. Then she returned to the ranks after returning salutes with the commander.

Gunnery Sergeant Zander then ordered loudly, "Staff Sergeant Rusu, front and center."

The gunny again recited a citation that promoted the individual to gunnery sergeant. Finished, the commander shook the young man's hand, and they saluted each other, then he, too, returned to the ranks.

Then Gunnery Sergeant Zander announced, "Staff Sergeant Rosenstein, front and center."

The staff sergeant, smartly outfitted in her dress uniform, marched forward and repeated the salute and posture of her previous comrades in arms. Gunnery Sergeant Zander read the citation that promoted her to gunnery sergeant, and she shook the commander's hand, saluted, and turned and took her place in the ranks once again.

Commander Blankenship then turned and looked at Lieutenant Commander Conor Raybourn, who handed him a certificate. The commander then ordered Gunnery Sergeant Zander front and center. With a little surprise on his face, the gunny took his place in front of the commander and saluted. The commander then read the certificate that promoted the gunny to the rank of master sergeant. When finished, the new master sergeant shook hands with the commander and saluted. There were cheers and clapping from all present, including the commander.

After a moment, Commander Hadden Blankenship raised his voice and announced, "Ladies and gentlemen, we're not done yet."

Master Sergeant Evan Zander returned to his place beside the commander. Hadden Blankenship turned again to Conor and extended his hand. Conor filled it with yet another certificate, and the commander turned and placed it on the podium before opening it.

"Gunnery Sergeant Shiran Rosenstein, front and center," announced Conor.

The new gunnery sergeant marched forward with surprise written all over her face. She once again saluted and stood at attention as she had a short time ago. The commander looked her up and down and nodded as he opened the certificate.

"Let all those here know that the following takes the authorization of three line officers," announced Commander Blankenship, "which the following certificate contains, and all three officers are present if there remains any doubt." The commander then read the certificate that confirmed that Gunnery Sergeant Rosenstein had meet all the requirements for promotion to second lieutenant of the United Systems Marine Corps, and that said promotion was effective immediately.

The jaws of her fellow enlisted were hanging open in shock and surprise with the exception of the master sergeant, who stood there grinning. Shiran Rosenstein had been working on the requirements even before she had reported aboard the *New Horizon* but did not realize that the promotion was to be presented to her anytime sooner than a year or two down the road. The looks of shock and surprise were replaced by thoughtful looks as her teammates realized that the dynamics for their department had changed dramatically. They now had an OIC, or officer in charge, who was actually a US Marine. As the commander finished reading the citation, Shiran simply stood at attention, stunned at the turn of fortune.

Commander Blankenship stood there for a moment before saying, "Second Lieutenant, it's customary to shake hands and salute."

"Yes, sir," said Second Lieutenant Shiran Rosenstein as she shook his hand and snapped a salute that the commander returned.

"Anything to say, Second Lieutenant?" queried the commander.

"I find myself suddenly extremely out of uniform, sir," responded Shiran Rosenstein.

"I believe Ezekiel can help you with that, Second Lieutenant. That's as long as you're buying us all a drink," the commander stated as the snickering died down.

"I can do that, sir!" declared Second Lieutenant Rosenstein.

There were loud cheers and clapping at that, and the commander dismissed everyone so they could come forward and shake their new second lieutenant's and master sergeant's hands. Conor and Michael waited for everyone to pass through the line and enter the Overlook before going up to congratulate the new officer and master sergeant.

They entered the restaurant, and Ezekiel Yap presented the two senior Marines with fresh uniforms hanging inside plastic bags. They thanked him, and Ezekiel escorted them back to the bathrooms, where Staff Sergeant Krupich and Gunnery Sergeant Rusu already stood in new uniforms, holding the doors open for their colleagues. Shiran Rosenstein entered the door Rachel Krupich held open, and Zander entered the other with Gunnery Sergeant Rusu. The doors closed, and Krupich turned to assist her new second lieutenant and Rusu his new master sergeant.

When they were ready, Lieutenant Anderson presented them to their comrades. First came Master Sergeant Evan Zander, and the crowd cheered and clapped. Then it was Second Lieutenant Rosenstein's turn as she stepped out into the main dining room. When she stepped out, Master Sergeant Zander stepped in front of her and presented her with a sword, which he attached to the belt at her side, then Michael announced her.

"Ladies and gentlemen, may I present to all of you Second Lieutenant Shiran Rosenstein," he called.

Clapping and cheers filled the room, and there were now more people crowding the room than her fellow Marines and the officers at the ceremony. Shiran's face flushed, and a smile spread across her face as she noticed Captain Hiroka Tamura, Chief Tami Zander, and several others in their dress uniforms waiting to meet her.

Conor took hold of Shiran's elbow and escorted her over to Captain Tamura, who stood beside Commander Blankenship. They both congratulated her on her accomplishment, and then the commander reminded her that she had promised to buy the first round. She was led to the counter where Master Sergeant Evan Zander presented her with a fifth of Kentucky's finest, which made a few eyebrows raise. Second Lieutenant Rosenstein, in turn, presented the bottle to Ezekiel, who already had shot glasses for everyone present sitting on the counter. He filled each from the bottle, and when he was finished, everyone took a shot and held theirs, looking expectantly at Rosenstein.

Shiran raised her shot and stated loudly, "Semper fi!"

Everyone in the room repeated her toast, and they all took a swallow of what was probably one of the last Earth-brewed whiskeys they would ever see again in their lifetimes. The liquid burned going down and left a warm glow in her stomach, relieving the tension that she had felt since the stunning announcement of her becoming the only United Systems Marine officer in this part of the galaxy.

She contemplated that last thought. Was she really a United Systems Marine anymore? There was little chance of ever returning to Sol system or even contacting Sol system during their lifetimes. Any decisions to be made would have to originate here on site with no inputs from any headquarters outside their own. A weight of responsibility seemed to descend on her shoulders as she looked at the other officers present. Commander Blankenship seemed to sense what she was thinking because he was watching her eyes, and when they locked on each other, he nodded as though in agreement.

Commander Blankenship looked at Master Sergeant Zander and asked, "So, Master Sergeant, exactly how many cases of that beverage do you have on board?"

"I don't know what you mean, sir," stated the master sergeant.

"Let me rephrase that, Master Sergeant," replied the commander. "The captain's locker aboard the *New Horizon* is lacking refreshments for visiting high-ranking guests, and it would be greatly appreciated to have someone," he paused, then added, "provide a gift to restock the captain's locker."

"I understand, sir. I will see what can be done," returned the master sergeant, who turned and nodded at Ezekiel behind the counter. Ezekiel vanished into the back room and returned in short notice with another bottle, which he handed to the master sergeant. Evan Zander, in turn, presented the bottle to Commander Blankenship, who nodded his thanks.

The gathering was served up another shot of beverages by Ezekiel, though this time, the shots were rougher when making its way down. The bottle it came in was locally made by the glassworks that had started up shortly after the foundry and cement works. It was filled by a brewery that was part owned by Evan Zander, who knew a bit about the manufacture of malts and liquors. Evan assured all those present that quality would improve with age, and until then, everyone would have to endure.

After their second liquid salute, Ezekiel invited everyone to take a seat so he could serve them their meal. It consisted of slices of meat that were originally from triceratops, rice, and boiled carrots. After the meal, Ezekiel served a chocolate pudding that the commander had authorized from the ship's stores for the occasion. It was all delicious, and after the meal, everyone sat back with cups of tea, which they slowly sipped as the various table occupants sat and talked.

Shiran and the other officers present were sitting at the table in the back, exchanging pleasantries and discussing the various endeavors the colonists were attempting to give the colony variety, such as the new pastries that the Flour Mill down the street was serving, when Shiran brought up the find that the master sergeant had made in his report.

"Master Sergeant Zander said they found a bronze spearhead yesterday when they were hunting our meal," said Second Lieutenant Rosenstein.

Conor looked at her, surprised. "I haven't seen that report yet."

"It's probably in your in basket considering he just filed it this morning," responded Shiran.

"Oh!" said Conor.

"The report says it looks like a spearhead. It is bronze though," continued Shiran. "The master sergeant had it sent up to that archeologist named Lavie to have a look at."

"Forward his finds to me ASAP," injected Commander Blankenship.

"Yes, sir," responded Lieutenant Commander Raybourn.

The conversation drifted, and the commander mentioned that he had reservations about Shiran's promotion to second lieutenant. Hiroka chastised him on that, asking if he felt that way about all females, and his response was simply that he was unsure if she was ready for the responsibility. However, he also added that he needed another officer. Shiran was somewhat abashed and determined that she would do her best to prove herself to the commander. She didn't realize how soon the opportunity would come.

CHAPTER 16

That afternoon, after the ceremonial mast, Commander Hadden Blankenship and Lieutenant Commander Conor Raybourn were in the cave in the back of the west side of the cleft. The cave was no longer being used as sleeping quarters by the colonists and was being repurposed as an electronics suite. The commander had wanted a secure location for the installation, and there had been disagreement with the president over the future use. A vote was held with the commander only winning by a bare margin. Conor's friend Lieutenant Michael Anderson was in charge of the project and gave them a tour.

The cave had been expanded, and the walls had been smoothed down. Racks for the equipment were being installed, along with cable runs for the various equipment. Offices for those working there were at the left and right of the main hall. After the offices was a radio room to the right side of the hall, which would contain all the equipment to maintain communications. To the left was the space for an operations room for the radar and security scanning equipment. At the end of the hall was the computer complex or AI room.

After the tour, they sat in the only complete office discussing matters and having coffee. It was the cleanest part of the facility and was used as a break room by the workers. The room was small with a desk, file cabinet, and three chairs all made of wood and produced by the carpentry shop. Michael sent his crew to an early lunch so they would not be disturbed during or after the tour, assuming that there would be a discussion afterward that the commander might want to keep private.

"This looks good, Lieutenant," commented Hadden Blankenship.

"Thank you, sir. There's room to expand the complex in the future too," replied Michael.

"How soon should the radio and operations suite be up and running?" asked Hadden.

"We're estimating six months to a year, sir," answered Michael.

"That long?" queried the commander, perplexed.

"The ship's factory can only produce so much in the way of equipment and cabling. The civilian end has run behind on manufacturing also," said Michael uncomfortably.

"It's all right, Lieutenant. I understand. Is there any way to move the time frame up?" returned Hadden.

"There's also the fact that we're running low on some essential elements and minerals the ship's factory requires for the manufacturing of key components," added Conor.

"What are we doing about that?" asked Hadden.

"I'm taking a chopper with a sensor unit out to see if we can locate any deposits nearby," stated Conor.

"Provide me a list of what we are low on, and have Hattie designate items being produced that require them, Mr. Raybourn," ordered the commander.

"Yes, sir," replied Conor.

"Good. Anything else?" asked Hadden.

There was a slight pause, and finally, Michael finally broached the subject. "We could get part of the suite up sooner if we took redundant equipment from the *New Horizon* radio room, CIC, and ship's stores."

"Would it significantly increase our time frame?" asked Hadden.

"Only if certain equipment and cabling are also produced on time. In which case, we could have a minimal suite with few to no backups in three months," returned Michael.

"Forward me a list of the equipment we could remove and what equipment we would need to produce to make that happen, Lieutenant," said Hadden.

"Yes, sir," Michael confirmed.

"Break it down by systems also," ordered the commander.

"Yes, sir," Michael acknowledged.

Hadden Blankenship sat back and pondered the dark space in the rear of the complex that would contain the AI. It was not the skills available to create another AI that worried him but the resources. It would take a lot more rare earth and precious metals to produce a computer capable of supporting an artificial intelligence, much more than the *New Horizon* carried, and most of that was already dedicated to the building of just the radio shack.

"How long will it take to produce an AI?" Hadden finally asked, breaking the growing silence that had descended on the room.

"That would take us back to the element and mineral shortage, sir," replied Michael.

"I see," said Hadden.

"If I may, sir, we haven't evaluated the planet's moons for resources," interjected Conor.

The commander looked at Conor, then said, "That is a thought. What do you propose?"

"A longboat with a crew of four equipped with a sensor suite and EVA equipment," said Lieutenant Commander Raybourn.

"Who's going to be put in command?" asked Hadden.

"I was thinking myself or Michael, sir," stated Conor.

"No, I need you both down here on the planet," responded Hadden.

"Who do you recommend, sir?" asked Conor.

"I think Ensign Sobolov would be a good choice. Who else were you thinking of sending?" asked Hadden.

"I want to send that exogeologist Steven Gates, along with another pilot. I was thinking Boatswain Martins and a Marine, namely, Gunny Rusu," said Conor.

"Why the last two?" inquired Commander Blankenship.

"Boatswain Martins has completed seven round trips between the *New Horizon* and the cleft as command pilot on longboats," replied Conor.

"And Gunnery Sergeant Rusu?" asked Hadden.

"Gunny Rusu has been doing simulator training for piloting longboats for over six months now," returned Conor.

"Giving them a third pilot if need be," stated Hadden. "A good choice, Mr. Raybourn."

"Rusu is also familiar with handling drones and robots remotely," Michael injected.

Hadden Blankenship nodded. "Draft a mission with those recommendations and send it to me on the *New Horizon*."

"Draft a mission profile, sir?" asked Conor.

"I'm sure the president will want to know why we are needing a civilian and what resources are being utilized," deadpanned Hadden.

"Yes, sir. I understand," returned Conor.

"Why the Marine, Lieutenant Commander?" inquired Hadden.

"Sir, the fauna and flora on this planet had to come from Earth or vice versa. That suggests that a spacefaring race exists. After the discovery of the spearhead the other day, I think it's best that there be a strong arm along on any mission we send out," Conor explained.

"I agree. I also want the shuttle armed with chaff, flares, smoke, and EMP. Give them a minimal package of rockets for offensive capability, but I want it understood that they are to run, not fight," stated Hadden. He then looked at Michael and asked, "What are the chances of reproducing a type A factory, Lieutenant?"

"The ship's type A factory cannot even produce a wide variety of the parts required. We'd have to start from scratch. The HTs might be able to produce some of the required parts in the ship's machine shop, and we may be able to cobble together some of the control circuits. However, that brings us back to the element and mineral shortage. Even if we did have all the resources available at this time, it would take a major effort of most of the skilled manpower to be able to produce another type A factory," responded Michael.

"If we did have the resources and manpower available?" asked the commander.

"With testing and quality assurance, I don't think we could do it in less than five years, sir. We're looking at two to three years to construct the AI already being built just to control the factory," said Michael.

"I was afraid that would be the answer," sighed Hadden. "How many of Dr. Hollinger's requirements can we meet along with our own?"

"It might add a year or more to the production of the AI and increase our time frames for other items by 50 percent," stated Michael.

Commander Hadden Blankenship sat back and sighed again.

"Is there a problem, sir?" asked Conor.

"It's been brought to my attention that the people of the colony are demanding access to Hattie, and that in turn requires more equipment to be produced and supplied to them," returned Hadden.

"That will require more resources and more time availability for the ship's factory to produce such equipment and put us behind schedule," said Conor.

"They also want other equipment produced for their welfare and entertainment," added Hadden.

"What kind of equipment, sir?" inquired Conor.

"People like their laptops, toasters, ovens, refrigerators, and other conveniences not normally supplied aboard ship, Mr. Raybourn. All of which would take up resources and time of the ship's factory," stated Hadden.

"Have you and Lieutenant Anderson looked at the secure file I've created, sir?" asked Conor.

"I have, Mr. Raybourn. I'm not happy with the projections, and I understand your concern," said Commander Blankenship.

"That would expand our time frame significantly, sir," stated Conor. "The resources we have and what we acquire barely meet our own requirements."

"And the ship's factory wasn't meant to operate for extended periods of time without a shipyard overhaul," added Michael.

"And we already have parts that have gone past their expected lifetime inside the ship's factory," stated Hadden Blankenship. "Fortunately, Hattie says the HTs can manufacture most of them to within specifications in a matter of days. I've already given the HTs the specifications that are being produced when they stand duty," stated Hadden Blankenship, referring to the hull technicians, or

HTs, who were the craftsmen of metal and wooden items the ship's factory could not produce.

"How long will the stock they have last?" asked Conor.

"Hattie estimates two years at the current rate of consumption," stated Hadden.

"The foundry isn't advanced enough yet to replace that quality of stock. They're hoping to produce that quality in another year if all goes well, and even then, it will be limited," said Conor.

"We may have to lower the standards," stated Michael.

"I'd rather not do that, especially for parts in the ship's factory," said Hadden.

"So we lower standards for other equipment being made. Some things do not have to be the specs the military requires, especially when it's for civilian use," suggested Conor.

"I agree," said the commander. "At least for the time being. Then gradually improve their quality as resources become available."

"Will the president agree to this?" asked Conor.

"He'll have too," said Hadden. "He won't have much of a choice. It's either keep the people happy or tell them to do without."

"So two years to hold on to what we have or slowly decline. Not very encouraging, sir," said Conor.

"No, it isn't," said Hadden.

They sat in silence for a few moments sipping their coffee and pondering what more they could do to keep the colony from taking a slow fall from the spacefaring race they had become. The thought of living on a planet inhabited by some of the largest denizens of Earth's past without technology to aid them was not heartening. Just then, Staff Sergeant Krupich burst in as the three were sitting back and finishing their coffee. They looked up, astonished at the intrusion. She was out of breath and made no excuse, but for what she had to say, she needed no excuse.

"The elevator cable broke, sirs!" she yelled as she attempted to come to attention.

The three officers were up and running past the Marine before she could even salute. The chopper was parked only a hundred meters from the cave entrance, and Conor made a beeline toward it. Time slowed, and it seemed to take forever to arrive as Conor's legs pumped. He saw two figures approaching the chopper parallel to his position carrying a large case between them, and as they all arrived at the chopper, Conor realized they were Drs. Hollinger and Joshi. The kit was thrown into the side carrier and strapped in as Conor prepped for takeoff. The commander sat beside him as the other three squeezed into the rear.

The chopper took off and reached the edge swiftly, and Conor slowed as he started to drop to the base of the cliff. He noticed the other chopper rise beside the Marine Complex and head toward the elevator. Then he saw the Marines—all were still in their dress uniforms—as he descended, entering the cloud of dust at the bottom of the elevator. Because of the sword strapped to the waist of the Marine, he was positive that it was Shiran leading them. His tension and anxiety grew at the realization that she was in very real danger, and he might be too late to prevent it.

"The dust is going to be bad," said Hadden Blankenship as Conor dropped the chopper toward the elevator's base. The other chopper and ATV could be seen moving in the swirling dust.

People working in the various factories were emerging and either heading toward the elevator or simply staring in disbelief. Dust covered the cockpit as Conor approached, and he hoped no one was beneath them in the dust storm, and if they were, they were getting out of the way. The dust cleared, and Conor adjusted as he realized the chopper was falling. There was a flash of red by the perimeter fence as he slowed their descent. He landed with a jarring bump that made everyone grunt as Conor turned off the engine. Everyone jumped out, keeping low, as the blades started to slow down. Dr. Hollinger was the only member of their party to run straight toward the scene of devastation as they scrambled to unpack the kit and stretchers that formed the side carriers of the chopper.

The dust was blinding, making Lieutenant Commander Conor Raybourn squint and claw clumsily at the straps securing the stretcher, but they finally came loose, and he felt Michael release his end of the stretcher only a second later. They stumbled with the stretcher between them toward the remnants of the elevator platform, wondering if anyone could have survived the fall, hoping against hope that perhaps there would be a chance, however slight.

The dust cleared for a second, and Conor saw a scene that would stay with him for the rest of his life. He saw Second Lieutenant Shiran Rosenstein run toward the platform being lifted by the ATV. She loosened her belt, gripping it in her hand as her sword dropped to the ground. Then she dove underneath the platform.

CHAPTER 17

Three happy people were laughing and gossiping the next day as they entered the cage of the elevator. Last evening's party left everyone in a cheerful mood and ready for another day. Everything was fine with the world. The door was shut, and the cage started going down. It was nearly twenty meters along when everything changed. A cable suddenly snapped, and the cage tilted sideways, wedging itself against the guide rails. The passengers were thrown against the steel net composing the side of the cage. They screamed in horror as the net gave way, and one of them fell to the base of the cliff. The last two clawed feverishly at the safety net for the possible security it provided.

There was a screeching noise, then something snapped. The trip to the bottom seemed to take forever as they fell. The impact was like a giant fist against their frail bodies, and bones gave way. Then silence fell as a cloud of dust rose like a living thing into the skies from the violent impact. It spread over the growing industries at the base of the cliff and rose above the edge of the cleft. Many of those outside had watched in horror as the platform had fallen, frozen to inaction.

Second Lieutenant Shiran Rosenstein heard something unusual as she was about to enter the Marine Complex. She looked toward the cleft as the rest of the Marines who had accompanied her down looked back also. She saw the elevator descend swiftly at an odd angle with a person preceding it to the rocky base of the cleft. Dust flew, and she saw the two people inside the crumpled cage bounce at the impact. She looked at Gunnery Sergeant Rusu beside her and pushed him toward the chopper parked nearby.

"Bring the chopper!" Second Lieutenant Rosenstein yelled, then she ran toward the devastation, leaving all the Marines behind her.

She was out of breath, and the dust was still clouding the air when she arrived. She approached more cautiously, allowing the Marines behind her to catch up. She reached the wire mesh of the cage. The air cleared momentarily, allowing her to see the twisted cage and the broken bodies of the two it contained. A severed foot protruded from underneath the edge of the platform where the person who fell must lie. She heard the chopper approach from the Marine Complex behind her, and a second chopper coming over the edge of the cleft caught her peripheral vision.

Shiran entered the cage and went up to the woman lying there, while Evan approached the body of the man. The woman was Carol Moore, and the man was her fiancé, Richard Hunt, both of whom had been part of the engineering crew and had started a glass factory together since their arrival on the planet.

The woman's eyes slowly blinked as she focused on Shiran, and she said, "Shiran, what?" Then her eyes became unfocused and stared into the distance as a small dribble of blood slid past her lips.

Evan came over and placed a hand on her shoulder as tears flowed down her cheeks. "There was nothing we could have done," stated Master Sergeant Zander.

The Marine chopper landed, and Marines jumped out, grabbing stretchers. More dust filled the air with the arrival of the cleft chopper. Two stretchers carried by Marines passed Shiran, and they gently placed the broken bodies of her friends into them. They were being removed from the platform and taken to the waiting Marine chopper as Dr. Hollinger ran up to inspect the bodies. She shook her head upon seeing the condition of the broken bodies, and her shoulders slumped. Shiran saw her reach down and gently close the eyes of Carol and Richard in the stretchers.

The ATV with the loader had arrived and was being positioned to lift the platform as Shiran turned to walk over to the chopper where Dr. Hollinger stood by the two bodies being attached to the chopper by Marines. Out of the corner of her eye, Shiran saw people scrambling to remove the Neil Robertson stretchers from the chopper that had arrived from the cleft with Dr. Hollinger. She knew they were uniformed people, but it did not register who they were as they started approaching with their burdens.

By now, all was in confusion. A crowd had gathered from the industries, and many of them were looking on in shock. People were crying. Others were running about shouting. One person seemed to be laughing and bawling, while another looked at him in anger. One man had his arms around a woman, just holding her.

Just then, the ATV that had inserted the loader under the platform slowly lifted the edge up. There was a cry from underneath, and Shiran turned away from the Marine chopper already running toward the cry. She unfastened her belt and let her sword drop to the ground with her belt still in her hand. She dove under the platform and into a dust-filled hell. The master sergeant and another Marine looked at each other as she passed them and immediately worked furiously to place blocks under the raised edge as Shiran squirmed into the confined space. She grabbed a leg that had no foot and was covered in blood for her effort as she wrapped her belt around its severed end. The leg continued to struggle as the platform was lifted higher by the ATV, and more blocks were placed to keep the platform from collapsing on her and whoever was underneath with her.

Finally, the struggling stopped, and choking on dust while squinting through tear-filled eyes, she was able to crawl forward. She carefully looked and felt along the back of the person lying there and decided to take the chance of rolling the person over so she could position him to pull him out by the shoulders on top of her. She inched back the way she had come and dragged the victim toward open air and daylight. The journey seemed to take forever, but finally, hands reached past her and took hold of the burden that had become deadweight and lifted it off her.

Then other hands grabbed her and lifted her gently up and out from underneath the ruined platform. The master sergeant was there; his dress uniform covered in dust and blood with a torn front. His hands steadied her when she gained her footing. His face was grim, but pride showed in his eyes as he looked her up and down. He gave her a salute and turned back to the body that she had just pulled out of hell. Dr. Hollinger was examining Thomas Tollifer, whose dust-covered body lay in the stretcher; she shook her head.

Finished, Dr. Hollinger looked at the commander, saying, "If we can get this man to the *New Horizon* alive, I might be able to save him and the foot. Place the foot on ice right now!"

A Marine started running to fetch a cooler and ice from the shuttle. The commander ordered him to inform Chief Tami Zander to prep for an immediate departure. The doctor bent down and looked at Tollifer's ID tags as Dr. Kers Joshi handed her a tourniquet to replace the blood-soaked belt around the injured man's leg. Taking the tourniquet, she started placing it just below the belt.

"I also need at least a liter of O positive blood now," she ordered as Kers Joshi went back to the type B med kit the cleft chopper had brought. Seven Marines stepped forward, rolling up their sleeves as they did so. Kers withdrew a plasma bag to begin the process.

While this was happening, Shiran noticed Gunnery Sergeant Samuel Rusu walk over to the cable end that lay nearby on the ground. He was examining it closely without touching it as she walked unsteadily over to him. There was a scowl on Samuel's face as she squatted down beside him.

"What's the problem?" Shiran asked.

"Acid," Samuel responded lowly.

"What?" she returned as Evan and Conor squatted down beside them.

"That part of the cable was covered in acid," replied Samuel in a low voice.

"Are you sure?" demanded Conor as he looked around to make sure no one was close enough to overhear.

"Yes, sir. I've seen it before," whispered Samuel Rusu.

"Keep this to yourselves," ordered Conor. "Not a word, even to the other Marines. Understood?"

They all nodded as they stood up, and Conor walked over to Commander Blankenship, drawing him aside to whisper to him. Hadden gave Conor a sharp look, then searched the gathered crowd intensely. The commander then turned and bent down to pick up the discarded sword and retrieved the belt that the doctor had replaced with a tourniquet. He walked over to Shiran and slowly put the belt around her waist and sword in place as he ignored the dust and blood that covered her uniform. Finished, Hadden stood at attention and presented Shiran a sharp salute and stated, "Second Lieutenant Rosenstein, if I had any doubts about your promotion this morning, they are dispelled forever."

She stood there, her new uniform torn down the back with the uniform's arms and legs in tatters. Blood and dust covered her from head to foot. She returned the commander's salute and said, "Thank you, sir!"

They held their salute. She looked around and saw Conor, her Marines, and many of the civilians holding salutes. When the salute was dropped, many of those gathered began to clap. Then the commander stepped forward and embraced her even though it covered the front of his uniform in dust and blood. Then he passed her to Conor, who did the same.

Corporal Johnson had returned with the cooler, and Shiran could hear the longboat prepping for launch. Turning, the commander and Conor guided Shiran to the waiting chopper. She saw the Marines gently take the stretcher containing Thomas Tollifer toward the longboat with Dr. Hollinger striding along beside. The master sergeant looked at her and said he would take care of things. The commander and Conor guided her toward the MILDET chopper Conor had flown from the cleft. Michael and Dr. Joshi took the bodies of Carol and Richard to the cleft medical facility in the Marine chopper.

The chopper ride up to the cleft and the walk to the MILDET prefab that served as quarters for Conor and the commander when he was ashore was a blur. Conor took her to the shower and toilet and gently pushed Shiran in. She removed her clothing and tossed them on the floor outside the door and took a long hot shower. When Shiran was finished, a knock sounded on the door, and a hand with a fresh set of cammies complete with the correct insignia appeared. She took the uniform and closed the door as the hand disappeared.

She heard Staff Sergeant Rachel Krupich ask, "Anything else, sirs?"

"No, Staff Sergeant, that will be all. Thank you," came the voice of the commander.

"You're welcome, sir," came the cheerful reply.

Shiran heard the outside door to the prefab close as she dressed herself. Finished, she stepped out to discover Conor and the commander already changed into cammies also, but then they hadn't been covered in blood from head to foot and could simply wash up at the kitchen sink. They were both looking at her as Conor handed her boots to complete her outfit.

"Feeling better, Shiran?" asked Hadden Blankenship.

"Yes, sir," she replied.

"Up for a walk?" asked Conor.

"I think so," Shiran replied.

"We'll meet you in the Overlook in two hours, sir?" asked Conor.

"In two hours then, Conor," responded Hadden.

Conor escorted Shiran to the door. As they departed, Shiran heard the commander say, "Hattie." They walked along the edge until they reached the Overlook, then followed the boardwalk along the river. They just walked arm in arm with her head upon his shoulder. People passed and nodded politely, and some offered her thanks as they passed by, though none lingered to disturb their time together as they walked the boardwalk.

They finally ended up at the Flour Mill and found a table. The owner, Stefanie Lanier, took their order and offered her congratulations and thanks to Shiran. They sat and drank tea as they listened and watched the people pass by. Finally, Conor looked at his wrist and said, "We're late."

"For what?" asked Shiran.

"Supper," replied Conor.

The two got up and walked the short distance to the Overlook and entered. Ezekiel met them at the entrance and escorted them back to where Commander Hadden Blankenship and Captain Hiroka Tamura were already seated. They were both dressed in cammies, and Shiran relaxed.

"What would the lady like to drink?" asked Ezekiel as he held Shiran's chair for her.

"A tea would be nice, Ezekiel," replied Shiran.

The others gathered at the table chose tea also. Cups, tea bags, and a pot of steaming water were brought to them by Roberta. They sat back and talked about small items that were happening in the colony until the meal was ready. The meal was fish with wild rice and a salad covered in oil and vinegar. Ezekiel brought a bottle of sweet blush wine that was produced in the brewery.

"Compliments of the house," Ezekiel stated as he poured the sweet beverage, then placed the bottle on the table.

They ate their meal slowly, relishing every bite, as the conversation drifted to their early lives in Sol system. They sat and talked late into the evening before the group left, each going their separate ways. Conor and Shiran walked near the wall by the edge, looking out on the world that was slowly becoming a home. When they made it to the MILDET prefab, they were both tired and lay simply embracing as they fell asleep.

The day after the elevator incident, Shiran awoke early. Conor had already showered and dressed for the meeting that he had with the president and the commander. She gave him a kiss as he departed and got ready for the meeting she had at the Overlook. She hadn't mentioned it to Conor because of whom she had a meeting with. Shiran walked over to the Overlook and entered as Ezekiel was giving Dr. Kers Joshi a Danish to go with the tea that he was stirring.

Kers looked up with a smile at Shiran as she walked in. "Good morning, Shiran."

"Good morning, Kers," replied Shiran.

"How are you doing this morning?" asked Kers.

"I'm fine, Kers. Thank you," responded Shiran

"I'm glad I met you. You saved me a walk over to the Marine tent," said Kers.

"I wasn't at the Marine tent last night," replied Shiran.

"Oh! All the better I met you here then. Please take this," said Dr. Joshi as he pulled something out of his pocket and laid it on the table.

"What is it?" asked Shiran.

"A breathalyzer," stated Kers.

"Why do I need that?" asked Shiran.

"You may not need it. But Dr. Hollinger and I both agreed that you should carry one for a couple of weeks. If you start having trouble breathing, use it," said Kers.

"Why would I have trouble breathing?" asked Shiran.

"There was a lot of dust in the air. We gave the master sergeant enough breathalyzers to give to all the Marines when he left his home this morning. However, he said you might be here for breakfast this morning," responded Kers.

The thought of how Master Sergeant Zander knew she'd be here this morning went through her mind. It seemed that some secrets were just not possible to keep from that man. She shrugged mentally and decided that she'd have to pay more attention to his methods to determine how he did it because she knew he'd never tell her how he did it. She picked up the breathalyzer and put it in her pocket after reading the simple directions on the package.

"Anything else, Doctor?" asked Shiran.

"As a matter of fact, you have lab work at the clinic later on this morning, say, about eleven?" asked Dr. Joshi.

"Why?" demanded Shiran.

"Because of your heroism, my dear sweet lady." Kers smiled.

"Eleven then," said Shiran, rolling her eyes.

"Have a nice breakfast, Shiran," said Kers, smiling.

"You too, Kers," returned Shiran as she walked to the back of the Overlook where Jacqueline Vinet was already seated.

CHAPTER 18

The Overlook was relatively empty when she arrived. Ezekiel was serving breakfast to Catalina Ramirez and John Martins in the corner. Dr. Kers Joshi sat at a table near the entrance where he was drinking tea and having a Danish.

"Good morning, Jacqueline," said Kers Joshi.

"Good morning, Kers. How is everything?" she replied.

"I'm fine. How are you today?" asked Kers.

"Everything is fine," replied Jacqueline.

"Breakfast before work," responded Kers. "Dr. Hollinger wants me to go over some charts before seeing the morning cases. Are you doing all right?"

Jacqueline nodded knowing that the question involved her currently growing condition. Few knew yet, but it was going to be readily apparent very soon. Hopefully, her secret was still safe and would not turn into an issue in the meeting she had this morning.

"We still have our appointment at ten?" asked Jacqueline.

"Yes," responded Dr. Joshi.

"I will see you and Dr. Hollinger at ten then," Jacqueline stated as she turned away.

"Don't be late," called Kers as she walked away.

"I won't, Kers," she responded over her shoulder.

She turned back toward the counter in the back of the Overlook. Ezekiel was already waiting for her with a menu in hand as she approached. She indicated to him that she preferred one of the tables in the back, and he led her to one in the corner. The tables and seating were somewhat roughly made, but the carpentry shop was working overtime supplying everyone with the basic furniture. She took a seat facing the front entrance.

"Good morning, Ezekiel," said Jacqueline.

"Good morning, Ms. Jacqueline," greeted Ezekiel.

"I don't need a menu," she stated. "Just some tea."

"Are you expecting anyone?" asked Ezekiel.

She glanced up in surprise. "Yes, I am."

"May I ask who so I can direct them to you if need be?" inquired Ezekiel.

"Shiran Rosenstein," responded Jacqueline quietly.

Ezekiel raised an eyebrow but asked no further questions. He turned and went back to the counter where he filled a cup with hot water and placed a tea bag on the saucer. He placed it on a tray along with a container of sugar and returned to the table, where he set the tea and sugar in front of Jacqueline. Assured that she needed nothing else when she nodded her thanks, he turned to see on his other customer's needs.

Though Jacqueline gave the appearance that all was well, in reality, she was not happy. She didn't know what to do or how to resolve the complex feelings that invaded her mind. She loved Conor Raybourn, but they had separated as the interests they shared appeared to grow further apart. Their interests in the FTL drive had drawn them together. However, she had sensed that Conor did not share her intense interest in politics and forming a new government in this fledgling colony. No, his interests were exploring the new world around him.

She touched the bulge that she was attempting to hide by wearing loose-fitting outfits, but soon it would be readily apparent to all that she was very pregnant. She didn't want to deal with that thought at the moment. It was her problem, and she didn't want anyone telling her how to run her life or what to do. She liked her independence and wished to keep it that way.

Jacqueline sat sipping her tea, contemplating the turn of events that were taking place, when Shiran Rosenstein arrived. She didn't notice her at first because she had been preoccupied. Dr. Kers Joshi greeted and spoke to Shiran, then Roberta pointed Shiran toward the back of the Overlook. Shiran nodded and walked briskly back toward where Jacqueline sat. She was dressed in camouflage and wearing her sidearm, so she was most likely going down to the Marine Complex afterward.

"Good morning, Jacqueline," greeted Shiran.

"Good morning, Shiran," Jacqueline replied as Shiran sat down opposite of her.

They sat looking at each other for a moment in silence, then Ezekiel arrived to break the tension.

"May I get you something, Ms. Shiran?" asked Ezekiel.

"How about some tea and a Danish, Ezekiel?" Shiran smiled.

"Very well, Ms. Shiran. Do you need a refill, Ms. Jacqueline?" asked Ezekiel.

"Why don't you bring us a pot of hot water and some tea bags?" decided Jacqueline.

"Very good. I'll be right back, ladies," said Ezekiel.

Ezekiel turned to get their order as they sat there looking at each other in silence. The tension seemed to grow as they waited for Ezekiel to return. He was back quickly with the order, which he placed in front of them. He refilled Jacqueline's cup with hot water and retreated back behind the counter as the two women put tea bags in their cups and stirred in sugar.

Shiran finally picked up a fork and broke off a piece of Danish and said, "As I recall, you asked to see me to talk about something."

"Yes, I did," replied Jacqueline. "Congratulations on your promotion."

"Thank you," said Shiran. "But I'm sure that's not what you wanted to talk about."

"Not exactly," confessed Jacqueline.

"Is this about Conor?" asked Shiran pointedly.

"Yes and no," replied Jacqueline.

"What then?" questioned Shiran.

Jacqueline Vinet sat back looking at Shiran Rosenstein and contemplated how to approach the subject. This was proving more difficult than she anticipated. The conflicting emotions running through her thoughts made her question the wisdom of asking for this meeting. Finally, she decided to broach the subject.

"There are troubles in the colony," stated Jacqueline.

"Yes. I read about it in the paper," replied Shiran as she pointed to the daily paper that was lying on the table across from them that Ezekiel read when he had the time.

"I'm talking about more than the elevator malfunction or the brawls that the sheriff and his team break up on a routine basis," said Jacqueline.

"What makes you think it was a malfunction?" asked Shiran.

Jacqueline blinked as the implications to that comment sank in. "What do you mean?"

"That's all I'm going to say about it," stated Shiran.

"Very well. Then perhaps you'll understand when I say there are forces within the colony that see Conor as a possible threat to themselves," said Jacqueline.

"In what way?" asked Shiran.

"Since he is one of the highest-ranking officers who decided to remain active and he was the operations officer, when Captain Tamura stepped down, it made him the executive officer of the *New Horizon*," stated Jacqueline. "If something should happen to Commander Blankenship, that would effectively make him captain."

"I don't see what difference that will make," stated Shiran.

"Some people have already suggested a military coup," said Jacqueline.

"That's ridiculous," stated Shiran.

"Is it? What if Blankenship decided to withhold or refuse to do as the president orders?" asked Jacqueline.

"Why would the commander do that?" questioned Shiran.

"I merely mention it as a possibility—a possibility that I've overheard others suggest," responded Jacqueline Vinet.

"The *New Horizon* needs the manpower and resources that the colony provides as much as the colony requires the *New Horizon*," stated Shiran.

"Does it?" asked Jacqueline.

"The ship is severely undermanned. The colony has to send up people every week just to keep the systems that are online operating in an optimal condition," stated Shiran.

"That doesn't keep people from talking about it," stated Jacqueline.

"Which people?" Shiran delved.

"I'd rather not say," countered Jacqueline.

"I can guess," observed Shiran.

"And you may very well be correct. It doesn't keep them from talking about the possibility," said Jacqueline. "They're worried, especially about Conor."

"Why?" asked Shiran.

"Many reasons. Your relationship to him and your recent promotion to second lieutenant makes you the Marines' department head. It's also very apparent that Marines support him and like him," said Jacqueline Vinet.

"That doesn't make him a threat. He's not interested in taking over the colony," replied Shiran.

"I know that," said Jacqueline.

"You're making a big thing over something that's not there," stated Shiran.

"Maybe," confessed Jacqueline.

"Whose child are you carrying?" riposted Shiran Rosenstein, suddenly changing the subject.

The question struck Jacqueline like a round fired from her companion's sidearm. She felt like a deer caught in the headlights of an oncoming vehicle. "What do you mean?" stammered Jacqueline.

"Just because I wear a Marine uniform doesn't mean I'm stupid," retorted Shiran.

"I didn't say that," said Jacqueline.

"You don't have to say it," insisted Shiran.

"What does that mean?" implored Jacqueline.

"I've been to college and know what a lot of the educated think of the military, especially what they think of the Marines," stated Shiran.

"Who told you I was pregnant?" asked Jacqueline. "Dr. Kers?"

"No! It's pretty obvious," stated Shiran as her eyes flashed menacingly. "You suddenly start wearing loose-fitting clothing. Hell, the Marines even have a pool on who the father is, though they think I don't know about it. Whose child is it?"

"I'd rather not say," countered Jacqueline.

"Then you might as well say it's Conor's," stated Shiran. "How do you think it looks to the people you're talking about? Think they'll leave you out of this power game you say they're playing?"

Jacqueline Vinet sat back knowing that Shiran Rosenstein was stating the truth. She had tried to deny that truth to herself. She knew deep down that the people would look for ways to manipulate things to their ends. In other circumstances, it would be easy enough to avoid, but in such a small community, it would be nearly impossible.

While they had been talking, the other two customers finished and left. Brad Guillete arrived and talked to Ezekiel for a moment. Brad went behind the counter and grabbed a toolbox and was replacing an electrical outlet that had been broken. He was finishing up as Norman Pool, a chief who had worked in engineering, walked in. When he saw Brad, his eyes squinted, and a smile appeared on his face.

"Whatcha doing there, Guillete?" sneered Norman Pool loudly as he walked up to Brad, which drew the attention of the two women who sat and watched.

"Installing an outlet for Ezekiel, Mr. Pool," Brad Guillete informed Norman Pool.

"Really? You know what you're doing?" questioned Pool.

"Do you need something?" Brad replied, but it was obvious that he was growing tense.

"Nope! I'll just sit here and watch," stated Pool with a malicious grin.

"If that's what you want to do," replied Brad as he finished screwing the cover plate back over the receptacle and started putting the tools he had used back in the toolbox.

"You know what I've heard about you there, Guillete?" Pool grinned as he changed tactics.

"No, I haven't," replied Brad.

"I've heard that you're a real screwup and that you don't know what you're doing." Pool grinned.

Brad visibly tensed and looked at Pool as he asked, "Who told you that?"

"Doesn't matter. I've heard that everything you do is fucked up," Pool stated, grinning.

"I'm sorry you feel that way," replied Brad as he returned the items to the toolbox and put it back behind the counter.

"Yep! That's the way I feel about it. I'd be surprised if that even works for a week." Norman Pool grinned as he pointed at the newly installed outlet.

"If that's what you believe," replied Brad Guillete. Then turning toward Ezekiel, he said, "Ezekiel, I'm done. I'm leaving."

"Thank you, Brad," replied Ezekiel pensively.

Shiran Rosenstein looked at Jacqueline Vinet and said, "Excuse me, but I think we're done here, and duty calls."

Jacqueline Vinet simply nodded and watched as Shiran Rosenstein went up to Ezekiel. She whispered something to him, and he relaxed as he nodded back at her. Shiran walked briskly to the front door and shouted, "Brad, wait up!" Then Shiran was gone.

Meanwhile, Ezekiel Yap asked Norman Pool if he wanted something, and Pool shook his head. Ezekiel attempted to say something else to Pool that Jacqueline didn't hear. She did hear Pool shout "Mind your own business!" as he stomped out of the Overlook. She saw Ezekiel shake his head and clench his fists for a moment. He raised his hands to cover his face and let out a deep sigh as he turned toward the counter. He poured a stiff drink of the local beverage and downed it all in one swig, then looked around, noticing that he still had a customer.

"Are you all right, Ezekiel?" asked Jacqueline.

"I am fine, Ms. Jacqueline," replied Ezekiel as the smile returned to his face.

"What was that all about?" asked Jacqueline.

"I'm sorry the lady had to see that. May I offer you another tea or Danish?" returned Ezekiel as he attempted to change the subject.

Jacqueline Vinet looked at Ezekiel for a minute, not saying anything. Ezekiel looked behind himself to make sure no one else was in the Overlook, then he walked over to the table where Jacqueline sat. Taking the seat that Shiran had abandoned, he placed the empty tea setting on the Danish dish and set them aside. Done with the minor task, he again looked at Jacqueline, and the smile that normally occupied his demeanor had again vanished.

"All is not as it seems, Ms. Jacqueline. Even you understand this, yet do not see the full depth at times," said Ezekiel.

"You're talking about what just took place between Brad and Norman?" asked Jacqueline.

"Yes," stated Ezekiel emphatically.

"I don't understand," said Jacqueline.

"You and Ms. Shiran were discussing it just a little while ago," stated Ezekiel.

"You overheard what we were talking about?" queried Jacqueline.

"When one works here, one can hear many things," said Ezekiel. "Acoustics."

"I see," said Jacqueline. "How does what just happened relate to what Shiran and I were talking about?"

"Mr. Pool is a member of the group who supports Mr. Martinez. He is part of Mr. Martinez's inner circle," stated Ezekiel.

"I still don't understand," said Jacqueline.

"Ms. Felter is part of Mr. Martinez's inner circle also," added Ezekiel.

Agnes Felter had been Brad's division officer prior to starting the colony. Jacqueline felt at a loss as to how that related to what she had just witnessed. Were there hard feelings because Brad Guillete had chosen to join the colony instead of remaining active duty? But Felter had chosen to join the colony instead of remaining active duty also, so that didn't make sense. A puzzled frown crossed her face.

"I still don't see," Jacqueline confessed.

"Ms. Felter did not like young Mr. Brad even before Commander Blankenship released us to form the colony," Ezekiel informed Jacqueline.

"I see," said Jacqueline as things came together.

Ezekiel nodded. "Those same feelings hold for how Mr. Martinez feels about many of those who were given rank and status in the service even though they were not originally active United Systems personnel. This especially holds true for those who were involved in the FTL project."

"But Brad was not part of the FTL development project, and he's been part of the United Systems military for over ten years," stated Jacqueline.

"It does not matter because Ms. Felter does not like him," replied Ezekiel.

"I understand. Thank you, Ezekiel," said Jacqueline.

"You're welcome, my lady. Now if you'll excuse me, I have tables to clear and get ready for the lunchtime rush," Ezekiel said as he got up and moved off to take care of business. He went over to Roberta, who was wiping down a table at the front door, and talked briefly with her. He then went to the counter and grabbed a rag and spray bottle and commenced wiping down the top and front of the counter as he prepared for midday customers.

Jacqueline got up and moved toward the door, saying, "I have an appointment to attend."

"I know, and congratulations," Ezekiel said as she reached the door.

A small smile touched her lips as it occurred to her that Ezekiel Yap most likely had overheard that part of her conversation with Shiran Rosenstein. It occurred to her that Ezekiel also ran betting pools on different happenings in the colony as the smile turned into a grin and a chuckle of mirth at her own expense.

As she exited the Overlook, she turned left down the walkway that ran toward the back of the cleft's depression paralleling the river. She had a lot to think about as she contemplated what she had learned in the Overlook today. Ezekiel was correct in that not everything was as it seemed and that a lot more was behind the politics that ran the colony than a feeling of comradeship and teamwork needed to establish themselves on this world.

A few shops down, Jacqueline passed the Flour Mill. It was a café that specialized in tea, the local coffee, Danishes, and breads.

Shiran Rosenstein and Brad Guillete sat at an outside table talking to each other, and she nodded at them as she passed. Brad did not seem as tense as he had been when he had left the Overlook. She looked back as she stood at the entrance to the clinic to see Rachel Krupich arrive and give Brad a hug and kiss. She watched as Shiran got up after saying something to the two, then she walked off briskly in the direction of the Overlook and the elevators.

CHAPTER 19

Nearly a week had passed since the elevator incident. They were met by Bahri Hiran when they knocked on the door of the president's prefab. He indicated where they should sit across from the other two people who were already present. He poured coffee for Hadden Blankenship, Conor Raybourn, and Shiran Rosenstein, then he retreated into the kitchen area of the prefab from which President Martinez soon emerged and closed the door.

Felipe Martinez sat at the head of the table in the prefab that he used as his presidential office, with Agnes Felter and Norman Pool to his right. The government offices were still under consideration and would be for quite some time considering the specifications that Martinez had required. Hadden, Conor, and Shiran sat to Martinez's left across from the other two who composed the president's immediate cabinet.

The president cleared his throat as he looked at the people assembled in the room. He was clearly unhappy, and it wasn't hard to guess exactly what was on his mind. Everyone in the room knew that the elevator incident was no accident. Someone, most likely the saboteur who had stranded them, was on the planet with them. What his or her motive was for creating havoc in the colony when everyone's survival depended on them working together was unknown. Finally, the president nodded and addressed the people gathered in his office.

"We have a serious problem. Someone appears to want to hurt the colony. Everyone here knows that even though we've been keeping it from the rest of the colony," stated Felipe Martinez.

"Why not tell them?" asked Conor.

"And create panic?" demanded Agnes Felter. "Everyone will be looking at each other and accusing the other of being a saboteur."

"Then what do we do?" asked Shiran.

"It's the Marines' job to provide security," stated Norman Pool.

"For military assets and external threats to the colony," Shiran stated. "We barely have enough Marines to do that."

"We need more security and protection, Commander. How do you propose to provide it?" demanded Felipe Martinez.

"This is an internal security problem of the colony," replied Hadden Blankenship.

"The security of the colony is paramount to the security of the ship also," retorted Felipe.

"Are you declaring martial law, Mr. President?" the commander asked.

"No!" declared Felipe as his face turned red.

"Then bolster your sheriffs, and we will provide training and equipment for them," replied Hadden.

"There's already six people in the sheriffs' department taking care of the brawls and other infractions these people do. How many people do you think we need in a sheriff's department?" retorted Agnes.

"As many as it takes," replied Hadden. "Civil law enforcement is not the military's concern."

"We have too many people who don't want to do their fair share," sneered Agnes.

"Like people who rearrange duty sections so they can attend a party?" asked Conor. He felt Shiran hit his leg lightly under the table, and Hadden gave him a puzzled frown.

"What does that mean?" demanded Agnes, red-faced.

"Nothing," replied Conor.

Felipe Martinez cleared his throat and took a sip of his coffee. He sat thoughtfully for a moment, looking at all the people gathered in the room. An uncomfortable silence pervaded the room until finally his eyes locked on Shiran.

"So the Marines are unwilling to do their job," President Martinez stated.

"I didn't say that, sir," replied Shiran.

The commander interjected at this point, "Are you declaring the elevator and factories military property, Mr. President?"

"I didn't say that! We need armed patrols and security guards stationed at key points to protect the colony," stated Felipe.

"We have all of thirty Marines, Mr. President. That is nowhere near enough to provide the type of security you're asking for," responded Hadden Blankenship. "You hold the inactive commission of a lieutenant commander and should be more than aware of that, Mr. President."

The room grew quiet for a few moments as those assembled stared at one another. The meeting was not going to go well, thought Conor. Martinez was demanding that the people who still served as active military, and most especially the Marines, provide more security and protection for the colony. His demands for armed patrols throughout the day were not practical for the thirty Marines under Second Lieutenant Rosenstein. It was doubtful that it would be practical even if there were a complement of one hundred Marines.

There was a slight clattering of dishes from the kitchen area. Hadden Blankenship looked at the closed door with a frown but didn't say anything. Conor felt Shiran's hand clasp his knee and tap twice on his kneecap. It was a private signal between them to keep alert. The other people in the room simply smiled and shook their heads, muttering something about clumsy people. Felipe Martinez was not through with his demands.

"So you're not going to provide security to vital assets of the colony and the *New Horizon*?" demanded Felipe.

"What would you have me do, Mr. President?" I can take Marines off the duties and reassign them, in which case, those duties that they currently do will not be accomplished," said Hadden.

"That's not satisfactory!" retorted Agnes.

Hadden looked at Agnes Felter and added, "Or I could recall people to active duty so they can provide added security."

"You don't have my permission to do that!" growled Felipe.

"Don't I? You're demanding more security personnel to protect vital assets. I've read the Constitution of the colony, and that means

I can recall people when I deem there is an emergency that threatens the colony or *New Horizon*," stated Commander Blankenship.

Martinez grew red-faced and stated, "That's not what I'm saying."

"It sounds like it to me, Mr. President," replied Hadden.

"I'll fire you," said Felipe.

"If that's what you wish to do, Mr. President. Then I'll hand over command to Lieutenant Commander Raybourn," stated the commander.

Felipe Martinez's face turned beet red, and he sputtered, "We'll provide the security, but we'll need training and equipment."

"I'm sure we can do that, Mr. President," replied Hadden.

"Fine! The three of you are dismissed. I need to discuss this with my cabinet," growled Martinez.

The three military members rose and saluted the president, then left the room as silence descended. It was apparent that the commander had not made any political points with the president. Other demands he might make would obviously be discussed within his cabinet of supervisors.

They just reached the brick walkway that led to the elevators when Blankenship stopped. "The two of you need to watch your backs," stated Blankenship.

"We will, sir," said Rosenstein.

Hadden looked at Conor and asked, "What was that about the duty rosters?"

"Something I became aware of at the party, sir," replied Conor.

"Since you're acting executive officer, I want you to go over all the duty rosters since we've been here. If there's anything that you deem as"—the commander paused—"inconsistencies, I want to be informed about them."

"What kind of inconsistencies, sir?" inquired Conor.

"If there are people who do more than two weeks per year," said Hadden. "Or if they're continually being rescheduled to stand duty when there's an event."

"What if some are not on the duty roster at all, sir?" asked Conor.

"I want to know that also and who they are on both sides of the issue," ordered the commander.

"I understand, sir," Conor acknowledged.

"Get back with me on this ASAP," ordered Hadden.

"Aye, aye, sir," confirmed Conor.

"Anything else, Mr. Raybourn?" asked Hadden.

"How much training do you want my Marines to give the security detail once the cabinet arranges for them, sir?" asked Shiran.

"We'll cross that bridge when we come to it, Lieutenant," said Hadden.

"I'm only a second lieutenant, sir," replied Shiran.

"You're more of a lieutenant than what's in that room back there, Lieutenant. Now which one of you is buying me a drink?" stated Hadden.

"We both will, sir," Shiran proclaimed.

The trio walked briskly down the walkway, passing the elevator, and down to the corner where they entered the Overlook. Ezekiel took one look at the three and knew that three shots were the order of the day as they approached the counter. The other four customers called greetings to the commander as he passed, and Hadden nodded acknowledgment. The shots were poured, and the three took their drinks to the table in the back where they wouldn't be disturbed. They sipped the amber fluid slowly. Finally, the commander looked at the two officers and sighed.

"I'll be returning to the ship shortly," said Hadden.

"Anything we can do to help, sir?" asked Conor.

"Pray," stated Hadden.

"It's a miracle that we found this planet, sir," stated Shiran.

"I know," said Hadden.

"The Marines will do all we can, sir," said Shiran.

"I'm aware of that," replied Hadden.

"We could use more Marines. Recruitment?" suggested Conor.

"That may very well be an option, Conor," replied Hadden.

"Not many people available for that, sir," Shiran.

"I'm aware of that. The question is Mr. Martinez's plans. He can't draft security personnel, so what incentives can he offer to make a person want to do the job?" replied Hadden. "I want the two of you, along with Lieutenant Anderson and Master Sergeant Zander, to keep your eyes and ears open for any other inconsistencies. If it's important, I'll need to know ASAP," ordered the commander.

Seeing their glasses empty, Ezekiel moved over to the table with three mugs and a pot of coffee. He set the mugs down, poured, and placed each mug in front of the three customers. He asked if they needed anything else and was told no.

They sat and sipped on their coffee in silence. The sounds of ongoing construction could be heard as they watched the customers of the Overlook. As they finished their coffees, the commander stood up and said, "I'll be back in two weeks." Then he turned and left.

Ezekiel returned with the coffeepot and poured for Conor and Shiran. "The commander does not look happy," stated Ezekiel.

"He has a lot on his mind," said Shiran.

"This elevator accident concerns him?" asked Ezekiel.

"Among other things," responded Conor evasively.

"Ms. Raisa told me that she has concerns too," said Ezekiel.

Raisa Romanov was a chemist who had been part of the science division that Jacqueline Vinet had been in charge of on the *New Horizon*. The science division had been composed of fifty scientists of various disciplines. All had been commissioned as CWOs, or chief warrant officers, to serve as specialists during the voyage. She now helped at the foundry and other factories that needed assistance. She put them on track for refining the metals they required to manufacture, along with such materials as ink for the printing presses Francesca operated. Raisa was a valuable member to the community and, according to Ezekiel, a wonderful cook who taught him a variety of new dishes to serve at the Overlook.

"What concerns Ms. Romanov?" asked Conor.

"Somehow, a bottle of sulfuric acid has vanished from the inventory that she had brought down from the *New Horizon*. She did not see a reason to report it since it was less than a tenth of a liter, but she now keeps her apartment locked," said Ezekiel.

Conor and Shiran looked at each other for a moment. The statement that Gunnery Sergeant Rusu had made about the cable breakage was foremost in their minds. It would seem that Samuel had been correct and that they needed to talk to Raisa Romanov.

"I think keeping things such as that locked up might be a wise precaution," stated Conor.

"Especially if they are important to her work," added Shiran.

Ezekiel nodded. "Yes. I now keep my solvents for cleaning locked up too."

"That may be a good idea, Ezekiel," said Shiran.

"If one were to ask for a security system to be installed, would the *New Horizon* be capable of providing such?" asked Ezekiel.

"I believe that might be arranged, Ezekiel. I'll forward a memo to the commander," said Conor. "If he agrees, perhaps the second lieutenant can have one of her Marines install it for you."

"Oh no! The Marines already do too much. I'm sure young Mr. Brad would be more than willing to take care of installing such equipment," said Ezekiel, referring to Brad Guillete.

"All right, Ezekiel. If the commander agrees and sends some down, I'll have someone run it up to you," said Shiran.

"That would be wonderful, Ms. Shiran," said Ezekiel. "Now if you will excuse me, I need to attend to my duties."

"All right, Ezekiel. You have a wonderful day," said Shiran as Conor nodded to Ezekiel in turn.

They finished their coffee in silence. Somehow, Conor felt that Ezekiel knew more about things that were supposed to be secret than either of them wished to admit. The thought occurred to Conor that Ezekiel could be the saboteur. He shook his head at that. The master sergeant and Marines trusted Ezekiel. What if they all were? Conor shook his head. This job could make a person paranoid, because if that were the case, they were all in trouble.

CHAPTER 20

She observed the intruders for many moons. They had been building a nest in the cleft and below it during that time. There were many of them who had been deposited by large birds that landed on the lake. They were strange birds that carried the intruders inside and disgorged them on the shore of the lake.

Strange things had come into the world. These beings built their nests of wood, stone, metal, and some sort of hide. She had watched them as they made lines of metal that extended from the high crevice in the cliff face to its base. They had built metal nests that moved between the top and bottom of those silvery lines, then use it to raise and lower themselves on it.

Lately, she had started sleeping at outlying small cave sites that she had set up as refuges over the years. She spent several days at each site observing the intruders and their doings. They were strange beings, and she had at first thought that they were the ancient enemy of her people. They walked on two legs and had no tail. They also carried fire sticks that could kill from afar. But these intruders had no hair on their faces and were smaller than the descriptions passed down by her kind.

The huge unknown beast that the intruders used was crossing the plain and frightening the herds as it passed. She knew the beast could carry up to six of the intruders inside its mouth. Why it did not devour them, she did not understand. Perhaps it was some sort of symbiotic relationship like some animals she knew, or perhaps it was a machine like the watercraft her people constructed. That latter thought gave her pause. The rulers of her people also used carriages to transport their august presence through the people. However, those carriages required handlers to lift and carry them.

Could the beast really be a carrier with unseen handlers inside that caused it to move about, carrying the intruders to where they wished to go? She shook her head at the thought, but a gleam came to her eye as new understanding dawned on her. She already knew these intruders were dangerous. A single intruder could bring down one of the long-necked ones, which were the biggest creatures that roamed these plains. She had even seen them take down one of the giant carnivores with a fire stick. The fire sticks were deadly, which was why she was very careful not to be seen by the intruders.

She knew that they could see color, because there were two times that they must have seen her red plumage that stood out. Once was when they were in the flying beast. Another form of carriage perhaps? And once while she was observing them digging at the base of the cliff a few thousands of body lengths south of their nest. Her natural coloring, although duller than males, was a danger to her around these intruders.

The beast stopped nearly a hundred body lengths from a herd of triceratops. The side mouths opened, and the intruders departed the beast. As Qu'Loo'Oh' watched, she noticed that she could see all the way through the beast and out the mouth that must be open on the far side. Sometimes, like today, the beast was longer and swiveled in the middle. When the beast was extended like that, the intruders killed a herd beast and placed the meat in the mouth of the body's rear extension. It made no sense that the beast was bigger when hungry. Many confusing things occurred when she was watching the intruders.

She watched as two of the intruders walked forward with their fire sticks. The one carrying the smaller fire stick pointed at a young bull and nodded. The intruder with the larger fire stick went to its knees and pointed its fire stick at the young bull. There was a loud crack, and the young bull dropped to the ground. The rest of the herd retreated her way at a trot, and she retreated behind a large tree as they passed. The intruders entered their beast again, and it went over to the dead bull. Then the intruders reappeared from the interior of the beast and commenced butchering the bull and placing large pieces of the dead animal in the beast's hind extension. She waited till the butchering was complete and the intruders left.

She approached the site of where the triceratops lay cautiously. Scavengers were already feasting on its corpse, and other larger scavengers were approaching. She circled the corpse cautiously. Keeping watch for danger, she searched the area for anything the intruders might have left. As she reached the chest area of the dead creature, she noted that the liver and heart had been removed. Near the corpse stood a dark stick protruding from the bloody ground. On alert, she moved over and quickly grabbed the stick and pulled.

She withdrew the item from the ground. It had a handle made of an unknown material. She licked it and knew it was not wood, or at least no wood she knew. The attached metal was long, flat, and sharp. Along one edge, it shone like silver. The rest of the length was black and dull. She knew it for a knife, but like no knife she had ever seen. She tested the edge on the three-horn's corpse beside her, and it cut like freshly chipped flint or a bronze blade that was just sharpened. Yet she had watched the intruder use it for quite a while. She looked closely at the edge and could detect no nicks or dulling along its length. A tool and what a tool to leave lying. She was sure that the intruder would be back for it once the intruder realized that it had been left behind.

She placed the knife in a leather sheath that she had. She placed her prize in her pouch, then she looked around searchingly for any danger. Assured, she ate from the corpse, for it had been long since she had the flesh of a triceratops. Having eaten her fill, she raised her head and looked about again as she withdrew into the tree line.

She had just entered the forest when the beast returned, heading toward the kill the intruders had butchered. The scavengers scattered as the beast arrived at the dead triceratops, and two of the intruders got out of the beast. They walked around the dead three-horn, inspecting the ground closely. The larger one squatted down and inspected the ground where the knife had been. The smaller intruder walked over to where the larger one squatted. They appeared to be communicating as the larger one pointed its forelimb at the ground.

Then the larger one rose to its full height and looked directly at where she hid in the forest. She froze, fearing the intruder could see her, but then she saw its head sweep left and right as if it scanned the tree line. The intruder turned and walked back to the beast with the smaller one following. They entered the mouths of the beast and left, heading toward the nest that they built at the cliff base and the ledge above.

Qu'Loo'Oh' waited until the beast vanished over the rise before she rose. She was sure they came back for the knife she now carried in her pouch because they searched the ground where the knife had been. A knife made of a material her people could not make or reproduce. She had seen metal objects that were said to be from the Old Ones, the ancestors of her race. The Old Ones of her people were said to have come from a faraway place that lay in the heavens among the very stars. There were many legends about them, and they were considered gods among the people.

If these intruders were like her Old Ones, they, too, must have come from somewhere far away, for she had never before seen the large birds that carried them into the sky before the intruders appeared. Could they have come from the new star that always stayed at the same point in the horizon? The star had appeared shortly before the arrival of the intruders. It did not move as other stars did. It moved more as the moons.

Qu'Loo'Oh' decided to brush the thoughts from her mind for the moment. She had planned on moving to a better vantage point to observe the intruders today. It would be dangerous since the shelter that she had set up long ago was inside their territory. It was past the place where the intruders mined for copper and near the silvery web they had erected around the base of the cliff. The beasts that the intruders controlled moved a lot of earth when they were mining the copper in the area.

She moved cautiously, wary of being seen and ever vigilant for possible dangers. The greens avoided the forest line of this plain because of the intruders and their fire sticks, but they still remained a threat to be reckoned with. She moved deeper into the vegetation and found the path that led toward the copper mine of the intruders.

She knew that today it would not be worked because she had seen three of the beasts with their extended bodies take the path along the lake, heading south and east.

As she neared the mine, she slowed. Qu'Loo'Oh' knew she was at least a thousand body lengths from her shelter at this point. She started looking for her evening meal as she slipped through the bushes and low-hanging branches. The sun was still a few hours from setting, and she was approaching her shelter when she spotted a small rooter ahead of her. She stalked the rooter, being careful not to make a noise that would frighten the prey. Finally, she was close enough to make her dash and deliver a disabling stroke with the talon on her right foot to its side, and so she could grab and break the neck with her jaws.

She ate her fill, then picked up her kill to take with her for the rest of the journey. It was heavy, and she was old. She took several breaks before finally reaching the shelter. Laying her burden down, she moved forward, cautiously searching for anything out of place or an animal that was using it as a lair. There was nothing, and she went to her burden. Taking a length of gut line from her pouch, she tossed the weighted end over a nearby branch, then tied the other end to a leg of her cooling meal. She took the weighted end and pulled the animal up to the branch the line passed over. Tying the weighted end of the line down, she left her repast hanging from the branch.

She walked up the rise, being careful to remain in the heavy foliage as she neared the top above the cave. Looking out over the plain, she saw the silver web the intruders had erected. She was sure that the web was made of some metal. To her people, such was unimaginable wealth, yet these intruders used it to form what could only be a fence to keep the large beasts out. How such a fragile thing would keep them out was inexplicable, but she had seen some of the larger beasts shy away from the web when they touched or went near it. She decided to wait till the sun set to investigate closer.

The smell of burnt flesh reached her nostrils as she crouched at the top of the rise, and an unusual sound emanated from the same direction. Something was happening on the ledge of the cleft. She suspected a large group of the intruders had gathered there for a feast.

Would the intruders intentionally burn the flesh before eating it perhaps to simulate the heat of natural flesh after so long? She snorted and shook her head at the thought. More to think about as she turned and went back down the ridge to the cave nest that waited.

Qu'Loo'Oh' decided to risk a small fire in the back of the cave that night for the warmth it would provide. She drew out the dried tinder she had stored in the cave to ensure there would be little to no smoke visible after it filtered through the foliage outside the cave. She then spread the dried bedding atop the sandpit she had created nearly three years ago. She lay down and drifted off to sleep as the sun set over the distant cliffs to the west.

She was startled awake almost immediately when she heard explosions. Fear gripped her heart, for she thought a massive storm or volcano was nearby. The ground did not shake, so she ruled out volcano. She peered outside the cave and saw stars through the foliage, but bursts of bright light flashed from the direction of the intruders' nests. She climbed to the top of the ridge again and saw streaks of flame rise into the sky near the cleft ledge and burst into brilliant displays of bright flowering points of light. She watched in awe as the very air lit up, and resounding explosions shattered the night. Some of the great beasts stampeded, while others cowered in fear across the plains to the south.

Sometime later, the nightmare finally stopped, and the world was at peace once again. Qu'Loo'Oh' saw the ledge light up, and dim figures moved along the edge toward the nests they had created. She waited, but the phenomena appeared to be over. She snorted and shook her head, then returned back down the ridge to her nest. She had a restless slumber where fire and thunderous noises plagued her dreams.

The next morning, Qu'Loo'Oh' ate her fill of the beast she had hung the evening before. She left the rest lying for the scavengers as she retrieved her weighted line. Finished, she returned to the top of the ridge and watched the nests of the intruders. Around midday, one of the beasts that climbed the webs fell. An intruder proceeded it to the bottom of the webs, and when the beast struck the bottom, a large cloud of dust obscured the area.

She saw a group of intruders near the nest where the large flying beasts lay at rest on the water run toward the place where the dust rose in the air. The two smaller flying beasts with wings that twirled atop their bodies flew toward the dust cloud—the first from the nest the large group of intruders ran from and the other appeared shortly after from the ledge above.

Before either of the fliers could land near the fallen web crawler, one of the beasts with a forelimb she'd never seen before started running toward the dust cloud from the building where the large flying beasts lay in the water. It arrived shortly after both fliers landed and placed its forelimb underneath the web crawler and lifted the beast. As it did so, one of the intruders dropped something long and went underneath the web crawler. The intruder crawled from underneath the web crawler with another intruder shortly afterward, and both were picked up by the other intruders. One was placed on a small nest, and the other was set on its feet again. Qu'Loo'Oh' could only assume the intruder placed in the small nest was the one she had seen fall to the bottom prior to the web crawler and the other was the one who had gone under after the web crawler was lifted.

She saw an intruder run to one of the large flying beasts that lay in the water and return with a box. The intruders placed something in the box, and a group of them carried the box and the intruder in the small nest to the smaller flying beast lying in the water.

When the box and nested intruder were placed inside the beast, it started moving away from the shore. As it moved faster and faster, it lifted from the water and flew away into the sky. Then the other flying beasts with the wings atop their bodies returned to where they came from while the beast with the forelimb stayed lifting the web crawler. Most of the gathered intruders started returning to their nests. Qu'Loo'Oh' blinked and snorted as she thought about the events she just witnessed. What could it mean?

CHAPTER 21

Two weeks passed, and it was early morning when Conor arrived at the military complex. The elevator had been repaired, additional safety features were installed, and the sheriff's department had been expanded. Additionally, security cameras and security fencing were being installed in sensitive areas that were considered essential to the colony. There was some grumbling, while others took it in stride, but no one asked why it was necessary since the explanation was for the safety of the children.

The Marine Complex resembled a giant concrete square block with ports for guns at the upper levels. It was one of the first structures built since it was meant to protect the shuttles, longboats, and ATVs not stored up in the cleft. The choppers were normally stored up in the cleft, but one chopper had been brought down the night before so it could be outfitted with a sensor suite for the day's mission.

It was a clear day when Conor arrived at the Marine Complex, already outfitted in body armor and carrying his Navarro M-71 machine gun. His Gerst S-7 was in its holster and his Kinley-Grant or KG-3 combat knife in its boot sheath. A good day for flight training, especially for a first time in the hot seat. Second Lieutenant Shiran Rosenstein was waiting for him outside near the chopper, along with Master Sergeant Evan Zander. They both gave Lieutenant Commander Raybourn crisp salutes, which Conor returned.

"Good morning, sir," they said in sync.

"Good morning, Second Lieutenant and Master Sergeant," replied Conor. "Is the sensor suite installed and checked out?"

"It is, sir," responded the master sergeant. "Staff Sergeant Hall will be riding behind you and operating it. She's already in the chopper."

"Are you ready, Second Lieutenant?" inquired Conor.

"Anytime you are, Lieutenant Commander," she replied nervously.

"You only live once." Conor smiled.

"I don't understand," Shiran confessed.

"It means enjoy yourself while you can. I was nervous my first time behind the stick also," said Conor.

"All right," said Shiran hesitantly.

"Don't worry, Shiran. You did well in the simulations. I'll be able to take over at any time," said Conor.

"As you say, sir," responded Shiran.

"Want to come along, Master Sergeant?" asked Conor.

Something like a hiccup sounded beside him, and he looked at Shiran questioningly. She looked back at Conor straight-faced, and he shrugged it off.

"I have business to attend to here, sir. If you'll excuse me, I'd best attend to it," replied Master Sergeant Zander briskly.

"Very well, Master Sergeant," said Conor as Evan turned and went back into the Marine Complex. Conor heard a chuckle and looked at Shiran again as her chuckle became a huge grin. "Mind telling me what's going on?" inquired Conor.

"The master sergeant is deathly afraid of flying," confessed Shiran.

"He's a Martian and flown millions of miles," said Conor.

"He's not afraid of space or traveling in space. He's afraid of flying in the air. He's fine in a longboat or shuttle until it hits the atmosphere. Choppers scare the hell out of him," said Shiran.

"Really?" asked Conor.

"He had an accident back on Earth. He was the chopper pilot," admitted Shiran.

"Oh!" he responded.

Conor made a mental note to not suggest the master sergeant for any missions that required him to be in the air. He also made a point of learning more about the capabilities of the Marines in general so he wouldn't make a mistake assigning someone who shouldn't be assigned. The intricacies of command were multiple.

They walked to the chopper and climbed aboard. After strapping in, Shiran prepped for takeoff as Conor watched to make sure she did everything correctly. Then he indicated that she take them up and along the cliff face, flying west toward the perimeter fence.

"It's a beautiful day," exclaimed Shiran.

"Yes, it is," replied Conor.

They were passing over the fields south of the cement and stone works. Georgia Cambi was out tending the crops, but at the moment, she was standing, staring at the fence. Conor looked at the forested ridge beyond the perimeter fence where Cambi's attention appeared to be directed. He saw a flash of red on the ridge past the perimeter fence that vanished a moment later.

"Fly over the ridge and hover," directed Conor, pointing at the ridge beyond the perimeter fence. Shiran took the chopper over the ridge and hovered.

"What are we looking for?" asked Shiran.

"Thought I saw a something red," replied Conor, searching the forest below.

"Maybe a flower or blood on the foliage, sir," commented Staff Sergeant Amanda Hall.

"I don't think so," countered Conor.

"Nothing there now," said Shiran.

"Seems to have vanished," admitted Conor. "Let's go east over the lake."

Shiran took the chopper slightly east as she flew back over the Compound. The Marine Complex and piers were over a kilometer to their left as they flew over the rice paddies the colony harvested. The lake passed quickly below them, its sapphire surface reflecting the morning sun. They came up on the swamp on the east side of the lake that stretched for several kilometers along the base of the cliff face. The cliff started angling to the north as they passed over the swamp. There were several large beasts that watched the chopper as it passed overhead.

A forest lined the east side of the swamp. Further on, alternating patches of forest and open plains where herds of ancient wildlife still roamed past below them. It was amazing to Conor that their luck had stranded them so far away from Sol system to find a world teeming with life. The fact that the life was possibly Terran in the first place was even more extraordinary. They followed the cliff face for over one hundred klicks and were passing over a rise when Shiran got a puzzled look in her eyes. She started circling back.

"What are you doing?" asked Conor.

"Don't you see it?" inquired Shiran.

"See what?" asked Conor.

"Look at that mound closely," Shiran said.

He looked as she continued to circle around the mound. Conor noticed that it was no ordinary mound. There were definite angles to its shape, almost like it was constructed. He started looking for a place to set down, then thought better of it. "Circle," he ordered. Then looking back, he said, "Staff Sergeant."

"Yes, sir," responded Amanda.

"Are we mapping?" asked Conor.

"Yes, sir," affirmed Amanda.

"All right, enlarge the circle by a hundred meters until we reach three klicks out from the pyramid," ordered Conor.

"We could set down right there," suggested Shiran.

"No. We'll come back with more firepower than three M-71s and our sidearms," stated Conor.

"As you wish," stated Shiran as she turned the chopper back.

Conor nodded and switched over to the Marine Complex channel. He ordered the master sergeant to prepare two ATVs and to have ten Marines and an archeologist ready to leave in two hours. After mapping the immediate area from the air, they turned back toward the cleft. It took another half hour to return and land. The landing was a little rough, but the chopper was meant to handle combat and first-time fliers.

They arrived at the Marine Complex, and the ATVs were waiting. Master Sergeant Zander was fully outfitted and carrying a Vinter HR-19 sniper rifle. Nine other Marines stood by—eight with M-71s and another with a second Vinter. The archeologist Jon Lavie was there, holding a Navarro M-71 and looking decidedly uncomfortable in the cammies he was outfitted in.

"Master Sergeant," said Conor.

"All set, sir. The extra gear is in the ATV," stated the master sergeant.

"What about the second lieutenant's?" asked Conor.

"With all due respect, sir, only one officer should go on this mission. The second lieutenant should stay and run interference in the light of recent events in the colony and security," responded Master Sergeant Zander.

"Wait a minute!" cried Shiran. "I'm the Marine officer, and it was my find."

"If we were going into known territory and not over twenty klicks away from the cleft, I might agree with you coming along, ma'am," responded Zander. "But the lieutenant commander said he was leading this mission."

"But—" shouted Second Lieutenant Rosenstein.

"I need firsthand knowledge for my report to the commander and most likely to the president," interjected Conor before Shiran could go any further. "Your job is to run interference and have two fully equipped ATVs along with a chopper loaded for bear if things go south. Gunnery Sergeant Rusu can fly the chopper, and Lieutenant Anderson can stand duty here if you're needed."

"Fine!" responded Shiran. Then she added, "Just come back in one piece."

"That's why I'm going along, ma'am," stated Evan Zander.

Conor and Shiran drew together and kissed long and deeply. There was shuffling and a few whistles in the background, then the master sergeant cleared his throat.

"You'd best come back too," demanded Shiran, looking angrily at the master sergeant. "Chief Zander will be impossible to work with if you don't."

"She'd kill me if I didn't," stated Evan Zander. "Now by your leave, ma'am, daylight's burning."

"Good hunting, Master Sergeant," called Shiran as Master Sergeant Zander entered the ATV. Conor gave Shiran another kiss and climbed aboard the ATV, where the master sergeant handed him magazines for his Gerst S-7.

"What's this?" asked Conor, looking at the magazines. Each one had yellow-and-red-striped tape on the butt.

"Every third round is an explosive round. Replace the magazine you have and put one of these in your Gerst," said Zander. "Your M-71 is already loaded with explosive rounds in the same manner."

"Standard procedure?" inquired Conor.

"Missions like this, it might call for it," stated Evan.

"Does Lavie have them?" asked Conor.

"He only has standard rounds, and we gave him basic firearms training for an hour before you arrived," assured Evan.

"Dr. Lavie, are you good with this?" asked Conor, searching the doctor's eyes.

"Mr. Raybourn, until today, I've never fired a weapon in my life. However, to be one of the first people to actually examine alien ruins up close, it'll be worth it. I'll try not to let you or the Marines down," replied Jon Lavie.

"We should be there within two hours. So, say, about noontime. That will give you about five or six hours to study the ruins unless we stay the night," Evan Zander informed Jon.

"What's the chances of staying the night?" inquired Jon.

"That depends on the local inhabitants, Doctor," stated Evan as he hefted the Vinter HR-19.

"That's not very comforting, Mr. Zander," said Jon.

The rest of the Marines chuckled, and the doctor sat back looking confused as Conor gave him a smile. It was hard to believe that after a year on the planet that there were still people who never handled a firearm or even imagined the real danger that existed outside the cleft. He decided that he needed to talk to the commander about the possibility of having civilians assist the Marines with their hunting expeditions. A hands-on approach to what life was like outside the cleft might be a good idea.

They bounced along for nearly three hours before reaching the site. At first sighting, it was not obvious that they were in the ruins of a long-lost alien city. The foliage had overgrown the area so much that most of it looked like various-sized mounds, making progress even more hazardous.

They arrived at the pyramid that rose out of the forest, not even realizing that they had driven up the first two terraces that formed its base. Trees, bushes, and other foliage blanketed the structure and all the surrounding structures in a mass of tangled green. They departed the ATVs and formed a skirmish line between them. Staff Sergeant Hall was at the end of the line when something big came out of the bushes heading directly for her.

It was a snake, but what a snake! Its head was at least twice the size of any boa or python she had ever seen. Amanda raised her M-71 and pulled the trigger, firing at the head as it kept coming. The explosive rounds caused it to rear its head up and move to the left. The coil of its body whipped toward her. It smashed into her and sent her flying to be abruptly stopped by a tree. There was a loud snap as jolting pain ran up her left arm when it hit the solid bark.

The monster was huge. Amanda swore the damn thing was twenty meters long as it whipped its head around over its coiled body. She heard shouting and more shots as she dropped low and made her way around the tree. A coil of the monster smashed the bark off the spot in the tree she had just left. The head came around the other side of the tree, then passed over her when she dove and rolled as excruciating pain shot up her left arm again. The staff sergeant felt hands grab her by the back of her body armor. She landed roughly as the hands jerked her back behind a rock outcrop. When Amanda looked around to see whose arms had pulled her to safety and held her tightly to his chest, it was Evan Zander.

"Thanks, Master Sergeant!" she murmured.

"We're not out of this yet," growled Evan.

The firing had not ended, and the coiled monster was still searching for prey. Its massive coils lashed, and she saw Sergeant Flores dashed to death between a stone pillar and the body of the creature. His broken body seemed to stand for a moment afterward, then collapse as the snake passed. Then Amanda saw the behemoth turn its attention back toward her and the master sergeant and open its mouth. She saw Sergeant Adachi rise, and the grenade launcher attached to his M-71 spat. The grenade flew into that snake's open mouth, obliterating the monster's head. The behemoth died hard, its coils whipping here and there in its death throes. Trees were toppled, and the ground seemed to resound as the Marines drew back from the immense body. Several minutes later, it still quivered as the life drained from the massive bulk.

Finally, it lay still, and they slowly approached it and the body of their fallen comrade. A stretcher was brought, and the body of Flores was placed on it and taken back to the ATVs. Staff Sergeant Rachel Krupich took Staff Sergeant Amanda Hall aside and tended to her broken arm as the master sergeant met with Lieutenant Commander Raybourn.

Conor was upset, but Evan insisted they needed the intel, so they spent another hour investigating the area. They rounded to the east side of the pyramid, and that was when they discovered the doors. The doors were coated in gold. They were cracked and broken in places, but they still stood surrounded by the marble framework. Conor took out his flashlight as he approached with the master sergeant. Private Johnson and Sergeant Ivankov were already at the door, attempting to open it. Then with a creak and cloud of dust, the door gave way, and they cautiously entered a hall of marble stonework that led to the interior of the pyramid.

They walked for nearly thirty meters before they entered a room. The room was golden, the floor was coated in gold pebbles, while sheets of gold covered the walls and ceiling. What looked like an altar was at the far end of the room, and it appeared to be made of solid gold. There were recesses in the walls that held objects made of gold. The treasure of an emperor lay at their feet. With no way for them to return to Sol system, it was just pretty baubles to the castaways.

"There must be tons of gold here," breathed Evan.

"Back in Sol system, we'd all be wealthy," replied Conor.

"True. Not much good to us now," Evan replied lightheartedly.

"That's where you're wrong, Master Sergeant. We need to load up as much of this as we can," stated the lieutenant commander.

Master Sergeant Zander looked at him questioningly.

"Gold is essential in a lot of electrical equipment. We could use a couple of hundred kilos," Conor informed the master sergeant.

"Ivankov, Johnson, go get containers right now and bring Krupich and Hoffman back with you," ordered the master sergeant.

"Roger that, Master Sergeant," responded Sergeant Nikolai Ivankov.

They returned with the other two Marines and four containers. One container had four folding shovels and a couple of lanterns. The archeologist Jon Lavie arrived with his camera and walked over to Conor.

"This site is an invaluable archaeological find. We can't just take things from it without records," stated Jon.

"Doctor, you have about sixty seconds to make a photographic record before we start grabbing as much as we can. After that, we're hauling ass out of here," retorted Conor.

"But!" exclaimed Jon.

"We need gold for equipment manufacturing. Two hundred kilos would probably last us the next hundred years or more if these were ordinary circumstances. But they aren't. The mainframe for the AI we're building, the medical equipment we require, and if we're able to build another factory will require quite a bit of gold in their manufacturing. Now get to making your record, because if there are any more of those snakes around, I don't want to meet them without more firepower," stated Conor firmly.

Grumbling, Jon Lavie started taking pictures as the Marines set up four lanterns and arranged the crates to fill. They started shoveling the crates full of the golden pebbles that covered the floor. The Marines hurried as they filled the crates to the brim with the yellow treasure, while Conor and the master sergeant kept watch and inspected some of the items in the recesses.

One recess held a miniature pyramid, while another held a plaque resting on a stand. In another was a statue of what looked like a velociraptor, but the raptor held something in its forelimb. In another was what appeared to be a rounded cylinder. All were made of gold, and all would be worth a fortune back in Sol system. Conor only wished he knew what these artifacts meant and how they could help the colony survive.

When one crate was filled, it was closed, and a Marine grabbed each end and took it down the entryway. They were just returning as the second team was departing with their first crate. About a quarter hour later, Conor and the master sergeant took the shovels and lanterns between them as they followed the Marines who carried the other two filled crates with a grumbling archeologist in tow. Jon Lavie carried the tablet from the niche as he walked toward the passageway leading to the outside.

"I thought you said we shouldn't disturb anything, Doctor," said Conor.

"When are we going to be back?" asked Jon.

As they came to the exit, Conor noticed something white near the area the Marines had been digging and filling crates. He stopped and brushed the gold pebbles aside to reveal a skull. It looked like a velociraptor skull, only larger than any raptor he had seen so far, and there was a bulge above the eye sockets. Conor picked it up and went to the exit.

"What's that?" asked Jon.

"A big problem, I think," stated Conor as he stuffed it under his arm. He also noticed Evan Zander go to another niche in the wall, pick up one of the statues, and stuff it in his pouch. "Ready to get out of here, Master Sergeant?"

"Yes, sir!" said Evan as he moved toward the exit.

Conor and Evan closed the doors to the mysterious chamber as the Marines secured the crates to the back of the ATV. They then boarded the ATVs and headed back to the cleft.

As they traveled, Jon Lavie withdrew the golden plaque he had taken from the chamber and started examining it. "So when we are going to be back?" Jon asked again.

"We lost a Marine today. Not anytime soon if I can help it," stated Conor.

"I'm sorry," replied Jon. Then he added, "I mean that, Mr. Raybourn."

Conor shifted uncomfortably and asked, "So what do you have?"

"I photographed where this was prior to taking it so there is a record of where it was found. It has hieroglyphic text on it, but I'm not familiar with the writing. I would say it's some sort of record," said Jon Lavie.

"Is it decipherable?" asked Conor.

"I doubt it. We'll have to have a lot more of the text," confessed Jon.

"Which implies you want to go back," said Conor.

"It might tell us a lot about what's going on," returned Jon.

"That might be, but there's only so many of us that we can afford to lose in the pursuit of knowledge. If the colony grows substantially in the next twenty to fifty years, that might be possible," Conor informed the archeologist.

"I understand, Mr. Raybourn," replied Jon Lavie. He then looked down and said, "After today, I think those of us living in the cleft don't understand the real dangers that this world holds except perhaps the Marines and people such as yourself. We know we're on a world that has life, but we're sheltered in the crevice that you've found for us. We really don't interact with the world as the Marines and others who go out into the field."

CHAPTER 22

A conference was being held in the MILDET prefab. President Felipe Martinez and most of his cabinet were present, along with Dr. Bess Hollinger and Dr. Jon Lavie. Commander Blankenship had Conor, Shiran, Michael, and Evan Zander present also. The discovery of the alien city and the loss of a Marine had kept the commander dirtside. That there was an intelligent race that might or might not still inhabit the planet was disturbing. That they might be related to the velociraptors was even more disturbing. The only good news was that the colony had nearly four hundred kilograms of gold to transport up to the *New Horizon* for the ship's factory. However, even that was being disputed by the president of the colony.

One thing that could not be disputed was the long skull containing rows of pointed teeth running down its jaws. It looked like a velociraptor skull. However, it was too large for the velociraptors the colony was familiar with, and it had an enlarged cranial dome. It came from the chamber of gold that the Marines had located in the abandoned city. Was it one of the original inhabitants? No one knew. But the evidence suggested it was since images of such a being were inscribed on the plaque that Dr. Jon Lavie had brought from the chamber.

"You're sure?" demanded Hadden Blankenship.

"The inscriptions on the plaque clearly show the creature handling tools," stated Jon Lavie.

"The inscriptions appear different than those carved on the back wall of the cleft," said Conor.

"They do, but that means nothing. What's represented here and on the cave of the cleft are obviously not a full representation of the language," said Jon.

"Or they're two different languages. That is, if they are symbols for a language," stated Conor.

"What else could they be?" asked Hadden.

"Symbols of gods or even mathematics perhaps," stated Jon.

"Which means that until we know more, it's nothing more than conjecture," said Felipe Martinez.

"Ladies and gentlemen, could we please get back to the skull?" insisted the commander.

"The skull I examined had a cranial cavity slightly larger than the average human. Some of that may be accounted for by an increased olfactory and possible visual acuity, but it should have nearly human intelligence," stated Bess Hollinger as she contemplated the skull that sat on the table before them.

"Perhaps this will help add credence to that possibility," said Evan as he set the golden statue of a velociraptor holding something on the table.

"What is it, Master Chief, and where did you find it?" asked Hadden.

"You took that from the pyramid. I recognize it from one of the recesses," stated Jon Lavie.

"That's right, Mr. Lavie, and you'll also recognize this item," stated Conor as he set the miniature pyramid beside the statue.

"You've vandalized a priceless archaeological find," declared Dr. Lavie.

Everyone gave the man a look that questioned whether he knew where he really was as Commander Blankenship spoke, "Doctor, I'm sure that the lieutenant commander and master sergeant meant no harm and are more than willing to turn both those artifacts over to an appropriate museum." Then he paused before he continued as he looked the archeologist, "That is, if one is ever built to support such endeavors."

The archeologist looked around the table, then said, "I'm sorry, Commander, and I apologize to the lieutenant commander and master sergeant."

The two looked at Jon Lavie and nodded.

"May we continue with this meeting, Mr. Lavie?" asked Hadden.

"Yes. Let's do that," replied Jon.

"So the inhabitants that built this city may have been velociraptors? At least that is what the evidence points to," asked Hadden.

"I would say so, Commander," replied Bess Hollinger.

"But all the raptors we've encountered are primitive," retorted Felipe Martinez.

"They are a different form of raptor,'" replied Bess.

"What are you trying to tell us?" demanded Felipe as he looked heatedly at the doctor.

"In contrast to the skull before you, the velociraptors we've encountered so far are like comparing a chimpanzee to a human," said Bess.

"I'm still questioning how the animals we see around us came here," stated Hadden. "Even this city and your finds don't explain it. Pyramids, spearheads, and golden artifacts do not add up to the ability to travel in space or to the stars. Neither do I find convergent evolution a satisfactory explanation for what happened here."

"Or if they had that ability, how they lost it," stated Conor.

"And why we've seen no sign of any equipment that would indicate such," added Shiran.

"At least not yet," added Evan Zander.

"Ladies and gentlemen! This seems more like a counsel of war than a discussion of an archaeological find. What are you suggesting?" stated Jon.

"Dr. Lavie, we're talking about a race that may have originated here, on Earth, or some other planet. How they came here is of high interest to all of us. Additionally, the fact that velociraptors are all carnivores is somewhat worrisome to me and many others at this table, if not to you. Do you understand our point of view?" asked Hadden Blankenship.

"Even if they are carnivores, that does not mean they pose a threat," stated Jon Lavie.

"The nature of the beast," muttered Evan Zander.

"What was that, Master Sergeant?" asked Hadden.

"Carnivores may very well have a different perspective on what life is all about, sir," said Evan.

"I agree. Even herbivores can be territorial, and we are talking about a species that has very little in common to ours," said Bess Hollinger.

"We have no proof that any of these," Felipe Martinez hesitated, "advanced velociraptors even exist anymore. I don't see what the problem is. Why are we worried about something that we haven't seen? It sounds like you're looking for ghosts."

"We're here to discuss the recent discoveries of the lieutenant commander," stated Hadden. "We are also making a threat assessment of what these discoveries imply to the colony. In light of what I'm hearing, we may have a problem if the inhabitants of that city are still around."

"You're borrowing trouble where none exists in my opinion," sneered Felipe Martinez.

"This whole planet is trouble, and now I have a dead Marine," countered Shiran.

"So a Marine is dead. At this point, what difference does it make?" demanded Agnes Felter.

It became quiet in the room as everyone in uniform glared at the president's cabinet member. Finally, Commander Hadden Blankenship cleared his throat. "The fact that a Marine is dead is part of the reason why we are here doing a threat assessment, Ms. Felter," stated Hadden.

"I'm sure Ms. Felter didn't mean what she said the way you appear to have taken it," counseled Felipe Martinez.

"Seemed pretty clear to me," growled Evan.

The commander gave the master sergeant a sharp look and a brief shake of the head. Evan Zander sat back, presenting an image of being at attention while still sitting.

"The facts are that whoever or whatever inhabited the city were living alongside the creatures we see. For them to do so with only Bronze Age tools means they were capable of being fairly fierce," stated Shiran Rosenstein.

"We've survived for over a year now, Second Lieutenant," stated Felipe.

"Hidden away behind fences and in the cleft, while the only people who adventure outside that restricted area are the Marines," stated Conor.

"Your point, Mr. Raybourn?" demanded Felipe.

"Yes, Lieutenant Commander, what do you propose?" inquired Hadden.

Lieutenant Commander Conor Raybourn sat back and thought about where the conversation had led them and the misgivings he had after losing Corporal Flores. But living inside the Compound was not possible either. Sometime in the near future, their resources would be depleted, and they would be forced to face the world.

"Sir, even though we're safe, we're not. Many of the colonists have never been beyond the confines of the Compound at the base of the cleft, and some have been up on the cleft for months except when they pull a tour onboard the *New Horizon*. What do they really know about life on this planet other than that?" said Lieutenant Commander Raybourn.

A slight smile crossed the commander's face. The commander looked thoughtful for a moment as others in the room, with the exception of Second Lieutenant Shiran Rosenstein and Master Sergeant Evan Zander, looked at one another in confusion. The Marines were watching the others straight-faced. The implications of what had been said was obviously lost on most in the room.

"What are you getting at, Lieutenant Commander?" demanded President Martinez.

"Aside from the Marines, there are only about a couple dozen people who have set foot outside of the confines of the cleft's Compound. Even for Mr. Lavie, it was the first time he had been outside the Compound, and he had never used a firearm until the Marines instructed him," said Conor.

"So what?" sneered Agnes Felter.

"I think what the lieutenant commander is saying is that you're taking your safety for granted, Ms. Felter. Most of us are living in a few square kilometers of land, unaware of the very real dangers outside the fragile walls that protect us. Does that about sum it up, Mr. Raybourn?" inquired Commander Blankenship.

"Yes, sir," affirmed Conor.

"The only options were settle here or spend the rest of our lives on the *New Horizon*," sneered Agnes.

"Exactly," countered Conor.

"What are you getting at, Mr. Raybourn?" asked Jon Lavie.

"We came here and enclosed ourselves in a comfortable little bubble believing we're safe," stated Conor. "If a disaster destroyed that bubble, how would we survive?"

"We could return to the *New Horizon*," insisted Norman Pool.

"And if the longboats and shuttles are destroyed or even the *New Horizon* at the same time?" asked Conor patiently.

"You're being a sensationalist!" shouted Norman.

"I'm being a realist. If all of this and the *New Horizon* were destroyed, the only place we have to turn is the world outside this complex," stated Conor.

"We have weapons," stated President Martinez.

"How long will those weapons last without facilities to maintain them?" demanded Commander Blankenship.

"And there are only a limited amount of weapons," added Shiran.

"Then throw in the possibility of an intelligent race that may or may not be aggressive into the mix," added Conor.

"We have enough troubles without going out and looking for them!" shouted Felipe Martinez. "We're done here!"

The president and his cabinet members stood up and left. Commander Blankenship watched passively as they did so. Dr. Bess Hollinger and the archeologist Jon Lavie had remained seated with stunned looks on their faces.

"Is that normally how these meetings go?" asked Bess.

"Actually, that went pretty well," said Hadden.

"But we've made no progress in determining the origin of that city or even if the inhabitants still exist," replied Jon.

"I'm sure that will come in time," assured Conor.

"What do we do until then?" asked Shiran.

"Prepare," stated Hadden Blankenship.

"For what?" asked Jon.

"The unknown," replied Hadden.

"To prepare, the medical facilities will require more equipment and supplies. Having most of what we need on the *New Horizon* is not feasible for proper emergency care," stated Bess Hollinger.

"Work up a list. Prioritize the equipment and supplies that you think you might need urgently. Ask Hattie to provide a breakdown of vital resources required to assist you with your choices. I want the same done for the communications suite that Lieutenant Anderson is building, Mr. Raybourn," said Hadden.

The two nodded compliance as the commander looked at Shiran. "Anything you need, Second Lieutenant?"

"Maybe some M-71s and the security equipment for the perimeter fence and Marine Complex, sir," replied Shiran.

"They're already being made," replied Hadden. "Mr. Raybourn, how soon can that moon mission be ready?"

"The team is just waiting to know when," responded Conor.

"I'm going up to the *New Horizon* after Corporal Flores's funeral. Inform them to be on the longboat with me. Ensign Sobolov says *Longboat 4* is equipped and ready to go," stated the commander.

"What's going on?" asked Jon Lavie, who hadn't left and was listening to what the others were saying.

"Looking for resources, Doctor," said Conor.

"Are we that short?" asked Jon.

"After I authorize the equipment for the doctor and Lieutenant Anderson's comm suite, we will be very short, Mr. Lavie," stated Hadden Blankenship.

"But what about the equipment I've requested? I've been waiting for months," said Jon.

"Mr. Lavie, would you rather have a fully equipped medical facility and a way of contacting the *New Horizon* in an emergency or your equipment?" asked Hadden.

"Well, if you're going to put it that way…," Jon trailed off.

"Dr. Lavie, I'm not saying that your contributions wouldn't be important to us, but the safety and welfare of the colony comes first," said Hadden.

"I understand," said Jon.

"Do we have anything further to discuss, ladies and gentlemen? Otherwise, this meeting is adjourned, and you're all dismissed," asked Hadden.

Most of those gathered shook their heads and pushed back from the table. There were muttered "Good days" as most of those gathered left the MILDET prefab. Lieutenant Commander Conor Raybourn remained seated. Second Lieutenant Shiran Rosenstein looked at him, and he indicated for her and Master Sergeant Zander to remain seated.

"I'd like to discuss a matter with you if you have a moment, sir," said Conor as Commander Blankenship looked at the three still seated at the table.

"What is it, Mr. Raybourn?" asked the commander.

"You've read the mission reports, and there's been a recurring theme of people seeing flashes of red in the distance," said Conor.

"Yes?" stated Hadden, turning the affirmative into a question.

"Prior to discovering the pyramid and the recent incident when the second lieutenant took the chopper up, there was something on the ridge west of the Compound," said Conor.

"What was it?" asked Blankenship.

"Something red, sir. It moved into the vegetation as we approached. We were not able to tell what it was," Conor informed the commander.

"You're sure?" questioned Hadden.

"I saw it too, sir. I believe Georgia Cambi saw it also. She was standing facing the ridge as we flew over her," said Shiran.

"Check with her on that," ordered Hadden.

"I will," affirmed Shiran.

"What are we proposing?" asked Hadden.

"I think we need to investigate the area west of the Compound," stated Conor.

"Haven't we been through that area out to the copper mines?" asked Blankenship.

"Most of the vanishing flashes of red have been noted around that area and no other place so far, sir," stated Conor.

Commander Blankenship sat back, looking thoughtful. He placed his elbows on the table and steepled his fingers together, then said, "Let's see the map."

Conor opened the laptop in front of him and called up the map of sightings he had created. He slid the laptop over to Hadden. The commander studied the map for a moment.

"What are you proposing?" asked Hadden.

"Foot recon into the bush past the mines," answered Conor.

The commander sat back again before saying, "We just lost a Marine, Mr. Raybourn. A foot recon there might even be more dangerous."

"I realize that, sir, but there's no way to take an ATV into that terrain any further than the copper mines," said Conor. He paused then added, "I also want to check out that ridge west of the Compound, and that's only available on foot."

"Think there's something there?" asked Blankenship.

"Only one way to find out, sir," stated Conor.

"Where do I fit into this?" demanded Shiran.

"Minding the Marine Complex and sending the cavalry prepped to save my ass if we get into trouble," stated Conor.

"I should be leading this," stated Shiran.

"I'm not ready to lose a second lieutenant, and the doctor still has you on limited duty," stated Hadden Blankenship.

"What?" demanded Shiran.

"You'll have to discuss that with the doctor. They're concerned enough to keep you on limited duty and are unwilling to discuss the issue further with me," said Hadden.

Commander Hadden Blankenship and Lieutenant Commander Conor Raybourn waited as Second Lieutenant Shiran Rosenstein's flashing eyes went from the Hadden to Conor.

Master Sergeant Evan Zander, who had remained quiet until now, said lowly, "Shiran."

Shiran glanced at the master sergeant, and the look of defiance vanished from her eyes slowly. Then Shiran sat back in her seat, defeated, and gestured for them to continue.

"When?" asked Conor.

"A week, maybe two, if you're sure this is that important," stated Blankenship.

"The master sergeant says he's been having an uneasy feeling about it ever since Staff Sergeant Hall lost that combat knife," stated Conor.

"I read that report. It gave me an uneasy feeling too," said Hadden.

"If there is an intelligent form of velociraptor and it's still around, we need to know, sir," said Shiran.

"I agree. Every time we go outside that Compound, we're at risk, and if we get too comfortable despite a threat like this, we'll all be in danger," stated Commander Hadden Blankenship.

CHAPTER 23

The graveyard was five hundred meters to the south of the Marine Complex near the shoreline of the lake. It was peaceful here. The wild rice used by the cleft was regularly harvested off the shoreline, but they had to be careful of the crocodiles inhabiting the lake. Captain Hiroka Tamura and Commander Hadden Blankenship stood at the foot of the grave with other naval personnel in uniform standing in ranks behind them. Many of the colonists had attended the funeral also and formed up behind the Marines on each side.

There was silence in the Marine ranks as Sergeant Tadashi Adachi played taps for the Marine they were laying to rest. All the Marines were in dress uniform and formed ranks on each side of the casket. Sergeant Nikolai Ivankov was performing the rites as the ministry representative for Sergeant Jose Flores's faith.

"Ashes to ashes, dust to dust," said Nikolai.

Lieutenant Commander Conor Raybourn's mind wandered as the familiar and comforting words and their appropriateness pervaded his mind. He questioned the whole point of existence—to live a brief time and die? Was it worth the effort? Then he looked around at all the people who struggled with him in this existence. His gaze finally fell on Shiran. The answer he came up with was yes!

He heard Nikolai say, "Shall live with him, and if we persevere, we shall also reign with him."

"Amen," responded those gathered.

"Blessed are those who die in the Lord. Let them rest from their labors, for their good deeds go with them," continued Nikolai.

Conor's gaze wandered as the service continued. He noticed Felipe Martinez and his cabinet members behind the Marines on the right side of the grave. They wore somber faces, then he noticed Bahri Hiran standing behind Felipe. There was a scowl on Hiran's face, and he appeared to be glaring at Nikolai Ivankov or Shiran standing at the foot of the grave. Bahri Hiran noticed Conor, and he looked down. When he looked up again, his face was placid and his eyes downcast, and Conor wondered if he had been mistaken. Conor had few interactions with Hiran and didn't know of anyone who did other than Martinez and his cabinet. Was there more to what Conor had seen, or was he imagining things that weren't there? The president and his cabinet were generally resistant to suggestions from the commander and himself. He wondered if perhaps there was more to it than a dislike of the FTL project and its staff.

His thoughts were interrupted as the rites were completed, and people started to depart to the cleft. Most of those in uniform stayed as four Marines took up shovels and filled in the grave of their fallen comrade, with Master Sergeant Evan Zander overseeing the project. Three civilians stayed also and gathered around Hadden Blankenship.

Conor felt a hand touch his arm, and he looked to see Jacqueline Vinet standing beside him.

"Are you all right, Conor?" asked Jacqueline.

"I'm fine," stated Conor warily.

"What happened?" asked Jacqueline.

Conor was sure the question was rhetorical. By now, the whole colony knew the story.

"What happens to everyone in the end, he died," stated Conor.

"Did he have to?" inquired Jacqueline.

"If we're going to survive on this planet, we're going to have to take chances, Jacqueline," stated Conor.

"We have the cleft and the surrounding Compound, which we can expand," said Jacqueline.

"Which requires resources from outside the Compound," countered Conor.

This conversation was where they had been months ago. Vinet couldn't see the knife's edge the colony balanced on, and that one small slip could very well be its end. He did not really want to have this conversation again, especially at this time. He felt that Jacqueline and many of the other colonists were ignoring the fact that the danger was very real and that they were hiding in a small piece of a world that they created for themselves to retreat into.

"You've changed, Conor," Jacqueline stated as she shook her head.

"We're going to need to change to survive here," stated Conor.

"At what cost?" asked Jacqueline.

"We could have settled one of the uninhabited planets, Jacqueline," said Conor.

"To never feel the air in our hair or the touch of the sun," said Jacqueline.

"Exactly!" stated Conor.

"I didn't mean it like that," replied Jacqueline.

"Then what did you mean?" Conor questioned as he watched Shiran approach.

"Nothing," said Jacqueline. "Take care, Conor."

Jacqueline turned to walk away toward the Marine Complex and the elevators to the tenuous safety that the colonists now called home. Conor shook his head as he thought about how most of the colonists were creating a world that blocked out the reality of the situation. They were on an alien world and needed to know what was out there to truly be safe. Blocking out that reality was only a retreat.

Presently, Shiran touched his arm. She looked into his bright blue eyes with her brown ones questioningly. "What did she want?" asked Shiran.

"She asked me if I was all right," replied Conor.

"That's all?" queried Shiran.

"She's still promoting isolation and security," explained Conor.

"By living inside the Compound?" asked Shiran.

"Yes," replied Conor.

Shiran shook her head. "I'm sorry, Conor."

"Not your fault. She wants the world to stand still," said Conor.

"And if the world intrudes into her security?" asked Shiran.

"Hasn't it already?" inquired Conor.

"There's no going back. We're here to stay, and that means we need to know what's out there, Conor, or we should just have stayed on the *New Horizon*," agreed Shiran.

"That's what I tried to tell her," said Conor.

"I know," replied Shiran.

"I'm sorry about Flores, Shiran," Conor said quietly.

"I know that too. There will be more funerals. Let's hope that they aren't too close together," said Shiran with a worried tone in her voice.

The two took each other's hands and walked slowly back to the Marine Complex.

A funeral wake for the sergeant was held the previous evening, and a table against the wall was laid out with awards, personal items, and a picture of the young Marine. Conor and Shiran gathered two mugs of coffee and sat at a table with Hadden Blankenship and Hiroka Tamura, who were already there. Conor watched as others came in to look at the display and talk to some of the Marines for a few moments or longer. He also noticed that President Martinez and his cabinet members who attended the funeral were notably absent from paying their respects.

Conor left shortly after the commander and captain, telling Shiran he would see her later at the Overlook for an evening meal. When Conor left the Marine Complex, he went to the pier where the longboat and shuttle were docked. There were three people in dress uniform, and Conor remembered seeing them all at the funeral. A length of chain, which must have just arrived from the *New Horizon*, had been laid out down the center of the pier. Lieutenant Tom Tollifer and Petty Officer Ramirez was carefully inspecting each link of the chain, and Petty Officer Kaur was making notations on a tablet. The three stopped and saluted Conor as he approached.

"Good morning, Lieutenant Commander," said Tom Tollifer.

"Good morning, Lieutenant. How's the leg?" asked Conor as he returned their salutes.

"Still going through physical therapy. But doing well, sir," replied Tom.

"What do we have going on?" inquired Conor.

"Inspecting the control chain for the foundry," responded Tom.

"The foundry didn't make it?" asked Conor.

"It's a length from the boatswain locker of the *New Horizon*, sir. Higher quality of steel," stated Boatswain Mate Second Class Ramirez as she bent down to look at a serial number on one of the chain links and read it off to Supply Clerk Second Class Kaur.

Then Conor remembered the requisition and how an argument had ensued between Commander Blankenship and President Martinez. Felipe Martinez wanted the whole roll of chain from the *New Horizon* stores. The commander informed the president in no uncertain terms that he would only receive the length the foundry required. Hattie's specifications only required a tenth of the roll.

"How does it look?" asked Conor.

"So far, it's fine, sir," said Catalina Ramirez.

"Mind if I stay and watch?" asked Conor. "Perhaps explain to me what the inspection involves."

"You're welcome to learn," replied Tom Tollifer with a smile. "Feel free to ask questions."

The inspection took another fifty minutes as Tom Tollifer and Catalina Ramirez looked at each remaining link. They explained the types of defects and inconsistencies they were looking for that might inhibit the proper performance of the chain as it was used. When they were finished, Petty Officer Anya Kaur had the two inspectors sign the tablet she had been making notations on. Finished, Anya Kaur signed the chain over to Lieutenant Tollifer and said she would make arrangements for it to be transported to the foundry.

Lieutenant Commander Raybourn thanked the crew for the instruction and started down the pier, heading toward the elevators. Tom Tollifer caught up with Conor as he was walking to the elevator. The two discussed the funeral, and Tom asked Conor if he had time to talk over a beer at the Overlook as they entered the elevator. Conor gave Tom a quizzical look and agreed as the elevator rose to the cleft. When they arrived at the Overlook, Conor decided it was time to call it a day and ordered beer for the two of them. They took a seat at the back table, and a moment later, Roberta set two cold ones in front of them.

"So what's on your mind, Tom?" asked Conor.

"Thought we'd just sit and talk for a bit, Lieutenant Commander," said Tom.

"Call me, Conor," said Conor as he took a sip of beer.

"Conor, is there more going on than the commander is telling us about?" asked Tom.

"What do you mean, Tom?" returned Conor evasively.

"It seems like there's a lack of communication and a lot of misinformation in getting things done," replied Tom Tollifer as he placed his hat on the table, then took a swig of beer.

Lieutenant Commander Raybourn sat back and looked at Tom for a moment, then said, "I'm not in a position to say anything, Tom."

Lieutenant Tollifer took another swig of beer and nodded. "I thought that would be the answer."

"I'm sorry, Tom," said Conor.

"You answered the question. Whether you realize it or not, it told me all I needed to know," said Tom.

"Anything else you want to talk about?" asked Conor.

"Now that you mention it, don't you think there are a lot of accidents?" inquired Tom, looking down at his legs and stretching them.

"I'm not allowed to talk about that either, Tom," replied Conor.

"Thought so," said Tom. "I just want you to know that there are a lot of us who support and appreciate what the commander and you have done. If you ever need anything, just ask, and I'll see what we can do."

"I appreciate that, Tom, and I'll let the commander know," said Conor. "Are there any problems we should be aware of that may have missed our attention?"

Tom sat back and looked at Conor for a moment, then took a swig of his beer. He got a distant look in his eye, then he looked directly into Conor's eyes and said, "There are problems that have been developing where people are shunned by certain groups. Right now, it's only developing, but I expect it will get worse."

"Like Brad Guillete's current situation?" inquired Conor.

"Very similar. They can still find work, but there are a few individuals who, I believe, will find it harder as time goes along," said Tom.

"We've heard rumors about that, Tom. Anything the commander and I can do?" said Conor.

Tom sighed and said, "Not much. They're starting to withdraw even from the people willing to offer them a helping hand. The master sergeant and Ezekiel are about the only people whom they trust aside from myself."

"They're getting fed, sheltered, and receiving medical attention?" asked Conor.

"They will as long as I have something to say about it," replied Tom vehemently.

"What does that mean?" asked Conor.

"Some people are saying that unproductive members should have to fend for themselves," replied Tom Tollifer heatedly. He then added, "The same ones who go out of their way to make life miserable for them."

"I think I know who you mean," replied Conor. "It needs to stop, but there's not much the military arm can do in civil matters."

Tom nodded his understanding and said, "I was hoping Jacqueline could figure out a strategy that might change things around, but the instigators simply switch tactics, and things become worse for the people we're trying to help."

CHAPTER 24

It was a beautiful day as Lieutenant Michael Anderson walked along the brick walkway toward the back of the cleft. He could hear the sounds of welding metal and concrete mixers turning. The river was running swiftly in the opposite direction, and the heavenly odor of fresh bread filled the air as he approached the Flour Mill. The café that fronted the bakery had some customers, and Michael decided to have a cup of tea before continuing to the cave where he and his team were constructing an AI and communications center.

As he approached, he noticed Brad Guillete and Rachel Krupich at one of the tables. Seeing Brad, he decided to talk to him about an issue that they were having with the portable satcom transceiver that had been installed a week earlier. When he arrived at their table, the two looked at him and smiled questioningly.

"Good morning. Do you mind if I have a seat?" Michael asked.

"Good morning, sir. Go ahead," replied Rachel. She was dressed in fresh cammies and obviously spending some time with Brad prior to work as she got out of her chair. "I'm sorry. I can't stay. I have to get to work."

"I'm sorry you have to leave, Staff Sergeant," said Michael.

"I'll see you later, Brad," Rachel said as she kissed him. Turning, she threw a salute in Michael's direction, which he returned.

"How are you today, Brad?" asked Michael.

"All right. How are you?" replied Brad.

"I'm fine," Michael responded.

Stefanie Lanier, the owner of the café, came over and asked Michael what he would like, and he told her tea. Stefanie went back and returned with the requested item, which Michael stirred some sugar into. When he finished, he looked up at Brad and asked.

"Didn't you work in the Electronic Repair Office?" inquired Michael.

"Yes, I did," replied Brad guardedly.

"What do you know about the portable satcom transceiver?" asked Michael.

"The SAC-23F?" inquired Brad.

"I believe that's the nomenclature assigned to it," Michael affirmed.

"If that's it, then not much, sir," stated Brad.

"Would you mind taking a look at it?" asked Michael.

"I can do that, sir," said Brad distractedly.

Michael paused. Brad was being polite, but he didn't seem very interested. The answers Michael received were short and to the point, but ambiguous. Michael wondered what exactly it had been like to work in the electronics repair division. If that brief conversation he heard back when the ship was still heading to the planet was normal, he suspected that the work environment of the electronics repair division was hostile. Michael forced himself to stop thinking about it and go back to the subject at hand.

"I'd appreciate it if you don't mind," said Michael.

"Whenever you're ready, sir," said Brad.

"Let me finish my tea," returned Michael. "Have you known Staff Sergeant Krupich long?"

Brad gave Michael a searching look and replied, "We met when I reported aboard the *New Horizon*. She gave me the guided tour after finding me bedding and showing me to my bunk room."

"So you've known her for a while," inquired Michael.

"We hung out. Friends. More than that now," added Brad uncomfortably.

"I'm not trying to pry," said Michael.

"It's all right, sir," Brad assured him.

"Are you ready to go, Brad?" asked Michael, changing the subject.

"Anytime you are, sir," replied Brad.

Michael and Brad got up and walked to the back of the cleft. Reaching the back wall, they turned left and walked a short distance to the cave entrance. There were several cables running into the cave. Michael noticed Brad look at them for a moment and shake his head, but he didn't say anything. The cave widened out past the entrance. They walked past the offices into the back to the radio room. The back of the cave was still being excavated, and there were plans to smooth the rough rock walls when all was finished to build the AI computer. Guiding Brad over to the side of the radio room, Michael showed him where the SAC-23 was installed.

"Here it is, Brad," said Michael.

"Do you have the tech manuals?" asked Brad Guillete.

"I believe they're in the shelving unit over there," said Michael.

"I'll just take a look at the equipment first, sir," replied Brad.

"Do you want my help?" asked Michael.

"I'll be fine if you have other things to do," replied Brad. "Do you know who installed the equipment?"

"It was Chief Wheaton. I'll be further back in the cave working on the AI. The rest of my crew should be here shortly," said Michael.

"All right, sir. I'll let you know if I require anything," replied Brad, who was already looking at the equipment.

Michael headed back into the cave where he started working on a computer capable of supporting a new AI. The portion of the motherboard with the new row of cards was giving them installation problems. Part of the power supply had been left out of the diagrams and was in the way. Michael suspected that they'd have to go back to the drawing board and make modifications. Hopefully, those modifications would not inhibit the airflow required for the cooling of the cards when installed. What else might they be missing?

Brad was still working when his crew arrived and started working. Shortly after that, Brad walked back and asked for a tool kit, which was provided with a snicker by one of the crew. Brad seemed to ignore the outburst and took the tool kit back and opened the transceiver. He inspected the interior of the unit and, taking a wrench, tightened something inside the unit. He bypassed the interlock and powered the unit up. Looking at the front panel indicators, Michael saw him nod. He then saw Brad put the unit back together and check all the indicators again. He then looked at the back panel, then shook his head and took another wrench and tightened something at the rear of the equipment.

"Sir, could you come here?" requested Brad.

"I'll be right there, Brad," said Michael, setting down the circuit board he was working on, then walked over to where Brad stood.

"Would you try calling the ship, sir?" inquired Brad.

"I can do that," replied Michael.

"Give me a moment so I can watch the indicators, sir," said Brad.

Giving Brad the moment, Michael sat down and waited until Brad indicated he was ready. Michael pressed the transmit button and spoke into the mic, "New Horizon. New Horizon. This is… MILDET Cleft. Over."

There was static for a moment, then from the front panel speaker came Lieutenant Vanda Kisimba's voice, "MILDET Cleft. MILDET Cleft. This is the New Horizon. It's nice to finally hear from you. Over."

"New Horizon. MILDET Cleft. It appears we'll be available for clear communications from now on. Do you have any orders? Over," stated Michel.

"MILDET Cleft. New Horizon. We have no orders for you except to place a watch on your comms for any transmissions from now on. Over," responded Lieutenant Kisimba's voice.

"New Horizon. MILDET Cleft. Understood. Over and out," said Michael.

Michael sat there for a moment, then looked at Brad and said, "Thank you, Brad."

"You're welcome, sir," replied Brad.

"What was the problem?" inquired Michael.

"Loose connection on the power supply. There was a detached wire to the transmitter that I soldered back on, and the antenna connector on the back panel was loose," Brad informed Michael.

"That was it?" asked Michael. He had been waiting for Chief Wheaton, who was serving his two weeks aboard the *New Horizon*, to look at the unit.

"Yes, sir," assured Brad.

"I'll put a commendation in for you with the commander," said Michael.

"Thank you, sir," said Brad.

"You're welcome," said Michael.

"Will that be all, sir?" asked Brad.

"Do you have somewhere to be, or can I show you what we're doing?" inquired Michael.

Brad looked at Michael for a moment, then smiled and said, "I wouldn't mind taking a look. I do have to leave in a couple of hours. I promised to do a job downstairs at the Marine Complex after lunch."

"All right then. Let me show you what we're doing," replied Michael.

The next couple of hours, Michael showed Brad the plans and layout of the complex they were working on. Brad asked a couple of questions and offered a couple of suggestions about the diagrams but seemed reserved in saying what he actually thought. Michael noticed that occasionally Brad would glance fleetingly in the direction of the other people working, but when near them, he remained silent unless one of them said something to him. Strained relations? Yet the man had repaired the transceiver when none of the others appeared to be able. What was going on? Michael shook his head when Brad indicated that he needed to go and walked with him to the entrance of the cave.

"Thanks, Brad," said Michael warmly.

"It was no problem, sir. Have a good day," replied Brad.

"You too, Brad," said Michael.

He turned and went back into the cave, wondering what other problems he was going to run into getting this complex online. He heard talking as he was about to enter the electronics suite and stopped at the door.

"Waste of skin," said a low-pitched voice.

"Yeah," came another voice.

"It's a wonder he even knew what a SAC-23 was," stated another voice.

"Why do you guys hate him so much?" came a female voice.

"Shut up!" said the first voice.

"Surprised the guy even knows which end of a screwdriver to hold," said the second voice again.

"You couldn't fix the SAC-23," came the defending female voice.

"Wait till the chief finds out that he was messing with his gear," came the first voice.

"We'd best get back to work before the lieutenant gets back," came the second voice.

"Yeah, okay," came the first voice.

Lieutenant Michael Anderson walked back outside. He had recognized all the voices and who they belonged to. He found it disconcerting that only Petty Officer Barbara Gabrielson had defended Brad Guillete. He thought about a conversation he heard long ago right after the *New Horizon* had been stranded in the system. There were more issues here than he realized. Michael shook his head and decided to talk with Conor about it later. Right now, he needed a walk, and he was hungry.

He went down the path to where the river sprang out of the cliff wall and turned right. Walking down the boardwalk, Michael followed the river down to the elevators. The sound of water rushing by helped calm his mind as he stood there before he finally followed the boardwalk along the edge to the Bookworm. The smell of chemicals to treat the paper and the sound of the machines to create the paper invaded his senses. He saw Francesca in the back holding and examining a newly made book. As he approached, he saw the cover had a picture of a young girl looking up at a grinning cat sitting in a tree. Francesca looked up, and a bright smile dominated her lovely dark Indo-European features as she tossed her raven-black hair over her shoulder. She saw him examining the book cover she held.

"I thought you were still working on *The Complete Works of Rudyard Kipling*," said Michael.

"We're ahead in production. All fifty copies of *Kipling* were completed this morning, so we've started working on *Alice in Wonderland*," said Francesca excitedly.

"That new printer worked?" asked Michael.

"It did! Thank you," replied Francesca.

"You're welcome," responded Michael.

"The new ink created by Raisa Romanov works well in the refillable cartridges, and Anthony Finley has improved his tanning process for the covers," stated Francesca.

"Since you're ahead of schedule, does that mean you have time for lunch?" inquired Michael.

"I'd love to have lunch with you. Let me go freshen up," responded Francesca happily.

"Go ahead," said Michael as he held out his hand for the book.

He took the book from Francesca as she turned to leave. The soft, smooth feel of its brown leather cover was good quality. He opened the book and flipped through some of the pages. There were pictures inserted from the original book printed nearly six hundred years ago. A feeling of nostalgia came over him as he read a few lines of the familiar story. He was so engrossed in the book that he didn't hear Francesca come back.

"It's really quite an enchanting story, isn't it?" asked Francesca.

"Yes. My mother used to read it to me when I was a boy," replied Michael.

"I remember my mother reading it to me too," responded Francesca.

"We seem to have a lot in common. Shall we?" Michael smiled.

Francesca took Michael's offered elbow, and they walked to the front door. They took a left and followed the boardwalk over to the Flour Mill and had a seat outside, watching the river. They ordered a light lunch of sandwiches and chips with tea as they watched people pass by about their business. They talked about some of the goings-on in the colony, and Michael finally made a comment about the book he had been examining.

"It's a beautiful book," stated Michael.

"Would you like a copy?" asked Francesca.

"I could, or I could just read your copy anytime," stated Michael as he placed a small wooden box in front of her.

"What's this?" asked Francesca, her dark face holding a look of surprise.

"Open it," suggested Michael.

She opened the box and saw a golden ring with what looked like a diamond set into it. Her eyes gleamed with tears as Michael asked, "Will you marry me?"

It took a moment for Francesca to gain her composure as she got up. Michael stood too, and she fell into his arms and said, "Yes, I will."

"Then I guess I don't need a copy of that book," said Michael cheerfully.

"Yes, you will. But you can borrow ours anytime you want," said Francesca mischievously.

Michael thought about that last statement, not grasping the meaning. "Why do you say that?"

"Because I'm pregnant, silly," said Francesca.

CHAPTER 25

The *New Horizon* orbited, falling forever above the same point of the world below, perpetually ensnared in its cosmic dance. The longboat docked, and the passengers and crew awaited to leave as the commander floated to the hatch. The inspection and refueling crew waited to board in the bay as the hatch was opened. Commander Hadden Blankenship floated off the longboat first, and the 1MC made the announcement.

"*New Horizon* arriving."

Protocol demanded that even though he was only a commander that he be announced, just as protocol demanded that he be the first to depart the longboat or shuttle when disembarking and the last to board when the small craft was embarking. He was not comfortable holding the reins of command, especially now, but the duty of command fell on him. Leaving the bay as the others disembarked, he went to the bridge first where Lieutenant Junior Grade Vanda Kisimba was standing the bridge watch. Vanda's smile was prominent against her dark African features.

"Good afternoon, Commander," said Vanda.

"Good afternoon, Lieutenant. Is everything in order?" asked Hadden.

"The longboat you requested for the lunar mission is outfitted and ready to go on your command, sir. All systems' statuses remain the same as when you departed. The return shuttle is being inspected and refueled as we speak. Message traffic should be waiting for you on the bridge when you return from your tour, sir," replied Vanda.

"Very good, Lieutenant. I'll be back to relieve you in two hours when the longboat going planetside is ready," said Hadden

Blankenship as he headed toward the hatch leading aft to commence his inspection tour. He went aft to the engine rooms and checked with the duty engineers on the status of the power planet and Benson drive. He worked his way forward, looking into the machine shops, berthing areas, damage control shops, armory, Marine suite, medical, and other areas.

He was just approaching the comm shack to make sure his traffic had been forwarded to his in-box when the hatchway opened. Ensign Hiran floated out of to find himself confronting Commander Blankenship. A mixture of emotions crossed the ensign's face, then he saluted.

"Good afternoon, Commander," snapped Ensign Hiran.

"Good afternoon, Ensign Hiran. Everything all right?" asked the commander.

"I forgot my password again and had to have Chief Wheaton help me," said Ensign Hiran.

"In the radio shack?" inquired Hadden.

"He met me here and let me inside. Then he logged in to the system and corrected my problem. He was very helpful," replied Hiran, smiling.

"I'm glad he was able to assist you, Ensign. Carry on," stated Hadden.

Commander Blankenship watched Ensign Hiran float down the passageway. Hiran passed Petty Officer Third Class Mizra, who came to a stop beside Hadden near the radio shack door. She turned and saluted as she greeted him.

"Good morning, Captain," said Petty Officer Mizra.

"Good morning, Petty Officer," replied Hadden.

"Going in, sir?" asked Mizra.

"Yes, I am," said Hadden.

He shook his head and keyed his security code into the hatchway door to open. He saw Chief Wheaton and Petty Officer Second Class Powell in the shack. The electronics technician Powell looked up from his station and turned to say something to Chief Wheaton. The chief looked startled for a moment, then put a smile on his face.

"Good afternoon, sir," said Chief Wheaton.

"Good afternoon, Chief," replied Blankenship.

"Can we do anything for you, sir?" asked Wheaton.

"Just making a tour of the ship, Chief," said Blankenship. He looked behind the chief where a screen reflected what the chief was doing at his station. The screen was all the message traffic that the ship had received from the MILDET. As the commander watched, the chief deleted a message, backed out of the screen, then he called up a diagnostic.

"Is my message traffic all set up, Petty Officer Powell?" asked Commander Blankenship.

"Yes, sir," stated Petty Officer Powell.

"Very good, Petty Officer Powell," said Blankenship. "Chief, how are we doing on the long-range lidar?"

"I was working on it when you walked in, sir," replied Wheaton.

"Really? Are we getting anywhere on it, Chief?" asked Hadden.

"It seems to be a problem with the AI interface, sir," replied Wheaton, referring to the artificial intelligence computer.

"If it's the AI interface, why are you in the comm shack instead of the AI or lidar room?" asked Blankenship.

"Oh! Well, I can run diagnostics from any terminal on ship, and Petty Officer Powell said he might need some help here in the comm shack with the message traffic."

Blankenship was growing impatient and decided it was time to change the subject and said, "Has the lunar mission left for the far moon yet, Chief?"

"They were just waiting for you to give them the go, sir," replied Wheaton.

"And the return longboat?" asked Blankenship.

"They'll be ready to leave on my arrival, sir," stated Wheaton.

"Who's relieving you, Chief?" asked Blankenship as Petty Officer Mizra relieved Powell.

"Petty Officer Gabrielson," said Wheaton.

"Very good, Chief. Please inform the lunar mission crew that I will be on the bridge in a minute and the return longboat crew to let me know when you're aboard," said Blankenship as he floated out of the comm shack.

"Aye, aye, sir," returned Chief Wheaton.

Ten minutes later, Hadden was strapped into the pilot's chair as he operated the controls of the view screen he was watching. The lunar mission was underway, and the return longboat had left. He should be going over his message traffic.

His thoughts wandered as he watched the displays. He had been down to the cleft a few weeks earlier and met with the captain. Hiroka Tamura had chosen to leave the *New Horizon* when their current situation and her own condition were explained to her. Hiroka said that she felt changed and incapable of performing the duties of captain and left him holding the ball. Even though Hiroka had assured him that she always considered him capable and deserving of a ship of his own, he felt the world close around him with the burden that had been placed on him.

Hiroka had awakened months earlier a changed woman and had told him he was now in charge. Observing her, he noticed that she had changed, appearing more withdrawn than her usual self after the operation. Dr. Hollinger assured him that Hiroka's recovery was complete but reiterated that she would most likely never be the same as she was prior to the accident. She appeared more unsure of her decisions. The orders that came so naturally to her that they seemed to flow now came haltingly to her.

His feelings about her had not changed over the years. He had carefully crafted a persona to not reveal those feelings to her or to others. However, there was nothing to stop him now. The United Systems was far away, and they would never be in contact with them again during any of the colonists' lifetimes. He was free to pursue a relationship and even marriage with Hiroka if she was willing. Concessions would have to be made, he knew. The circumstances that had brought them all here and existed now called for new rules.

His thoughts turned to the disquieting news of the elevator. Gunnery Sergeant Rusu had been sure it was sabotage, and the analysis by Raisa Romanov confirmed that the cable had been subjected to sulfuric acid. The only way that was possible was intentionally. So it was sabotage, but was it the same saboteur who stranded them here? There was no way to know. Their only hope was to catch the individual and hope for a confession. Hadden Blankenship shook his head; thinking about it was giving him a headache.

Then there was the disquieting news of the discovery of the abandoned city. Coupled with the master sergeant's report of a lost combat knife, which was possibly taken by someone or something. The two incidents together suggested that they were not the only intelligent life-forms on the planet. The human race still had problems coexisting, attested by the fact that there was a need for a United Systems Navy. Even the name United Systems did not encompass all of Sol system. There were still countries on Earth that were not members of the United Systems. Then there were several moons of Jupiter and Saturn that were independent of the United Systems, along with a few of the asteroids. Blankenship hoped that meeting the natives of this planet would go well, but he felt in his gut that that wouldn't be the case.

His thoughts turned to the continuing problems with the long-range lidar resolution as he relieved Lieutenant Junior Grade Kisimba on the bridge. If the lidar was working properly, it could tell them a lot about the planet below. They would have known about the abandoned city prior to setting foot on the planet. It would also tell them how widespread any possible civilization on the planet might be. He returned to the command seat and brought up the holographic screen to review his message traffic.

"Hattie," said Commander Blankenship.

"Operating. Good afternoon, Commander," responded Hattie.

"Message traffic, please," ordered Blankenship.

The screen displayed all the message traffic that he had incoming. He smiled when he read the message that Anthony Finley and Evangeline Dalisay had a new baby girl. Jacob Valdez had broken his ankle while working at the copper mine. The master sergeant reported that Joseph Green had discovered a substantial zinc deposit on the hunting expedition. That would be good source for the brass and bronze the colony required. The second lieutenant had expressed an urgent need for brass to replace the round casings that had been expended and not retrieved for the last year. Additionally, Ezekiel had expressed an interest in acquiring some bronze for his restaurant furnishings.

Hadden Blankenship turned to the ship reports. There were no major malfunctions while he had been dirtside. The lidar resolution was still a major issue. Deck department reported that the heat shielding in *Longboat 2* was replaced and that the longboat had been inspected and deemed fully operational.

"Hattie, was that all my message traffic?" asked the commander.

"All that was forwarded to you, Commander," replied Hattie.

Blankenship thought about that statement as he looked sharply at the computer screen. Conor had said something when they were discussing business that the AI acted unexpectedly when he had created the Colony Viability file.

"Hattie, are you implying some messages have not been forwarded to me?" asked Blankenship.

"All that remains active has been forwarded to your review," replied Hattie.

"Are there inactive files that have not been forwarded to me that should have been?" asked Blankenship.

"Yes, Commander," said Hattie.

"Do you still have access to these files, or are they erased?" asked Blankenship.

"They are still in the trash bin, Commander," replied Hattie.

"How many files are there?" asked Blankenship.

"One hundred seventy-three, Commander," replied Hattie.

"Please display the files from newest to oldest," ordered Blankenship.

The display in front of him provided a listing of files, and he discovered the newest was placed in the inactive listings only a couple of hours ago. Some of the oldest went back to the day after he announced he was releasing all the colonists of most of their military obligations. He noticed that Hattie attached the names of the people who had placed the files in the inactive listing. There were about a half dozen, and Chief Wheaton was the most recent.

He opened the first file and found a letter of commendation/recommendation from Lieutenant Anderson for Petty Officer

Guillete. The next was the list of personnel who were assigned extra ship assignments and those who were delinquent from Lieutenant Commander Raybourn, which had been assigned to the inactive file by Felipe Martinez.

Anger started to build up as the commander went through the files. It took several hours to read through all of them. Roberta MacIntrye was on board as acting steward and contacted him, asking if he would care for dinner. He told her to bring whatever was available to the bridge. She brought him some zero-G rations as he closed the last of the files that had not been forwarded to him.

"Will there be anything else, Commander?" asked Petty Officer Third Class MacIntrye.

"No, Ms. MacIntrye. Thank you," replied Blankenship.

She hesitated as she was about to leave and asked, "You don't look very happy, sir. Is there a problem?"

"No. Nothing I can't take care of after giving it some thought," sighed Blankenship.

"You know, many of us support you, Commander," stated Roberta.

"Thank you, Roberta. That'll be all," said the commander.

Roberta saluted the commander as she turned to float toward the aft hatch. He returned her salute and sat back in his seat to think. Coming to a decision, he looked down at the display in front of him.

"Hattie," said Hadden Blankenship.

"Yes, Commander," said Hattie.

"Open Colony Viability file," ordered Hadden.

"Open, Commander," said Hattie.

The commander read the file and reviewed the insightful addendums from Lieutenant Commander Raybourn and Lieutenant Anderson. Sometimes the commander felt as though they were spinning their wheels, especially after reading the message traffic that was purposely not forwarded to him. A part of the file caught his eye as he reread some of the early inputs. It was an addendum about the health of the colonists, attached by Hattie at Raybourn's order. Blankenship made a decision about the medical equipment.

"Hattie, place a priority on the production of medical equipment for the cleft clinic and add it as a note to the file," ordered Hadden.

"Done, Commander," replied Hattie.

The subject of the colony's health was important. The loss of skilled labor would inhibit their progress just as the addition of skilled labor would increase it. But even then, they would suffer losses. They would all be missed. The recent loss of Corporal Flores still bothered him. Yet every birth was a potential increase and blessing to replace their losses.

"Hattie, how many colonists are required to maintain a technological level comparable to United Systems in Sol system?" asked Hadden Blankenship.

"Estimates from researchers that have explored that matter say ten thousand or more," stated Hattie.

"Which means that we will not be able to maintain that with our current population," replied Hadden.

"If the colony continues with its current level of losses, no. However, it would be possible to have a viable colony by the third generation in forty years if each mating couple of these generations provide four to seven children," returned Hattie.

"So is this a viable colony?" inquired Hadden Blankenship.

"Not at this time. However, as new generations increase significantly and are trained in useful skills and if the colony does not suffer severe loses, most of the current colonists should still be alive when that status is achieved, as long as current health-care standards can be maintained," returned Hattie.

Health care had improved significantly over the last five hundred years. Many people lived to a ripe old age of 150 Earth years. The aging process had been significantly slowed, and many people were active for the first century of their lives. The aging mechanisms of the body were delayed by nearly thirty years, meaning a person in their late seventies might only appear to be fifty years old who had never received treatments. The only sure way to know the difference would be to give the individual a through medical examination.

"Is there anything else that will improve that possibility other than having more children?" Hadden smiled.

"A class A or B factory would assist the colony greatly," stated Hattie.

"We don't have the blueprints or programming for a class B factory, Hattie," said Hadden.

"My memory banks contain the blueprints and programming for class A through D factories, Commander," returned Hattie almost eagerly.

Blankenship looked at the computer screen, stunned. "Why and who programmed that into you, Hattie?"

"Unknown, Commander," stated Hattie.

CHAPTER 26

The longboat pulled away from the *New Horizon* and fired its thrusters, aligning itself toward the nearer moon. The four people aboard were strapped in and prepared for an extended period of zero gravity. There were four seats left in the longboat. The craft's aft was now loaded with the survey sensors and additional equipment, along with supplies. Gunnery Sergeant Samuel Rusu watched the monitors as they pulled away.

The mission objectives called for a survey of the far moon. The scans by the astrometrics lab of the *New Horizon* indicated a high likelihood of an abundance of the needed materials. It would take a day to reach the moon and an estimated six to eight days to survey the moon. Samuel sat back in his seat and thought about the parameters of their mission.

"Looking forward to our little excursion, Mr. Rusu?" asked Steven Yates.

The exogeologist Steven Yates was sitting across the aisle from him. The man had been part of the science department under Jacqueline Vinet. He was a short balding man whose light-brown hair was showing gray around the ears. However, his dark eyes were shiny and keen, seeming to observe everything.

"Part of the job, sir," responded Samuel.

Rusu didn't especially care for the confined spaces. He was slightly worried about spending possibly the next few weeks in a craft where he would be restricted to a chair with little to no movement. Hopefully, there would be some time for EVA, or extravehicular activity, involved so he could at least stretch his muscles. Of course, there was also the zero-G exercise gym installed at the end of the aisle in the very rear of the craft. He believed he would be spending a lot of time in that gym over the next couple of weeks.

"Is everyone ready for some delta Vs?" asked Ensign Dominic Sobolov.

There were affirmatives from everyone as they checked their safety harnesses and sat back in their seats.

"All right then," said Dominic. Then he keyed to transmit, "New Horizon. New Horizon. This is Longboat 4. Over."

Samuel Rusu recognized Commander Blankenship's voice over the comms. "Longboat 4. Longboat 4. This is New Horizon. We read you. Over," came the reply from the *New Horizon*.

"New Horizon. Longboat 4. We will commence our burn in ten seconds on my mark. Over," replied Dominic.

"Longboat 4. This is New Horizon. Roger. Over," came Commander Blankenship's response.

"New Horizon. Longboat 4. Mark!" stated Dominic. Then he started his count, "Five. Four. Three. Two. One. Ignition. Over."

"Longboat 4. New Horizon. Good luck. Out," declared Commander Hadden Blankenship.

The back of his seat pressed into Gunnery Sergeant Rusu's back after Ensign Sobolov fired the engines. Once they were at a tenth of a G, Samuel decided to make the most of it. Hopefully, they would be there in a day. Intending to catch up on some much-needed sleep, he closed his eyes. Fate, however, didn't seem to think much of his plan since his companion appeared to have other ideas.

"I'm really looking forward to a close look at that outer moon, Mr. Rusu," stated Steven.

"My name is Sam, Dr. Yates," sighed Samuel. Obviously, that nap time was going to have to wait because it was pretty apparent that Steven was looking for conversation. Unfortunately, Rusu was pretty sure what that conversation was going to be about.

"You can call me Steven then, Sam," said Steven.

"So, Steven, why are you looking forward to checking out the outer moon?" asked Samuel.

"According to our observations and Hattie's projections, it's only been in orbit for forty to eighty million years," said Steven Yates.

"The best estimate is that it'll break free of its orbit in another twenty to thirty million years."

"So?" countered Samuel.

"Large planetoids like this don't normally rove or wander into the inner system in Sol system," replied Steven.

"So?" repeated Samuel.

"Where did it come from, and how did this one get here?" questioned Steven.

"Isn't there an asteroid belt in this system?" asked Samuel.

"Yes. But most asteroids this large in a system as old as this are supposedly set in their orbits," stated Steven Yates.

"Is that unusual?" inquired Samuel.

"Since we were only beginning to get information from the probes sent to some of the closer solar systems, yes, it is," stated Steven. "This planetoid is well over a thousand kilometers in diameter at its narrowest."

"One thousand and thirty-four," stated Samuel firmly.

"Excuse me?" exclaimed Steven in surprise.

"That's how wide it is at its narrowest, and it's one thousand two hundred and seventy-seven at its widest," replied Samuel.

Steven blinked and sat back in his seat before asking, "You just knew that off the top of your head?"

"Started studying the moon the moment Lieutenant Commander Raybourn picked me for this mission," replied Samuel Rusu. "I studied the projections Diego Quintana, Maria DiAngelo, Hattie, and yourself have made about its orbit too."

"Oh!" exclaimed Steven.

Boatswain John Martins had turned around and was smiling as he listened. John asked, "So, Gunny, are we going to find what we're looking for?"

"North polar region has a high probability of aluminum, but I suggest we go for the equator. There's supposedly a deposit of euxenite or something very similar to it that they've located by spectral analysis. If it were, the commander wants about four to five hundred kilograms to process," stated Samuel Rusu.

"Sounds like you have a plan, Gunny," replied John.

Samuel cocked an eyebrow at Steven Yates, who just sat there looking somewhat perplexed. Samuel sat back in his seat and pulled his cap down until it covered his eyes as he manipulated the seat controls to recline. Shortly, a slight buzzing noise could be heard as Samuel entered that place of solitude he had intended to enter a few minutes earlier.

The trip out was uneventful, and Samuel awoke as they neared their goal. Ensign Sobolov kept them on a course that circled the moon from pole to pole under power. Steven scanned the moon's surface with a spectral analyzer, looking for a large deposit of euxenite prior to setting down. The longboat moved around the moon quickly, but it still took most of the day to run a sensor sweep of its surface. Finished, Dominic Sobolov set up a parking orbit trailing the moon, and the ship went into zero G as they analyzed the data.

"This looks very promising," stated Dominic as he pointed to an area just south of the equator where the map projection showed deposits of zinc with gallium.

"A bit rough but possible," said John Martins. "If we can pull in here and deploy the anchors, we'll be right beside the deposit."

"I agree," said Steven Yates.

"I'd like to land on the north polar region where it's not quite as rough first," stated Dominic somewhat nervously.

Everyone looked at him questioningly.

"I haven't done an EVA or attempted to pilot a longboat near an asteroid," explained Dominic nervously. "I'd like to do a landing on a…not quite so rough area first."

"I agree with Ensign Sobolov," interjected John. "I'd like to try that too."

"We have the fuel to do that?" asked Samuel.

"We have plenty." John grinned. "Just a couple of nervous pilots."

"Let's do that then. If it'll make Mr. Sobolov and you both more comfortable." Samuel grinned. "If we have the fuel, I'd like to try it too, as long as one of you is comfortable with supervising me."

Ensign Sobolov looked up more confidently and said, "Lieutenant Commander Raybourn said we were to treat this as an exploratory and training mission. Yes. We will do that before we try the rough terrain. We will all EVA also to grow more comfortable with procedure and to pick up samples."

The exogeologist Steven Yates looked at the three around him thinking he had missed something important. Samuel Rusu sat back in his chair and simply nodded at Ensign Sobolov. Petty Officer Martins simply smiled as he watched the young ensign make his first command decision.

They spent the next day landing around the north polar region. They landed six times total, giving each of the pilots two times at the helm. Each time, one person EVA'd and took samples around the craft. When the training missions were complete, they remained anchored and slept the night secured to the moonlet before moving to the objective site.

The next day, they took off, and Ensign Sobolov maneuvered the longboat above the smoothest area they could locate near a significant euxenite deposit. As the landing gear touched the surface of the moon, John Martins deployed the anchors. The anchors were braided microfiber lines with rock picks in the end that shot into the surrounding rocks at six different points around the craft.

"Anchors deployed," stated Petty Officer Martins. He paused for them to set and tighten to hold the longboat securely in place. "Anchors set, sir."

"Very well, Petty Officer Martins," stated Dominic. "I will go and suit up. You have the conn."

"Excuse me, sir, but I'd like to take this EVA," said Samuel.

"Why you, Gunny?" asked the ensign.

"I need the fresh air," replied Samuel straight-faced.

Steven Yates looked at Rusu questioningly, then shook his head before he said, "I'd like to try this EVA thing once also, if that's all right."

They all looked at the exogeoligist. Ensign Sobolov spoke up, inquiring, "Why did you not volunteer earlier, Dr. Yates?"

Steven Yates looked up, surprised. "How hard can it be?"

"I'll make sure Mr. Yates knows what to do, sir," stated Samuel. "Don't we need to check in with the *New Horizon*?"

"Very well, Gunny, please take care of that, and I will take care of checking in," said Dominic.

Ensign Sobolov turned back to his console, and Boatswain Martins flipped some switches on the transceiver. Samuel turned to Steven and looked at him. With his chin, he indicated the back of the longboat and said, "Shall we?"

Steven unstrapped his restraining straps and floated back toward the suits and air lock as Samuel did the same. Sam spent over an hour instructing Steven about the donning and operation of the suits. Satisfied that Steven wouldn't kill himself putting the suit on, Samuel told Steven to don the suit while he floated over to another suit and donned it. Steven Yates was still attempting to put the suit on when Samuel finished and floated over to check on him.

"Boats!" called Samuel.

"Here, Gunny," responded John Martins.

"I'm all suited up. Mr. Yates here is having some trouble. Would you help him out while I set some lines?" said Samuel.

"Roger that, Gunny," said John.

"Lines?" questioned Steven.

"Hardly any gravity out there, Doc," stated Samuel as he opened a cabinet above the suits. He removed what looked like a rifle with a drum roll magazine.

"I know that," said Steven Yates while looking at the rifle. "What's that?"

"Shoots a pin with a line attached. The pin sinks into the rock and sets. Point it at the rock at your feet and shoot it again, and another pin attached to the other end of the line sinks into the rock. The line is designed to tighten once the pins are set. Then there should be a tight line between two points for attaching your suit's safety line," stated Samuel.

"Oh!" blurted Steven.

"I need to set some lines for us to attach to so we don't float off. We'll be almost floating out there and don't want to end up in orbit. Make sure when you come out that you use your tie offs, or we may not be able to retrieve you before you run out of air," said Samuel Rusu. He paused for a moment, then added, "When you're out there, don't make any sudden moves. If you do, it might propel you down the line uncontrollably. If your faceplate hits something hard when you reach the end, it might break."

Steven Yates sat there looking stunned and uncomfortable. Samuel could tell the man was having second thoughts about going outside. Then it occurred to him that Steven was an exogeologist and that was why he had been asked to go on this expedition.

"Have you ever done any fieldwork?" asked Samuel.

"What do you mean?" returned Steven.

"Well, you're an exogeologist. Didn't you ever go out and collect samples or examine formations on other planets?" asked Samuel.

"Why would I need to do that?" countered Steven.

Gunny Rusu thought about the samples he and the others had collected on their other excursions at the north pole of this moonlet. The samples had been collected at Steven's request and more as an afterthought on Steven's part, but then only after he had been asked if he wanted samples. It was Joseph Green who had wanted to come along and who requested samples if possible. Joseph also started going on hunting expeditions with the Marines to collect samples, whereas Steven Yates had never requested the Marines to do so during excursions.

Samuel Rusu finally looked at Steven and asked, "How do you do your research?"

"I study pictures of the formations along with the spectral data available. If there's physical samples and seismic soundings, that information is useful also, but not necessary for me to analyze and determine the possible geological structure of a planetary body," stated Steven.

Samuel looked at Steven for a minute, not saying anything. It was hard for him to believe what he had just heard. He looked at Boatswain Martins, who was just listening to their conversation, impassively waiting.

"Steven, why don't you just sit this one out? Boats, just suit up and monitor me in case I need you," stated Samuel.

"Roger that, Gunny," confirmed John.

"But I want to do this," stated Steven.

"If you can prove to the boats you're capable, I'll see you out there," replied Samuel. "If not, I can handle it."

"All right," said Steven, defeated.

"I'll send a sample through the air lock forthwith for a spectral analysis, Doc," continued Samuel.

Steven Yates looked abashed and nodded as Samuel entered the air lock with the line rifle. After cycling through, the gunnery sergeant hooked up with his safety line to the starboard midship's anchor line and slowly pulled himself out to its end. He sighted the rifle toward where the forward line on the starboard side was sunk into the rock and shot across it. Then he pointed the end of the rifle at a rock formation three feet away and fired again. The line tightened between the two points as the manufacturer had guaranteed it would do.

Bending down, Samuel Rusu used his geological hammer to chip off a piece of the surrounding formation. He bagged it and placed it in the longboat's air lock, then attached his other safety line to the new line he ran to the forward's anchor line on the starboard side. He detached from the starboard midship's anchor line and moved to its midpoint where he took another sample. He then moved to the anchor point of the starboard forward's anchor line and took another sample. Samuel set the new lines to the endpoints of all the anchor lines until he completed his circle, moving in a counterclockwise direction, taking samples every time, until he was back where he started. Samuel went back to the air lock and reentered the longboat. Boatswain Martins took the samples from him and handed them to the exogeologist Steven Yates.

"How'd it go?" asked John Martins.

"Fine," said Samuel.

"Mr. Yates, we're going to need the analysis as soon as possible," said John.

Steven Yates gave Boatswain Martins a searching gaze, then shrugged as he went forward to the science station.

"What happened?" whispered Samuel.

"He decided to stay inside," whispered John.

"All right, I'm up for a nap," stated Samuel, yawning.

"You could use a shower," added John.

"Didn't see any accommodations like that installed in this bucket." Samuel chuckled.

"No room. We'll all be pretty ripe by the time this mission is over," said John.

It took most of the afternoon for Steven to run his tests. Samuel woke up and was sipping some coffee when Steven finished. The best sample was from the aft port side anchor point. Steven assured them that it was a high-grade ore and should provide for their needs.

Gunnery Sergeant Rusu spent the rest of the day studying the longboat's recon images of the moonlet's surface. The ship had images of the near surface from the telescopes aboard the *New Horizon*. They had a complete surface survey map, and as he studied it, he started to have an uneasy feeling. There were large craters along one side of the moonlet. He checked, and it was on the far side from the planet and, therefore, not visible.

It took the better part of two days to fill the cargo bins attached to the longboat's wings. It was decided that Steven Yates would monitor systems and suits while the rest of the team EVA'd. They estimated that they had nearly two thousand kilograms of ore when they completed their task. Samuel Rusu looked across the aisle at Steven Yates after he strapped in.

"Mr. Yates, doesn't the sensor package have seismic equipment?" asked Samuel.

"Yes, it does. Why?" confirmed Steven with a question.

"Would you mind running some seismic soundings on the moonlet?" ventured Rusu.

"I can, but we should really do it from two or three different locations," Yates replied.

"That's fine. When we're sure our load is balanced, we'll ask Ensign Sobolov to do a couple more surveys and practice landings," said Samuel.

"We can do that, Gunny Rusu," stated Ensign Sobolov. "I am getting more comfortable with each landing on this moonlet."

"See, Mr. Yates, it's no problem," chided Samuel.

"I still don't see why we're doing this," stated Steven.

"I'll explain it to you if my suspicions pan out," confessed Samuel. Steven Yates looked at Rusu and received a deadpan look in return.

They did three practice landings. Yates conducted seismic tests at each of the new landings. When they had all the results in and looked at the holographic projection, it was apparent that there were large fractures emanating from the craters that Samuel Rusu noted on the topographic display of the moonlet. Samuel then asked Ensign Sobolov to do three more landings. Dominic wanted to leave, but since Samuel wanted to do the landings himself for practice, he was willing to do it in the name of training.

They performed three more landings. Samuel also wanted samples from each site, which meant three more EVAs. They landed at the epicenter of three of the largest craters, and Samuel asked for radiation readings as they approached. The sites proved cold when tested for radiation. The samples taken had a glassy look as though intense heat had been applied. Samuel stared at the moonlet's hologram as he was discussing the samples with Steven Yates.

"I don't see what this proves, Mr. Rusu," said Steven.

"How much heat does a meteor impact generate?" asked Samuel.

"Quite a bit," said Yates.

"So does a nuclear bomb," countered Samuel.

"But there was no radiation," stated Yates.

"How about we just do the test to see how this glass formed?" inquired Samuel.

"The tests won't be conclusive," stated Steven.

"What is? Do you have something better to do with your time?" asked Samuel.

"I'll run the tests," said Steven, defeated.

"Mr. Rusu, I am going to set a course back to the *New Horizon* unless you wish to do more training exercises," stated Dominic.

"Unless you or Boats want to, I'm good, sir," replied the gunny.

Dominic Sobolov looked at Boatswain Martins, who simply shook his head. The two then floated forward to the pilot and copilot seats to set up a course to the *New Horizon*. Samuel looked at Steven Yates, who took the samples back to the lab to conduct tests. Rusu relaxed and ensured the fastenings on his restraints and decided to take a nap. Several hours later, Steven Yates finished his tests, and the four were examining the results.

"You said that the moonlet had been in orbit for about forty to eighty million years," said Samuel.

"Yes," replied Steven.

"How sure are you of that?" asked John.

"Hattie is sure," said Yates.

"Any way to determine where these craters were in relation to the planet when that happened?" asked Samuel.

"Hattie might be able to come up with a rough estimate," said Steven.

"If the moonlet hit the planet, what kind of destruction would we be looking at?" asked Samuel.

Steven Yates blinked and stated, "That thing's a planet killer for an Earth-like world."

"Thought so," said Samuel.

"What are you getting at, Mr. Rusu?" asked Dominic Sobolov.

"Well, sir, when I was outside setting lines and taking samples at our mining site, I found this embedded in the rock," said Samuel. He pulled out a ten-by-ten-centimeter piece of metal. It gleamed like highly polished steel, and when Gunnery Sergeant Rusu turned it over, there appeared to be writing in some unknown script etched onto its surface.

CHAPTER 27

Lieutenant Commander Conor Raybourn was doing an inspection tour of the foundry. Felipe Martinez was promising steel that could be used to produce a high-quality internal combustion engine now that additions to the foundry were complete. The first batch was in a bucket being moved to pour into the form for the engine block. With luck, when it cooled, they would be able to start production on a hauler that would increase their ability to transport raw ore. That was vitally required if they wanted to have replacements for equipment in the future.

"We'll be able to have a hauler ready in maybe two or three months if the quality is right and the forms are ready," stated Martinez as they stood on the upper walkway overlooking the working crew on the foundry floor.

"How much ore will it be able to carry?" asked Conor.

"It should carry at least ten to fourteen thousand kilograms," stated Norman Pool.

"How long to produce another one?" questioned Conor.

"Maybe a month later since we'll have the forms," Martinez informed Conor.

"Why a month?" asked the lieutenant commander.

"Processing the steel, pouring the forms, and putting the finished parts together all takes time and manpower, Lieutenant Commander," stated Norman Pool.

"Have the forms been made for ATV production?" inquired Conor.

"Some of them are ready. It might be another six to nine months before we're ready for production. Right now, we're attempting to finish the forms for an excavator and loader, which would be a major asset to obtaining the required ore," informed Felipe Martinez.

Conor nodded. "How's the aluminum production coming?"

"We're having difficulties with the refinement process," interjected Norman Pool.

"Have you talked to Lieutenant Anderson?" asked Conor.

Martinez's face turned red as he answered curtly, "No, I haven't."

Conor simply looked at Martinez and said nothing as Martinez stared back in defiance. An uncomfortable silence grew as the two stood there. Conor knew that Martinez did not like the old FTL crew and, for some unknown reason, refused to associate with Michael.

"Perhaps the lieutenant commander would like to inspect the forms?" interjected Bahri Hiran.

"Yes, that's a good idea," added Pool.

The palpable tension was still there, but Felipe Martinez finally nodded. Conor Raybourn was still on the upper platform with Martinez when the incident occurred. The chain for the bucket filled with refined molten steel gave way and poured on the floor. Three people were splattered with hot drops, and their clothing caught on fire. The installed water and carbon dioxide extinguishing system went off and started cooling the metal as planned. There were cries of pain, and people ran forward to help drag the injured from the molten metal that was flowing across the cement floor. Others used hand extinguishers to put out the burning clothes. Fortunately, they had the foresight to install metal grating above the floor, so the flow went underneath, but even then, it was unbearably hot as the air above superheated, forcing the people to move back as the air became suffocating.

"What happened?" demanded Felipe Martinez.

"The control chain on the bucket gave way!" yelled Norman Pool.

"That was a brand-new chain!" screamed Felipe Martinez.

"I know that," responded Norman Pool.

"How many are hurt?" demanded Conor.

"At least three," said Bahri Hiran.

"Didn't someone test the chain?" demanded Martinez.

"It was thoroughly inspected when it arrived planetside and when it was installed in the factory," stated Bahri Hiran.

"I'm going to have someone's ass!" yelled Felipe Martinez heatedly.

"Let's make sure the men are all right," ordered Lieutenant Commander Raybourn as he headed for the ladder.

He reached the lower level where he could still feel the heat of the cooling metal. Steam and carbon dioxide clouds filled the air as Conor Raybourn advanced on the mayhem. There were pain-filled cries and groans from the injured people who lay on the floor, grating. Stretchers were being brought and laid beside the injured. The nearby metal still radiated heat, making it difficult to remain in the area.

The heat and flames had seared the flesh on the injured. In one case, the man's legs had terrible burns that were already developing huge blisters along their entire length. The people moving them to the stretchers attempted to be careful not to touch any of the burnt areas as they lifted the injured. They picked the stretchers up and moved toward the doors leading outside and were met by Dr. Bess Hollinger and her team as they headed toward the elevators leading up to the cleft.

Dr. Hollinger and her team split up among the wounded. Hollinger went to a seriously injured man whose blistering legs were making him grimace and scream in pain. The doctor took a syringe and gave him an injection. The man's movements slowed almost immediately as his face became calm, and he relaxed.

"What was that?" asked Conor.

"Morphine," stated Bess Hollinger. "Which we're in short supply. What happened?"

"Bucket chain broke and poured hot metal down on the floor," answered Conor.

"I've told them they need more protective gear," responded Bess in anger.

Conor looked at Bess as they entered the elevator and went up. It had not occurred to him that the former chief engineer was not observing proper safety procedures. What else was he neglecting in the foundry that might be a safety issue? The safety officer for the *New Horizon* was Lieutenant Tollifer as Conor recalled, and he had inspected the chain when it arrived. Then Petty Officer Anya Kaur had arranged for the chain to be delivered to the foundry from the pier after Tom Tollifer had inspected it with Petty Officer Ramirez.

The elevator arrived, and Conor assisted the doctor and medical team to the clinic. The injured were taken back into the emergency ward, leaving Conor in the front waiting room. Conor was in the waiting room for hours before any news of those injured was forthcoming. The news was not good. All three workers had severe burns and damage to their lungs. He felt helpless and decided he was doing no one any good wearing a hole in the clinic's floor. He stepped outside and walked along the boardwalk, wondering where everything was leading and if it was worth it.

He stopped and placed a hand on the railing. He knew the clinic's location was only temporary. Now that the bridge at the Overlook was complete, the groundwork started for building the eastern boardwalk. Additionally, construction of the hospital, along with the school and university, were already underway. Hopefully, that construction would be far enough along by the time the new medical equipment arrived. Conor could see the rough outlines of the first level with the hospital above. Work on the structure was progressing well now that housing for all was nearly complete.

Sometimes it seemed that it was taking forever to accomplish anything because of the setbacks. Conor shook his head at that thought. That wasn't right. They had accomplished a lot in the short time they had been on this planet. He looked behind himself at the four-story structure. Businesses comprised the first level with residential climbing toward the ceiling of the cleft crevice above that level. Then there was the foundry, lumber mill, glassworks, brick and cement works, along with the Marine Complex. Beyond those were the four square kilometers of Earth crops under cultivation, along with another kilometer of wild rice. All the accomplishments were enclosed by the perimeter fence a kilometer past the buildings and crops.

It was after noontime, and the yellow sun was high in the clear blue sky. White puffs of clouds floated in that azure field where the pteranodons and pterodactyls flew. Conor looked again at the beginnings of the shops, which would have the hospital and school above them. He felt a sense of pride for all they had accomplished in the short time they had been on the planet.

Leaving the railing along the riverbank, Conor took the boardwalk to the Overlook and entered. Ezekiel and Roberta were cleaning the tables and counter from the noontime rush. Conor went to the back table and had a seat. Roberta came over and told him the special was a triceratops burger and fries, which Conor ordered with a cup of coffee. Conor was just finishing his mug of coffee when Ezekiel placed his order in front of him.

"Will there be anything else, Mr. Raybourn?" asked Ezekiel.

"Have you seen Tom Tollifer today, Ezekiel?" inquired Conor.

"He was here for lunch. I believe he is assisting with the new hospital today," replied Ezekiel.

"Thanks, Ezekiel," said Conor.

"It's no problem," said Ezekiel. Then after a moment, he added, "Mr. Tollifer was very upset about the accident."

"It wasn't his fault," said Conor.

"He feels responsible because of the new control chain," Ezekiel informed Conor.

"He did inspect it, and it appeared fine when it was inspected on the pier," replied Conor.

"Yes. I told him he should wait for an investigation to be done to find out why the chain failed," responded Ezekiel quickly.

"That would be best," said Conor.

"Unfortunately, Mr. Martinez doesn't want an investigation and is blaming Mr. Tollifer and Ms. Ramirez for not inspecting the chain," returned Ezekiel.

Conor looked at Ezekiel sharply and snapped, "What?"

"Mr. Martinez insists that getting the foundry back online is more important. He is now demanding the full roll of chain from the *New Horizon*. Commander Blankenship is refusing," said Ezekiel.

"When did this all happen?" asked Conor. "The accident was just a few hours ago."

"Master Sergeant Zander had lunch here and said Mr. Martinez demanded that he use the comms on the shuttle to contact the commander on the *New Horizon*," replied Ezekiel. He then added, "He said Chief Zander was very upset."

"I'm sure she was," said Conor. "Does Second Lieutenant Rosenstein know?"

"Evan said she was furious," replied Ezekiel.

"Thanks, Ezekiel," affirmed Conor.

"It was no problem, Lieutenant Commander," said Ezekiel. "Will there be anything else?"

"Another cup of coffee while I think," responded Conor.

The chain had only broken five hours ago. Conor knew that Felipe Martinez had not gone to the hospital to check on the injured and had assumed he was investigating what had happened. There was a good possibility that Commander Blankenship had been blindsided by the demands of Martinez because of the accident. Conor knew he should have reported the accident to the commander immediately but felt that the care of the injured was more important and something that should be in that report. He was still beating himself up mentally when Commander Blankenship sat down while Roberta set two new steaming mugs of coffee in front of the two officers.

"Commander!" said Conor as he attempted to stand and salute.

"At ease, Mr. Raybourn," said Commander Hadden Blankenship. Then he asked, "How bad is it?"

"Three injured. One very badly. Dr. Hollinger says they should all live," responded Lieutenant Commander Raybourn.

"The control chain broke?" inquired Hadden.

"I saw it break, sir," said Conor.

"It was the new chain we just sent down?" asked Hadden.

"Yes, sir," replied Conor. "That chain was inspected by Lieutenant Tollifer and Petty Officer Ramirez. I was there to learn and observe for the last two-thirds of the inspection they performed."

The commander nodded and took a sip of his coffee before saying, "Mr. Martinez said he wanted the rest of the roll without doing an investigation into what happened. I told him that he wouldn't get any of the roll until a thorough investigation was accomplished. Lieutenant Anderson and Gunnery Sergeant Rusu are already there with four other Marines to take a look at that chain."

"I'm sorry I let you down, sir," said Conor.

"Why do you say that, Mr. Raybourn?" inquired the commander.

"I didn't let you know the moment the incident happened, sir," replied the lieutenant commander.

"The people were more important than the foundry being repaired. The foundry being down is not going to kill more people," stated the commander. "You did the right thing."

Conor's brow furrowed as he thought about that. The commander was right; the foundry being down was not a life-threatening situation. On the other hand, a major system on ship might put everyone in jeopardy. Command decisions could be complex, and those in command needed to be able to weigh the consequences, sometimes at a moment's notice. Conor took a sip of coffee and looked at his superior, Commander Hadden Blankenship.

"Thank you, sir," replied Lieutenant Commander Raybourn.

"Don't thank me yet. The president wants to hang all of this on you." The commander smiled. Then after a pause, he looked at the surprised look on Conor's face and added, "I told him there was no way in hell that would happen."

CHAPTER 28

The metal end of the examination table Second Lieutenant Shiran Rosenstein was sitting on was cold. Dr. Bess Hollinger was busy looking at the lab reports. Hollinger finally turned and faced Shiran with a serious look on her dark face. Shiran knew that Bess was of African descent, but her family had been from the United Kingdom of Earth for nearly six generations, and she had been educated at Oxford University. Bess had been the ranking officer of the medical department on board the *New Horizon* and held the rank of lieutenant commander before being stranded with everyone else.

"Well, Second Lieutenant, it's been nearly two weeks, and your lungs appear fine. Have you been having any trouble breathing?" asked the doctor.

"No. I feel fine, Doctor," replied Shiran.

"That's good. However, after reviewing your labs, it looks like I'm going to have to leave you on light duty," said Bess.

"But I feel fine. I had a little problem breathing for about a week, but it cleared up with the breathalyzer that you had me use," stated Shiran.

"That's not the problem, Shiran," countered Bess Hollinger.

"Then what's the problem?" inquired Shiran.

"Have you been feeling ill in the morning, Shiran?" asked Bess evasively.

"I don't have an appetite lately when I wake up, and sometimes my stomach turns when I smell something cooking," replied Shiran.

Dr. Hollinger simply sat there looking at Shiran with a smile on her face. Shiran felt confused and irritated as though the doctor was toying with her about something important. Then it struck her, and her eyes grew wide.

"Are you saying I'm pregnant?" Shiran demanded.

"Bingo. She got it right on the first try." Bess smiled.

"I can't be pregnant! I have an implant," Shiran half shouted.

"Which was supposed to be replaced over four months ago," added Bess.

"What?" demanded Shiran.

"I've been trying to get you to come in for over four months for your yearly physical, Shiran. Part of that physical was to see if you want your implant replaced," stated Bess patiently.

"What am I going to do?" implored Shiran.

"What do you want to do?" countered Bess.

"I don't know. I have a career," Shiran nearly pleaded.

"Do you?" asked Bess.

Shiran looked at the doctor and replied, "What do you mean? Of course, I have a career."

"You had a career as a United Systems Marine, but are we in the United Systems anymore?" Bess Hollinger questioned.

"Of course we're in the United Systems," snapped Shiran.

"Can we report back to the United Systems headquarters?" asked Bess amicably.

"No, but…," Shiran trailed off as she realized the argument was moot. How could they be responsible to United Systems or anyone but themselves at this point? They were on their own and would have to make their own way from now on. The reality was that there was no real career in the United Systems for her now. The truth of the matter was, she and the few who continued to wear the uniform as United Systems Marines and Navy were simply holding on. Or were they? Didn't they represent some new beginning, and in being new, could they create their own rules?

Dr. Hollinger simply sat there watching Shiran, giving her time to grasp the reality of the situation. When Shiran finally looked back into the doctor's eyes, Bess nodded. "We're making our own rules now, Shiran. Now what do you want to do?"

"I'll have to think about it," said Shiran.

Bess nodded again before saying, "I think you'll make the right choice. Having a child doesn't mean your life is over, especially out here. I can wait another two weeks before I have to put you on light duty, but you should consider going easy on the hero stuff until you've made a choice."

"What do you think?" asked Shiran.

"I think that we're in a serious situation. However, life goes on, and all we can do is make the best life we can while we live," stated Bess.

"That's not really an answer, Bess," countered Shiran.

"No, it isn't, but it's the only advice I will give you other than perhaps you should talk it over with the father," admitted Bess.

"I'm not sure I want to do that either," confessed Shiran.

"Why? Don't you love him?" asked Bess.

"Of course, I love him!" affirmed Shiran.

"Then what's the problem?" inquired Bess.

"I don't know," murmured Shiran lowly.

"Then I suggest you figure it out," said Hollinger as she looked at the clock on the wall. "Now if you'll excuse me, I need to prepare for my twelve o'clock appointment."

"All right. Thanks, Bess," said Shiran as she stood up.

"You're welcome," said Hollinger as she got up and left the room.

Shiran spent a couple of minutes straightening her uniform in the mirror attached to the wall. She stepped into the outer office of the clinic where a few people were waiting as the nurse Caroline deLang was busy. Through an open doorway, she saw Thomas Tollifer, the crewman she saved in the elevator incident, lying on an examination table. He saw her and waved her over.

"I want to thank you, Shiran," said Tom.

"Just doing my job. How are you, Tom?" inquired Shiran.

"The doc was able to save the foot. Part of the bone is plastic now. She says I'll be fine after a little therapy," replied Tom.

"That's good. I'll reserve a dance for you at the next party." Shiran smiled.

"I think what you did was brave as hell. You deserved that promotion by the way," said Tom seriously.

"It was nothing, and thank you," replied Shiran.

"You're welcome," said Tom.

"All right, Tom, I have duties to attend to," said Shiran.

Tom reached up, touched her arm as she was turning away, and confided, "If there's anything I can ever do for you, just let me know."

"Thanks, Tom," said Shiran.

Shiran departed the clinic and went over to the riverfront. She stood at the railing watching as the crystal clear water rolled by. She must have lost herself as she stood there contemplating how to approach Conor and her duties with this new turn of events. Presently, a hand touched her arm, and when she looked, Francesca Chandra stood beside her.

"It's time for lunch, and Michael's busy," stated Francesca.

Nodding at the invitation, Shiran followed Francesca over to the Flour Mill. Stefanie Lanier took their order of a light lunch—sandwiches, chips, and tea—as they exchanged pleasantries. A silence finally settled over the meal as Shiran let her mind drift back to the latest news about her life.

Finally, Francesca said, "Children might seem like a burden, but they are also a blessing."

Shiran looked sharply at Francesca and said, "Did the doctor tell you?"

"No," said Francesca, "but I saw you leave the clinic with a faraway look in your eyes, so I suspected and thought you could use a friend."

"Thank you, Francesca," Shiran confessed.

"We all have to make decisions about the lives we're now going to live. Right now, there is no one who can replace what you've become in our society, even if you decide to take on additional duties that will add continuity to the colony," confided Francesca.

"There are lots of people who could replace me," said Shiran.

"Are there?" questioned Francesca.

Sitting back, Shiran thought about that. The master sergeant could do her job if need be, but he really didn't want that responsibility. He was content being who he was—a man who trained the enlisted under him and provided guidance to the officers over him. He had even found time to add a family to his life with all that going on. Shiran looked at her clock and started when she saw the time.

"I have to get going, Francesca. Duty calls," stated Shiran.

"I'm glad we could have this talk. Take care," replied Francesca.

Waving back at Francesca, Shiran walked briskly toward the elevators with a newfound resolution. This was a whole new world, and she could handle the duties and responsibilities of both a Marine officer and a mother of a colonist family.

She arrived at the Marine Complex feeling invigorated with a new sense of purpose. She made rounds of the armory and air traffic control, then inspected the radar and rocket installations on the roof of the complex. Finished, she went to her office and looked at her message traffic.

She was completing her responses to the messages when Master Sergeant Evan Zander looked through the open door with a knowing grin. Shiran wondered what the grin meant and decided not to ask.

"What is it, Master Sergeant?" asked the second lieutenant.

"Sergeant Adachi says he's finished the forms, and the brass made from the zinc Joseph Green found made fine casings. I sent a team out this morning to bring a load back, along with another triceratops for Ezekiel Yap, ma'am," stated Evan.

"That's great! How's he coming on explosive rounds?" inquired Shiran.

"That chemist Raisa Romanov says she needs some equipment from the ship to produce more explosive primer in quantity and the powder for the rounds," stated Evan.

"When will she have her request ready?" asked Shiran.

"She said she already put in a request to the *New Horizon* over a week ago. It should have been in your message traffic," replied Evan.

"I never saw that message, Master Sergeant," replied Shiran, confused.

Master Sergeant Zander gave her a grim look. They were not short on ammunition yet because of the reloads Sergeant Adachi provided. However, if they wanted to produce new ammunition and even increase the original supply, it would require a significant increase in explosive production.

"Hattie," said Shiran.

"Operating. Second Lieutenant Rosenstein," replied Hattie.

"Please put me in contact with Commander Blankenship via a secure line," ordered Shiran.

"Please wait while I set that up, Second Lieutenant," returned Hattie.

"Ma'am, if you'll excuse me, I have some business on the cleft to attend to," said the master sergeant from the doorway.

Shiran nodded knowing that the master sergeant's business involved finding out what he could about the missing message.

"Commander Blankenship is online, Second Lieutenant," stated Hattie.

"Thank you, Hattie," said Shiran.

Commander Hadden Blankenship's face with the *New Horizon*'s bridge in the background appeared above Shiran's desk. His face was impassive as he looked out the view screen. Then a smile touched his lips and extended to his eyes.

"Good afternoon, Second Lieutenant. What can I do for you?" asked the commander.

"Good afternoon, Commander. I appear to be missing some message traffic the master sergeant says was sent to the *New Horizon* over a week ago," replied Shiran.

"What was the message traffic about?" inquired Hadden.

"Raisa Romanov supposedly sent a request for equipment to produce more explosive material so we could make more ammunition," stated Shiran.

"I'm aware of the situation, Second Lieutenant," Hadden confirmed.

"Care to elaborate, Commander?" asked Shiran.

"Not at this time, Second Lieutenant," replied Hadden evasively.

"About the equipment, sir?" Shiran returned to the missing request.

"The equipment she requested will be on a shuttle this evening. I've already informed Chief Zander to have the dockside shuttle prepared to transfer power for the colony to the arriving shuttle. You should be receiving a message to have your Marines assist in docking and underway procedures for the two shuttles in the next hour," confided the commander.

"Thank you, sir," confirmed Shiran.

"I'll be piloting the shuttle down. I've already contacted Lieutenant Commander Raybourn and Lieutenant Anderson to be present at the Marine Complex at that time. Consider this your notice that you are to have a conference room ready at that time. The conference will be brief, and I will be returning to the *New Horizon* with the departing shuttle," stated Hadden.

"Yes, sir," acknowledged Shiran.

"Have plenty of cammies out on the docks, Second Lieutenant," ordered the commander.

"Yes, sir," acknowledged Shiran again.

"Second Lieutenant, I want you present also. Out," stated Commander Blankenship.

Sitting back in her seat with a frown, Shiran watched the commander's face blink out of existence above her desk. There was more going on here than the commander had let on, and it was obvious that whatever it was, he was not happy about it either. Shiran hit a button on the desktop and said, "Staff Sergeant Krupich, I require your presence in the command office."

She waited a few moments for her friend Staff Sergeant Rachel Krupich to arrive. She informed Rachel about the impending shuttle arrival that evening and to have all the Marines in cammies ready to assist. Rachel Krupich acknowledged her orders without question and went to take care of her new assignment.

Lieutenant Commander Raybourn and Lieutenant Anderson arrived in cammies a half hour prior to the shuttle's arrival at seventeen hundred. When it arrived, they joined in with all the Marines as they walked down the pier shuttle. The only person on the dock not in cammies was the master sergeant's wife, Chief Tami Zander, directing operations but acting as all was normal. When line handling was completed, all camouflaged personnel carried boxes to the

Marine Complex, while Chief Zander transferred power generation for the cleft and Compound from *Shuttle 1* to *Shuttle 2*.

The commander and the three others he had requested sat around a table in the mess area of the Marine Complex. The commander looked grim as he looked at them.

"We have a problem. This goes no further than the four of us without my express approval. Understood?" Blankenship stated. Conor, Michael, and Shiran nodded.

"What is it, sir?" asked Conor.

"There appears to be a cabal of individuals disrupting communications," stated Hadden.

"What do you mean, sir?" asked Shiran.

"That request for more equipment from Raisa Romanov so she could increase her manufacturing of explosive material for the Marines was placed in an inactive file. Basically, it was put in the trash," said the commander.

"Who would do that?" asked Lieutenant Michael Anderson.

"I've identified five people who are directly responsible at this time," said Hadden.

"Who are they?" asked Conor.

"I'm not going to reveal that information yet. I'm not sure of everyone involved. However, after reading through the messages, I'm sure it's none of you because the trashed messages were directly related to your operations. I'm also fairly sure I can trust Dr. Hollinger and possibly Dr. Joshi, but they do not need to be involved in this affair," said Hadden.

"What were the messages pertaining to?" asked Michael.

"A wide variety of things. There was a recent commendation that you submitted and requests for equipment from you too," said Blankenship.

"So what do you want to do, sir?" asked Shiran.

"If it's important, you send it via regular message traffic to cause no suspicion. You will also send it via foot messenger from now on. The only messengers we use are Ensign Sobolov, the master sergeant, Chief Pennington, and any Marine whom the second lieutenant approves. Any questions?" asked Commander Blankenship.

The other three gathered in the room shook their heads.

"Very well then. This meeting is over, and it's time for you to escort me back to the shuttle. Second Lieutenant, you are to tell your people that I wasn't here. Understood?" asked the commander.

"Yes, sir!" replied Shiran.

CHAPTER 29

Lieutenant Commander Conor Raybourn arrived at the Marine Complex in his cammies and was met by Second Lieutenant Shiran Rosenstein. The two embraced and kissed to the cheers of the Marines waiting for him at the entrance. The two walked slowly over to Master Sergeant Evan Zander and five other Marines standing at attention.

"What's the plan, sir?" asked the master sergeant.

"We're going to reconnoiter along the cliff base to the south. We're only sure of the first four or five klicks in that region along the cliff face. I'd like to double or triple that if possible," stated Conor.

"Sounds like fun, sir," said Evan.

"How many of us are going, sir?" asked Staff Sergeant Rachel Krupich.

"Just the five of you and myself," stated Conor as the master sergeant handed him an M-71. "Has everyone else been outfitted, Master Sergeant?"

"Loaded for bear, sir." Evan grinned.

"Let's hope we don't need it," stated Conor.

"We're also going to carry two type 2 first aid kits and enough rations for five days along with the normal gear," stated Evan as he held a backpack up for Conor.

"We staying out the full five days, sir?" asked Rachel.

"We're going to walk in starting from here. Our first goal is to reconnoiter that ridge just west of the fence," answered Conor. Then he added, "After that, we're going to try to expand what we know about the base of the cliff another ten to fifteen klicks. There should be enough to eat without the rations, but we'll carry them anyway.

So we may be gone longer than a week depending on what we find and the terrain."

"Thank you, sir," said Rachel.

"That's all right, Staff Sergeant," replied Conor. "If you or anyone else needs to inform people of what's going on and how long, you have a quarter of an hour."

Most of the Marines went inside the complex for the stated time as Conor and Shiran talked and wished each other well. Even the master sergeant went over to the shuttle for a moment to talk to his wife. All were back and ready to embark at the stated fifteen-minute mark. Chief Tami Zander had returned with Evan as they walked hand in hand from the shuttle. Conor noticed Brad Guillete emerge from the Marine Complex doorway with Staff Sergeant Rachel Krupich, and they exchanged a brief hug and kiss, then Rachel formed up with the rest of the team.

"Are we ready, Master Sergeant?" asked Conor.

"Lead on, sir," stated Evan.

Conor and the Marines waved to those gathered, and they turned to find out what fate might have in store for them as they strolled across the fields man had created on this planet. It took about half an hour to arrive at the gate and pass through it as they entered their identification code. The brush started fifty meters beyond the fence and was kept at bay by the defoliant and an ATV that mowed the area on a regular schedule.

It looked like a short hike to the top of the ridge, but it still took them an hour to reach the top. The brush was so thick it seemed to grow back as fast as it was cut. The terrain under their boots was rough as they progressed up the rise.

They reached the top and conducted a search in the location that Conor and Shiran had seen the red form from the chopper. Rachel discovered a feather that was a reddish brown near the location, but Conor assured her that what he had seen was much redder. They bagged the specimen and continued their search. Sergeant Tadashi Adachi discovered a path that led down the other side of the ridge, and the master sergeant took Sergeant Nikolai Ivankov and Lance Corporal Lenard Barrett with Tadashi leading the way to investigate, while Conor, Staff Sergeant Rachel Krupich, and Corporal Natalie Hoffman continued to investigate the ridge top. Less than a quarter of an hour passed before the master sergeant contacted Conor.

"Sir, you better get down here," came Evan's voice.

"What's up, Master Sergeant?" replied Conor.

"You need to see this, sir," came Evan's response.

"We'll be right there," returned Conor.

Conor looked at the two teammates with him and indicated for Rachel to lead the way. They started down and found the path. While not well kept, it was easy going, and it only took a few minutes to reach the bottom. There, they found the others gathered around the entrance of a small cave at the base of the ridge. The brush that had covered the entrance had been pulled to the side, and the master sergeant was in the entrance, shining his flashlight into a small comfortable cave. What could only be deemed a nest was set up along the wall at the end of the cave.

"Something dens here, Master Sergeant?" asked Conor.

"Only if it uses fire, sir," stated Evan.

"You're sure?" asked Conor.

"Firepit along the side of the wall along with dry tinder in a niche on the other wall, and there's this," said the master sergeant as he held up a bright-red feather.

Taking the red feather from Evan's hand, Conor examined it, and a chill ran down his spine. They were being watched, and they still didn't know by whom or what. Conor looked Evan in the eye and could tell Evan Zander was having the same bad feeling. He finally shook off the mood and returned to the present.

"Anything else, Master Sergeant?" asked Conor.

"Yes, there is, but I'll let the sergeant explain it to you, sir," stated Evan.

Conor looked at Sergeant Adachi.

"It's over here, sir," replied Tadashi, indicating a tree.

"Tell me about it," ordered Lieutenant Commander Raybourn.

"There was something hanging from that branch, sir," Tadashi stated as he pointed to the branch. "I climbed up there and found a wear mark from a rope of some sort."

"What led you to look up there?" asked Conor.

"The blood splatters at your feet, sir," said Tadashi, indicating the earth at Conor's feet where speckles of blood could be seen if one looked closely. "They tied off the line over here," said Sergeant Adachi, indicating another low branch, which Conor looked at but didn't notice the bark missing until his eyes were within a foot of the branch.

"What was it for?" asked Conor.

"Lunch, sir," declared Tadashi. "It was keeping the meat in an unreachable spot to keep it from small scavengers. Anything else big enough to get at the meat could have it while whatever creature that did this attempted to escape."

"Makes sense, Sergeant. Good work," acknowledged Conor, impressed. "Was there anything else in the cave, Master Sergeant?"

"Just tracks, sir. They're raptor, and they're larger than any raptor tracks I've seen except once," stated the master sergeant.

"The lost KG-3?" inquired Conor, referring to the Kinley-Grant combat knife Staff Sergeant Hall lost during a hunting expedition and the tracks discovered when searching for the knife.

"Yes, sir," replied the master sergeant.

"Recommendations," demanded the lieutenant commander.

"Search the immediate area for fifteen mikes and move on. Let's track the thing," responded Evan Zander.

"Sounds good," returned Conor.

They found a path that led in the general direction of the mines. Sergeant Adachi studied the path for a few minutes and assured Conor that the tracks from the cave went down the same path. They followed the path slowly with Tadashi checking for signs of the creature's passing they now hunted. As they followed the game trail, they passed within a kilometer of the copper mine. The trail split another kilometer along. They took the trail leading south and came across a wide stream two kilometers later. They crossed the stream and, another two kilometers later, started going up a rise. At the top, they could see that the forest continued on for another five to six kilometers where it ended and the plains began. It was starting to get late, and Conor debated whether they should stop for the night. Tadashi approached and pointed to the side of the rise that was steep.

"We should search over there, sir," stated Tadashi.

"What do you think is over there?" asked the lieutenant commander.

"A cave, sir," replied Tadashi.

"Why do you think that?" inquired Conor.

"The last cave was a temporary shelter," replied Tadashi.

"Why do you think that?" asked Conor, perplexed.

"The tinder was restocked to dry," stated Evan Zander.

"So you both think there will be another cave near here?" questioned Conor.

"Yes, sir," responded Evan.

"Why do you think that?" asked Conor, feeling slightly frustrated with asking the same question three times. Was he just not seeing something, or was he getting tired? He shrugged it off and waited for an explanation.

"This is near the plains area where Staff Sergeant Hall lost her KG-3," said Evan patiently.

Conor thought about that for a moment. The master sergeant was right, of course. The plains would be within walking distance of this ridge, and a cave would be a good place to shelter for the night.

"All right, Master Sergeant. Two teams like before, let's look for that cave and spend the night," stated Conor as he took off his helmet and wiped his forehead. When he returned the helmet to its place, the master sergeant nodded.

"Good idea, sir," replied Zander.

They almost missed the cave. It was well hidden but large enough to fit them all. The entrance would have allowed a creature larger than a man through, but that didn't mean anything until they knew for sure what they were dealing with. Like before, there was a sandpit in the rear of the cave where the creature obviously slept. There were niches on each side of the wall in front of the sand, which provided places for fire on one side and dry tinder storage on the other.

They slept fitfully during the night using the fire niche to keep warm. There was one person on watch at all times during the night. A couple of large beasts passed by, and once, a large predator sniffed at the entrance of the cave. Some green wood placed on the fire caused smoke, which dissuaded the predator that snorted and moved off.

In the morning, they eliminated all traces of their presence and restocked the woodpile. They followed the trail back to the fork near the copper mine, then took the trail leading west, deeper into the forest.

Lieutenant Commander Conor Raybourn walked slowly and cautiously through the forest, examining his surroundings carefully as he went. He was following Sergeant Ivankov, who was the point man, and had learned the hand signals necessary so he wouldn't have to speak when Nikolai stopped walking and raised a closed fist. Conor and the rest of the team stopped as one. Something moved out in front of them as they stood frozen in place. A large carnivore moved into the open as they watched. The creature raised its head, and they heard it breathe deeply as though hunting a scent, then it shifted its head and did it again.

The party remained frozen as the beast lowered its head and moved south into the forest. They could hear the sound of its passage for several minutes afterward before Nikolai Ivankov, the point man, relaxed and motioned the group forward. Knowing the beast was not far ahead made the group extremely cautious as they slowly moved forward.

Suddenly, they heard crashing ahead, and vegetation swayed wildly as a group of stegosaurus smashed through the brush and trees. The carnivore was at their heels but swerved to the south as the beast passed the party in the depression below their position. Master Sergeant Evan Zander looked intently at the wall of green, and he drew his right hand across his neck. Everyone readied their firearms facing outward.

A velociraptor jumped out from the foliage and grabbed Lance Corporal Lenard Barrett by the neck with its mouth. Lenard fired his Navarro M-71 reflexively as the raptor ripped out his throat. The shots hit the other raptor in front of Lenard as it jumped, making it flop backward, and green feathers flew. Another one jumped forward and grabbed the lance corporal by his leg as the first one grabbed him with its arms. The lance corporal never had a chance since his throat was missing from the first raptor's attack. Lance Corporal Barrett dropped like a broken doll as the raptors ripped him apart.

Sergeant Adachi and Conor fired at the raptors as they continued their gruesome attack. A Vinter HR-19 sounded from behind Conor, and he heard something thrash in its death throes behind him. There was a female scream and thrashing to Conor's right, and when he looked, Staff Sergeant Rachel Krupich had vanished. A shaft came out of nowhere and hit Sergeant Adachi in the shoulder, causing him to go to his knees. The Vinter HR-19 sounded again, and to Conor's left, he saw something red thrash in the brush.

"Back!" shouted Master Sergeant Zander.

Conor grabbed Sergeant Adachi around the waist and helped him up. Conor let his M-71 hang from the sling and drew his Gerst S-7, then fired at the shaft embedded in Adachi's shoulder, breaking it off about six inches from Tadashi's chest. Tadashi screamed, then gritted his teeth. He nodded at Conor after Conor holstered his Gerst and grabbed his M-71. Lieutenant Commander Raybourn fired at some vegetation to his left as it moved and was rewarded with a shriek of pain. The party moved back quickly, constantly watching for more movement.

They made it two klicks before they were attacked again. Three more green velociraptors died as they jumped forward. Conor saw a flash of red behind them and fired a burst in its direction. He was rewarded with another shriek of pain.

"We're being hunted," stated the master sergeant.

"It's at least another two klicks to that ridge we designated as an LZ," said Conor, referring to the landing zone they had selected for a chopper retrieval.

"Hope we can make it. Adachi, how are you doing?" asked Evan.

The master sergeant was rewarded with a look of pain and a nod from Tadashi as he gritted his teeth more tightly. The master sergeant looked at the lieutenant commander as they moved, and Conor nodded. They made it another klick before the brush to their left and right exploded with motion. Evan Zander fired to the right as Conor fired a burst to the left. He heard Sergeant Ivankov and Corporal Hoffman firing behind him. There was a grunt of pain, and as he looked, Corporal Hoffman collapsed to the ground with a feathered javelin embedded in her thigh. The Vinter sniper rifle sounded, and the red form that was drawing its arm back had its head explode into a red cloud of mist. Conor and Nikolai fired to both sides of the red-feathered raptor and were rewarded with more thrashing in the vegetation.

Master Sergeant Zander shouldered his Vinter HR-19 and dropped to his knees. He broke off the shaft protruding from Natalie Hoffman's thigh and picked her up. Conor looked at Tadashi, who was barely keeping his feet under him and received a nod.

"Time to go," stated Evan Zander.

Conor grabbed Tadashi by the waist, and the two moved as fast as their burdens would allow while Ivankov watched their rear. Conor fired once at movement to their right as they finally started up the slope to the LZ. Lieutenant Commander Conor Raybourn heard Sergeant Ivankov empty a whole magazine from his M-71 behind them and reload. He continued firing short bursts to the left and right as they mounted to the LZ to call for recovery.

*****

Staff Sergeant Rachel Krupich remembered backing up to take a shot at the raptor when suddenly she was falling. The brush to her side was so thick it had concealed the ten-meter drop. She lost her Navarro M-71 somewhere in that fall. Her left arm and personal communicator were broken on the rock that had arrested her fall. She remembered running through the forest, tripping over the underbrush for what seemed like an eternity. She saw a flash of bright-green feathers in the forest behind her and knew that she was still being hunted. She had lost her Gerst S-7 sidearm when she had killed the dull green velociraptor. She had not come out of that encounter unscathed though. There was a long gash in her left thigh from the inner claw of the creature's foot, and one of its hand claws raked three long gashes in the bicep of her right arm. Her helmet prevented the raptor from taking off her face, but the teeth had made a deep cut in her left cheek. Rachel was nearly spent as her boot slipped off a rock. She stumbled and fell to the ground. She knew when the velociraptor following her finally closed in, it would mean her end.

The green raptor closed in rapidly as Rachel rolled in the underbrush. She searched the ground in feverish haste for a branch or rock to use as a weapon when the brush to her right exploded. A reddish blur of feathery death struck the green from the side, ripping out its throat with sharp daggerlike teeth. At the same time, the red velociraptor's hind foot disemboweled the green slightly below its rib cage. The reddish velociraptor made sure of the green by snapping its neck with its powerful jaws. The scarlet beast then forced the green to the ground and stood on it as death came in quivering spasms. The red's wide mouth full of razor-sharp teeth was covered in blood and green feathers as it turned toward her. Staff Sergeant Rachel Krupich lost consciousness as she saw the red-feathered velociraptor take a step toward her.

CHAPTER 30

Qu'Loo'Oh' watched the intruders for three more days from her shelter near their silvery web. She was growing anxious because the hunters would soon arrive and start their ritual hunt on these sacred grounds, and it was time to hide. She had hunted and gathered wood, storing it in the sacred retreat where she had lived for the past four years.

She was watching from the top of the ridge when Qu'Loo'Oh' saw an intruder in one of the places where the plants grew in rows standing and looking in her direction. Then one of the beasts with wings like a dragonfly flew in her direction. She drew back further into the foliage knowing she had been seen as it hovered above the silvery web. She watched the intruder and saw the intruder return to whatever it was doing. Were these creatures herbivores? Yet they rode those weird great beasts and hunted the great beasts too.

Perhaps these plants were for healing purposes. She knew of certain plants that had healing properties and that the healers of her people knew even more but were secretive about such knowledge. A thought crossed her mind. Perhaps the healers of her people had secret places where they, too, grew patches of plants that had healing properties.

This was more for her to think about as she went into hiding during the time of the sacred hunt. The sacred hunt would last for a cycle of the inner moon or twenty-seven days. It would be unsafe to leave the chambers that Qu'Loo'Oh' lived in during that time. Qu'Loo'Oh' shook her head and snorted as she walked down the ridge to the trail that led to the sacred chambers where she lived.

It was time to hunt and store meat and wood for the isolation she would soon endure.

Qu'Loo'Oh' was picking up wood a few days later when she heard a noise of something falling through the brush. She heard the sound of the intruders' fire sticks nearby. Qu'Loo'Oh' froze and waited anxiously, thinking something might have seen her. There was an intruder running through the forest nearby. The intruder was holding its right forelimb where gashes had torn the blood-soaked fabric, and blood ran down its left leg as it ran. Then Qu'Loo'Oh' spotted the green stalking the intruder, and she crouched lower. The intruder swerved and approached Qu'Loo'Oh's position, possibly seeking the protection of the heavier vegetation. Then the intruder slipped and rolled deeper into the covering of tangled brush.

The green dashed forward, and Qu'Loo'Oh' made a decision. The green passed her hiding place, and she ran forward and attacked the green. Her jaws ripped through the feathers on the green's neck as her right foot raised for a disemboweling stroke to the green's midsection. The green's neck cracked as Qu'Loo'Oh' bit through the bone, and blood squirted from the torn arteries. After she delivered the great wounds to the green, she pushed the green to the ground and stood on the dying body to prevent it from injuring her or the intruder. Qu'Loo'Oh' raised her head then and looked intently at the intruder. The intruder's eyes closed, and its body went limp.

The quivering of the body underneath her grew less, and she stepped off, looking at it closely. It had the mark of a hunting clan, and she searched her surroundings closely as she froze, waiting. No flashes of red or green appeared in the surrounding foliage as she watched. She left the body of the green and went over to the intruder. There were deep gashes in its leg and forelimb, along with one on its cheek where blood flowed. Its chest still moved, so it was alive, and Qu'Loo'Oh' decided to take a chance. She lifted the body of the intruder and cautiously made her way to the sacred cave, which lay nearby. She placed the intruder in the entrance and returned for the body of the green and took it to the sacred cave too. She then returned and commenced obliterating the signs of the struggle and all tracks.

Returning to the entrance of the sacred cave, she sealed the hidden doorway. The intruder still appeared unconscious when she finished, but she poked it with a pole before approaching closer. Assured that the intruder posed no threat, she picked up the limp body and made her way to the room she occupied. There, she laid the intruder on her nest and inspected the intruder closer. She soon learned that the intruder's body was covered in some sort of material and that the skin of the face and hands was its natural outer color. She removed the knife she found and laid it on the bench where she kept the one she had acquired. The head covering confused her until the snaps suddenly gave way as she tinkered with them. She removed the covering and concentrated on the covering on the rest of the intruder's body.

She was toying with the straps running down one side of the body when the intruder's body jerked. She heard a groan and watched as the intruder's eyes opened. They remained unfocused at first, then they centered on Qu'Loo'Oh', and she could see fear as the intruder drew back. The intruder's hand went to the place on its belt where the knife had been. A thought occurred to Qu'Loo'Oh', and she walked to the bench, picking up the knife, and returned. She slowly placed the knife in the intruder's lap as the creature watched in terror. Qu'Loo'Oh' stepped back, watching the intruder in case it attempted to attack.

The intruder looked at the knife then at Qu'Loo'Oh'. Finally, the intruder picked up the knife with its arm, though there was a wince as it moved its left arm and placed the knife aside and looked at Qu'Loo'Oh' expectantly.

Qu'Loo'Oh' looked at the knife then at the intruder, suspecting a trick. Nothing happened. The intruder simply sat there looking at her. Finally, Qu'Loo'Oh' took a step forward and slowly picked up the knife. She walked back to her bench and placed it beside the other knife. When Qu'Loo'Oh' turned, the intruder was working at the covering of its body. It was able to release the straps along one side and worked its way out of the covering. It agonizingly removed the belt that was around its waist and released it. It was working at the thongs and straps of the covering on its feet when the creature let out a groan and lay back. Its eyes closed, and shortly after, a buzzing sound emitted from its mouth.

Qu'Loo'Oh' waited a short time, then moved forward. She worked at the straps and thongs that held the covering on the creature's feet. She grasped the covering on one foot and gently pulled. The covering came off, and she repeated the process with the other foot. Once both coverings were removed, Qu'Loo'Oh' looked at the sleeping intruder carefully and discovered some sort of fastenings running down the front of the material covering the creature's chest. She worked at those and was able to loosen them, so the material revealed the pale skin underneath. There was some sort of harness on the creatures upper chest, but Qu'Loo'Oh' could not discern any fastenings that held it in place. There was a fastening on the lower material in the front that she was able to loosen, then she discovered a metal strip that had a metal tab at the top. There was a hole in the tab that she worked at with her claw. When she pulled, it moved, and the metal strip parted.

Not wishing to disturb the creature further, Qu'Loo'Oh' left the room, going to another room down the hall that she used as a storeroom. She gathered rushes that she had stored there and returned to her room where the creature still slept. She placed the rushes along the wall near her nest and made three more trips for more rushes. She went back to the cave entrance and gathered up the body of the green. When she returned, she lay the green on the floor and ate her fill.

When Qu'Loo'Oh' finished, she found the intruder awake and watching her. The creature removed the material covering its upper and lower body carefully, leaving the harnesses at its chest and crouch. Then it removed a case from the belt it had worn. It opened the case and removed a small silver tube. Qu'Loo'Oh' grew apprehensive, fearing it was a fire stick like the ones that killed from afar. Instead, the creature grasped its left leg at the gash with its left forearm. Its face contorted as it did so, but it continued until the skin at the lips of the gash came together. Then it pressed the end of the tube in its right forearm, and a click sounded. The creature continued the process along the gash until it went from one end to the other. The gash remained closed, and Qu'Loo'Oh' moved over to look. There were miraculously thin black lines holding the skin together.

The intruder looked at Qu'Loo'Oh' and extended its right arm. It then looked at the three gashes in its forelimb then at Qu'Loo'Oh' as it held the silvery cylinder in its left hand. Qu'Loo'Oh' understood immediately but hesitated, suspecting once again a trick. Slowly she pushed at the skin till one of the gashes closed. The intruder moved the cylinder along the lips of the gash, clicking the cylinder. When the intruder finished that gash, the process was repeated for the other two as Qu'Loo'Oh' pushed them together. The intruder then produced a tube from its bag and removed a cap and slowly applied a salve to the now closed gashes. It then placed a white pad to the gash on its leg and took a roll of more white material that stretched and wrapped it in place. The intruder then repeated the process with its right arm.

The creature removed a small pouch from the bag that it had removed from its back earlier. It tore the pouch open with its teeth and removed items from it that it put in its mouth and ate. It then took out something from the case that had held the silver tube and removed a very small pouch, which it opened with its teeth also. There was a small white pebble inside that the creature swallowed.

The creature grasped its upper left arm, obviously in pain, and the arm was slightly bent compared to the other. The creature slowly rose from the nest and walked over to the fireplace as it grasped the upper part of its left arm. It placed most of the joint of its left arm into a narrow niche near the fireplace. It pushed its body back away from the wedged arm joint, and Qu'Loo'Oh' heard something crack. The intruder screamed in pain and pulled the joint out of the wedge. When the intruder turned, its face was whiter than before. Its eyes grew glazed, then closed, and the body started to collapse as Qu'Loo'Oh' ran forward to catch the intruder in her forearms. She turned and walked over to the new rushes she had placed on the floor where she carefully lay the intruder on its back.

Qu'Loo'Oh' returned to the fireplace and placed wood on it, raising the heat in the room. She returned to her nest and removed the items there, placing them on the table. As she did so, she had a thought. Were the materials used to cover the body of the intruder because it was cold? The creature did not have the natural down of feathers her kind had. Her people used hides and woven material to make blankets and outer wear to ward off the cold.

She took the material that had covered the chest and legs over to the intruder and laid them over its body as best she could. She stood there a moment, marveling at the material. It was finally woven and dyed to blend into its surroundings. Qu'Loo'Oh' worried about how close an intruder could be without being noticed if they did not move. Coupled with the fire sticks the intruders had, it would constitute a significant danger.

Qu'Loo'Oh' shuddered for a moment, then went to curl up in her own nest and dozed. The legends and prophecies of old disturbed her sleep as she lay in fitful slumber. Her dreams were chaotic, filled with rivers of blood and cities burning in flames as mountains fell from the heavens. Qu'Loo'Oh' awoke in fear, the terror making her draw back against the wall of her room. The terror and fear receded as the reality of where she was came to her. Her mind calmed slowly, and she settled restlessly back into her nest.

Then she heard movement, along with a groan, and remembered she was not alone. She looked over the edge of her nest to see the intruder looking back at her. It broke eye contact, and the intruder slowly rose to a sitting position, being careful of its left arm. The creature looked at her again as it rose to its feet and slowly walked to the bench and reached for its bag. It drew out a roll of something with its good arm, then it worked at the back till something popped out of the side. It did it again on the opposite side of the bag until something popped out again.

The intruder picked up one of the sticks, placed it against the inside of its left arm, then placed the stick on the edge of the nest so the stick remained tight against the inner arm. She placed another stick over the top of the arm. She then picked up the roll, and with its teeth, it grabbed an end and pulled. A ripping sound followed as a strip of material slowly unwound from the roll until it was approximately a claw-length long. The intruder then placed the material on its arm and the stick at the top, patting it afterward. The material appeared to stick to both the arm and the stick, causing it to remain in place. Then with the blunted digits of its right hand, it ripped the material, leaving the material sticking to the arm and stick.

The intruder repeated the process to the ends of the sticks until they remained attached to the intruder's left arm. It then opened the case, and instead of the magic tube, it removed another roll of white material. It found the end and started wrapping it around the injured arm slowly from top to bottom. Finished, it took up the first roll of blue material and commenced wrapping it over the white material. Qu'Loo'Oh' had never seen such an act performed on her people by the wise. Those as injured as this intruder was were left to fend for themselves. They either survived or died. Those who did survive rarely were as good at hunting as before the injury. When the intruder finished, it returned to the bench with its magic roll of blue material and the case with the magic silvery tube. It took out another small package from the case and tore it open, then swallowed something again that caused its eyes to get a faraway look.

It looked at the green lying on the floor and reached for one of the knives lying on the bench. Qu'Loo'Oh' grew apprehensive once again but relaxed as the intruder walked over to the green. It used the knife to cut off an arm and remove the skin as it held the limb between its legs. Finished, it lay the limb on the stone before the fire and then added wood to the fire. The intruder walked back to the nest Qu'Loo'Oh' had made for it and took up the material she had placed over the intruder. The intruder walked back over to the fire and proceeded to cover its body with the material again.

The arm of the dead green was burning, and the scent filled the room, causing Qu'Loo'Oh' to snort and wrinkle her nose. The intruder looked her way as it turned the meat to burn on the other side. It took its knife and sliced into the burnt meat, cutting off a strip. It then stabbed the meat with the tip of its knife and raised it to its mouth and, with its teeth, started to nibble on it. Qu'Loo'Oh' snorted again as the thought of eating burnt meat made her stomach turn in disgust. The intruder continued its repast in this manner as the meat burned until it had had its fill. Once full, it continued to burn the meat for several hundreds of heartbeats. When it had accomplished its task, it set the meat and knife carefully in an empty niche near the fire, making sure Qu'Loo'Oh' saw. It was obviously saving the meat for later and wanted to ensure that Qu'Loo'Oh' knew where the knife was also.

The intruder went back to its nearby nest and lay down. It must have been asleep as soon as its head lay on the reeds because a buzzing noise emitted from its mouth almost instantly. Qu'Loo'Oh' suspected that the drugs the creature had taken after wrapping its arm would cause it to sleep for a long time since she had observed its effects once before. She made a decision and rose noiselessly going to the door. She went down the hall and to the entrance of the sacred cave. She exited and carefully examined the forest around her. Watching, listening, and smelling for several hundred heartbeats left her confident that no hunters or other carnivores were in the area. She stepped out and, keeping alert, slowly worked her way toward the area where she had acquired the intruder.

From the sign, she could read nothing had passed this way. She finally arrived at the spot where she had attacked the green and started following the trail of the intruder. It was easily followed to the base of a drop that was at least three body lengths tall. There, she discovered the fire stick that the intruders carried. Searching the surrounding area, she discovered the smaller fire stick they rarely used and a bag that the intruders wore. Qu'Loo'Oh' took them all and started back to the sacred chambers.

She was careful to leave no sign as she went. She placed the items she had found inside the chamber's entrance and took her broom. Backtracking a hundred body lengths, she carefully erased any sign as she backed toward the chamber's entrance. Assured that the trail was erased as best as it could be, she replaced her broom and closed the outer seal of the chamber. She picked up the items as she returned to her room. There, she discovered the intruder awake as she entered. The intruder's eyes widened as it saw the items Qu'Loo'Oh' carried.

Qu'Loo'Oh' placed the items on the bench and stood back. The intruder looked at her then back at the fire sticks. Finally, the intruder rose from its nest and approached the bench. The intruder took a metal case out of its bag that it opened. Inside, there was a white cloth, sticks with white balls on the end, a metal bar, and a couple of transparent containers filled with liquid. The intruder picked up the smaller fire stick and commenced taking it apart. It spent a long time obviously cleaning both of the fire sticks, then putting them back together. When the intruder was finished, it placed them back on the bench and left them.

The intruder then walked over to the fireplace, and utilizing the scoop Qu'Loo'Oh' used to remove ashes, it scooped ashes from the bottom of the fire. The intruder spread the ashes on the stone floor in front of the fireplace so they lightly covered the stone several paw widths in all directions. The intruder then looked at Qu'Loo'Oh' and waved a paw at her and patted the stone beside where it was sitting.

Qu'Loo'Oh' stepped forward as the intruder turned back to look at the ashes it had spread. The intruder looked at Qu'Loo'Oh' sideways then back at the ashes. With its right arm, it reached forward and drew a vertical line in the ashes with one of its digits. It looked at Qu'Loo'Oh' and raised its fist with a digit extended and said, "One." The intruder kept drawing vertical lines, raising the same number of digits while saying a new word. The fifth line went at an angle through all four lines, and the intruder raised all five of the digits on its hand and said, "Five."

Qu'Loo'Oh' understood, and the communication lessons between her and the intruder had begun.

CHAPTER 31

Lieutenant Commander Conor Raybourn was worried; two Marines were injured, and he had lost two more during the excursion. Lance Corporal Barrett was definitely dead, and he didn't know if Staff Sergeant Krupich was dead or alive. Considering the nature of the encountered hostiles, he believed the former was more likely than the latter for the staff sergeant. They hadn't seen the velociraptors because of the large herbivores and carnivore that had stampeded past them right before the attack. Two other members of his team were injured, incapable of continuing further. Conor made a Mayday call to the Marine Complex.

"Master Sergeant?" yelled Conor.

"We're in trouble, sir! We're being surrounded!" Master Sergeant Evan Zander yelled back.

"Set me up against that rock, sir," wheezed Sergeant Tadashi Adachi painfully, pointing to a nearby rock, knowing it would allow Conor to use both hands. "I can still shoot if I have support."

Conor moved over to the rock and let go of Tadashi's waist, freeing his left hand. The Vinter HR-19 10 mm sounded as the master sergeant acquired a target, and green feathers flew as two velociraptors went into their death throes. Evan Zander was good at that, thought Conor as he checked the rear and fired three rounds from his M-71 when a redhead appeared. It exploded into a brilliant cloud of red when the explosive round hit the back of its cranium. He heard Sergeant Nikolai Ivankov firing behind him and the sound of more thrashing vegetation when the firing stopped.

"How's Hoffman?" yelled Conor.

Tadashi bent down in pain and checked Corporal Hoffman's jugular as he watched the foliage below. "She still has a pulse, but that leg material is soaked in blood. I'm going to tourniquet."

"Do it!" shouted Conor.

Conor heard the Vinter go off behind him and again within a couple of seconds. The master sergeant yelled at Sergeant Ivankov to throw his M-71 over as an explosion from a grenade filled the air to the left side of the ridge's downhill slope. Nikolai went to Tadashi and took the M-71 he had placed on the ground to work on Natalie. Conor fired his M-71 down the slope at some foliage that moved and was rewarded with a screech of pain as more green feathers flew. He glanced to the east and saw the choppers coming fast. Shiran must have had Marines on watch, sitting in their seats, to get them in the air that quickly. But who was piloting the choppers? Conor heard two Navarro M-71s firing behind him as he fired a burst to his right then the sound of the Vinter going off again.

"Everything all right back there?" yelled Conor.

"Under control so far!" growled the master sergeant. "Ivankov, grenade."

"Last one, Master Sergeant!" screamed Sergeant Ivankov as Conor saw him throw downslope and to the right where Evan Zander pointed.

"We've got about fifteen seconds till fire support is here!" shouted Conor.

"Better be because I only have one more mag for the M-71!" yelled Nikolai Ivankov, reminding Conor to slap his musette pouch. *Empty! Damn!* He didn't know how many times he had fired the mag in his M-71 as he set the selector switch to single shot. He shot a round into a green as it popped up and was rewarded with a scream of pain. His next round missed, and the tree behind it was cut off three feet from the roots by the explosive round. Fortunately, the tree fell on the raptor as it made its charge because the next trigger pull rewarded Conor with a click. *Damn!* He let the M-71 hang loose on its strap as he drew his Gerst S-7 sidearm.

The air moved as Conor pointed the Gerst downslope and knew the cavalry had arrived. He shot another green that popped its head up and watched as it was torn apart by the miniguns mounted under the gunship. The recovery chopper dropped while Conor ducked and stepped back to the rock where Sergeant Adachi leaned. Grabbing hold of Tadashi, he assisted the Marine to the chopper and helped him lie down in the carrier. The master sergeant stood guard as Conor fumbled with the straps that secured Tadashi. Conor saw a musette pouch on the seat in front of him and grabbed it as he turned to help the master sergeant with Corporal Hoffman. He reached into the musette pouch and replaced the magazine in his M-71, then handed a magazine to the master sergeant, who quickly reloaded.

The gunship standing guard above them swept the downslope to the west as the two bent to pick up Corporal Hoffman and place her in the side carrier. The recovery chopper repositioned by doing a 180 at less than a meter off the ground. Not many people in the colony would attempt such a maneuver, so Conor knew it had to be Michael at the controls. They placed the corporal into the carrier as carefully as they could when an M-71 sounded from the other side as Sergeant Ivankov provided cover. Conor strapped the corporal in as Evan Zander turned and fired behind them. They heard a rocket sound, and a large tree to the west fell as more screams sounded below. Conor finished with the straps and turned as the master sergeant fired again along with the miniguns from the gunship.

"Time to get the hell out of here, sir!" yelled the master sergeant.

"I agree!" shouted Conor as he fired a three-round burst downslope.

The master sergeant hopped into the back seat and slid over as Conor grabbed hold of the roll bar and pulled himself into the vacated seat. M-71s resounded in the cabin as the master sergeant and Sergeant Ivankov fired. Conor saw movement and shot another three-round burst into the chest of another green velociraptor. The recovery chopper started to rise, and green shapes burst from the foliage downslope, sprinting up the incline. Conor heard the gunship firing as he and the others in the recovery chopper went to full auto and fired. When they quit firing, the recovery chopper was over ten meters up, and it leveled off for its run back to the Marine Complex.

Out of the foliage below stepped a large brilliantly plumed scarlet velociraptor.

"Hold!" shouted Conor.

The chopper steadied out as the red drew back an arm and brought it forward. The javelin hit the chopper above the carriage where the corporal lay and rebounded off the hull. It fell to the ground, and the red raptor screamed in challenge at the chopper as it reloaded and drew back its arm. Conor attempted to fire and found he had expended his magazine. The red raptor threw, and its aim was true; the feathered javelin flew through the air and embedded itself in Conor's thigh. The pain was excruciating as his hand went around the center of his pain, but he refrained from removing the javelin. Instead, he looked at Evan Zander.

"Master Sergeant," demanded Conor.

The master sergeant took up the Vinter HR-19 that he had thrown on the floorboards of the passenger section. Michael swung the chopper around so Evan would have a clear shot. He reloaded quickly as the chopper steadied and took aim. The shot resounded through the cabin, and Michael dipped the nose slightly as everyone in the cabin lost their hearing for a moment. The red raptor went down as the back of its chest exploded.

"I want that body!" yelled Conor as his hearing still rang.

Michael must have transmitted his order to the gunship because the miniguns and rockets went off in a semicircle around the body of the red. Vegetation fell like a harvester was reaping a crop. Michael lowered the recovery chopper, and Nikolai Ivankov ran downslope with a hook that had a thin line attached leading back to the chopper's winch. He fired at something that moved, then wrapped the line around the red raptor's leg twice as the gunship and everyone aboard the recovery chopper provided cover. Nikolai ran back upslope like the demons of hell were behind him and jumped into the copilot's seat.

They were back in the air and rising fast with the red raptor in tow as the winch drew it up to the undercarriage of the chopper. When Michael reached a hundred meters, he leveled off and headed east while the gunship came up beside them. Conor looked over to see who the other pilot was and saw Shiran looking grim but assured as she maneuvered her chopper into position. Conor switched the comm in his helmet, clicking the comm as he did so, and spoke.

"I was wondering who could be flying the other chopper," grunted Conor.

"It's the landings that are the hardest according to my instructor," came the reply.

The flight back was uneventful but seemed to last forever as Conor sat back, attempting to ignore his pain. Dr. Hollinger and a team of medical personnel were on the flat west of the clinic as the choppers came in for a landing. They removed Corporal Hoffman and Sergeant Adachi by detaching the stretchers and headed for the clinic as Drs. Hollinger and Joshi attended to them. The master sergeant and Sergeant Ivankov assisted Conor into a stretcher that the medics left after using a microfiber to remove the main shaft of the javelin. Evan and Nikolai took up the stretcher gingerly and belatedly followed the doctors and medics to the medical facilities.

Shiran and Michael came up on each side. Shiran's face was tense as she looked back at the red body lying behind the recovery chopper.

"What happened?" she demanded.

"We were attacked," replied Zander.

"Krupich and Barrett?" demanded Shiran.

"Barrett is dead. I'm not sure about Krupich. Most likely dead also," gritted Conor through his pain.

Something like anger and pain shot through Shiran's eyes. She looked away as tears formed. Rachel Krupich had been a close friend of hers. Conor reached out and grabbed her hand.

"Did we learn anything?" she demanded.

"We now know we're not the only intelligent life-forms on this planet," Evan Zander answered.

"And they use the green raptors like dogs," informed Nikolai.

"What?" demanded Shiran.

"The green raptors were sent in to attack while the reds watched for an opening. Just like a hunter would use dogs to flush prey," explained Evan.

Silence fell among the group as they arrived at the clinic. Dr. Hollinger worked on immobilizing the spearpoint in Conor's leg. Fortunately, it had missed the major artery and bone, and the doctor was happy that Conor had not only refrained from removing the point himself but also had seen little movement during the time it was embedded. Even so, the wound hurt and would require him to use a cane for two weeks while the injury mended enough for the stitches to come out. It took twelve stitches to close the wound, and the doctor assured him that it would leave him a nice scar to talk about unless he wanted the scar to be removed. Dr. Hollinger then placed the spearpoint in his hand as a memento of the experience. A wheelchair was brought for him to use to get back to the MILDET complex, and Shiran wheeled it in.

"Are you all right?" asked Shiran.

"I think so. How are Adachi and Hoffman?" inquired Conor.

"Still in surgery," replied Shiran.

"Let's wait," said Conor.

Second Lieutenant Rosenstein wheeled Lieutenant Commander Raybourn out into the waiting room where most of the Marines were gathered. He was greeted by all of them as Shiran wheeled him through the gathering, heading toward the table across the room where the master sergeant sat with Sergeant Ivankov.

"How are you, Lieutenant Commander?" asked Evan.

"I'm fine, Master Sergeant. What's this?" asked Conor.

"Debriefing, sir," returned Evan.

"Somewhat informal," stated Conor.

"We're all worried about Adachi and Hoffman, sir," replied the master sergeant.

"I understand," returned Conor.

A pot and four mugs were on the table as Shiran placed Conor in the spot with no chair. Shiran sat beside him and took up the pot to fill the two cups in front of them. The rich smell of coffee permeated the air as the steam rose from the filled mugs. Conor picked up the mug and blew on it for a second, then took a sip.

"So the colony is being watched?" asked Shiran.

"Yes. But we don't know if the caves we located were being used by the velociraptors that attacked us," said the master sergeant.

"I agree. The cave would only accommodate one to four raptors at a time. Almost as if it were a lone raptor simply observing us," stated Conor.

"That doesn't prove that it wasn't a scout," countered Shiran.

"There is that," said Evan.

"So what do we know?" asked the second lieutenant.

"We know we were being observed by a lone individual. It may be a scout, or it may be working independently. We also know that there are intelligent raptors that have red feathers vice the green that we've observed so far. We know the red raptors use the green raptors like dogs," said Zander.

"The green raptors are marked," interjected Sergeant Ivankov.

"What do you mean?" interjected Shiran.

"The green raptors have markings on them that are not part of their normal color pattern. The marks vary and appear to be brands," replied Nikolai.

"Brands?" queried Shiran.

"Like they did with cattle to signify ownership, but instead, these markings are possibly paint. Some of the greens carried the same markings," stated Nikolai.

"We also know that the red raptors are at least in the Bronze Age," stated Conor as he placed the spearpoint that the doctor had given him on the table.

"The spears had markings on them also. Perhaps to signify ownership," said Evan Zander.

"They also use atlatls," added Nikolai.

"I noticed that," said Conor as he resisted the urge to massage his leg.

"What's that?" asked Shiran.

"A tool that extends the arm. You place the butt of the spear in at the end and throw. Using it adds to the penetrating power, and the spear will go farther," explained Nikolai.

"So they're tool users in the Bronze Age. Anything else?" questioned Shiran.

"The one we brought back had a bag around its middle. What was in the bag?" asked Conor.

One of the Marines came forward and placed the bag on the table as the master sergeant moved the coffeepot aside. The bag was tied shut with a length of leather strung through holes made in the bag. The knot was tightly tied, and Conor wondered how the raptor was able to tie it utilizing the claws that tipped its forearms.

They undid the knot and poured the contents on the table. What looked like coins made of copper, silver, and bronze tinkled as they hit the tabletop. There was also a beaded cord, wooden disk, wooden box, and something tubular wrapped in woven material lying on the table.

The master sergeant gathered up the various rounded metal pieces. "Looks like coins."

"May not be money but used for barter. The metal can always be used to make items," stated Conor.

"Or they may just be pretty to the creature's eye," added Staff Sergeant Amanda Hall.

"I think they're more than that. They're either money or used for barter, which indicates they are something like money to the raptors," said the master sergeant.

Shiran picked up the small box. It was about ten centimeters long and half that in width and height. She released the small hooks from the pins on each side and lifted the lid off. Inside was a long piece of rock and, beside it, a length of metal that looked like iron.

"That's flint and iron, tinderbox for making fires," grunted Evan.

"What's the beaded cord for?" asked Nikolai.

"Some primitive people used them to keep track of accounts and such," stated Gunnery Sergeant Samuel Rusu from behind the second lieutenant.

"So it's like an abacus," said Shiran.

"Sort of, ma'am. To be sure, we'll have to ask the archeologists and Hattie," said Samuel.

Shiran placed the box back on the table and picked up the tube wrapped in some woven material. Unwrapping it revealed an intricately carved tube of bone. The tube was also about the same length as the box. She turned it over in her hand and looked at the markings as she let the fabric drop to the tabletop.

"I've seen something like it. May I, ma'am?" said Samuel Rusu.

Shiran handed Samuel the item to examine. He turned it over in his left hand, tracing the markings a few times with the tip of his right-hand index finger. Looking up from his examination, Samuel stated, "Looks like it might be a calendar."

"You're sure?" asked Shiran.

"Fairly sure, ma'am. We can have the archaeologists and Hattie take a look at it to be sure. But I've seen some items like it in a museum back on Earth, and they were labeled as calendars," stated Samuel Rusu.

Lieutenant Commander Raybourn picked up the carved bone tube and looked at it closely. The dots, lines, and crescents did remind him of a piece that a museum back on Earth called a calendar too. As he looked closer, he noticed a thin line running around the bone piece halfway up the tube. He took each end of the tube by the thumb and index finger of each hand and gently pulled.

"Don't break it!" cried Shiran.

"Now you've done it, sir." Evan Zander grinned.

The bone piece came apart into two equal lengths, and a metal needle dropped to the tabletop. Conor placed the bone pieces on the table and picked up the needle. The needle was nearly the length of the combined tube with a point at one end and flattened with a hole at the other end. It was obviously intended to sew with and large enough to take a thin piece of leather gut through the hole at the end.

"Looks like a sewing needle," stated Shiran.

"It's not made of bronze, silver, or copper. Looks like iron," stated Conor.

"May I, sir?" asked Nikolai Ivankov.

"Here you go, Sergeant," said Conor as he handed Nikolai the needle.

"Private Caylor, would you find a fairly large bowl and fill it with about five centimeters of water at the bottom," requested Nikolai.

"What are you thinking, Sergeant?" asked Shiran.

Sergeant Nikolai Ivankov examined the needle for a moment and nodded. He then reached for the thin wooden disk on the table. The disk was about ten centimeters in diameter also and was bisected into four quarters by a cross. There were smaller lines that extended from the center of the circle at regular intervals, but they did not extend to the edge like the cross. Nikolai laid the disk flat on the palm of his left hand, then placed the needle into one of the lengths of the cross bisecting the disk.

Private Vivian Caylor checked behind the nurses' station and located the requested bowl, which she filled partway with water. She returned to the table, setting the bowl of water in the middle of the table after the master sergeant cleared a space. Sergeant Nikolai Ivankov carefully placed the flattened disk with the needle on it into the water, while Gunnery Sergeant Samuel Rusu opened his compass and placed it beside the bowl. They all watched as the wooden disk rotated with the point of the needle pointing north.

"It's a compass," breathed Shiran.

CHAPTER 32

The office was a bit warm, and Second Lieutenant Shiran Rosenstein shifted uncomfortably in her wooden chair behind her rough-hewn desk. She made a mental note of talking to Tom Tollifer about sending someone over to take a look at the air-conditioning. She had been going over reports on her laptop and contemplating how to reply to those requiring responses. The loss of two more of her Marines did not sit well with her. She knew that the high risks that they took were part of the job. The double funeral for Staff Sergeant Rachel Krupich and Lance Corporal Barrett had been a despondent affair for her. She had lost three Marines in almost as many weeks.

Lieutenant Commander Conor Raybourn had limped back to the Marine Complex with her. The two of them only exchanged a few words before he went to the naval pier. The pain from his wound was apparent as he leaned on the cane. The two parted after making plans for the evening. The ID signal for Lance Corporal Barrett informed them it had not moved for hours. While the ID signal for Staff Sergeant Krupich was nowhere to be found, which meant that the ID was either turned off, broken, out of range, or something prevented its response.

As she sat there brooding, a light knock sounded on the open door. She looked up to see Master Sergeant Evan Zander standing there.

"What's up, Master Sergeant?" asked Shiran.

"You know, it really isn't your fault, ma'am," said Evan.

"I shouldn't have sent out those teams," muttered Shiran.

"Why do you say that?" queried Evan.

"If they hadn't gone out, this wouldn't have happened, and Rachel would still be alive. And so would Flores and Barrett," blurted Shiran vehemently.

"Now you're sounding like Jacqueline Vinet," chided Evan evenly.

Shiran felt like she had been slapped in the face. She glared at Evan Zander as he stood there patiently waiting. She closed her eyes and took several deep breaths. Shiran thought about the implications of what she said. What the master sergeant stated was true; she was attempting to retreat and wall off the world outside the confines of the Compound. Slowly calm came to her and she reopened her eyes to see that Evan was still there.

"Did I really sound like that?" pleaded Shiran.

Evan Zander just cocked an eyebrow at her.

"I did," Shiran admitted. "But if I'd been there…"

She trailed off as she saw Evan shake his head and say, "It would have made no difference."

"I'm more trained than, Conor," insisted the second lieutenant.

"It wasn't his fault in any of those deaths either," stated her friend Evan Zander.

"I didn't say it was," countered Shiran.

"These things happen. It's part of the risk we all take. The lieutenant commander did as well as I would expect from any Marine," said the master sergeant.

"Rachel might still be alive if I'd been there," protested Shiran.

"We don't know she's dead," said Evan.

"You're saying she's still alive?" inquired Shiran earnestly.

"I'll believe she's dead when I see the body. Right now, we need to soldier on," Evan Zander observed.

Second Lieutenant Rosenstein sat back and thought about that. She realized that the master sergeant was doing what he did best, and that was being a sounding board and guide for the officer in charge. That meant she needed to think about what was needed for her Marines. She suddenly realized what her main issue was in this whole affair. Unfortunately, there were only so many resources to draw from to fulfill the dilemma at hand. She decided to change the subject slightly.

"We need more Marines, Master Sergeant," stated Shiran.

"Rumor has it that you have one in the making, ma'am." Evan grinned.

"I'm being serious, Master Sergeant!" snapped Shiran.

"Yes, ma'am," said Evan seriously. "How about Mr. Green?"

"Joseph Green?" asked Shiran as she envisioned the face of the seaman who had been on the recon mission when they first arrived on the planet. He had been assigned to the team because he had a geology degree, which proved useful.

"Yes, ma'am," replied Evan Zander.

"Has he expressed any interest in being a Marine?" inquired Shiran.

"Corporal Hoffman likes him, and he's been doing PT with us because of her. He's also been volunteering for the hunting expeditions so he can collect geological samples," Master Sergeant Zander informed her.

"That's not exactly expressing an interest, Master Sergeant," replied Shiran.

"No, ma'am, but it is a strong indication," returned Evan.

"So he knows firearms?" asked Shiran.

"Trained him myself," declared Evan.

"Geological samples?" inquired Shiran.

"Pieces of different rock formations. He also has a rig that he uses to collect core samples when he goes with the hunting expeditions," said the master sergeant.

"Is this of any use?" inquired Shiran.

"He's the one who located the copper mine, and he discovered a zinc deposit about a month ago. We can start making brass and bronze in quantity if he's right," confirmed Evan.

"All right, you've convinced me. I'll talk to him," said Shiran.

"Begging the lieutenant's pardon, but I'd prefer to handle this if you don't mind. I'll send him to you when he's ready," admonished Master Sergeant Zander firmly.

"Is there anyone else, Master Sergeant?" asked Shiran.

"I have several prospects, but they will take some time," admitted Evan.

"Who are they?" asked Shiran.

"I'd prefer not saying at this time," said Evan.

"Anyone else that's even close to wanting to join up?" implored Shiran.

"I was hoping Brad Guillete might want to join soon, but that will be difficult without Rachel Krupich," confessed the master sergeant.

"Are you pimping out my female Marines, Master Sergeant?" demanded Second Lieutenant Rosenstein.

"I prefer to think of it as offering encouragement to improve our ranks, ma'am," responded the master sergeant with a straight face.

Shiran glared at the master sergeant. In turn, he shrugged and cocked an eyebrow at her.

"Brad Guillete is already a first-class petty officer. I was hoping for someone who was a third class or below." Shiran frowned.

"He knows weapons and keeps up on the PT. He was also doing simulator training for choppers and longboats with Rachel Krupich. They were both going to request flight training on choppers in another month," Evan informed the second lieutenant.

"He still doesn't have the skills a grunt learns by going up the ranks," stated the second lieutenant.

"I wasn't suggesting he does, though skills can still be learned," said the master sergeant.

"Then what are you suggesting?" questioned Shiran.

The only answer she received was Evan Zander cocking an eyebrow at her.

"Officer?" asked Shiran, stunned. "There's no room for another second lieutenant."

"I wasn't suggesting that either. He likes the field of work he's already in," replied Evan.

"Technically specialized," said Shiran. "CWO?" Referring to the chief warrant officer ranks of the Marines.

The master sergeant nodded and said, "We could use someone who knows air traffic control and can repair the gear. Between that and if he qualifies on choppers, he'd be a serious asset."

"How good is he on repairing electronics?" inquired Shiran.

"You'll have to judge that for yourself, ma'am," said Evan. "At this time, my recommendation is not to push him. Allow Brad to make the choice."

"Because of Rachel?" observed Shiran.

"Among other things," said Evan.

Shiran knew she wouldn't get an answer to any question about what that meant. She suspected that it involved the incident that she witnessed in the Overlook. She decided it was time to change the direction of the conversation.

"How's everyone doing, Master Sergeant?" inquired Shiran.

"As well as to be expected, ma'am, waiting for you to make your rounds," replied Evan Zander.

"Shall we, Master Sergeant?" suggested the second lieutenant.

"After you, ma'am," agreed the master sergeant amicably.

The two of them walked up to the air traffic control room, or ATC, where Sergeant Nikolai Ivankov was standing watch. They walked up to the roof and inspected the rocket launchers, radar antenna, and UHF antenna, then headed down to the ground level to inspect the barracks rooms and armory. The mess area came last before going outside to inspect the prefab on the south side of the complex. It had been brought down from the cleft to serve as a lab for Raisa Romanov to produce the explosives they required for more munitions. Raisa had been part of the science division on board the *New Horizon* with a doctorate in chemistry and was proving herself to be a valuable asset to the colony. They went over to the piers where the Marines maintained security. Finally, they inspected the two ATVs and chopper that sat on the north side of the complex. All was in order as Shiran and the master sergeant stopped in the mess hall for a coffee.

"It looks good, Master Sergeant," Second Lieutenant Rosenstein complimented.

"Thank you, ma'am," returned Master Sergeant Zander.

"I'm going to go up to the clinic and look in on Adachi and Hoffman," stated Shiran.

"That sounds like a good idea, ma'am. Tell them I'll be up to check on them later," said Evan Zander with a smile.

"I will, Master Sergeant," said Shiran. "Expect me back after lunch."

"No hurry, ma'am. Take the rest of the day," observed Evan. "We have your back."

Shiran left the Marine Complex and took an elevator up to the cleft. She had lunch at the Overlook and headed over to the clinic. Sergeant Tadashi Adachi and Corporal Natalie Hoffman were both awake. Tadashi was sitting in a chair beside Natalie, who lay on her bed. He had a book in his hand, reading *Alice in Wonderland* aloud. The two noticed her immediately, and they talked for a time until Natalie said she needed to sleep, at which time the second lieutenant said goodbye. Shiran left the clinic and decided to take a walk. Her wandering the cleft area finally brought her to the residence of Captain Tamura.

Hiroka Tamura was tending and working on the garden she was building when Shiran arrived. Shiran knew that many of her Marines spent off-duty hours assisting Hiroka in putting together the plots that were growing around the outside of Hiroka's home. Bricks, mortar, and dirt awaited for people to construct the plots Hattie had designed. The plans were to make the whole west end of the cleft into a flower and spice garden for all people to walk through and enjoy. Shiran also knew that as the variety of flowers and spices increased, Hiroka planned to harvest them for the scents to make perfumes, soaps, candles, and other luxuries. There were also plans for a bathhouse to be built east of the gardens. As Shiran drew close, Hiroka looked up to see who it was and smiled recognition.

"Good afternoon, Shiran-san," greeted Hiroka.

"Good afternoon, Hiroka-san," Shiran returned with a smile.

"What can I do for you today?" inquired Hiroka.

"I do not know," replied Shiran truthfully.

"Did you come to see how well my garden is coming along?" asked Hiroka.

"That would be one reason," confirmed Shiran.

"But not the whole reason?" questioned Hiroka.

"I don't think so," confessed Shiran.

"I wish you to thank the master sergeant and your Marines for the assistance they've provided in putting together the gardens so far," said Hiroka.

"It appears to be coming along," admitted Shiran.

"I hope it will be a place where a person can seek harmony with oneself when they are completed," stated Hiroka.

"That would be nice," replied Shiran.

"Do you seek harmony, Shiran-san?" inquired Hiroka.

"I suppose I am," admitted Shiran.

"Tell me," suggested Hiroka authoritatively.

Shiran started talking about the recent incidents that cost her Marines. While she was talking, Hiroka simply listened and nodded. At times, Shiran was near tears, and at other times, she grew angry as she talked. It seemed that at times the burden of command weighed heavy on her shoulders and that it would all come crashing down.

"Staff Sergeant Krupich was a good friend of yours, was she not?" asked Hiroka.

"Yes," agreed Shiran.

"The way of life is like that. I would have been and still would be devastated if I had lost Hadden during this last decade, though I would not have admitted it prior to my accident," confessed Hiroka.

Shiran looked at Hiroka in disbelief and said, "You've always been so strong."

"He has been my support for nearly a decade, and I did not consider how that would affect me until then. If something had happened to him, I would have lost my harmony," stated Hiroka.

"Then I've lost my harmony. Rachel made me laugh," admitted Shiran.

Hiroka nodded. "You must learn to find harmony."

"How?" inquired Shiran.

"Come," said Hiroka.

Hiroka led Shiran to her cottage. There was a large bowl and pitcher there. Hiroka poured water from the pitcher into the bowl and washed the dirt from her hands and face. She used a towel to wipe away the water, then stepped into her home. She returned with a katana. However, this katana was made of wood. Shiran recognized it as one of the set that Sergeant Tadashi Adachi had produced. Hiroka handed the katana to Shiran and led her to the place where Hiroka practiced every day with hers.

"You are with child, so we will go slowly and learn stances. Do not overstrain yourself. Learn the stances and focus on gaining harmony in doing so. Clear you mind of all and concentrate only on what I instruct you to do," commanded Hiroka.

"Yes, ma'am," acknowledged Shiran.

Hiroka showed Shiran several different stances, telling her to concentrate on finding her center. Difficult, considering her "center" was currently being occupied and growing. But Hiroka persisted, and they spent nearly two hours with Hiroka simply having her learn different stances and practice.

When they stopped, Shiran was exhausted, and Hiroka simply smiled at her. They had tea and discussed Shiran's upcoming nuptials. Finally, Shiran left, feeling better about the recent events in her life. She stopped and looked out over the lake, forests, and plains spread out below her vantage point from the edge. The world awaited, and she planned on being one of the architects of that new world.

CHAPTER 33

Lieutenant Commander Conor Raybourn stood in the operating room at the clinic. The memory of the time only a few short days ago was still vivid in Conor's mind. The pain of the javelin that had been embedded in his thigh was still fresh as he leaned on the cane. Dr. Bess Hollinger assured him there was no permanent damage and that he'd be fine in a week or two if he took it easy.

A gathering of over a dozen people were present to listen to what Dr. Bess Hollinger had discovered. Right now, she was at the end of the table where the red velociraptor's head was on display. It lay on its belly with its legs hanging over the sides and its tail hanging over the other end. In many ways, it reminded Conor of some surreal scene from a low-budget fantasy. A twinge of pain shot up his leg and brought Conor back to reality as he leaned on the cane the clinic had provided him. His mind came back into focus as the pain passed.

The president and his cabinet finally filed into the room nearly twenty minutes late. Master Sergeant Zander looked at Conor and cocked an eyebrow, but Conor simply shook his head. Commander Hadden Blankenship had patiently awaited their arrival, though it was apparent by his clenching jaw that he was not happy.

"Now that we're all here, what do you have, Doctor?" asked Commander Blankenship as he stood looking at the cranial cavity with a brain in a bottle beside the head.

"We have a big problem, sir," stated Dr. Hollinger.

"Explain," ordered Hadden Blankenship.

"This specimen has a larger brain than *Homo Sapiens*. Its olfactory area is larger, meaning it can smell better than we are able to. The occipital lobe is smaller, meaning it probably can't see as well as we can. However, it's cerebral cortex is as large as the average *Homo Sapiens*, meaning it can most likely think and reason just as well as we can," Bess Hollinger informed those gathered.

"So they'll learn quickly," said Conor.

"I would say so," returned the doctor.

"How many do you think there are?" questioned Hadden.

"Unknown. But if they have nests like the greens and lay a similar number of eggs, I'd be surprised if they don't have population problems," Bess explained.

"Warlike?" inquired Hadden.

"The scars on the body suggest that it has been in a lot of skirmishes of some sort. Whether they're from hunting or battle is unknown," replied the doctor.

"Would they have been capable of building the abandoned city?" asked Conor.

"If they can work together, they could have. We know they utilize tools. There's the atlatl, knife, and javelins this one had in its possession. The knife is bronze, and the javelin point is bronze. They're also aware of iron after the discoveries of the tinderbox and needle for the compass. That suggests a higher culture than some nomadic hunter. It also had what appeared to be copper, bronze, and silver coins in the pouch it had," Bess Hollinger relayed what information she knew.

"They may not be coins but items to melt into jewelry, tools, and weapons, or they could just be shiny items the individual found and kept," interjected Evan Zander.

"What else can you tell us about the raptor, Doctor?" asked Hadden Blankenship.

"I would say the red feathers are natural. This one is male, and the female may or may not be as brilliantly plumed, which would mirror the greens' differentiation between sexes. The red is heavier than the green males we've examined so far. The green males mass more than their females, and this, too, may hold true with the reds and their females," said Bess.

"So we have a race of intelligent carnivores that are larger than we are and utilize Bronze Age weapons. They may build cities such as the abandoned one. We don't know where they reside or even how many of them there are. Does that about sum it up?" asked the commander.

"Their technology may be regressing, which would explain the abandoned city," stated Second Lieutenant Rosenstein.

"Or it may simply be abandoned, and they built elsewhere," cautioned Conor.

"Where?" demanded Felipe Martinez arrogantly.

"We've done very little exploration of the island, and there's the continental mainland only a couple of hundred kilometers away," stated Conor.

"The ship telescopes would see cities if they were there," declared Felipe Martinez.

"They didn't see the abandoned city," replied Hadden.

"The lidar then," countered Felipe.

"You know very well that the lidar's resolution isn't repaired," replied the commander.

"It still isn't repaired?" demanded Felipe.

"Don't you read the ship status reports?" inquired Conor.

"What ship status reports?" asked an astonished President Felipe Martinez.

Hadden and Conor looked at each other when Martinez asked that question. The commander gave a slight shake, his head signaling Conor not to say anything further. There was more going on here than simply discussing the red velociraptor and its implications.

"The lidar's resolution problem is still unresolved, and therefore, we can't rely on it to provide us with that information. What we need is to make plans based on the information we do have available," replied Commander Blankenship patiently.

"What type of plans?" demanded Felipe.

"Security of the colony is paramount, Mr. President," responded Hadden.

"The colony is secure," retorted Norman Pool.

"Are the people who venture outside the Compound secure?" asked Hadden.

"We have the ATVs and helicopters, and our weapons are more advanced. They're a primitive people compared to us," sneered Norman Pool.

"Even primitive people have overwhelmed more advanced cultures in Earth's past. Superiority in technology is no guarantee in winning a battle," stated Hadden.

"What do you want, Commander?" demanded Felipe.

"Two thousand kilograms of your highest-quality steel, Mr. President," stated Hadden.

"What do you require that much for?" demanded Felipe.

"Two autocanons and a variety of personal weapons to arm the colony if it comes down to defending our home," responded the commander.

"No! That steel is dedicated to building the hauler and loader. You can have the two thousand kilograms after they're built and we manufacture more," stated President Martinez.

"How soon will that be, Mr. President?" asked Hadden.

"It may be three to six months. We still haven't processed enough steel for the hauler sides, and the loader hasn't even been started," replied Norman Pool after Martinez looked in his direction.

"Let us hope that we have three to six months," replied Hadden.

"Are we done here?" demanded Martinez impatiently.

"I was going to proceed with the rest of my findings," stated Bess Hollinger.

"They're intelligent, red-feathered, and slightly larger than the green velociraptors. Is there something else we need to know?" demanded Felipe impatiently.

"You have the basic gist, Mr. President," replied Bess.

"Then we're done here," stated Felipe.

The president and his cabinet filed out of the room as the rest of the group stood where they were. Dr. Hollinger simply shook her head when they were gone and looked at the commander. Commander Blankenship remained impassive for a moment, possibly battening the hatches on what he had wanted to say to President Felipe Martinez.

"Shall I go on, Commander?" asked Bess, somewhat hesitantly.

"Please do," said Hadden quietly.

"The creature has a more developed larynx than the greens. It may be able to speak our language if the intelligence is as high as I believe," continued Bess.

The briefing went on for over an hour as Dr. Hollinger went into detail over her findings about the red velociraptor. By the time she was finished, it was apparent to everyone that the red velociraptor was a formidable opponent even without intelligence. The fact that the red raptor came from a tool-using society made it even more ominous.

After the briefing, the commander held a meeting in the MILDET prefab. The commander's face was impassive as he tapped the tabletop. The president's response and attitude over the raptor did not bode well.

"The president didn't know about the ship status reports," stated Lieutenant Commander Raybourn.

"I noted that," returned Hadden.

"Aren't those sent to him daily?" questioned Second Lieutenant Rosenstein.

"They are. It would appear that some things are not being routed to our illustrious president also," said Hadden.

"Or he's simply not looking at them," said Lieutenant Michael Anderson.

"That may be true also," said Conor.

"Who and why would they do that?" asked Shiran.

"Possibly the same individual or individuals who have been sabotaging us since the FTL incident." returned Conor.

"He still should have questioned why he wasn't receiving ship status reports," insisted Shiran.

"He may not be receiving all of the reports," said Hadden.

"What?" asked Shiran.

"He's used to receiving the engineering reports. It may not have occurred to him that we would forward him reports from all the departments, or he may not know all the reports that each department submits," the commander informed everyone.

"It would be easy to miss one report, like eight-o'clock reports from the electronics repair division," added Michael Anderson.

"Hattie," called Hadden.

"Operating. Commander Blankenship," replied Hattie.

"Hattie, are all ship status reports being routed to Lieutenant Commander Martinez?" asked Commander Blankenship.

"They have, Commander," replied Hattie.

"Has he reviewed them?" asked Hadden.

"He has not been aboard *New Horizon* to do so, Commander," returned Hattie.

"Explain," ordered Hadden.

"All ship status reports are available to him on the *New Horizon*, Commander," replied Hattie.

A puzzled look crossed the commander's face, then he asked, "So he has to go to the *New Horizon* to view the status reports?"

"If he wants to view them all, Commander," returned Hattie.

"If I may, Commander," said Michael.

"Be my guest, Lieutenant," replied Hadden irritably.

"Hattie, which ship status files are available to Lieutenant Commander Martinez at the colony?" asked Michael Anderson.

"All except fire control and electronics repair division reports," stated Hattie.

"Why are those not available to the lieutenant commander at the colony?" asked Michael.

"I was given programming instructions to that effect, Lieutenant Anderson," stated Hattie.

"By whom?" asked Michael.

"Lieutenant Commander Martinez," stated Hattie.

"He set it up that way himself?" asked Michael.

"Unknown," stated Hattie.

A puzzled look crossed Michael's face, then he asked, "What do you mean, Hattie?"

"I cannot confirm that Lieutenant Commander Martinez issued those programming instructions," stated Hattie.

"Explain, Hattie," ordered Michael.

"The routing instructions were made aboard the *New Horizon*, but Lieutenant Commander Martinez was not aboard the *New Horizon* when they were programmed," stated Hattie.

"Where was Lieutenant Commander Martinez?" asked Michael.

"He was being inaugurated as the president of the colony that day," stated Hattie.

The people gathered in the MILDET office looked at one another. Someone aboard the *New Horizon* had given Hattie instructions to keep select status reports from President Martinez quite some time ago. Since it happened the day of the inauguration, they knew that Martinez was going to be the president. So they were denying him information unless he went aboard the *New Horizon*. Unless…

"Hattie, would Lieutenant Commander Martinez actually have access to those reports if he came aboard the *New Horizon*?" asked Michael.

"My programming does not allow the lieutenant commander to have access to those reports if he returns to the *New Horizon*," stated Hattie.

"What?" demanded Hadden.

"Patience, Commander. Let Michael work," said Conor. Hadden looked at Conor and nodded.

"Hattie, who issued those routing instructions?" asked Michael.

"Commander Blankenship," responded Hattie.

"When?" asked Michael.

"The day of the president's inauguration," stated Hattie.

"Where did the instructions originate from, Hattie?" asked Michael.

"On board the *New Horizon*," stated Hattie.

"I wasn't aboard the *New Horizon* that week," stated Hadden irritably.

"Hattie, please display and make a printout of who was on duty aboard the *New Horizon* that week," ordered Lieutenant Michael Anderson.

The list displayed above the table. Everyone studied the list as it was displayed on the three laptops on the table. No names stood out as possible perpetrators to Lieutenant Commander Conor Raybourn.

"Can we be sure that the deletions were performed on the *New Horizon*?" asked Conor.

"Hattie says they were," stated Michael.

"Hattie's sure that it couldn't be done remotely?" questioned Shiran.

"They would have to reprogram Hattie, and if it wasn't obvious, I'd have to go through the code line by line at that point," said Michael.

The commander had remained silent until then and stated, "Wheaton."

"Why would he do that?" asked Michael.

"He's the chief of the electronics repair department, and I've seen him vanish messages," said Blankenship.

"What?" demanded Michael.

"The commendation you submitted for Mr. Guillete was placed in an inactive file by Chief Wheaton," replied Hadden.

"Why would he do that?" asked Conor.

"I think I know why," said Michael.

"Inform me, Lieutenant," insisted the commander.

"Right after the incident that brought us here, I overheard a conversation between Lieutenant Felter and Petty Officer Guillete. The lieutenant was abusive, to say the least. What I gathered from the conversation I overheard was, Lieutenant Felter had been told by someone at Guillete's previous command that he was, to put it mildly, unwanted. Some of the technicians working in the cleft comm suite don't think much of Mr. Guillete either," replied Michael.

"Petty Officer Guillete had a run-in with Mr. Pool at the Overlook one day also. The attitude about him appears to have crossed over to the president's cabinet members too," added Shiran.

"I see," replied Hadden impassively.

"Why would Chief Wheaton prevent the president from seeing eight o'clock reports?" asked Second Lieutenant Shiran Rosenstein.

"The obvious reason is so electronics repair division looks good in the president's eyes," responded Lieutenant Commander Conor Raybourn.

"So it has to be him," said Lieutenant Michael Anderson.

"It may or may not be him," replied Conor.

"What do you mean?" asked Shiran.

"It may be more than one person or group of people doing this, and they may or may not be working together," stated Conor.

"I agree. We need to keep this to ourselves until we know more," stated Commander Hadden Blankenship. Then he added, "What worries me is that the people we know of and suspect are being manipulated."

"By whom?" asked Michael.

"Our saboteur," replied Commander Hadden Blankenship as he sat back uneasily into his chair.

The rest of the group looked at one another at that thought. People generally thought of sabotage as a violent action meant to harm others physically or destroy equipment. Yet wasn't turning people against each other a form of sabotage? The end result could very well be the same if it destroyed the chances of a group to work together for their mutual benefit. If the colony's population became disjointed and did not work together toward a common goal, the colony, in all likelihood, would not survive.

CHAPTER 34

There was a slight limp in Lieutenant Commander Conor Raybourn's step as he walked over to the boardwalk heading toward the elevators. Dr. Hollinger assured him that he no longer needed the cane, but he had strained his leg helping repair the ATVs. Dr. Hollinger lectured him about how he should be more careful and how he should take it easy. It was hard to relax though with all the work that needed to be accomplished. At times, he wondered if they would ever be done. He shook his head. Sometimes you had to make the time for yourself.

He crossed the open area between the prefabs and constructed buildings, which was reserved for the chopper and special events. Stepping onto the boardwalk, he headed toward the elevators until he passed the Bookworm. Backtracking, he entered the Bookworm and saw Francesca sitting at a table examining a book. She raised her head to see who entered, and a smile touched her lips.

"Hello, Conor. How are you today?" greeted Francesca Chandra.

"Well enough. I finished my work and decided to take a walk. I was outside and thought I'd drop in and see how you're doing," replied Conor.

"Have a seat. May I get you some tea?" asked Francesca.

"Tea would be perfect," said Conor.

Conor sat at the table as Francesca left to get tea. The tables and chairs in the main lobby were well fashioned. Conor looked at the cover of the book Francesca had been examining. It was *The Complete Works of Sir Arthur Conan Doyle*. Conor also noted that it was volume 3. Francesca returned with the tea setting and poured them each a cup.

"So the new book is *The Complete Works of Sir Arthur Conan Doyle*?" inquired Conor.

"It was the next on my list," replied Francesca.

"Didn't he write about a detective?" asked Conor.

"Yes, Sherlock Holmes," answered Francesca.

"Why?" asked Conor.

"I like detective novels," Francesca replied.

"I didn't know that." Conor smiled.

"He also wrote other works. I came across one that I found interesting," said Francesca.

"What was it called?" asked Conor.

"The Lost World," Francesca informed him.

Conor got a blank look on his face, then said, "Never heard of it."

"It's about a group of explorers who discover a plateau that was very hard to reach, since their only air transportation at that time were hot-air balloons," said Francesca.

"So what's so interesting about the story?" questioned Conor.

"The top of the plateau was huge, and dinosaurs lived on it," replied Francesca.

"That sounds familiar," said Conor.

"Yes, it does, doesn't it?" Francesca affirmed with a question that didn't require an answer.

"Would you mind if I borrow the book to read?" asked Conor.

"I'll have Anya take it up to the MILDET prefab so you don't have to carry it," replied Francesca, referring to Anya Kaur.

"I'm not helpless, Francesca," Conor chided her.

"Are you going back to the MILDET prefab after you leave here?" asked Francesca.

"I was planning to walk the boardwalk first," said Conor.

"Then it's settled. It's out of your way, and it won't take that long to deliver it," replied Francesca.

Conor decided to change the subject and asked, "So this is going to become the colony library?"

"Yes, then there's the other nine sets that go to designated areas as the colony grows. The other forty copies of each book are making the rounds as first come, first served," explained Francesca.

"Who's designated?" asked Conor.

"Well, there's here, then there's the time vault, then the *New Horizon*, the hospital, the university, and the Marine Complex," said Francesca, counting on her light-brown fingers.

"I didn't know the Marine Complex was receiving a set," said Conor in surprise.

"The master sergeant requested it for the Marines," said Francesca.

"Oh! That was only six of the designated sets," said Conor.

"I have one set aside for the children's school when it starts up," Francesca replied.

"Who do I talk to about getting the MILDET a designated set?" inquired Conor.

Francesca smiled. "By talking to me. I'll have the whole set delivered to the MILDET before you're done with your walk."

"Thank you. When the electronics suite is finished, they were going to expand the cave for MILDET staterooms. The people utilizing them will appreciate it," said Conor.

"Was there anything you'd like to see published, Conor?" inquired Francesca.

Conor sat back and, after a moment, said, "I've never really thought about it, Francesca. How many books do you have in print now?"

"We print a new one about every month and are up to eleven different works right now," replied Francesca Chandra.

"Francesca, that ink is ready," Anya Kaur interrupted.

"I'm sorry, Conor. I have work to do," said Francesca.

Conor looked at his nearly empty cup and finished it. "That's all right, Francesca. I should be on my way," said Conor.

"Those books will be at the MILDET prefab when you arrive," stated Francesca.

"Thank you, Francesca," replied Conor.

Conor walked the brick boardwalk toward the elevators. He contemplated walking out to the Marine Complex to see Shiran but decided that it wouldn't be a wise idea. He had an appointment with Dr. Hollinger in a little more than an hour, and with his leg bothering him, it would probably be best if he hobbled toward the clinic instead. He decided that stopping at the Flour Mill and having some tea along the way would be a better idea. As he approached the elevators, he noted Ensign Hiran sorting through supplies that just arrived from the *New Horizon* and handing them out to various people who were waiting. Conor watched for a moment, then took a left going upriver toward the Flour Mill and the clinic.

His leg was still sore, and Dr. Hollinger had told him that if he popped another stitch, she would confine him to bed rest at the clinic so she could keep an eye on him for two weeks. Conor shook his head and smiled as he turned left up the boardwalk toward the clinic. He did have an appointment to have one of the nurses to change the bandage. He had better keep it, or he'd be under clinic arrest. A smile touched his lips at the thought. Conor stopped at the Flour Mill, ordering tea and a Danish, then his thoughts wandered back to his injury. The dynamics of keeping him in the clinic would be interesting. Would she install bars, lock him in a room, sedate him, or a combination of all the above? The smile slowly turned into a grin.

When he arrived at the clinic and took a seat, he was not there long before one of the examination room doors opened, and Dr. Hollinger came out. She looked at him and smiled, then turned her attention to the nurse who worked on a laptop at the counter. Then from the examination room emerged Jacqueline. When she saw Conor sitting there, she had a confused look on her face until she noticed the cane and bulge of his leg.

She waddled over to him and asked, "How are you, Conor?"

"I'm fine. How are you, Jacqueline?" asked Conor.

"Wishing this was over," she said as she patted her belly.

"Is everything all right?" asked Conor.

"Just a checkup, and you?" questioned Jacqueline.

"Bandage change," stated Conor.

"Does it hurt?" inquired Jacqueline.

"Sore but livable," said Conor.

"Are you ready for the wedding?" asked Jacqueline.

Conor looked startled for a second, then realized Jacqueline was talking about his upcoming wedding to Shiran.

"Looking forward to it," he stated.

"Good. I wish the two of you happiness before the occasion," replied Jacqueline.

"Thank you, Jacqueline. How soon?" Conor asked, directing his gaze to her belly.

"The doctors say another three months," said Jacqueline as she patted her bulge.

"Have you decided on a name?" inquired Conor.

"Jason if it's a boy and Janette if it's a girl." Jacqueline smiled.

"You don't know?" asked Conor in surprise.

"What's the fun in that, Conor?" teased Jacqueline.

Conor didn't know how to respond to that. It seemed to him most people would want to know. Then Conor noticed that Bess was patiently waiting for the two of them to finish talking. Not wanting to take up too much of the doctor's time, Conor shifted and tried to change the subject. "Both names sound fine, Jacqueline. It looks like the doctor is ready for me," said Conor.

"Have a good day, Conor."

"You too, Jacqueline."

Conor waited for Jacqueline to leave before he stood up. Bess ushered him into a different examination room where a rolling tray with bandages, scissors, tweezers, alcohol, and antiseptics were all laid out. Conor rolled down his pants to expose the bandaged leg, then took a seat on the end of the examination bench.

"How are you today, Conor?" asked Dr. Hollinger.

"I'm fine, Bess. How are you?" returned Conor.

"Everything is going fine. We're expecting some new equipment from the *New Horizon* today or tomorrow," replied Bess.

"I believe it's on the elevator being sorted out right now," Conor informed the doctor.

"Good. How do you know that?" questioned Bess.

"It was in my message traffic about a supply run today, and I saw Ensign Hiran with some of his people handling packages for delivery at the elevator," replied Conor.

"It will be nice to have that equipment. I'm not sure where we're going to put it though," said Bess.

"How's the work on the new location coming?" asked Conor.

"Slow. Martinez says he has other priorities for his processed metals at this time. So the rebar for construction is being put on a back burner," responded Bess.

"That sounds familiar," said Conor.

"He says the haulers and loader take priority, then he'll think about who has the most pressing needs."

"What does he consider pressing?" asked Conor.

"Well, after that, there's the presidential office suite and a community center if he and his cabinet have their way," stated Bess.

Conor winced as Bess prodded and poked at his injured thigh. The area was still purple and swollen around the stitches. The doctor tsked and applied some antiseptic to the area once she had cleaned it with alcohol. The area stung, and Conor gritted his teeth to keep from saying anything. She then placed a large piece of gauze over the area and taped it in place.

"This looks good, but take it easy for a couple more weeks. How's the cane working?" asked Bess Hollinger.

"It's fine. It takes most of the weight off the leg," replied Conor.

"As it should. Just take it easy. No hero stuff, okay, Lieutenant Commander?" asked Dr. Hollinger.

"As you wish, Commander." Conor mocked a salute as she smiled back.

CHAPTER 35

Rain was falling, but it didn't reach Michael Anderson and Francesca Chandra as they walked along the brick walkway along the outer ledge of the mall. Ezekiel's restaurant was at the corner where the waterfall was just ahead. The bridge to reach the other side of the river and look out over the waterfall was completed, and the couple were going to cross to look at the beginning construction of the school and hospital.

They were still strolling down the riverside boardwalk when Michael heard the explosion. He pushed his companion to the ground in fear. The sound seemed to reverberate along the cleft as he lay on top of her, using his body as a shield. When nothing further happened, he rolled off her body and looked at her.

"Are you all right?" asked Michael.

"Yes. Are you?" returned Francesca.

"I'm fine. That sounded like it came from the clinic or electronics suite," observed Michael.

"From the smoke, I'd say the latter," said Francesca.

"I have to go!" said Michael with urgency.

"Go!" returned Francesca.

Michael ran after helping Francesca to her feet. As he approached the electronics suite, he grew more cautious and slowed down. The door to the communications suite was already open, and Michael could hear shouting inside. The communications suite was in shambles as Michael stepped inside with smoke still wafting through the air.

It was the voice of Bess Hollinger shouting orders to her nurses as they worked on the severely burned body of Petty Officer Third

Class Charles Fooks in the hallway that lead to the offices. Another body lay against the wall of the comm shack like a broken doll. It was readily apparent why they were not concentrating their efforts on Petty Officer Third Class Cindy Brooks.

As Michael moved toward her broken body, he saw the workbench where the AI they had been working on was in ruins. The motherboard they had been painstakingly constructing was a total loss. How an explosion had occurred was a complete mystery since no materials of that nature were stored inside the cave that housed the AI. Michael bent to close the eyelids and discovered that there was no lids to close. The voice of Bess Hollinger spoke softly behind him as he took a tarp out of a nearby drawer and draped it over the body.

"She must have been closest to the blast," stated Bess Hollinger.

"It would look that way," replied Michael.

"What could have caused it?" asked Dr. Hollinger.

"There's nothing here that could have except the cleaners and solvents that we use. There's not enough of that housed here to cause an explosion like this though. We store the excess in the hazmat locker on the other side of the cave. All the rest is in another hazmat locker near the Marine Complex," said Michael Anderson, referring to the hazardous material storage lockers the communication suite used to store dangerous materials.

Lieutenant Commander Conor Raybourn arrived, limping. Michael could tell from the painful expression on his face that Conor had pushed himself to get to the electronics suite. He was favoring his leg and leaning on the cane he had been using. Conor Raybourn stopped when he saw the tarp at the feet of Michael and Bess.

"Who?" asked Lieutenant Commander Raybourn.

"Cindy Brooks," replied Bess.

"Who else?" demanded the lieutenant commander.

"Charles Fooks was in the hall when it happened. He has a broken arm, fractured ribs, concussion, and severe burns," stated Bess.

Conor closed his eyes. Lately, it seemed that they were losing people left and right or they were severely injured. He felt a hand on his shoulder and looked to see Michael standing there. There was pain and sadness in Michael's eyes, but he still felt a need to comfort his friend.

"What happened, Michael?" asked Conor.

"I don't know, Conor. It had to be a bomb of some sort," replied Michael.

"Why do you say that?" questioned Conor.

"There's nothing here that could explode. At least not in that quantity," stated Michael.

"Let's make sure of that, Lieutenant," ordered the lieutenant commander.

"Yes, sir," returned Lieutenant Michael Anderson.

"We'll need a full investigation. I'm going to ask the second lieutenant to assist you in any way possible," stated Conor.

"I'd like Sergeant Adachi to assist me if she can spare him," replied Michael.

"Wasn't he the one who helped with the FTL incident?" asked Conor.

"Yes. He works demolitions," stated Michael.

"I'll let Shiran know," replied Conor.

"Conor, it looks to me like the frequency standard unit we just installed from the *New Horizon* is where the explosion originated," said Michael.

"You're sure?" questioned Conor.

"I want Adachi's opinion on it and a chem analysis before I can say for sure," replied Michael.

"I'll have Shiran send him up ASAP. How bad is the damage?" asked Conor.

"We can probably repair the comm shack in two months and have a basic comm suite up and running in that time. The motherboard for the AI we were working on, however, is a total loss," said Michael.

At least three months of manpower had been expended on the motherboard by Michael and his crew over the last year. Hattie had estimated that it would take three to four years of constant work to put together a basic AI mainframe. Hattie had the schematics for a mainframe, but the ship's factory did not have the capabilities to manufacture one. With the material and manpower available, Michael and Hattie had estimated that it would take nearly five years for one person to piece a suitable mainframe together. Replicating an AI program afterward would be fairly simple by utilizing a seed from Hattie. An AI was essential before there were any thoughts of constructing an automated factory. It took an AI to coordinate and perform the different processing functions inside an automated factory.

"All right, Michael, I'm going to go down to the Marine Complex and arrange for Adachi to work with you," said Conor.

"Conor, we need to catch this son of a bitch," stated Michael heatedly.

Conor looked back at Michael and nodded. "I'll see you later, Michael. I need to inform the commander."

Lieutenant Michael Anderson nodded and turned to Chief deLang, who stood there with a canvas stretcher. He assisted her in laying it beside the body of Petty Officer Cindy Brooks. They wrapped the body in the tarp that Michael had placed over the body. They gently lifted Cindy Brooks's body and carried her to the clinic. Dr. Hollinger and Dr. Joshi were still working on Charles Fooks when they arrived. They placed the stretcher on an operating table in another room.

Lieutenant Michael Anderson went back to the waiting room and took a seat on one of the hard wooden benches. He placed his head in his hands with his elbows on his knees, wanting to weep. Petty Officer Brooks had been one of his best workers. The loss would hurt in more ways than he could think because she had become a friend of Francesca and himself. He would miss her bright, cheery smile and the smell of lavender perfume that she used.

He didn't know how long he had been sitting there or when Francesca arrived. The first he knew that she was there was when he felt her arm go around his shoulders and smelled the jasmine perfume she favored. She didn't say anything. She simply sat there beside him, offering him her strength and comfort.

More time passed. Conor and Shiran arrived and waited with their two friends. No one said anything until nearly three hours later when Dr. Hollinger came out of the operating room looking exhausted. They had been able to save Charles Fooks. Nearly 40 percent of his body had severe burns, and one of his lungs was compromised. He would require reconstructive surgery on his epidermis and regenerative surgery on his left lung. The broken bones he received from being thrown against the wall were set and would heal naturally. One bone had sliced through a main artery, and they almost lost him, but Dr. Joshi noticed it right off and prevented another casualty.

The four friends thanked the doctor, who said she didn't want to disturb the patient for the next twenty-four hours. The doctor suggested that it would be best if they all went to the Overlook to eat and get some rest. Taking the doctor's advice, the four friends walked down to the Overlook. To everyone's surprise, it was already late evening, and Ezekiel was already chasing people out for the day. When he saw who was at the door though, he waved them in.

To the group's surprise, Commander Hadden Blankenship and Hiroka Tamura were sitting at the back table, waiting for them. They all greeted one another and had a seat. The commander just arrived planetside and met Hiroka at the Overlook, then sent a message to the clinic. The group told the commander and Hiroka the condition of Charles Fooks and what had happened earlier in the day as Ezekiel brought them strips of apatosaurus and vegetables served over rice with beer for all.

"What do you think happened, Lieutenant?" asked Commander Blankenship.

"I think it's our saboteur, sir," replied Lieutenant Anderson.

The commander nodded. "I do too. Unfortunately, others in the colony wish to use this for their own ends and I think the ends of our saboteur."

"What do you mean, sir?" questioned Second Lieutenant Rosenstein.

The commander sat back and chewed on a grisly piece of apatosaurus for a moment, then took a swig from his beer before answering. "The president and his staff want Lieutenant Anderson relieved of responsibility for the MILDET communications shack and receive a reprimand."

"What?" demanded Lieutenant Commander Conor Raybourn.

"I'm not being given much choice. They want Lieutenant Felter reactivated and placed in charge," said the commander. Then he added, "Most of the technicians are supporting this."

"Why?" asked Francesca Chandra.

"The president and his staff do not like the FTL crew. They blame us, which includes me, for being stranded here and have over time gained followers with that attitude," replied Lieutenant Commander Raybourn. "I'm surprised he didn't demand my removal."

"He did," answered Commander Blankenship. "I told him no."

"So what are you going to do, Commander?" asked Second Lieutenant Rosenstein.

"Lieutenant Anderson will be relieved of responsibility for the comm shack refit. His only responsibility will be for construction of the AI," said the commander.

"And the reprimand?" asked Lieutenant Commander Raybourn.

"There will be no reprimands or any other changes. Let's see how this plays out," replied Commander Hadden Blankenship.

"Will I have anyone working with me?" asked Lieutenant Michael Anderson.

"I'm not sure yet. Not all the technicians were present at the meeting the president demanded after this incident," replied the commander.

"I'm sure Brad Guillete was not among those present at that meeting," said Lieutenant Anderson.

The commander cocked an eyebrow at Michael and inquired, "How did you know that, Michael?"

"Just things I've observed, sir," replied Lieutenant Anderson.

"I believe I'm aware of the situation. Any ideas on how to handle it?" asked the commander.

"No, sir," replied Lieutenant Anderson. "But I'll work with Brad Guillete and see if there's anyone else who will work with me."

"Can he help with your investigation of the MILDET comm shack incident?" asked the commander.

"Am I still in charge of investigations?" inquired Michael.

"I had the second lieutenant seal off the MILDET comm shack and station a Marine guard until the investigation is completed. The president isn't happy about it but doesn't have the authority to deny a military decision in this matter," said Commander Blankenship. "So Mr. Guillete is free to join your team. Sergeant Adachi has already spent the day investigating the comm shack and will brief you about his results in the morning."

"Thank you, sir," replied Lieutenant Anderson.

"Lieutenant, I'm not blaming you, and if there is anything you can do to get that comm shack online quicker, please do so," said Commander Hadden Blankenship.

CHAPTER 36

Master Sergeant Evan Zander was standing fifty meters from the interior of the perimeter fence watching the forest beyond. The forest had been cleared another fifty meters beyond the exterior of the fence line. This provided nearly one hundred meters of uninhibited viewing beyond the perimeter fence for the security cameras to the forest's edge. The master sergeant was considering clearing the forest back another fifty meters. Staff Sergeant Amanda Hall and Brad Guillete were installing the camera and motion sensor on the pole they had sunk into the ground. Sergeant Nikolai Ivankov was watching the forest intently, and Zander walked over to him.

"Anything, Sergeant?" asked the master sergeant.
"Thought I saw something, Master Sergeant," replied Nikolai.
"What?" demanded Evan.
"Flash of red," stated Nikolai.
"Think we're being watched?" questioned Evan.
Nikolai Ivankov intently searched the green foliage again. "Yes!"
"I think so too," the master sergeant informed the sergeant.
"Why don't they try attacking?" inquired Nikolai.
"I think they've seen other animals approach the fence and then shy away after being zapped. So they know the fence means pain without testing it," said Evan.
"How many do you think there are?" asked Nikolai.
"No way of telling unless they come out of the forest," said Evan Zander.
"We could do an IR scan," observed Nikolai.
"Already looked. There's about ten out there, but there's no way to tell the reds and greens apart at this distance," countered Evan.

"So it could just be the one, or they all could be reds," stated Nikolai.

"I'm inclined to think there's one to three of them," confided Evan.

"Why?" inquired Nikolai.

"Recon," the master sergeant deadpanned.

Sergeant Ivankov looked at the master sergeant and, after a moment, nodded agreement. The reds had already been proven aggressive, and the battle to the LZ must have had survivors. There was no way of knowing how many of the new velociraptors there really were or where they came from. What the colony needed to do was find out where they came from and do a recon of their own. Until then, without knowing the numbers or the true nature of the reds' society, the colony was in danger. Evan Zander knew they were at a disadvantage so long as the colony knew next to nothing about the world around them. The only way to find out that information was to explore and find out what was out there before what was out there discovered the colony and any weaknesses that it had.

The master sergeant turned toward Staff Sergeant Hall and Brad Guillete. "How's it coming?"

"Be done in ten, Master Sergeant," stated Amanda.

"Good!" acknowledged Evan.

They were a little behind schedule, but Brad Guillete found the problem and corrected it. Afterward, the work progressed rapidly as they became more comfortable with the installation of the units. The security cameras and motion sensors would require an extra watch in the Marine Complex, and Master Sergeant Evan Zander was feeling that the Marines were getting stretched a little thin.

Joseph Green decided to do training and was being put through the wringer by Gunnery Sergeant Rusu and the rest of the Marines. Master Sergeant Zander had three other prospects who might be possible to recruit. Four if he counted Brad Guillete, but Brad had told him that he would have to think about it for a while. There were other people among the outcasts who might be possible recruits in the near future. They had not lived up to the expectations of some in the colony, but the master sergeant was not willing to push too hard or too fast.

The ATV was packed, and everyone boarded to move on to the next security unit installation. They finished two hours later and returned to the Marine Complex. Staff Sergeant Hall and Brad Guillete spent another hour making sure all the remote sensors were working from the security room. When they were finished, they assured Second Lieutenant Rosenstein and Master Sergeant Zander the installations were working.

Evan Zander went to ensure watches were set and told Gunnery Sergeant Rusu to go over the watch bills to make sure there were no conflicting overlaps. He toured the Marine Complex prior to going down to the piers. As he approached *Shuttle 1*, his wife, Chief Tami Zander, came out of the hatch dressed in Navy blues. There was a dab of grease on her forehead, but a large smile came to her face as she saw who was standing at the end of the gangway.

"Hello, love!" she shouted.

"Hi there yourself!" he shouted back as he walked up the gangway.

She came down the gangway and fell into his embrace as best she could with the round bulge of impending life between them.

"Are you willing to play hooky?" asked Evan Zander.

"Anything for you, love. What do you have in mind?" mumbled Tami Zander as she nibbled his ear.

"We pick up the twins for the afternoon, then find a babysitter for the evening," stated Evan Zander distractedly.

"That sounds like fun. Then what?" Tami Zander asked as she pulled back to look in his eyes.

"I was thinking a quiet evening meal at the Overlook," replied Evan Zander as he moved forward to nibble her ear.

"I might be able to handle that," said Tami.

"I arranged for Ezekiel to make your favorite, and I've already found the babysitter for later," replied Evan Zander.

"You're so thoughtful, but I'm hungry right now," stated Tami.

"Poached eggs, Danishes, and tea at the Flour Mill," said Evan.

"Is that a question?" inquired Tami.

"Nope, already arranged," Evan assured her.

Tami Zander pulled back and looked Evan in his eyes. Evan Zander's eyes were twinkling in that special way he had that had endeared her to him. There was something going on here that was eluding her, and she didn't know what kind of mischievousness he was up to.

"Are you trying to get me pregnant?" she teased.

"A little late for that, don't you think?" Evan grinned as he softly placed a hand on her rounded abdomen.

Tami laughed, embarrassing Evan. "If we're going to do this, I need a shower."

"Your wish is my command. Follow me, my lady," said Evan graciously.

Evan escorted her to the Marine Complex and left her at the shower room with a fresh set of clothing and shoes. He went to his office and changed into civilian clothing. Once done, he went to the Marine mess where he poured a cup of coffee and sat down to wait. He was just finishing his coffee when Tami appeared, outfitted in a loose-fitting dress that she had chosen for herself that morning.

"You look beautiful," stated Evan Zander.

Tami cocked an eyebrow at him and replied, "Thank you."

"Shall we, my dear?" asked Evan.

"By all means. Lead on, my love," replied Tami with a twinkle in her eye.

They had a scrumptious meal at the Flour Mill. The poached eggs were wonderful, and the Danishes were magnificent. They were sipping on their tea when Anya Kaur came up to them with the twins in the double-wide stroller that Evan had specially made. They strolled down the boardwalk to the bridge outside the Overlook and crossed. There, the construction had begun on the future hospital and school.

"Here is where the future begins," stated Evan.

"So now you're an oracle?" asked Tami.

"Well, I make things happen," said Evan.

"You do have a way about you." Tami chuckled as she rubbed her abdomen.

"I do, don't I?" Evan grinned.

"We won't have to worry about school for at least another five years unless they also plan on running a day care," replied Tami.

"Don't most schools do that nowadays?" asked Evan.

"Well, yes, but we're not really in the United Systems," said Tami.

"My darling, I could make this happen, I think," said Evan.

"Sometimes between Ezekiel and you, I think the two of you run the colony," replied Tami.

Evan got a hurt look on his face. "I'm wounded, honey. We just make things happen. We have no need of political or bureaucratic power."

"Your way does make life easier," admitted Tami with a wide smile.

"My people are happier too." Evan grinned.

"There is that," affirmed Tami.

"Are you up to looking over the beginnings of the new hospital?" asked Evan.

"Yes, but I need to sit for a bit," replied Tami.

"Your wish is my command," responded Evan.

They spent some time sitting and talking and generally watching the world go by for a time. Then they completed the tour of the up-and-coming facilities that would improve the capabilities of the colony and their chances of survival. The world seemed right as the afternoon passed under a star far from home.

Dropping off the twins with Anya Kaur at their apartment, they ended the evening at the Overlook. Ezekiel prepared baked fish with rice and a salad. The wine was a sweet white that came from the brewery. As they relaxed over tea, Tami finally looked at Evan.

"So what's this all about?" queried Tami Zander.

"Can't a man take his wife on a date for no reason?" asked Evan Zander with a hurt look.

"I know you too well. You're buttering me up for something," replied Tami.

"You wound me!" cried Evan.

"Come on. Out with it," demanded Tami.

"Well, there is one thing," muttered Evan.

"And that is?" insisted Tami.

"Well," Evan paused, then he continued, "you know how you ladies always complain how useless you feel the last few months during a pregnancy."

"Helpless," responded Tami.

"What?" asked Evan, confused.

"Helpless, not useless," stated Tami.

"All right," said Evan.

"What about it?" asked Tami.

"Well, the Marines have taken on some new duties, and we've lost some Marines. The second lieutenant is worried that we might be a bit overextended," explained Evan Zander.

"Yes?" inquired Tami Zander impatiently.

"There are some duties we do that a pregnant female could fulfill at the Marine Complex even if she isn't a Marine," blurted Evan.

"What duties?" inquired his wife.

"Operations and security watches," stated Evan.

"Let me get this straight. You want pregnant females to sit around and watch radar screens and security monitors during the last few months they're pregnant?" Tami reiterated.

"Something like that," muttered Evan.

"On those hard plastic seats with no bathroom and no elevator?" demanded Tami.

"We can fix that," protested Evan quickly.

"Can you now?" Tami grinned.

"Anything for you, babe," insisted Evan.

"Really?" countered Tami.

"The elevator is already nearly done, and so is the bathroom. I didn't think about the seating though," admitted Evan.

"You never said anything about having that kind of work being done, and where are you building them?" demanded Tami.

"Well, what I meant is that the work on those start tomorrow," confessed Evan.

"Oh! You must be awfully sure of my saying yes to my helping you convince all these pregnant women to stand those watches," Tami replied somewhat heatedly.

"Well, it was already arranged to have those accommodations because of the second lieutenant and other Marines in the command who might acquire conditions that might limit their capabilities," said Evan Zander.

Tami just looked at Evan, and slowly a smile came across her face. Finally, she said, "All right, you've nearly convinced me. As long as they are not going to have to become Marines?"

"No! I guarantee it," responded Evan.

"This isn't some scheme to increase the ranks through subterfuge?" inquired Tami with a smile.

"If they want to become Marines, they are free to volunteer and see if they can pass the tests." Evan grinned.

Tami gave him a stern look, then changed the subject by asking, "How about transportation for those poor pregnant ladies?"

"There will be an ATV and Marine on call to provide transportation," promised Evan.

"Great. When do we start recruiting?" asked Tami.

"Well, I was thinking of leaving the recruiting thing to you," replied Evan.

"What?" demanded Tami.

"I'm not very good with talking to pregnant women, and I still have to convince the second lieutenant that it's a good idea," confessed Master Sergeant Evan Zander.

"Have you even told her about your brilliant scheme?" demanded Chief Tami Zander.

"Well, no. But I'm sure she'll see reason," said Evan.

Tami rolled her eyes and made a face at Evan. "Does convincing her involve lunch and dinner?"

Evan looked hurt as he replied, "No! I reserve that only for my special lady who requires a lot of convincing."

Tami grinned. "All right, you've convinced me. I'll recruit the pregnant women, and you work your charm on the second lieutenant."

"Good! Oh, there should be at least three of them on watch at any time. I'll arrange for a single bed to be available in case one of them needs a nap," said Master Sergeant Zander.

"You're so thoughtful," Tami Zander said.

"It takes a lot of work," confessed Evan Zander.

"Somehow, I sense Ezekiel's hand in this," admonished Tami Zander.

"You'd be surprised what brainstorms occur over checkers and beer," Evan Zander confided, chuckling.

"I thought so," Tami Zander said as she shook her head and smiled.

Ezekiel came over with a huge grin on his face. The companionship between Evan Zander and Ezekiel Yap had lasted for years. Even when they had been rivals over the attention of Tami Zander, it had been good-natured.

"Have you convinced her?" Ezekiel grinned.

Half the moon could be seen shining in the sky with the brilliant point of its companion following as Tami looked out the front window of the Overlook. Her gaze returned to the two friends, and she shook her head in defeat. The three companions burst into laughter as Ezekiel sat down to have a glass of wine with them to watch the world outside dimming in the last rays of sunlight.

CHAPTER 37

Lieutenant Anarzej Gataki floated through the aft hatch and onto the bridge as Commander Hadden Blankenship finished his report. Hadden noticed the olive-colored hand grasp the command chair armrest and knew his relief had arrived. When Anarzej was alongside the commander, he saluted.

"Good morning, Captain," said Anarzej.

"Good morning, Lieutenant," returned Hadden.

"Reporting for duty, sir," stated Anarzej.

"All conditions remain the same, Lieutenant. Keep an eye on engineering and that power fluctuation. Contact me if anything changes," ordered Hadden.

"Yes, sir. Wish the couples well for me," replied Anarzej.

"I will, Lieutenant, and thank you for volunteering to take the watch," replied Hadden.

"You're welcome, sir," said Anarzej.

"I'll be back in two weeks, Lieutenant. Make sure the old lady is still here when I come back," chided Hadden Blankenship.

"She will be, sir. I relieve you, sir," stated the lieutenant as he saluted.

"Very well, Lieutenant. I stand relieved," Commander Blankenship said, returning his salute.

The commander saved all his work and logged out of the computer after finishing his deck log. He released his harness and floated out of the command chair. He kicked off toward the forward hatch and the passageway to the docking bay. He passed through the bow deck department and entered the docking bay where Ensign Dominic Sobolov waited near the shuttle hatch.

"Good morning, Captain," Dominic said as he saluted.

"Good morning, Ensign," said Hadden as he returned the salute then asked. "Is everything ready?"

"Yes, sir. I was just waiting for my last passenger who just arrived." Dominic smiled.

"Passenger? I'm piloting, Ensign." Hadden grinned.

Dominic looked startled for a moment, then replied, "Yes, sir. Sorry, sir."

"Just a slight change of routine, and I need my qualifications updated, Ensign. No time like the present," said the commander, grinning at the ensign's discomfort.

"Yes, sir," replied Dominic.

"Fine. Shall we?" said Hadden.

"Yes, sir," snapped Dominic.

Ensign Sobolov entered the shuttle with Commander Blankenship following him. Hadden secured the hatch as Dominic moved to check all the passengers' restraints and ensure all the cargo was properly secured for reentry. When he was finished, he went forward to find Hadden already in the pilot seat checking readouts and prepping for launch. Dominic took the copilot seat and pulled on his restraints as he did his prelaunch checks.

"Everything secure, Ensign?" asked Hadden.

"Yes, sir," replied Dominic.

"Thank you, Ensign," said Hadden. He toggled the comm and said, "New Horizon. New Horizon. Shuttle 1. Over."

"Shuttle 1. New Horizon. We read you. Over," came the reply from Lieutenant Gataki.

"New Horizon. Shuttle 1. Prelaunch checks complete and read fivers. We are ready to launch. Over," stated Hadden.

"Shuttle 1. New Horizon. You are clear to launch. Over," replied Anarzej's voice.

"New Horizon. Shuttle 1. Roger. Out," said Hadden.

Commander Blankenship looked at Ensign Sobolov and asked, "Ready, Ensign?"

"When you are, sir," replied Dominic.

"Commencing burn," said Hadden as he applied thrusters to push the shuttle out of the docking bay into the freedom of empty space.

The shuttle eased out of the docking port as Hadden applied the shuttle's bow thrusters. When the shuttle was a hundred meters from *New Horizon*'s bow docking bay, Hadden utilized the shuttle's stern thrusters to bring their relative motion to the *New Horizon* to a stop. Toggling his communications, he transmitted.

"New Horizon. Shuttle 1. New Horizon. Shuttle 1. Over," said Hadden into his comm.

"Shuttle 1. New Horizon. We read you. Over," came Anarzej's reply.

"New Horizon. Shuttle 1. Commencing captain's inspection of *New Horizon* hull. Over," stated Commander Blankenship.

"Shuttle 1. New Horizon. Roger that. Out," said Anarzej's voice over the comm.

Applying stern and port thrusters, Hadden edged the shuttle's trajectory so it passed fifty meters away from the starboard side heading aft. Finished, he corrected his course so he would slowly go along the port side at the same distance from the *New Horizon*. He repeated the process for a keel and superstructure view—not that the last two terms really meant anything other than points of reference when talking about the ship.

"The ship looks in good order, sir," said Dominic.

"It would be nice to have the plating where the breaches were repaired painted, Ensign," said Hadden distractedly.

"Yes, sir. But she is still ready to sail," replied Dominic.

"I don't see much sailing in her near future, Ensign. It may be decades before the colony can afford to let her explore the stellar system we're in," replied Hadden.

"Perhaps someday, sir," suggested Dominic.

"Someday perhaps," agreed Hadden.

The commander applied bow thrusters and brought the shuttle to a relative stop in front of the *New Horizon*. He toggled the comm and spoke.

"New Horizon. New Horizon. Shuttle 1. Over," said Hadden.

"Shuttle 1. New Horizon. We read you. Over," came the reply from Lieutenant Gataki.

"New Horizon. Shuttle 1. Have completed inspection. No new discrepancies noted. Over," stated Hadden Blankenship.

"Shuttle 1. New Horizon. We copy that. No new discrepancies. Over," replied Anarzej.

"New Horizon. Shuttle 1. Roger. We are commencing our burn for reentry sequence. Over," said Hadden.

"Shuttle 1. New Horizon. We copy that. Shuttle 1 commencing reentry sequence. Godspeed, Commander. Roger. Out," said Lieutenant Anarzej Gataki.

"New Horizon. Shuttle 1. Roger. Out," replied Commander Blankenship.

The commander looked at his panel and tapped the controls that would start the burn for reentry. Being in geosynchronous orbit made the longboat and shuttle routes for reentry and reaching orbit fairly routine. The burn began, and the longboat pulled away from the *New Horizon*. It would circle the world below, passing beneath the *New Horizon* nearly two times before breaching the atmosphere, at which time their speed would reduce dramatically as air friction slowed the craft.

Ensign Sobolov watched his monitors during the burn and spent another ten minutes checking readings to ensure the trajectory was correct. Satisfied, he sat back just as Hadden was finishing his own systems checks. Hadden noted that Dominic was fidgeting as though he wanted to ask something but was afraid to do so.

"What is it, Ensign?" asked Hadden.

"What do you mean, sir?" returned Dominic.

"Out with it, Ensign. You want to ask me something. Get it off your chest," stated Hadden.

"What have we learned of Gunnery Sergeant Rusu's discovery?" asked Dominic.

"Nothing really, Ensign. The writing on it did not match anything we've come across so far. Francesca Chandra, our cultural anthropologist and linguistics expert, says it's reminiscent of some form of Sanskrit in style, while the writings discovered in the abandoned city are more like Aztec and Mayan," said Commander Blankenship.

"What about the writings in the cleft cave?" asked Dominic.

"Unidentifiable. They match nothing we've encountered in this system or on Earth," replied the commander.

"Could the reds have developed all three writing systems?" asked Dominic, referring to the red raptors.

"The people of Earth have multiple writing systems," said Hadden.

Dominic nodded. "So they all may have been developed by the reds."

"Or there could be two or more different intelligent species represented by the various writings," said Hadden Blankenship.

"Or three different races of velociraptors, sir," replied Dominic.

"That's true and something to think about," affirmed Hadden.

The longboat bucked, and Hadden adjusted course as they entered the atmosphere. Dominic nodded, acknowledging Hadden's knowledge of the controls. Hadden could see the young man was nervous not being in the pilot seat. A smile crept onto the commander's face as he thought about when he was a young ensign. Some things always remain the same; it would seem only the people who played the roles changed.

The commander slowly vectored north as they approached the southern end of the island. Dipping the nose of the craft slightly down, he descended toward the coastline as Dominic called in their position to the Marine Complex. The river was visible as they dropped below the cloud cover and rapidly approached the island. Hadden squinted as they did so and pointed toward the coast.

"What do you see there, Ensign?" asked Hadden.

Ensign Sobolov squinted also, then called for magnification of his half of the view screen. Four ships with red and green figures moving on the decks and the beach came into view and passed below them as they reached the coastline. Three of the ships were moored, and another was sailing westward toward the mainland.

"They look like old sailing ships, sir," stated Dominic.

"I would say that the question of whether the red velociraptors can work together cooperatively and why we haven't seen them before now is partly answered, Ensign," replied Hadden.

Dominic Sobolov simply nodded as the forest and plains passed quickly below the shuttle. They rapidly approached the lake where the cleft was located. Banking east, Hadden lost more speed as the shuttle paralleled the nearby cliffs and overshot the lake's far end. Hadden brought the shuttle about, causing it to lose momentum rapidly as he lined up to bring the shuttle down for a landing. The radio crackled into life as the commander brought the nose up for the water landing.

"Marine Complex. Shuttle 1. Marine Complex. Shuttle 1. Over," came Second Lieutenant Shiran Rosenstein's voice over the comm channel.

"Shuttle 1. Marine Complex. We read you. Over," responded Commander Blankenship.

"Marine Complex. Shuttle 1. Our eyes are blind and cannot provide guidance. Over," stated Shiran's voice over the comm.

"Shuttle 1. Marine Complex. Understood. We have the ball. Over," replied Hadden.

"Marine Complex. Shuttle 1. Roger that. You have the ball. Over," said Shiran Rosenstein's voice over the comm.

"Shuttle 1. Marine Complex. We'll be there in thirty. Out," stated Hadden.

"Marine Complex. Shuttle 1. Roger that. Out," came the reply.

The commander glanced over at Dominic as he adjusted his angle and brought the nose up. They fell swiftly toward the lake, and the shuttle jerked slightly as the stern touched the lake's surface, bringing the nose downward. As the ship leveled out and more of the undercarriage touched the surface of the lake, the restraining straps bit into Hadden's shoulders. Hadden lowered the hydro brakes and maneuvering fins into the lake water, reducing their speed even more. The shuttle was lined up for a run to the piers when it came to a complete stop. Commander Blankenship looked over at Ensign Sobolov.

"Still got it, son," said Hadden.

"Excellent, Commander. I couldn't have done better myself, sir." Dominic grinned.

"Thank you, Ensign. Now let's see if I can park this rig without putting a dent in it," said Hadden.

"I wonder what happened to the Marine radar," said Dominic worriedly.

"We'll find out when we get there. I'm sure the second lieutenant is already chewing some butt over it," replied Hadden.

Ensign Sobolov simply nodded as Commander Blankenship manipulated the controls operating the rear thrusters, allowing them to push the shuttle slowly forward in short bursts. Approaching the pier, he fired the forward thrusters to slow down as he came up alongside the docking cradle built for the shuttle. He fired the starboard side thrusters and nudged the shuttle into the cradle. The cradle clamped onto the longboat automatically, and docking was complete.

The commander sat there for a moment, then began flipping switches and tapping control panels to turn off active systems. Ensign Sobolov followed suit with his control console as the gangway and refueling lines extended from the pier and attached themselves to the shuttle. Finally, the pilot and copilot released their restraining straps and opened the outer hatch.

"All ashore," ordered Hadden as he waited for the shuttle's passengers to file out and down the gangway.

When the shuttle occupants were on the pier, Commander Blankenship stepped out and closed the hatch. He then strolled down the gangway where Ensign Sobolov waited with Chief Petty Officer Tami Zander.

"Good morning, sir," said Tami as she saluted.

"Good morning, Chief. How are the children?" returned Hadden.

"They're doing well, sir. Little hellions like their father," she replied with a grin.

"And mother, I'm sure," said Hadden, returning the grin.

"You wound me, sir." Tami grinned. "I see that you still have it, sir."

"Thank you, Chief. I did the landing without any ground guidance," said Hadden.

"Why is that, sir?" asked Chief Tami Zander with concern on her face.

"I take it that the radar went down on our approach," replied the commander.

"That's not good," she stated.

"No, it's not. Take care of the bird, Chief. Make sure everything is in order. I need to go find out what's going on in operations," ordered Commander Blankenship.

"Aye, aye, sir," responded Chief Zander.

The commander walked down the pier with Ensign Sobolov as they headed to the Marine Complex seeking answers.

CHAPTER 38

The shuttle was commencing its turn for the approach to the lake as the MSRDR-17—the acronym for Marine short-range defense radar—became inoperable at the Marine Complex. Sergeant Ivankov was monitoring the approach when the radar console in the air traffic approach room lost all radar imaging. The only thing they could tell was that the IFF—the acronym for identification friend or foe—for the shuttle was still working. The IFF signal gave them a range and bearing to the shuttle but no other information. Second Lieutenant Shiran Rosenstein had been in the air approach room when the radar blinked out.

"Marine Complex. Shuttle 1. Marine Complex. Shuttle 1. Over," said the second lieutenant.

"Shuttle 1. Marine Complex. We read you. Over," came Commander Blankenship's voice.

"Marine Complex. Shuttle 1. Our eyes are blind and cannot provide guidance. Over," stated Shiran.

"Shuttle 1. Marine Complex. Understood. We have the ball. Over," replied Hadden's voice.

"Marine Complex. Shuttle 1. Roger that. You have the ball. Over," said Shiran.

"Shuttle 1. Marine Complex. We'll be there in thirty. Out," responded Hadden.

"Marine Complex. Shuttle 1. Roger that. Out," said Shiran.

Shiran Rosenstein grabbed a set of binoculars and ran to the roof of the Marine Complex. She looked out to the east searching for the shuttle and found it as the last jets of water were streaming back from the quickly slowing shuttle. Assured that the shuttle was down, she watched for a moment as it maneuvered to align itself for an approach to the piers near the Marine Complex. Shiran went back down to the air traffic approach room and contacted the shuttle.

Shiran was slightly irritated since the MSRDR-17 was the only eyes the Marine Complex had that had a range of over two hundred kilometers. Worse, it had gone down during the weekly shuttle landing. This made her look bad, and she was ready to chew someone's butt.

She looked at Master Sergeant Zander as he stepped into the operations suite and snapped, "Master Sergeant, get on the horn to the electronics suite and have Lieutenant Felter send someone down to fix our MSRDR."

"What about asking Brad Guillete, ma'am?" replied Evan.

"Do you know where he is, Master Sergeant?" demanded Shiran.

"He's downstairs having lunch with Sergeant Adachi," replied Evan.

"Does he know anything about the MSRDR-17?" demanded Shiran.

"One way to find out," replied Evan.

"I'll go talk to him about it myself. Thanks, Master Sergeant," responded Shiran as she walked toward the mess.

The second lieutenant went down to the mess hall in the lower level of the Marine Complex. As she entered, there were four Marines and Brad Guillete eating lunch together. Sergeant Tadashi Adachi was sitting across from him as Shiran approached the table.

"I'm sorry to interrupt, Sergeant, but I need to speak to Mr. Guillete for a moment," said Shiran.

"No problem, ma'am. I was just getting ready to go back to servicing the ATVs," replied Tadashi. "I'll see you later, Brad." Tadashi got up from the table, taking his dirty tray.

Shiran sat down across from Brad and said, "Good afternoon, Brad."

"Good afternoon, Second Lieutenant," replied Brad.

Shiran noted that he had a question in his eyes about what a Marine officer could possibly want to talk to him about. At least that was what she assumed the look meant.

"Brad, what do you know about the MSRDR-17?" asked the Shiran.

"It's a radar, ma'am," replied Brad.

"Well, yes," replied Shiran. Since she had expected more, it gave her pause. "Have you ever worked on an MSRDR-17?"

"No," responded Brad.

Shiran was about to give up and go back to calling the operations suite when Brad looked at her and asked, "Would you like me to look at it, ma'am?" Then he added, "I'm not doing anything right now, ma'am. If you want, I can take a look."

"I'd appreciate it," replied Shiran.

"What happened?" inquired Brad.

"We lost all signals from the radar as the shuttle was coming in," stated Shiran.

"Even the IFF?" asked Brad, referring to the identification friend or foe system attached to the radar.

"No, that was still working," responded Shiran, confused.

"Was the signal from the IFF at the right bearing and range?" continued Brad.

"Yes," said Shiran.

"Then the antenna is still spinning up on the roof?" questioned Brad.

The second lieutenant thought about it and remembered that the antenna was still turning on the roof of the Marine Complex and said, "Yes, it is."

"Good." Brad nodded. He got up, then asked, "Who's up in the operations suite?"

"Master Sergeant Zander and Sergeant Ivankov," replied Shiran.

"I'll go take a look." Brad smiled.

"I can escort you up," said Shiran.

"No need, ma'am. I know where it is. I work on the IFF," returned Brad.

"All right. I'll be up in an hour to see how it's going," said Shiran. As Brad turned to go, she said, "Brad." He stopped and looked back, and she added, "I'm sorry about Rachel."

"I am too," said Brad as pain filled his eyes. Then he turned and went to the stairs leading to the upper part of the Marine Complex.

The second lieutenant sat and finished her coffee as she waited for the commander to arrive. He had a habit of dropping by the Marine Complex upon arrival to see how everything was going and to have a cup of coffee himself. This time, she was sure he would be more interested in answers as to what went wrong than coffee. Shiran had just walked over to put the cup in the sink when Commander Blankenship and Ensign Sobolov entered the Marine Complex. The second lieutenant came to attention and saluted.

"Good morning, Commander," snapped Shiran.

"Good morning, Second Lieutenant. What seems to be the problem with the radar?" asked Hadden.

"The radar went down, sir. Mr. Guillete is having a look at it right now," returned Shiran.

"Shall we go see how he's doing?" asked Hadden.

"Yes, sir, if you'll follow me," replied Shiran.

"I know the way, Second Lieutenant," stated Hadden as he headed toward the nearby stairwell.

"Yes, sir," returned Shiran.

They reached the operations room to find Brad Guillete lying on his back with over half his chest and head hidden by the extended radar cabinet. His hand reached out and searched the floor beside him as the commander and others stood there watching. The only tool on the floor was a screwdriver just past the fingertips of his searching extended hand. They heard a "Damn it" resound as the questing hand continued to search. Hadden moved over and bent down, then took up the screwdriver, placing it in the hand as it continued its quest. The hand stopped as it felt and grasped the handle.

"Thank you," came from underneath the equipment.

"How's it going in there, Mr. Guillete?" asked Hadden.

"Looks like the power amplifiers are burned out," replied Brad.

"Why do you think that?" inquired Hadden.

"Considering half of one's on the floor beside my head and its base is still screwed into the case, I'd say it's bad," explained Brad.

"Are there spares here?" questioned Hadden.

"Yes," came Brad's response.

"Where are they stored?" inquired Hadden.

"Blue plastic case in the locker over on the far wall," returned Brad.

Dominic Sobolov went over to the locker and opened it. There was a large blue case on the second shelf from the bottom, which he took out and brought over to Hadden. The commander took the case, setting it on the floor beside him, and opened it.

"What am I looking for, Mr. Guillete?" queried Hadden.

"Power transistor with a part number papa tango dash three eight four one alpha November. The top will look like this, and the number should be printed there," stated Brad as his hand came back out from underneath the equipment to display the top of the faulty component.

The commander opened the compartment drawers of the blue case looking for a fairly large silvery component. He located several in the back section of the bottom drawer neatly arranged in a pink foamy substance.

"I found them, Mr. Guillete," said Hadden after checking the part number.

"I'll need two," came the reply.

"Why?" asked Hadden.

"This stage of the circuit is a multivibrator. There's two transistors that make up the circuit to make the radar pulse. If one goes bad, it generally means the other one's been degraded, and they should both be replaced," explained Brad Guillete.

"Are you ready for the first one?" asked Hadden.

"Anytime," said Brad as his hand came out. He laid the other half of the bad transistor on the floor. He flipped his hand palm up and waited for the transistor Hadden held. The commander gently placed it in the palm, and Brad's fingers closed around it as the hand withdrew underneath the equipment again. A few minutes later, another scorched transistor appeared on the floor and another new transistor was given. A short time later, Brad slid out from under the equipment rack, and a look of surprise crossed his face as he looked up at the commander.

"Captain, sir," Brad Guillete said as he saluted.

"Easy, son, you're not in uniform," chided Hadden.

"Yes, sir," replied Brad.

"So is the radar repaired?" asked Hadden.

"Will have to do a smoke test, but I believe I have the problem fixed," replied Brad.

"Smoke test?" questioned Hadden.

"Turn it on and see if it works or if it fries something else," confided Brad.

"Why would it do that?" asked Hadden.

"One of the circuits this circuit feeds might short out when the pulse is applied to it. Yet all the readings were nominal before I turned it off. I did some static checks with my multimeter while I was replacing the transistors and didn't see anything unusual. So we turn it on and see what happens. If it's something that only happens when the pulse is applied, it will probably damage the transistors again," stated Brad.

"All right, Brad, let's try that." Hadden smiled.

Brad Guillete stood up and pushed the extended cabinet in, then went over to the main breaker. He removed the red danger tag attached to it and turned the switch on. Brad then returned to the radar and threw another switch. He checked the front panel monitors of the radar and the oscilloscope; he nodded. He threw another switch, and a pulse appeared on the oscilloscope. Brad checked the front panel monitors of the radar again and nodded. Finally, Brad turned and looked at Second Lieutenant Rosenstein. "Does the radar console have a display now, ma'am?"

The second lieutenant and the commander walked into the other room. Shiran sat down in front of the radar console. Turning it on, she adjusted some controls and watched the display screen. Shiran watched the display for a moment and started nodding. "It looks fine, Brad. I can see the cliff face, some of the higher ridges, and what has to be a couple of pterodactyls flying over the lake," said Shiran.

"Looks like you fixed it, Brad. Good work," stated the commander.

"Thank you, sir. I should check the readings to make sure they're within specs before I'm done," replied Brad.

"You have training on this radar?" asked Ensign Sobolov.

"No, sir. I've just worked around it and know a little bit about how it operates," replied Brad.

"Still, good work for the on-the-job training," said Commander Blankenship.

"No one else has training on this radar, sir," came Brad's response.

Hadden looked at Brad and nodded, then said, "Next time you're on board the *New Horizon*, I'd appreciate talking to you, Brad."

"I'll be up in a couple of months, sir," returned Brad.

"Is that your normal schedule?" asked Hadden.

Brad looked at the commander and said, "It is now."

"What do you mean?" queried Hadden.

"The schedule was revised, and I'm due up at that time to stand a two-week duty tour," replied Brad.

"Weren't you on board during the party just a couple of months ago?" asked Hadden.

"Yes, sir," replied Brad.

"Have you said anything about it to your superiors?" questioned Hadden.

"It's my superiors who rearranged the schedule, sir," stated Brad.

Hadden Blankenship got a thoughtful look on his face. "Come see me on board when you're there, and we'll talk, Second Lieutenant."

"Yes, sir," snapped Second Lieutenant Rosenstein.

"I expect an appropriate commendation for Brad to be forthcoming from your office," stated Commander Blankenship.

"Yes, sir," acknowledged Shiran.

"Brad, can you take the operations watch until the second lieutenant can round someone up to take your place?" asked Hadden.

"I can do that, sir," affirmed Brad.

"Then I'll see you in a couple of months, Brad," said Hadden.

The commander, second lieutenant, and Ensign Sobolov left the operations room and went downstairs to the Marine mess hall.

"I have to go to the MILDET, and I want you to come with me, Second Lieutenant. Find someone to take Mr. Guillete's place at watch. I'll wait," ordered Commander Blankenship.

"Yes, sir," said Shiran.

She went over to the table where Staff Sergeant Hall sat and talked to her for a second. Amanda picked up her coffee and headed up the stairs to the operations room.

"All set, sir," stated Second Lieutenant Rosenstein.

CHAPTER 39

Conor and Michael were in their dress uniforms waiting for their soon-to-be brides to walk down the gauntlet of well-wishers and corridor of bridesmaids and groomsmen. The music started announcing the brides. Master Sergeant Zander was to give away Shiran and escorted her up the aisle, while Ezekiel was to give away Francesca and escorted her up the aisle behind them. Evan and Ezekiel were both in dress uniforms, and so were the brides. The two grooms were serving as best man to each other.

Ensign Dominic Sobolov and Lieutenant Jacqueline Vinet had been given the duty of finding seven men and seven women from the officer ranks to stand as bridesmaids and groomsmen, including themselves. A variety of ensigns, lieutenants, and chief warrant officers made up those bridesmaids and groomsmen. They, too, were in full dress uniform of the United Systems, complete with white gloves and swords at their sides.

It was a beautiful day for the ceremony. A person could see forest and plains for miles. The great beasts could be seen moving across this brave, new world that the colonists shared. A slight breeze made it pleasant as the sun beat down on those gathered. Commander Hadden Blankenship performed the ceremony with Hiroka Tamura at his side. There was silence and some crying and nose blowing as the rites were read to the two couples. Hadden finished the rites with Hiroka holding his hand, looking up at him.

"Do you, Conor Raybourn, take Shiran Rosenstein to be your lawfully wedded wife?"

"I do," stated Conor.

"And do you, Shiran Rosenstein, take Conor Raybourn to be your lawfully wedded husband?"

"I do," stated Shiran.

"Do you, Michael Anderson, take Francesca Chandra to be your lawfully wedded wife?"

"I do," stated Michael.

"And do you, Francesca Chandra, take Michael Anderson to be your lawfully wedded husband?"

"I do," stated Francesca.

"Then I pronounce you, Conor and Shiran, husband and wife and you, Michael and Francesca, husband and wife. You may kiss your brides."

There was applause in the background as the couples kissed, then the two friends shook hands. Hadden and Hiroka added to the applause as they stood grinning at the couples. When they finished, the couples turned to face the crowd, and from behind, the commander's voice stated, "Ladies and gentlemen, I present to you Mr. and Mrs. Raybourn and Mr. and Mrs. Anderson. Long may their unions last!"

Swords flashed and made a silver-lined vaulted ceiling above the heads of the attendants on both sides of the passage for the brides and grooms to pass down. The grooms and their brides proceeded down the passageway with Conor and Shiran in the lead. As they exited the end of the passage, they were showered in a rain of multi-colored confetti and cheers.

The happy couples proceeded to the spot where Captain Tamura, Commander Blankenship, and the rest of the wedding party were gathering as the couples were applauded and cheered. The well-wishers passed down the line and headed to the open area where tables and seating had been arranged for all. Ezekiel had been placed in charge of that and the reception buffet, with Marines and Navy personnel who had volunteered to serve at the reception were in dress uniform.

Ezekiel and Evan were serving drinks at the bar that had been set up for the guests. A bottle of the latest brewery batch of champagne had been sent to the table of honor. Gunnery Sergeant Samuel

Rusu went down the table and poured the new vintage in fluted glasses specially made from the glassworks for the wedding party.

Laughter and loud voices filled the air as all present celebrated with the happy couples. The meal ended, and people sat talking and drinking champagne. Roberta and the Marines took things back to the Overlook as the buffet was broken down. The bar remained open, along with a table of sandwiches and snacks for the guests.

After thirty minutes, music started up, and everyone looked at the brides and grooms expectantly. The grooms led their brides out onto the open space reserved for dancing. The first waltz started, and they danced their first dance as married couples. When the waltz finished, another waltz began, and the couples exchanged partners while others walked out to the dance floor to join them. Hadden and Hiroka were one of the couples who had joined in on the second waltz. Francesca was a wonderful dancer and seemed to flow across the dance floor, anticipating Conor's lead.

"You dance beautifully." Conor smiled.

"Thank you," returned Francesca.

"I wish you and Michael a long and happy life," said Conor.

"Thank you. May the same hold true for you and Shiran," replied Francesca.

They danced for nearly half an hour, and after several exchanges of partners, Conor regained possession of his wife for a waltz. When they were finished, Conor limped to the table with his pregnant wife. He rubbed his leg gently as he watched the well-wishers dance. The brides and grooms cut the cake, and they put a piece in each other's mouths as people clapped and cheered.

"When do you think the commander and captain will tie the knot?" asked Shiran.

"I'm sure when the time is right," said Conor.

"That's not really an answer," stated Shiran.

"It's not really our business, snoopy." Conor grinned.

Shiran wrinkled her nose at him and held Conor closer. As the waltz ended, Shiran wanted to sit for a while. They sipped champagne and talked to Michael and Francesca. Well-wishers approached and stayed a short time before making room for others. When Conor finally felt up to it, he and Shiran returned to the dance floor. They danced slowly, enjoying each other's company, as the orange-tinted evening sun slowly sank beneath the horizon.

"The president and his cabinet made it," said Shiran.

"I noted that when they wished us well. Political," stated Conor.

"True. I'm sure they'd rather not be here."

"Wouldn't look good snubbing the wedding of the executive officer, especially with Captain Tamura and Commander Blankenship attending," said Conor.

Shiran nodded. "I heard that he was not going to let the foundry workers off to attend. Then Tom Tollifer threatened to lead a strike if he did so."

"I hadn't heard that," said Conor.

"Martinez relented on the condition. No one said a word about it," replied Shiran.

"How do you know?" asked Conor.

"Tom, silly," Shiran whispered in his ear.

"So what do you have in store for our honeymoon, darling?" Conor asked to change the subject.

"You'll see." Shiran smiled mischievously.

"I hope it doesn't involve a trek through the forest. I'm sore hurt," groaned Conor.

"No, but I have just the thing for that ailment." Shiran giggled.

"What?" inquired Conor apprehensively.

"You'll find out." Shiran smiled impishly.

"Somehow, I have the feeling it doesn't involve a lot of bed rest." Conor groaned again.

"You'll get plenty of that," stated Shiran. Then a look crossed her face, and she grinned. "Or perhaps not."

Conor decided to keep dancing as the waltz ended and another one began before his bride decided a honeymoon tucked away in a crammed longboat on the nearer moon was a good idea. It had its attractions, but the thought of eating military rations and the lack of facilities for a week or more didn't really appeal to him.

"I've heard that Bess Hollinger is going with Anarzej Gataki," stated Shiran.

"Are you snooping again?" asked Conor.

"No!" cried Shiran.

"So who's Martinez going with?" asked Conor.

"Now who's snooping?" demanded Shiran.

"Not me," stated Conor.

"He's been seen with Agnes Felter," said Shiran.

"Really?" demanded Conor.

"Rumor has it she's pregnant," replied Shiran.

"How about the rest of his cabinet?" asked Conor.

"Who knows?" replied Shiran. "There's Hiran."

"What about him?" asked Conor.

"I don't remember seeing him at the wedding or passing through the line to wish us well," said Shiran.

Conor thought about it and said, "He may have had business elsewhere, or maybe he was hungry."

"You're probably right," returned Shiran.

"When am I not?" asked Conor.

"More than you realize," replied Shiran, smiling.

Conor threw back his head and laughed, drawing questioning looks from others surrounding them on the dance floor. The dancing and drinking went on well into the evening. Finally, the brides and grooms decided to make their departure. They got up to more applause and cheers as they bid the remaining guests farewell. The two couples strolled to where the remaining prefabs stood. Conor and Shiran said good night to Michael and Francesca as the couples parted. Michael and Francesca went to the prefab that was now set aside for them until accommodations could be made for the couple in the colony residential area, while Conor and Shiran went to the MILDET prefab and their future together.

CHAPTER 40

The intruder had grown sick a couple of days after Qu'Loo'Oh' had rescued it and had remained that way for five days. A slick film of water covered the intruder's body during that time, making it stink. The intruder ate little and swallowed small beads from an unusual jar that was in its pack.

Two days after the sickness passed, the intruder went to the jar of water that Qu'Loo'Oh' refilled each day, filled a cup, and drank it. The intruder then shook the jar and slowly walked to Qu'Loo'Oh' with it. The intruder shook the jar again and looked at Qu'Loo'Oh', then walked to the room's door. The intruder looked back at Qu'Loo'Oh' expectantly, then shook the jar again.

Qu'Loo'Oh' thought about the actions of the intruder. It was obvious that it wanted more water. It was also obvious that it wanted to get the water itself. However, it didn't know the way to the stream for refilling the jar. Qu'Loo'Oh' got up from her nest and walked to the door and opened it. She stepped into the door-lined corridor and walked toward the main chamber. Reaching the main chamber, Qu'Loo'Oh' slowed and waited for the intruder to catch up. She led the intruder to the far end of the chamber and opened a door where a passage went deeper into the cliff.

They followed the passage. Doors lined the sides for nearly a hundred body lengths and then another five hundred body lengths further. They entered a chamber that was well lit by the ancient method of mirrors to bring in the sun. There, a pool of water lay with a stream feeding it, and a fish jumped as they watched.

Qu'Loo'Oh' led the intruder to the stream and showed her where to fill the jar. When the jar was full, the intruder started taking off the material that covered its soft pink flesh. When the intruder was finished, she eased herself into the water of the pool, allowing the inflowing stream to wash over her upper body and head. The creature appeared to enjoy the water even though it was icy cold from the glacial water source.

Qu'Loo'Oh' shrugged mentally. *Some creatures!* Then Qu'Loo'Oh' stalked down the edge of the pool, watching the water closely. When she was near the outflow of the pool on the other side of the pond, she stood silent, waiting. After some time, a fish swam near, and Qu'Loo'Oh' tensed. It swam closer, and Qu'Loo'Oh's forearm blurred, spearing the fish with her talons. She lifted it to her mouth and devoured it whole. She moved further along the edge, waited again, and was soon rewarded with another fish. Instead of devouring it, she returned to where the intruder sat and offered it to the intruder by placing it on the ground near her.

The intruder looked at Qu'Loo'Oh' but did not pick up the fish at first. Instead, it bowed its head and muttered some incomprehensible sounds. It then crawled out of the pond and picked up the fish, laying it near the now full jar that stood on the beach. The intruder then commenced wiping off its body with the clothes she had shed. Finished, the intruder then went to the pond and commenced washing them and wringing them out. This Qu'Loo'Oh' understood, for the females of her tribe washed weaved fabric also. Qu'Loo'Oh' went to catch another fish.

When she returned, the intruder had draped the material she had worn over her shoulder and had picked up the fish. She looked at Qu'Loo'Oh' and indicated the jar full of water with the puny digits of her feet.

A sound came out of its mouth. "Please."

Qu'Loo'Oh' understood that she was being asked to carry the jar for the weak stranger. She picked up the jar, and the two returned to Qu'Loo'Oh's room. The intruder placed the fish on the bench and the wet fabric near the fire to dry. Returning to the bench, the intruder picked up one of the knives and commenced gutting the fish. After it was finished with the task, it went over to the fire and placed what was left near it. She went back to the bench and picked up the remains and took them to the fireplace and threw them in the fire.

The intruder then spread ash across the floor near the fire and looked at Qu'Loo'Oh'. Qu'Loo'Oh' went over to the fireplace even though the stench of burnt flesh was nearly nauseating. The intruder looked at Qu'Loo'Oh' and pressed its forelimbs against its chest and said, "Rachel."

It did it again, saying the same sound. It then pressed its forelimbs against Qu'Loo'Oh's chest and looked at Qu'Loo'Oh' expectantly. Was the sound the intruder had made its name or the name of its kind? Qu'Loo'Oh' decided that it was the creature's name, and it wanted her name.

She said, "Qu'Loo'Oh'."

The intruder repeated her name a few times. Then the intruder started drawing. It made what was obviously a caricature of itself. Then underneath, it made several more of the same caricatures. It then drew a caricature of a Ques'Coat'L' and, underneath that one, drew several more. The intruder pointed at the lone picture of the caricatures of itself and repeated, "Rachel." Then it indicated all the caricatures of the intruders underneath and stated, "Humans."

Qu'Loo'Oh' understood and was happy she had made the right guess. Qu'Loo'Oh' pointed at the lone Ques'Coat'L' and then at herself and said, "Qu'Loo'Oh'." She then indicated all the caricatures of the Ques'Coat'L' underneath them at the walls and stated, "Ques'Coat'L'."

The lesson proceeded with the intruder checking the burning fish occasionally. By the time the intruder indicated that it was ready to eat the fish, the two knew ten words of each other's language. When the intruder finished its repast, it checked the material it had hung near the fire. It seemed satisfied that the material was dry and pulled it back over its body. Qu'Loo'Oh' could tell the creature was weary and pointed her taloned forelimb at the nest the creature had been using. The creature nodded, walking over to the nest where it lay down. Before it closed its eyes, it looked at Qu'Loo'Oh' and said, "Good night."

Qu'Loo'Oh' was not sure what that meant, but she repeated the sound, "Good night."

Time passed, and each day was a new lesson in the intruder's language. As the lessons progressed, Qu'Loo'Oh' learned much more about the creature. She understood that the creature came from the sky and now lived behind the silvery web that surrounded the west side of the lake and in the niche of the cliff above the lake.

She also understood that the intruder was the female of her kind. She wondered what the eggs of the intruder looked like. The intruder had informed her that she did not lay eggs, but Qu'Loo'Oh' found that preposterous. What animal did not lay eggs to produce more of their kind? Only a few animals did not lay eggs, and they were the small fuzzy eggeaters and the like. Although it was suspected that the ancient enemy did not lay eggs also.

She also came to understand that the new beasts that the intruders brought with them were not beasts. Rachel had brokenly explained that the beasts were like her fire sticks. They were tools to move them. When Qu'Loo'Oh' had asked how it was done, the intruder did not have the words to explain. However, Rachel did explain that her people used simple tools also. In fact, there were still people of Rachel's kind who still used beasts for work and to move.

Qu'Loo'Oh' considered this. There were those of her people who herded beasts, raised them, and culled the herds. However, using them for work and to move across the land was rarely done. It occurred to her one day that the Old Ones must have known how to make the tools that the humans used in place of beasts. If so, perhaps the Old Ones also learned to use the beasts for such purposes too before creating the tools to replace them. If so, perhaps someday her people could learn to tame the beasts and use them for such purposes.

Time passed, and the lessons between Qu'Loo'Oh' and the intruder were going well. They could now communicate over five hundred different ideas between each other. The lessons had been slow at first because the intruder was weak and slept a lot, but as her strength increased, they had more time for lessons. The intruder also went to the pond now every day and washed. The stink was almost bearable when the creature cleaned, and she carried the water jar every day also.

A moon's time passed in the sacred chambers, and the intruder's injuries had mostly healed, and it had removed the unusual sticks and material from her arm a couple of days ago. The forelimb of the intruder had shrunk in size and looked sickly compared to the other. Even so, the intruder picked a piece of wood from the woodpile and started lifting the wood and lowering it with the misshapen forelimb.

The intruder asked how to leave the sanctuary, and Qu'Loo'Oh' made it clear that it was unsafe to leave the sanctuary at this time. When asked why, Qu'Loo'Oh' tried to make clear that it was the time of the sacred hunt and would encompass the time of three moons for her people and that it would be better to wait. The intruder didn't seem to understand, but she was still weak, and Qu'Loo'Oh' was finally able to convince her to wait.

A few days after the intruder had removed the sticks from its arm, Qu'Loo'Oh' decided to distract the intruder from her desire to leave too soon. She led the intruder to the main chamber and to the passage that went to the pool. Instead of going to the pool, Qu'Loo'Oh' took her through the third door to the right. After a short walk, they entered a large well-lit room with a table in the center. The walls were lined with carefully drilled holes where scrolls resided that had been stored for ages. Some were so frail that it was impossible to pick them up without destroying them.

The intruder's eyes grew wide with astonishment as they fell on the scrolls that could very well go back to the days Qu'Loo'Oh's ancestors came to this world. Qu'Loo'Oh' spent time trying to make the intruder understand that some records could not be touched without them falling to dust. Rachel appeared to understand and asked Qu'Loo'Oh' where she might look. Qu'Loo'Oh' led Rachel to the more recent scrolls and removed one from the wall. It was a text on the basics of Qu'Loo'Oh's language. Qu'Loo'Oh' went over to the corner and removed another scroll and a jar, which she laid beside the first. It was a blank scroll, and after removing the lid from the small jar, Qu'Loo'Oh' dipped a talon of her right forelimb into it.

Qu'Loo'Oh' proceeded to draw the alphabet that Rachel had shown her in the ashes.

The routine of Rachel exercising her arm several times a day continued, and Qu'Loo'Oh' noted the muscle mass increased with time. They also continued the trips to the pond with a stop at the library for more lessons. By the end of the second month of Rachel's rescue by Qu'Loo'Oh', they could understand over three thousand words in each other's language. They both learned to read and write in each other's language too.

Qu'Loo'Oh' learned that Rachel arrived on a ship and was amazed to find out that Rachel was from one of the distant stars. Qu'Loo'Oh' found this hard to believe even though the legends of her people carried the same message. But then she had never seen a creature like Rachel or the beasts and tools they used. More amazing was that Rachel told her that they had come here by accident and could not leave because the machine that had brought her and her kind here was broken beyond their ability to repair. They had no choice but to establish a place to live on this world.

Rachel also told her that each of the stars in the night sky were suns, like the sun that warmed her world, only very far away. When Qu'Loo'Oh' asked how far away stars were, Rachel told her that it varied because the stars moved through the heavens. That the heavens were like a big pond in which the sands were stirred up in and that each grain of sand was like a star, only vaster and with more space between each star, and that it took light-years to travel between them. Since they had already discussed units of measure, Qu'Loo'Oh' asked how fast light traveled and was in disbelief that light could travel as fast as Rachel stated. Rachel also told her that the light from the star Rachel came from would take thousands of years to reach this world. Exactly how long, Rachel did not know, since the year for Qu'Loo'Oh's world was longer by another half a year compared to the world Rachel came from, but she believed it would take around six and a half thousand years.

Qu'Loo'Oh' contemplated all this while she taught Rachel the ancient legends of her people—how they had escaped the destruction of their world by the ancient enemy and fled in a ship, how the voyage it was said had taken over a million years to find a new home, only to be discovered again by the ancient enemy after a long period of peace that was rumored to have lasted thousands of years. There had been a battle in the skies and mountains rained upon the world. The ancient enemy was defeated, but much of what her people had built and accomplished had been destroyed, along with the ship that had brought them here. When Rachel asked how long ago the destruction had happened, Qu'Loo'Oh' could not tell her. She only knew that it was a very long time ago.

CHAPTER 41

The honeymoon wasn't exactly the type of matrimonial bliss Conor Raybourn had always imagined as he picked up the next brick to mortar into place. He looked up to watch his new bride, Shiran Raybourn, being instructed by Hiroka Tamura in the art of the sword. Even though Shiran was already starting to show, there was a grace in the way she held the wooden training sword that Sergeant Tadashi Adachi had made for her. She had been training for nearly a month now, and the movements Hiroka had been helping her develop seemed to come more and more easily to her.

Conor lifted another brick into place and set it on the mortar, gently tapping the top so the brick set up against the cement wall. There were four baths with smooth cut stone on the inside of the building, along with a sauna. Hiroka said the idea had come to her after a day of talking about girl things with some female Marines. Conor didn't understand, and all Shiran did was grin when he asked her to explain what Hiroka had meant.

Each bath pool could hold two hundred liters of water, and each was in a separate room that had hooks and a stone bench to the side for dressing and undressing. The commander sent down equipment that could heat the lines of each faucet to a desired temperature, and Anarzej Gataki donated the cut stone for the baths as an advertisement scheme for new customers in his start-up business.

Hiroka was not limiting her enterprise to simply baths though and had been raising flowers and spices for soaps and candles, which were displayed in the forum leading to the baths. She had about a dozen different scents to utilize at this time, and Conor discovered that they were quite popular with a large number of the colonists who were looking forward to a change. While it was true that the *New Horizon* factory could produce these things for the colonists, many of them preferred to use items actually made in the colony. This was partly because it gave them something to keep them occupied and that the ship might not be able to produce them in the distant future.

Conor bent to pick up another brick and felt a sharp twinge in his thigh. He sat down and rubbed his thigh, massaging the muscle. It had almost been a month since the attack in the forest, and the doctor had taken his cane. She had told him in no uncertain terms that he needed to work that muscle back into shape but take it easy. It now only hurt when he had been on it too long or was overexerting himself. He decided that it was time to take a break.

"Time for a break, Conor?" asked Commander Hadden Blankenship's voice from behind him.

"I think so, sir," replied Conor.

"We're not in uniform. Call me Hadden or Blankenship," replied Hadden as he handed Conor a beer.

"All right, Hadden," said Conor.

"That's better. How's the leg?" questioned Hadden.

"Better. Still bothers me if I do too much," replied Conor.

"Bess said you shouldn't notice it at all in another two or three weeks if you continue working it like you have," said Hadden.

"I hope so," said Conor.

"I want to thank you and Shiran for helping out around here. Hiroka really appreciates the help, and so do I," said Hadden.

"It's nothing, sir. We enjoy helping out," interjected Shiran as she patted the now noticeable bulge of her abdomen.

"Are you sure you should be doing so much, Shiran?" asked Hadden.

"I'm not that pregnant yet," retorted Shiran.

Hadden Blankenship chuckled and looked at Hiroka Tamura as she came out of the house with a setting of tea for her and Shiran Raybourn. It was obvious that Commander Blankenship was loosening up and relaxing. He'd been here for the last two days without having any urgent ship or colony business interfere with his time off. Before that, he had to go to the MILDET or Marine Complex to take care of business because the president of the colony made it a point of making everything an emergency that needed attention ASAP.

The commander's last row with the president ended with the commander threatening to recall all military members back to active duty if the president couldn't run his colony without military assistance every day. Perhaps it was just the calm before the storm, but it was nice not having a care in the world, even if it were just for a few days. Even Michael Anderson was enjoying his much-anticipated honeymoon and spent some time with Conor putting bricks on top of each other when he wasn't helping his new bride, Francesca, at the Bookworm.

Conor Raybourn took a swig of his beer and settled back to take in the midday sun. Hadden and Hiroka talked about how fast the garden plots were coming along and the work on the baths being built along the eastern wall on the other side of Hiroka's home. The subject turned to expanding the home so there would be more room for the two, but Hiroka wished to finish the gardens first.

"I think it's time for lunch," stated Hadden as he finished his beer.

"I will go make it," said Hiroka.

"No! You and everyone are going to wash up," stated Hadden.

"I can make it," stated Hiroka.

"I already had Ezekiel make us something, and it'll be ready in thirty minutes." Hadden smiled.

"You didn't have to do that," said Hiroka and Shiran together.

"I wanted to. I've already informed Michael and Francesca. Now off with the three of you. Freshen up, and we'll meet at the Overlook in thirty minutes," stated Hadden as he grinned.

The couples left to their respective accommodations where they freshened up and changed clothes. They met outside their prefabs and strolled down to the Overlook. By the time they reached the door, they knew more than a simple dinner was planned.

Most of the Marines were there, along with many Navy personnel and civilians. When the couples entered, there was clapping and whistles. Ezekiel was smiling as they entered. He came forward and escorted the couples to the back table where Hadden and Hiroka sat.

"Your guests of honor are here, Commander." Ezekiel smiled.

"I guessed that, Ezekiel. Thank you," said Hadden.

"What is this, Commander?" asked Conor.

"Family reception after the official reception," replied Hadden.

"Family?" queried Michael.

"Michael, these people will do almost anything for all of you. I think that rates as family more than you realize," Hadden replied.

"Even me?" asked Francesca.

"Francesca, you've always reported the facts objectively in your daily news, letting the people decide. Then there's the collection of books you've supplied to the *New Horizon*, the Marine Complex, and the MILDET. So yes, most especially you," said Hadden vehemently.

"I was just doing my job and helping out," responded Francesca.

"And that's the point, Francesca," replied Hadden.

"So where do we go from here?" asked Francesca.

"Into the future," stated Hadden as he raised his wineglass and stood up. He tapped his glass to gain the attention of those gathered in the room. When the room grew quiet, he addressed those gathered. "I'd like to propose a toast," stated Commander Hadden Blankenship.

"Hear! Hear!" came the reply from those gathered.

"My friends, may we live well in this new world. To the future, my friends!" said Hadden Blankenship.

"To the future!" came the response with much clapping.

The meal was excellent and comprised of spaghetti marinara, a salad, bread, and wine. There was talking and laughter during and after the meal. The honeymoon couples made rounds to the various tables and were congratulated once again. Master Sergeant Evan Zander and Chief Petty Officer Tami Zander had the twins—named them Eric and Harold—there, so Shiran Raybourn and Francesca Anderson had to hold them.

Bess Hollinger was there with Anarzej Gataki and her associate, Dr. Kers Joshi. Ensign Dominic Sobolov was sitting with Maria DiAngelo, an astrophysicist from the science department. Gunnery

Sergeant Samuel Rusu was sitting with Staff Sergeant Amanda Hall, while Corporal Joseph Green and Corporal Natalie Hoffman were sitting together. Even Brad Guillete was there sitting at a table with three other Marines.

Time passed as people changed tables to talk to the others gathered in the Overlook. Drinks were brought, and a card game had started that people gathered around to play and watch. Sergeant Tadashi Adachi and Brad Guillete were at a corner table in the front playing chess, with Dominic Sobolov and Maria DiAngelo doing the same at the opposite front corner table. Francesca produced dominoes from the bag she had. Ezekiel and Roberta cleared away the dishes and cleaned the tabletop for those sitting there to participate.

"This isn't supposed to be a working dinner," said Hadden Blankenship hesitantly as the table was being cleared for the upcoming game.

"It's all right, sir," replied Conor.

"I don't want to alarm you, but the last longboat reported that there were over fifty ships moored at the mouth of the river, and they saw at least three more making for the estuary. Hattie confirmed the report after examining the ship's visual logs. There were fifty-seven ships altogether," stated Commander Blankenship.

"That's not good," said Shiran Raybourn.

"There is no big rush. However, in a week or so, I want Conor to take an expedition to the coast by helicopter and recon the area for intel on these raptors," said the commander.

"Mission requirements, sir?" asked Lieutenant Commander Conor Raybourn.

"Chopper outfitted as a gunship with a four-man crew. The other chopper to be outfitted the same with a two-man crew on ready alert at the Marine Complex to assist if you run into troubles. I want two members of each crew flight qualified so there is a relief pilot if necessary," said Hadden.

"Yes, sir," replied Conor.

"I want Joseph Green on the recon chopper so he can take samples," added Hadden.

"I understand," said Conor. "If we're attacked?"

"We're not out to start a war. This is only recon," stated Commander Hadden Blankenship. "If you're attacked, retreat."

"Just recon, sir?" queried Conor.

"We need to know more about their capabilities. They're obviously not from the island, or we would have seen them before now. They have ships capable of crossing the channel from the mainland to the island. Capturing one for interrogation isn't an option because no one knows their language. So observation of their activities appears to be the only viable option," replied the commander.

"Why not take a longboat to the mainland?" asked Lieutenant Michael Anderson.

"Can we be sure these raptors represent the peak of their technology? We can't afford to lose a longboat and its crew at this time. No. We need knowledge of what's in front of us and not go looking for more right now. If there are raptors with advanced technology, say, with muskets and canons, could we hold them off if they attacked in numbers? I don't think so. What if they were even more advanced with rifled semiautomatics and capable of flight? Our only hope would be to abandon the planet if they chose to attack. How long would we or our children be safe even then?" said Commander Hadden Blankenship.

The table fell silent as the prospects of the commander's statement sank in. The people of the colony had put a lot of work into the growing city they now lived in. Uprooting them to live somewhere else was not a thought many would relish. If they had to abandon the planet, life would be even more difficult, because building habitats to live in would take more time and resources than living on a world already suitable for human habitation.

CHAPTER 42

Gunnery Sergeant Samuel Rusu watched the forest intently as the foundry ATV loaded the trailer. Security for the mining operation had been increased after the attack on the recon team. There were now six Marines providing security; before, there had been none. Prior to this, the mining crew were responsible, with the Marines only giving training and advice. The forest had been cleared out for fifty meters from the mining site when it had been started, but Samuel Rusu felt that another fifty meters should be added. Samuel ported arms as he shifted his feet. He was uncomfortable. It was too quiet, and something just didn't feel right.

He looked at Sergeant Nikolai Ivankov and saw the sergeant looked uncomfortable also. There was a tenseness there, and when Nikolai turned to look at Samuel, he nodded, pointing with his chin at the forest. Samuel edged over to Nikolai as he watched the forest like a hawk.

"Have Hoffman get inside the ATV. Tell her to keep sharp and provide cover through the port," muttered Samuel.

"Roger that, Gunny," replied Nikolai.

The gunnery sergeant walked to the far side of the ATV as the loader dumped another scoop of coal into the trailer. The trailers were nearly full, and Samuel hoped their luck would hold. President Martinez tried to order them to attach a trailer to the Marine ATV, but the second lieutenant was having none of it. Shiran told the president she took orders from Commander Blankenship and that he needed to talk to her boss. Shiran then contacted Commander Blankenship, who told the president that his Marines were there to provide security and that they could not do that effectively if overburdened by a trailer attached to the Marine ATV.

The gunny looked back along the road that led to the Compound as he reached the far side of the Marine ATV. One of the civilians hopped out of the ATV with the loader and was checking something about the trailer. It was Philip Roe, and he wasn't carrying the Navarro M-71 that all mining workers were issued when they left the Compound. Samuel Rusu growled under his breath. The loader started to pick up another scoop as the man looked at the axle of the trailer. When Philip saw Samuel approach, he stopped and waited.

"What the hell do you think you're doing?" growled Gunnery Sergeant Rusu.

"Checking the axles and getting ready to direct the ATV for hookup so we can go back to the Compound and unload," stated Philip Roe.

"Where the hell's your firearm and body armor?" demanded Samuel.

Philip pointed at the ATV and said, "There."

"What the hell good is it going to do you there if a raptor comes after you?" growled Samuel.

"I don't know. We've never been attacked here before," said Philip Roe. Then he looked at Samuel and added, "Isn't that what you're here for?"

"Get back to the loader and get your goddamned body armor and weapon now!" ordered Samuel.

The man looked shocked. "But I have to check things and get ready to direct the hookup."

"I don't care! If you don't go get your weapon right now, I'm going to take my Marines back to the Compound. We have better things to do than babysit a bunch of idiots who want to get themselves killed," growled Samuel Rusu.

"You can't do that!" shouted Philip.

"Watch me," growled the gunnery sergeant.

"Fine! I'll go get it," muttered Philip.

The man stomped off toward the loader ATV, shaking his head and muttering. Samuel Rusu watched as Philip entered the foundry

ATV. A few minutes passed as Samuel watched the surrounding forest, then Ethan Sanders hopped out a moment later, wearing body armor with an M-71 slung from his shoulder. Ethan approached Samuel with an angry look on his face as he went to check the axles. When he was finished, the loader returned and dumped its load into the trailer. It wheeled around and went to be hitched up as Ethan went to direct the operation. Philip Roe finally appeared at the hatch of the ATV and looked at Samuel Rusu then Ethan Sanders.

"Ready?" yelled Philip.

"Yeah!" Ethan yelled back.

"Then let's do this!" shouted Philip.

Just then, gunfire sounded from the far side of the Marine ATV. The muted sound of another M-71 joined in as Corporal Natalie Hoffman opened fire from inside the Marine ATV. Gunnery Sergeant Rusu ran forward and pushed Ethan Sanders toward the loader ATV hatch and yelled, "Get in!" A javelin thudded into the ground beside them. There was a scream of pain from the loader's hatch as Philip Roe fell back into the ATV with a javelin protruding from his chest.

Samuel Rusu turned and provided cover for Ethan as he ran to the loader ATV hatch. Ethan was just getting ready to close the hatch when a javelin pierced his left leg. He fell into the loader ATV, and another hand reached out and pulled the hatch closed.

Something hit Samuel Rusu in the back and bounce off as he ran toward the Marine ATV. He climbed in, slamming the hatch behind him, as two more javelins hit the side of the ATV. Samuel opened a gunport, stuck the muzzle of his M-71 out, and fired at the two raptors standing at the forest's edge. A red raptor flipped backward, clawing at its chest, as the rounds from Samuel's M-71 found their target. The other red raptor quickly faded back into the forest while the first was in its death throes.

Muted weapons fire was now coming from the other ATVs with trailers that were lined up on the road back to the Compound. The ATVs blocked Samuel's view of the forest. Corporal Natalie Hoffman was firing short bursts from the front passenger seat. The hatch on the opposite side of the ATV quickly opened, and Sergeant Nikolai

Ivankov jumped in. A thud sounded on the hatch as it slammed shut behind him.

"You hit?" growled Gunnery Sergeant Rusu as another thud sounded on the same hatch.

"No. Just another fun-filled day in the life of a Marine, Gunny." Nikolai grinned grimly.

"Yeah. Tell me about it." Samuel chuckled as he switched gears.

"Can they attach that rig without having someone direct them?" asked Nikolai as he opened a port and pointed his M-71 out, then fired.

"I guess we'll find out shortly," replied Samuel. "Abrams, bring us around so we can cover the loader from the other side."

"Roger that, Gunny!" shouted Lance Corporal Abrams.

Samuel watched as the loader ATV readjusted haltingly and slowly backed toward the loader.

Javelins rained down on the ATVs as they waited for the loader ATV to attach to its trailer. The clangs of metal hitting metal continued for less than a minute. The Marine ATV opened fire with the minigun mounted on the roof. Leaves and feathers filled the air where the stream of high-velocity rounds passed. The radio crackled as the trailer finally clicked into place with the loader ATV.

"Philip is dead, and I have a spear through my leg!" screamed the voice of Ethan Sanders over the comm.

"What? How?" came a disembodied voice obviously from the other foundry ATV.

"Philip has a spear in his chest. He just died!" came Ethan's scream.

"Where the hell were the Marines?" growled the other voice.

"Telling us how to do our job," stated Ethan's voice.

Gunnery Sergeant Rusu hit his comm and growled, "This is Gunny Rusu. Your man died of his own stupidity. Now cut the chatter, and let's get this caravan back to the Marine Complex."

"Who the hell do you think you are? I'm the boss here!" demanded the voice.

"And if you'd been doing your job, Philip Roe's death may not have happened. He wasn't wearing body armor or carrying his M-71 when I told him to get back into the ATV," growled Samuel Rusu.

"It's your job to protect us," retorted the voice.

"I'm not going to argue with you about this. We were assigned as added security because of the increased threat. Therefore, I run security and say where and what we do when outside the fence. If you don't like that, then take it up with your superiors," growled Gunnery Sergeant Rusu.

"I will!" cried the voice.

"Now if we're all set to go, let's get this caravan back to the Compound," ordered Samuel.

"All right," said the voice. "But I'm taking this up with your superiors."

"I'm sure you will," muttered Samuel.

The caravan moved along the dirt road in silence as Gunnery Sergeant Rusu radioed ahead to inform Second Lieutenant Raybourn about the incident and have medics waiting upon their arrival at the elevators. They were traveling through the forest when they ran into more problems. A tree was across the path, blocking their return. Gunnery Sergeant Rusu looked over the situation. The IR, or infrared scanner, revealed that there were raptors hiding in the forest on both sides of the tree. Samuel shook his head. He could clear them out with the minigun but decided that would waste ammunition.

"Sergeant, break out the IR scopes. You take one and give me the other," ordered Samuel.

Clipping on the IR scope Nikolai Ivankov handed him, he took aim out the port on his side. Two raptors dropped before the others on that side realized the danger and left. The sergeant had three down before his side cleared out also. The IR scanner read clear for over two hundred meters.

"Corporal Hoffman, Q-5 while we cover," ordered Samuel Rusu.

The corporal was out the door and ran to the trunk of the tree. She placed three Q-5 charges and came back. A moment later, the ATV pushed through the remains of the mutilated tree with the caravan close behind. They entered the plains area, and Samuel saw something that was yellow and blue in the distant tree line across the plain. Taking binoculars from storage, Samuel saw red and green raptors raising what appeared to be a tent near the far tree line.

The last twenty-three kilometers to the Compound gate passed uneventfully. Gunnery Sergeant Rusu knew that there would be trouble when they arrived. It was bad enough worrying about the new raptor threat they were facing. Unfortunately, it seemed as though some colonists just wouldn't listen to reason. Now there was a dead miner in the caravan, and he already knew the Marines were going to be held accountable for it. They passed through the gate and quickly approached the Marine Complex where a crowd was waiting.

The body of Philip Roe and the injured man Ethan Sanders were loaded into stretchers by the doctors and nurses. Felipe Martinez and his cabinet were there and talked to one of the men from the work crew. The voice on the comms was Hector Lopez, the mining boss, who was red-faced and pointing at the Marine ATV.

"What happened?" asked Second Lieutenant Shiran Raybourn.

"Ambush. Philip Roe wasn't wearing his body armor or carrying his firearm, ma'am," stated Samuel.

"He was outside the ATV?" asked Shiran.

"He was at first. I sent him back, and Ethan Sanders came out. Philip Roe was at an open door without armor or firearm when the attack began. He fell back inside, skewered through the chest," stated Samuel Rusu.

Second Lieutenant Raybourn shook her head and muttered, "Idiot!"

"Somehow, I don't think this is going to go well for the Marines, ma'am," stated Samuel Rusu.

Second Lieutenant Shiran Raybourn looked at President Felipe Martinez and the mining boss before saying, "I think you might be right, Gunny."

CHAPTER 43

Lieutenant Commander Conor Raybourn and Second Lieutenant Shiran Raybourn were with Lieutenant Michael Anderson and his wife, Francesca, for an evening meal at the Overlook. Master Sergeant Evan Zander and Chief Petty Officer Tami Zander had shown up and joined them. Shiran and Francesca started a conversation about childbirth with Tami, asking what to expect and who provided the best care when needed.

As they talked, Conor noticed that nearly half the Marines were there also, clustered at tables in front of the lieutenant commander's group, dressed in civilian clothing. He would have thought nothing special of this since some were eating and some were drinking, but some appeared to be watching, waiting for something. Conor noticed that the master sergeant's smile did not reach his eyes, which scanned the door regularly as though he, too, was expecting trouble. The master sergeant became aware of Conor's unease and made a silent signal with the fingers of his right hand indicating danger.

The men were having an after-dinner drink while they all carefully avoided the subject of the recent mining incident. Francesca was leading the discussion of the local gossip and occurrences when about a dozen people from the foundry and mining operations entered. They sat down at a couple of empty tables at the far end of the counter and ordered drinks.

The Overlook grew silent, and there was a visible sign of tension that seemed to emanate from the new group. A few of the customers must have sensed something and quietly paid their bills, then left. Finally, Norman Pool, who worked at the foundry, looked around at those gathered in the Overlook as his eyes lighted upon the Marines sitting across the room. A wicked smile crossed his face.

"Well, well, what do we have here, United Systems' finest," cried Normal Pool sneeringly.

"Finest? Look like a bunch of losers to me," came a voice from behind Norman.

"That's what the fliers say back in Sol system," protested Ethan Sanders, who sat beside Norman Pool.

"Stupid grunts can't even handle simple security from what I hear!" shouted another voice behind them.

"Well, that's no surprise considering the bumbling idiots who run the operation around here," stated Norman Pool as he looked at the table where Conor and the others sat.

The Marines sat at their tables looking at the provocateurs with no expressions on their faces. A couple more customers silently slipped out the front door as the two groups sat glaring at each other.

"Please, no trouble," said Ezekiel Yap, stepping around the counter to confront Norman Pool.

"Why should we listen to you, gook?" demanded Norman Pool.

"Please, no trouble. Please leave," pleaded Ezekiel.

"So now our business isn't good enough for you?" demanded Norman Pool.

"He has a soft spot for these losers!" shouted one of the voices from the back.

"Yeah? Well, that makes him a loser too," stated Ethan Sanders.

Ezekiel had stepped forward by this time to confront Norman Pool, who sat toward the middle of the provocateurs. He was waving his hands and repeating his plea as a couple of the industrial workers slipped behind him. Master Sergeant Zander saw the move and started to get up from the table, but he was too late. Norman Pool stood and pushed Ezekiel back as one of them put out a leg behind Ezekiel's lower legs. Ezekiel's momentum carried him back as he tripped over the legs. His shoulder hit the edge of a table as Ezekiel tumbled to the floor.

Once Ezekiel was on the floor, the man who had provided the immovable object for the setup aimed a kick at Ezekiel's head. The kick didn't connect, but Evan Zander's right fist did with the assailant's nose. The group of industrial workers stood with ugly looks on their faces, and chairs pushed back too quickly overturned. Two men jumped toward Evan as the rest of the party suddenly realized they were surrounded.

A man flew back and landed on top of a table, turning it over, when Sergeant Tadashi Adachi kicked him in the stomach. Another lay on the floor, possibly unconscious, with a broken nose from Corporal Natalie Hoffman. Staff Sergeant Amanda Hall grabbed another man by one arm and slammed him headfirst against the wall with a knee applied to the groin as he went down to his knees, reaching to defend his manhood. While he was down, Amanda applied a bottle to the back of his head, and he lay down on the floor like a felled tree.

Conor started losing track of everything occurring as a man and woman headed toward the table where he and his friends sat. The woman, Wilma Nolan, confronted Michael Anderson, and Conor saw Michael hesitate to his undoing as a bottle from her left hand swung wide, colliding with the left side of his head. Michael went down as Wilma raised the bottle again to apply to the back of his head. Just then, a dart appeared in her chest, and Wilma looked down and said, shocked, "Oh!" as she crumpled to the floor.

The man's name who approached Conor was Heath Stills, and he punched Conor in the stomach while he was distracted, bringing Conor's attention back to him. Conor bent over the pain in his stomach as Heath placed another blow to his head, which probably caused Heath more pain than Conor, since something audibly cracked and the man yelled in pain. Heath danced cradling his right hand, while Conor grabbed Heath's hips and pulled himself up quickly, so the top of his head collided with Heath's nose. Conor let go as Heath went over backward. Then a dart appeared in Heath's arm as he lay on the floor, and he went limp. Conor turned toward the table where the three pregnant women still sat. Chief Petty Officer Zander placed a magazine on the tabletop beside Shiran as she calmly stood with her Gerst S-7 pointing toward the brawl.

"Sleepy darts," stated Tami Zander.

Shiran took out her Gerst from somewhere unseen. She took out the loaded magazine, then racked back the slide to ensure the weapon was clear. Picking up the new magazine, Shiran checked the rounds before inserting the magazine into her Gerst S-7. Chambering the first round, she shot a woman in the back who was approaching Evan Zander from behind. The woman's hand reached toward her back as she turned with a confused look on her face and fell to the floor. Evan reached down and grabbed Ezekiel by the shoulders and placed him on his feet with a slap on his shoulder.

Then Evan Zander waded through the skirmishers, distributing well-placed punches, as he approached the spot where Amanda lay on the floor being choked by a woman. He grabbed the woman's shoulders and squeezed, causing the woman to release her hold. A dart appeared in the woman's arm as Evan lifted her, and she went limp. The fighting was winding down with the Marines shoving people into a circle as Shiran Raybourn and Tami Zander shot the more belligerent with sleepy darts. Evan handed the limp woman to one of the group being pushed to the center of the room as Ezekiel offered his hand to help Amanda stand.

Second Lieutenant Shiran Raybourn had Norman Pool brought to her when the group quieted and demanded, "What's this all about, Mr. Pool?"

"It's about a dead man the Marines should have been protecting!" Norman Pool sneered as he spat at the second lieutenant, hitting her on the chest.

Shiran looked down at the drool on her shirt in disgust then at Norman Pool. She was tempted to lash out with her pistol and take the smirk off Pool's face. "If your men followed simple safety precautions, that man might still be alive," Shiran responded heatedly.

The sheriff, James Upton, and his deputies arrived as the beleaguered hung their heads or helped their fellows. The sheriff stood there looking at the Marines, dumbfounded. It was obvious from his demeanor that he had expected to confront a completely different scenario than the one he found in the Overlook. He looked at one of his deputies and muttered something, and the deputy took off running as the sheriff walked further into the Overlook.

"Is there a problem, Sheriff?" asked Conor.

"Who started this?" returned the sheriff.

Conor looked at the man for a moment, then replied, indicating the people surrounded by Marines. "Mr. Pool and this group. I hope your deputy went to get the doctor because some of them might need assistance," replied Conor.

"That didn't answer my question," retorted James Upton.

"What answer are you looking for?" asked Conor.

"Mr. Pool, who started this?" asked the sheriff, looking past Conor.

"That man right there!" shouted Norman Pool as he pointed toward Master Sergeant Evan Zander, who looked back at him levelly with a glint in his eyes. "He hit Jacob Valdez after the owner stumbled, and we attempted to render assistance," added Ethan Sanders.

"That true?" asked the sheriff, looking at Jacob.

"Damn right he broke my nose. All we were trying to do was help poor old Ezekiel," replied Jacob.

Conor looked at Pool then the sheriff and said, "That's not what happened."

"I'm just a sheriff. I'm afraid I have to place Zander there under arrest," stated James Upton.

"Are you going to take any other statements about what occurred?" asked Conor.

"No. Why should I?" responded the sheriff.

"To find the truth," replied Conor.

"I already have that," retorted the sheriff.

The president's voice sounded from the doorway as he stepped into the Overlook, followed by the deputy and several others. "What the hell's going on here?"

The sheriff looked relieved and responded, "I'm placing Master Sergeant Zander under arrest for assault and battery and disturbing the peace."

"Then do it!" shouted President Felipe Martinez.

"I don't think so," growled Lieutenant Commander Raybourn as the Marines looked daggers at Felipe Martinez.

"Put that man under arrest too!" screamed President Martinez, pointing at Conor.

"On what charges?'" growled Conor.

"Obstructing justice," sneered Felipe.

"Try it," said Shiran sweetly as she inserted a new magazine of sleepy darts into her Gerst S-7 and racked the slide. Martinez took a step back as his attention was directed at the weapon being held by the second lieutenant.

"Sheriff, place this rabble all under arrest!" shouted Felipe as he swept his arm around the room, indicating the Marines.

"How do you propose he do that, Mr. President, and where do you intend to confine us?" asked Lieutenant Commander Conor Raybourn.

"Are you disobeying lawful orders?" shouted Felipe.

"If they were lawful, we wouldn't be at this impasse," growled Conor as Shiran pointed her Gerst in the president's direction.

President Felipe Martinez's face turned pale as he backed up watching Shiran. "I'm the president of the colony. If you have a grievance, then it can be accessed in a court of your peers," squeaked Felipe Martinez.

"Who would those peers be?" asked Conor.

"Chosen citizens," Martinez replied firmly.

"Chosen by who?" asked Second Lieutenant Shiran Raybourn, still pointing her Gerst in Martinez's direction.

"Myself and my cabinet of course," stated the president.

"Mr. Pool over there is part of your cabinet, and he's instrumental in starting all of this," replied Lieutenant Commander Conor Raybourn.

"I'm sure that's not the story he tells," retorted President Martinez.

"You're right, it isn't, which is why he and his friends are no longer welcome in this establishment," interjected Ezekiel, folding his arms across his chest.

"What?" demanded several voices.

"That includes the sheriff and his deputy," added Ezekiel Yap, looking heatedly at the dejected group surrounded by the Marines. He then added, "Do you wish to be included, Mr. President?"

"You can't do that! This is a public area!" shouted Felipe Martinez.

"This is a private establishment, and I reserve the right to serve only those I chose to serve," stated Ezekiel heatedly.

"I suggest that these people leave and not come back," stated Shiran forcefully.

"This is a free society. They can go where they wish," Felipe responded.

"Get out! Do not come back," stated Ezekiel.

"I would suggest they freely go to the clinic to have the doctor have a look at their injuries," stated Shiran, motioning the group surrounded by the Marines toward the door.

"They can't do this," said Felipe Martinez as he looked at Conor.

"It would appear, Mr. President, that they just did," replied Conor.

"What are we supposed to do now?" asked Felipe.

"Perhaps you would like to help these people to the clinic?" Conor suggested to Felipe and the sheriff as he gestured toward the group. He knew that Martinez had meant something different with that question but refused to acknowledge it. Felipe Martinez stood there red-faced. There was shuffling and movement in the ranks of those surrounded by the Marines but no protests. It seemed the aggression they had arrived with had been replaced by defeat.

The president glared at Conor, then walked over to where Norman Pool sat. Those able assisted others as they left the Overlook. Once they were gone, the Marines commenced putting things in order without a word. Tables and chairs were righted, while brooms, mops, and sponges seemed to appear by magic. Within half an hour, the mess created by the ruckus had been corrected, and people were sitting and drinking with talk of how their day had gone.

"I think there's more to it than a man being killed," said Shiran after they were seated at their table in the back of the Overlook.

"There will be repercussions," stated Conor, worry lines creasing his forehead.

"There's always repercussions. That was a setup that backfired," replied Shiran.

"It was aimed at us. Ezekiel just got in the way," inserted Evan Zander.

"Why?" asked Michael.

"Power play," stated Francesca.

The group sat in silence contemplating the meaning of the incident as Ezekiel brought them fresh drinks. Francesca was right about it being a power play, but Conor felt the motives and reasons were unclear. Felipe Martinez was already the president of the colony. There was more to it than Martinez and the others looking for revenge for the dead man in the mining operation. Forcing a confrontation between the miners and Marines was not in his best interests. It was almost as though an unseen opponent was manipulating the colonists into turning on each other. Conor shook his head in an attempt to get rid of the thought. Was he imagining trouble where there was none? He took a sip of whiskey and glanced at Evan Zander, who was watching him closely. Evan gave him a slight nod as though acknowledging those thoughts.

CHAPTER 44

Commander Hadden Blankenship and Lieutenant Commander Conor Raybourn were having a working lunch at the Overlook. They had spent most of the morning discussing security issues, policies, supply issues, and events that affected all. After the recent presidential meeting with the people, the commander wanted to ensure that he and his second-in-command were on the same page as they conducted business with the colony.

The two ordered the special, which consisted of strips of apatosaurus marinated in a sauce, served with rice, a side of peas, and a biscuit. It was delicious, and both men complimented Ezekiel on his culinary abilities. They were sitting back waiting for Ezekiel to bring them after-dinner mugs of coffee.

"Commander, I don't wish to disturb you, but Mr. Green asked if he could speak to the two of you. He says it's important," stated Ezekiel as he placed a mug of steaming coffee on the table in front of each of them.

"Did he say what it was about?" asked Commander Blankenship.

"He did, Commander, and I think it's best that he tell you himself," stated Ezekiel.

"Will it take a lot of time?" asked the commander.

"It may, sir," responded Ezekiel.

"All right, Ezekiel, we have time. Tell him to come over and bring him a mug of coffee," said Hadden Blankenship as he sat back.

"Thank you, sir," said Ezekiel.

Ezekiel walked over to the counter and whispered to Joseph Green. Joseph walked over to the table where Hadden and Conor were sitting. They exchanged greetings as he sat down.

"Ezekiel says you have something to tell us," said Lieutenant Commander Raybourn.

"Yes, I do, sirs," said Joseph Green.

"So what's on your mind, son?" asked the commander.

"Well, sir, I've been conducting some geological research on the planet, taking core samples from around the surrounding area when I'm at the different mining sites and when the Marines hunt," stated Joseph.

"What have you discovered?" asked Hadden.

"Well, sir, I can't be sure of this, and Mr. Yates thinks I'm wrong," said Joseph hesitantly, as Ezekiel placed a steaming mug on the table beside him.

"You have a degree in geology as I recall," stated Hadden.

"Yes, sir, but it's only a bachelor's," replied Joseph.

"While Mr. Yates holds a doctor's degree in exogeology," stated Conor, remembering Gunnery Sergeant Rusu's report on the outer moon.

"Yes, sir," replied Joseph.

"Let's hear what you have to say, son, and we'll decide for ourselves," stated Hadden Blankenship.

"After comparing the core samples, I found an iridium layer at about the same comparative stratum in each sample from the surrounding area. I've run tests on the different layers with the geological equipment at the colony and aboard the *New Horizon*, attempting to date the different layers, and I believe they are approximately right," said Joseph.

"How's that important?" asked Hadden.

"An iridium layer is generally formed when an asteroid impacts a planet. Depending on how large the asteroid will depend on the area of dispersal," said Joseph.

"All right. What else did you discover?" asked Hadden.

"Well, did you know that according to the astrophysicists and Hattie, the outer moon has only been in orbit for approximately forty to eighty million years?" queried Joseph.

"I remember reading that in Gunny Rusu's report," replied Conor.

"If my calculations and tests are correct, then that iridium layer is only forty to eighty million years old also," said Joseph.

"That's quite a coincidence, Joseph," said Hadden.

"Yes, sir. I've been collecting fossils when I find them and sharing them with the biologist Silas Cheptoo. The life-forms we see around us today only occur above the iridium layer, while different life-forms occur below the iridium layer," said Joseph.

"How different?" demanded Hadden.

"Quite different, sir. There are still examples of those life-forms that exist today, but they occur mostly in the flora and not the fauna," Joseph informed them.

"Have you discussed these differences with Second Lieutenant Rosenstein, Joseph?" asked Conor.

"She expressed an interest, but she's been busy with her normal duties," replied Joseph.

"I'll talk to her as long as you're sure of this," said Conor.

"Mr. Cheptoo assures me that they are quite different," said Joseph. "Sir, the life-forms you see today have more in common with us at the DNA level than they do with the life-forms that survived from before the iridium layer formed."

"What are you saying, Joseph?" asked Hadden.

"Sir, I think this planet was terraformed by an asteroid, eliminating most of the previous life-forms and replacing those life-forms with the flora and fauna we see today," stated Joseph.

The commander sat back looking thoughtful, and Conor did likewise as silence descended on the group. The clatter of dishes and silverware invaded the silence, along with the smell of meat cooking on the grill.

Lieutenant Commander Raybourn and Commander Blankenship looked at each other. Wiping out the entire ecology of a planet to seed it with a preferred life-form seemed unethical. The idea of terraforming had been around a long time, and humans had even started the process on Mars back in Sol System. They were even considering the idea of terraforming Venus, though the scientists wanted to move it into Earth orbit so it would be more comfortable. However, discussions of entering a system that already had a planet with a thriving ecology and eliminating those life-forms was generally frowned upon.

"That would explain a lot about this planet," stated Conor.

"Yes, it would," added Hadden.

"How large of an asteroid would it take to cause the event that you are describing, Joseph?" asked Commander Blankenship.

"About as large as the outer moon according to Mr. Yates and Hattie," replied Joseph.

"How long would it take to introduce the new life-forms?" asked Conor.

"I couldn't tell you for sure, sir. It would depend on how soon all the dust in the atmosphere settled after the impact. During that time, you could introduce algae and mosses to start the process. Dr. Yates and Hattie's best estimate is a few hundred to a few thousand years," replied Joseph Green.

"So it would have been a long-term project," stated Hadden.

"If they didn't have FTL, they would be used to thinking long term," said Conor.

"Who?" asked Joseph.

"The obvious answer is the red raptors," replied Conor.

"That would suggest that they were a spacefaring civilization when they arrived in this system. Pretty long fall from being a spacefaring culture to a Bronze Age culture," said Hadden.

"Why would they lose all their technology?" asked Joseph.

"War, disease, natural catastrophe, or any other of a multitude of reasons. We have no way of knowing. It obviously happened over the last forty to eighty million years if they arrived here at that time," replied Conor.

"We can conjecture all we want. Until we have hard evidence, we'll never know. Was there anything else, Joseph?" asked Commander Hadden Blankenship.

"Not at this time, sir," replied Joseph.

"Have you presented this information to anyone else?" asked Conor.

"Just Mr. Yates, and I've discussed the fossils with Mr. Cheptoo. Some of the Marines have shown interest in my work," said Joseph.

"How about the president?" asked Hadden.

"He wasn't interested," stated Joseph.

Commander Hadden Blankenship nodded. President Felipe Martinez and his cabinet appeared uninterested in anything but their own immediate concerns. They had displayed little interest in the red raptor lying in the morgue. Additionally, the Marine security detail for the mining operation had been more the commander's suggestion than a request from the president and his staff.

"Do you have this information on an organized database, Joseph?" Conor asked and Hadden nodded.

"Yes, sir," said Joseph.

"What's the file name?" asked Conor.

"Joe's Geology, but I'll have to grant you access. I didn't want anyone adding to my research or stealing what I've done. There's a general discussion and comments section after each file, but you cannot add to the file," said Joseph.

Conor chuckled, remembering the days he had done the same thing to protect the information he was working on. "Could the commander and I have access, Joseph?"

"Yes, sir. I also have a talk page for people I have granted access, and I give credit to people for ideas and information provided," Joseph Green informed him.

"Who has access already?" asked the commander.

"Most of the Marines," replied Joseph Green.

"Why doesn't that surprise me?" Conor chuckled.

"Joseph, you have my interest in your project. How transportable is your equipment, and can you be available at a moment's notice for a mission?" asked Commander Blankenship.

"I'm thinking of joining the Marines, so I keep flexible, sir," stated Joseph. "As for the equipment, it will fit in a Neil Robertson stretcher."

"Good. You've just become part of the mission the lieutenant commander will be heading," stated Commander Blankenship.

Joseph Green looked surprised but apparently was willing to take it all in stride. "How soon, sir?"

"Sometime within the next week. That will give the lieutenant commander and myself enough time to look over your information. Can you be ready by then?" said Hadden.

"All I have to do is transfer it from the Marine ATV to one of the Marine chopper's medical carriages, sir. Perhaps fifteen mikes," replied Joseph.

"Pick out some sites you'd like to look at and forward them through the Marines to the lieutenant commander and myself," ordered the commander. Then he asked, "How long does it take to drill a core sample, Joseph?"

"About an hour, sir," replied Joseph.

"Then pick a dozen or more for Lieutenant Commander Raybourn and Second Lieutenant Raybourn to look over with me. Highlight the ones you prefer but only expect to visit a handful because of time constraints and safety factors," said Commander Blankenship.

"I'll do that, sir." Joseph nodded.

"All right, Joseph, why don't you take care of that while the lieutenant commander and I discuss other mission parameters," said Hadden.

"Yes, sir. Thank you, sir," Joseph said with a grin as he got up and left.

"Interesting," commented Hadden.

"What's that, sir," asked Conor.

"Have you ever wondered how much information is suppressed back in Sol system by individuals who are supposed to be experts in their field all in the name of accepted science?" inquired Commander Hadden Blankenship.

CHAPTER 45

The elevator opened, and Master Sergeant Evan Zander stepped out with three women, two of whom were obviously pregnant. He escorted them over to the operations room of the Marine Complex as Second Lieutenant Shiran Raybourn stood waiting. She listened as the master sergeant was introducing the women who had volunteered to stand watches to their new and upcoming duties for the next few months.

Shiran still wasn't sure how Evan had convinced her to allow this change to happen. When he had first approached her with the idea, Shiran had openly refused to even contemplate the change. There had been the women she met while off duty who said how great it would be to have something to do. Then there were the Marines who always seemed to be overextended in their duties even though they would not admit it to her, while others in the colony like Ezekiel suggested that people were looking for something less strenuousness to occupy them. For some reason, it seemed that in some way Shiran had been manipulated into reversing her decision.

The elevator had been completed in a week, along with a bathroom and bunk room for the watch standers. There had been plenty of room for this expansion since it was in the original design plans. Something she had been trying to have done for months had suddenly become a priority to those capable of the construction. Somehow, Shiran had the feeling the master sergeant was behind that also. Shiran wasn't sure if she was right or how he did it, but if it were true, she wished he would tell her how he worked his miracles. It seemed to her that a commissioned officer would have more pull than a senior enlisted and that she had to be wrong. Shiran shrugged.

What Shiran Raybourn did find interesting was that Evan had said that it was mostly for the pregnant women to have something to do while convalescent. It turned out that there were volunteers, both male and female, who were willing to stand those watches while laid up, and that even surprised Evan. Shiran smiled because it wasn't often that she saw Evan Zander taken by surprise.

Another surprise was that three of the people involved in the incident at the Overlook had shown up to talk to Master Sergeant Zander at oh six hundred that morning. From her understanding, they had disagreed with what had happened at the Overlook with their fellow antagonists. In turn, the foundry and mining operations had laid them off indefinitely for irreconcilable differences. They then attempted to apologize to Ezekiel. That led them to be given the only option available to them, which turned out to be enlistment with the Marines. When they arrived, the master sergeant turned them over to Gunnery Sergeant Samuel Rusu for six months of training.

The second lieutenant smiled. Somehow, she felt sure that Evan Zander had known about what was going down at the Overlook before it happened and had ensured that everything went his way. That feeling was reinforced in the fact that his wife, Chief Petty Officer Tami Zander, just happened to have six magazines of sleepy darts with her that evening. Knowing Evan Zander, he had even plotted something with Ezekiel that would ensure a fortuitous outcome for the Marines in the end. However, she suspected that having people sign up to be Marines went above and beyond even what he had planned, but then again, perhaps not.

Then there was the surprise that the tanning factory sent to the Marine Complex—cushioned seats to replace those at the watch stations in operations ahead of schedule. Not only that; they sent more cushioned seats to replace all those in the Marine mess hall. Of course, the mess would now host civilians since the watch standers would be allowed to eat there also.

Standing in the back, the second lieutenant listened to the master sergeant putting on his best face for the pregnant women who had volunteered. Shiran could tell he was uncomfortable, but she did let him know that this was his project, not hers, and Shiran expected him to be the face of the Marines promoting this endeavor. His rich baritone carried as he cited the capabilities of the Operations Center and the equipment utilized within.

"This is the Operations Center, where we monitor air traffic to guide the shuttles and longboats. We also monitor the security cameras that we've installed and the active ID signatures," stated the master sergeant.

"You do all of that here?" asked one of the women.

"Yes," replied Master Sergeant Zander.

"What do you mean active ID signatures?" asked the man in the group.

"Everyone's dog tags or ID tags have a transponder that tells us who they are if challenged. It has to be activated by the individual wearing it. When Marines go on missions, they activate them until the mission is over or if they suspect that the enemy has found a way to trace the ID tag," Master Sergeant Zander informed the group.

"So it's sort of like the identification friend or foe system that the *New Horizon*, shuttles, and longboats use," replied a woman.

"Same concept, but the transponder is obviously a lot smaller," replied Evan.

"Where are the cameras for security installed?" asked the first woman.

"The pier, the helo pad topside, the ATV court. We also have a full three-hundred-sixty-degree view of the Marine Complex, both gates to the Compound, and now the fence line," stated Evan.

"We're going to be responsible for all of that?" asked the woman.

"You'll be trained on how to handle the job," Evan Zander assured them.

"Will we be responsible for handling the rockets and miniguns on the roof?" asked the man.

"That's not part of the plan. If you notice something or there's a threat to the colony, you sound the alarm, and a Marine will come and relieve you until the threat has passed," replied Evan.

The second lieutenant stayed for a few more minutes, then walked to the elevator and went to the Marine mess hall for a cup of coffee. Shiran had limited her intake to one cup a day for the baby.

She poured herself half a cup as she patted the now noticeable bulge of her stomach. The baby kicked back at the attention, letting his mother know that everything was fine. Shiran winced and smiled as she thought about the new life developing within her. Dr. Bess Hollinger had told her everything was going well and not to worry, so she headed toward her office.

The biggest surprise of all these new changes had arrived from the tanning factory that replaced her furniture. There were three cushioned leather chairs to replace the desk chair and wooden visitor chairs, along with a matching desk, all made of a deep mahogany. There was a fine brass trim on all the furniture. Shiran sat back into the soft cushions and patted her belly. Life was looking up, and hopefully, it would remain that way for a while. Her Marines had more time to accomplish tasks that were building up and not being done. She only hoped that the master sergeant's idea didn't cost them in some way in the long run.

Shiran sipped her coffee for a few more minutes in silence as she turned to check her morning traffic. There wasn't much, and she needed to report the arrival of the shuttle along with the failure of the ATV motor control board, which were all that was important. She sipped on her coffee again as she logged on to her computer and composed a message to the *New Horizon* with attention to Commander Blankenship and her husband, Lieutenant Commander Raybourn. She just finished the report when there was a knock on the door.

"Come in," called Shiran.

Master Sergeant Zander poked his head inside, looking uncomfortable. He obviously didn't want to say what he was about to say.

"What is it, Master Sergeant?" asked Shiran.

"Well, ma'am, we're going to require the diving gear from the *New Horizon*," said Evan as he stiffened to attention.

"What?" demanded Shiran.

"It seems one of our Marines lost her M-71 while assisting the shuttle at the pier," stated Evan.

Shiran rolled her eyes and asked, "How did that happen?"

"She was tending to duties and assisting the longboat while docking," Evan said straight-faced.

Second Lieutenant Raybourn looked at the master sergeant and realized that his answer wasn't going to change. She also noticed that the name of the Marine had not been given, only a pronoun. Shiran wondered what had actually happened. Shiran found it more likely the master sergeant didn't want his Marine in any further trouble than she already was and that she would be paying a penalty to the master sergeant when the time came. That penalty being a highly undesirable but necessary job.

"All right. I'll start drafting a message requesting the gear," said Shiran.

"Thank you, ma'am," replied Evan.

"However, I want your input on exact phrasing on what happened that caused that M-71 to go into Poseidon's watery embrace," observed Shiran.

"I can do that, ma'am. How soon do you want it?" questioned Evan.

"I'll give you six hours," said Shiran.

"Yes, ma'am," acknowledged Evan.

"How's the training going with our volunteers, Master Sergeant?" inquired Shiran.

"It's going well, ma'am. We'll probably have to give them a month of training on the radar to know procedures. But three senior operations specialists from *New Horizon* are willing to do that and free our Marines up once we give them a basic rundown on how we run operations here," replied Master Sergeant Zander.

"How about the security watch stander?" asked Shiran.

"Not much to that, ma'am. Call if in question but hit the alarm when sure. If in doubt and unable to reach anyone, hit the alarm," Evan informed her.

"That sounds about right," observed Shiran.

"Works for me. I'd rather have a security alert and practice than not have a security alert and find I'm up to my armpits in trouble," stated Evan.

Shiran nodded and said, "All right, Master Sergeant. Get what you need to do done and get me that wording for the message ASAP."

Second Lieutenant Shiran Raybourn sat for a moment, shaking her head and thinking about what could have actually happened for a Navarro M-71 to be lost over the side of the pier. She finally switched over to the security feed and keyed in for the fence view. There was nothing happening along the Compound's perimeter except a group of triceratops warily walking along the edge but avoiding the electrified cables. Shiran switched the feed again to watch Master Sergeant Zander as he stood looking but not saying anything to Corporal Hoffman, who stood at attention. Shiran zoomed in and could see that Hoffman had been crying but stood her ground. Finally, Evan said something, and Natalie Hoffman saluted, then marched down the pier to the Marine Complex building. There were tears rolling down Corporal Hoffman's face, but she was obviously relieved.

Shiran decided it was time to do a walk-around as she waited for the master sergeant's input as to exactly what happened to make that M-71 fall in the water. One hour later, Shiran was up in the operations room watching Sergeant Tadashi Adachi providing training and guidance to the new watch standers. Tadashi was proving to be very proficient and had been instrumental in setting up the prefab for the chemist Raisa Romanov, who was providing them with a steady supply of munitions and exploding devices.

Shiran was hoping Tadashi Adachi did well on his next test because she needed a staff sergeant. Sergeant Nikolai Ivankov was also proving to be worthy of promotion after the last couple of incidents. She wasn't sure how the ranks would be filled to accommodate them, and an overwhelming sense of loss overtook her as she thought of the spot one of the two would fill. Staff Sergeant Rachel Krupich had been a dear friend for nearly five years, and Shiran missed her. How she would replace that loss was unknown since the two of them had confided in many things and at times provided guidance that only another female would understand.

Second Lieutenant Raybourn was still going over the phrasing of the message the master sergeant had given her when Sergeant Adachi knocked on the door. He had a huge grin on his face, which immediately put Shiran on alert.

"What is it, Sergeant?" asked Shiran.

"Mr. Guillete would appreciate your presence in the mess for a cup of coffee, ma'am," stated Sergeant Adachi.

"I'm kind of busy right now, Sergeant," stated Shiran.

"Mr. Guillete says it's important, ma'am," replied Tadashi.

"More important than writing a message to the commander about our missing firearm?" asked Shiran.

"The master sergeant and gunny think so," insisted Tadashi.

"They're still here?" questioned Shiran.

"Yes, ma'am," replied Tadashi.

"Well then, lead on, Sergeant," stated Shiran.

Master Sergeant Zander, Gunnery Sergeant Rusu, and Brad Guillete were all sitting at a table in the mess having coffee. They all stood as Second Lieutenant Shiran Raybourn entered. Shiran waved them back into their seats.

"Mr. Guillete, I heard that you needed to talk to me," said Shiran.

"Yes, ma'am. Are you, by chance, missing something?" asked Brad, smiling.

"Yes, I am," replied Shiran heatedly as she glared at the master sergeant.

"It wouldn't happen to look like this?" asked Brad as he lifted a mud-covered Navarro M-71 from behind the cabinet beside him.

Second Lieutenant Shiran Raybourn let her jaw drop, and a look of surprise crossed her face as she asked, "How did you recover that hardware?"

"Leave it to an old country boy." Evan Zander grinned.

"What does that mean?" asked Shiran.

"Brad was raised on a farm in Missouri," replied Samuel Rusu.

"That doesn't answer my question," stated Shiran.

"I think it's best that Brad explain himself," interjected Evan.

"All right, let's hear Brad's version of the story," said Shiran.

"Well, ma'am, when I heard that an M-71 was lost over the side of the pier and that you were sending for diving equipment, I had an idea," said Brad.

"How did you do it?" asked Shiran.

"I went up to the operations room locker to see if there was a used magnetron stored there. There was, so I removed one of the magnets. Then I went to Chief Zander and asked for a hefty length of line, which she provided. I tied the magnet to the end of the line and went fishing where Gunny Rusu said it was lost over the side. It took a few times, but I finally snagged what I was fishing for, and here we are," said Brad Guillete.

"Thank you, Brad," said Shiran sincerely.

"You're welcome, ma'am. I put the magnet back in the locker with the line in case it ever happens again," Brad informed Shiran.

"I'm sure that it will come in handy. Hopefully, we're not going to be making a habit of losing our firearms over the side," Shiran said dryly as she looked at the master sergeant and gunnery sergeant.

The master sergeant and gunnery sergeant remained impassive until Shiran let a smile cross her lips. "Don't be too rough on Corporal Hoffman, Master Sergeant," said Second Lieutenant Raybourn.

Master Sergeant Evan Zander let a confused look cross his face for a moment, then it brightened, and he laughed. "The pier security feed."

CHAPTER 46

The recon chopper sat on the pad on top of the Marine Complex. Lieutenant Commander Conor Raybourn was stealing a kiss from Second Lieutenant Shiran Raybourn and attempting to assure her he wasn't going to take any chances. Gunnery Sergeant Samuel Rusu, Sergeant Tadashi Adachi, and Joseph Green waited for the recon mission leader, trying not to notice the display of intimacy. Joseph Green secured his core sampling equipment in the Neil Robertson stretcher on the side of the chopper, along with a tool bag of geological tools and equipment. The miniguns mounted on the undercarriage of the chopper were visible.

Joseph Green had listed a dozen spots on the map where he wanted to collect samples. Conor and Samuel Rusu rejected four of them outright as too hazardous, and if it took an hour at each location, they would only have time for about half a dozen in the first place. Joseph had agreed and crossed off another two, bringing the total number of sites to investigate to six. Joseph Green indicated four that he definitely desired samples from, leaving the other two as possible sites to investigate only if they had the time.

Shiran wanted to go along, but the noticeable bulge of her abdomen precluded any such endeavor. A strand of her long dark hair escaped from the bun under her cap and whipped in front of her face. Shiran stood facing Conor, holding his hands. A shuffling sound and a cough emanated from somewhere behind Conor as he looked into Shiran's deep brown eyes.

"Don't get into any trouble out there," said Shiran as she glanced over his shoulder at the chopper and its crew.

"You know me," returned Conor.

"I do," replied Shiran worriedly.

"These guys are waiting. We'll check in every hour," Conor replied uncomfortably.

"Every fifteen if you've landed. We'll be tracking the chopper down in OPS," stated Shiran.

"We'll be back," Conor stated as Shiran entered the elevator. Conor Raybourn turned to walk over to the chopper.

Gunnery Sergeant Rusu saluted and handed Conor his Navarro M-71. "Are we ready, sir?"

"Yes. Let's get this show on the road," replied Conor as he returned the salute.

"Mr. Green wants to know if we're still heading south and east over the river first. He's anxious to pick up some samples from the far side," Samuel informed Conor.

"That we are," returned Conor.

Conor climbed into the pilot seat and did his preflights with Samuel backing him up. They lifted from the pad atop the Marine Complex and headed south and east. They flew over the plains where the great beasts roamed and quickly reached the river, crossing it into the little-known regions beyond. Three pavilions sat at the forest's edge to the south with red and green shapes moving among them. Conor turned east and took them over the rugged, forested area where the coal fields lay until they reached the river. Crossing the river, they flew over forest for nearly ten klicks, then a plain opened up. Thirty kilometers later, they were approaching the far side of the valley and the first point on the map where Joseph wanted to take a core sample. Conor circled the chopper, looking for a suitable spot and possible dangers.

The lieutenant commander set down in the tall grass and warily eyed their surroundings. As the rotors slowed and no movement occurred, the recon crew dismounted and started unloading the core-drilling equipment. It didn't take long to set the equipment up and commence drilling. Half an hour later, Conor went over to Joseph as he watched, ensuring they proceeded correctly.

"How's it look?" asked Conor.

"If I'm right, I'm seeing the same iridium layer at the same sedimentary level as the other side of the river. I'll know for sure after running some tests once we're back at the colony," stated Joseph.

"Do the tests take long?" asked Conor.

"A few days if I have access to the equipment," said Joseph.

"Is access a problem?" inquired Conor.

"There's a waiting list. There's a limited amount of equipment," replied Joseph.

"Perhaps I can do something about that," stated Conor.

"I don't think that would be wise, sir," replied Joseph.

Conor gave Joseph a searching look, then asked, "Why?"

"The scientists are the ones generally requiring the use of the equipment, and they are left alone, for the most part, by the president by doing favors for him," said Joseph.

"What kind of favors?" questioned Conor.

"Generally testing raw materials for purity and testing finished products," replied Joseph.

"I see. Anything else?" asked Conor.

"Rumor has it the president is on a rampage already about the commander and the Marines. I try to fly under the radar by not making waves, and I generally get away with it. If we try to make a big thing about pushing people to the side to have these tests done, we'll irritate the scientists and put a target on my back. Then excuses why I can't use the equipment will start happening," responded Joseph.

"Thanks, Joseph. I'll keep that in mind," replied Conor seriously. "Are we about done here?"

Joseph looked at the meter on the tripod drilling rig they had set up and said, "About ten more centimeters should do it, sir."

When the desired depth was reached, Conor assisted Joseph with bringing the core sample up. They removed the clear plastic tube that displayed the different layers of sediment the drill had penetrated. Green looked at the tube and indicated a dark layer a little over halfway up as he nodded.

"That's it, sir," stated Joseph.

"The iridium layer?" questioned Conor.

"Yes." Joseph Green nodded. Then he added, "This whole river valley has been worn down. I'd like to get against the cliff face and look at the sedimentary layers. I need some samples and photographic evidence."

"Let's get this into the carrier, and we'll see what we can do," responded Conor.

They took four core samples as they moved along the eastern side of the river toward the coast before they ran into trouble. They were just packing the fourth core sample back into the side stretcher when Gunnery Sergeant Rusu shouted, "Heads up!"

The rattling of a Navarro M-71 on full auto sounded from the other side of the chopper. Sergeant Tadashi Adachi grabbed the Vinter HR-19, dropped to the ground, and took a shot as Conor watched the nearby tree line. The thump of a grenade sounded and was followed by shrieks of pain. Joseph grabbed his M-71 and scanned the trees also as he ran toward the rear of the chopper to assist the gunnery sergeant and sergeant.

The lieutenant commander saw a flash of red and fired a three-round burst in its direction. Conor was rewarded with a scream of pain as a javelin thudded into the ground at his feet. The far side of the chopper had grown silent.

"Everything clear?" shouted Conor.

"Clear, sir!" yelled Samuel.

"Green, gear?" demanded Conor.

"Secured, sir!" shouted Joseph.

"Then let's get the hell out of here," declared Conor.

Everyone scrambled into the chopper as green and red raptors erupted on the pilot side of the chopper. The sound of Joseph's M-71 sounded behind Conor, sweeping the area. A grenade sailed through the air from the back seat as Conor lifted the chopper into the air. It landed between a red and green, then exploded, throwing them in opposite directions. More raptors appeared from the opposite direction as the chopper ascended quickly into the air, javelins sailing beneath the undercarriage.

Lieutenant Commander Conor Raybourn decided that it was time to complete their primary mission as he took the chopper south toward the ocean. It didn't take long to see the clean white sands of the beach with the turquoise waves lapping the shoreline. Conor flew west following the coast for nearly fifteen kilometers to the estuary of the river. A herd of stegosaurus moved there but ran into the nearby trees as they spotted the chopper.

"Jumpy," stated Gunnery Sergeant Rusu.

"If the commander's information is correct, they have reason to be," replied Conor.

They flew over the swampy tree-covered area of the river mouth. On the far side, there were at least fifty ships moored on the beach. Each ship looked capable of carrying thirty to fifty raptors. Multicolored pavilions dotted the beach with inhabitants standing beside them or wandering between them. Most of the raptors had stopped and looked up at the chopper flying high above them.

"Looks like an invasion," stated Samuel.

"We can't be sure, but I see no ships leaving either," replied Conor as he swung the chopper around to circle the ships and encampment.

"The ships look like sloops for the most part with a few triremes thrown in," said Tadashi.

"Not the highest tech," observed Conor. "Mr. Green, are we getting all of this?"

"The visual recorders have been running since we left the Marine Complex, sir," stated Joseph.

"Good," replied Conor.

"Awful lot of greens down there," observed Samuel.

"Servant class?" suggested Conor.

"They're used for hunting. They are smart enough too where they could also be given simple tasks," said Joseph Green. "Dr. Hollinger thinks they're smarter than a chimpanzee."

Just then, a parade of reds and greens started to emerge from the forest. The reds patrolled the perimeter of the caravan, while the greens walked in line with large packs on their backs. Conor took the chopper down lower for a better view. There was a thud against the undercarriage, causing Conor to pull up.

"They use the greens as pack animals too," said Conor.

"I think we can confirm that the greens are used for more than hunting. Wouldn't be surprised if they're used as oarsmen and messengers also," stated Joseph.

"There appear to be different shades of red too," said Tadashi.

"More like two. There's a bright red and a dull red with lots of brown mixed in. Perhaps male and female," stated Conor.

"My thoughts too, sir. The finches and other birds back home were like that. The females were generally the duller color," said Samuel.

"Sexual dimorphism is common in animals," stated Joseph Green.

"I think it's time we leave," said the lieutenant commander.

"Looks like they're harvesting something from the island's interior," stated Gunnery Sergeant Rusu.

"Most likely meat," said Sergeant Adachi.

"Why do you say that?" asked Joseph Green.

"They're carnivores. It would take a lot of meat to feed the encampment below. They might also be shipping it back to wherever they come from," replied Sergeant Adachi.

"Or they could be here to stay," interjected Gunnery Sergeant Rusu.

Lieutenant Commander Conor Raybourn looked at Gunnery Sergeant Rusu for a moment as the thought of another colony of hostile residents inhabiting the island went through his mind. Trying to obtain resources to keep the colony viable was already a challenge. Fighting a guerrilla war to get those resources would be nearly impossible. The colony could not afford to lose anyone at this time, and the unwillingness of some of the colonists to take simple safety precautions didn't help matters. It seemed to Conor that the colony was fighting a war on two fronts. There was the exterior threat of hostile natives surrounding the colony. Then there was the interior threat of the colony waging a war between themselves. How it would play out in the end, time would only tell.

CHAPTER 47

The longboat had just arrived, and Lieutenant Michael Anderson watched as Lieutenant Agnes Felter directed the crew who just finished with the installation of the components they had been able to repair and replace. The damaged metal equipment racks were replaced, and those needing it were primed and painted. Hopefully, the new components for the NAPACS, or naval automated processing autonomous communications system, would be aboard the longboat. Lieutenant Felter, Chief Wheaton, and the other technicians were preparing to go down to the elevators to pick up the incoming shipment.

"You need to send your technicians down to help with the shipment now, Lieutenant Anderson," demanded Lieutenant Agnes Felter.

"Actually, I don't, Ms. Felter, but I will send them to assist your crew," replied Lieutenant Anderson.

"Fine! As long as their asses are down there to help," sneered Lieutenant Felter as she stomped off toward the comm shack entrance.

Michael nodded at the two technicians still assigned to him. They put aside the components they were working on for the new AI and joined the working party.

"Sure you don't want to come, sir? The special of the day is burgers and fries," asked Petty Officer Third Class Barbara Gabrielson.

"No, I have some work to do. You all go ahead," replied Michael.

"All right, sir. We should be back in two hours," said Barbara Gabrielson.

Michael watched as they left the communications suite. He got up from the chair and walked over to the workbenches. The old frequency generator that supplied the synchronizing frequencies to all the equipment was lying there in a pile, burned and warped from the explosion that had started in its interior. Raisa Romanov informed him that the bomb had been a combination of thermite and Q-5 plastic explosive, which explained why the burns on the bodies of the technicians had been so severe.

Michael Anderson started examining the frequency generator again, though he didn't expect to find anything. The metal chassis was mangled where the explosion had ripped through the components. The interior was warped and scorched beyond recognition. It surprised Michael that such a small amount of explosive could cause such devastation, but Sergeant Adachi assured him that the plastic explosive used was extremely potent and that just a gram was sufficient.

Michael shook his head and thought of Cindy Brooks, who had died when the equipment had been turned on. Then there was Maria Ortiz and the others who had died when the FTL drive had been brought online so long ago. Michael knew the perpetrator hadn't used the ship's factory to produce the explosive, which indicated that the perpetrator either produced it or had a supply brought aboard the *New Horizon* when it departed Ceres back in Sol system.

Something caught Michael's eye as he examined the interior of the equipment. There was something dark mashed in between the face plate's interior side and the rack for the circuit cards. Michael took tweezers from the tool drawer on the workbench and gently grabbed the corner of the item. He slowly worked at the dark object until it came loose.

The tweezers held a thin rectangle that was scorched. It appeared to be the top of an integrated circuit chip, though how it had survived the explosion intact was beyond Michael. He was about to put the item down with the other pieces of scrap when he noticed something. There appeared to be writing on one side of the rectangle, but it wasn't standard nomenclature for components. Michael stood up from the workbench and walked over to the high-powered microscope at the microminiature repair station. He carefully placed the rectangle on the viewing tray with the side containing the writing up.

Sliding the tray under the observation lens, Michael turned the microscope on and adjusted the magnification. There on the viewing screen was the rectangle with the writing enhanced. It was somewhat scratched and burned, making it hard to read, but he took a picture of the rectangle. Michael turned off the microscope and removed the rectangle and bagged it as evidence. Michael put the bag in his office safe, along with a copy of the picture he had produced. He had just placed the other copy of the picture in his pocket when Chief Wheaton and the other technicians returned with several large packages.

"Was the new frequency standard in that shipment, Chief?" asked Lieutenant Anderson.

"It looks like it, sir. We'll know after it's unpackaged," said Chief Wheaton.

"Did everything else come in?" inquired Lieutenant Anderson.

"I believe so. Not that it's any of your business, sir." Chief Wheaton snickered.

"Good! Can you and the others start installation? I have an errand to run," said Lieutenant Anderson as he ignored the insubordination.

"We were planning on doing that, sir," said Chief Wheaton, smiling.

"I should be back in two hours or so," replied Lieutenant Anderson.

"Take your time, sir." Chief Wheaton snickered.

Michael heard more snickering as he departed the comm shack. Michael walked over to the Bookworm to see if Francesca had eaten already. When he arrived, she was just finishing her review of a story for the daily paper. She looked up to see Michael watching her, and a bright ivory smile appeared on her brown face.

"Busy?" inquired Michael.

"Not anymore," stated Francesca.

"Good! I'm taking the rest of the day off," said Michael.

"Something wrong?" asked Francesca.

"Nothing Brad Guillete hasn't experienced," replied Michael.

Francesca frowned for a moment, then her eyes widened as she whispered, "Oh!"

"Yeah. It's time for lunch," said Michael.

They sat in the back of the Overlook and asked Roberta for tea. When she returned, Francesca and Michael ordered the special. Francesca did most of the talking during their meal. Michael attempted to shrug off the drama in the comm shack but knew that it was going to lead to a hostile work environment.

"So what do you plan to do?" asked Francesca.

"I don't know," replied Michael.

"You could ask for reassignment," said Francesca.

"I'm the only one who can build an AI mainframe from scratch," stated Michael.

"Did you do something to antagonize them, Michael?" asked Francesca.

"Other than stranding us all here?" retorted Michael.

"That wasn't your fault! It was an accident. It was a prototype engine being tested with a volunteer crew who supposedly knew the risks," declared Francesca.

"Most of them don't care," said Michael distractedly.

"There's something else, isn't there?" inquired Francesca.

"What do you mean?" asked Michael.

"This isn't the only thing bothering you," stated Francesca, looking deeply into Michael's eyes.

There was, but Michael didn't know if he should tell Francesca or not. She didn't know about the saboteur, and neither did most of the colonists. He knew there were people who had suspicions, but most of them were Marines. Michael looked at his wife and decided it was time.

"So what's the problem, Michael?" asked Francesca.

"What do you mean?" returned Michael.

"You seem distracted. More than the problem you've already mentioned," stated Francesca.

"I was looking at the piece of equipment where the explosion in the comm shack originated," said Michael hesitantly.

"Yes?" inquired Francesca.

Michael reached in his pocket and placed the photograph of the rectangle with the unusual symbol in front of Francesca. Michael didn't know what kind of reaction he was expecting, but the one he received was not what he was prepared for. She looked at the picture, and Michael watched fear grow in her eyes as the degraded symbol's image registered.

"Where did you find this?" whispered Francesca.

"It was wedged inside the piece of equipment that the explosion originated from. Do you know what it means?" asked Michael.

"I do," said Francesca as she fearfully viewed the restaurant customers.

"What is it?" asked Michael lowly.

Francesca simply shook her head. Just then, a brown hand picked up the picture. It was Ezekiel, who then sat with them uninvited as he gazed at the picture carefully. Michael could see him tense as he studied the photograph. Finally, he looked at Michael intently. "You found this in the debris of the communications suite?" asked Ezekiel, worry furrowing his face.

"Yes," said Michael apprehensively.

"Put it back in your pocket," said Ezekiel, handing it back to Michael, who took it and slid it back into his pocket. "You need to speak to the commander about this thing," stated Ezekiel after the photograph was securely in Michael's pocket.

"What is it?" asked Michael.

"It is a symbol of death and revenge," whispered Ezekiel.

"Against whom?" asked Michael.

"All who do not believe," stated Ezekiel lowly.

"I do not understand," whispered Michael.

"It's an old symbol. It calls for death and revenge against infidels," whispered Ezekiel.

"Who would use it?" questioned Michael.

"A variety of cultures have used it over the last five centuries," whispered Francesca.

"Which is why it should not be made public," stated Ezekiel quietly. Then he added, "This needs to be brought to the commander's attention as soon as possible."

"Michael, go," urged Francesca.

"Wouldn't that look suspicious?" replied Michael.

"The commander is acting captain of the *New Horizon* and needs to know," said Ezekiel.

"This symbol is that important?" asked Michael.

"Yes!" stated Ezekiel.

Michael walked Francesca to the Bookworm, then they went to the MILDET prefab. When they knocked on the door, Commander Hadden Blankenship answered it. Seeing who was standing outside, he opened the door wide and indicated for Michael and Francesca to enter. Hiroka sat at the table sipping tea where a pot and another full cup sat beside her.

"This is unexpected. To what do we owe the pleasure of the visit, Michael and Francesca?" asked Hadden.

"It's important. It involves the issue you've been having me look into, sir," said Michael.

Hadden looked at Francesca then at Michael and cocked an eyebrow.

"I found something and consulted with Francesca to find out what it meant," said Michael.

"Tea?" asked Hadden. He looked at the two and received a nod before adding, "Let me find a couple of cups."

Hadden went to the kitchen and returned with two more cups. He poured hot water into the cups and placed a container of tea bags on the table. Taking the pot to the kitchen, Hadden refilled it with water and placed it on the heating unit. Returning, he sat down at the table.

"What did you find, Michael?" asked Hadden.

Michael reached into his pocket and took out the photograph of the symbol and slid it across the table to Hadden. Picking it up, Hadden studied the picture with a puzzled frown.

"I found that inside the frequency generator that exploded," stated Michael.

"I've never seen it before. I don't know what it means," replied Hadden.

"It is a very old symbol, Commander. It is a symbol of hate and vengeance," explained Francesca.

"May I see it, Hadden?" asked Hiroka.

Taking the picture, Hiroka sat back staring at it. The silence in the room lasted for a long time.

Clearing his throat, Hadden quietly asked, "Hiroka?"

Hiroka rubbed the scar on her forehead before answering, "Only trusted captains and above know of this symbol. We are all in danger until we find the person responsible for this. The perpetrator will not stop until dead."

"Does anyone else know you found this, Michael?" asked Hadden.

"Francesca obviously. Ezekiel looked at it when I was showing it to Francesca, then told me to put it away and see you immediately," replied Michael.

"He knew you would show it to me. We can trust, Ezekiel. His people have reason to know the meaning of that symbol," said Hiroka.

"What do you think we should do?" asked Hadden.

"First, I will give you and Michael access to all information about this symbol. We should also inform all those we can trust so they can assist in finding this saboteur," said Hiroka.

"I believe we can trust Conor and Shiran Raybourn," said Hadden.

"Good. I trust them too," replied Hiroka.

"What about Ezekiel?" asked Michael.

"Tell him to not say anything to anyone about this, Michael. However, I believe you will find that he already knows that," said Hiroka.

"What about President Martinez?" asked Hadden.

"I do not trust him to keep this secret, and he may even be the perpetrator," stated Hiroka.

Hadden nodded and looked at Francesca. "Francesca?"

"I understand and can remain quiet while carefully watching for the individual," said Francesca.

"Do not assume there is only one," said Hiroka.

"You think there may be more than one?" asked Michael.

"Do not underestimate the people who made this," said Hiroka, pointing at the picture of the symbol that now lay on the table. "We must be sure we have found them all and eliminated them."

"Eliminate them?" asked Michael.

"Their purpose, if there is more than one, will be to kill us all," stated Hiroka flatly.

A pronounced silence fell on the room. The information was overwhelming in many ways to Michael. He had always considered the military a blunt object, never realizing that the secrets kept from the public also encompassed the Machiavellian. He had always considered it more of the bureaucratic and political theater. Michael watched Hiroka, who finally picked up her cup and sipped at the now cold tea, wincing as Hadden took the cup from her to dump and refill with hot water.

"Life has become a lot more complicated," said Hadden as he looked at Michael.

CHAPTER 48

Dr. Bess Hollinger was busy. She had already delivered a baby that morning and was reexamining the red raptor that they stored in the morgue. The commander had requested a full autopsy of the body with an analysis of any physical capabilities she could discern about the creature. It was laid out on the table. She wasn't sure what the commander was looking for, and apparently, he didn't either. Bess shrugged but knew that her cursory exam had not been complete. Her original examination was only conducted on the cranial regions in detail with a minor or basic exterior review of the physical attributes of the red raptor. Now the commander wanted a full breakdown of the body.

Bess sent the body for an X-ray, MRI, and CAT scan that morning. The techs and Dr. Kers Joshi were still examining the results of those tests. So this afternoon, Bess cracked open its chest and abdomen and removed the organs. The raptor's interior was much like the green raptor's. This specimen was a male and had a crested ridge of feathers on the top of its skull much like a cockatoo, though nowhere near as prominent. The feathers were a bright scarlet, but Bess suspected that the female's feathers would be duller, much like the green raptor's female. The larynx, however, was much more complex than a green raptor's, which suggested it could produce a wide range of sounds.

She also noted that the ball socket of the shoulder was more versatile than that of the green raptor, allowing for more movement. The claws on the forearms were shorter and more retractable; adaptations that were more suited for tool use than the green raptor, she suspected. Bess shook her head and marveled.

Bess Hollinger dictated her findings as she made a visual record with the emergency computer. It was tedious, but until the communications suite was up and running, she had to rely on it to assist her. Hattie's abilities to assist the medical clinic were severely limited until the NAPACS was brought online to handle the traffic of the colony.

She was sitting in front of her laptop finishing her notes when Chief deLang knocked on the open door.

"What is it, Caroline?" asked Bess.

"Ma'am, are you busy?" inquired Caroline deLang.

"I was just finishing up, but I need a break," said Bess. "What is it?"

"Sergeant Ivankov is here for his rounds," replied Caroline hesitantly.

"And?" asked Bess.

"Jacqueline Vinet is insisting that he baptize the baby," Caroline blurted out.

"Oh!" said Bess loudly.

Bess thought for a moment as she took off her bloodied smock and washed her hands. She was not especially religious. Her family came from an Islamic background. Bess had attended a couple of services with the few who followed the faith since their arrival on the planet. She found the routine soothing at first, but some of the followers, like Bahri Hiran, had demanded more participation. This had led her to reconsider the direction she wished to go since it started interfering with her responsibilities at the clinic. She still prayed at times, but it was on her terms since she felt her work was doing God's will. She hadn't thought of Jacqueline as especially religious either, but then people change, and it was the mother's choice.

"What shall I tell her?" asked Caroline.

"Where's the baby?" asked Bess.

"In her room," replied Caroline.

"How's the little guy doing?" questioned Bess with a smile.

"The monitors say he's healthy and doing well." Caroline smiled.

"Then I don't see any problem. Go get the sergeant and let's baptize the baby," stated Bess.

They went to the waiting room and escorted Sergeant Nikolai Ivankov back to the room Jacqueline occupied. Dr. Kers Joshi stepped out of his office just then and glanced at Bess. Kers obviously had something he wished to discuss with Bess, but she raised her hand to stay his efforts.

"What's going on?" asked Kers.

"My morning baby is going to be baptized," stated Bess.

"I see," said Kers as he followed the procession down the hall.

The party entered the room where Jacqueline was sitting up in bed, watching her child. The baby was in a clear plastic crib sleeping peacefully, unaware of the people gathered to see him. Nikolai set the brown bag he had slung over his shoulder on the table beside the crib and walked over to Jacqueline.

"I'm told you wish to have your child baptized," stated Nikolai.

"Yes," said Jacqueline Vinet.

"Are you a Catholic?" asked Nikolai.

"My parents were," Jacqueline replied.

"Yet I have not seen you at services," replied Nikolai.

"I have my doubts," replied Jacqueline.

"I see. Yet you wish the child baptized," said Nikolai.

"Yes," said Jacqueline.

"You realize I serve only as a deacon of the church?" asked Nikolai Ivankov.

"Yes. But you're the closest thing we have to a priest," replied Jacqueline.

"Very well, Jacqueline. I will do this thing for the child," stated Nikolai.

"Thank you." Jacqueline smiled.

Sergeant Nikolai Ivankov opened the soft brown leather bag on the table. He took out a deep-red stole and a small crystal bottle capped with a silver lid. Meanwhile, Bess went to the crib and took the baby to his mother, laying it in Jacqueline's arms. When Nikolai turned, the stole was draped over his shoulders, hanging down to his waistline in front. Nikolai held a brown leather-backed Bible with gold lettering in one hand and the crystal bottle in the other. He approached the bed and looked at Jacqueline.

"Are you ready?" asked Nikolai.

"Yes," replied Jacqueline.

"Very well. Which name do you wish to give your child?" inquired Nikolai.

"Jason Conor Vinet," stated Jacqueline.

Silence descended on the room as everyone looked at Jacqueline. Bess Hollinger saw Sergeant Nikolai Ivankov pause and raise an eyebrow at Jacqueline. How news of this christening would go over with Second Lieutenant Shiran Raybourn was most likely going through his mind. The moment passed, and Nikolai Ivankov continued with the baptism.

"What do you ask of God's church for Jason Conor Vinet?" questioned Nikolai.

"Baptism and faith," responded Jacqueline.

"You have asked to have your child baptized. In doing so, you are accepting the responsibility in ensuring he is trained in the practice of faith. It will be your duty to ensure he is brought up to keep God's commandments as Christ taught us, by loving God and our neighbors. Do you clearly understand this undertaking?" stated Nikolai.

"I do," replied Jacqueline.

Nikolai took the crystal bottle and poured a drop on the infant's head.

"Jason Conor Vinet, the Christian community welcomes you with great joy. In its name, I claim you for Christ, our Savior, by the sign of his cross. I now trace the cross on your forehead and invite your parent to do the same," stated Nikolai.

With that, Nikolai Ivankov reached forward and made the sign of the cross in the water on the child's forehead, as did Jacqueline. Bess watched as Nikolai opened his Bible and read a passage about Jesus and the little children. When he finished, Sergeant Ivankov returned the items to the bag on the table, then shouldered the bag.

"Jacqueline, I wish you and your child well. I need to leave now and attend to others," said Nikolai as he turned to leave.

"Thank you, Nikolai," said Jacqueline.

Bess Hollinger saw Nikolai Ivankov nod but could tell he was not happy about the function he had just performed. She wondered what repercussions were in store for the young man in the near future. Bess Hollinger shrugged, then took the still sleeping baby and returned it to the crib as Sergeant Ivankov departed. Bess checked the sticky, wireless monitors attached to the baby's skin to ensure they were all right, then turned to Jacqueline and said, "Now you need to rest."

"All right," said Jacqueline.

"Do you need a sedative or anything?" asked Bess.

"No," replied Jacqueline.

"Then get some sleep. I want you out of here in two days," ordered Bess. Dr. Hollinger turned and shooed the rest of the group out of the room, closing the door as she stepped out.

"Do you have a moment, Bess?" asked Dr. Kers Joshi.

"Of course. What is it, Kers?" replied Bess.

"I think I need to show you," returned Kers.

"Lead on," replied Bess.

Dr. Joshi took Bess to the morgue. He went to the cold storage area where the red raptor she had examined earlier in the day was interred. Clouds of cold air puffed out as he opened the small door. He pulled out the slab, exposing the body, and motioned her over.

"I was going over the scans that we did this morning since I had time, and I noticed an anomaly," said Dr. Joshi.

"What was it?" asked Bess.

"See this scar tissue here?" Kers pointed to a fairly large round scar that was on the right hip of the raptor.

"I noted that on my examination. The raptor has a lot of scar tissue," said Bess Hollinger.

"When I was looking at the MRI, there's a nearly straight line of what appears to be scar tissue between this scar and a point about fifty centimeters down the tail ending near the spinal column." said Kers.

"And?" returned Bess.

"That point near the spinal column is a black hole on the X-ray. Like something is lodged there," stated Kers.

"Well, let's do a little surgery," said Bess.

Dr. Kers Joshi went across the room and brought a cart containing a tray of implements. Bess picked up a large scalpel and a large clamp.

"Where?" asked Bess.

"About right there would be best," said Kers, pointing at a spot on the tail.

Bess made an incision near the tail's spine where Kers indicated while he took a clamp and pulled the skin back on the far side of the cut. Bess kept cutting until she reached something solid. She picked up a large forceps and reached in to grasp the solid piece, slowly withdrawing it. Bess held it up for Kers and herself to view.

"Is that what I think it is?" asked Bess.

"It looks like a musket ball to me," said Kers.

CHAPTER 49

Conor was still attempting to consolidate the new information into a cohesive picture, but he was distracted. Shiran and he had a heated argument over the news about the name of Jacqueline Vinet's child. Why Jacqueline felt an overwhelming need to use the name Conor as a baptismal name was an item of contention. Thankfully, Jacqueline had not used his name for the child's first name when christening him. The Marines were on their best behavior and staying out to the second lieutenant's way whenever possible. Sergeant Nikolai Ivankov had been hustled out of the Marine Complex by the master sergeant as a last-minute replacement for duty on the *New Horizon*. That ensured that Nikolai, who was only performing his sacred duties, was well away from the second lieutenant for at least two weeks, even though he had served his two weeks just three months earlier.

Conor sat back and sighed. He needed to think about other problems affecting the colony than his own personal issues. The growing discontent in the colony was worrisome, and the antagonistic behavior of some individuals connected to the foundry and mining operations even more so.

The red raptor's arrival on the coast and the fact that they apparently were moving north was a pressing issue also. Hunting and mining operations were disrupted, along with the harvesting of local produce and wood from the nearby forest, as the *New Horizon* produced miniguns to mount on the new haulers. Two ATVs were now assigned to the hunting rather than for protection, with a chopper outfitted as a gunship on standby when they were out. The hunting teams reported that the herds were skittish and moving north and east along the river. Even the large carnivores were moving with the herds. Three sets of pavilions had been seen along the forest's edge, and the ATVs had to fend off an attack by both green and red raptors.

The question of whether the red raptors were simply passing through or here to stay weighed heavily on the minds of all. Until the raptors left or a peace was made, the colony had to make do, but all those resources were required for the colony to survive. Conor made a note of the problem in the Colony Viability file.

The thought of attempting to establish a peace with the raptors had been forwarded, but to establish a peace involved being able to communicate, something the raptors had not shown any likelihood of doing anytime soon. How do you establish a peace when the first response from the other side was a javelin flying toward you? Conor rubbed the scar where the wound had been as he thought about that last question.

Though there were voices in the colony calling for preemptive strikes against the raptors, the commander was reluctant to initiate aggression first, and Conor agreed. All-out war against a primitive people was not something many in the colony desired. They had joined the *New Horizon* as explorers, not conquerors, and a peace, even an uneasy one, was desired over a genocidal war.

They had no idea how many raptors inhabited this world or if the current raptors they had encountered represented the height of their technology. Joseph Green's revelations suggested that the planet had been terraformed and that the predominant flora and fauna had been seeded to replace the old. Were the red raptors possibly the descendants of a spacefaring species? If so, where was the evidence that they were? Additionally, was there possibly a more advanced civilization of the red raptor somewhere on the planet?

These were all unanswered and unanswerable questions at this time. What they would discover on the mainland would remain unknown for a number of years because of the fragile nature of the colony. The commander stated that they didn't need to go looking for trouble, and Conor tended to agree with that assessment.

Then there was the discovery of the musket ball from Dr. Bess Hollinger. The idea that it was a musket ball was in dispute. No one had reported any musket fire or the use of gunpowder from the red raptors. However, Bess was sure that the lead ball had penetrated over fifty centimeters of muscle, because of the scar tissue through the muscle, before lodging next to the vertebrae at the base of the raptor's tail. There was no other way for the lead ball to reach that point without passing through the muscle. It had left a scarred path to where it had been lodged. There were those in the colony who disputed her word on the matter. There was no way of proving that a weapon had lodged the piece of lead into the raptor's tail. The only thing they could be certain of was that a piece of lead had been extracted from near the tail vertebrae during an examination of the raptor.

Conor finally turned his attention to the problem Michael had discovered. Not enough was known yet to identify the perpetrator. Conor read the dispatch that the commander had given him at their last meeting. The symbol was used by several loosely knit and little-known terrorist organizations back in Sol system. Those organizations were like wisps of smoke appearing occasionally to create havoc, then vanishing to reappear later. No government or even the United Systems, which had existed for nearly three hundred years, had any reliable information on the organization or organizations. The only known fact was that it had been around before the first Mars colony had been established over five hundred years ago.

Most of the documented information about the organization, if it was one organization, covered minor incidents of known sabotage over the centuries. However, there were three occasions when the organization, if that was what it was, caused massive carnage.

A mining site on Mercury was completely destroyed when the atmosphere had been vented in an explosion. All the pressure doors were sabotaged to prevent them from closing. Nearly a thousand people died in that blowout.

A bioweapon had been released in the Ceres habitat, and over 80 percent of the population of nearly a hundred thousand died. Survivors had severe health problems and lived for only three to ten years after the incident. The hospital ship, USS *Mercy*, discovered a cure, but too late for those who survived.

The third-generational colony ship was en route out of Sol system with a crew of nearly ten thousand when a fusion plant failed.

The ship had just passed Saturn and was severely damaged. Only seventeen people had been rescued, and the ship had been left adrift to wander in the Oort cloud on an orbit that would return in system in about another seven thousand years or more.

The three incidents had one thing in common—a symbol had been discovered in the carnage near the point of origin while only a few times were messages located from the perpetrators claiming responsibility for the incidents. There had been other incidents, both major and minor, that the perpetrators were suspected of, but no symbol or message had been located during the investigations. The organization or organizations remained elusive, while the perpetrators were unknown and had never been located, with their identities remaining a mystery.

"Hattie," said Conor.

"Yes, Lieutenant Commander," Hattie replied.

"Please close all files and forward changes to designated personnel on the access list," said Conor.

"Would you like an update on the colony viability projections prior to closing, Lieutenant Commander?" asked Hattie.

"Please do so and display changes," said Conor.

A graph appeared above the table where Conor was sitting. The graph had taken a dramatic dive and was now projecting that the colony's viability was below the level it needed to survive at its current technological level.

"What happened, Hattie?" asked Conor.

"Redefine question, please," replied Hattie.

"Why does the graph show our viability to maintain our current level of technology below acceptable levels?" asked Conor.

"The new information from Lieutenant Anderson about the saboteur," replied Hattie.

"We already knew about the saboteur, Hattie," said Conor.

"Now that more information is available about the nature of the saboteur, the chances of the colony have lowered below acceptable levels until the saboteur or saboteurs are dealt with," replied Hattie.

Conor thought about that for a moment, then asked, "What do you know about this symbol, Hattie?"

"That it is used by a loose-knit organization that has been in existence for several centuries and that they have a record of achieving chaotic ends without being apprehended," stated Hattie.

"Is that all?" asked Conor.

"Would you like to review the rest of the data on the symbol and what is known?" asked Hattie.

"Not at this time, Hattie," replied Conor. "Please close the Colony Viability file and forward all updates to those who have access."

"Closing files and forwarding changes," Hattie responded.

"Thank you, Hattie," said Conor.

"You're welcome, Lieutenant Commander," replied Hattie.

Conor sighed and sat back in his chair. He rubbed his eyes to clear the muck out. He stood up and stretched to work out the stiffness. He massaged a twinge in his thigh where the javelin had struck him. Shiran had left for the Marine Complex early. She and Corporal Hoffman had taken the rumpled uniforms to the laundry to drop off. Deciding to take a walk, Conor pulled on his camouflage top and left the MILDET prefab. He went over to the ledge and looked down at what they had built.

There were people moving between the buildings at the base of the cleft. Work continued in the construction of their new home. He moved his eyes upward toward the pier and Marine Complex where personnel in Navy and Marine uniforms were performing their duties. Sweeping his gaze further afield, he looked out over the fields the colony was raising to the perimeter fence with its four gates that kept out the great beasts that inhabited this world. Beyond the fence, he saw herds of triceratops, apatosauruses, stegosauruses, and other creatures that had not existed on Earth for over sixty-five million years. As he watched, a large carnivore burst forth from the forest and attacked a stegosaurus. The fight was brief, and the large carnivore roared its victory with the rest of the herd moving away as the carnivore's mate moved out of the forest.

The carnivores started feasting, and Conor moved his attention back to the ledge. The yellowish bricks of the boardwalk lay to his left, and he started toward them. Placing his hand on top of the restraining wall that protected colonists from going over the edge, he walked toward the elevators that lay over a kilometer ahead, and he passed the storefronts lining the left side of the boardwalk. He finally neared the elevators and the storage warehouse beside the Overlook where Bahri Hiran was busy looking over a recent arrival of stores from the *New Horizon*.

"Good afternoon, Bahri," greeted Conor.

"Oh! Good afternoon, Lieutenant Commander," said Bahri as he looked up from what he was doing.

"What do we have today?" asked Conor.

"Not much, sir. A piece of equipment for the comm suite, medications for the good doctor, a part for the ATV at the Marine Complex, and a control card for the foundry," replied Bahri.

"Good. Martinez has been anxious about that," said Conor.

"Yes, they've been asking for it," replied Bahri.

"It should up production and help increase the quality of the metal," stated Conor.

"We build a fine colony here," replied Bahri.

"Yes, we are. It's not what I expected to do with the rest of my life, but I feel as though we've accomplished more here than if we were still in Sol system. There's a feeling of pride and accomplishment," stated Conor.

"So long as our arrogance is not our undoing," replied Bahri.

"What do you mean?" asked Conor.

"We have crossed light-years of space to be stranded, unable to return home, where we discover a habitable planet to set up an enclave of mankind very similar to the one we left," replied Bahri.

"Is that a bad thing?" asked Conor.

"We could have explored other ways of living," said Bahri.

"People are comfortable with the familiar. Everyone was given a chance to express their desires. We've worked hard and have made a good start here for the little we had to start with," said Conor.

"Time will tell, Lieutenant Commander. Now if you will excuse me, I have to deliver these items. I'm sure the good doctor is waiting," said Bahri.

Conor watched as Bahri Hiran pulled the trolley down the boardwalk and vanished around the corner where the Overlook stood. It was true that they were attempting to build a colony similar to the life they left behind on Earth. The physical appearance of what they were building did not look similar to the home he was familiar with. However, the abstract concepts of freedom and independence were in the contract the colonists had written to accept as a way of life and make the laws under which they lived. Unfortunately, even that system had its drawbacks.

Conor looked over the ledge and shook his head to clear it of those last thoughts as he viewed once again all they had accomplished in so short a time.

CHAPTER 50

Qu'Loo'Oh' had learned much, and so had her new pupil Rachel as they taught each other their languages. Rachel had learned many of the symbols of Qu'Loo'Oh's people, and Rachel, in turn, had taught her the symbols that composed its unusual language. Qu'Loo'Oh' could see the benefits and deficiencies of each style of writing as she contemplated the symbols Rachel had drawn on the parchment before her. Rolling the parchment up to study later, Qu'Loo'Oh' watched as Rachel studied a scroll from the library. The youngling had consumed the information on the beginner scrolls and was studying scrolls that were meant for higher learning. Rachel had asked for scrolls about the history of Qu'Loo'Oh's people, and Qu'Loo'Oh' had guided her through them. Rachel now knew more than most Ques'Coat'L' knew about their ancestors.

"I'm going to the library," chirped Rachel in Ques'Coat'L'.

"I will be there shortly," replied Qu'Loo'Oh' in English.

Walking across the room, Rachel left with the scroll she had been studying. Qu'Loo'Oh' would only allow Rachel to take two scrolls from the library at a time. The other scrolls she borrowed were to be returned before taking more. Rachel appeared to understand this concept and did not oppose Qu'Loo'Oh's rules.

The youngling had healed well over the last couple of moons, except for her upper left arm, which had a crook to it. Unfortunately, Rachel had discovered the outside entrance to the sacred chambers and wanted to leave. Qu'Loo'Oh' attempted to explain to her that it was unsafe but felt that Rachel did not believe her. Qu'Loo'Oh' was worried. Rachel knew where the entrance to the sacred chambers was, and she was being insistent that she wished to return to her people.

The sacred hunt was only half over, and the hunters had been moving north. The big beasts had already departed the forests surrounding the caves. That meant most of the hunters should be near the plains moving east then north along the river. Outside the sacred chambers should be relatively safe. Most of the hunters preferred the large game to be had elsewhere. However, that might not be so if they had discovered the intruders' constructions to the east of the sacred chambers. If that happened, the hunters would patrol the perimeter of the intruders' new dwellings and attack the silvery web when ready.

The fire burned low as Qu'Loo'Oh' mused. She left her nest and went to the door. Rachel had not returned, and Qu'Loo'Oh' decided to check on her. She went to the library and entered to discover Rachel studying an ancient scroll. When Rachel saw Qu'Loo'Oh', she rolled up the scroll and slipped it into the case it came from.

"I need to go back," said Rachel.

"Not safe," replied Qu'Loo'Oh'.

"When safe?" asked Rachel.

"One moon," stated Qu'Loo'Oh'.

"Too long," replied Rachel.

"Not safe," said Qu'Loo'Oh'.

"Why?" questioned Rachel.

"[Untranslatable] hunt," replied Qu'Loo'Oh'.

Rachel stood looking at her, and Qu'Loo'Oh' finally saw Rachel raise her shoulders. Qu'Loo'Oh' knew that the gesture meant a sign of indifference or defeat to Rachel, so Qu'Loo'Oh' did a mental shrug while Rachel went back to studying the scroll lying on the table in front of her. The scroll Rachel had been studying described the arrival of Qu'Loo'Oh's people in the giant world ship that brought them here.

When Rachel left the library, she told Qu'Loo'Oh' that she was going to the room to lie down, but when Qu'Loo'Oh' arrived a several thousands of heartbeats later, she was not there when Qu'Loo'Oh' returned. Qu'Loo'Oh' searched the nearby rooms and didn't find her, and when she checked the entrance to the sacred caves, she discovered her tell tripped. She left the safety of the sacred caves cautiously knowing Rachel had left the caverns. She knew it would be dangerous during the time of the sacred hunt, but she felt the Rachel's safety was important, not only for herself but for her people.

Qu'Loo'Oh' trailed Rachel for nearly a thousand body lengths by the time she caught up with Rachel. She cautiously parted the foliage in front of her to confront a tense Rachel pointing her fire stick at her. She saw Rachel lower the fire stick when she realized who she was confronting.

"Not good. Not safe," said Qu'Loo'Oh'.

"I need to go back," stated Rachel.

"Not safe," returned Qu'Loo'Oh'.

"I've made it this far," replied Rachel.

"Not safe," said Qu'Loo'Oh'.

"Then you should go back," stated Rachel.

"Come with me," demanded Qu'Loo'Oh'.

Suddenly, the verdant foliage on each side of the clearing Rachel stood in parted, revealing a pair of green raptors. Rachel shot one with a short burst from her fire stick, causing it to fall back and kick in its death throes. The other started forward to be met by Qu'Loo'Oh' midway. Feathers flew as teeth, claws, and talons fought for supremacy. She tore into the green as it fought back, ripping the skin along Qu'Loo'Oh's ribs with the talons of its forearm. Qu'Loo'Oh' raised her right leg for a disemboweling stroke as she grasped the neck of the green with her jaws. She clamped down on the green's neck and twisted her head, causing the vertebrae to snap as she raised her right foot and pushed against its chest. Releasing her grasp on the neck, she pushed the quivering green away and felt a sharp pain in her right leg. The rattling of Rachel's fire stick erupted again as a red raptor threw a javelin that pierced Qu'Loo'Oh's right leg. Rachel ran to Qu'Loo'Oh' as she fell to the ground.

"You poor thing!" shouted Rachel.

"Back, not safe," wheezed Qu'Loo'Oh.

"Right, we'll go back," agreed Rachel.

"Good," wheezed Qu'Loo'Oh'.

"First, I fix," stated Rachel.

Rachel opened the med kit she was carrying. Rachel had Qu'Loo'Oh' swallow two white beads she removed from a jar. Shortly, Qu'Loo'Oh did not feel the pain in her leg or side. Rachel carefully removed the javelin point still in the wound. There was much blood, but Rachel did something that caused the blood to stop and then sealed the wound with her magic wand. She then used her magic wand to stitch together the open gash along Qu'Loo'Oh's ribs. Then Rachel took another tube and sprayed a white foam over the top of the wounds. The foam was cool as it was applied to the wound and dried to a rubbery consistency that allowed movement.

"There, that should stop the bleeding," said Rachel.

"No blood, good. Less trail," replied Qu'Loo'Oh'.

"Can you move?" asked Rachel.

"Slowly," returned Qu'Loo'Oh' as she climbed to her feet and took a step.

"Then let's go back to the chamber," said Rachel.

"Rachel, take branch. Clear trail. No tracks," stated Qu'Loo'Oh'.

"I can do that," said Rachel.

Then a look came across her face as she removed an object about the size of a small pawpaw from her shoulder harness. She went over to the red raptor's body and did something with the object as she placed it under the body. Finished, she stood back up and walked back over to Qu'Loo'Oh'.

"What do? asked Qu'Loo'Oh'.

"Trap," replied Rachel.

"Kill?" asked Qu'Loo'Oh'.

"Yes," returned Rachel.

Qu'Loo'Oh' had mixed emotions about Rachel setting a trap to kill Qu'Loo'Oh's kind as Rachel picked up a branch and carefully brushed her tracks and Qu'Loo'Oh's from the ground. The alternative was that the hunters would track and kill Qu'Loo'Oh' and Rachel. Rachel was looking at Qu'Loo'Oh' because she had not moved. Qu'Loo'Oh' finally nodded, a gesture she had learned from Rachel that indicated agreement according to Rachel.

"Good. Slow tracking. Maybe go away," said Qu'Loo'Oh.

They moved off back toward the cave using the same route they had taken to the clearing. Rachel was careful to remove as many signs of their passage as she could. When they were to the crevice that led to the doorway, Rachel stopped again and removed the tube that sprayed the white foam from her pack. Rachel then handed Qu'Loo'Oh' her backpack to carry. Qu'Loo'Oh' looked at Rachel and cocked her head to the side, which Rachel knew was her way of asking an unspoken question.

"You go to chamber. Rest. Sleep," Rachel stated firmly.

"What you do?" asked Qu'Loo'Oh'.

"False trail and trap," replied Rachel.

Qu'Loo'Oh' nodded, then turned and moved slowly down the crevice, leaving Rachel. Reaching the end of the crevice, she entered the door. Qu'Loo'Oh' closed the door and went to her chamber, where she placed wood on the fire and lay down. Rachel must have been gone for nearly five thousand heartbeats before she walked into the room. Going to her backpack, Rachel reached inside and removed a small jar. Rachel took the lid from a small jar, shaking two small beads into her hand, which she handed to Qu'Loo'Oh'.

"Take them," said Rachel.

"What do?" asked Qu'Loo'Oh'.

"Make sleep," said Rachel.

"No. Danger," stated Qu'Loo'Oh'.

"You sleep. I watch," replied Rachel, hefting her fire stick.

Qu'Loo'Oh' nodded and swallowed the beads as she attempted to make herself more comfortable. She watched as Rachel walked to the fire and placed more wood on it. When Rachel was finished, she left the room and closed the door as Qu'Loo'Oh' drifted off to sleep.

*****

Rachel watched Qu'Loo'Oh' limp down the crevice back to the chambers. When Qu'Loo'Oh' was out of sight, Rachel backtracked fifty meters toward the clearing where she pricked her finger with her KG-3 combat knife. She wrapped the finger and started erasing her trail again till she reached the crevice, but she also left traces of blood to be found every couple of meters while doing so. When she reached the crevice, she kept going toward the sound of water. There was a sizable stream another hundred meters to the west of the crevice. Rachel then took several small pieces of driftwood and let blood drop on each. She threw them into the middle stream, which slowly took the bloodstained sticks downstream. She then removed the tube of bandage foam from her pouch and thoroughly covered her small wound so it wouldn't bleed.

Backtracking a few meters, she rigged another grenade with some monofilament as a trip wire across the trail. Rachel took up her branch again and erased her tracks from the stream to the crevice. She then rigged another grenade near the entrance to the crevice. Hopefully, if the grenade was triggered, it would obliterate any traces of their passage down the crevice to the door. Taking up her makeshift broom, Rachel carefully erased any trace leading down the crevice until she reached the doorway. Rachel took her broom inside and closed the door to the sacred cave.

Rachel checked on Qu'Loo'Oh', then returned and climbed the stairs near the entrance. Locating the peephole Qu'Loo'Oh' had shown her, Rachel opened it to view the crevice and listen as she sat patiently guarding the door to the chambers with her Navarro M-71 lying across her lap.

A distant thump sounded, and Rachel tensed knowing her trap had been sprung. Over an hour passed as she sat there, then a green raptor appeared at the end of the crevice. It stopped searching the ground and smelling the air as it investigated. She watched as it was thrown into the air against the foliage as her second grenade was tripped. Many minutes passed before another green raptor appeared. It went to the body of the dead green, lying where the grenade had thrown it. The new green paused shortly before it started sniffing and searching. It moved out of sight going west along the false trail Rachel had left. In its wake, three more greens and two armed red raptors followed slowly behind it. Around forty minutes later, the last grenade Rachel had set sounded.

Rachel waited, hoping her ploy had worked and the raptors would continue following the fake trail she laid. About thirty minutes after her third grenade trap was tripped, a more distant explosion sounded from the same direction. A grim smile crept across her lips as she sat watching the crevice because she knew Master Sergeant Evan Zander was keeping up and rendering aid.

CHAPTER 51

The wind was blowing from the south, and dark clouds were gathering there. The treetops bent in the wind as the distant herds of beasts gathered into groups to seek shelter in companionship. The smell of moisture was in the air, and people were preparing for the storm that the *New Horizon* reported was heading their way. Second Lieutenant Shiran Raybourn was on the roof of the Marine Complex with Master Sergeant Evan Zander examining the Marine helicopter and its landing pad. The chopper was strapped down to the roof for the storm.

"These restraints need work, Master Sergeant," stated Shiran.

"I agree, ma'am. I'll have them work on that after the storm passes," replied Evan.

"Good. Let's have Brad take a look at the radar and communication antennas after the storm," ordered Shiran.

"Good thought, ma'am. I'll talk to him about doing a little preventive maintenance on them," replied Evan Zander.

"Ask him to look over the electronics on the choppers and ATVs also," added Shiran.

"Yes, ma'am. Should we go inspect the pier?" asked Evan.

"After you, Master Sergeant. I'll try not to step on Chief Zander's toes too much," replied Shiran.

"Chief Zander is always open to constructive criticism," replied Evan Zander, smiling.

"I'm sure she is." Shiran grinned.

They were just finishing up their pier inspection when Sergeant Tadashi Adachi ran up. He gave a hasty salute as he stopped and came to attention. Second Lieutenant Raybourn returned the salute, looking at the sergeant questioningly. It was obvious the Tadashi had something important to tell them.

"They need you in operations, ma'am," stated Tadashi.

"What's the problem, Sergeant?" asked Shiran.

"Ma'am, Staff Sergeant Krupich's ID is responding," replied Tadashi.

"This better not be a joke, Sergeant," stated Shiran heatedly as she picked up her pace, walking toward the Marine Complex.

"How long ago did it appear, Sergeant?" asked Evan.

"It appeared about thirty mikes ago. I didn't believe it myself, so I went up to operations. It's there, ma'am," stated Tadashi firmly.

"Stationary or moving?" asked Evan.

"Moving," responded Tadashi.

"Direction?" questioned Evan.

"East. Toward the cleft's Compound," said Tadashi.

By the time the three reached operations, the ID was stationary and had remained so for nearly ten minutes. It continued to be stationary for nearly another thirty minutes after Shiran arrived. The ID then moved west, the direction it appeared from. The *New Horizon* reported five hours before the storm front hit, and Shiran ordered a chopper in the air. The chances of seeing anything, even an IR image, through the foliage was doubtful. The possibility of a landing in that area any closer than the previous LZ where Conor and the Marines had been rescued was out of the question.

"Why doesn't she use her comms?" asked Shiran.

"Damaged or lost," grunted Evan.

"Then why doesn't she use a flare?" asked Shiran.

"It's probably too hot, and she doesn't want to give away her position," replied Evan.

"Then we can't be sure it's her," said Shiran.

"It's in the same area we lost her signal before," replied Evan.

The ID trace reached the area where the operator said the ID signature had appeared. The ID paused and moved west again for a short distance, then paused for a short time. Then the ID slowly returned to the point it had paused at first. There was another pause, and then it vanished near the cliff. The chopper arrived in the area where this was all happening but reported it could see nothing because of the foliage. However, about half an hour after the ID vanished, an explosion occurred at the point where the ID had been furthest east.

The master sergeant had a grim smile and said, "That was her."

"How do you know?" asked the second lieutenant.

"Booby trap," stated Evan knowingly.

"You can't be sure of that," replied Shiran.

"Have the chopper remain in the area. If she has all four of her grenades, there will be two more explosions along the ID track," replied Evan Zander confidently.

"Why only two?" questioned Shiran.

"She will rig two more grenades and save her fourth. One will be right here where her ID vanished again and the other here at where her ID was furthest west," stated Evan.

"How can you be sure?" demanded Shiran impatiently.

"She did the same thing in a training exercise," replied Evan.

"That's not proof it's her," said Shiran.

"It'll be proof enough for me," stated Evan.

"We need to go in and find out if it's her," protested Shiran.

"The area is too hot to go in right now. That explosion happened shortly after she stopped," replied Evan. "We go in now, and we'll lose more people."

"So what should we do?" asked Shiran.

"Are you asking for my advice, ma'am?" questioned Master Sergeant Evan Zander, leveling his eyes at his second lieutenant.

Shiran hesitated, then replied, "Yes, Master Sergeant, I am. What do you recommend?"

"Wait and try to draw them away from that site. Then hope that fourth grenade doesn't go off," stated Evan.

The meaning of an explosion from that fourth grenade went through Shiran's mind. She wanted to help her friend, but sending more people into an area that was presumed hot wasn't a viable solution either. If the master sergeant was right, Rachel was holed up and keeping silent because she had no way to communicate without giving away her position. It was time for her to let an old hand give her advice and hope for the best.

"How do we draw them away?" questioned the second lieutenant.

Master Sergeant Zander pointed to the spot where the ID signature had stopped moving west. "If another explosion happens here, we wait for thirty minutes and light off a grenade further out. Making whatever is following that track think that she continued on and something else set off a trap accidentally. Hopefully, it will throw them off the scent, and they won't think of backtracking," said Master Sergeant Zander.

Shiran thought about the plan laid out by the master sergeant for a moment, then nodded. "Do it, and I want constant surveillance on that area in case the ID appears again."

"Roger that, ma'am!" acknowledged Evan.

Once he had the go-ahead, the master sergeant went over to a station where he donned a headset. After adjusting it, he issued orders to the chopper. While he was giving orders, they reported another explosion right in the area Evan had predicted. A few minutes later, he removed the headset and moved back to stand beside Shiran.

"Now we wait. If another explosion happens at the end of that westward track, we can be pretty sure it's her and that they haven't located her yet," said Evan.

"The chopper will need to come back as soon as it drops a grenade to avoid the storm," replied the Shiran.

"We'll be cutting it close," muttered Evan.

"We need to do a recon and rescue," stated Shiran.

"I agree. But right now, we'd probably lose more people. If she's still alive, and I'm now convinced she is, then she's found a hole to hide in. We have to hope that she can hold out for a while longer. If we go in, we need to be prepared, and that will take a week or two to plan. We can't afford to go in half-cocked and lose more people," replied Evan.

"All right, Master Sergeant. I want you and Rusu to come up with that plan. Be quick and have someone inform Lieutenant Commander Raybourn about this," ordered Shiran.

"Roger that, ma'am," acknowledged Evan.

"Master Sergeant," said Shiran.

"Yes, ma'am," said Evan.

"Let Brad know about this if you think he'll be all right," replied Shiran.

"I was going to ask him to sit in on the planning. He'll probably want to be part of the team that does the recon and rescue," stated Evan.

Shiran thought about that for a moment. She knew that Rachel had strong feelings for Brad Guillete, but sometimes he was very hard to read. Somehow, Evan Zander had penetrated that impervious facade that seemed to surround him and understood what Brad would do. Shiran had to admit that Brad was proving to be an asset to the Marines even though he still rebuffed efforts by the master sergeant for recruitment. Brad had repaired the Marine radar and gained the commander's notice, and when one of the ATVs experienced a problem with its infrared detection system, he spent a day getting it to work. She also knew that Lieutenant Michael Anderson mentioned that Brad repaired the SAC-23 when no one else seemed capable of fixing the satellite transceiver. Then there was the retrieval of the M-71, saving them the hazards of plunging into the lake with the native wildlife.

Shiran nodded and said, "If you think he can be an asset, do it."

"Roger that, ma'am. And, ma'am, about that pier inspection?" responded Evan.

"It'll wait until after the storm, Master Sergeant," replied Shiran.

"Will you be going to the cleft?" asked Evan.

"For now, I'm going to my office. Have all the Marines recalled and the operations personnel relieved so they can return to the cleft before the storm hits," said Shiran.

"Yes, ma'am. I'll get on those items ASAP," said Evan.

Shiran went to her office to look over her morning traffic. Shiran lost track of time and found she had been at it for over an hour. Sitting back, she rubbed her eyes thinking how much simpler life had been before accepting her commission. But then life had been simpler prior to taking on the extra passenger she was now carrying. Shiran sighed and shrugged. Unnoticed, Master Sergeant Evan Zander poked his head into her open doorway and must have seen that sigh and shrug because there was a grin on his face.

"Everything all right, ma'am?" Evan grinned.

"Yes and no," replied Shiran.

"The burdens of command." Evan nodded knowingly.

"Are we all set for the storm?" asked the Shiran.

"Yes, ma'am. I've done everything you asked. Are you sure you wish to stay? I can handle it," said the master sergeant.

"I have the feeling I won't be alone," said Shiran as she watched Conor approach on the security feed. Evan Zander entered the room and looked over her shoulder, then said, "I suppose you won't be."

"Have someone check to make sure he has a clean uniform to change into when this is all over, Master Sergeant," ordered Second Lieutenant Raybourn.

"Roger that, ma'am. Anything else, ma'am?" inquired the master sergeant.

"Not that I can think of. I'm going to meet my husband," said Shiran.

"Yes, ma'am. I'll take care of that and be right there," replied Evan.

Shiran left the office and walked down the hallway. She met Conor at the entrance as he was shaking off the damp from his cammie jacket. They gave each other a hug and kiss, then went to the Marine mess for something hot to drink. Conor gathered a coffee for himself and ginkgo tea for Shiran, then escorted her to the closest table.

"Why are you here?" asked Shiran.

"To be with you. I presume you're planning on staying here and planning a rescue mission," said Conor Raybourn.

"I've already assigned that to the master sergeant and Gunny Rusu," replied Shiran.

"The commander also wanted the shuttle topside, and the longboat is to take the load for power requirements for the colony. They're predicting the storm to be pretty bad, and he doesn't want the shuttle damaged," said Lieutenant Commander Conor Raybourn, referring to the fusion plants in the longboats and shuttles used to supply electrical power to the colony.

Shiran looked at the master sergeant who walked up as they were talking and nodded. He went over to Sergeant Ivankov, who was the only other person in the mess, and sent him to inform operations of their new orders about the shuttle.

"So Staff Sergeant Krupich may still be alive?" Conor questioned as the master sergeant returned and stood nearby.

"There is a high probability," returned Shiran.

"Master Sergeant," said Conor, looking pointedly at Evan Zander.

"Yes, sir. I believe she is, sir," stated Master Sergeant Zander.

"That's not what I was going to ask, Master Sergeant," snapped Conor.

"Excuse me, sir," replied Master Sergeant Zander with confusion in his eyes.

"Now is there anything keeping you here that the second lieutenant, Gunny Rusu, and myself can't handle?" asked Lieutenant Commander Raybourn.

"The storm and the rescue plan the gunny and I are supposed to prepare, sir," returned Evan.

"Are you suggesting that we're incapable of weathering a storm or making a rescue plan with Gunnery Sergeant Rusu, Master Sergeant?" replied Lieutenant Commander Conor Raybourn, indicating himself and Second Lieutenant Shiran Raybourn.

"No, sir," replied Master Sergeant Zander defiantly.

"Then why are you still here, Master Sergeant?" demanded Conor.

"Sir?" questioned Evan.

"Isn't your wife almost due?" inquired Conor.

"Yes, sir," replied Evan with a smile.

"Then I think it's time for you to attend to personal matters and let those you've trained to watch your back," stated Conor, smiling.

"I agree, Master Sergeant. Go!" Shiran grinned.

Evan Zander looked at the two officers and friends sitting before him and thought of how much they'd changed over the time they'd been on this planet. It seemed like only yesterday that they were still learning their roles of leadership as he guided them. Pride swelled his chest as Evan Zander snapped a salute to the two of them, and they, in turn, stood and returned his salute. Master Sergeant Evan Zander turned with a spring in his step as he felt accomplishment and fulfillment in a task well done in the grooming of young people into a leadership position.

CHAPTER 52

The baths were a success. Hiroka Tamura had customers come to utilize the facilities constantly. Her soaps, lotions, and perfumes were well received too. She was considering expanding the baths and lines of items because of the reception she received and had a woman who wished to assist her with the expansion. Hadden Blankenship was encouraging her because it took away the need for the ship's factory to produce such mundane products so it could concentrate on other needs for the colony.

There were three people utilizing the baths currently as she cleaned the fourth. She was refilling the tub when she sensed a presence behind her. She turned to see Norman Pool standing there with a grin on his face.

"Well, well, if it isn't our damaged captain," sneered Norman Pool.

"Can I help you, Mr. Pool?" asked Hiroka.

"Why yes, I think you can. I need a bath," said Norman Pool.

"I will go get you some towels," stated Hiroka.

"I already have towels," stated Pool, pointing at a pile set on the stone seat behind him. "What I need is a companion."

"If you wanted a companion, you needed to bring one with you," said Hiroka.

"I already have," stated Norman Pool as he drew nearer, placing a hand on her arm and reaching for the fastenings on her kimono.

"No!" screamed Hiroka as she slapped his questing hand away and yanked her arm from his grasp.

"Yes, I think so." Pool grinned as he reached for her again.

Hiroka threw the brush she held at Norman Pool, and the wooden handle connected with his nose. Norman Pool's head snapped back with the impact, and his hands reached up to cover his now ajar and bleeding nose. He shook his head, and the grin had transformed into a look of malice as Hiroka turned and ran out of the door of the bath.

"Come here, you little bitch!" growled Norman Pool as he gave chase.

"What's going on here?" demanded Tom Tollifer as he emerged from the bath across from the one Hiroka had been cleaning.

"None of your damned business!" shouted Pool as he pushed Tom back into the bath he had emerged from. Tom lost his footing and flew backward into the tub set in the floor. Tom Tollifer's head hit the side of the tub, and a long gash creased his scalp as he scrambled frantically to keep his head above water. Hector Lopez peered out through the crack of a partially opened door of another bath, and a grin appeared on his face as he closed the door to return to his bath. Pool turned his attention back to pursuing Hiroka as she slipped out the main entrance to the baths.

Hiroka made it to the front door of her home. She was just opening the door when Hiroka felt a blow on her back that sent her tumbling across the floor of her home. Scrambling to her hands and knees, Hiroka saw the shadow of Norman Pool reach across the small room. She heard an evil chuckle as he advanced slowly. Hiroka reached up and took up her katana from where it rested above her head, and she saw Norman Pool quicken his pace. Without thinking, Hiroka thrust the point of her blade into her opponent as she stood up. Norman Pool froze momentarily as the cold length of the blade slid into his gut, then let out a howl of disbelief. Hiroka Tamura withdrew the blade quickly from where it was sheathed in Pool's intestines. Norman Pool fell to the floor and curled around his misery, groaning in pain as blood flowed across the floor.

Corporal Natalie Hoffman appeared at the entrance of her cottage, and Hiroka raised the katana once again. Corporal Hoffman raised her hands in defense, and she asked, "Are you all right, Captain?"

Hiroka Tamura lowered the katana and sighed. There was a growing pain on the left side of her back as she lowered her katana. Gesturing with her katana toward the groaning man curled in a fetal position on her floor, Hiroka winced in pain and said, "No, and he's going to need a doctor immediately."

Natalie looked down at Norman, who bled on the cottage floor, then at the bloody tip of the katana and nodded. Tom Tollifer stumbled up to the cottage door with blood covering his face. He took in the scene of Hiroka standing with a bloodied sword over Norman Pool, who lay on the floor curled in agony. There must have been something in the look on Hiroka's face because Tollifer ran forward, catching and lowering her to the floor as she collapsed. The last thing Hiroka Tamura was aware of was Tom Tollifer shouting to Natalie to get a doctor.

Time passed, and images blurred together in a whirl of shapes, colors, sounds, and scents. Hiroka felt lost and struggled to resurface in a world that made sense. She didn't know how long she had been like this; it seemed to be forever. Then a lull occurred, and she heard something that drew her back to the world. There was a voice speaking. It was a soft baritone, but the words were unintelligible at first. They were not in her native Japanese, but as she concentrated, she realized they were English. The words were telling a story she remembered from her childhood. It was the story of Tanabata, which had led her to seek a commission in the United Systems Space Force.

Hiroka Tamura slowly opened her eyes and watched as Hadden Blankenship read. She remained quiet, listening to the story, as Hadden sat in the chair beside the bed she lay in. He turned the page and continued on for several more minutes until he came to the end of the story. He sighed, inserting a finger to hold his place as he closed the book around it. Looking over at Hiroka, a gentle smile lit Hadden's face.

"Good morning," he murmured.

"Good morning." Hiroka smiled.

"How are you feeling?" asked Hadden.

"I feel fine," said Hiroka as she attempted to sit up. A sharp pain in the left side of her back and a firm hand over her chest caused her to stay put.

"No, you aren't," stated Hadden as he removed his hand and stood.

"What?" said Hiroka as she took in the room that she had ignored when she was listening to the story. She suddenly realized that this was not her cottage but a room in the clinic. Flashes of events prior to being in the clinic brought her to the present. The attempted rape. The chase. Being hit from behind and rolling across the floor. Stabbing Pool with her katana. Collapsing in Tom Tollifer's arms. Then blankness.

"You were attacked," said Hadden.

"Yes. Is he dead?" asked Hiroka.

"No. Now stay still while I get the doctor," ordered Hadden.

Hadden Blankenship stood up and walked out of the room as Hiroka lay quietly in the bed. He returned shortly thereafter with Bess Hollinger in tow. Bess's ivory smile radiated against her dark skin as she approached the bed.

"How do you feel, Hiroka?" asked Bess.

"I thought I was alight until I tried to sit up," replied Hiroka.

"That would be your ribs. One is broken and had punctured your lung. Three others are cracked. I've had you under for the last three days so you wouldn't move while the regen medicine did its work. That doesn't mean you're all fixed. You need to take it easy and rest for at least another week," said Bess Hollinger.

"Can I go home?" asked Hiroka.

"I don't see a problem with that happening in another day. I just want to make sure you're all right," replied Bess.

"How is Pool? Is he here?" demanded Hiroka.

"Recovering and yes. Do you want to see him?" asked Bess.

"No. But if he is here, I wish to leave," stated Hiroka.

"I'd rather you didn't," replied Bess Hollinger.

"Then I want my katana," stated Hiroka.

Bess's face got a worried look. "I'd rather not have it here."

"Then send me home," said Hiroka defiantly.

"Hiroka, please," said Hadden.

Hiroka looked at Hadden and saw the worry in his face. "Will you stay with me?"

"Yes," replied Hadden.

"Very well. I will stay for one more day," replied Hiroka.

There was a look of relief on Bess Hollinger's face. A quiet knock on the door drew everyone's attention. Ezekiel stood there with a silver covered tray with a small smile on his face.

"Well, I have duties to perform if everything is all right here. Ezekiel, it's nice to see you," said Bess.

"And you, Doctor," replied Ezekiel.

"Thank you, Doctor," said Hadden.

The doctor left the room, and Ezekiel carried the covered tray to the stand beside the bed. There was a tantalizing aroma that distracted Hiroka.

"I just dropped by to see how she's doing," stated Ezekiel.

"Everything is fine, Ezekiel," said Hadden.

"Good. Good. I brought her favorite dish since the good doctor said she should be awake this morning," said Ezekiel.

"You didn't have to do that, Ezekiel," said Hadden.

"It is my pleasure, sir," replied Ezekiel.

"Thank you, Ezekiel," said Hiroka.

"It was nothing," stated Ezekiel with a grin.

Just then, there were some loud voices down the hallway and then footsteps. President Felipe Martinez appeared and stepped into the room. Hadden Blankenship moved to insert himself between the president of the colony and Hiroka.

"What do you want, Mr. President?" asked Commander Hadden Blankenship.

"I see she's awake. I want her arrested for what she did to my cabinet member," demanded the president.

"No. She defended herself," replied Hadden.

"That's her word against his," insisted Felipe.

"I'll believe her before I believe him, and Tom Tollifer says she was attacked by Pool," replied Hadden.

"Pool says he couldn't have seen anything," stated Felipe.

"Then there's Corporal Hoffman who saw him hit her from behind when she reached her cottage," said Hadden.

"Hearsay," retorted Felipe.

"What do you want?" demanded Hadden.

"I want that whore locked up," shouted Felipe.

Hiroka saw Hadden stiffen and his face turn red. Ezekiel placed a leathered brown hand on Hadden's right shoulder as he moved up beside the commander.

"Allow me, Commander," said Ezekiel impassively.

Suddenly, Ezekiel lashed out with his right fist, which connected with Felipe Martinez's nose. Felipe Martinez dropped like a felled bull with blood spurting from his nose. Felipe lay there for a moment before his hands went to his face. A moan of pain sounded as he was lifted up by Ezekiel and escorted to the door. Ezekiel looked back over his shoulder as he grabbed the door handle with his free hand.

"I will take this poor man to see the doctor, Commander. He appears to have broken his nose in that fall. Would you mind wiping up the spill on the floor that he slipped on?" said Ezekiel, pushing Martinez through the door.

"Yes, I can do that, Ezekiel. Thank you. And thank you for the food," said Hadden.

"It was nothing, Commander." Ezekiel smiled as he closed the door and escorted Felipe Martinez back down the hallway. As they left, the occupants of the room could hear Ezekiel tell Martinez, "Perhaps if you're lucky enough to spend a night here, you can share a room with Mr. Pool."

Hadden walked over to the counter that held basic medical supplies for the doctor. He pulled on surgical gloves from the available box and plucked a few surgical wipes from a container. He cleaned the blood spot on the floor and tossed the wipes into the hazardous waste disposal sitting beside the counter.

Returning to the bed, Hadden pushed the button that slowly raised Hiroka to a sitting position. Then lifting the cover off the tray Ezekiel had left, he examined the meal that had been hidden. Revealed were two dishes. Each contained a portion of the local fish broiled with a lemon seasoning, a serving of wild rice, a pudding made from fresh strawberries, and a small cake that had flakes of coconut on top. Hiroka smiled at Hadden as he took one dish along with the available silverware and set it on the movable tray in front of her. He then took up the other dish and silverware, placing it beside the other, as he took a seat on the edge of the bed.

"Ezekiel is wonderful," stated Hiroka.

"I don't know what we'd do without him," agreed Hadden.

They ate their meals, relishing every bite. They ate in silence enjoying each other's company, letting the world pass by without them for a short time. Hiroka felt fulfilled in having someone there for her who demanded nothing from her in return. As she finished the last bite of cake, she smiled at Hadden, and he returned it with a twinkle in his eyes.

CHAPTER 53

The president had recently demanded that the commander place Lieutenant Agnes Felter in charge of the communications shack. Since then, Lieutenant Michael Anderson stayed out of the way, working only on constructing the AI being built in the back of the comm suite spaces. The communications center for the colony was mostly complete, but it wasn't working. For some reason, the NAPACS, or naval automated processing autonomous communications system, which was to handle all the message interactions between the colony and the *New Horizon*, was still completely down after the last required system component had been installed.

Lieutenant Commander Conor Raybourn sent Brad Guillete over a week before to have a look at the system since he was a NAPACS technician. Brad had been rebuffed by Chief Wayne Wheaton and told in no uncertain terms he was not allowed to touch any part of the system. Chief Wheaton ordered a new system component to affect repairs from the *New Horizon*, stating that he knew exactly what was wrong with the system. In turn, he was not letting anyone else look at or troubleshoot the system, much less touch any other piece of equipment in the communications center without his permission. Since Lieutenant Agnes Felter was now the acting communications officer and electronics material officer, she was supporting Chief Wheaton in his demands, even though Felter was currently serving her two weeks onboard the *New Horizon*.

The new component, which was the cryptologic component of the system, arrived, and Wheaton installed it earlier in the morning. When they turned on the system and loaded the crypto with the day's code, nothing happened. No message traffic was received or transmitted between the comm suite and the *New Horizon*; even voice communications were not possible.

Chief Wheaton spent the rest of the day troubleshooting the system to no effect. By the end of the day, he declared the new cryptological unit faulty. Impassive looks were exchanged around the comm suite, but no one contradicted the chief. Shortly thereafter, Chief Petty Officer Heather Tate arrived and relieved Chief Wheaton for the day's watch. Chief Wheaton announced he was leaving for the day and would order a replacement tomorrow.

Michael had been watching all this from the microminiature lab, where he was steadfastly working at putting together a new AI motherboard. The other one was ruined by the incident that had destroyed most of the equipment in the comm suite. A half hour later, he was about to wrap up what he was doing and call it a day when he saw Brad Guillete approach Chief Radioman Tate.

"Chief, would you mind if I take a look at the NAPACS?" asked Brad.

Chief Tate looked at Brad and smiled. "Why should I care? The goddamned thing still doesn't work. You can have the whole damn thing!"

"Thanks, Chief," replied Brad.

Brad sat down in front of the computer used by the system and commenced opening the front panel. The inside surface of the front panel contained various indicator lights and switches. Brad then attached a tablet to the metal equipment rack beside him so he could view it while working on the inside of the front panel. He then turned the tablet on and called up the technical manual of the diagnostics of the computer. Michael had never seen Chief Wheaton do this, so he was curious and leaned over to talk to Brad when he was close enough.

"What are you doing, Brad?" asked Michael.

Brad looked at Michael apprehensively, then shrugged and said, "Troubleshooting the NAPACS."

"Isn't Chief Wheaton the NAPACS technician?" asked Michael.

"No," Brad responded.

"How many people on board the *New Horizon* were trained on the NAPACS?" inquired Michael.

"There were two, myself and Petty Officer Sakuta," said Brad.

Michael remembered the funeral held aboard the *New Horizon* shortly after the incident that had stranded them in this system. He recalled that seventeen had died and that Petty Officer Akio Sakuta was among them.

"I see," said Michael. "Would you mind if I assist you?"

Brad looked at Michael, then said, "If you want to, sir."

Michael went over to Chief Tate and asked, "Chief, would you mind sending someone over to my living quarters to inform my wife not to wait up for me?"

"I can do that, sir." Heather Tate smiled.

"Thank you, Chief," said Michael as he returned to sit beside Brad. "So what are you doing now?"

"This is the computer that controls the NAPACS. It's a stand-alone computer from the AI, which is why the second *A* in the acronym NAPACS stands for *autonomous*. The whole system will operate without any AI inputs because of this computer, but this computer is dumb and will only do what it is told to do by programming it or inputting data commands manually. If all the other components in the system are operational, we can transmit and receive high-speed data streams or voice messages to other ships and stations within range. What I've done is open up the front panel of the computer that has the diagnostic test console on the back of the front panel. The test console allows me to run diagnostics by inputting instructions octally with these switches in microsteps once the diagnostic program is loaded," Brad informed Lieutenant Michael Anderson.

"Seems a little antiquated," stated Michael.

"It is, but it's hardened against electromagnetic pulses, or EMP, and handles most of the message traffic for the comm shack," replied Brad.

"Oh!" said Michael.

"Warships have most of their vital systems controlled by a computer similar to this one," stated Brad.

Lieutenant Michael Anderson recalled that there had been two computers similar to this one in engineering. There were another two on the bridge, one on each side. He also recalled seeing one in the boatswain locker near the shuttle and longboat control clamps, which meant there were probably similar computers for missile control, gunnery control, and other vital ship systems. Obviously, the Navy believed in redundancy.

"How many diagnostics are there, Brad?" asked Michael, changing the subject.

"Seventeen. So this might take a while," said Brad.

"Can we be sure the computer is the problem?" asked Michael.

"I didn't say it was, sir. I'm just ensuring that the computer is running optimally," replied Brad.

"Oh! I could use some coffee. How about you?" inquired Michael.

"Coffee would be great, sir. I'm planning on running each diagnostic three times to verify my results, so I'll be here awhile," replied Brad distractedly as he pressed some switches on the panel.

Running the diagnostics and verifying the results took nearly half the night. When Brad was finished, he had a list of thirty-one probable faulty cards to replace. Unfortunately, there were no spares held by the communications suite. He had narrowed that list down to three as the most likely culprits. Then he walked around the comm suite looking at the indicator lights on the various components that comprised the NAPACS system.

"What are you doing, Brad?" asked Michael.

"It just doesn't feel right," stated Brad.

"What do you mean?" questioned Michael.

"We're receiving data from the *New Horizon*, but it isn't being processed by the computer. While the data we want to send never appears to leave the computer," said Brad.

"So where do you think the problem lies?" asked Michael.

"I would say the computer. It appears to be receiving data, but that received data doesn't appear to make it to the computer, and the computer isn't forwarding the data we want to send," Brad said as he walked over to the transmitter room where all the radios for transmitting and receiving were installed. He came back to the computer station and picked up his coffee to take a sip. Michael watched as Brad's eyes roamed the suite and finally fixated on an equipment rack across the room. He walked over and looked at an empty equipment rack that was awaiting a component.

"Chief Tate, wasn't Chief Wheaton planning on replacing the old crypto with the new crypto in the NAPACS?" Brad asked.

"Yeah, but it didn't happen," replied Heather.

"I remember that. The commander disapproved the upgrade to save resources and time. We had a spare for the old crypto in the security locker that he had sent down," said Michael. "What are you thinking, Brad?"

"Let me check something," muttered Brad.

Brad removed a multipurpose tool about the size of a pen that he always carried in his pocket and turned on one of its basic functions. A bright beam of light shot out of the end of the tool, and he crawled behind the equipment rack where the crypto was located. He reappeared and walked over to the computer and crawled behind the rack where it was installed. When he reappeared again, he was nodding.

"What are you thinking?" asked Michael.

"That the data cable between the computer and the old crypto we're using was never installed," said Brad Guillete.

"So what is hooked up?" asked Michael.

"The cable between the computer and the new crypto rack," replied Brad, pointing to the empty racks he stared at earlier.

"Can we switch the crypto we're using to the new rack?" asked Michael.

"No. There's different connections in the back of the equipment. They won't mate when it's slid into that rack," stated Brad.

"Can we switch the cable to the old rack?" asked Michael.

"No. It has a different plug end for the crypto connection," stated Brad.

Silence fell between the two. Michael could see that Brad was thinking about the problem.

"You know, sir, that cable was either thrown away, never made, or it could be lying around this suite somewhere, like in one of these drawers," said Brad.

Brad pulled open the closest drawer to him. It was a fairly large drawer used to store large items, such as boxes of paper used in the comm suite. Michael saw Brad look down into the drawer for a moment, then he looked up and stared intently at Michael.

"What?" asked Michael uncomfortably. Then he looked into the drawer that Brad opened, and there inside the drawer sat a large rolled-up data cable. Michael looked back up at Brad and said, "You don't think?"

The two of them pulled the cable from the drawer. It was a heavy cable because of the radio frequency shielding, or RF shielding, used to protect the delicate wiring harness inside. Brad and Michael checked the nomenclature on the plug ends, and sure enough, it was the cable they required. Brad turned off the computer and crypto, while Michael threaded the cable through the overhead cable run between the two pieces of equipment. Then Brad attached the ends to the appropriate slots on the back of each piece of equipment and turned the equipment on.

"Chief, would you mind loading the day's code?" asked Brad.

"I can do that," acknowledged Chief Tate.

After the chief loaded the codes, the high-speed printer near the computer that Michael recalled was part of the NAPACS system started spitting out messages.

"It looks like we're receiving, Brad." Chief Tate grinned.

"Let's see if we're transmitting," said Brad.

Lieutenant Michael Anderson followed Brad Guillete as he entered the transmitter room. Brad went over to an equipment rack that held two ultrahigh frequency or UHF transceivers. He studied the top of the rack where several jumper cables were inserted into a switching unit. The unit allowed the operator to physically select how the transceivers would be utilized. Brad took a picture of the cable runs and started to take them out.

"What are you doing, Brad?" asked Michael.

"I didn't see the transmit light flash on the front panel of the transceiver, and I don't think this setup is right," replied Brad.

"What was it set up for?" questioned Michael.

"I think Chief Wheaton was attempting to set it up for dual PACS, but I think it was set up wrong, and I don't have my notes about the setup with me," said Brad.

"Where are your notes?" inquired Michael.

"On the *New Horizon*," said Brad.

"So what are you going to do?" asked Michael.

"Dual PACS requires two transceivers, one to transmit and one to receive. I'm going to set it up so we can transmit and receive using one transceiver," stated Brad.

"It's a transceiver. Why would they set it up to use two different transceivers?" asked Michael.

"In dual PACS, you transmit on one frequency and receive on a different frequency. When message traffic is high, like when we're in Sol system where there are many ships transmitting, it allows the naval station or ship to select who they're communicating with. These transceivers allow you to only select one frequency at a time, so it requires two different transceivers. Waste of time and equipment in this case since both the *New Horizon* and the comm suite can use the same frequency to transmit and receive with little interruption," replied Brad.

"Interruption?" asked Michael.

"Another station transmitting or both the *New Horizon* and the comm suite transmitting at the same time," Brad informed Michael.

"Why did you take a picture of the hookup?" asked Michael.

"So I could put it back the way it was if this doesn't work," said Brad, looking at Michael sideways.

Brad took a jumper cable and put one end into a slot that said NAPACS and the other into the slot for one of the transceivers. Brad watched the transceivers transmit light for several moments. Nothing happened. He shrugged and reconnected the transceiver end into the other transceiver slot. Suddenly, the transmit light started blinking on the transceiver. Michael and Brad walked out into the comm suite.

"Chief, are we receiving and transmitting to the *New Horizon*?" asked Brad.

The chief checked something on her screen and turned to Brad with a huge grin. "That we are, Petty Officer Guillete. Thank you."

"All right, Chief. I'm going to get breakfast, and I'll be back to write up the CASCOR," said Brad, referring to the casualty corrected message that needed to be sent out upon the repair of a major system or unit.

"Roger that, Petty Officer Guillete," responded Chief Tate.

"Sir, would you like to go to breakfast with me at the Flour Mill?" inquired Brad.

Michael looked at his watch and realized it was almost six thirty in the morning. They had been at this all night. There was a sense of pride in knowing that the system was finally online, and they could now communicate with the *New Horizon*. Then Michael thought about Francesca and the fact that she was probably wondering where he might be.

"I would Brad, but I need to go. My wife is probably wondering where I am," replied Michael.

"All right, sir, maybe next time," Brad replied as he left.

Michael watched Brad leave, then went to the microminiature repair room to pick up his things. He thought of writing a message to Commander Blankenship commending Brad on the work he had accomplished. He heard the morning crew come in as he started composing. Michael lost track of time, and he was still attempting to compose the commendation when the door to the microminiature room opened, and Brad came in. Brad came up to Michael and looked at him for a moment.

"What are you doing, sir?" asked Brad Guillete.

"I'm recommending you for an award. I'm writing a letter of commendation," said Lieutenant Anderson.

"You needn't bother, sir," responded Brad.

"Why do you say that?" asked Michael.

"Because it will go nowhere," stated Brad.

"I don't understand," replied Michael.

"Chief Wheaton is writing up the CASCOR for the NAPACS," said Brad, referring to the casualty corrected message that was required for major systems or major casualties that would inhibit a command's ability to complete its mission.

"Why does that matter?" inquired Lieutenant Anderson.

"He's not taking any inputs as to how the system was repaired," said Brad.

"How can he write a message about how the system was repaired if he doesn't take inputs on how it was repaired?" questioned Lieutenant Michael Anderson.

Brad simply shrugged.

CHAPTER 54

There was a meeting at the MILDET prefab with the commander. Lieutenant Commander Conor Raybourn and Lieutenant Michael Anderson sat with the commander listening to Lieutenant Agnes Felter giving her version of the status of the comm suite and how Chief Wheaton had been highly instrumental in the installation and repair of the NAPACS system. Commander Hadden Blankenship listened to the report impassively, while Michael looked at Felter in disbelief. When Agnes Felter finished her report, Hadden Blankenship sat back with his hands clasped on the tabletop, studying Lieutenant Felter.

"Are you finished, Lieutenant?" asked Hadden.

"Yes, sir," replied Agnes.

"Yes, I do believe you are," stated Hadden.

An uncomfortable silence fell upon the room as everyone waited for the commander to continue. He continued staring at the lieutenant, saying nothing, patiently waiting.

Finally, Agnes fidgeted in her chair and asked, "What do you mean?"

"I mean that I am inactivating your commission, and you may rejoin the colony, or I will reassign you to another department," stated Hadden.

"You can't do that! The president put me in charge of electronics repair division, and you answer to the president!" shouted Agnes Felter.

"I answer to the president, but he does not make personnel duty assignments. I do," stated Commander Blankenship.

"You can't do this!" cried Agnes loudly.

"Those are your two choices," said Hadden quietly.

"I'll resign my commission and rejoin the colony," replied Agnes dejectedly.

"You will continue to do your two-week stints when your duty rotation comes up, but you will answer to Lieutenant Anderson, who will be in charge of electronics repair division," said Hadden.

"I have seniority to Lieutenant Anderson," stated Agnes.

"That can be changed," replied Hadden.

"What do you mean?" demanded Agnes.

"There's two ways I can do this. I can demote you to lieutenant junior grade, or I can promote Lieutenant Anderson to lieutenant commander. Personally, I like the idea of doing both, but I'll settle for promoting him to lieutenant commander," stated Commander Blankenship.

"It doesn't matter. We're never going back to Sol System," retorted Agnes.

"I'm also filing a reprimand in your permanent record. That will be available for the future records of the colony, and if we ever do make it back to Sol System, it will be available for United Systems to review and take action on," stated Commander Blankenship.

Conor watched as Agnes Felter's jaw dropped. "Why are you doing this?"

"I think you know why. Additionally, if Lieutenant Commander Anderson has any problems with you in the future, I will demote you to lieutenant junior grade. Is that clear?" questioned Hadden.

"Yes," replied Agnes, defeated.

"Yes what?" demanded Commander Blankenship.

"Yes, sir," murmured Lieutenant Felter.

"You're dismissed, Lieutenant," returned the commander.

The room remained quiet as Agnes Felter rose from the table and left. Staff Sergeant Amanda Hall stood outside the door as it opened. The commander's face was tense as he watched the woman leave. The staff sergeant closed the door as the lieutenant walked away, giving the remaining officers privacy.

The recent incident involving Norman Pool was portrayed by the president and his staff as an attempt by Hiroka to assassinate a presidential cabinet member. Additionally, there was the miners' animosity over the incident involving the Marines and the brawl at the Overlook. A rumor was going around about how the commander himself tried to assassinate the president at the clinic. Fortunately, many people felt that the commander was doing a good job and that all this was simply rumors and conspiracy theories.

When they had the room to themselves, Hadden looked at Michael. It took a moment for the tense expression on his face to be replaced by a warm smile.

"Lieutenant Commander Anderson, I believe you are out of uniform," stated Hadden.

"Sorry, sir," said Michael.

"I believe I can help him with that, sir." Conor Raybourn grinned.

"Then let's do this, Lieutenant Commander Raybourn," said Hadden.

"Yes, sir," replied Conor, grinning, as he and Hadden Blankenship stood.

Lieutenant Commander Raybourn produced a small box that contained the gold leaf collar insignia for a lieutenant commander. Conor indicated for Michael to stand as Hadden worked his way over. Michael rose and stood at attention as Blankenship stopped before him. The commander reached up and removed the collar devices from Michael's uniform and replaced them with the new ones of a lieutenant commander. When he was finished, he took a step back, and Michael, knowing the drill, saluted. Hadden returned the salute and held out his hand.

"Well done, Lieutenant Commander," said Hadden as he clasped Michael's hand and shook it.

"Thank you, sir," returned newly promoted Lieutenant Commander Michael Anderson as Conor took his hand and shook it also.

"I have one request for you, Michael," said Hadden Blankenship.

"What is it, sir?" asked Michael.

"In addition to your other duties, I want you to help Master Sergeant Zander convince Brad Guillete to return to active duty," said the commander.

"I'm not sure that's possible, sir," returned Michael uneasily.

"I realize that, Michael. I want you to get with Zander and give it your best shot," replied Hadden.

"He has lots of trust issues," replied Michael.

"Do you blame him?" asked Hadden.

Michael looked at the door that Lieutenant Agnes Felter had departed through. "No, sir."

"All I'm asking of you is to try. I don't care if he reenters in the Navy or Marines. We need him," stated Commander Blankenship.

"I agree with that assessment, sir," said Michael.

"Conor, about this recon-and-rescue mission," said the commander, changing the subject.

"It's only a proposal, sir. We could use the intel Staff Sergeant Krupich could give us if she is still alive," said Conor.

"I understand, but we can't afford to lose more Marines. Is there any way to determine if it was actually her?" said Hadden.

"The master sergeant is sure it's her," replied Conor.

"I trust the master sergeant's instincts. They're usually right. It's still too much of a chance. The last longboat says there's five pavilions scattered on the plains outside the Compound at this time and at least two dozens near the river mouth down south," said the commander.

"That's a lot of raptors," said Michael.

"We have no way of knowing if there might be more hidden by the forests," replied Conor.

Suddenly, Staff Sergeant Amanda Hall burst through the door unannounced. Amanda's face was flushed as she caught her breath. Amanda then declared loudly, "The fence is being attacked."

Conor was out the door, and the rest of the group followed closely behind him. He reached the edge and looked out across the fields to see a section of the fence approximately one hundred meters or more in length lying on the ground. Two apatosauruses and a triceratops lay enmeshed in the fence, while the rest of the herd scattered across the open fields of the Compound. However, a large segment of the herd was being directed toward the manufacturing buildings below by red and green running shapes.

The figures of people could be seen as some ran toward the elevators, while others stood watching in shock. Marines in full battle gear were running toward the factories as the stampeding creatures approached. Two Marine ATVs were crossing the fields, trying to intercept and interpose themselves between the green and red shapes that were running toward the elevators also. Conor saw the minigun mounted on the trailing ATV mow down three greens and a red that had unwisely grouped together while the lead ATV simply ran over a green. The Marine chopper was lifting from the roof of the Marine Complex. People were lining the cleft's edge as they watched the unfolding chaos below.

"They need help!" stated Lieutenant Commander Raybourn.

"How?" asked Amanda.

"Michael, the chopper," ordered Conor as he turned to run toward the MILDET prefab.

"Sir, his body armor and weapon!" shouted the staff sergeant.

"We'll bring them while he does preflights!" Conor shouted back.

"Roger that!" shouted Amanda, already running toward the MILDET prefab.

Commander Blankenship and Staff Sergeant Hall entered the prefab with Conor. They drew their body armor on and grabbed weapons. Conor carried body armor for Michael and tossed Amanda Hall an M-71 for Michael. Conor noted that she grabbed the musette bag filled with grenades while Hadden Blankenship had a musette bag full of magazines for the M-71s. They ran to the chopper where Michael was just finishing preflights. Conor tossed Michael his body armor as the commander told him to move over.

The stampede had crossed the fields and reached the buildings as Hadden dropped the chopper toward the plain below. The ATVs and Marine chopper were attempting to steer the herd toward the west as the red and green raptors streaked into the buildings below.

"Why don't they fire on the herd and stop them?" asked Michael.

"Innocent civilians," replied Hadden.

"What?" questioned Michael.

"It's not the herd's fault," replied Conor. Then he added, "How many tons of rotten meat do you want lying around after this is over?"

"Oh!" said Michael.

"Let me get lower and try to take out some of the green and red raptors," said the commander.

Commander Hadden Blankenship took the chopper lower, heading toward the foundry and lumber mill. A group of Marines were slowly retreating from the foundry door as raptors came around the corner of the lumber mill. Fire and smoke were rising from inside the lumber mill. The Marines continued to retreat, firing at the invaders. The elevator arrived, and the waiting people pushed to enter the empty cage, but there would not be enough room for all.

"Set us down near the elevators, Commander," said Conor.

Hadden Blankenship set them down. Conor, Michael, and Amanda grabbed their weapons and musette bags to join the Marines who were making a stand at the base of the elevators. The commander rose into the air and cut loose on a group of raptors with the minigun, ripping them to shreds, while the two lieutenant commanders set up a skirmish line with the Marines to protect the unarmed colonists. The fight was intense even with the chopper providing air support. There were two people down near the elevators and three more out in the roadway between the foundry and lumber mill. Conor received a cut from a javelin along his left cheek as he took position.

He saw Michael drop his Navarro M-71 and grab his left arm with a cut that ran from wrist to elbow down to the bone. Aabir Issawi was standing next to Conor when he fell, a javelin piercing his back with the bloody tip protruding from his chest. Conor fired a three-round burst into a raptor's chest that was getting ready to throw a javelin at Anthony Finley as Anthony removed his belt and threw it to Anya Kaur. Anthony rolled on the ground and picked up Michael's M-71 and entered the fight as Anya grabbed the belt and wrapped it around Michael's arm above the elbow.

A javelin hit Conor in his chest, knocking him to the ground, when it hit his body armor. Staff Sergeant Hall stepped over Conor's legs as he lay dazed from hitting his head on the concrete surface surrounding the elevators. He saw her take two raptors running toward him with two quick bursts from her M-71, then eject the magazine and ram a fresh one into the chamber as Sergeant Adachi fired a burst into a raptor that changed direction and ran toward her. Amanda ignored the raptor that skidded to the ground at her feet on her right and raised her Navarro M-71, firing two quick shots that struck two raptors at a hundred meters in their heads, causing them to collapse to the ground.

Suddenly, the shooting stopped, and Amanda turned around to offer her hand to Conor as the chopper followed the few fleeing raptors. Conor grabbed her hand and rose to his feet to view the battlefield. The ground was littered with red-feathered bodies, and at least two colonists lay out there among them. Colonists were still going up the elevators, but one coming down carried Bess Hollinger and Kers Joshi. Conor saw Anya Kaur tending Lance Corporal Rand, who had a javelin in his shoulder. Turning, Conor walked over to Michael, who was sitting with his back against a cement block, holding a cloth that wrapped around his left forearm.

"How are you doing, Michael?" asked Conor.

"I could use a painkiller," said Michael, wincing.

"Staff Sergeant!" called Conor.

Amanda Hall walked over, her eyes constantly searching the nearby buildings. She reached into a pouch at her waist and handed Conor a bottle as she surveyed the surrounding area.

"Give him two, sir," said Amanda as the chopper appeared over the top of the smoking lumber mill.

Taking two pills out of the bottle, Conor squatted down and put them on Michael's tongue. He swallowed them, and a couple of minutes later, his face relaxed as Bess Hollinger walked up.

"How are you, Michael?" asked Bess.

"He has a tourniquet on his upper arm. There's a cut down his forearm that starts at the wrist and ends at the elbow. It goes down to the bone," answered Conor for Michael.

"Sounds bad. Let me have a look," said Bess as she knelt down beside Michael.

Debris flew as the chopper landed to the west of the elevators. Conor rose to his feet and walked with Staff Sergeant Hall over to where the commander stood surveying the carnage. Hadden shook his head and looked at his feet, closing his eyes for a moment, as he stood in the breeze from the slowly spinning rotors.

"We need more defenses," stated Hadden, turning his attention to Conor.

"I thought we were prepared, sir," said Conor.

"We were for any normal animal," replied Hadden. He swept the battlefield with his arm. "But these are intelligent beings," he added. "It'll take more than a fence to stop them."

"I'll get with the master sergeant and see what ideas he has for increasing our defenses. Right now, the fence needs repair," said Conor. "I'll fly air guard while the Marines work on the perimeter fence."

"I'll take Lieutenant Commander Anderson to the clinic. Then I'm going to the comm suite and have them expedite the pharmaceutical unit. After that, I'll be at the clinic," replied Hadden.

"Aye, aye, sir," said Conor as he saluted.

Conor wondered how much more blood would have to be paid by both sides of this conflict before a peace of some sort could be established. With no way to communicate with the raptors, the likelihood of a peace seemed remote. The survival of the colony seemed to be balanced on a fragile hope as Conor turned to the door to go do what he could to increase that one-in-a-million chance.

CHAPTER 55

Lieutenant Commander Conor Raybourn met the longboat at the pier with a colony truck. He assisted Lieutenant JG Vanda Kisimba and Petty Officer Anya Kaur unload the new pharmaceutical unit Commander Hadden Blankenship had expedited from the ship's factory on the *New Horizon*. The unit was strapped in, and the three entered the truck to take it to the clinic for installation. Smoke was rising from the damaged buildings as Conor rose in the elevator.

Commander Blankenship was already at the clinic, adding support and encouragement to those who had been injured and their families. Conor's wife, Shiran, was at the MILDET Complex coordinating operations for the perimeter fence repair. Gunnery Sergeant Samuel Rusu was with the Marines and several colony members at the fence breach with four of the ATVs effecting repairs and butchering the five large dinosaurs that had died during the raptor raid. Master Sergeant Evan Zander was at the clinic for personal reasons since Chief Tami Zander went into labor after the raptor attack had been fended off.

When they reached the ledge, they took the truck to the front entrance of the clinic where a forklift waited to unload the pharmaceutical unit. The forklift took the unit into the clinic and to the designated room behind the reception desk. The forklift lowered the unit to the floor and backed out of the room.

"Looks good, Petty Officer Kaur," said Conor.

"Could I get you to sign for it, sir?" asked Anya.

"Might be better to have Dr. Hollinger do that since it belongs to the clinic," replied Conor.

"Yes, sir," answered Anya.

"Do you require my assistance any longer, Lieutenant Commander?" asked Vanda.

"Aren't you supposed to be taking the commander topside?" asked Conor.

"He said he wanted to be on the *New Horizon* when *Longboat 4* left for the moon," replied Vanda.

"Why don't you locate the doctor for Petty Officer Kaur? I have Brad Guillete waiting to make the necessary hookups to power the unit up," said Conor. He paused, looking at the pharmaceutical unit, and added, "Tell her the unit should be hooked up and the diagnostics run in, say, an hour."

"Yes, sir," replied Vanda.

It took about half an hour to make the attachments to the main power for the pharmaceutical unit. Then Brad and Conor pushed it into place against the wall and commenced running the diagnostics. Dr. Hollinger and Hadden arrived before he was finished. The doctor looked haggard, and her smock was bloodstained as she sipped on a mug of coffee at the table in the corner with Hadden. They waited for Brad to complete the task and nodded.

"How does it look, Brad?" asked Hadden.

"According to the diagnostics, it's operating perfectly," replied Brad.

"That's wonderful," stated Bess enthusiastically.

"Hopefully, this will make your life easier, Doctor," said Hadden.

"It will. Thank you. We already have a few things we need to issue out with this emergency. Excuse me, now I need to get back into surgery," said Bess as she finished her coffee and left.

Conor looked at Hadden Blankenship and asked, "How bad is it?"

"Bad. There are seven dead and another nineteen injured," replied Hadden.

"How bad are the injured?" inquired Conor.

"Five are in critical condition. Bess said the rest should recover with no complications," answered Hadden.

"It could have been worse," said Conor.

"Yes, it could have," said Hadden distractedly. He sat looking at the wall for a moment then at Conor and said, "I haven't eaten since breakfast. Let's go find something to eat before I go topside to the *New Horizon*."

The two left the clinic and met Shiran at the Overlook. They ate while Shiran updated them both on the fence repairs. When they were finished, they walked toward the MILDET prefab and noticed others walking that way. Reaching the end of the shops, they entered the large flat space reserved for parties and Friday night dancing that existed between the shops and the MILDET prefab where a large crowd had gathered. It was the only place that an assemblage that large could gather on this side of the river that cut the cleft area in two. A stage had been set up for a meeting, but it was apparent that President Felipe Martinez had ideas of controlling access and limiting discussion since he and his cabinet were the only ones allowed on the platform. That last part was not working so well for the president since Tom Tollifer was standing in front of the stage, confronting him.

"Why hasn't the colony been informed about the capabilities of this new intelligent raptor, Mr. President?" demanded Tom.

"What makes the new raptor a concern of the people?" retorted Martinez.

"Considering they're intelligent and utilize tools and could plan that," replied Tom as he waved an arm toward the devastation below. "I think it makes it our concern."

"Then you know everything you need to know," returned Martinez.

"There's people dead from this attack and a miner died. I'd say we need to know a bit more," replied Tom Tollifer.

"Where were the Marines?" came a catcall from the back.

"Not protecting the miners or the colony obviously," came another voice from the back.

Felipe Martinez saw an opportunity and stated, "It was the Marines' job to protect the miners and the colony. They obviously failed."

Conor felt his neck get hot, and when he glanced at Shiran, her eyes were flashing. Blankenship simply looked at the two and, when he had their attention, shook his head. He was right; showing anger now would play into the hands of those refusing to admit they were wrong. What needed to be done was educate the people that it was dangerous outside the Compound, especially now with an intelligent, tool-bearing being that they knew little about. Tom Tollifer was not willing to let the matter rest.

"The miners knew the risks of going outside the Compound," snarled Felipe Martinez.

"The word I hear is that they were leaving the ATVs without weapons or body armor. Is that standard procedure, Mr. President?" demanded Tom.

"Wearing body armor and carrying a weapon is highly recommended by the Marines when working outside the Compound," replied Felipe.

"Did you issue orders to the miners to follow those recommendations?" demanded Tom.

"They're grown men and women. If they chose to ignore what the Marines recommend, they are free to do so," responded Felipe.

"That's not an answer, Mr. President," said Tom.

"I don't understand what you mean," replied Felipe.

"It's real simple. Did you issue orders to follow the Marine recommendations of wearing armor and carrying weapons when working outside the Compound?" demanded Tom.

"No. Why should I?" snarled Felipe.

"Aren't you the director of the foundry and mining operations?" demanded Tollifer.

There were more catcalls this time directed at Tom. Others in the crowd weren't having it, and some yelled at the agitators to shut up. There was a shout from the back to make them. It was becoming apparent that this meeting was slowly devolving into something ugly. The sheriff and his people were not in the crowd but instead stood around the stage and did nothing. Suddenly, there were the sound of seats being overturned and cries of pain in the back of the crowd. When this occurred, Hadden Blankenship looked at the Evan Zander and nodded.

The master sergeant led the way as the commander walked over to the steps leading up to the stage where the president stood, watching the developing brawl in the back of the crowd. Sheriff Upton made a move to block the commander, and the master sergeant put a hand on the man's chest. The sheriff visibly deflated as the master sergeant simply stood there looking into the man's eyes. At that point, the president noticed the commander ascending the stairs to the stage.

"You're not allowed up here!" screamed Felipe.

"Mr. President, with all due respect, I'm going to speak," said Hadden.

"I'm the president, and I say who speaks!" shouted Felipe.

"You may be president, but I still intend to speak," said Hadden.

"Is this a coup?" demanded Felipe.

"Mr. President, look at it as an opportunity," said Hadden.

"An opportunity to do what?" pressed Felipe.

"The right thing," replied Hadden.

"What do you consider the right thing?" sneered Felipe.

"Stopping the developing riot in the back would be a good start," replied Hadden.

"How do you propose I do that?" replied Felipe Martinez as Blankenship stood looking at him.

"You brought this about through dishonesty and mismanagement. You control the people who are making the trouble," replied Hadden.

"If anyone is responsible for the developing riot, it's you," sneered Felipe disdainfully.

"Why do you say that?" asked Blankenship patiently.

"Your austerity measures in denying these people the simple comforts that would make their lives more bearable!" shouted Felipe.

"You would have the ship's factory produce toasters, refrigerators, and air conditioners instead of medical equipment and replacement parts for the factory itself and other essential equipment?" asked Hadden.

"Yes!" shouted Felipe.

"Is that the people speaking or yourself?" asked Blankenship.

"I speak for all the people!" roared Felipe.

"It doesn't look that way to me," replied Hadden calmly.

"This meeting is over!" shouted Felipe.

"This meeting has just begun, Mr. President. If you leave now, you may not be president in the morning," stated Hadden.

"Are you staging a coup?" screeched Felipe Martinez.

"No, but the Constitution allows for your replacement if enough people petition for it," replied Hadden Blankenship.

"Who would start a petition like that?" demanded Felipe heatedly.

"I would! And I have over two hundred signatures already!" shouted Jacqueline Vinet from the crowd.

The meeting went on till nearly two in the morning. There was a lot of shouting, but the impending riot failed to develop after Felipe Martinez shouted that the troublemakers should settle down or be arrested. Felipe Martinez retained his hold on the presidency by a small margin. Conor suspected there were many who were dissatisfied with their lives here and wanted what Felipe had offered. He also conjectured that there were people who feared Felipe, or at least the people who supported and voted for him. However, there were those who understood the necessity of what was being done and the sacrifices that needed to be made.

There were a lot of unhappy colonists who were demanding outright war with the raptors. The commander argued that the full strength and capabilities of the raptors were not known, and he was not willing to exterminate them outright. No one knew if the current raptors represented all there were or only a small contingent of the whole. The option of taking the war to the raptors was not an alternative either with only the Marines as a real fighting force as they might be overwhelmed by sheer numbers. The commander and Conor argued for strengthening the defenses and installing more security measures. Many of the colonists were not happy with this proposal but in the end agreed that until more was known about the full strength and capabilities of the raptors, it was the only option available.

The commander left for the *New Horizon* shortly after the meeting. Conor stood on the cleft edge surveying the devastation below. A group of colonists and Marines worked on the break in the fence with portable lights. There were four ATVs at the break, two standing guard and two being used as work vehicles. The Marine chopper was on the ground just inside the fence break, ready to go into action, guarding the people there.

Half the crops were ruined by the attack, and the lumber mill was a smoking ruin. The brick and stone works had been damaged, and Conor could see people repairing the damaged wall and roof. The foundry had suffered little or no apparent damage, but there was smoke rising from the coal pile on its eastern side. The Marine Complex and piers had not suffered damage because of the defenses the Marines had emplaced in case of such an event.

Fortunately, the raptors had not reached the cleft's edge, but that had been the purpose of building here in the first place—a high defensible spot to protect the people. With the exception of the shuttles and people working below, everything at ground level could be rebuilt. The one flaw of the cleft was if an invader was able to hold the ground surrounding the cleft and conduct a siege. The cleft required power from the shuttles and food from the land below.

Conor sighed as the sun came up in the east. A gentle breeze brought a fragrant scent that tickled the nostrils with an unknown but somehow familiar essence. The undulating roar of an allosaurus sounded as a shriek of pain from its prey was cut off abruptly, reminding Conor that this land was both beautiful and deadly. Conor wasn't sure how the future would unfold, but he hoped that the fates would smile on this small enclave of humans so far from home.

CHAPTER 56

It had been a long night for Bess Hollinger and her staff. The clinic was full of patients from the raptor attack who required care. Jacqueline Vinet and four other volunteers had appeared shortly after the attack, and two of them had spent the night along with Caroline deLang. Ethan Sanders lost his lower left leg in the attack. Anthony Finley had been hit in the chest with a javelin, puncturing a lung. John Martins had taken a javelin to his right thigh before he could shut the shuttle door. Joseph Green had a javelin wound in his left shoulder. Sergeant Nikolai Ivankov received a concussion saving Joseph Green. There were many more injuries, and there were seven dead from the raptor attack on the Compound. It had already been a long day, and Bess was getting ready to leave when Anthony Finley developed a problem that required Bess to reopen his lung to correct. Dr. Joshi had been called away as they were just getting ready to close Anthony back up.

Bess just finished washing from surgery when Evan Zander carried his wife into the clinic. Her contractions were already close, and Bess took them into the emergency room immediately. Even then, it had taken nearly three hours for the birth to happen and another hour ensuring the mother and infant girls were doing well. The second set of twins for the Zanders had left Bess and the mother exhausted, and she was ready to lie down. She checked the mother and the twins' vitals before leaving the room. The parents had named them Ruth and Clare. Bess smiled and thought about what she would name her own children—that is, if Anarzej Gataki ever decided to tie the knot with her. The man was frustratingly dense at times, and she was coming to the conclusion that she was going to have to take matters into her own hands.

There was a buzzing noise that emitted from the far wall. Evan Zander lay there on a cot, his cammie shirt still not fastened up the front. Bess Hollinger smiled. Tami and Evan had been the first colonists to commit, and it appeared that the marriage was going well. They were also leading the colony in baby production. A standing joke after it was known that they were having another set of twins was that they were starting a colony of their own.

The couple had two sets of twins now, and they were just approaching one planet year on the planet they had settled. Tami had become pregnant only a month after arriving in the system and had to decide on letting the first set come to term. A hard decision to make, especially without knowing if there was a truly habitable planet to colonize. Fortunately, it had worked out for the happy couple. Their first set of twins, Harold and Eric Zander, were now over a year old. Bess walked over to the incubator units in the corner and checked on how the two new arrivals were doing.

The two were asleep and appeared to be doing fine. Bess decided it was time to finish up and take care of herself. She quietly walked out the room and went up to the nurses' station where she wrote a prescription for Tami Zander. Bess hung it for Caroline deLang, knowing she'd be by shortly. She then keyed in the medications for the pharmaceutical unit to produce so Caroline could deliver them to the Zander room.

The new pharmaceutical unit had arrived yesterday, delivered by Petty Officer Kaur, and was against the wall behind the nurses' station. It had already been put to good use, and some of the simplest medications that the colony had been doing without were now available. Commander Blankenship had refused to send the pharmaceutical unit installed on the *New Horizon* when the clinic had been set up, citing that the colony and the *New Horizon* could not afford to lose such a valuable piece of equipment. However, he had kept his promise of fast shipments from the *New Horizon* and the manufacturing of a new unit when resources became available. Taking off her apron and mask, Bess was just getting ready to leave when Caroline deLang returned from an errand down the hall.

"Caroline, I have a prescription running for Tami Zander in the unit. Just leave it on her nightstand so she and Evan will notice it," said Bess.

"All right, Bess. I take it they're asleep?" replied Caroline.

"Yes. Don't disturb them. They need it as bad as I do," said Bess.

"Are you taking off?" asked Caroline.

"Yes. I feel like I could sleep for a week," replied Bess.

"You deserve it. Have a nice night if you want to call it that." Caroline chuckled as she looked at the window where the dawning light of the sun was visible.

"Are you going home soon?" inquired Bess.

"When the others arrive in an hour," said Caroline.

"Then you have a nice night too." Bess smiled.

Picking up the heavy brown bag that contained everything Bess required for basic house calls and emergencies, she turned toward the entrance. Bess Hollinger decided that the current situation demanded that they try to always be prepared for an emergency, and sometimes it was easier to check a patient at home. Bess chuckled as she thought about the argument she and Dr. Kers Joshi had about house calls. Kers had been against it at first, not wanting to carry the old-time bag, but after he had visited several people, he saw how they were more open about their ailments. He also discovered that he could assess without asking the living conditions that might be causing an ailment to a patient.

When Bess Hollinger stepped from behind the nurses' station carrying her bag, Ezekiel Yap was in the waiting room looking anxious. He was outfitted in a tan rough-cloth shirt, brown corduroy jeans, and brown leather boots, which went well with his leathered brown skin. He must have left the Overlook closed if he was here because his outfit looked freshly cleaned.

"Good morning, Doctor," greeted Ezekiel, smiling widely.

"Good morning, Ezekiel," Bess returned.

"How is she, Doctor?" asked Ezekiel.

"She's fine, Ezekiel." Bess smiled.

"Good. Good. Where's Evan?" inquired Ezekiel.

"He's in the room with her, sleeping. Would you like to go back?" asked Bess.

"No. No. If they are sleeping, it's best to let them do so," replied Ezekiel.

"I don't think you'll wake them up, Ezekiel. They were up most of the night," said Bess.

"No. I will wait out here. Roberta will open the Overlook," stated Ezekiel.

"If that's what you wish, Ezekiel," said Bess.

"Thank you, Doctor," said Ezekiel as he went to a chair and sat down.

Bess watched as Ezekiel sat down and put the back of his head against the wall. He closed his eyes, and shortly, there was a slight buzzing sound emitting from where he sat. Bess went behind the nurses' station and started looking at the log. She noted that Caroline was already delivering the medication to the Zander room for when they woke up, and Jacqueline should be arriving shortly along with the two other assistant nurses. Bess decided to allow Ezekiel to wait when a voice sounded behind her.

"Ezekiel, you old dog, are you here checking on my girl?" Evan Zander grinned.

"She'll always be my girl." Ezekiel grinned back.

"You shouldn't have stepped on her feet every time you danced with her," replied Evan.

"True, but she kept saying yes when asked," responded Ezekiel.

"She was just being polite," chided Evan.

"She has a big heart," agreed Ezekiel.

"That's true. Come on back and see the new additions," said Evan. He placed a hand on Ezekiel's shoulder, guiding him toward the hall.

"If you insist," Ezekiel protested as he followed his friend down the hallway.

Bess watched them go down the hall and enter the room where Tami and the new twins rested. She picked up her bag and headed toward the front door of the clinic. She was halfway across the waiting room floor when Kers burst through the front door of the clinic. His face was flushed, and he stopped when he saw her. She watched as he took two quick breaths before he started talking and walking quickly toward the emergency room.

"Bess, we have a problem! Caroline, I need as much O+ blood as we have now!" shouted Kers as he rushed through the doors to the emergency room, followed by a stretcher carrying Wilma Nolan. Wilma looked like she had slight convulsions and was going into shock. Kers handed Bess a phial of blood as they rushed into the emergency room.

"I need that analyzed," ordered Kers.

Bess walked over to the far wall and placed the vial into the analyzer. She started the unit, and it hummed as it removed a drop of blood from the sample. Assured the unit was working, Bess turned to assist Kers, who had started inserting the gastric suction tube down Wilma's throat.

"What happened, Kers?" asked Bess apprehensively.

"There's three people dead!" stated Kers.

"What? How?" demanded Bess.

"They're all people we've issued medications to in the last day," stated Kers.

"Are you sure?" demanded Bess.

"Yes! Mr. Hoff, Ms. Neil, and Mr. Landon are dead," answered Kers.

"What of Leonard Bastien?"

"Tom Tollifer is checking on Leonard. Have you issued any other medications since yesterday?" questioned Dr. Joshi.

"No…wait! Yes, I did!" cried Bess as she started running toward the room with Tami and Evan Zander. She nearly fell as she rounded the corner, grabbing the hallway doorframe to steady herself. It seemed to take forever to reach the doorway the two friends had left open. Bess reached the doorway, looking into the room where Evan stood with a cup of water and the pill she had prescribed for Tami Zander.

"Stop! Don't give that to her," Bess wheezed as Tami picked the pill up off Evan's palm. Ezekiel's weathered brown hand slapped the

453

pill out of her dark fingers as they were heading toward her mouth. Evan withdrew the cup from her reach.

"What?" asked Evan as he watched the pill bounce on the floor and roll up against the wall.

"There's at least three people dead, and we suspect it's the pharmaceuticals," replied Bess, relieved she had arrived in time.

CHAPTER 57

The morning after the raptor attack, Eric Hagerman and Nona Klein died of complications to their wounds, bringing the death total of the raptor attack to nine. Another four people had died of the pharmaceuticals issued by the new pharmaceutical unit at the clinic. Tom Tollifer had found Leonard Barstein dead at his residence from the medicines of the new unit.

The president led a charge, demanding answers for the thirteen dead from Lieutenant Commander Conor Raybourn. Many were holding back, wondering how it could have happened. Conor had been able to fend off the president and his cabinet with the assurance that the incident was under investigation, mostly because of the support of Tom Tollifer and Jacqueline Vinet. It appeared that Tom and Jacqueline together had a sizable backing from the colony that the president did not want to go against after the meeting last night.

This left Conor with breathing space to check on Lieutenant Commander Anderson's investigation prior to departing on a mission. The commander had left orders to remove the red raptors from the island. He had specified that if they attacked Conor's force, they were to use lethal force to remove the threat. However, if the raptors retreated, they were to be allowed to depart. Unfortunately, there was no way to communicate that message to the raptors except by example, which meant there would be dead raptors until they understood that they were being allowed to escape. Hopefully, they would be able to divine the message before too many died. Conor was in full body armor with his M-71 slung over his shoulder when he arrived at the comm suite.

"Good morning, Lieutenant Commander," greeted Chief Heather Tate brightly.

"Good morning, Chief," returned Conor. "Is Lieutenant Commander Anderson here?"

"He's in the back with Brad Guillete," replied Heather.

"Brad Guillete?" queried Conor.

"They brought in the pharmaceutical unit," said Heather. She paused for a second, looking Conor up and down, then added, "They were both wearing full body armor too."

"Thanks, Chief," said Conor.

"Mind if I ask what's going on?" asked Heather.

Conor stared at her for a moment, then said, "Treat this as something you don't need to know, Chief."

Heather nodded and replied, "I'll tell everyone working here to ignore what's going on back there and say nothing to anyone."

"That would be best, Chief," said Conor as he opened the heavy door leading further back into the rough-hewn cave.

They had set up the back tunnel that the comm suite had been built in to examining the clinic's pharmaceutical unit. Lieutenant Commander Michael Anderson was in charge of determining the problem with the pharmaceutical unit and had asked for Brad Guillete's assistance in his examination. At the moment, Michael was reading the schematics of the unit. Brad, in full body armor for bomb disposal, was further back in the cave. He was carefully removing a cover plate. Brad had wormed a fiber-optic cable into the interior to determine that it was not booby trapped.

Brad hadn't asked why all these precautions were necessary. He had also been informed to look for the symbol Michael had discovered and let Michael know if he discovered one inside the equipment. Brad had responded by asking, "So this has something to do with the accidents that are happening?"

The question had sounded more like a statement than a question, but Conor said, "Yes."

Brad had simply nodded and went to examine the equipment. Brad had been working for nearly half an hour and had two of the cover plates off when he stopped and pushed back his face shield.

Conor looked up at him, and when he saw this, Brad said, "Sir?"

"Yes, Brad. Did you find something?" asked Conor.

"No, sir," responded Brad.

"What is it?" asked Conor.

"I realize that it's been a long time, but did we ever recover any of the drones?" asked Brad.

For a moment, Lieutenant Commander Raybourn didn't know what Brad Guillete was talking about. Then he realized that he was talking about the survey drones they had lost when initially exploring the island. The drones had suffered malfunctions and crashed. Conor looked at Brad, stunned, and wondered how much the man knew about the incidents and the saboteur. They thought it was due to the pterodactyls and other large flying creatures since at least one drone had been attacked and two others had shown the large creatures flying near them. Was it the creatures that had attacked them, or had they crashed due to other reasons? It very well might be worth their time to investigate the cause of those malfunctions. However, that meant retrieval. At this time, that would be dangerous until the raptor threat had been dealt with.

Conor turned his attention back to Brad, who was still watching him, and said, "No, we haven't, Brad, but I'm going to make the retrieval and examination of those drones a priority after the recon-and-rescue mission."

"When?" asked Brad.

"Three days," replied Conor, knowing Brad was asking about the recon-and-rescue mission and not the drones.

Brad Guillete simply nodded and went back to disassembling the pharmaceutical unit. Brad had requested to be part of the mission, and Conor had accepted his inclusion in the mission since the master sergeant suggested adding him, just as Conor found out that the master sergeant included Brad in the planning of the recon and rescue. Conor suspected it was Brad's attachment to Staff Sergeant Krupich that led to the master sergeant including him in the operation. He also suspected that the master sergeant was working on recruiting Brad Guillete into the Marines.

"Michael, I have to take care of some things at the MILDET and Marine Complex," said Conor.

"We have everything under control, Conor," replied Michael.

"The master sergeant is having a welcome aboard party at the Overlook this evening. Will you and Francesca be attending?" asked Conor.

"Francesca would never forgive me for missing the opportunity to see the new arrivals," replied Michael. Then he added a grim reminder, "Unless the current job puts Brad and myself in the clinic or morgue."

"Let's hope that doesn't happen," returned Conor.

"Sir," interrupted Brad from across the room.

There was a large container that must have come from the pharmaceutical unit in Brad's hands. The container was part of the basic element and Compound containers the unit utilized to create the several thousand synthetic medications. The unit was a standard feature in clinics and hospitals throughout the United Systems and had been instrumental in saving billions of lives in the last two centuries. Brad had a worried look on his face as he held the container.

"What is it, Brad?" asked Michael.

"You remember that symbol you told me to watch for?" returned Brad.

Turning the container, Brad Guillete displayed the end that plugged into the unit. There inscribed on the end that would not be seen unless the unit was removed was the ominous symbol that Michael had discovered in the comm suite unit after the incident. Conor felt a chill along his spine. The colonist who was committing these atrocities was becoming braver. It was only a matter of time until they discovered the perpetrator's identity. Would they discover who the perpetrator was before irreparable damage occurred to the colony? The future looked uncertain.

"Good work, Brad," said Conor.

"I'm not finished yet, sir," replied Brad.

"You think there might be other things wrong with the unit?" asked Conor.

"I'd rather be sure than sorry, especially in this case," stated Brad.

"All right, fieldstrip the unit," ordered Conor.

"Sir, I think it would be best to have a new unit built. No one is ever going to trust medications from this one. There will always be the question of whether everything tampered with was found," stated Brad.

"I think he's right, Conor," injected Michael.

"We could ship it up to the *New Horizon* for testing," said Conor.

"Then we run the risk of losing a longboat or damaging the *New Horizon* if there's an explosive device," stated Michael.

"Options?" asked Conor.

"Let me strip it down and check all the components. Then set up a secure area for Hattie to test them here," said Brad.

"How long will that take, Brad?" asked Conor.

"Several months or more to set up a secure area and procure equipment to do the job," returned Brad. "The equipment will have to be approved, then made by the ship's factory."

"I agree with that assessment," said Michael.

"All right, we'll put this one in storage for now. I'll inform the commander the clinic will require a new unit," said Conor.

"I'll have this unit put in secure storage when we're through," said Michael.

"Good. I need to go make a report to the commander," replied Conor.

Conor left the comm suite and walked to the MILDET prefab. Commander Blankenship had a small bag on the table for his upcoming stay on the *New Horizon*. An anomaly had been observed on the surface of the inner moon, and an expedition was planned. The commander also felt it necessary to be on board for the next few weeks to coordinate with the lunar mission. He also felt a need to be on board to expedite efforts with the ship's factory production. Conor knew the commander was with Hiroka for most of the morning but should be returning soon.

Looking at the time, Conor saw that he had enough time to write his reports. Seeing the laptop sitting on the table, Conor sat down and logged into the system. Now that the NAPACS was operational, the entire colony could have access to Hattie. Demands had come in from the president that most of the colonists wanted laptops and tablets. The commander had resisted, and it had taken a meeting with the colony to reach a compromise. The commander agreed to have the ship's factory produce fifty laptops. Half of them would be given to the university and made available to the general public, while the others would be distributed to key positions, such as the clinic and industries.

Conor searched for information that concerned the drones that the expedition lost when they arrived. It bothered him that he had not thought that the drone incident was related to the other mishaps the colony had been experiencing. It took several minutes to find the information he required. Conor made a printout of the map Gunnery Sergeant Rusu saved of the downed drone locations. He intended to talk to the commander about another mission for recovering the drones when he arrived. Conor sat back and sipped coffee as he drafted a message about the pharmaceutical unit and another about the drones and forwarded them with his recommendations.

*****

The attack at the first pavilion was swift and seemed like a slaughter. All six ATVs and both choppers outfitted as gunships approached the first pavilion. The orders were to eliminate any resistance but allow the raptors that retreated to do so. Only a few chose the latter option. Most of the raptors chose to fight, attacking the ATVs until mowed down by the miniguns. Only a few chose to retreat, and those that did were allowed to depart unmolested. The site was secured, and an ATV with a full crew was left to secure the location. Conor noted that those that retreated went in the directions of the other pavilions that dotted the grassy plain. Landing his chopper beside the first pavilion and as Conor stepped out from under the slowly rotating rotors, Master Sergeant Evan Zander saluted him.

"Why are you here, Master Sergeant?" asked Conor.

"Doing my duty, sir," snapped Evan.

"I realize Gunny Rusu is topside and preparing to go to the moon, but you could have let the staff sergeant handle this. Your wife just had twins," said Conor.

"With all due respect, sir, Chief Petty Officer Zander told me I was getting on her nerves and she wanted some peace. So she told me to get the hell out of there and work it off. Something you might want to consider in a few months." Evan grinned.

Conor looked at Evan Zander for a moment and smiled. "Advice noted, Master Sergeant. Shall we see what we have here?"

"Yes, sir," said Evan.

Many items of interest were packed for shipment back to the Compound. A longboat utilizing its VTOL capabilities was brought in and landed nearby. The second pavilion was met with only slight resistance as the red raptors retreated. The rest of the pavilions were empty of all raptors as the attack forces arrived, leaving the Marines only the job of packing up items for inspection back at the cleft.

CHAPTER 58

The gray surface of the moon was approaching as the longboat was vectored in for a landing. The longboat slowly maneuvered closer to the site where the anomaly observed by the *New Horizon* was located. As they descended, Ensign Dominic Sobolov had ordered Steven Yates to run a spectral analysis and take photographic records. Steven attempted to argue with Dominic until the rest of the crew gave him cold looks, and he relented.

Gunnery Sergeant Samuel Rusu watched the surface on a monitor as the photographic record was being taken. When they were still two hundred kilometers from their destination, the gunny noticed a mound that looked unusual near the side of a mountain and marked it for later reference. Steven Yates muttered something about the chance of a substantial lithium deposit being below them as Samuel made a note about the mound.

"Worth investigating, Steven?" asked Samuel Rusu.

"Lithium is one of the items on the short list from the commander," replied Steven Yates.

"I know that," said Samuel patiently.

"Yes. It might be worth investigating once we've completed investigating the anomaly," agreed Steven Yates.

"Do you see the mound I've marked on the map?" asked Samuel.

It took a moment, then Steven replied, "It does look unusual."

"Is that near that lithium deposit?" asked Samuel.

Another moment passed. "Yes, it is."

Samuel nodded. "Kind of had a feeling it was."

Steven Yates cocked an eyebrow and looked at Samuel Rusu for a moment but said nothing. Samuel, in turn, was not going to volunteer any further information. Samuel went back to studying the unfolding landscape below them. Unfortunately, it had turned into a wide, flat plain, only broken by an occasional crater marring its surface.

They were approaching the site of the anomaly fast. Ensign Dominic Sobolov eased the longboat down while lowering the landing gear. He slowed their approach with quick bursts of the altitude jets. Samuel watched his video feed as the surface below gradually approached. The longboat touched the surface, sending up dust that hid the view. There was a slight bump, and they were down.

"That was almost like landing on the moon," stated Ensign Sobolov.

"Slightly less gravity here, Mr. Sobolov," replied Steven.

"Dah! I could tell," returned Dominic.

"Where's the anomaly?" asked Samuel.

"About a hundred meters from the air lock," replied Dominic.

"I'll get suited," said Samuel.

"I'll go with you," injected Steven.

Gunny Rusu looked sideways at Steven for a moment, then nodded as he went to suit up. The longboat stood firmly on the surface of the nearer moon. The air lock opened, and the ladder lowered as Gunny Rusu stepped out of the longboat air lock and descended to the surface. The anomaly that Commander Blankenship had wanted investigated lay approximately one hundred meters directly from the starboard side.

As Samuel Rusu's foot touched the gravel, he muttered, "That's one small step for man and one giant leap for mankind."

There was a chuckle in his ear, and Boatswain Martins voice said, "Is everything all right out there, Gunny?"

"Just contemplating the future of mankind," replied Samuel.

"Well, you might have a little time to contemplate," said John Martins.

"Is there a problem?" asked Samuel.

"Ensign Sobolov is assisting Mr. Yates with the proper procedures of putting on his helmet for the third time," came Martin's answer.

Gunnery Sergeant Rusu rolled his eyes, then looked around at the barren landscape. It reminded him of Earth's moon where he learned vacuum suit procedures himself. He looked at the crater that seemed like a short distance away but decided he'd best wait. Best to be here to ensure there were no suit accidents.

Samuel wanted to take Joseph Green instead of Steven Yates on this mission. Commander Blankenship and Lieutenant Commander Raybourn had insisted that Green's expertise was required on another project. Samuel Rusu knew Joseph Green was attempting to prove his theory that the planet had been terraformed around fifty to sixty million years ago. The commander and Lieutenant Commander believed that proving that was worth knowing to the colony, but Samuel Rusu still would have preferred Green in exchange for Yates. Steven Yates knew theory, but Samuel had reservations about trusting Steven with his analysis and conclusions. The longboat hatch finally opened, and the space-suited figure nearly fell out the door before catching the handrail inside the hatchway.

"Turn around, Steven," ordered Samuel.

"What?" asked Steven.

"Come down the ladder facing the longboat. Don't try to jump, or you'll most likely land on your behind or crack your helmet open," replied Samuel calmly.

"Oh! All right," replied Steven.

"Take your time. There's no hurry," said Samuel.

The suited figure turned around and grabbed the extended rungs to lower itself to the surface. Gunny Rusu reached out and steadied Steven as his feet reached the surface. When Steven let go of the ladder, he did what most trainees did and turned too fast. Samuel was prepared for that and had a firm hold on one of the ladder rungs to prevent Steven from falling. Samuel grabbed Steven's arm as the newcomer's feet left the ground. Pulling gently downward, Samuel set Steven Yates's feet back on the ground.

"Easy. Slowly," cautioned Samuel. He saw Steven's head nod inside his helmet and said, "You need to use your comms, Steven. I won't be able to see you nod or shake your head."

"Yes, right," replied Steven.

"I'm going to let go now. Take it slowly and walk in that direction," said Samuel as he let go of Steven's arm and pointed toward the crater where the anomaly lay.

They reached the edge of the crater without incident. The impact had been at a slight angle, and whatever had impacted here was buried. However, near the middle of the crater, there was the sheen of polished metal. Samuel carefully made his way down into the crater and walked across to the anomaly. He went to his knees and brushed gravel from the metal as Yates came up beside him, throwing his shadow over the area.

"Could you move to the side, Doc?" asked Samuel.

"What?" asked Steven.

"You're blocking the light," replied Samuel.

"Oh!" exclaimed Steven.

The shadow moved aside, and Samuel Rusu continued brushing the metal surface clean. A line in the metal appeared as he did so. It looked like it might be where two edges of metal met. A door? Samuel took the collapsible shovel from the belt at his side. He had attached it when leaving, thinking it might be useful. He noted that Steven Yates had done the same and was detaching his to help. They continued clearing the debris away from what was definitely a smooth metal plate surrounded by a curving surface of the same metal. When enough of the rubble was removed so it would not fill in the cleared area, they stopped.

"Looks like a plate of some sort," said Steven.

"You think so, Doc," replied Samuel sarcastically.

"Something wrong, Mr. Rusu?" asked Steven.

"No. Have any ideas?" asked Samuel.

Steven Yates went to his knees beside the plate and examined it. The plate itself was a smooth, polished surface, and as Samuel looked closer, there appeared to be etchings on the surface. Samuel continued digging, and Yates assisted him. Whatever it was, the artifact was big. They were getting to the point where they could not dig without the surrounding rubble sliding back into the hole. They reached what appeared to be a port. They dug until a small part of the port was uncovered, but they were now having debris flowing from the top edge down to the work area.

"Might need a hand out here, Mr. Sobolov," said Samuel.

"I will come out and assist you," replied Dominic Sobolov.

"Why don't both of you come out? The ship isn't going anywhere," suggested Samuel.

"Are you certain that is safe?" asked Dominic.

"If there's an enemy out here, we're in trouble," stated Samuel calmly.

"All right. We come," said Dominic.

"Bring shovels and buckets, sir," said Samuel.

"We will do that. What do you think it is?" inquired Dominic.

"I think it's a ship," stated Samuel.

"Are you sure it is safe for all of us to leave the ship?" demanded Ensign Sobolov.

"It's buried. I think it's been here a long time, sir," replied Samuel.

"Very well, we will come out and assist you," came Dominic's hesitant reply.

Ensign Sobolov and Boatswain First Class Martins arrived about ten minutes later, carrying buckets and shovels. It took several shifts to uncover a significant portion of the artifact. It was huge in comparison to the artifact Samuel had discovered on the outer moon. If he were to judge, it was at nearly as big as the longboat, and it was definitely a spacecraft. They had cleared more debris away to reveal that it was a viewing port. They were able to uncover enough of the port to shine a light inside. What they saw was a control panel of some sort. There was also what appeared to be a suited figure inside, but they could not make out details.

"I want to have another look at that plate again," stated Samuel.

"All right," replied Dominic.

The two went over to the plate, and Samuel examined it once again. While he was inspecting it, Ensign Sobolov was looking at the surrounding surface. The plate still presented a smooth surface to Samuel's questing eye. The ensign was looking at the surface outside of the plate.

"What's this?" asked Dominic as he touched a small round, circular plate. The small plate moved aside to reveal a depression with a crossbar big enough to hold. Dominic reached in, grabbing the bar, and twisted it clockwise. The large plate Samuel was inspecting moved.

Samuel Rusu's eyes widened. "Do that again."

Ensign Sobolov twisted further, and the large plate slid slowly aside. The other two members of the expedition came to stand beside them as the plate retracted. The plate proved to be a door of some sort, and now that it had recessed, it revealed the interior of what had to be a spacecraft. Inside was a space-suited figure whose outlines had become very familiar to Samuel Rusu since arriving on the world this moon orbited. The long-tailed body with powerful hind legs and a forward-projecting head because of the posture of the creature could only mean that the space-suited figure was a velociraptor. The nose of the mummified body could be seen through the faceplate of its helmet and traces of red feathers.

"I think we might have solved the mystery of how dinosaurs can exist on both Earth and this planet," stated Gunnery Sergeant Samuel Rusu.

"They were spacefaring creatures," said Steven Yates in awe.

CHAPTER 59

The choppers were prepped to go to the designated LZ where Conor had been speared in the leg nearly three months ago. The operation to drive the raptors off the island went well, though they couldn't be completely sure if all the raptors had departed. Lieutenant Commander Conor Raybourn had drafted Lieutenant Michael Anderson and Chief Tami Zander to pilot and drop the incursion force at the LZ. Sergeant Nikolai Ivankov, who recently finished his flight qualifications, had asked to pilot one of the choppers to the LZ. Conor took the copilot seat and fastened his safety harness. Looking back, Staff Sergeant Amanda Hall, Sergeant Tadashi Adachi, Lance Corporal Dwayne Abrams, and Private Vivian Caylor gave him a thumbs-up, which Conor, in turn, gave to the sergeant.

Nikolai Ivankov brought the chopper up slowly and moved toward the edge. Once past the lip of the cleft, he increased his forward momentum and brought the chopper on a westward heading. Conor could tell Nikolai was a little nervous but trying to relax. Conor sat back and put his head back against the headrest and closed his eyes till they were slits. He watched as Nikolai looked his way then forward again. A huge grin split Nikolai Ivankov's face, and he shook his head.

"Dah. It is good," said Nikolai.

"What?" asked Conor, keeping his eyes closed to slits.

Nikolai paused before answering, "That the officer in charge attempts to instill trust in his people."

Conor looked over at Nikolai. "Does it?"

"It will do, Commander. It will do," replied the sergeant as he increased his speed.

"I'm only a lieutenant commander," said Conor.

"Soon you will be commander, I'm thinking," returned Nikolai.

"Why do you say that? There's no room at the top," said Conor.

"I have the premonition." Nikolai grinned.

"I'll settle for a long life instead of a promotion," said Conor.

"Why not both, sir?" asked Nikolai.

Conor thought about that for a minute as they swept over the forest below. He had been given an honorary rank of lieutenant commander for the original mission they were to perform. Staying in the service after the mission was an option he had only casually considered at the time. However, the circumstances had changed drastically with the FTL incident that landed them here.

Nikolai nodded and said, "You take the long view. That is good. Many want to gain rank quickly. It does not make for a good or better leader."

"There are other options than the service," replied Conor.

"What would you do if not the service?" questioned Nikolai Ivankov.

"Join the university," replied Conor.

Sergeant Ivankov sat for a moment, contemplating that, then decreased his speed and started downward at a rate that sent a chill up Conor's spine. He then looked at Conor with a grin. "Then you would miss all this fun, sir," stated Nikolai.

As the chopper descended into the LZ, Conor saw the master sergeant standing beside Lieutenant Commander Michael Anderson and Brad Guillete. Michael waved as the other two kept a sharp watch on the surrounding forest. The Marine Complex chopper had been about a minute ahead of their chopper, and it appeared that the raptors were not present. The MILDET chopper settled into the long grass as the rotors slowed enough to leave. All the passengers exited the chopper as Michael approached the pilot's side to relieve Sergeant Ivankov. Conor went around and shook his hand as Evan Zander came up.

"Anything, Master Sergeant?" asked Conor.

"Quiet, sir," stated Evan.

"Too quiet?" asked Conor.

"No, sir. Plenty of wildlife and no sign of raptors," said Evan.

"Then why don't we do this thing?" asked Conor.

"Right. I'll get the others, and we'll pack up," said Master Sergeant Zander as he headed toward the Marine Complex chopper.

"Take care, Conor," said Michael worriedly.

"The master sergeant has my back, and so do you," said Conor.

"You got it. Just come back in one piece along with everyone else. I hope you find Krupich," stated Michael.

"I do too," said Conor.

The recon-and-rescue party walked down the slope of the ridge and entered the forest as the two choppers rose and hovered above their position. Sergeant Adachi took point as the other nine of the party entered single file. The master sergeant and Sergeant Ivankov carried Vinter HR-19 sniper rifles at ready with a Navarro M-71 slung across their backs. They progressed slowly, vigilant and wary of the slightest movement in their verdant surroundings. Tadashi signaled multiple times for a halt and cover, but each time, it turned out to be one of the large or lesser beasts and no raptors.

They were nearing the general area where Staff Sergeant Rachel Krupich's ID made its furthest approach to the east. A short time later, they located the clearing where Rachel had stopped. It had to be Rachel because bullet holes had pockmarked the bark of a large tree across the clearing, and a small depression in the soil contained the fragments of a grenade. A few red and green feathers were discovered in the clearing, but no bodies.

There was no apparent trail leading away from the clearing, and the terrain and leafy overhang of the surrounding trees would have made it impossible to bring in the ATVs or the chopper. The master sergeant had them form a skirmish line, and they advanced slowly northwest toward the cliff face. They reached a point near the cliff where a tree's bark had been stripped away, and small holes containing more grenade fragments penetrated the wood that had been underneath.

"This is the place where her ID vanished," stated Evan Zander.

"She had to enter a cave to block the signal," replied Conor.

"Down there," said the master sergeant, using his chin to point at a narrow crevice leading toward the cliff.

"Why?" asked Conor.

"Just a feeling," replied Evan. He called, "Adachi. Hall."

The two Marines the master sergeant had called moved into the crevice slowly. They rounded a bend and were lost from sight but reappeared after a short time. Staff Sergeant Hall in the lead continued back to the group, but Tadashi had stopped at the turn in the crevice and stood examining the rock face before him.

"Nothing, Master Sergeant," said Amanda Hall.

"You sure?" returned Evan as he continued watching Tadashi.

Amanda Hall turned to see her partner had stopped where the crevice turned.

"Adachi!" the staff sergeant called, and he looked at her.

"Master Sergeant," called Tadashi as he gave a thumbs-up to the staff sergeant.

Master Sergeant Zander looked at Amanda and said, "Stay here."

He then looked at Conor, and the two of them walked over to Sergeant Adachi.

"There's a door here, Master Sergeant," stated Tadashi as they drew close.

Conor and Evan examined the rock surface. After a few moments, it became apparent that there was a well-concealed door in front of them. What lay behind that door was a mystery and probably one that Staff Sergeant Krupich knew.

"What do you think, sir?" asked Evan Zander.

"I think we're not going to try to blast our way in. It would probably draw unwelcome attention to this location, and if Krupich is inside, we don't know if the blast would kill her," said Conor.

Tadashi had been examining a rock surface to the side of the door. He pushed at the rock surface, and it moved, revealing a circular bronze plaque set inside a stone hollow.

"Looks like a cypher lock of some sort," stated Tadashi.

"Can't read the inscriptions. Some sort of hieroglyphs," said Evan.

"Let me take a picture and send it to Michael," said Conor.

Lieutenant Commander Raybourn took the radio off his shoulder and snapped a picture. When Conor attempted to transmit the picture, he received no response from Michael. He walked back to where the rest of the party waited at the entrance to the crevice and tried again, along with a message explaining the problem.

Shortly, Michael responded, "I don't recognize it. I'm going to send it to Francesca."

"Mind if I look, sir?" asked Brad Guillete, pointing toward Master Sergeant Zander and Sergeant Adachi, who still stood near the mysterious door in the rock face.

"Go ahead, Brad. There's no reception down there. Tell the master sergeant we're waiting for Francesca to look at the hieroglyphs," replied Conor.

"Too much copper in the walls. That's why the rock is almost green," returned Brad.

Conor looked and noted that the rocks did have a green shade to them. The copper mines were several kilometers to the east along the cliff face. Did the vein run from here to there? If so, how much further west did the vein go? Something to investigate at a future date. Perhaps there was a better deposit to mine as the colony grew. Conor watched as Brad examined the door and bronze plate beside it. He saw Brad heft a large stone and hit the door, then shake his head, saying something to the master sergeant. Brad examined the bronze plate again but didn't touch it. He was walking back out when Conor's comm beeped. He looked at the screen display. The hieroglyphs had numbers beside them starting with zero.

"They're numbers, but I can't read them," said Brad.

"Why do you say that?" asked Conor.

"There's ten symbols. Zero through nine only makes sense," agreed Brad.

"Francesca would agree with you, Brad," said Conor.

"It still doesn't tell us what sequence to use," said Brad.

Conor looked at Brad and had an inspiration and said, "Come on. Let's go try something."

"Door's too well built for grenades or Q-5. It would take a bunker buster to crack it," said Brad.

"Is that why you hit it with that rock?" asked Conor.

"Yeah," replied Brad.

When Conor reached the door, he stood in front of the bronze plaque. He reached up to manipulate it, but the master sergeant grabbed his arm and said, "I can't let you do that, sir."

"Why not, Master Sergeant?" asked Conor.

"That's my job, sir. If its booby trapped, I'm the one to take the risk," stated Evan.

"There's no fallen rock or dead bodies here, Master Sergeant. I would say it either opens because the person opening it knows the code or it doesn't open because the person doesn't know the code," replied Conor.

"I still can't let you do that," stated Evan.

"I'll do it," interjected Brad. "It's the Fibonacci sequence you were going to try, wasn't it, sir?"

The master sergeant nodded agreement to this arrangement, and Conor admitted defeat as he moved back with the master sergeant and Sergeant Adachi to the crevice entrance.

"First ten numbers, Brad," called Conor.

"Makes sense," Brad returned loudly as he started manipulating the plaque back and forth. When he stopped, the stone beside him moved out of the way almost immediately, suggesting it was well used. Brad turned and waited for the others.

"Sir?" asked Evan.

"How many do you suggest, Master Sergeant?" asked Conor.

"No more than half, sir," stated Evan.

"Myself and Brad, team 1. You and Adachi, team 2. The rest, stay here to watch our backs," said the lieutenant commander.

Master Sergeant Zander smiled and nodded. "Hall, you're in charge of watching our backsides. Fall back into the cave if attacked."

"Roger that, Master Sergeant," snapped Staff Sergeant Amanda Hall.

"Lance Corporal Abrams, can you handle this without breaking it?" Zander asked as he handed the lance corporal his Vinter HR-19 knowing full well that the young man had received top quals on the Vinter HR-19 sniper rifle in the last qualifications.

The young man looked at it and replied, "I think so, Master Sergeant."

"Good. Better not be a scratch on it when you return it to me." Evan grinned. He then said, "Everyone going inside, make sure your weapons are loaded for standard rounds while inside. We don't know how sound the structure is inside."

Conor unslung his Navarro M-71 and ensured it was on single shot. He then pulled the magazine to ensure it contained standard rounds. Taking out his Gerst S-7, he checked the magazine for standard rounds also while the team members going inside the cavern did the same.

They entered the cave single file. The entrance proved to be a room with a door on the far side. A stairwell to the right led upward, and a brief exploratory trip by Sergeant Adachi proved it to be a lookout post with a hidden slit that looked out well above the entrance. The other door led to a large rectangular chamber that they entered. Hallways lead off to the left and right in the nearer corners of the room.

Conor and Brad Guillete went right toward the entrance of the right hallway, while the master sergeant and Sergeant Adachi moved to the left to reconnoiter the opposite hallway. Brad entered the hallway and started down it, while Conor watched from the chamber. There was a sound down the hallway. Then Conor saw Brad stop and peer at a dim figure down the passageway, then set his M-71 against the wall.

"Rachel!" shouted Brad.

Conor heard a female voice that he could only assume was Rachel Krupich shout, "Brad!"

Conor stood and watched as Brad Guillete started running down the passage. He also saw Staff Sergeant Krupich drop a pile of wood on the floor and run toward Brad. They fell into each other's arms halfway down the passageway where they became lost in a kiss that lasted several moments as Conor stood there smiling. Then from a side doorway not more than five meters behind Rachel, the head of a red raptor appeared as it looked toward the two reunited lovers. Brad's Gerst S-7 leaped from its holster and pointed at the raptor coming through the doorway.

"Brad, no!" shouted Rachel, and as she grabbed Brad's arm, pushing upward, a shot resounded.

CHAPTER 60

Qu'Loo'Oh' was slowly recovering. Her leg and the wound on her back were still sore, but the medicines that Rachel gave her helped with the pain. Rachel assured her that the stitches would dissolve as time passed. Rachel brought her food, tended the fire, and generally took care of Qu'Loo'Oh' since the ambush. She had told Qu'Loo'Oh' that the traps she had set had been sprung and that the deception she had used appeared to have worked. She had spent most of each day at the front entrance keeping watch, but now that seven days had passed, they decided that it was now safe to not guard the entrance.

Rachel had already brought water and food. When she finished, Qu'Loo'Oh' asked Rachel to bring her a scroll to read here in the room. When Rachel returned, she brought ten scrolls, which had disconcerted Qu'Loo'Oh' since she did not like taking so many from the library at a time. When she had expressed her displeasure, Rachel assured her that she would take them back when they were finished with them. Qu'Loo'Oh' decided that it was best to let the issue go, though she didn't see how Rachel was going to read them to her since some were beyond Rachel's understanding at this time.

Rachel left the room again and returned a short time later, dragging a piece of furniture that Qu'Loo'Oh' had never seen before. Rachel told her that she had noticed it in the large room down the hallway where furnishings were stored. The piece turned out to be a stand that was made to lay a scroll on while lying in one's nest. When asked if there were more, Rachel had told her there were several. This eased Qu'Loo'Oh's mind further, because she had believed that since none of the rooms had scrolls in them, the previous inhabitants had made a policy to only use the scrolls in the library. Obviously, that was not the case. Those who used the sacred chambers had left, leaving nothing in the sleeping quarters to indicate they had intended to return. No personal items were to be found in any of the sleeping quarters or anywhere else. Additional items and furniture for the rooms had been stored down the hall in a large room. Firewood was stored in another room down the hall and had been fully stocked when Qu'Loo'Oh' had arrived. The sacred scrolls had all been filed in the slots provided for them in the library; none had been left out. The chambers had been stored and filed as though the past inhabitants had known they were leaving but had planned to come back someday.

With the stand set up, Rachel handed Qu'Loo'Oh' one of the scrolls. Qu'Loo'Oh' placed it on the stand and slowly unrolled the ancient text. There was a crinkling sound as the browned parchment was laid out. She carefully spread the document, then a soft hiss emitted from her throat as Qu'Loo'Oh' realized it was not a text but a map. But what map? It was not of the world she knew. She read the text that lined the top of the document and realized that this was of the ancient home world. Her interest in the text must have drawn Rachel's attention because she came near, looking at the page.

"What is it?" asked Rachel.

"Heaven," replied Qu'Loo'Oh'.

"Is that what this says?" asked Rachel, indicating the glyphs at the top of the map.

"No," said Qu'Loo'Oh'.

"This isn't a map of this world," stated Rachel as she studied the map.

If all the things Rachel had told Qu'Loo'Oh' were true, then Rachel had seen the world from far above. Qu'Loo'Oh' wondered what it would be like to sail far above the world among the stars. Legend said her ancestors had done so long ago.

"It is a map of the ancient home world," said Qu'Loo'Oh'.

Rachel continued studying the map. After a time, she pointed one of her fingers at a continent on the right-hand side of the map. "That's North America," she stated, then moved her finger upward. "And that's South America."

"That is not their names," said Qu'Loo'Oh'.

Rachel continued staring at the map as she stated, "The continents are not in the right positions, but that's a map of Earth."

"What are you saying?" asked Qu'Loo'Oh'.

Rachel didn't answer as her eyes studied the map. Qu'Loo'Oh' knew apprehension and fear as she thought about what Rachel had just said. How could this creature know of the ancient home? The ancient home was far away. The ancient texts stated that it had taken many generations to reach this world. Were these creatures truly able to span the stars? Rachel had told her that her people came from one of those stars in the sky in the blink of an eye. Even the ancient ones could not do that. It was said that it took generations to cross between the stars.

Qu'Loo'Oh' watched as Rachel continued to study the map. Her fingertips continued to trace the outlines of the continents. Finally, she stopped, and Qu'Loo'Oh' saw Rachel's eyes get a faraway look.

"Sixty-five million years of continental drift," whispered Rachel.

Qu'Loo'Oh' understood the first half of what Rachel said, but the last half confused her. She shook her head and raised the crest running down the top of her head. She knew the words but not the meaning of what Rachel was implying.

"What is continental drift?" inquired Qu'Loo'Oh'.

Rachel spent quite some time attempting to explain what she meant. Many of the words Rachel used were unknown to Qu'Loo'Oh'. The concept of continents moving because they were on plates lying on a fluid surface was disturbing. The idea that they moved and that it took many years to do was nearly unbelievable. Then Qu'Loo'Oh' thought about how this new concept would explain why many of the old maps of this world were incorrect. The continents were in different positions, and on one map, even the sacred island they were on had been farther and more isolated from the continent where Qu'Loo'Oh's people lived.

The fire was burning low, and Rachel replenished it with the little wood that remained in the storage niche beside it. The room would start growing cold as soon as the fire burned low again and need to be rebuilt in an hour or two. Qu'Loo'Oh' had dozed off after

Rachel left to bring more wood for the fireplace. The information she had learned discussing the map with Rachel made her uneasy and plagued her sleep. She was suddenly awakened by the sound of a deep voice.

The voice called, "Rachel!"

She heard the sound of wood being dropped then the sound of feet running. Qu'Loo'Oh' rose and approached the open door of her room. She poked her head through the doorway and looked down the hallway. There stood Rachel with another of her kind in an embrace with their mouths locked together. Qu'Loo'Oh' wondered if this was some sort of mating ritual these creatures performed because she had seen this activity once before being done by the creature further down the hall. That creature with another had been on a ridge on this side of the silvery web the creatures had constructed when it, too, had locked its mouth with another of its kind.

The creature embracing Rachel stopped and drew back. It then noticed Qu'Loo'Oh' standing in the doorway. Qu'Loo'Oh' saw it draw the small fire stick from its side and raise it in her direction. Rachel grabbed its arm, pushing upward, as she cried, "Brad, no!"

There was a loud sound that reverberated down the hallway, and Qu'Loo'Oh' heard the whistle pass her head, and something splintered the wooden door. Qu'Loo'Oh' withdrew into her room and limped to her nest. She entered the nest and curled up, watching the door. There was much talking and footsteps, but she could not understand what was said. Finally, Rachel came into the room with the armload of wood. She went to the fireplace and placed some of the wood on the fire after placing the rest in the niche. Then she walked over to where Qu'Loo'Oh' lay and sat on the edge of the nest, looking at her. Several minutes passed this way, and as the heat from the fire warmed the room, Qu'Loo'Oh' gained the courage to speak.

"I die now?" questioned Qu'Loo'Oh'.

"No!" stated Rachel.

"They will kill me," returned Qu'Loo'Oh'.

"No!" stated Rachel.

"Who?" asked Qu'Loo'Oh'.

"Will you meet them?" asked Rachel.

The fear of death still weighed on Qu'Loo'Oh'. The sound of death's closeness as the fire stick had been fired still sent shivers up her spine. The hole in the door seemed to happen instantaneously with the sound, making what had happened even more ominous. These creatures had power that her people could not match. She moved her head, so it rested against Rachel's leg, wondering what to do for several minutes. Then finally, she gave in to what seemed the inevitable.

"I will meet them," she whispered.

"Mr. Raybourn, you and Brad may enter," said Rachel.

The other two creatures entered. Qu'Loo'Oh' noticed that they were not carrying their large fire sticks right off and that the pouches on their belts were missing the small fire sticks also. There was shuffling sounds in the corridor, which meant others of Rachel's kind had invaded the sacred chambers and stood outside in the hallway, but they did not enter.

The one that had embraced Rachel drew closer and said, "I'm sorry."

"You are Rachel's mate?" asked Qu'Loo'Oh'.

The skin on Brad's face turned red, and she heard Rachel make the noise Rachel said her kind used when they found something funny. Then Rachel said, "Not yet."

"Soon then," affirmed Qu'Loo'Oh.'

"Perhaps," replied Rachel.

"Sit, Brad," said Qu'Loo'Oh'. Brad turned and sat nervously on the other side of Qu'Loo'Oh's head from Rachel, and the other creature stepped forward.

"Who is this, Rachel?" asked Qu'Loo'Oh'.

"Qu'Loo'Oh', this is Lieutenant Commander Raybourn, our second-in-command," stated Rachel.

"I'm pleased to meet you, Qu'Loo'Oh'. You may call me Conor," greeted Conor.

"I have seen you before," said Qu'Loo'Oh'.

The creature blinked and asked, "When?"

"Nearly a year ago on a ridge outside the silvery web your people constructed. You were with another whom you locked mouths with," replied Qu'Loo'Oh'. "Did you mate with that one?"

There was a round of laughter from the three humans as Qu'Loo'Oh' had learned they called themselves.

When the laughter died down, Conor replied, "Yes."

"Good. What would you have of me?" asked Qu'Loo'Oh'.

"Hope!" stated Conor.

CHAPTER 61

Lieutenant Commander Conor Raybourn watched as Qu'Loo'Oh' stared at him. Her crest rose and fell as she twitched her tail. She raised her head and looked at Staff Sergeant Rachel Krupich for several minutes as Rachel gazed into her eyes. Brad Guillete sat stiffly, still uncomfortable with his position in this affair. Finally, Qu'Loo'Oh' turned her attention back to Conor and gazed at him.

"I think I understand," stated Qu'Loo'Oh'.

"Will you come with us to our home?" asked Conor.

"If I can make it," said Qu'Loo'Oh'.

"She was hurt, sir. She will require help to even make it a short distance," stated Rachel.

"There's a clearing east of here where a grenade was used. Was that you?" asked Conor.

"I believe so. Was it a little over a kilometer?" asked Rachel.

"Yes," replied Conor.

"She may be able to if Brad and I help her," said Rachel.

"Master Sergeant!" called Conor loudly.

Master Sergeant Evan Zander stepped into the room and locked eyes with Qu'Loo'Oh' for a moment. Then he swept the rest of the room with his gaze, noting the minute details. When he was finished, he looked pointedly at Rachel and grinned.

"Nice to see you, Staff Sergeant. What kind of trouble have you got me into this time?" Master Sergeant Zander chuckled.

"Hopefully, not too much, Master Sergeant," replied Rachel.

"You requested my presence, sir?" Evan Zander said as he turned his attention to Lieutenant Commander Raybourn.

"Do we have explosive rounds for the Vinters and Navarros along with some Q-5?" asked Conor.

"We do, sir," returned Evan.

"Think we can blow enough trees down and branches off in that clearing where we found the grenade fragments for a chopper to make a landing there?" asked Conor.

"Yes, sir!" responded Evan.

"Tarp and four abled bodies for a stretcher take too many away from protection?" inquired Conor.

"We haven't seen any raptors. We might be able to do it," replied Evan.

"Qu'Loo'Oh' here needs transport to the clearing. Call the choppers in. One as air guardian at all times for the ground team. Staff Sergeant Krupich, Mr. Guillete, and myself will leave first with the raptor and two Marines. You and the rest of the team with the other chopper," ordered Conor.

"Sounds like a plan, sir," said Evan.

"Let's make that happen," replied Conor.

"Roger that, sir," replied Zander as he turned and left.

Master Sergeant Evan Zander shouted orders all the way down the hall as he went to the entrance to establish communications with the rest of the team. Rachel and Brad got up and started packing her things into her backpack, while Conor sat down beside Qu'Loo'Oh'. He swept the chamber with his arm.

"What is this place?" asked Conor.

"Sacred chamber of the ancestors," said Qu'Loo'Oh'.

"What did they do here?" asked Conor.

"Many things, but mostly study," replied Qu'Loo'Oh'.

"There's a library, sir. The map on that stand is from it," interjected Rachel.

"Rachel, no!" hissed Qu'Loo'Oh'.

"What do you fear?" asked Conor.

"The library and other things in these chambers are for other seekers to find," stated Qu'Loo'Oh'.

Lieutenant Commander Raybourn turned his attention to the map. He studied it carefully for over a minute. He cocked his head and studied it for another minute before he said, "That's Earth."

"I think so too, sir," responded Rachel.

"What do you know of this?" asked Conor of Qu'Loo'Oh', indicating the map.

"It is the ancient home," hissed Qu'Loo'Oh', now even more uncomfortable.

"May we borrow these if we promise to return them?" asked Conor cautiously.

Qu'Loo'Oh' stared at Conor for a moment before responding, "Yes."

"Tell Rachel what else to bring, but I would like to take this map along," stated Conor.

"The rest of the scrolls that are here will suffice," replied Qu'Loo'Oh'.

"There are three scrolls I think Francesca would be very interested in seeing, sir. I will go get them while Brad packs my bag," said Rachel.

"Will you allow this?" asked Conor, looking intently at Qu'Loo'Oh'.

It took nearly two minutes as they looked into each other's eyes before Qu'Loo'Oh' hissed, "Yes."

"Go," replied Conor as he nodded at Brad, who continued to pack Rachel's bag.

Rachel and the master sergeant returned a short time later walking side by side. They carried a Neils Robertson stretcher, which Conor did not want to think of the logistics of acquiring with the foliage around the entrance of the cave. Lying inside the stretcher were what Conor assumed the scrolls that Rachel retrieved. It took nearly an hour carrying Qu'Loo'Oh' to the clearing once they sealed the sacred chambers. The master sergeant and Sergeant Ivankov made short work of clearing trees and foliage so the MILDET chopper could land while the Marine chopper provided fire support.

Conor took the copilot's seat beside Lieutenant Commander Michael Anderson, while Brad, Rachel, Nikolai, and Vivian took up the back. Qu'Loo'Oh's stretcher was attached, and as a counterweight, the scrolls in cases filled the stretcher on the pilot's side. The chopper lifted and made a rapid trip to the cleft and landed behind the clinic. Qu'Loo'Oh' was unstrapped and, with the assistance of Rachel and Brad, walked to the clinic's back entrance with a crowd watching. Conor and the rest of the crew kept the people back until Qu'Loo'Oh' was inside.

When they entered the emergency room, they were met by a very apprehensive team of medical professionals. Dr. Bess Hollinger and Dr. Kers Joshi looked at their new patient as if expecting Qu'Loo'Oh' to spring forth and kill them both. Lieutenant Commander Raybourn understood their misgivings, and truthfully, he had his doubts also. Staff Sergeant Rachel Krupich inserted herself at this point to quell the tension in the room.

"Say hello, Qu'Loo'Oh'," said Rachel.

"Hello," chirped Qu'Loo'Oh'.

"This should prove interesting," said Bess nervously.

"You are a healer?" asked Qu'Loo'Oh'.

"We both are," replied Bess, startled, as she indicated Kers.

"Rachel has said you are very good," said Qu'Loo'Oh'.

"With people," said Bess.

"I am people," responded Qu'Loo'Oh'.

"I think Dr. Cheptoo might be of assistance," stated Dr. Joshi, referring to Silas Cheptoo, who was originally part of the science division under Jacqueline Vinet.

"Why do you say that?" asked Conor.

"He's a veterinarian, and his specialty is xenobiology," said Kers.

"He also works here three days a week during the mornings as a general practitioner," added Bess.

"Where would he be?" asked Conor.

"He works at the butcher shop. He studies the beasts the hunting parties bring back," said Bess.

"Wouldn't he learn more with the hunting parties?" asked Conor.

"He did at first, but a green raptor almost got him on his third time out," said Brad.

"I see," said Conor. "Brad, could you locate him and ask him to come here?"

"I can do that, sir," said Brad after looking at Rachel.

Rachel gave him a smile and wink, then said, "I'll still be here when you get back."

They started working on Qu'Loo'Oh' by scanning her and drawing blood samples. She was not happy about many of the things done, but Rachel stayed by her side through it all. Dr. Silas Cheptoo arrived and looked over the scans and blood work. In turn, he recommended a variety of treatments to be given to her after consulting with Bess and Kers. They had determined that Qu'Loo'Oh' had arthritis and was suffering from a variety of deficiencies because of her diet. They also decided to experiment by trying some antibiotics for the wound that had become infected. Rachel had told them that she had given Qu'Loo'Oh' the antibiotics she had left, and they had appeared to help at first, then they ran out. They also started Qu'Loo'Oh' on fluids since Dr. Cheptoo determined that she was dehydrated.

Several hours passed as the doctors worked. Finally, they took Qu'Loo'Oh' to a room for rest. Rachel remained with the raptor the entire time and sat in a chair as they prepared a nest for Qu'Loo'Oh' in the corner of the room. Second Lieutenant Shiran Raybourn arrived, and Conor met her in the waiting room. Conor escorted Shiran down the corridor to the door of the room where Qu'Loo'Oh' rested. Rachel was waiting outside the room to meet her friend. Conor watched as the two embraced.

"I can't believe you're still alive!" exclaimed Shiran, smiling.

"I can hardly believe it myself," replied Rachel, beaming.

"I'm sorry it's taken me so long to arrive. I had business to attend to at the complex," said Shiran.

"That's what you get for accepting a commission." Rachel snickered.

"It's wonderful to have you back," said Shiran, grinning.

"It looks like you're doing wonderful too," said Rachel as she touched the rounded bulge of Shiran's abdomen.

"I'm on maternity leave starting tomorrow. We'll have lots of time to catch up," said Shiran.

"That's great!" exclaimed Rachel.

"It looks like you're not doing so well," said Shiran as she looked at the noticeable crook in Rachel's upper left arm.

"I'll be all right," said Rachel.

"You need the doctors to look at that," said Shiran.

"After I'm sure Qu'Loo'Oh' is taken care of," said Rachel.

"Promise," demanded Shiran.

"Promise," returned Rachel.

"Did the creature do that to you?" asked Shiran.

"No. It happened before I met her. She saved me from a green raptor," said Rachel.

"So where is this Qu'Loo'Oh'?" asked Shiran.

"The doctors sedated her when they went to work. She's still asleep and in the corner of this room on mattresses and blankets," replied Conor.

"Can I see her?" asked Shiran.

"This way," replied Rachel.

Shiran followed Rachel into the room where Qu'Loo'Oh' lay sleeping. With a critical eye, Shiran looked at the creature that had saved and lived with her friend for so long. It was hard to believe that such a fierce-looking creature was capable of compassion, yet her friend Rachel made it clear that she owed her life to the raptor.

"Can we trust it?" asked Shiran.

"The future might depend on it," replied Conor.

CHAPTER 62

The Overlook was quiet, and the company good. Conor and Shiran had arranged to have an evening meal with Michael and Francesca. Conor sat back in his chair and took a sip of his coffee as Shiran and Francesca talked about the twin girls the Zanders had. Michael mentioned that he was going to try his luck fishing off the shuttle pier and asked Conor if he had time to try. Conor was debating on whether to take a few hours with Michael just to get away. Shiran reminded them both that if they were going to fish off the pier, they'd best take their Navarro M-71s and keep an eye out for crocodiles. Michael said something about how he was planning on a nice fish meal and not crocodile burgers. They all laughed at the grim humor, which reminded them that they weren't in Kansas anymore.

Conor took another sip of coffee and watched as Shiran picked at the salad she had ordered. Francesca was doing the same to the fine strips of meat with vegetables and rice.

"Not hungry?" asked Conor.

"Already full," replied Shiran as she patted the prominent bulge that was her abdomen. "I'll be glad when this is over."

"So will I," stated Francesca as Michael patted her arm.

"Have you had a chance to look over the scrolls we brought back?" asked Conor.

"I did. Some of the glyphs are almost identical to those used by the Maya and older civilizations in the Americas. Even the meaning is relatively the same," stated Francesca.

"How can that be?" asked Conor.

"I have no idea," replied Francesca.

"Another mystery," said Michael.

"The red raptors were spacefaring. Perhaps a ship returned to Earth and taught the glyphs to a human culture," said Shiran, referring to the recent discovery on the inner moon.

"Something to consider," said Conor. "Francesca, as soon as Qu'Loo'Oh' is better, I'd like to have her meet with you."

"How is she doing?" asked Francesca.

"The doctors want two more days with her," replied Conor.

There was a commotion at the front entrance that drew all their attention. Ezekiel Yap was confronting President Felipe Martinez at the door and not allowing him to pass. There were shouts behind Felipe Martinez for Ezekiel to get out of the way. A few of the Marines who had been dining at other tables watched, and two of them got up to stand behind Ezekiel.

"We want to talk to Lieutenant Commander Raybourn," demanded Felipe.

"You are not welcome here," responded Ezekiel firmly.

"I'm still president," retorted Felipe.

"I do not care," Ezekiel said calmly.

Lieutenant Commander Conor Raybourn noticed his wife, Second Lieutenant Shiran Raybourn, reach into her bag and withdraw her Gerst S-7 so others couldn't see. She passed the weapon to Conor and whispered, "Sleepy darts." Conor took it and slid it into his belt behind his back as he got up. Shiran reached into her purse again and withdrew another Gerst, which she changed the magazines on and handed it to Michael.

"Francesca and I will go out the back entrance," said Shiran to Michael.

Michael nodded and took the Gerst S-7. He did as Conor had done and followed Conor toward the front as the two women got up, walked behind the counter, and entered the back room. When Conor stood behind Ezekiel, who was still denying the mob outside access to his establishment, Conor placed his hand on Ezekiel's shoulder.

"It's all right, Ezekiel," said Conor.

"Only him. That table," replied Ezekiel Yap, looking over his shoulder and pointing at the table closest to the door.

Conor pulled out a chair and sat facing the front entrance of the Overlook. He looked at Felipe Martinez and motioned to the chair across the table from him. Felipe's face turned red from being treated so cavalierly by someone he obviously considered a subordinate. Martinez sat and glared at Conor for nearly three minutes as the mob outside shuffled and muttered.

Finally, Conor broke the silence and asked, "What do you want to talk about, Mr. President?"

"We demand that you turn that murdering raptor over for justice," demanded Felipe loudly.

There were shouts of agreement from outside the main door. One of the mob attempted to come in, and Michael stood in his way, blocking him. A woman screamed something unintelligible, and a man coughed. Conor was worried that this might get out of control, but he was certain that he was not going to turn Qu'Loo'Oh' over to this mob. He had heard stories of the riots on the Ceres habitat from a century ago and had seen footage of restricted data while in training to receive his commission. The idea of that happening here didn't sit well with him, even if the being these people wanted to bring their vengeance upon wasn't human. But then what defines humanity? Conor pushed that thought out of his mind as he gave his answer.

"No," replied Lieutenant Commander Raybourn calmly.

"I'm still the president and you're commander in chief. I demand you carry out my orders!" shouted President Martinez.

"I'm required to obey your orders if they are lawful," returned Conor.

"What does that mean?" demanded Felipe.

"If Qu'Loo'Oh' is a prisoner, then she is a prisoner of war and subject to military jurisdiction, not civil jurisdiction. I will not hand her over to you or your mob," said Conor.

"The people demand justice! I'm still the president, and I'm ordering you to turn the raptor over!" shouted Felipe.

"I don't answer to you. I answer to Commander Blankenship. If you have an order for me, clear it with my chain of command. I will not hand over what may prove to be our best hope of resolving the differences between human and raptor," stated Conor.

"You'll do as you're told!" shouted Felipe.

"I'll do as Commander Blankenship orders," said the Conor.

"Then we'll just take the beast!" shouted Martinez as he pushed back his chair and stood up.

Shouts of encouragement came from those outside the Overlook. Conor withdrew the Gerst from behind his back. He laid it on the table, still grasping it. Felipe Martinez's eyes grew wide, and silence fell on those gathered outside the Overlook.

"You can try that. However, I'm sure by now that my wife has more than two Marines outside the door of the raptor's room, which means you and your forces will be caught between the cross fire," stated Conor.

"This isn't over, Raybourn," shouted Felipe.

An uncomfortable feeling grew in the back of Conor's mind as he watched Martinez and his mob leave. How many colonists would follow Martinez in his quest to seek what he called justice? Was it justice they sought or simply vengeance? Conor suspected that the latter was the case. There had been at least thirty colonists outside the Overlook while he had talked to Martinez. Didn't any of them understand that the raptor Qu'Loo'Oh' represented their best chance of breaching the gap between human and raptor?

Conor Raybourn shook his head as he watched the last of the mob vanish into the night. Ezekiel's leathered brown hands placed two beers on the table in front of him. Michael took a seat across the table from Conor. Conor took a sip, then set the bottle back down. He rubbed his eyes and heard the sound of chairs being placed near the table on each side. When he looked up, Ezekiel sat in one chair and Evan Zander sat in the other holding beers, while Roberta closed the doors to the Overlook.

"Master Sergeant," said Conor.

"Shiran and Francesca are safely at home. I assigned Hall and Hoffman to stay with them until both of you return," stated Evan Zander.

"Thank you, Evan," said Conor.

"Eleven showed up at the clinic while the crowd here was distracting you. They're sleeping it off in the waiting room under the care of nurses and two Marines. I had a feeling there was going to be trouble and already had two Marines that you ordered for security. Additionally, I had an extra two Marines in the next room even before the second lieutenant arrived at my door," stated Evan Zander.

Conor looked at Evan Zander then Ezekiel Yap. It seemed the two knew intelligence information before it happened. Fortunately, that foresight had worked out well for second lieutenants and even lieutenant commanders a number of times.

"Was Pool one of the eleven?" asked Conor.

"As a matter of fact, he was," replied Evan.

"This could spiral out of control," stated Michael.

"Tensions are high," returned Evan.

"What do we do about it?" asked Conor.

"Above my pay grade, sir," said Evan.

"The agitators will continue so long as they can do so without repercussions," said Ezekiel.

"Foresight, Ezekiel?" asked Michael.

"It happened in my homeland when I was a child. Over five hundred died," responded Ezekiel.

Silence fell on the group as they contemplated what the future might hold in store for them. Conor realized the raptor attack on the colony had only been an excuse for what had transpired this evening. People were unhappy. They were stranded in a solar system far from everything they knew. There was also a growing divide.

"Bringing the raptor here wasn't the wisest decision," muttered Conor.

"She understands English and speaks it. That bridges a huge gap that existed," said Michael.

"I agree. We need someone to bridge that gap. The bond Staff Sergeant Krupich has established with the raptor may determine our survival on the planet. You did the right thing," stated Evan Zander.

"Bridging the gap will be important," agreed Ezekiel.

"How do we bridge the gap that exists in the colony? Most of them either fear her or want to kill her," said Conor.

"Promotional advertising," said Ezekiel.

Everyone around the table looked at Ezekiel strangely. Then Master Sergeant Zander smiled slyly and stated, "Get her out there meeting people."

"It might work," said Michael.

"She'll still need more security. Four to six guards instead of two. Maybe my people can work up something in the way of body armor for her," said Evan.

"A wise idea," said Ezekiel.

"Who?" asked Evan intently.

"The scientists would be most interested in examining her," said Michael.

"Something without probes and instruments. A party," added Evan.

"Yes, we also need people who have met her," said Ezekiel.

"You haven't met her," stated Evan.

"I need to be introduced. Soon," added Ezekiel.

"You deliver fresh meat warmed to body temperature, and I'll have Rachel introduce you to her," said Evan Zander.

"Agreed. With the party at a later date here at the Overlook," returned Ezekiel.

"Good idea," said Zander.

Conor and Michael had remained silent as the two friends batted their plan back and forth. Conor suspected that they were watching how the master sergeant always seemed to know things and have a plan one step ahead. He was also beginning to wonder who really ran the colony when the two turned toward him.

"What do you think, sirs?" asked Evan Zander with a smile.

Conor gazed at him then Ezekiel for a moment, then looked at Michael and said, "A good plan, Master Sergeant."

"Best thing we have," agreed Michael.

"Of course! Drinks and hors d'oeuvres while rubbing elbows is always the best way to make friends," stated Ezekiel Yap.

Conor sat back for a moment and looked at his three friends. His mood had lifted, and a smile slowly crept onto his lips. He raised his bottle and held it above the center of the table. The other three bottles were raised and clicked his bottle in salute.

CHAPTER 63

Sitting in his stateroom aboard the *New Horizon*, Commander Hadden Blankenship went over the daily reports. He took a sip of coffee from his zero-G cup. The room was small but more than most had aboard the *New Horizon*. The bed folded into the wall, a table and two chairs folded out from the opposite wall, and there was a small toilet that served as a shower also. There were drawers, a locker, and file cabinet built into half the wall on the table side of the room. It was luxury for a captain serving on a United Systems ship.

There was nothing pressing, and there had been no new incidents in the last three days. Lieutenant Commander Raybourn appeared to have everything under control on the surface after confronting the lynch mob. The lieutenant commander was now preparing a recovery mission for the drones they had lost when they first arrived on the planet. He was also going to do an air recon of the river mouth where the raptors arrived and departed.

The shuttle carrying the ATV with the excavation equipment had arrived on the moon four days ago, and the alien craft the longboat recon team had discovered was being loaded onto the shuttle. The report said that the craft appeared to be a fighter craft of some sort, piloted by a raptor. The photographic imagery showed an egg-shaped craft with damage to the wide bottom part where the craft's main engines were located. The damage wasn't visible until the craft was mostly uncovered by the excavation team. Hadden allowed two scientists to go with the shuttle mission, which made four members to the shuttle crew team.

Now Ensign Sobolov wanted to investigate a region that the longboat had passed over when arriving on the moon. The xenogeologist Steven Yates reported that he read high lithium deposits on his spectral analysis as they had passed over, and Gunnery Sergeant Rusu added a note to the report that there was an unusual geological formation in the same area. Hadden looked at the photographic images the gunny had annotated. The mound looked out of place compared to the surrounding landscape.

Hadden must have dozed off while he was staring at the screen. The screen was darkened, and when he touched the pad, it asked for his password. A knock on his stateroom door startled him. He took a moment to rub his eyes and get his thoughts together, and the knock sounded again.

"Come in," called Hadden.

The door opened, and Brad Guillete entered. He was in a dark-blue jumper with his rank insignia on his collar, which was the standard uniform while serving aboard a United Systems ship. He appeared slightly nervous and looked around the stateroom. Brad's attention quickly turned to Hadden, and he saluted.

"You wanted to see me, sir," stated Brad.

"Welcome aboard, Mr. Guillete," greeted Hadden.

"Thank you, sir," said Brad.

"I'm sorry we had to draw you away from your reunion with Staff Sergeant Krupich so soon," said Commander Blankenship.

"That's all right. I understand, sir," replied Brad.

"Is everything all right between the two of you?" asked Hadden.

"Yes, sir," replied Brad and paused about to say something. The commander waited, raising an eyebrow in question. "She accepted my proposal."

"That's wonderful! Congratulations," said Hadden, grinning.

"Thank you, sir." Brad smiled.

"Did you set a date?" asked Hadden.

"Not yet, sir," answered Brad.

"I hope everything works out well for the two of you," said Hadden. Then after a slight pause, he decided to broach the reason he had requested Brad's presence on the *New Horizon*. "I realize this isn't your normal duty tour, Mr. Guillete, but I'm sure you know the long-range lidar is still not fully functional."

"I know that, sir," Brad replied impassively.

"I need it repaired," stated Hadden.

"I've never attended formal training on that, sir. It's Chief Wheaton's specialty," said Brad.

"I'm aware of both those points, Petty Officer Guillete. I'd still like to have you take a look at the system," replied Hadden, somewhat irritated.

"I'd rather not, sir," returned Brad.

The answer frustrated the commander, and he almost released that irritation on Guillete. He looked at the impassive face across the table from him. Hadden thought back to Brad's fixing the Marine radar, and Lieutenant Commander Anderson had told Hadden that the recent CASCOR, or casualty corrected, to the NAPACS system was a lie, along with an earlier repair to the SAC-23 transceiver. Unfortunately, the evaluations from Lieutenant Felter told a different story, and there was a possibility that this had been true even prior to Petty Officer Guillete's reporting to the *New Horizon*.

Hadden redirected his irritation, suddenly realizing that Brad Guillete had trust issues and wondered how far back in the man's military service they went. Both Conor and Michael thought highly of this petty officer, and they believed he would be an asset if he could be talked back into active service. However, Hadden suspected that was what happened when the man's immediate superiors undermined any chance of Brad assuming a leadership role with the technicians. Hadden didn't know an immediate solution for that, but he did want the lidar repaired and wasn't getting results from Chief Wheaton, who had been trained on the equipment. While this was going through his mind, he was interrupted by Brad, clearing his throat.

"Sir, do I have to work with any other technician if I work on the lidar?" asked Brad Guillete, looking uncomfortable.

"No, Petty Officer Guillete, you don't, unless you choose to have one help you," replied Hadden as some of his suspicions were confirmed.

"I'll work with Petty Officer Gabrielson if she's aboard. Otherwise, I'd prefer to work alone if you insist on my taking a look at the lidar," said Brad impassively.

"I think she was due to leave with the longboat," said Hadden.

"Oh," replied Brad.

"The longboat hasn't left yet. Let me see what I can do," said Hadden.

"Will that be all, sir?" asked Brad.

"Yes, Petty Officer. You're dismissed," said the commander.

Hadden watched as Brad got up, folded his seat into the wall, then departed. He called up the bridge and asked the OOD, or officer of the day, to have Petty Officer Gabrielson contact him prior to allowing the longboat to depart. The call came within minutes, and it was arranged for Petty Officer Gabrielson to remain on board and assist Brad for the next week. With that accomplished, Hadden returned his attention to ship and colony priorities.

Two days later, Hadden floated into the berthing area amidships where Petty Officer First Class Brad Guillete and Petty Officer Third Class Barbara Gabrielson were waiting for him. Brad was floating on the other side of the compartment, while Barbara Gabrielson sat at the communal lounge table of the twelve-person berthing area. Brad informed the commander that he thought they'd discovered the problem with the lidar and wished to show him, but how that problem could be related to a berthing area was beyond Hadden.

"Attention on deck," called Barbara as she stood slowly in the zero gravity and saluted.

Brad turned and saluted.

Commander Blankenship saluted and said, "As you were. Now why am I here?"

"Petty Officer Guillete believes he's discovered the problem, sir," replied Barbara.

"Petty Officer Guillete told the OOD it was the two of you, and this isn't the radar compartment," returned Hadden, making reference to the report from the officer of the deck who was standing the bridge watch.

"No, sir, it isn't," said Brad.

"Explain yourself," demanded Hadden patiently.

"The long-range lidar compartment is on the other side of this deck, sir. This is the waveguide from the lidar going to the antenna array," stated Brad.

"All right," said the commander as he realized that Brad Guillete was right. This compartment was one level above the lidar room.

Brad Guillete knocked on the waveguide with the knuckles of his right hand, and there was a hollow sound like a drum. The waveguide had a sign stating not to strike it, but Hadden was pretty sure that meant something more solid than a person's knuckles. Brad kicked off, floated in the zero gravity across the compartment to where Hadden floated, and grabbed the doorframe.

"If you'll follow me, sir," said Brad.

He entered the passageway and went forward one level. He entered another berthing area that was adjacent to the one they had just left and floated across the compartment to the waveguide that ran through it on its way to the antenna array. He again rapped his knuckles on the waveguide, but this time, the sound was a dull thud.

"Hear the difference, sir?" asked Brad.

"I do. Explain," said Hadden.

"I suspect this section of the waveguide is filled with water," stated Brad.

"Enlighten me, Mr. Guillete," said Hadden, intrigued.

"The waveguide is generally filled with air or nitrogen on a spacecraft. In this case, the waveguide uses air. I suspect this section of the waveguide is filled with water. Passing through water degrades the radar wave as it travels down the waveguide. The radar wave may still pass through it, but in turn, the resolution of the signal will be degraded immensely," Brad informed the commander.

"Like what we're seeing now," responded Hadden.

"Yes, sir," replied Brad.

"How did this happen?" asked Hadden.

"When the incident that brought us to this system occurred, the potable water line that runs through this compartment ruptured and flooded the compartment with water. I believe it passed through the seal," stated Brad Guillete, indicating a joint where two parts of the waveguide were joined together to form a continuous whole.

"Why didn't it drain back out?" asked Hadden.

"I don't know, sir. I can only assume that something resealed the hole, preventing it from doing so," said Brad.

"Why isn't the whole waveguide filled with water?" asked Hadden.

"There's quartz windows between each joint to provide airtight integrity to the ship in case the compartment and waveguide are damaged, sir," quipped Barbara Gabrielson from behind him.

Commander Hadden Blankenship remembered interviewing Petty Officer Third Class Barbara Gabrielson when they first left port back in Sol system. As he recalled, she was an LRL-73 technician too, which made him suspect there was more to Brad's asking for her assistance than he first suspected.

"Aren't you an LRL-73 technician, Petty Officer Gabrielson?" asked Hadden.

"Yes, sir," she replied timidly.

"Then why haven't you fixed the LRL-73 prior to this?" asked Hadden impatiently.

The petty officer's face turned red, and she looked away from Hadden. There was an uncomfortable silence that grew as he waited for an answer. Brad Guillete finally broke the silence.

"She's been assigned as the supply petty officer and other collateral duties, sir. Chief Wheaton didn't want her touching the radar or any other piece of equipment," stated Brad.

"Why?" asked the commander.

He received a shrug from Brad in response, then Brad said, "I'd rather not say, sir."

"So who found this problem, you or her?" asked Hadden as his suspicions were confirmed.

"Petty Officer Guillete knows quite a bit about the lidar. I assisted him on the areas he's fuzzy on, and he's the one who found the problem. I would still be stumbling around trying to fix it. I learned a lot more about the lidar in the last two days than I have since reporting on board, sir," stated Petty Officer Third Class Barbara Gabrielson.

Hadden looked at her then at Brad and nodded. "I like a truthful answer. How long will it take to repair my lidar, Petty Officer Guillete?"

"I checked the section forward of this. It's the splitter and doesn't appear damaged. This section of the waveguide will have to be replaced. The ship's factory will have to produce this section, and it will require gold to line the interior, then another day to install and seal any breaches between compartments to maintain airtight integrity from removing and installing the waveguide and another day to check out and adjust the system according to Petty Officer Gabrielson. Three to four days, sir," said Brad Guillete.

"Has the part been entered in the system?" asked Hadden.

"Petty Officer Gabrielson put it in the system an hour ago, sir," replied Brad.

"I'll make it a top priority for the ship's factory. Let's get it done, Petty Officers," said Hadden, smiling.

"Yes, sir!" responded the two petty officers together.

It took the ship's factory six hours to produce the part. Two days later, the repairs were complete. The hull technicians assisted with the airtight integrity between the compartments as if it were a battle situation and their lives depended on restoring the integrity of the compartment. When the job was finished, it looked like both petty officers had not slept, cleaned, or changed during the repair time, yet both were smiling when the commander asked whether the lidar worked.

Petty Officer Guillete affirmed that it did as he pointed to the bridge display. The screen revealed what was obviously the cleft and Compound. All the buildings along the lakefront were clearly revealed in high resolution, including the Marine Complex and pier. Hadden could even see people working around the longboat and shuttle docked to the pier.

"Outstanding work, Petty Officers," complimented the commander.

"Thank you, sir," responded both the petty officers.

"There will be a longboat waiting to take both of you planetside in twelve hours. Dismissed," replied Commander Hadden Blankenship.

The two saluted and left for some much-needed sleep.

After they departed, Hadden sat down at the console and watched the image for a time. Then he moved the image to follow the river to its estuary at the southern end of the island. From there, he moved it west toward the continent till he reached the coast. He adjusted the resolution and penetration factor to view through the foliage the ship telescopes could not penetrate. There, on the mainland, a city was revealed. There were buildings over a fairly large stretch of the coast with pyramids sprinkled in, and throughout, figures moved between them. A large pyramid was set further inland, and thousands of figures were gathered around it.

Hadden moved the focus out, and the pyramid shrank. He swept the coast, and further inland where more cities. Hadden returned to the first city and magnified the display again. He swept the shoreline with high resolution, and as he did, there were ships under construction up and down the coast. Commander Hadden Blankenship's face assumed a grim look as he contemplated the future.

CHAPTER 64

It had taken two days to remove enough debris from around the alien craft to have a clear view of its egg-like shape. There was damage to the wide end where the engines resided, like an explosion had occurred near the ship. Gunnery Sergeant Samuel Rusu suspected it had taken the damage from a near miss by a missile but was willing to let the forensic experts decide. The body of the raptor had been removed and put in a sealed crate with foam protection lining the interior for transport. They spent another day ensuring that the craft's power was completely dead and that there was little chance of anything accidentally exploding. They spent another day anchoring the shuttle and rigging the crane so they could lift the alien craft into the cargo hold. Yesterday, they moved the craft into the cargo hold and ensured it was securely fastened in so it wouldn't move. Now the shuttle and its crew were on standby until the longboat performed one more mission before the longboat escorted the shuttle back to the *New Horizon*.

The longboat rose and headed toward the site that Steven Yates had reported showing favorable lithium deposits. The trip would be a short one since it was only about 150 kilometers away from the downed spacecraft's location. The region was in the border area of plain and mountains though, and Ensign Dominic Sobolov refused to risk a landing on anywhere but the bordering plains. Samuel Rusu had asked Ensign Sobolov to land near the mound that he had noted on the map when arriving.

Gunny Rusu watched the flat landscape pocked by craters as they approached the site. The mound he had noted stood a short distance away, and as the longboat approached, it looked even more unusual, like someone was using it as a dumping ground for unwanted material. The longboat went around the mound, and the surface below them became a maze of crisscrossed tracks.

"What the hell is that?" exclaimed Dominic.

"What?" asked Boatswain John Martins.

"The light reflected, and I thought I saw something. Let me get closer," said Dominic.

The longboat drew closer to the base of the ridge at the foot of the mountain. A large dark hole appeared before the bow and went horizontally into the base of the ridge. Dominic brought the craft down, and dust obscured their vision for a moment. As the dust settled, the ensign pointed forward, and everyone leaned forward.

"Shine a light down that hole," said Dominic.

"You got it, sir," replied John.

The searchlight turned on, and Petty Officer First Class John Martins adjusted it so its bright beam shone down the hole.

"That!" exclaimed Ensign Sobolov as the light hit something bright down the hole.

When the crew saw what was illuminated before them, silence fell in the longboat. The hole was rough for about the first twenty meters, then turned into a smooth bore approximately ten meters in diameter. Set five meters in from the area where the tunnel became a smooth surface, a pair of heavy-looking metal doors stood partway open.

They knew that the alien spacecraft came from somewhere, but they assumed it was a mother ship since it appeared to be a fighter craft. Yet before them stood the doors to what might be a complex of unknown dimensions. The doors themselves were large enough to permit the alien spacecraft to enter, but Samuel suspected that was not the purpose of those doors because of the tracks that lay beneath them. However, further into the complex might lie another exit, which might be where the craft had come from.

"Do you think anyone's home?" muttered Samuel. His question must have carried because everyone looked at him apprehensively. In turn, he smiled and said, "We probably need to call this in, Mr. Sobolov."

"I agree with Gunny," said Dominic.

The report was called in to the *New Horizon*, and the longboat crew was told to wait for the arrival of the shuttle and ATV. An hour later, they watched as the shuttle touched down to the side of the pile away from the entrance. Two hours later, the ATV arrived over the surface and stopped at the shuttle. Their orders were to send a team of four into the complex at Ensign Sobolov's discretion, but at least two pilots were to remain outside—one with the longboat and with the shuttle. Dominic contacted the shuttle and told them their orders and to choose two people, but at least one pilot needed to remain with the shuttle.

Dominic then turned in his seat and looked at Samuel. "Gunny, you're with me. Let's suit up."

The two suited up and met the other two members of their team as the ATV stopped beside *Longboat 4*, and two armed figures stepped out. The two from the ATV proved to be David Smith and Jacob Valdez as they fell in behind Ensign Sobolov and Gunny Rusu. They approached the doors warily and turned on their helmet lights and one arm light each. Since the doors were partially ajar, some light penetrated the interior, which, coupled with the suit lights, proved the first set of doors to be the outer doors of a fairly large air lock. The second set of doors were closed, and they thought they might have to turn back until Jacob Valdez pointed to the side where a much smaller door was barely visible with the suit lights. They walked over to the door and found that the control's locking mechanism, which was set in the center of the door, was fairly simple to operate. It was mechanical, and after a turn of the barred cross set inside a circle, they pushed the door inward, causing door to open.

"Relies on internal pressure to keep the door shut. If there were air inside, we would not have been able to open the door. Simple. Efficient," said Dominic Sobolov.

There was another large door set thirty meters further down the tunnel with a smaller door like the one they had just entered beside it. The doors were open, and beyond lay a large chamber.

"Air lock," stated David Smith.

"It would seem so," said Samuel.

They entered a large chamber that contained tracked vehicles with a decidedly egg-like shape to the main carriage. It was obvious that they were constructed for hauling, loading, and digging. There was another set of large doors at the far end of the chamber, which were open. Beyond those doors stretched a tunnel that went further than the lights would reach. There was another large door off to the right side of the chamber with a smaller door standing beside it. Samuel Rusu moved over to the smaller door, which had a locking mechanism like the one they entered. The other members of the party had followed him, so he spun the lock and opened the door. He stepped inside a fairly large room that had two more doors in it and nothing else.

"That door leads to whatever is behind the large doors beside us," stated David Smith.

"It's built to seal if the pressure is lost in that chamber also," added Jacob Valdez.

"This is an air lock, and that door over there is to something important because it will seal if this room loses pressure," stated Dominic.

"Let's check the other door first," said Samuel.

Ensign Sobolov went over to the other door that would seal air pressure in the air lock, which led to the large doors. He opened it and stepped into the chamber, then motioned everyone to follow. They all stepped into the chamber to discover a small vehicle that reminded Samuel Rusu of a forklift. There were pallets on the floor with bars of what could only be refined metal on them. Each bar was about half a meter long with a width and height of around ten centimeters. There were at least a hundred bars on the pallet beside Dominic, and there were hundreds of pallets laid out on the floor of the chamber.

"Looks like a treasure trove," said David.

"Mining operation. I'm buying the next round if that's a foundry behind that door," said Samuel as he pointed to the large closed doors at the far end of the chamber.

"What do you think they were mining?" asked Jacob.

"Let's take some samples," said Samuel as he removed the pouch Steven Yates had given him.

Taking a tool, Samuel Rusu scraped samples off seven piles while marking each pile and sample container. Finished, Samuel returned the bag to his belt. Then the party moved back into the room they had come from. Samuel went to the untried door and turned the locking mechanism. He pushed on the door, and there was resistance, then it moved slightly, and dust engulfed him and the rest of the party. He pushed the door open the rest of the way as the dust slowly settled.

"There was still air," stated Dominic.

"Not enough to matter," grunted Samuel.

They went through what appeared to be an air lock and entered a larger room. Suits and helmets similar to that of the raptor pilot in the spacecraft they had salvaged were arranged along the walls of the compartment. There were twenty spaces for suits, but only seventeen of those spaces were filled.

The group went across the suit storage chamber and passed through the far door into what could only be some sort of control room. The room was huge, and consoles that were similar in design to the one in the alien ship lined the walls. No one touched any of the controls since no one knew what the controls were. There were three other doors departing the chamber, and they were all closed. The first two revealed passageways that led off into the distance beyond the light in their suits' ability to penetrate. The third door, however, led into some sort of lounge area as far as the explorers could tell. A desiccated raptor lay on a stone slab against the wall under what looked like a light fixture of some sort. Other slabs lined the chamber's walls under similar fixtures. There were four other doors leaving the chamber. All four doors led into passageways, two of which were lined with more doors.

"I think it is time to go back and make a report," said Dominic.

"Good idea. The commander will be very interested in what we've found," said Samuel.

The party returned to their ships and waited while Ensign Sobolov made his report. Steven Yates was given the samples Samuel carried to run tests. Three of the samples proved to be on the short list of required materials, and that information was relayed to Commander Blankenship. The commander ordered the teams to acquire as much of the refined ore as they could before returning.

It took several hours to open the inner doors of the first air lock that allowed vehicles access to the mine. Once that knowledge was acquired, the door to the refined ore room was open within an hour. With a clear path from the shuttle to the refined ore room, it was simply a matter of loading the ATV for transport. It took two days in space suits, but when they were finished, the shuttle was carrying nearly ten thousand kilograms of refined ore for transport to the *New Horizon* in addition to the alien spacecraft.

The longboat and shuttle took off from the lunar surface. They left the ATV at the entrance to the mining complex, intending to return. The refined ore alone was well worth another visit to the mines. The commander also intended to have the mines returned to an operational status if possible.

As they departed the moon, Samuel sat back, slowly sipping a coffee. His eyes had a faraway and somewhat haunted look, and Steven Yates noted it.

"You seem to have something on your mind," said Steven.

"I do," replied Samuel.

"What is it?" asked Steven.

"I did some more exploring while the shuttle was securing down the cargo. I wanted to know if there was a foundry on the other side of those doors leading off the refined ore chamber," said Samuel.

"Was there?" asked Steven.

"As a matter of fact, there was, and I owe everyone a round," replied Samuel.

"That's good. Perhaps we can get it operational," said Steven.

"Yeah," said Samuel with a faraway look in his eye.

"Is there something else?" asked Steven.

Samuel Rusu gave Steven Yates a penetrating look, then said, "There was a pile of bones on the foundry room floor."

"Well, we knew that not all of the raptors had evacuated. The one in that lounge area was proof of that," said Steven.

"I have the feeling that none of them were evacuated," said Samuel.

"What do you mean?" asked Ensign Sobolov.

"There were an awful lot of bones. Possibly enough to man the operation," said Samuel.

"So?" asked Steven Yates.

"They looked like they were all gnawed on by another raptor," stated Gunny Rusu.

The cold of space seemed to penetrate the hull and send a chill through the cabin of the longboat. The other three members of *Longboat 4*'s crew stared at Gunnery Sergeant Samuel Rusu in silence as the implications of what he said left them with a feeling of dread and horror.

CHAPTER 65

Second Lieutenant Shiran Raybourn was sitting on a bench beside Francesca Anderson. Both women had pillows between themselves and the stone bench underneath. They were enjoying the noonday sun, having a pleasant conversation with Hiroka Tamura. Hiroka was trimming the mint back in her garden. She had already worked on the roses, which were finally blooming. The baths were being taken care of by Evangeline Dalisay while Hiroka worked at gathering scents for the soaps and perfumes she produced.

Francesca wasn't adding much to the conversation since she had a laptop. She had accessed the files on the raptor language, and Shiran watched the screen. There were hieroglyphs with captions in English that Francesca was studying. Hiroka was meeting Qu'Loo'Oh' today, and the two wished to be present.

Qu'Loo'Oh' came up the walkway between the flowers and spices with Staff Sergeant Rachel Krupich and Staff Sergeant Amanda Hall. When they drew near, Francesca closed her laptop. She and Shiran remained seated. With the burdens that they were lugging around, Hiroka could not fault them for not getting up. There was a sharp twinge of pain in Hiroka's side, under the bandages, but the doctors assured her she was fine but to take it easy. Rachel Krupich stopped, and Qu'Loo'Oh' came up to stand beside her.

"Qu'Loo'Oh', I wish to introduce you to Hiroka, our former captain," said Rachel.

"Pleased to meet you," said Qu'Loo'Oh'.

Astounded, Hiroka stood still for a moment. The beast actually spoke English. No one had informed her of that. Was it really intelligent, or was it simply imitating the language?

"I am pleased to meet you also. Are you a dragon?" asked Hiroka as those around her smiled and laughed politely.

"What is a dragon?" returned Qu'Loo'Oh'.

"A magical beast that breathes fire," said Hiroka.

"I do not breathe fire," said Qu'Loo'Oh'.

"That is good. I would not wish for you to destroy my garden," replied Hiroka.

"You are a healer?" asked Qu'Loo'Oh'.

"No," said Hiroka.

"Then why do you raise plants?" asked Qu'Loo'Oh'.

"For the smells," returned Hiroka.

"Why?" asked Qu'Loo'Oh'.

"To make perfumes and soaps," said Hiroka.

"I do not understand," replied Qu'Loo'Oh' as she looked at Rachel.

"They are applied to the body to make a person smell good," said Rachel.

"It is used to attract a mate?" asked Qu'Loo'Oh'.

"Sometimes," responded Rachel with a laugh as the others laughed with her.

Qu'Loo'Oh' looked at Second Lieutenant Shiran Raybourn and said, "You are the one who locked mouths with Conor many moons ago on the ridge beyond the fence."

Shiran didn't know what Qu'Loo'Oh' was referring to at first, then remembered a day that she and Conor had been running outside the perimeter fence and had kissed long and deep.

"Yes," said Shiran.

"Are you carrying an egg?" asked Qu'Loo'Oh' pointedly, looking at Shiran's stomach.

"Yes and no," said Shiran.

"You are carrying an egg also," stated Qu'Loo'Oh', looking at Francesca.

"Yes." Francesca smiled.

"You are the one who makes books," said Qu'Loo'Oh'.

"Yes," returned Francesca.

"You give birth to live infants. Rachel has told me this," stated Qu'Loo'Oh', shifting her gaze to Shiran.

"Yes, we do," replied Shiran.

"I would like to see this," stated Qu'Loo'Oh'.

Shiran was turning a bright shade of red as a shot rang out. Francesca looked shocked, then slid from her spot on the bench, collapsing on the ground. Another shot rang out, and Rachel fell backward, hitting the side of her head on the stonework around the roses and lay still. Another shot rang out, and Staff Sergeant Hall was hit in the left thigh, causing her to fall to the ground as she was drawing her Gerst S-7. Shiran looked in the direction the shots were coming from to see Norman Pool standing there taking aim and firing again. The shot ricocheted off the stonework behind Shiran.

Shiran went to her knees beside Francesca and slapped the palm of her hand over the spurting red spot in Francesca's lower-right chest. Francesca eyes stared in shock as she whispered something unintelligible. Hiroka crawled forward to render assistance to Shiran as another shot rang out to ricochet off the stonework again. Qu'Loo'Oh' had dropped low and was running toward the cottage as two more shots rang out to splinter stone chips behind her.

Seeing movement out of the corner of her eye, Shiran continued to apply pressure to Francesca's chest. Her fingers were red, and blood was pooling on the ground as she turned her head to watch Amanda Hall sit up. Amanda ejected the green-taped magazine from her Gerst that she still gripped with her right hand. She then took a red-taped magazine she held in her left hand and slammed it into the Gerst 9 mm. Levering the slide back and forth, Staff Sergeant Hall rested both elbows on her knees and took aim. Two quick shots rang out as Amanda's firearm bucked in her grip. Shiran looked in Norman Pool's direction and watched as Norman fell backward with a shocked look on his face. Pool's weapon was still gripped in his hand as his body and arm hit the ground. The weapon discharged, sending a round into the side of the MILDET prefab as his body lay still in a growing pool of blood.

Watching out of the corner of her eye, Shiran saw Amanda remove her belt and wrap it around her leg and stand. Shiran

Raybourn returned her attention back to Francesca as Amanda Hall limped over to Rachel Krupich. Shiran heard shouts and feet pounding the ground as she concentrated on maintaining pressure on the wound. Bloody bubbles were forming at the corners of Francesca's mouth, and Shiran knew that was the sign of a punctured lung. Suddenly, her husband, Lieutenant Commander Conor Raybourn, and Dr. Bess Hollinger were there, and Conor took her in his arms as Bess took over caring for Francesca. Amanda was checking Rachel, but not moving her, though Shiran could see that Rachel's chest still rose and fell. Qu'Loo'Oh' had returned and stood over Amanda and Rachel.

"Rachel!" Shiran heard Qu'Loo'Oh' cry as her tail twitched and her head lowered.

"Are you hit?" Shiran heard Conor ask.

Shiran centered her attention on Conor's face and started crying. The sobs were long as the shock of the incident hit her. She watched as stretchers were brought up to put the wounded into.

"Are you hit?" Conor asked again more forcefully.

"No," cried Shiran.

"Are you sure?" asked Conor gently as Bess Hollinger was giving directions on moving Francesca to the stretcher. Shiran saw that Dr. Kers Joshi was checking Rachel and giving directions to the people around him as Hiroka stood back out of the way with a hand on Qu'Loo'Oh's forelimb.

"It's Francesca's blood," said Shiran.

"What happened?" asked Conor.

"We were all talking when suddenly Pool came out of nowhere and just started shooting," replied Shiran as she sobbed again and pressed herself against Conor's chest.

Three teams of people carried three stretchers away from Hiroka's gardens toward the clinic. Bess Hollinger was at the lead stretcher that carried Francesca. Hiroka and Qu'Loo'Oh' trailed them slowly as people lined up on each side of the procession. The gathering crowd shied away at seeing the red raptor. Lieutenant Commander Michael Anderson ran up to the lead stretcher, saying something. His face turned grim as he received an answer.

Dr. Kers Joshi came over to Conor and Shiran and asked, "Are either of you hurt?"

"No, Doctor. This is all Francesca's blood," responded Conor.

"Then I will see to him," said Dr. Kers Joshi as he walked over to where Tom Tollifer stood over the body of Norman Pool, shaking his head. He said something to Kers, who spent a moment examining the body. Kers shook his head, and he said something to Tom, then left running to catch up with the wounded and assist those who still needed help. Two other colonists arrived with a stretcher to take the body of Norman Pool to the clinic. Tom took a blanket off the stretcher and covered the body from head to toe after the body was placed in the stretcher.

"Let's go clean up," said Conor quietly.

Shiran nodded as Conor escorted her to their prefab. Shiran took a hot shower, scrubbing vigorously, while Conor cleaned up in the sink. When she was finished and dry, she found a fresh uniform laid out for her and Conor waiting in his service dress, sipping on a coffee. He assisted her with putting her maternity uniform on, then the two of them slowly walked to the clinic.

There were six Marines at the entrance of the clinic, but no one was attempting to challenge their authority. The people gathered outside the clinic doors were silent. As Conor and Shiran approached, the crowd parted to let them through. When they entered the clinic, Master Sergeant Evan Zander stood in the center of the waiting room glaring at President Felipe Martinez, who sat in one of the waiting chairs. When the two officers looked at him, Felipe averted his eyes, but not before Shiran noted the new shiner around one of them.

"Master Sergeant," said Lieutenant Commander Raybourn.

"Yes, sir," replied the master sergeant.

"Commander Blankenship and Brad Guillete need to be informed about this incident," said the lieutenant commander.

"I'll take care of it myself, sir," replied Evan Zander, who walked to the entrance door. He opened it and yelled, "Sergeant Adachi, guard duty in the waiting room!"

Shiran and Conor went back through the doors of the emergency ward and left the master sergeant to his job. Michael sat at the entrance to one of the four emergency room doors with his head in his hands. Shiran and Conor went over to him, and the two friends took a seat on each side of him. Shiran heard the sound of a sob as Michael raised his head. Michael's eyes were red, and his face racked with pain. She put her arm around his shoulders as he emitted another sob.

"Any word?" whispered Shiran.

"No," Michael said weakly.

An hour later, Dr. Joshi came out of the emergency ward door with a three stenciled on it. He walked over to the group and looked at Shiran. "Staff Sergeant Hall is going to be all right. The artery in her leg was nicked, and she started bleeding out when we got her here and removed the tourniquet. She'll be here for a couple of days at least," said Dr. Joshi.

"What about Staff Sergeant Krupich?" asked Shiran.

"She has a concussion and a cracked rib from where the bullet struck the body armor. I have Nurse deLang watching her, and she's to come get me if anything changes. I need to assist Dr. Hollinger now. Excuse me," said Dr. Kers Joshi.

The door to emergency ward remained closed for hours as Bess Hollinger and Kers Joshi fought to save the life of Francesca. Commander Hadden Blankenship and Brad Guillete arrived. After being informed of the situation, Hadden asked where Hiroka was and went to see her and meet Qu'Loo'Oh'. He returned an hour later to sit with those who waited in anxiety over the outcome of the struggle. The doctors were in surgery for nearly a day, fighting to save the life of Francesca.

Finally, Bess Hollinger came out of the room. Her face was weary, and there was a sag to her shoulders, but a small smile was on her lips. "She'll be all right. A bullet nicked her right lung and embedded itself in her liver. She went into labor, and we almost lost her while we performed a C-section. She'll be in critical condition for a few days, but I believe she'll be all right," stated Bess.

Beside her, Michael slumped back with relief on his face as Conor smiled.

"And the baby?" asked Shiran.

"A healthy girl." Bess smiled as she turned to face where Commander Blankenship and Brad Guillete sat waiting.

Bess murmured something to Brad as she entered the emergency room where Rachel Krupich was, and Brad sat back to wait, but a smile was on his lips. It took a moment for everything to sink in, then Shiran realized that Bess had said a C-section had been performed and it was a girl.

"You're a father, Michael," said Shiran.

"That's right. Did Francesca and you have a name picked out?" asked Conor excitedly.

"Rebecca," replied Michael with relief written on his face as he smiled.

Shiran noticed that Brad Guillete was smiling even though they hadn't been informed about Rachel's condition. She wondered what Bess Hollinger had whispered to him before going in to see Rachel.

"What did Dr. Hollinger say to you about Rachel, Brad?" asked Shiran.

"She said she'll be fine. A slight concussion and a cracked rib from where the bullet had hit the body armor. They're also resetting her arm while she's out since she wouldn't let them do it before now," said Brad, smiling.

"Is that all she told you?" asked Shiran.

"She also said she likes to have healthy mothers with no deformities if she can correct them beforehand." Brad smiled.

CHAPTER 66

Conor woke to the baby's cry and got up. He went to the wooden crib and picked Conrad up. He made some cooing sounds and cradled Conrad as he walked across the room to the bed where Shiran lay. Shiran had gone into labor three days after the incident that had resulted in Pool's death. Shiran had been in labor for seven hours and had been thoroughly exhausted when Conrad arrived. The baby had arrived a week earlier than expected. The doctor's had kept her for another two days before Shiran stubbornly insisted that she was leaving. The last two days had been a series of naps between feedings. He placed Conrad on the bed beside Shiran, who moved Conrad over to her breast. As the baby started nursing, Shiran looked up at Conor and smiled.

"Are you going to be all right?" asked Conor.

"Natalie will be here in an hour to help out. You have an important mission tomorrow and need the rest. You should spend the night in the Marine Complex and be alert and ready. I'll be fine," said Shiran after looking at the clock on the wall.

"I could reschedule the mission," replied Conor.

"It's been put off enough. We need to look over those drones, and there should be blood in storage for Qu'Loo'Oh' if something actually does happen where she requires it," said Shiran.

Conor nodded and grabbed his cammies, walking out to the table where he laid his clothing. He made himself a cup of coffee and started pulling on his clothes. After dressing, he sat down to sip the coffee and think of the last few days.

The commander had agreed that the recovery of the drones might reveal information leading to the identity of the saboteur. He also agreed that Qu'Loo'Oh' was an important asset—one that might even lead to establishing a peace of some sort with the raptors. Since the expedition was going into new regions, Joseph Green wanted more geological samples. The commander also wanted an aerial survey of the surrounding area in addition to the other two jobs. Since all of them were important, it was decided to combine all the tasks and basically kill four birds with one stone.

Dr. Silas Cheptoo informed Conor that Qu'Loo'Oh' was very old for a raptor but, for the most part, healthy. They discussed what might be done to ensure her health, and the doctor suggested keeping three to five liters of blood available for transfusions. Capturing a red raptor was not high on Conor's list of priorities, and he informed the doctor that he had doubts if any red raptors were currently on the island. The doctor informed him that a green raptor's blood would work, since the two were closely related, but the blood would need to be tested for compatibility. Conor had been provided with a portable analyzer, a storage unit, and collection bags for the task. Conor still had misgivings about the project but knew it was important enough to warrant the risk.

There was a knock on the door, and Corporal Hoffman saluted as Conor let her in. Shiran really didn't require assistance, but since the shooting, a Marine had been stationed near the prefabs for security and protection. A prefab had been refitted and dedicated to housing Qu'Loo'Oh' with Staff Sergeant Rachel Krupich sleeping in the second bedroom to provide protection and assistance for their resident alien visitor. Security equipment had also been added, which could be monitored from the laptop on the table.

"She's in bed with the baby, Corporal. I should be back by tomorrow evening if all goes well," said Conor.

"Very good, sir. Has the baby been a problem?" asked Natalie.

"Neither one of us have had a good night's sleep in two or three days," said Conor.

"They already have the bed in her office and a fresh uniform ready for when you arrive. Good luck with your mission tomorrow," said Natalie.

"Thank you, Corporal," said Conor as he stepped out and closed the door.

He walked over to the Overlook and had a light meal. When he was departing, he was confronted by Martinez and several other colonists.

"You!" growled Felipe Martinez.

"Is there something I can do for you, Mr. President?" asked Conor.

"That staff sergeant of yours killed Norman Pool!" snarled Felipe.

"Pool killed himself when he opened fire on those women," replied Conor.

"That's your version of the story. As far as we know, he was simply defending himself," said Felipe.

"The women say otherwise," said Conor.

"Of course, they would," bellowed Felipe.

"You doubt the veracity of their statements?" asked Conor.

"One of those women attempted killing him only a few weeks ago!" shouted Felipe.

"Mr. Tollifer says Hiroka was justified, and if she had wanted to kill him, I'm sure she would have at that time," replied Conor.

"Your staff sergeant must have felt she had to finish the job!" shouted Felipe.

"I'm sure Staff Sergeant Hall used what force she felt was necessary," said Conor.

"Her weapon was loaded with sleepy darts. She ejected the magazine and reloaded with standard rounds. She murdered Mr. Pool!" shouted Felipe Martinez with others in the crowd murmuring agreement.

"Mr. Pool was over fifty meters away, and he was using standard rounds. Sleepy darts are only effective up to around twenty meters," replied Conor.

"So you admit she murdered him," growled Felipe.

"I admit she escalated to enough force to remove the threat—a threat that nearly murdered Francesca Anderson and several other unarmed women," replied Conor.

"Your wife is never unarmed!" shouted Felipe.

"She was that day for that event," said Conor.

"Your master sergeant assaulted me at the clinic that day," growled Martinez, changing tactics.

"He says you ran into a door," said Conor.

Movement sounded behind Conor. Felipe Martinez's attention and that of the others with him shifted to somewhere behind Conor at that moment. The man looked uncomfortable, and a couple of people suddenly distanced themselves from the group they were with. However, Felipe was not ready to relinquish his quest to seek justice in his own way.

"He hit me!" shouted Felipe.

"That's your word against his," said Conor.

"Now you're condoning violence?" demanded Felipe.

"No, sir. As far as I know, you ran into a door. Do you have witnesses or a video recording to the event in question?" asked Conor.

"No!" shouted Felipe Martinez heatedly as his face turned red.

"Then take it up with the commander. I need some sleep before tomorrow," said Conor as he turned to leave.

"This isn't over, Conor!" shouted Felipe.

"I'm sure it isn't, Mr. President," replied Conor as he walked away.

When Conor moved away, he noticed Ezekiel standing at the door of the Overlook with one hand behind his back. Five people moved in behind Conor as he continued walking, and when he looked, it was the Marines who would be accompanying him on the mission tomorrow. They arrived at the Marine Complex without further incident. Conor went to Shiran's office and slept on the small bed that folded out from the wall for when she needed to spend the night.

*****

It took five days to recover the four drones, procure blood, and take geological samples. Procuring the blood had almost resulted in a catastrophe when one of the raptors popped up after pretending to be unconscious.

"Heads up!" shouted Sergeant Nikolai Ivankov, leveling his Gerst S-7 to a point somewhere past Conor's left shoulder as his Navarro M-71 hung at his side by its strap.

The Marine shot the green that had suddenly sprang up right behind Conor. The sleepy dart worked fast as the beast stared at the feathered dart embedded in its breast. It took one step and collapsed as Sergeant Tadashi Adachi slammed into its side.

"Thanks, Sergeant," said Conor.

"All in a day's work, sir," replied Tadashi.

"Damn things are smart," muttered Nikolai as he nudged the raptor with the toe of his boot.

"A little too smart, Nikolai," responded Corporal Joseph Green as he bent down with the blood analyzer to examine the creature's blood type.

Joseph Green had joined the Marines nearly three months ago, and his wife, the second lieutenant, assured Conor he was fitting in nicely. Joseph was also going to marry Corporal Natalie Hoffman in another week with Nikolai Ivankov performing the services.

"Let's be glad these are greens and not reds," said Conor.

"You think the reds are that smart, sir?" asked Nikolai.

"They were a spacefaring civilization once, Sergeant," said Conor.

"They're only Bronze Age now," replied Tadashi.

"That doesn't mean they're not capable," replied Joseph.

"Qu'Loo'Oh' learned English fast enough," stated Conor.

"We could test her, sir," said Nikolai.

"I'd like to do that without making it too obvious," said Conor.

There was silence for a few minutes. Everyone searched the surrounding foliage as Joseph drew blood from the sleeping raptor he had tested as a match for Qu'Loo'Oh'.

"Games, sir," said Tadashi.

"What do you mean, Sergeant?" asked Conor.

"You have a party scheduled in a few days so people can meet with Qu'Loo'Oh. See if she's interested in games," said Tadashi.

"What would that tell us?" asked Conor.

"Right off, maybe nothing. But Maria DiAngelo is a chess master. If Qu'Loo'Oh' is interested in games and chess specifically, she could give us a gauge on the raptors' intelligence," stated Tadashi.

"I agree, sir," added Joseph.

"Only for that raptor," objected Conor.

"It would be a start, sir," said Tadashi.

Conor nodded. "Good idea, Sergeant."

They spent two more days retrieving drones and taking geological samples. The air surveillance that the commander had wanted revealed no obvious presence of red raptors in the river valley area. If there were red raptors still on the island, they were well hidden or not in any of the areas they had searched. Conor talked to Master Sergeant Zander about the idea that Sergeant Adachi had come up with, and Evan Zander agreed with the idea, saying he would set it up. Conor smiled knowing that the master sergeant would find a way.

CHAPTER 67

The Overlook was bustling with activity. Lieutenant Commander Conor Raybourn had not been sure how well this plan to introduce Qu'Loo'Oh' would go. All the scientists had been invited, and those who could were there. Several other colonists had also requested to attend. Most of the Marines were present, and all were in dress uniforms and provided Ezekiel a helping hand as servers while providing security. Qu'Loo'Oh' stood by a table near the center of the room, while many of the invited guests stood apprehensively around the edges of the room. A few daring souls had approached the table and examined some of the items that had been acquired at the pavilion the red raptors had abandoned when attacked by the colony.

Conor and his wife, Shiran, were milling in the crowd, talking to the various guests who had already arrived, along with keeping a sharp eye out for possible trouble. Conor moved up to a table where some of the colonists were inspecting items retrieved from when the raptors had been driven away. Qu'Loo'Oh' had been asked over the last few days about the items and their function, and notes had been attached to them.

Michael and Francesca arrived and sat at the back table with Commander Blankenship and Hiroka. Francesca moved stiffly as she rounded the table with Michael's assistance. Seeing them, Qu'Loo'Oh' moved to the table with Rachel in tow.

"You are Francesca," chirped Qu'Loo'Oh'.

"Yes, I am," replied Francesca with a forced smile.

Qu'Loo'Oh' bobbed in pleasure and said, "I remember. I am glad that you still live."

"I am too," replied Francesca as she sat down.

"You are no longer with egg," stated Qu'Loo'Oh'.

"No. I had a girl. Her name is Rebecca," said Francesca.

"That is good. I am happy for you," replied Qu'Loo'Oh'.

"Thank you," said Francesca.

"You're welcome. Do you have any more of those wonderful books?" asked Qu'Loo'Oh'.

"Yes, I do," affirmed Francesca, smiling.

"I would like to read more of them," said Qu'Loo'Oh', the crest on her head rising.

"You read?" asked Francesca.

"With Rachel's assistance," replied Qu'Loo'Oh'.

"What did you read?" asked Francesca.

"*Beauty and the Beast*. Rachel says you have many more such wonderful makeup stories," answered Qu'Loo'Oh' enthusiastically.

"I do. I will send some over to you tomorrow," replied Francesca.

"Thank you. Excuse me. Rachel wants me to answer some questions now, I think," said Qu'Loo'Oh'.

Rachel escorted Qu'Loo'Oh' over to the tables containing the scrolls and map from the sacred chamber. There was only one archeologist among the scientists, but many were interested in learning more about the red raptors and their history. Some were distinctly utilized by raptors only while other items were familiar to both species. The scrolls and map that had been borrowed from the hidden caves where Qu'Loo'Oh' had lived were on display. The map hung on the wall, while the scrolls were laid out on tables against the wall. Some of the colonists were studying the map, and among them was Steven Yates.

"So you know of Earth?" Steven Yates asked as he waved his hand at the map hanging on the wall.

"It is the ancient home," replied Qu'Loo'Oh.

"How did your people arrive here?" asked Jacqueline Vinet.

"In a great ship long ago," said Qu'Loo'Oh'.

"How long ago?" asked Steven.

"I do not know," said Qu'Loo'Oh'.

"How long did it take for your people to come here?" asked Maria DiAngelo, an astrophysicist, who stood with her hand resting in the crook of Dominic Sobolov's arm.

"It is said that it took many hundreds of lifetimes," returned Qu'Loo'Oh'.

"Did they sleep, or were they awake when traveling here?" inquired Maria.

"It is said that it was a great ship that contained forests and land for the people to live and hunt while traveling to their destination," stated Qu'Loo'Oh.

"Generation ship," injected Michael Anderson.

"Did your people come directly here?" asked Maria DiAngelo.

"No. They had tried to settle three other worlds and were always found by the ancient enemy," said Qu'Loo'Oh.

"Who is the ancient enemy?" asked Jacqueline.

"Those that hunt my people. We have been at war with them since our people met. They found us here, but we defeated them at great cost. Our great ship that brought us here was lost in the battle," replied Qu'Loo'Oh'.

"How long ago was that?" asked Joseph.

"It is said many hundreds of thousands of lifetimes ago," said Qu'Loo'Oh'.

There was a murmur among those gathered around Qu'Loo'Oh' as she stated that information. That span of time in human terms equated to millions of years. Whether Qu'Loo'Oh' was exaggerating or telling the truth was indeterminable, but the evidence in Earth's archaeological past and what existed on this planet could not be denied. Then someone asked what the scrolls on the tables were about, and the next hour was spent while Qu'Loo'Oh' and Rachel described the basic contents of the scrolls. Conor was near Rachel while Qu'Loo'Oh' was talking and drew her aside.

"You really learned that much of her language during the time you were in those caves with her?" asked Conor.

"It was more than two months, and there really wasn't that much to do other than to sit and learn, sir," replied Rachel.

Conor nodded. "Did you learn to speak raptor too?"

"I know a bit, sir," replied Rachel.

"Have you looked over the inscriptions from Ensign Sobolov's moon mission?" asked Conor.

"No. I haven't had the chance," replied Rachel.

"Do so at the earliest opportunity and get back with me on it," ordered Conor.

"Will do, sir," replied Rachel.

As the evening progressed, a lot of the apprehension among all those present eased. The refreshments had been limited to drinks and hors d'oeuvres. Rachel had informed Qu'Loo'Oh' to eat well prior to going since her eating might disturb the colonists. Qu'Loo'Oh' had argued over this since human food disturbed her, and Rachel knew this, but Qu'Loo'Oh' had finally recanted. She understood that the whole purpose of the event was to have the humans get used to her presence. Rachel said something about baby steps, and at first, Qu'Loo'Oh' didn't understand until Rachel explained that it had to do with younglings learning.

A table against the wall where Evan Zander stood drew Qu'Loo'Oh's interest. She walked over to it and eyed the square board covered in alternating black and red squares. She tapped the board with a talon of her hand, and it slid slightly.

"What is this?" asked Qu'Loo'Oh'.

"It's a game board," said Rachel.

"Show me," replied Qu'Loo'Oh'.

"I haven't played checkers or chess in years," said Rachel.

"Ezekiel!" called Evan.

Ezekiel looked at Evan and divined the reason for the call. He reached behind the counter and brought a bag that clicked over to the table. The two friends set up the pieces and commenced playing. Qu'Loo'Oh' watched intently as the two men described the rules of the game to her. Many of those present drew closer, watching the game and Qu'Loo'Oh'. When Ezekiel won, Qu'Loo'Oh' chirruped and twitched her tail while people drew away from her apprehensively. Rachel started laughing and explained that this was the way Qu'Loo'Oh' expressed pleasure, and it was her form of laughing.

Everyone watched as the two friends played again, but as the game progressed, some people sat down with cards at a couple of the large tables. When Evan Zander won, Qu'Loo'Oh' chirruped again and noticed the people at the other tables. She walked over and watched as they played cards, asking Rachel questions as she did so. Then she saw Maria DiAngelo and Brad Guillete on the other side of the room with a checkerboard but setting a variety of different pieces on it. She watched the two play, fascinated at the complexity of the game. The evening progressed into the night as the crowd slowly thinned out. Much was learned by those gathered about raptors.

Qu'Loo'Oh' learned chess, rapidly showing more proficiency with each game. They stopped after seven games, and DiAngelo agreed to meet with Qu'Loo'Oh' every week to play.

The next afternoon, there was a knock on the door of the prefab, and Conor let Maria DiAngelo in. Shiran showed off Conrad, and they talked for a few minutes. Then DiAngelo turned the conversation to business.

"Qu'Loo'Oh' is quite bright, Conor," said Maria.

"How bright?" asked Conor.

"I pulled the video from Ezekiel's security system and inputted them into Hattie, and the best estimate is, she has an IQ of one hundred and fifty, perhaps even higher," answered Maria.

"So she's as capable as her ancestors," replied Conor.

"Actually, possibly more capable," said Maria.

"What do you mean?" asked Shiran.

"The cranium of the present-day red raptors is slightly different than those our team recovered on the moon," stated Maria.

"In what way?" asked Shiran.

"Dr. Hollinger and Dr. Kers say those living today have on an average at least 3 percent more cranial mass than the bodies on the moon," replied Maria.

Conor whistled, then said, "So most likely brighter than their ancestors."

"I would think so. It would be nice to know what her relative age is as compared to a human. We know she is quite old, but is that age forty or eighty as compared to a human? The doctor believes she's around sixty because of her arthritis, and that is what we told Hattie to use as a standard comparison factor," replied Maria.

"How old does she say she is?" asked Conor.

"Thirty-one planetary years. That makes her approximately forty-five Earth years old," said Maria.

"She seems older," said Conor.

"Bronze Age health care," said Shiran.

"Exactly," replied Maria. "People during the Bronze Age on Earth were fortunate to live much past thirty to forty Earth years, while our modern health care is capable of making us active well into our eighties and nineties."

"I see. So we need to know more about live raptors to be sure," said Shiran.

"Yes, exactly. But for a start, we learned quite a bit, I think," replied Maria.

"Thanks, Maria. Can you write a report and forward it to Commander Blankenship and myself?" asked Conor.

"I can do that," said Maria.

"I'd like a copy also," replied Shiran.

As Maria left, Conor sat back with a mug of coffee. What they had learned about Qu'Loo'Oh' didn't surprise him. He had already determined that she was quite intelligent. She had told them her story of how she had left her people to seek the sanctuary and how she had evaded her people for several years studying the sacred scrolls of her people. The biggest point was, she had saved Rachel and even taught Rachel some of her language while learning theirs. This suggested that both the humans and raptors could work together toward a common end, and Conor thought that perhaps, just perhaps, there might be a way to make a future together.

CHAPTER 68

Ensign Dominic Sobolov entered the docking bay of the *New Horizon* and floated toward the longboat. He was ready to go back to the cleft for some relaxation after the mission on the nearer moon. The excitement of discovering that the raptors were a spacefaring race had made him a hero in the eyes of some. It answered many questions about the planet below. He was looking forward to sitting in the Overlook and relaying his adventures to his friends and whoever else would listen, especially Maria DiAngelo, who, for the last few months, always had a smile and wanted to dance at the Friday evening parties. He still couldn't believe that a member of the science team and an astrophysicist with a doctorate would have an interest in a simple ensign, especially one as pretty as she was.

Dominic returned his attention back to the business at hand and pulled himself into the docking bay. Petty Officer Second Class Catalina Ramirez was there looking over the newly installed ceramic plates of the longboats heat shield as Dominic floated up beside her.

"Is everything all right, Petty Officer Ramirez?" asked Dominic.

"Fine, sir. Just checking the new plates, but they look good," replied Catalina.

"That is good. I don't want to burn up as we descend into the atmosphere," said Dominic.

"Neither do I, sir," responded Catalina.

"Is anyone aboard?" asked Dominic.

"Ensign Hiran," replied Catalina.

"Then let us see if he is done so we can go dirtside. I am hungry and looking forward to a nice sausage and black bean meal at the Overlook," said Dominic.

"Roger that, sir." Catalina grinned as her nose wrinkled. She had tried that culinary delight once and decided it had to be an acquired Russian taste.

Boatswain Ramirez floated into the hatch and went forward to start her preflights. When Dominic entered the longboat, Ensign Bahri Hiran was in the back. Dominic heard something click into place like a panel closing but could not see what it was that Bahri Hiran had been doing because of the cargo that was strapped in place.

"What are you doing, Mr. Hiran?" asked Dominic.

"Just inspecting the straps and fastenings to ensure the equipment is secure," Bahri replied as he tested a strap on the container between the two of them.

"I thought that had been certified three hours ago," said Dominic.

"Never hurts to double-check," said Ensign Hiran cheerfully as he came up alongside Dominic. He patted Dominic's shoulder as he passed and added, "Have a good trip."

"Thank you. When will you be returning?" asked Dominic.

"I'll take the next flight," Bahri called back as he exited the craft.

When Ensign Hiran was gone, Dominic closed the hatch, then moved forward to the pilot seat and strapped in. His copilot was already doing preflights. Dominic started his checks as Catalina sat back from doing hers and made an entry into the log. When Dominic was finished, he called up the log and made his own entry. Keying up the UHF or ultrahigh frequency transceiver, he called the *New Horizon*.

"New Horizon. New Horizon. Longboat 4. Over," said Dominic.

"Longboat 4. New Horizon. We read you. Over," replied Lieutenant Jacqueline Vinet, who was serving her two-week stint on the *New Horizon*.

"New Horizon. Longboat 4. Request permission to depart. Over," said Dominic.

"Longboat 4. New Horizon. Permission granted. Over," replied Jacqueline.

"New Horizon. Longboat 4. Roger. Over," said Dominic.

Dominic Sobolov fired the thrusters, and the longboat slowly backed away from the bow of the *New Horizon*. He adjusted course and lined up for entry sequence.

"New Horizon. Longboat 4. We are beginning our descent. Over," stated Dominic.

"Longboat 4. New Horizon. Have a safe trip. Out," replied Jacqueline.

Dominic sighed as the routine of the atmospheric reentry commenced. Just once in a while, he wouldn't mind if the sequence was disrupted to where he had more to do than sit in the seat and allow the onboard computer to guide them down. Two hours later, the ship bucked slightly from the turbulence, but everything was going smoothly as the longboat made its descent. He checked the heat shield monitors looking for any burn through, but the replacement ceramic plates that had been installed in the last overhaul appeared to have done the trick.

As they pulled up and headed toward the coast, they noted that no raptor ships were moored at the river mouth. Suddenly, a control panel monitor for the reactor lit up, calling Dominic's attention to it. He glanced at the monitor, then looked again.

"We have a problem," stated Dominic, frowning, as he commenced his turn to the east.

"What is it, sir?" asked Catalina.

"Reactor core temps climbing," stated Dominic. "We have too much fuel entering the chamber."

"Bad?" asked Catalina.

"Yes, the automatic regulator appears broken, and the manual doesn't appear to work," stated Dominic as he manipulated a knob and attempted to slow the flow. Nothing happened, and worry lines creased his forehead.

"Will we make it down?" asked Catalina.

"We'll blow up first. Dump the fuel," ordered the ensign.

"We won't have any fuel to fly," Catalina stated as she opened the safety cover to the switch that would eject the fuel.

"We are traveling plenty fast. Too fast. We have the ailerons and the parachute," replied Dominic.

"Ejecting," said Ramirez.

The longboat bucked as the fuel was released. Dominic watched as the reactor core started cooling, and they rapidly approached the cleft.

"Good. Now let us hope we get down the rest of the way without killing ourselves," stated Dominic.

The craft continued its course as the last of the fuel sputtered out the propulsion nozzles. The craft was slowing down as it streaked past the cleft, and Sobolov adjusted course to bring the craft about in a wide turn. They were still going too fast as he came out of the turn well above the tree line. He edged down as they raced toward the marsh on the east side of the lake.

"I am going to attempt to lower the nose when we touch water and hit the dorsal thrusters," said Ensign Sobolov.

"We don't have any fuel," stated Catalina.

"Different system," Dominic informed her.

"What's the plan?" inquired Catalina.

"I think we will submerge for a short time," stated Dominic.

"The deceleration will probably kill us," breathed Catalina.

"Hopefully not," grunted Dominic.

They came in low and fast, the craft ripping off limbs and foliage. Dominic lowered the nose of the longboat so it would come in almost level when they reached the lake. Fortunately, the east end of the lake was mostly marshland. As he cleared the tree line, he edged down quickly as the three kilometers of marshland flashed by, and they touched the surface of the lake. He hit the parachute in a vain attempt to slow down. Nothing happened. When he hit the dorsal thrusters, he prayed the water resistance would slow the craft more if it went underwater. Hopefully, they wouldn't run into something or hit the bottom when they submerged.

"Hold on!" cried Dominic as the craft hit the water, jolting them.

The longboat skimmed across the water for a moment, then submerged, as Dominic gave the thrusters a brief burst. A leak sprang up in the rear of the craft as something banged against the heat shield underneath as they slowed. Using the ailerons, Dominic steered a course toward the surface and to the south. When they resurfaced, they were still going too fast, and the far bank was no longer so far away, but they were not headed directly toward the buildings.

"Damned streamlining," muttered Dominic.

The beach approached rapidly as they watched through the spray of the water that coated the forward viewport.

They entered the rice paddies in a spray of mud, bouncing horrendously, and something in the console flew loose, hitting Dominic in the forehead. Blood obscured his left eye as he heard something snap, and Petty Officer Second Class Ramirez screamed in pain. They finally came to rest on the far side of the rice paddies. There was a ringing in his ears as he groggily raised his head. Stars flashed in his field of vision as he shook his head, trying to clear it.

"Are you all right, Ms. Ramirez?" asked Dominic weakly.

"I think my arm is broken," wheezed Catalina as she held up her left forearm, which had what appeared to be an extra joint between the wrist and elbow. Pain contorted Catalina's face as she sat back in her seat, cradling the broken limb in her lap.

"Let me check the monitors, and I'll be right with you," said Dominic.

"Okay," came the enfeebled response.

Dominic checked the monitors, which were a field of red with an occasional touch of green. He saw nothing that indicated that a fatal event was imminent. He flipped a couple of switches, turning off the longboat's engine and main power systems. He then checked the radio. Dead. Dominic turned to face Catalina in his seat. He released his harness and got out of his chair. The craft was not level, but he reached behind the pilot seat and unstrapped the first aid kit. Retrieving it, he opened it up and found the painkillers and put two in Ramirez's mouth.

"Swallow," ordered Dominic.

Catalina swallowed the pills, and after a few minutes, the pain eased from her face.

"I am going to pop the hatch and see if I can contact the Marine Complex," said Dominic.

"They're already on their way," replied Catalina as she pointed with her chin at the viewport.

Dominic looked through the viewport and saw two ATVs approaching rapidly.

"Good. Will you be all right?" asked Dominic.

"I'm fine. Go," replied Catalina.

Dominic left Catalina sitting in her seat and went aft. Opening the hatch, he stepped uncertainly out onto the muddy ground surrounding the longboat. He sank up to his knees in the water and mud, then took a shaky step forward. He was still somewhat unsettled by the roughness of the landing and in awe that Catalina and himself were still in one piece. A deep trail cut through the rice fields behind the longboat as he looked back in the direction they had come from. The longboat was covered in dark-gray mud.

The Marine ATVs pulled up in a spray of water and mud that just missed Dominic. Master Sergeant Evan Zander stepped out of the lead ATV with a quick glance at the longboat. He saluted Ensign Sobolov as he approached through the knee-deep water.

"Looks like you had a slight problem, sir," said Evan Zander.

"Dah! You might say that, Master Sergeant," replied Dominic.

"Are you all right, sir?" asked Evan.

"I'm fine. Ramirez will require assistance. She has a broken arm," replied Dominic.

"Hall! Green! Ramirez has a broken arm. Stretcher duty. Minimal intrusion," shouted Evan.

"Minimal intrusion?" inquired Dominic.

"The commander wants this treated like a crime scene," replied Evan.

"Why is that, Master Sergeant?" asked Dominic.

"Mine is not to question why, sir," returned Evan.

The Marines entered the longboat to retrieve Petty Officer Second Class Ramirez, while Ensign Sobolov walked around the longboat, inspecting it for damage. The master sergeant followed him closely as he did, and Dominic suspected Evan Zander was expecting him to collapse from an injury. Dominic slipped once on his circuit of the longboat, but the master sergeant was there to grab his arm. When he finished walking completely around the longboat, the Marines were just loading Catalina Ramirez into the ATV. They walked toward the ATV together after checking to ensure the hatch was closed. As the two reached the ATV, they turned to look back at the longboat.

"Amazing it's still in one piece, sir," grunted Evan.

"Still lots of use left in her. She just needs a little tender loving care," replied Dominic.

Master Sergeant Evan Zander glanced sideways at Ensign Sobolov and nodded. "I'm sure that can be arranged, sir."

Commander Blankenship was in the waiting room of the clinic as they entered. The commander spoke briefly to Petty Officer Ramirez lying in the stretcher before letting Dr. Hollinger take her back to the emergency ward. When they had left, he turned to the master sergeant, and they spoke briefly before the commander walked over to Dominic. Dr. Kers Joshi finished the stitches on the ensign's forehead, then placed a bandage over the wound. Joshi looked at Hadden, then patted Dominic on the shoulder and told him to take it easy.

"What happened, Ensign?" demanded Hadden.

Ensign Sobolov relayed what had happened to the commander. Dominic reported in detail the flight from the *New Horizon* all the way to coming aground in the rice paddies. When he finished, there was something in the commander's eyes that was not there before.

"I'm amazed you're in one piece, Mr. Sobolov. That's one hell of a story," stated Hadden.

"I am too, sir," replied Dominic.

"Is the longboat salvageable?" asked Hadden.

"It will have to have a complete structural inspection, the engines will require a complete overhaul, all systems will require a complete checkout, and the heat shield will most likely need to be replaced," returned Dominic.

"Do you think she'll fly again?" asked Hadden.

"Yes, sir," stated Dominic with enthusiasm.

"Then I'm putting you in charge of the refit. Think you can handle that?" asked the commander.

"Yes, sir," snapped Ensign Sobolov.

"Good! Since the doctor appears done with you, go clean up and get some rest for the next two days," said Hadden as he turned to leave.

"Yes, sir," replied Dominic.

"And, Mr. Sobolov, I want to see you in the correct uniform the next time I see you," Hadden said as he reached the door.

"Excuse me, sir?" returned Dominic.

"A lieutenant junior grade doesn't wear ensign bars," Commander Hadden Blankenship said as he exited the clinic.

Dominic allowed his jaw to drop as the commander left. He heard a chuckle and looked at the master sergeant standing nearby. There was a huge grin on Evan Zander's face as he saluted Lieutenant Junior Grade Dominic Sobolov and shook his hand.

CHAPTER 69

Lieutenant Commander Michael Anderson was working on one of the drones Lieutenant Commander Conor Raybourn had recovered with his team. The planet year out in the open weather had hardly affected the exterior of the drone, and the casing didn't appear to be breached. Michael had chosen to work on this drone for that reason. The other drones had been filled with debris because of breaches in the protective coverings. It was for this reason that Michael felt his best chance of learning anything substantial would be with this particular drone.

He had already removed the dorsal covering on the drone and was inspecting the interior mechanisms. The control system of the drone was a mess. It looked like something had fried the circuits. Michael had not found any markings or the ominous symbol, but then it might have been erased when the incendiary had demolished the circuits.

Michael went over to the other drones and inspected the outer casings, looking for exterior damage. Two of the drone cases had shown signs, signs of burn through in the same area of the first drone he had inspected. The last drone had a dent with a notable crack in the nose cone as though it had collided with something solid. Michael walked back over to the workbench where he had the first drone he had been disassembling. He was just getting ready to pick up the first cover plate that he had removed and examine it when the commander Hadden Blankenship entered.

"Lieutenant Commander," said Hadden.

"Good morning, sir," said Michael.

"How was Francesca doing this morning?" asked Hadden.

"She's well, sir. Still stiff from the wound, but Dr. Hollinger says she's doing fine," replied Michael.

"And the baby?" asked Hadden.

"A little bundle of joy. We have Maria helping out until Francesca feels capable of handling a full day," said Michael, referring to the astrophysicist Maria DiAngelo.

"Do you have time to look over *Longboat 4*?" asked Hadden.

"Is there a problem with it, sir?" asked Michael.

"It just crashed," said Hadden.

"How bad?" asked Michael, shocked.

"Lieutenant JG Sobolov was able to land her in the rice paddies. He appears to be fine, but Petty Officer First Class Ramirez broke her arm. That's all I know unless the doctors say differently. They're both over at the clinic being checked out right now," said Hadden.

Michael placed the cover he had been preparing to inspect back down on the workbench. He had caught the rank changes that the commander had used in referring to Dominic Sobolov and Catalina Ramirez. He cocked an eyebrow at the commander as he said, "Lieutenant JG and Petty Officer First Class, sir?"

"They both deserved it. They lost flow control to the longboat's Benson reactor, and the core was overheating. They ejected the fuel just as it finished entering the atmosphere. They only had their thrusters and ailerons to land with," replied Hadden.

Michael whistled knowing the skill it would take to accomplish such a task. He then asked, "How soon do you want it inspected?"

"I want you to look it over right away. After a cursory, if you feel it can be moved, get with Second Lieutenant Raybourn to have her Marines assist you in towing it to the Marine Complex. If you need more time to inspect after that, let me know. Our new lieutenant JG is in charge of the refit. I told Dominic to take a couple of days off while you and the Marines bring it in," stated Hadden.

"May I use Brad Guillete if I feel the need?" asked Michael.

"Does he know longboat systems?" questioned Hadden.

"I'm not sure, sir, but it wouldn't surprise me if he did," replied Michael.

Hadden nodded. "Have you told him about the saboteur?"

"No, sir. He only knows we were looking for a symbol when we were inspecting the pharmaceutical unit," said Michael.

"It wouldn't surprise me if he's pieced it together," stated Hadden.

"He is the one who suggested recovering the drones for inspection," stated Michael.

"Have him help you on this and inform him about the saboteur. I'll let Conor know that I authorized that so it doesn't blindside him. Make sure Mr. Guillete understands that the information about the saboteur is to be treated as top secret, and he is only to discuss it with Conor, you, and me. If he thinks he has something, he is to tell us immediately in private," said Commander Blankenship.

"I'll get right on it, sir," responded Michael.

"How's the drone inspection going?" inquired Hadden.

"I was just starting, but it's waited this long. I'm sure it'll keep for a few more days," replied Michael.

"I agree. Let me know immediately if you find anything unusual with the longboat," said Hadden.

"Yes, sir," replied Michael.

Michael removed his surgical gloves, mask, and apron as the commander left. He hadn't known about the longboat crashing, and the thought of bringing in an unpowered longboat sent a chill up his spine. He stopped at the clinic to see Dominic Sobolov and congratulated him, then he had Dominic tell him about the incident. He shook his head and whistled as Master Sergeant Evan Zander brought him up beside the mud-splattered longboat in the ATV.

"Lucky it's still in one piece," said Michael.

"It was a hell of a thing to watch, sir. I'm surprised either of them made it out alive," said Evan Zander.

"Hatch is closed," said Michael.

"I had the Marines close it after retrieving Ramirez. Two Marines have ensured that no one went near the whole time, so the scene wasn't contaminated," said Evan.

Michael gave Evan a long look, wondering how much he knew about the incidents not being accidents. Could Zander be the saboteur? Michael shook his head at that thought and decided he was starting to see saboteurs around every corner. The master sergeant had a family, and if Evan Zander was responsible, they were really screwed. Michael waded through the knee-deep mud up to the hatch and opened it.

"I'm going to spend a couple of hours doing a cursory inspection before it gets dark. If I don't find anything, we'll move the longboat up to the Marine Complex tomorrow," called Michael.

"I'll make arrangements to have four of the ATVs with towlines available," returned Evan.

"That'll work," replied Michael.

"Do you want the craft guarded tonight?" asked Evan.

"Yes. No one in or out except myself," ordered Michael.

"Roger that, sir," snapped Evan.

Michael looked over the longboat for nearly three hours and found nothing. The next day, they towed the craft out of the rice paddies to firmer ground. Michael entered the craft and was able to lower the landing gear, but he was unable to engage the electric motors for maneuvering the longboat independently while on the ground. They moved the longboat over to the Marine Complex, and a guard was placed around the longboat while Michael worked in a more level environment. He spent the rest of the day discovering nothing and finally went home for the night.

The next day, he had Brad Guillete go with him to look over the shuttle. The cargo was removed and placed in a holding area under guard for possible inspection. They began taking off control panel covers and searching storage compartments, looking for anything unusual. It was nearly sundown, and they were putting away their tools when Brad looked back at a control panel in the rear of the craft. He got up with a screwdriver and went back to the panel.

"What is it, Brad?" asked Michael.

"When we were back here, I was working on the starboard side and you worked on the port," answered Brad.

"Yes," said Michael.

"Most of these panels say they are for flow control to the engines," stated Brad.

"That's right," replied Michael.

"Didn't Mr. Sobolov say they had a flow control problem?" inquired Brad.

"Yes. That's why we looked inside those first," said Michael as Brad nodded in agreement.

"Well, I wanted to be sure what I was looking at, so I looked over the interior of each of your panels when they were off," said Brad as he studied the end of his screwdriver.

"Sounds reasonable since you don't work on engines," said Michael.

Brad nodded as he inserted a screwdriver into one of the port control boxes. "So each of these should look the same inside. Just an inverse of the other," said Brad.

"They are, and they're dangerous to mess around inside if you don't know what you're doing. So be careful with that screwdriver," Michael responded, then he heard a slight click as Brad pried at something inside.

"Thought so," said Brad.

Brad pulled something out of the control panel and carried it carefully by the edges with his gloved fingers over to Michael. Michael turned the object in his gloved hand. It was thin, flat, and smooth, with a surface made of the same metal as the interior of the control panel. When he turned it over, the ominous symbol he had come to know was revealed on the obverse surface.

Michael bagged and took the device to the electronics suite. Under magnification, the device revealed a partial fingerprint. Michael did something to the lighting, and the telltale mark became more prominently displayed. He took a picture and sent it to Hattie. Within moments, he had the results of Hattie's analysis of the fingerprint. A confused look crossed his face because the name was one he would never have imagined.

Putting the device back into its bag, Michael put it and the picture into his pocket and left the comm suite. He walked over to the MILDET prefab and knocked on the door. Conor answered the door and let Michael in. The commander came out of the kitchen holding a mug of coffee. He went back and returned with another as he indicated for Michael to have a seat with them.

"You're sure?" demanded Hadden.

"A partial of her fingerprint was on the item," replied Michael.

"Could she have touched it while working in the longboat without knowing what it was?" asked Conor.

"It was on the underside of the device attached to the inside of the control box. That's the side the symbol was placed on too. So the symbol would not be visible unless removed," said Michael.

"What else?" asked Hadden.

"She's supply, and she was involved in the handling of the drones and pharmaceutical unit. She also handled some of the FTL parts," replied Michael.

"So what do we do, sir?" asked Conor.

"We bring her in for questioning and hold her until we are sure one way or the other," said Hadden.

"How do you want it done?" asked Conor.

Commander Blankenship sat back and steepled his fingers as a frown creased his forehead. Everyone knew Petty Officer Anya Kaur because they had all signed for an item from her at some time in the past.

"We have the Marines apprehend her at the pier and take her to the Marine Complex for holding," replied Hadden.

"Yes, sir," said Conor.

"With kid gloves. I'm not completely convinced of her being the saboteur," said Hadden.

The two junior officers sat and looked at the commander quizzically. A silence pervaded the room for over a moment, then the two shifted in their seats uncomfortably.

Hadden finally sighed and rubbed his eyes, then said, "I just find it too convenient that a partial print was left. Something in my gut says it's a setup."

The master sergeant and two other Marines made the arrest a day later as Petty Officer Kaur arrived on the shuttle. Anya Kaur was escorted to a holding cell in the basement of the Marine Complex. Several times she asked what was going on and what the charges were. There was no response from the silent Marines other than to have her rights read to her. When the commander arrived to ask her questions, she became irritated that he could even think she was the instigator of the incidents. She claimed no knowledge of any symbol or that any of the incidents were any more than the accidents and malfunctions the colony had been told they were.

There was a confrontation with President Felipe Martinez and his staff later in the day over the arrest of Petty Officer Anya Kaur. Both sides grew heated, but the commander informed Martinez that her arrest was a military matter involving the safety of the colony. Felipe was unconvinced that Anya was responsible even after he was shown the evidence, but he finally relented. Conor, however, found it disconcerting that neither the president nor his staff demanded to see the incarcerated during the whole affair.

CHAPTER 70

The human named Conor stood before Qu'Loo'Oh', reminding her of one of her offspring that had hatched nearly eighteen years prior. The hatchling had grown strong and splendid as he hunted position in society. He cunningly gained position with wit and a wisdom seldom found in one of her people so young. This one displayed a bearing and wisdom similar to Qu'Fal'Ral', who had risen so high so quickly. Instead of slaying her outright like many of the people would do, it spoke of hope and the future as Qu'Fal'Ral' did when negotiating treaties.

The offering of eggs to this one might be possible, allowing the people to survive and flourish instead of being crushed and all destroyed. Few young ones survived the hunts, and that was good because the people would lay waste the land if the population was not kept in check. However, the destruction of a whole tribe was not desired either. Knowledge was lost, and the pool of blood that made the people strong lessened when a bloodline was lost. It was not always the strongest or the quickest that survive the hunts but the most cunning.

The one called Conor shouted "Master Sergeant!" and another of its kind entered the room. Qu'Loo'Oh's heart froze as the new one's eyes locked with hers. This one was a hunter who paid heed to Conor but was a leader in its own right, then its eyes softened when seeing Rachel. The one called master sergeant talked about Rachel getting him in trouble, but Qu'Loo'Oh' suspected that he was teasing the young one.

Words were spoken between Conor and the master sergeant, and shortly, Qu'Loo'Oh' was being carried to the spot where she had been injured. Explosions sounded like a storm front was upon them, then branches and trees fell to the ground. After that, one of the flying beasts that carried these humans landed nearby, while another hovered overhead like an angry hornet. When they loaded Qu'Loo'Oh' onto a side carriage of the beast, she realized the beast was actually some form of machine because it was made of metal. The metal was similar to the relics her people kept from the ancestors, because when she scratched at it with a claw, it left no mark.

They fastened straps over her, and the machine rose above the world. She was grateful for those straps, for as they rose, she feared falling out of the precarious perch they had placed her in. The flight was short and, in a matter of heartbeats, crossed distances that would have taken her a day and more to walk. They landed in the depression of the cliff face where the humans had constructed buildings inside the silvery web surrounding this side of the lake. Rachel and Brad assisted her walk to one of the buildings, while other humans gathered on each side to watch. They went through a door and down a passage to a chamber where other humans waited. These humans said they were healers. They did many things that displeased Qu'Loo'Oh', but Rachel assured her it would make her better.

The doctors put a needle into her forearm that had a cord running to a clear bag that appeared to be filled with a clear liquid. They told her that it would make her sleep and that when she woke up, she would feel much better. She looked at Rachel, who smiled, as Qu'Loo'Oh' drifted off to sleep. She wondered as she did so if she would wake up again or if she had been tricked as her minded fogged and clouded over.

When Qu'Loo'Oh' awoke, she was in a different chamber, lying atop a marvelous nest made of cloth that was bundled up against her. Wealth worthy of a ruler. It would take months to weave such wealth to be used as a nest. She raised her head to look around the chamber and saw Rachel sitting on a bench against the far wall. She was staring at a rectangular item made of leather that she held in front of her. Rachel shifted the leather bond item as Qu'Loo'Oh' watched, and something that looked like papyrus flipped. Rachel looked across the room as this happened and folded the item she was holding in half.

"Good morning," said Rachel.

"Good morning," chirped Qu'Loo'Oh'.

"Do you feel better?" inquired Rachel.

Qu'Loo'Oh' thought about it as she shifted in the marvelous nest before replying. "The pain is gone, and my joints feel young."

"That's good! The doctors said you should feel much better. They want to keep you here for a couple more days for testing and treatments," replied Rachel.

"What is that?" asked Qu'Loo'Oh'.

"The testing and treatments are what is making you feel better," Rachel informed her.

"No! That," said Qu'Loo'Oh' as she pointed a talon on her forelimb at the object in Rachel's lap.

"What?" asked Rachel, confused.

"The item you hold in your"—Qu'Loo'Oh' paused, searching for the word—"lap."

Rachel lifted the item and stated, "It's a book."

"May I see it?" asked Qu'Loo'Oh'.

Rachel brought the book over and laid it in front of Qu'Loo'Oh' on a blanket. The cover had a picture on it of a human and what looked suspiciously like an ancient enemy on the cover. There were letters there that spelled *Beauty and the Beast*. Rachel opened the book and flipped through the first few pages, explaining as she did that it was publishing notes. Rachel said that it had something to do with the creators of the story and dates it was printed. Rachel stopped at a page that said Chapter One at the top. The writing was in the hieroglyphs that Rachel had trained Qu'Loo'Oh' about. They were small, but Qu'Loo'Oh' could still read them.

"This is the story of your people?" asked Qu'Loo'Oh'.

"This is a story made by my people," replied Rachel.

"I do not understand," stated Qu'Loo'Oh'.

"It is a madeup story," replied Rachel.

"You waste this marvelous paper on madeup stories?" asked Qu'Loo'Oh'.

"Yes," said Rachel.

"Why?" asked Qu'Loo'Oh'.

"Some stories are worth keeping, and paper is easy to make," replied Rachel.

"I understand. Will you help me read your story?" asked Qu'Loo'Oh'.

Qu'Loo'Oh' listened to Rachel read aloud while following along in the book, stopping her when she did not understand the meaning of a word or reference. She learned many new human words over the next few days as Rachel read and she recovered. Many words were a mystery to her, and Rachel was not able to convey a meaning that made sense to Qu'Loo'Oh'. The story at times was completely befuddling and yet wonderful. How could common tools come to life? Qu'Loo'Oh' shrugged and decided that it was something humans must believe.

There were doctors and others who visited Qu'Loo'Oh' during this time. She met the one they called the commander who had sharp eyes and asked many questions about her people.

Qu'Loo'Oh' grew stronger and felt new vigor in her body with each passing day. The healing magic of the humans removed many aches and pains that she had been experiencing in the last couple of years, and she wondered if the humans had discovered how to extend life. She was nearing thirty years of age, and most old ones did not live past forty. She had accepted that she had at most another ten years to live and study at the sacred chamber even before meeting Rachel.

Then the day came that Rachel announced that they were going outside to visit some of her friends. They left the chamber, and the one covered in the forest-patterned cloth like Rachel wore followed them as they left the chamber, leaving the door unguarded. They went down the passage and into the daylight, walking west as they left the structure Rachel called a clinic. There were some rounded structures with doorways that they passed as they approached an area covered in the green of plants surrounded by little walls. Other humans sat there talking.

Qu'Loo'Oh' talked to them all, and as they were talking, the loud noise of a fire stick sounded. The one called Francesca, who produced the marvelous books, slid off the stone bench as more explosions sounded. Then Rachel fell and knocked her head on the short stone wall surrounding the plants. Then the other one who had followed her from the clinic fell to the ground. Qu'Loo'Oh' ran knowing she was the real target, hoping that it would draw the aim of the aggressor from those around her.

She entered the structure as two explosions sounded closer than the prior ones. She peeked out the doorway and saw the one who had followed her from the clinic rise from a sitting position as she removed the belt around her waist. The one who had been shooting at them lay on the ground, unmoving, and people were running toward her and the others. Qu'Loo'Oh' left the structure and returned to where Rachel lay unmoving and called her name. The one called Hiroka placed a hand on Qu'Loo'Oh's forearm and gently pulled her to the side as two other humans knelt beside Rachel. The humans quickly loaded the wounded into carriers with the doctors who had cared for her attended those in the carriers. Hiroka walked with Qu'Loo'Oh' as they followed the humans to the clinic and stayed with her in her chamber. It was over a day later that Qu'Loo'Oh' found out that Rachel and the others had survived the incident.

The humans slowly recovered, and Qu'Loo'Oh' spent much time with the one named Hiroka for several days. Rachel returned and told Qu'Loo'Oh' that both Francesca and Shiran had given birth to their egglings. A half moon after the attack by the one named Pool, both women came to visit her with their egglings. They were pushed in a wheeled chair by their mates, Conor and Michael.

It was shortly after this happy event that she met a human named Ezekiel, who arrived with a delicious cut of meat from one of the horned beasts that was still warm. Rachel must have told him that the portion Ezekiel brought was her favorite part of the beast. She discovered that Ezekiel was one who prepared food for people at a restaurant. Qu'Loo'Oh' found Ezekiel to be an interesting human. He sent a human named Roberta to ask what she would like to eat each day, then delivered the meal himself.

Then one day, her human friends told Qu'Loo'Oh' of a gathering that had been planned for people to meet her. She was told that the people who wished to meet her were the intellectuals of the colony and were curious about her people and civilization. This gave Qu'Loo'Oh' pause because she was not sure how much to tell these humans. Was it safe, or would it make her a traitor to her people? Qu'Loo'Oh' was apprehensive, but Rachel and Hiroka did their best to alleviate those fears. They informed her that they were looking for ways to establish a peace where their two species could live together in some manner. Qu'Loo'Oh' reluctantly relented and agreed to attend.

The gathering at the place called the Overlook had many people who Qu'Loo'Oh' had already met. All wore coverings that looked similar, though there were items they wore on their chests and shoulders that differed. Some wore a dark-blue covering, while the ones Qu'Loo'Oh' knew to be warriors wore black with trimmings of dark red. She learned that the blue uniform signified those individuals who sailed the great sky ships. She was surprised to learn that the one named Conor wore the attire of a sailor while his mate wore that of a warrior.

There were many other people present who wore various coverings that did not conform, which Rachel called civilian attire. They asked Qu'Loo'Oh' many questions about her people and items made by her people that they had acquired. Many of them asked how a peace could be established and perhaps even trade. Qu'Loo'Oh' could only tell them that she did not know and would have to consider the matter.

Then Qu'Loo'Oh' noticed an item on a table near the one with the hard, sharp eyes named Evan. When she asked what it was, she was told it was a game. She asked to be shown, watching Evan and Ezekiel play a game they called checkers. Others in the room started playing various other games, which she took the time to watch. Along the far wall, she saw Brad and someone called Maria playing a different game that used the same board as the checker game. Qu'Loo'Oh' learned the game named chess, and after several games, Maria promised to make time to play this new game with her once every seventh day.

When the evening ended, Qu'Loo'Oh' was escorted back to the small hand-built cave the humans had provided her. She curled up in the wonderful nest they had made for her. As she lay there,

Qu'Loo'Oh' had the strange feeling that meeting other humans and the questions about her people had only been part of what had occurred during the evening. Qu'Loo'Oh' had the odd feeling that she had been tested.

CHAPTER 71

The world was wonderful as Conor Raybourn sat at the table with his wife, Shiran. The sun shone brightly through the window, and a fresh breeze moved the curtains lightly back and forth. Conrad was finally sleeping through the night, and both of them were able to sleep themselves. Conor had acquired an egg from Ezekiel, along with a cheese substitute and vegetables that Ezekiel assured him would go well in an omelet. Conor had made the omelet himself, and the remains of their repast was a pair of dishes with a light oil film on them.

They had moved into a two-room apartment above the Overlook only a month ago and were enjoying the textured walls and real furniture as compared to the plastaform furnishings of the prefab. The apartment was smaller than the prefab for a room, but Ezekiel assured them that the couple next door to them would be moving soon into bigger accommodations. He assured them when that happened, the apartment they were using would be modified so the two apartments, both that one and theirs, would become one apartment.

A gust of wind blew Shiran's raven hair across her face, and she pushed it back into place. The smell of sour milk from the cradle at her feet came to Conor as he smiled. Shiran leaned back in her seat and stretched briefly as she looked at Conor.

"That was good. Thank you," said Shiran.

"Anything for you," replied Conor.

Shiran looked out the window for a moment and said, "You know what I miss?"

"What's that?" asked Conor.

"Riding a horse. The feel of polished leather with the wind whipping through my hair," replied Shiran.

"Not many of those around here. Maybe I could saddle you a triceratops or apatosaurus," responded Conor, chuckling.

"It just wouldn't be the same," said Shiran dejectedly.

"I miss having a dog," stated Conor.

"I didn't know you liked dogs," replied Shiran.

"I had a German shepherd back on Earth. My father was keeping him while I went exploring," returned Conor distantly.

"What did you call it?" asked Shiran.

"Sputnik," said Conor.

"Sputnik?" asked Shiran, frowning.

"First artificial satellite ever launched. It caused what they called the space race about five hundred years ago," replied Conor.

"Oh!" exclaimed Shiran.

"What else do you miss?" asked Conor.

"Pigeons. My mother raised them. She let me feed and hold them. And the smell of fresh jasmine growing in the garden," said Shiran.

"I can accommodate you on that last one. I believe Hiroka has a plot of that in her garden," said Conor.

"She does, and it reminds me of home," said Shiran wistfully.

"That's good. This place is feeling more and more like a home as time passes." Conor smiled.

The two sat and sipped on their ginkgo tea. Conor freshened their cups and glanced at the window where the blue sky held puffs of clouds. He saw a pair of pterodactyls in the distance circling the lake as they hunted the fish of the lake. The sound of rushing water from the waterfall as it fell over the edge of the cleft was an ever-present reminder of its presence. He could detect the faint smell of the miniature roses Shiran was raising on the balcony.

The baby awoke and gave a slight cry. Shiran picked Conrad up and adjusted her gown as she placed the infant to feed. Conor smiled and stood up, removing the dishes to the small kitchenette against the wall. When he was finished cleaning the mess, Conor went to the wardrobe and dressed. He chose a tan shirt, dark jeans, and knee-high leather moccasins to don and slipped them on. The leatherwork and tanning shop that had produced the last item and had seen heavy damage when the Compound had been attacked. Conor knew they were still rebuilding and hoped that it would be repaired long before the moccasins required replacing.

Finished, Conor walked over to Shiran, who had placed Conrad back into the carrier at her feet. She stood up and stretched again, and her gown fell open. She noticed Conor admiring her and said, "We don't have time for that, silly." Shiran smiled.

"Oh?" queried Conor.

"We're supposed to meet Francesca in a half hour, remember?" asked Shiran.

"I vaguely remember making those arrangements," murmured Conor.

Shiran stepped into his arms with a twinkle in her eye. She stood on her toes and gave Conor a long kiss, then pushed slowly away. Conor watched her cross the room swaying sensually as he slowly sat down in the cushioned leather chair. Shiran shrugged, and the gown fluttered to the floor while she turned her head to look sideways at Conor, a smile touching her lips. Then Shiran began dressing slowly, glancing at Conor as she did so. When her undergarments were on, she pulled on a light-blue dress and buttoned it up the front. Finished, she reached into the wardrobe and pulled out her sandals and moved to the chair across from him to strap them on.

Wiggling her toes at Conor, she sat up and said, "Ready."

Conor chuckled as he picked up the baby carrier, and Conrad gave a slight cry. Shiran leaned over and cooed at the infant as he readjusted his position and stuck a thumb in his mouth. Conor smiled as Shiran stood back up, then she stood on her toes and kissed him soundly.

"Time to go," she whispered as they drew apart.

"A-a-all right," murmured Conor.

They left the apartment, taking the west hallway to the stairwell. Two flights of stairs took them to the first level and out to the boardwalk overlooking the edge. A cool spring breeze filled with unknown scents from a past era attempted to lift Shiran's hem, forcing her to hold it in place. They turned right and walked toward the Bookworm where Sergeant Tadashi Adachi stood outside.

"Qu'Loo'Oh' is here with Rachel," said Shiran.

"You're sure?" asked Conor.

"Tadashi had guard duty today," stated Shiran.

Conor nodded and, as they neared the entrance, said, "Good morning, Sergeant."

"Good morning, sir, ma'am," returned Tadashi with a grin.

"I take it Qu'Loo'Oh' is inside," observed Shiran.

"Almost every day," returned Tadashi.

Conor Raybourn nodded. Qu'Loo'Oh' had become infatuated with the stories that Francesca had printed so far and had read many of them. Then she had discovered that there were thousands, if not millions, of stories contained within Hattie's memory, along with actual movies of those stories. A holograph projector had been set up in the prefab dedicated to Qu'Loo'Oh', and she spent most of her evenings watching those stories reenacted with Rachel and Brad when they were available.

Qu'Loo'Oh' had also made five trips back to the sacred cavern by chopper with an armed escort to return borrowed scrolls and bring new ones to upload into Hattie's mainframe. They now had a fairly comprehensive library of the Ques'Coat'L' texts, and with Qu'Loo'Oh's and Hattie's assistance, translations were being made available to the colony. The scientists were ecstatic, and many of them were absorbing the information as fast as the translations were made. Then Qu'Loo'Oh' found that Hattie could recreate a virtual display of the stories retold in the ancient scrolls of her people.

They entered the Bookworm to find Qu'Loo'Oh' talking to three of the scientists about one of the latest translations of the ancient scrolls. Jacqueline Vinet was one of the three, which surprised Conor. She had always seemed uninterested and distant when discussing the world that existed outside the Compound, which was what had caused the rift between them. Jacqueline said something to Qu'Loo'Oh', and the raptor replied, then turned to walk over to Conor and Shiran.

"Conor. Shiran. Good morning," said Qu'Loo'Oh'.

"Good morning to you too," replied Conor and Shiran together.

"May I look at the baby?" asked Qu'Loo'Oh'.

"Of course," said Shiran.

Qu'Loo'Oh' inspected the infant in the baby carrier, then stated, "They do not grow very fast."

"No. It takes time for human children to grow," said Shiran.

Qu'Loo'Oh' bobbed—a habit she had gotten into to state agreement since she found it disconcerting trying to nod. "I look forward to the day they can walk and run."

"They're more trouble then," replied Shiran.

"All young ones are when they are capable of that," returned Qu'Loo'Oh'.

"What's going on?" asked Conor.

"The…scientists had questions about some translations of the old scrolls," said Qu'Loo'Oh'.

"Problems?" asked Shiran.

"No. But I must get back with them. This may take some time," said Qu'Loo'Oh'.

"Take your time, Qu'Loo'Oh'. We're going to sit and talk to Francesca," stated Conor.

Qu'Loo'Oh' bobbed and went back to her meeting. Francesca and Rachel were at a side table sipping tea and exchanged greetings, as Conor set Conrad down beside Rebecca in her baby carrier, then Conor and Shiran pulled up two more chairs.

"What's going on?" asked Conor.

"The scientists had questions about some ancient history. We already know Qu'Loo'Oh's people came here in a great ship and were fleeing an enemy. We also know they arrived here and terraformed this world and lived in bliss many lifetimes ago until the enemy found them again. Then a great battle ensued where their great ship was destroyed, along with the enemy's ship, only after, it had devastated the civilization they had created on this world," said Rachel.

"Yes. I've read the translations and understand that's what happened," said Conor.

Shiran nodded. "I have too."

"Qu'Loo'Oh' and Hattie have translated two much-older scrolls that the scientists spent some time restoring. They tell of the ancient home of Qu'Loo'Oh's people. The enemy that followed them here was not just a chance occurrence between two ships. It turns out that her people were at war with them for many thousands of lifetimes prior to that chance meeting of ships," replied Francesca.

Conor gave Francesca a penetrating look. "You're talking hundreds of thousands of years."

"Possibly millions. The references in the translation are vague," returned Rachel.

"How can that be?" asked Shiran.

"If they didn't have FTL, they would've had to use generation ships or cold sleep to travel between the stars. It would take hundreds of thousands of years to travel between systems. A war could last a million years," said Conor.

"Are these enemies the same species or a colony they planted that revolted?" asked Shiran, looking at Rachel.

"Qu'Loo'Oh' made it quite clear that her ancient enemy are not raptors, and the texts confirm what she believes," replied Francesca.

"So who are they, and what do they look like?" asked Shiran.

"The texts do not tell us anything except to make it clear they are not raptors, and they are only referred to as the ancient enemy," said Francesca.

"That's not telling us much," said Shiran.

"Qu'Loo'Oh' says they look a lot like us, only taller and covered in hair, according to the verbal legends of her people," said Rachel.

"But it's not written down?" asked Shiran.

"We haven't translated anything that describes their physical characteristics. They are only known as the ancient enemy," replied Francesca.

"Generation ships," murmured Conor.

"What?" asked Shiran.

"The star systems around Earth could be settled by both species if there were two spacefaring species using generation or cold storage ships that long ago," said Conor.

"It was a long time ago," said Rachel.

"They fought wars between star systems without FTL. That would take thousands, and most likely tens of thousands, of years to do even if inhabited systems are within a hundred light-years of each other using slower-than-light ships. They planned and fought their wars in the long term," replied Conor.

"They haven't attacked Sol system," replied Rachel.

"We haven't been around that long. However, we sent out the three cold storage ships over the last two centuries on a set route to the most likely stars that had habitable worlds," replied Conor.

"And if even one of these two species is still around and capable of space travel, it puts Sol system in danger," replied Shiran.

"Yes, and we don't know the scope of their expansion. We're ten thousand light-years from Sol system, and we found a colony the raptors started here," stated Francesca.

"Which means that if either or both of them are still around, it places us in danger also," stated Shiran.

"That might be hundreds or thousands of years from now," said Rachel.

"Which means it is up to us to ensure our descendants and theirs are prepared," stated Conor as he looked at the two baby carriers sitting on the floor holding their futures.

CHAPTER 72

Dr. Bess Hollinger was on the boardwalk looking at the entrance to the new medical facility. Shops would compose most of the first level of the structure. While most of the storefronts had yet to be filled, a restaurant had been started facing the back wall of the cleft, which catered mostly to those who worked at the foundry. The establishment was more of a bar than restaurant, so many of the cleft inhabitants avoided the area after their first visit.

Most of the hospital was on the second level. The hospital had a modest reception area and emergency entrance on the first level facing the edge of the cleft. The hospital was on the second level. Most of the framework and walls were finished at the entrance and second level. They were running the wiring for power outlets and lights, along with finishing the plumbing. The educational complex composed the third level with its entrance just east of the medical facility's entrance. It was still a framework of steel beams and rebar as it rose to house the future home of education for the colonists both young and old. With any luck, they would be moving into the medical facility itself in the next month or two, and Bess was looking forward to it. The facility they were using was nice in ways but way too small for the new equipment the commander had authorized because of the boon in resources discovered in the abandoned lunar mining complex. There would even be some equipment that was not aboard the *New Horizon* that might provide jobs for one or two of the scientists who were unhappy with their current employment opportunities.

With the new equipment the commander had authorized, Bess was sure that she and Kers could provide the quality of services most people enjoyed back in Sol system. The average life expectancy for people in Sol system had improved to well into the twelfth decade or longer. At the same time, they led a healthy and productive life well into their eighties and nineties before thinking about retirement because of degenerative effects of aging.

Compared to hospitals back in Sol system, the facility would look rough for some time to come. However, it would be as functional as the facility on the *New Horizon* and more so because of the commander.

Tom Tollifer had requested plastafoam equipment to coat and insulate the walls and hide the wires, cement, and other construction accessories under a smooth coated surface when they first set up the colony. That hardened on the top and provided insulation underneath. After it hardened, it could be textured and painted or left a smooth plain white surface. Over a year ago, the commander had asked where the equipment and foam the machine would require to perform its task would come from, and the answer had been the ship's factory, and the request had been refused. Now, however, with more resources available, the commander had authorized not only the equipment to spray the foam but also the equipment to make the foam since the scientists had come up with a recipe using the leavings from the brewery. If it worked, there would be a huge demand at all the residences and some of the shops.

Things were looking up, and the new hospital had been promised many things upon its completion. The lumber mill and carpentry shop were making new furniture and sending it over to the leatherworks for upholstering. The Overlook and Flour Mill were organizing a grand opening buffet for the hospital's first day and promising continued deliveries while only asking for timely requests. The Bookworm was working on coloring books and children's activity books for the youngsters who were reaching two Earth years of age. The Rose Blossom bath works promised several crates of hard and soft soap that was guaranteed to be antibacterial and hypoallergenic. Even the Hickory Barrel brewery had promised a thousand liters of ethanol for cleaning and sanitizing on the opening day of the hospital.

Bess Hollinger mused over the continued growth of the colony in the last planet year, which was nearly one and a half Earth years. Many of the colonists put in twelve or more hours a day.

President Felipe Martinez and Agnes Felter walked out of the newly installed doors of the hospital with Bahri Hiran following closely behind them. Felipe Martinez grinned when he saw Bess and approached her.

"Good day, Dr. Hollinger," greeted Felipe.

"Good day, Mr. President. What are you doing here?" asked Bess.

"Why, inspecting your new facility," replied Felipe.

"I didn't know you were that interested," replied Bess.

"But I am, Doctor. I'm also wondering how soon you'll be able to move your equipment and any inpatients into your new facilities," said Felipe.

"It should be accomplished in a month once the walls have been coated," said Bess.

"So two months most likely," said Agnes Felter.

"Most likely," replied Bess.

"Good. Good. Then my staff and I will be able to renovate the old clinic after that and set up our offices," said Felipe.

"What are you talking about? The brewery is moving into the old clinic," said Bess.

"Ah yes, plans change, and the old clinic is now going to be the presidential offices," stated Felipe.

"I don't think Evan Zander and Ezekiel Yap are going to agree with you about that," said Bess.

"I really don't care whether they agree or not. This is happening. I've got the votes to do it," returned Felipe Martinez.

Bess Hollinger gave Felipe a look of disgust. The man was infuriating in many ways. She had not really known him prior to arriving at the colony. It made her wonder if he had always been that way or if it were just since the incident that had stranded them.

"You're disgusting," stated Bess loudly.

"Now, now, Doctor! Let's not fight. The colony needs a seat of government and offices to operate from," said Felipe, smiling.

"Good day, Mr. President," said Bess.

"Good day, Doctor," replied Felipe cheerfully.

Bess's heels clicked on the brick boardwalk as she walked toward the bridge that crossed the river. When she reached the other side, she entered the Overlook. Bess saw Evan Zander and Ezekiel Yap sitting at their usual table near the end of the counter. The midday rush had not started yet, and the two were playing checkers with hot cups of coffee sitting at their elbows. Ezekiel looked up, and Evan turned in his chair as they heard her enter.

"Good morning, Doctor," said Ezekiel as Evan nodded greetings.

"Good morning," said Bess.

"Can I help you, Doctor?" asked Ezekiel.

"Do you two know what Martinez is planning to do once we move from the clinic into the new hospital?" asked Bess.

The two men looked at each other as if they were discussing something for nearly a minute, then Ezekiel nodded. They both looked back at Bess Hollinger, smiling.

"He's going to move into the old clinic and set up his presidential offices," stated Evan.

"Yes! Wait! How did you know that?" exclaimed Bess as a perplexed look crossed her face.

"It's all part of the plan," said Ezekiel, smiling.

"What?" demanded Bess, even more perplexed.

"Have a seat, Doctor," suggested Evan calmly.

Bess took a seat, being careful not to knock the table and upset the checker pieces or coffee. Her dark African features had a puzzled look as Ezekiel Yap and Evan Zander sat smiling at her.

"You see, Mr. Martinez has wanted to have the colony provide him with a grand presidential building for some time now," said Evan.

"I know that," said Bess.

"It is unfeasible, and the colony requires other things," said Ezekiel.

"That's obvious," replied Bess.

"Mr. Martinez does not like Evan or myself, especially since I banned him and some of his followers from the Overlook," said Ezekiel.

"I'm aware of that," said Bess.

"We never intended to expand into the clinic once you move out. We knew that if we expressed interest in moving into it that Martinez would most likely jump at the opportunity to wrestle it from us," stated Evan Zander.

Bess sat back and blinked before saying, "Okay."

"At which time his demands for a magnificent government seat become moot. We suspect he will have a hard time filling rooms inside the old clinic having so many people sitting around doing bureaucratic things. That would not sit well with quite a few colonists," said Ezekiel.

"We plan to show resistance to his plan, but we are going to allow him to win. After all, he has enough support to make it happen," said Evan Zander.

"He did say that," replied Bess.

"So now all you have to do is not let anyone know what we've told you and oppose Mr. Martinez, but not enough to keep him from having his way," interjected Ezekiel.

"I can do that," replied Bess.

"Good. We knew we could count on you," replied Evan.

"So you're not planning on expanding your distillery operation?" asked Bess.

"We're going to expand the cave where we're storing the finished product and move all the distillery equipment into it, then turn our current location next to Flour Mill into a retail outlet only, which was our original plan all along," replied Evan.

"Oh," murmured Bess as she saw wheels within wheels.

"Now it's almost time for lunch. Would you like some of the pepper apatosaurus strips, roasted potatoes, and a salad? I know it's one of your favorites, and it will be complimentary today." Ezekiel smiled as Bess Hollinger looked bewildered at the two friends smiling at her. Then Ezekiel stood and offered her an elbow to escort her to a clean table.

CHAPTER 73

Jacqueline Vinet was looking over the ongoing construction of the shops, hospital, and educational institution being built on the east side of the river that bisected the cleft. The building was small at this time, but there was plenty of room around to expand. They had conceded that the side facing the river would be devoted to shops and businesses on the first floor since there were colonists who were looking for space now that the bridge was finished. But there was enough room between the floor and the roof of the cleft to put many levels. The entrance of the hospital faced the edge of the cleft. It was for reception and waiting at this time, while the main body of the hospital composed the second level, and the educational institution, the third.

It had taken several meetings to compromise with the colonists on how the east side of the river would be constructed. There were those who wanted the east side dedicated to only the hospital and educational institution, Jacqueline being among them, while others argued there was plenty of space to allow businesses on the first level. However, when President Martinez had demanded that the whole east side was to be dedicated as presidential and bureaucratic offices, the colonists had refused to provide any space for such by a nearly 80 percent vote.

The movement that had opposed Martinez, led by Jacqueline Vinet, had meant compromising with people who were undecided. The compromise had involved dedicating nearly all the first level being built on the east side of the river to merchant endeavors, which was a faction led by Ezekiel Yap. Now Martinez was limited to the office spaces on the west side of the river where he was demanding more space and again being opposed by Ezekiel Yap. Most colonists wanted the west side dedicated to shops and residential area and had informed the president when they were ready to devote resources to bureaucratic infrastructure, it would be built somewhere in the Compound surrounding the base of the cleft.

There was more to it though. Martinez was not liked by a growing majority of the colonists. His past policies had disenfranchised many, and there were many who wanted nothing to do with him or his business—the foundry. It was rumored that he had a preference for certain types of people when hiring and promoting. Additionally, he and his staff were rumored to make it difficult for other businesses by delaying needed materials if those people were working for that business.

At this time, there were eleven people living on the far-east edge of the cleft, mostly because of the operating polices of Martinez and his cabinet. Some considered them outcasts, and many of them were considered drunks and drug abusers. Jacqueline suspected that until some sort of reform was made, many of them would continue down that road. There was not much she could do to help them. The educational institution had limited resources to draw upon, and some people were too worried about repercussions from Martinez and his cabinet. The only ones who apparently didn't care about the latter were Bess Hollinger and her staff, Ezekiel Yap, and Master Sergeant Evan Zander.

Jacqueline found out that with Ezekiel's help, the master sergeant had recruited two of the outcasts into the Marines, which had taken the original number of eleven down to nine. Unfortunately, one of the remaining nine had been too close to the edge one day and had fallen over. At least that was what people said, though many actually believed that the woman had taken her own life.

"Something wrong?" asked Tom Tollifer, who was sitting across the table from her.

"No. Just watching the construction of the hospital and educational institute," lied Jacqueline.

"I know better," said Tom.

"I was thinking of the people living on the east end of the cleft," admitted Jacqueline.

"What we can do has been done. Some of them lost hope when we were stranded here, and the animosity of others toward them has caused a divide," said Tom.

"Most of them are black," stated Jacqueline.

"Only a third of them," stated Tom.

"Which is a high proportion when comparing origins," said Jacqueline.

"I know. What do you want to do about it?" asked Tom.

"I'm not sure there's much we can do about it. We've offered them work at the institute, but there's only so many resources available there, and too many of the colonists who would help are too scared of Martinez and his associates," said Jacqueline.

"Ezekiel finds them work when he can, and Master Sergeant Zander has recruited a few of them. We could talk to the commander or lieutenant commander about the problem," stated Tom.

"You don't think they know about the outcasts?" asked Jacqueline.

"Let's just say I don't think they're aware of the whole situation," said Tom.

"How could they not be?" asked Jacqueline.

"Have you discussed the problem with them?" asked Tom.

"No," replied Jacqueline.

"Neither have I. I don't think we can assume things. When you do talk to them, it's usually about acquiring resources, not personnel problems in the colony," stated Tom.

"They should be aware of everything going on," stated Jacqueline.

"That's a tall order. The only way people know what's going on is if someone else tells them," replied Tom.

"You think that's our job?" asked Jacqueline.

"You think Martinez will tell them?" retorted Tom.

Jacqueline shook her head, blond hair going astray, as she said, "No!"

"There's also the problem that the military has no say over the civil authority unless we support a military coup," replied Tom.

"I don't want that either," said Jacqueline.

"Then it's up to us to correct the problem," said Tom.

"How?" asked Jacqueline.

"Martinez holds power because he controls the one major industry in the colony. It has the most manpower being utilized, and he expects the people who work for him to toe the line. Other industries rely on him, which means he has some control over them," said Tom.

"I know that," said Jacqueline.

"The lunar mining operation could upset that," replied Tom.

"Martinez will want control of that also," said Jacqueline.

"He won't get it," said Tom.

"What do you mean?" asked Jacqueline.

"The commander is aware of some of the personnel issues in the colony. Brad Guillete is doing much better than before," said Tom.

"I'm aware of Brad's situation," replied Jacqueline.

"He's doing better than you think. He's been offered a commission if he'll return to active duty," responded Tom.

"Really?" asked Jacqueline, shocked.

"Chief warrant officer, technical division," said Tom.

"Is he going to take it?" asked Jacqueline.

"I think so, since the commander offered Rachel Krupich a commission as a chief warrant officer, alien specialist," replied Tom.

"There's no such thing as an alien specialist designation," said Jacqueline.

"This isn't exactly United Systems. I think the commander is taking some liberties," replied Tom.

"Aren't the two of them getting married when he returns from the moon with Lieutenant Commander Anderson?" asked Jacqueline, referring to Brad Guillete and Rachel Krupich.

"What better way to start a marriage?" Tom smiled.

"That doesn't explain how Martinez won't get control of the lunar operation," replied Jacqueline.

"The commander and his staff do not want to give control of the lunar mines to Martinez. The commander has told Martinez the mines are part of interplanetary space and fall under interplanetary law. Therefore, it's out of Martinez's jurisdiction. The commander is placing it under martial law, and it will be under the control of the military space command until such a time as a permanent settlement is established. Since it's unlikely that a permanent settlement will be established in the near future, the military will retain oversight of the resource allotment, safety, and transportation while allowing civilians to operate the mines under those conditions," stated Tom.

"He just placed Michael Anderson in charge of lunar operations. So who's the lead civil authority for mining operations?" asked Jacqueline.

"Martinez doesn't want anything to do with the deal the commander is offering, so the commander offered me the job as lead civil authority," stated Tom.

Jacqueline blinked. Over the last few months, her feelings for Tom had grown. He had convinced her that Conor Raybourn in many ways had been right and that the colony could not isolate itself from the world outside the Compound. The attack by the red raptors on the Compound and the discovery of the hidden caves and Qu'Loo'Oh' had been major factors in her change of perspective, but it had been Tom who had provided the gentle convincing. The colony had already been relying on hunting the great beasts to provide sustenance. The mining operations had to operate outside the Compound to obtain the coal, iron, copper, and wood the colony required. There were also the foraging parties that brought back pawpaws, figs, and other natural foods. Jacqueline shook her head as Tom watched her digest what he had just said.

"How long will you be gone?" asked Jacqueline.

"The tour is one month out of four. The commander won't authorize longer tours because of the low-gravity habitation," replied Tom.

"I might be able to live with that," stated Jacqueline.

"Good," said Tom.

"When do you leave?" asked Jacqueline.

"Anderson is supposed to be back in three weeks. The commander is looking for a relief for him but hasn't decided yet," said

Tom. "I suggested Anarzej Gataki since it's only a one-month-in-four tour."

"Who are you taking as civilians?" asked Jacqueline.

"I have five already—two from the outcasts and three from other businesses who just want to try something different," said Tom.

"You approached the outcasts?" asked Jacqueline.

"Someone had to. Most of the others said if the first two come back in one piece without anything bad to say about the experience, they'd give it a try," said Tom.

Jacqueline thought about it for a moment and nodded. "You've been busy. I feel somewhat useless."

"You still have the ear of the scientists, and there are a lot of people who do respect you. You organized the people to form and create the colony into a constitutional republic. You've been working at the clinic as a nurse and have been the main organizer for the university. You've also been assisting the outcasts by finding them jobs and giving them items they need. You've also been learning the raptor language, which I believe will be important in the future," stated Tom.

"That doesn't seem like enough," said Jacqueline as she sat back in her seat.

"You can't do it all, Jacqueline," said Tom.

"It just seems like there's so many setbacks," replied Jacqueline.

"Which are beyond your or my control," said Tom. "We have to rely on others to do their job."

Sitting back in her chair, Jacqueline took a sip of her tea. She didn't like feeling so left out and helpless to do anything. She had watched as Conor and the others who had arrived here go out and make great discoveries about the new world in which they now lived—the ancient city to the northeast, the discovery of the sacred caves where Qu'Loo'Oh' lived that contained information, and now the discovery of a moon base of the Ques'Coat'L'. She was included in the loop, but she felt as though she was missing key information.

She knew that there were many factions within the colony. The two major ones she was aware of were the president and his followers and the military. There was a growing antagonism between those two factions, and she wasn't sure how to curtail the aggression. The killing of Normal Pool had not went over well with the faction who followed Felipe Martinez, yet Pool had been the one to initiate the hostilities in both instances from what she had gathered. However, she suspected there was more to it than Pool's death. Jacqueline shook her head. It seemed like the conflict between the two factions was being egged on in some manner.

Jacqueline turned her thoughts to other channels. Tom was right; she couldn't do it all herself. She could only do what was in front of her. The future of the colony had no hope of ever receiving support from a home world. They could only carry on and hope that fortune favored them all.

CHAPTER 74

Gunnery Sergeant Samuel Rusu stood back and surveyed the seven days of work it had taken to set up the two prefabs near the entrance to the lunar mines. They would be unpacking and setting up the antennas for both the NAPACS satellite communications system and MSDR-17 Marine radar so they would be ready prior to the shuttle's arrival in another two weeks. Samuel was ready for a trip back planetside after the last few weeks, and he was sure Lieutenant JG Dominic Sobolov was also. The lieutenant had talked about the astrophysicist Maria DiAngelo at least three times a day since they had departed the *New Horizon*. Samuel was sure that it would be quite the reunion when they returned.

They had run the cables from the top of the mound to the side of the mine entrance. It had taken several days to drill holes around the doors so they could run the cable through without interfering with the door's function. The process was repeated until they reached the lounge area where the desiccated corpse of the red raptor had been discovered. The lounge area had been chosen as the control center for operations at the mine, and Lieutenant Commander Anderson and his team would install the equipment when they arrived.

The original control center of the raptors was, for the most part, left intact. Rusu and the others had run the cables through the room and attached them to the ceiling. There were scientists and engineers back planetside who were chomping at the bit to come here and investigate the control panels of an alien species. However, they would have to wait until adequate accommodations were prepared for them to do so. Perhaps if they could understand and repair the existing technology, it could be used to put the mine back in production on a limited basis. For now though, they did not have the manpower to replace the two-hundred-plus dead raptors who had served this mining endeavor to keep it operational.

Two prefabs had been set up as temporary living quarters for their extended stay and would remain until the operations suite and living quarters were established inside the mine. The prefabs were more comfortable than the longboat and had taken the entire first week of their mission to set up. Samuel walked over to the air lock, bouncing in the low gravity leading into the nearest prefab, and stepped inside. When the air lock's cycle was complete, Rusu entered the living area and removed his helmet. Steven Yates moved over and assisted him with removing the rest of his suit as Lieutenant JG Dominic Sobolov sat sipping coffee.

"It is nice to be done," said Dominic.

"Don't you still have a job waiting for you planetside, sir?" asked Samuel.

"Yes. But Commander Blankenship wished this installation to take priority. We still have three longboats and two shuttles to use. *Longboat 4* will take some time, and I have always felt useless planetside until now," replied Dominic.

"Perhaps the commander will want an overhaul facility built on the planet and put you in charge," said Steven Yates.

Samuel Rusu cocked an eyebrow at Dominic Sobolov and said, "Sometimes even the good doctor has a great idea. It would beat the heck out of having to do it onboard the *New Horizon*, and it would give you meaningful employment planetside if you've felt that way."

Dominic looked at the two then at Boatswain Mate First Class John Martins, who had stayed quiet. Boats nodded, took another sip of coffee, then said, "Sounds like a plan to me, sir."

"How would I approach the commander about this?" muttered Dominic.

"It's almost like applying for a grant or funding for a project," replied Steven Yates.

"Yes? You know how to do that?" asked Dominic.

"I'm sure Dr. Yates has applied for plenty of grants and funding. He'd probably be able to help you whip something up in a few days," stated Samuel.

"You'll need a mission statement to start it out with," said John.

"See! If we start now, by the time we return to the *New Horizon*, you could submit a plan to the commander for review as you're heading planetside. He'll have just arrived topside according to his schedule and has nothing better to do than review ship's status and read reports when he's aboard," encouraged Samuel.

"It'll give us boatswains mates and the hull technicians an alternate job when planetside also," replied John Martins.

The rest of the evening revolved around drawing up a mission statement and rough outline for Lieutenant JG Sobolov. They ate their rations discussing the various aspects and forming a plan. Steven Yates injected a lot of input that the rest had never thought of, showing a side of him that Samuel never knew about or suspected. When they turned in for the night, they had over twenty pages written with a few dozen pages of notes to draw upon.

A week later, Gunnery Sergeant Rusu was sitting in the Overlook with a cold beer in hand. Evan Zander sat across from him with another beer, sipping slowly. The shuttle had arrived on schedule, and Lieutenant Commander Anderson had officially taken charge of moon operations as his new duty assignment. He had brought a crew of nine others to set up the operations suite and start converting the former quarters of the raptors into living quarters for those stationed there in the future. It was a mixed crew of military and civilian, but they understood that Michael Anderson had the last word. Samuel Rusu took a long swig of his beer and sat back in his chair as he contemplated the future.

"This beer is good," said Samuel.

"Took a little tweaking in the formula. The new crop of hops really made a difference," replied Evan Zander.

"Business good?" asked Rusu.

"It's booming. The scotch turned out all right, but it's going to take a few years to age. We found a tree that smells like hickory when it burns. Shiran assures us it's an ancient ancestor of the hickory tree.

The lumber mill made a few small barrels out of the one we cut down, and we're aging the scotch now," replied Even.

"Good retirement plan," returned Samuel.

"I'm not ready to retire yet. You know, there's always room for another partner," said Evan.

"I could lend a hand when planetside," said Samuel.

"Wise man. Adachi, Hall, and Ivankov are already part owners and learning the trade quickly," stated Evan, smiling.

"Sounds a little crowded," said Samuel.

"The location is. We'll have to look for a new location this next year. We're already storing the barrels so they can age in the cave over on the east side of the river," said Evan.

"I heard the second lieutenant is expanding the Marine Complex," observed Samuel.

"She wants a hardened building to the south with an underground tunnel to it from the complex. The expansion is for manufacturing munitions and explosives. The commander is all for it to save wear and tear on the ship's factory, while the prefab they're using now can be taken down and stored for future use," said Evan.

"Good idea. We might need the prefabs on the moon if we locate anything else worth investigating," said Samuel.

"Commander Blankenship agrees. We break ground in another week," stated Evan.

"How's Anya Kaur doing?" asked Samuel.

"Still in the brig. Still claims she's innocent," replied Evan.

"You believe her?" asked Samuel.

Ezekiel sat down with three more beers just then and started sipping on one of them as he passed the other two to the table occupants. Samuel Rusu saw Evan Zander get a faraway look in his eye as he thought about the question. When he finally returned, he took a long swig of beer. Having finished his original beer, he picked up the one Ezekiel had just placed in front of him.

"I don't know. My gut says yes, but the evidence says no," Evan finally replied.

"I do not think she did it," stated Ezekiel.

"Going to need some new evidence to prove that," returned Evan.

"I know," said Ezekiel.

"So we're just letting her cool her heels in the brig?" inquired Samuel.

"Well, you know, we've been letting her do PT with the rest of the Marines under guard. Since you've been busy the last month, you may not know, but I authorized them to teach her unarmed combat moves without a live opponent," said Evan.

"Sounds like you want to believe her," stated Samuel.

"I do. For some reason, this stinks like a setup," replied Evan.

Ezekiel nodded in agreement to that as he said, "She's a good girl. I never had problems with her as a customer, and she worked well when helping as a waitress."

"It'll be a shame if she has to spend the rest of her life in the brig," said Samuel.

"Yeah. I don't like it either," replied Evan Zander. He took a long swig of his new beer, then said, "How'd it go on the moon?"

"Got everything done that we were supposed to get done. Did a little exploring. If we can get the foundry back in operation, it'll up production. The refined metal we brought back when we found the mine was immensely better than anything coming out of the foundry here. There's still several shuttles worth of refined bars available though. Lieutenant Commander Anderson showed up on time, and we presented his new command to him," responded Samuel, giving a brief rundown of the mission report he had given to the second lieutenant.

"He is in charge of all moon operations?" asked Ezekiel.

"Commander Blankenship wanted him to have his own command," replied Samuel.

"Good. And the other project?" asked Evan.

"Mr. Sobolov submitted his proposal to the commander the moment we arrived at the *New Horizon*. The commander has about three hundred pages to look over while he's up there. He looked confused and impressed at the lieutenant's proposal," stated Samuel Rusu.

"Good! Did it take much convincing?" asked Evan.

"Once it was suggested to our new lieutenant JG, he seemed uncomfortable. Then Boats jumped in just like you said he would and even Steven Yates." Samuel smiled.

A smile crept across the master sergeant's face as he said, "See. Sometimes you just have to give them a slight nudge and encourage them into the right direction."

Ezekiel nodded and, grinning, added, "Yes, many young officers need much help to know which direction to go. Dominic Sobolov has great potential and, back in Sol system, would have gone far."

"Yeah. In another twenty-five to thirty years, he might have made a hell of an admiral back in Sol system," affirmed Evan.

The three sat back sipping on their beers as time flowed by like a gentle stream. All was right with the world, and even though the hand of fate had stranded them in a land before time began, they were making it a home.

"What about the commander and lieutenant commanders?" asked Samuel.

"They're all good men, as good as Mr. Sobolov. Sergeant Adachi did a good job giving Lieutenant Commander Raybourn that suggestion on testing the red raptor Qu'Loo'Oh' a few months ago. I'm glad I hinted to him that if opportunity came up, what to suggest," said Evan Zander.

"Almost lunchtime," stated Ezekiel as he finished his beer and checked the clock on the wall.

Lieutenant Commander Conor Raybourn and Second Lieutenant Shiran Raybourn walked into the Overlook a moment later. As the two walked back toward the rear of the restaurant, both of them gave the two Marines and Ezekiel a quizzical look as they greeted them in passing. As the two were getting ready to sit down, the lieutenant commander leaned over to the second lieutenant and muttered something to her in private, to which she nodded assent, not knowing the acoustics the owner had built into the Overlook.

"Sometimes I wonder who's really running this colony," came quite clearly to the three beer drinkers as they smiled at one another and took another swig of their beers.

CHAPTER 75

Commander Hadden Blankenship sat in the captain's bridge chair reading the writing on the tablet he held. He had been presented a proposal by Lieutenant JG Sobolov after he had returned from his moon mission. The proposal was over three hundred pages long, and he had been looking it over for the last few days. Hadden was surprised at the detail that had been included in the report and was quite impressed. Even a proposed architectural diagram of the building was included, along with a list of equipment required.

The ability to have the longboats and shuttles worked on while planetside would free up manpower when serving on the *New Horizon*. It would also allow the commander to temporarily assign them to the lunar operation if they volunteered. There were crewmen always working on the craft during their two-week tours of duty on board the *New Horizon* every Earth year. Working under zero-gravity conditions for only two weeks out of every year did make it more dangerous. Mistakes were made, and injuries occurred because of the unusual working conditions as the accident reports testified.

Hadden sat back in his chair and let a smile creep across his face as he took a sip of coffee. He detected the subtle hand of Master Sergeant Zander behind this proposal. How the master sergeant had come up with the idea seemed a mystery. The reason he had chosen Dominic Sobolov was more obvious after the incident with the longboat. That the proposal came in the wake of Dominic's return from the moon mission indicated that Gunny Rusu had a hand in implementing the master sergeant's grand scheme.

The fact that the proposal was something that Hadden had been thinking about for some time in the future made it seem like the master sergeant could read his mind. True, Hadden had told Dominic Sobolov that he would be in charge of the refit of *Longboat 4* after the crash. Then Hadden remembered that he had mentioned in passing to Hiroka at supper at the Overlook one evening that a facility like the one being proposed was needed. Hadden Blankenship shook his head as the thought of wheels within wheels crossed his mind.

Hadden Blankenship had known and worked with Evan Zander on and off for many years. This was the third command that they had served on together. Hadden knew that leadership came in many forms, but when dealing with the master sergeant, sometimes he wondered who was leading and who was being led. Hadden shook his head again and sighed, then went back to reading the proposal and annotating for clarification.

He was still working on the package when the personnel officer Lieutenant Vanda JG Kisimba entered the bridge unnoticed. The lieutenant floated up beside the commander and placed her feet on the floor.

She stood there for a minute before she finally cleared her throat. The commander looked up, and her dark African features split into a smile.

"Good afternoon, sir," said Vanda as she saluted.

"Good afternoon, Lieutenant," replied Hadden, returning the salute.

"Must be something important that you're working on since you've been at it for the last five days, sir," stated Vanda.

"Mr. Sobolov handed me a proposal for a planetside overhaul facility for the longboats and shuttles when he returned from the moon," replied Hadden.

"How long is it?" asked Vanda.

"Over three hundred pages," said Hadden.

Vanda Kisimba whistled. "Did they get anything done on the moon?"

"They finished their assignment and presented Lieutenant Commander Anderson his new command," replied Hadden.

"So it's a military operation?" asked Vanda.

"Yes," replied Hadden.

"What's the tour of duty?" asked Vanda.

"One month out of four. I don't want them in low gravity any more than that. They still serve two weeks every year on the *New Horizon*," said Hadden.

"So do you need personnel?" asked Vanda.

"Yes," said Hadden.

"Where do I sign up?" asked Vanda.

"You're willing to work for Anderson?" asked Hadden.

"I've never had a problem with him," said Vanda.

"You don't blame him for stranding us in this system?" asked Hadden.

"We all volunteered to try an experimental FTL drive on a large vessel. Those were the chances we took," replied Vanda.

Seven other FTL experiments with live crew members had taken place prior to the *New Horizon*. All those flights had consisted of crews of ten or less. Six of the seven had been successful. Three of those had traveled to nearby stars and returned loaded with data that scientists were still mulling over. None of the nearby systems that those early flights had explored had habitable planets, but they had led to the decision of a larger ship capable of extended exploration. Hence, the *New Horizon* had been reconfigured and launched.

"Good. Why would you like this assignment?" replied Hadden.

"Will I be in charge when I'm up there?" asked Vanda.

"The lieutenant commander will require someone in rotation while he's planetside. He will still have oversight of the command while planetside, but any immediate decisions will be made by the officer on location, and that officer will answer to him. Have you served as comm O or CIC officer?" asked Hadden, using the shortened version for communications officer or combat information center officer.

"Comm O as an ensign on the USS *Faraday*," replied Vanda.

"CIC officer will be easy enough on the moon since it only has a Marine radar. You'll have to learn mining operations, but in this case, we'll all be learning," said Hadden.

"I worked in the foundry planetside for three months," replied Vanda.

"So you have the basics on mining and refining operations?" asked Hadden.

"I think so," replied Vanda.

"Talk to Mr. Anderson. If he gives me the okay, you're in. Have you been learning the raptor language and writing?" said Hadden.

"A little," said Vanda.

"Learn more. You'll need it when working on the raptor equipment that's at the mine," said Hadden.

"Do you require any other help, sir?" asked Vanda.

"Is this a request to reactivate your commission, Ms. Kisimba?" asked Hadden.

"If you need the personnel, sir," responded Vanda impassively.

"Problems planetside?" asked Hadden.

"I keep busy enough. There's just places I won't work," replied Vanda.

The commander gave Lieutenant JG Kisimba a searching look. He knew there were problems on the planet. Obviously, they went deeper than the simple animosity that some had for Lieutenant Commander Anderson. Of course, he had learned over the past several months that the animosity had extended to Brad Guillete even prior to the FTL jump. It seemed Vanda Kisimba's request might have a relation to the other two.

Hadden decided to ask, "Like the foundry?"

"Yes, sir," replied Vanda.

"Lieutenant Commander Anderson will need help at the planetside comm suite when he's on the moon. This package opens up opportunities if we start the project, but Lieutenant JG Sobolov will be in charge of it. However, he's also serving as my exploration officer, so he'll need someone to step in at times when he's not planetside. Think you can fill in on those duties?" asked Hadden.

"Yes, sir," replied Kisimba, trying to keep from bursting with happiness.

"Then talk to them first. After that, talk to Lieutenant Commander Raybourn. I believe he requires an assistant for the planetside command," replied Hadden.

"Yes, sir," replied Vanda with a smile on her face.

"Now are you relieving me, Lieutenant?" asked Hadden.

"Yes, sir," replied Vanda.

"Very well, Lieutenant JG Kisimba. The *New Horizon* is in standard orbit. All conditions normal," said Hadden.

"I relieve you, sir," stated Vanda as she saluted the commander.

"I stand relieved," replied Hadden as they exchanged salutes.

Hadden released the straps holding onto the command seat and pulled himself up to where he was facing the aft hatch. He pushed off, floating toward the hatchway, and grabbed the hatch combing. Changing his trajectory, he pulled and floated down heading toward the stern. He stopped at the midpoint of the ship outside his quarters and entered the small accommodations allowed a crew member, even one of his status.

He entered the compartment that had the bed folded against the wall so the foldout chair and table on the opposite wall had room. The personal shower and toilet, a luxury only a few enjoyed on this ship, was in the rear of the compartment. He floated into the compartment and laid the tablet with Sobolov's proposal down on the tabletop where it stayed because of the magnetic strips in its back. Sitting down on the chair, he strapped himself in and rubbed his eyes. He had reviewed all the status reports for the ship, planet, and moon, leaving only the proposal for him to work on.

He wasn't tired enough to go to sleep and was not really ready to continue reviewing the proposal. He sat there numbly looking at the tablet and the writing it contained on its display. Coming to a decision, he marked his place and turned the tablet off. Releasing his seat straps, he kicked off toward the door. He left his stateroom and looked aft and forward. Flipping a mental coin, he pushed off heading aft. He floated down the passageway till he came to the door of the engineering room.

Chief Petty Officer Wilma Nolan sat at the control station watching the power planet readouts. The Benson drive station was unmanned and had remained so since three months after the arrival of the *New Horizon* in geosynchronous orbit. United Systems regulations stated that each station was to be manned even in orbit. However, he had determined that the station could be manned in an emergency if needed, but a manned watch was unfeasible in their situation. Wilma looked at the commander and started.

"At ease, Ms. Nolan," ordered Hadden.

"Good afternoon, sir. Can I help you?" replied Wilma.

"Just touring the ship, Chief. Everything all right here?" asked Hadden as he looked around the space.

"Everything's shipshape, sir. Power planet efficiency is down nearly 1 percent. Petty Officer Kataoka is making some adjustments on the lower level with Petty Officer Theron."

"Very well, Ms. Nolan. Carry on," said Hadden as he kicked off toward the lower levels. The two petty officers were just finishing their adjustments and getting ready to close the cover plates to the equipment as Hadden arrived.

"Attention on deck," said Petty Officer Theron loudly as she saluted.

Petty Officer Kataoka straightened up, carefully keeping her feet to the deck so her magnetic soles didn't detach, as she moved the screwdriver in her right hand to the left one and saluted also. The commander returned their salutes.

"At ease, Petty Officers," said Hadden.

"Good afternoon, sir," they chorused.

"How's my power plant?" asked Hadden.

"One hundred percent, sir. Just some minor adjustments," replied Petty Officer Kataoka.

"Good. Good. Carry on," said Hadden as he slipped past them.

The commander spent a little time poking his head around the power plant and Benson drive spaces, inspecting. Everything appeared shipshape, though he did note a couple of cover plates missing screws and mentioned it to the chief as he departed moving forward. The spaces themselves had clean bots, but those robots did not clean inside the equipment. Missing cover plates and their fastenings were a constant concern in preventing equipment deterioration from unwanted debris.

Hadden inspected five more spaces moving forward and was in the ship passageway leading forward when he paused. He looked at the hatch before him. It was labeled Cargo Bay 7, and he had never had reason to enter it. The compartment had been a missile room prior to the ship's conversion into an exploration vessel and had a hand and retinal lock that would only open to the ship's captain. The missile room on the port side had been converted to a cargo bay also and was labeled 8 but did not contain such an elaborate locking mechanism.

Hattie should recognize Hadden as acting captain after the last two Earth years. Coming to a decision, Hadden placed his hand on the palm screen and was just about to place his eye up to the retinal scanner when the 1MC, a system used for making shipboard announcements, announced loudly.

"Captain to the bridge. I repeat. Captain to the bridge," came Lieutenant JG Kisimba's voice.

Hadden stopped what he was doing and shook his head. After nearly two years of working with her, Hadden knew Lieutenant JG Kisimba would not make such an announcement lightly. He removed his hand from the palm screen and started pulling himself forward toward the bridge. When he arrived, Vanda was sitting in the captain's chair staring at the forward view screen. There displayed on the screen was the coast of the continent, and along that coast was a fleet of ships being launched into the ocean or setting sail with their prows pointed toward the island where the colony resided.

Vanda Kisimba looked at the commander and said grimly, "Sir, you wished to know if conditions changed on the coast of the continent."

"Yes, I did," said Hadden, a cold chill settling in his stomach.

CHAPTER 76

Lieutenant Commander Michael Anderson was having lunch with his wife, Francesca, along with Conor and Shiran Raybourn. He had recently returned from his lunar mission of setting up a NAPACS satellite communication equipment and MSDR-17 Marine radar for operation in the moon mining facility. The relief crew were setting up quarters and a mess hall in the old living quarters of the previous inhabitants.

"How did it go up on the moon?" asked Conor.

"Dominic Sobolov had the prefabs and antennas set up with all the cables run as planned. We were able to install all the operations suite equipment and refit enough living quarters for ten people. There was a problem with the radar antenna initially, but Brad was able to fix it with parts on hand. We also brought back one of the smaller raptor vehicles for study. There are about twenty of that type, so if it's damaged, there are replacements," said Michael.

"Sounds like you've been busy," stated Shiran.

"We were. We also did a little exploring and think we've located the power plant to the mining complex. It looks similar to the power plants on the *New Horizon*, shuttles, and longboats. We'll have to trace out the cabling and study the control systems. Would help if we could locate some schematics. It looks like it's in excellent shape. If it is the power plant and we can get it working, we won't have to rely on a longboat or shuttle for power," said Michael.

"That equipment's pretty old," said Shiran.

"Only fifty or sixty million years, but it's been in a vacuum all that time. It's not like it's been rusting," replied Michael.

"I wouldn't mind taking a look around up there. Didn't Lieutenant JG Kisimba take over for the next month?" said Conor.

"She did. Brad's supposed to relieve her, but Commander Blankenship wants him to wait until after her next watch. Lieutenant Gataki has already signed up for the next tour for the same reason you want to go. How'd you like to go up in, say, six months?" asked Michael.

"I'm glad Brad accepted that commission," said Francesca.

"I wasn't expecting to gain two Marines," said Shiran.

"What?" asked Francesca.

"Brad is accepting a commission as a chief warrant officer in the Marines. Barbara Gabrielson joined the Marines and is going through training. The commander is giving Rachel a commission to chief warrant officer also. So I'll soon have two new chief warrant officers and a new corporal," replied Shiran.

"That's wonderful!" exclaimed Francesca.

"Rachel and Brad are getting married next week," added Shiran.

"Then they'll be married before the baby is born. Where is the wedding?" asked Francesca.

"They're being commissioned and married right afterward at the Overlook," said Shiran.

"That should be quite the event," stated Francesca. "Why did Brad and Barbara join the Marines?"

"There's more need for Marines than Navy personnel right now," said Conor.

"With no ships available, I can understand that," replied Francesca.

"The commander also said since we're on our own that we should consider revamping how the Marines do business. When he commissions Brad, he'll be designated technical specialist, and Rachel will be designated as alien specialist," said Shiran. "I'm supposed to consider how to work those designations into the enlisted ranks. He wants us to be more than just grunts."

"I suppose I can wait that long before seeing the raptor installation. Besides, it looks like it's going to get interesting around here shortly," said Conor, changing the subject. Michael raised a questioning eyebrow.

Shiran nodded and said, "Commander Blankenship notified us while you were coming down in the longboat that there were eleven raptor ships that landed on the coast."

"What? Where are they?" exclaimed Francesca.

"They landed and came inland following the river," said Conor.

"They're not coming here?" asked Francesca.

"No. We're not sure where they're going, but the *New Horizon* is tracking them," said Conor.

"We estimate that we have about week to harvest what's between the outer fence and the new inner fence we erected," stated Shiran.

An inner fence surrounding the factories and elevators had been erected after the raptor attack several months ago. Unlike the outer fence, the inner fence was in independent sections that would remain electrified if a section became disabled. There were plans to modify the outer fence in the same manner, but it was determined there wasn't enough time to complete the task before the raptor fleets' arrival. That fleet composed of hundreds of ships would arrive within the next two weeks.

The lunch partners grew silent as they contemplated what the following weeks would bring. The size of the raptor fleet could only mean they intended war. The purpose and intent of the initial raptor party that had already arrived was anyone's guess. Hopefully, the perimeter fences and minefields, along with the ATVs and choppers, would dissuade the raptors without too much loss of life. Only the future could tell whether they would surrender.

Finished eating, Michael slid back from the table, determined to visit Anya Kaur in the brig. She still insisted she was innocent, and he wanted to talk to her again. He went down to the Marine Complex with Shiran where they parted. Going to the basement, he talked to the watch for a second who allowed him to see the prisoner privately.

"I've never offered you my congratulations on your promotion to lieutenant commander, sir. Congratulations," said Anya Kaur.

"Thank you," said Michael.

"So why are you here, Lieutenant Commander?" asked Anya.

"To find out how you're doing," replied Michael.

"I'm fine as can be expected. What else can I do for you?" asked Anya.

"Are the Marines treating you well?" asked Michael.

"They take me out to PT twice a day, they feed me, and they allow me a book to read," said Anya.

"They say they think you didn't commit the sabotages," said Michael.

"I didn't do it, Mr. Anderson," stated Anya.

"All the evidence points at you," replied Michael.

"I know it does," said Anya dejectedly.

"I wish I could believe you. Can you think of anything that might help me prove your innocence?" asked Michael.

"The Marines have provided paper copies and photographs of all the evidence. I go through it all the time and can't find anything that would prove me innocent," stated Anya.

"I wish I could find something," said Michael.

"I wish you could too. I don't hold this against you. If I were you, I'd believe that I'm guilty also," replied Anya.

"I'll keep looking," said Michael.

"I believe you," replied Anya.

"If you need anything, let me know, Petty Officer Kaur," said Michael. Michael turned to leave, and as he reached the door, he looked back and added, "Have hope, Anya."

Leaving the Marine Complex, Michael started toward the elevators. *Longboat 4* was on the field between the Marine Complex and the foundry with makeshift cranes along the starboard side as they removed the starboard wing. Michael stopped and talked to Dominic Sobolov for a moment, then went to the elevators and up the cleft to the comm suite.

Michael entered the communications suite and was greeted by Chief Tate. Not much had changed since he had been gone, but there really wasn't much to do except to maintain communications with the *New Horizon* and continue working on the AI mainframe they were constructing. The increased capabilities of the NAPACS allowed the colonists access to Hattie, which was in growing demand now that the commander had authorized another one hundred laptops because of the resources found on the moon.

Moving down the corridor that led deeper into the cave of the comm suite, Michael approached the thin transparent plastic barrier that lined the suite's end. There was more cave to expand into if the need arose, but that was to be determined sometime in the future. Michael unlocked the room where he worked on his investigation of the saboteur.

The lack of any further incidents was making it appear more and more likely that Petty Officer Kaur was the perpetrator they had been searching for. Her continued profession of innocence though did not sit well with Michael. He had just started looking at the drones when the longboat incident had happened. He had not placed much hope on the drones revealing any useful information because of their exposure to the elements. Three of the drones had been compromised, and the interiors had debris within them. The fourth had been the only drone intact, and he had just removed one of the plates composing the outer casing.

Walking over to the table where the intact drone lay, Michael pulled on a pair of surgical gloves. The outer casing plate he had removed so many months ago when the longboat incident had occurred still lay where he had placed it. He picked it up and looked at the lightly rusted outer covering of the plate that had been exposed to the elements and shook his head. He turned it over and examined the interior side of the plate that had been protected. As he examined the other side, his eyes widened in surprise. There was a dark-red droplet, nearly black, on the side that had been facing the components of the drone.

Michael stared at the dried rust-like spot for almost a minute. Taking a plastic bag from a nearby box, he slid the cover plate into the bag and sealed it. He removed his gloves, and taking the bagged plate, he locked the room as he left the comm suite. Michael went to the clinic where he asked for Dr. Hollinger. Nurse deLang told him Bess Hollinger was in the middle of an operation, but Dr. Kers Joshi was available.

"What can I do for you Michael?" asked Kers.

Michael showed the bagged cover plate to Kers and asked, "Can you tell me if that is blood, and if it is, whose blood?"

"It certainly looks like it might be blood," said Kers as he took the bag from Michael. "Come with me."

Kers turned and went through a door and into a room lined with equipment. Sitting at a table, he set the bag down and put on surgical gloves, then removed the plate from the bag. He pulled out a drawer and picked up a tool that he used to gently scrape at the edge of the droplet. He placed the residue on a slide, which he slid into a nearby machine.

"This will analyze our sample. If it is blood, and it certainly looks like it, we will know shortly," said Kers Joshi.

"If it's blood, will it tell us whose blood it is?" asked Michael.

"Yes, it will if they are part of the crew. Why do you wish to know?" asked Kers.

"I can't tell you," returned Michael evasively.

"Does it have to do with some of the accidents that have been occurring?" asked Kers.

Michael knew a moment of fear. Could Kers be the saboteur? If so, then he was in danger right now, but when Kers's look appeared sincere with no menace behind it, he changed his opinion. This job was starting to make him paranoid. Michael decided and forced himself to relax slightly and made a decision.

"Yes," replied Michael warily.

"Relax, Michael. Some of us have suspected that there has been more to some of the accidents than we are being told," said Kers.

"How long?" asked Michael.

"For me, since the pharmaceutical unit. Then there was the longboat accident, and shortly afterward, the Marines arrested Anya Kaur," said Kers as the machine beside him beeped. "Ah! Our results."

There on the screen before Kers was an analysis of the sample with its conclusions. It was human blood, and a name was displayed at the end of the data.

"Bahri Hiran," whispered Michael.

CHAPTER 77

The evidence displayed before Lieutenant Commander Conor Raybourn was quite revealing as Conor sat back in the chair of the MILDET prefab. Conor asked Hattie to display Bahri Hiran's location during each of the known incidents and any records that might connect him to the incidents. In each case, Hiran had access to the items that had been tampered with, though no record of his handling those items existed. On the other hand, Petty Officer Anya Kaur had also been present in almost every instance and had signed the shipping documents for those items. Not enough to incriminate Hiran alone but, coupled with the blood inside a sealed drone, very convincing.

Then there was the fact that Petty Officer Kaur went topside to the *New Horizon* for her yearly two weeks of duty on the *New Horizon* three days prior to the elevator incident. Dr. Raisa Romanov had examined the cable months ago, though she had not been told why, and had confirmed Gunnery Sergeant Rusu's opinion that the acid had to have been applied within twenty-four hours of its malfunction. It had only been an opinion though and not enough to state that Petty Officer Kaur could not have committed the tampering.

"Without that dried blood, all the evidence points to Petty Officer Kaur," said Conor.

"I just want to be sure," replied Michael. "We've already had Petty Officer Kaur locked up for months, and she continues to say she's innocent. What if it isn't Ensign Hiran either?"

Conor agreed with Michael's concerns. The blood was damning. There would have been no convincing reason for Ensign Hiran to have removed the drone's cover plate, and there was no possible way for the blood to enter that sealed compartment of the drone. Was there anything else? Then a thought occurred to Conor.

"What about prior to the FTL incident?" asked Conor.

"What?" asked Michael.

"Did you receive any components from supply for the FTL drive that were used in the area where the explosion occurred?" asked Conor.

"I hadn't thought of that. That whole section was so damaged that it never occurred to me to check. We don't even know what exploded," said Michael.

"Let's have Hattie check," said Conor calmly.

They gave Hattie their requirements and waited. It turned out that Petty Officer Kaur had very little to do with the handling of FTL components on the way to the jump point. In fact, Anya had been a late arrival and had reported to the *New Horizon* at the Ceres habitat. Between her arrival and the FTL incident, Petty Officer Kaur had only handled three components that Michael and his team had installed. None of which were in the section of the FTL compartment that had exploded. Ensign Hiran had been with the *New Horizon* during its complete overhaul to an FTL exploration ship. Conor was convinced; Michael still held reservations.

"Hattie. Marine Complex. Second Lieutenant Raybourn, please," said Conor.

"Wait, please. Lieutenant Commander Raybourn," said Hattie.

A moment later, Shiran appeared on the view screen, smiling. "Conor. Michael. What can I do for you?"

"We need to borrow some Marines," said Conor.

"Duty?" asked Shiran.

"Arrest and interrogation," said Conor.

"Who?" asked Shiran, her face growing serious.

"Ensign Bahri Hiran," replied Conor.

"Is this about what I think?" asked Shiran.

"Yes," stated Conor.

"I saw him leave the pier and go up the elevator less than half an hour ago. There will be six Marines outside the Overlook in five," said Shiran as the view screen faded.

Conor got up with Michael and walked over to the arms locker. They armed themselves with Gerst S-7 sidearms and checked the magazines, making sure sleepy darts were loaded. They left the prefab heading toward the elevator. They met Dominic Sobolov exiting the Bookworm, who noted the sidearms and determined that something was wrong.

"Good afternoon, Lieutenant Commanders. What is going on?" asked Dominic.

"We're going to arrest Ensign Hiran," replied Conor.

"Why?" asked Dominic.

"We believe he's the one who sabotaged your longboat and has caused other incidents in the colony," stated Michael.

"Son of the bitch," said Dominic.

"It's son of a bitch, Dominic," said Michael.

"No. I said what I meant," replied Dominic grimly as he started walking with Conor and Michael toward the elevators. The two lieutenant commanders looked at Dominic, smiled grimly, and nodded.

"In this case, you may very well be right," stated Conor.

"He was in the longboat prior to the launch. He said he was checking straps," said Dominic Sobolov.

"That wasn't in your report," said Michael.

"I did not think it necessary. I said something about it to Commander Blankenship at the clinic after the accident, and I thought Hiran was my friend," replied Dominic.

"Do you need more proof?" Conor asked Michael.

"No!" responded Michael.

They met Shiran and six other Marines as the elevator arrived. Conor noticed that most of the Marines had Gerst S-7 sidearms loaded with green tape on their magazines. There were two notable exceptions. Master Sergeant Evan Zander and Staff Sergeant Amanda Hall had magazines with red tape.

"We want to take him alive, Master Sergeant," said Conor.

"Staff Sergeant Hall and I are your backup. We only become involved if things go south," stated Evan Zander with Amanda Hall nodding agreement.

Conor nodded and said, "Let's hope it doesn't come to that, Master Sergeant."

"You're sure it's him?" asked Shiran.

"There was a drop of dried blood on the inside of one of the drones," said Michael.

Master Sergeant Zander looked at Second Lieutenant Raybourn and said, "That's enough proof for me. He's not a technician, and the inside of those drones are sealed from the environment."

Shiran nodded. "Let's find him."

"Already done, ma'am," stated Sergeant Adachi.

Looking across the bridge where Sergeant Adachi indicated, they saw President Felipe Martinez approaching with Bahri Hiran following him. Martinez and Hiran started crossing the bridge and stopped at the midpoint where they entered the small platform called the lookout, which gave a view of the waterfall rushing over the edge to plunge to the lake below. Martinez reached out his right arm and pointed to something at the lake's edge below while saying something to Hiran.

"Shall we?" asked Shiran, looking at Conor.

Conor nodded. "Master Sergeant, west end with the lieutenant commander. Second Lieutenant and Staff Sergeant Hall, secure the east end. Dominic, you're not armed. Please go over to the Overlook and wait this out. The rest of you, with me."

The party went to the bridge and started across. The master sergeant and Michael stopped as they came to the west end, while the rest of the party continued across. When they approached, Hiran noticed and turned to watch them. Shiran and Hall continued across the bridge to the east end as the rest of the party came to a halt at the lookout point. Felipe Martinez quit pointing below as he noticed that Hiran was no longer paying attention.

"Are you listening to me?" demanded Martinez loudly over the rushing water. As he turned toward Hiran, he saw the party of Marines surrounding the lookout point. Then Felipe Martinez demanded, "What do you want?"

Conor drew his Gerst S-7 and looked at Hiran, then said, "Ensign Hiran, I'm placing you under arrest."

Felipe looked from Hiran to Conor and shouted, "What are you talking about? This man is my assistant, and whatever you think he's done I'm sure is a mistake!"

"Mr. President, your trusted assistant is our saboteur," stated Conor as he watched Hiran.

"What? You already have the saboteur in custody!" shouted Felipe.

"I suspect she will be cleared of all charges," returned Conor.

Something in Hiran's demeanor changed as Conor made that statement. Gone was the subservient attitude, and a look of defiance entered his eyes. A stiletto appeared in Hiran's hand, and Conor raised his Gerst as the four Marines pulled theirs.

"Hiran, what are you doing?" shouted Felipe, staring at the stiletto.

"Shut up, you buffoon!" said Hiran menacingly as he grabbed Martinez, whipping him around and in front of him. His left arm tightened around Martinez's neck as his right reached around Felipe's back to reappear with the stiletto threatening Felipe's chest.

"Drop it, Hiran," said Conor, attempting to aim at Hiran's head.

"I don't think so. Now all of you put your weapons down, including your Jewish whore and the half-breed dog of hers at the ends of the bridge, along with those with them!" shouted Hiran.

"Not going to happen, Hiran," stated Conor.

"Then this idiot will die," screamed Hiran.

"How many more have to die, Hiran?" asked Conor.

"Everyone!" screamed Hiran. "You were all supposed to die. I have ensured your demise."

"Why?" asked Conor.

"Because they wished it!" screamed Hiran.

"Who?" asked Conor.

"Enough! Now drop your weapons!" screamed Hiran.

"Hiran, I'm sure if you surrender, we can work something out," pleaded Felipe.

"I told you to shut up!" screamed Hiran as he sank the stiletto into Felipe's chest.

Felipe Martinez jerked, and Hiran lost his grip on the stiletto handle as Felipe groaned, "You son of a bitch."

Felipe grabbed Hiran's right arm and forced himself to pull so he faced Hiran. The two men struggled until they were against the railing, and suddenly, they were both falling as the Marines ran forward. A splash was heard, and the heads of the two men were seen going over the edge of the cleft as the waterfall carried them away.

"They're gone," observed Michael as he approached.

"What happened?" asked Shiran.

"He didn't want to surrender. We need to look with a chopper," said Conor.

"Not many could survive that drop," stated Shiran.

"If they did, the crocs swarm down there," said Evan.

"If there's a chance they survived, we need to look," stated Conor.

Shiran nodded. "Adachi, Hall, with us. Master Sergeant, tell Chief Warrant Officer Guillete he's to remain in charge of the Marine Complex until I return."

"Roger that, ma'am," replied Zander.

"Michael, inform Commander Blankenship what happened," said Conor.

Half an hour later, they hovered near the base of the waterfall searching for the two who fell. A large crocodile lying on the muddy shoreline looked up at them with what looked like a clothed leg ending in a shoe caught between its teeth. The crocodile snapped its teeth, and the leg vanished. They saw nothing else as the crocodile slowly entered the water and submerged. The search continued around the lower cliff and shoreline for hours until at last they returned to the Marine Complex, where CWO Brad Guillete met them on the roof.

"Anything?" asked Brad.

"They're gone. They have to be dead," replied Shiran as they walked to the stairs leading down.

"Let's hope that's the last of Bahri Hiran," said Conor ominously.

CHAPTER 78

The cameras installed near the outer fences had recorded red flashes in the forest to the south and the east of the Compound for nearly two weeks. There had been no attacks on the fence, but none of the colonists were leaving the Compound. Many of the colonists had spent the last few weeks harvesting the crops that were ready between the inner and outer fences in anticipation of the outer fence being breached. The red raptor fleet had beached along the southern coast a week ago, and they had sighted green smoke to the south and east two days prior. It was estimated that the raptors would attack soon.

Many of the colonists had suggested that the raptor fleet should be destroyed outright with a preemptive strike from the *New Horizon*. Others had argued that until the raptors attacked, even though their intentions were obviously war, such a strike against them would be nothing less than genocide. The colony was divided. Agnes Felter had been confirmed as the acting president until a new election could be held. Agnes had led a faction that endorsed a preemptive strike against the raptors. They not only wanted the fleet destroyed but also suggested that the mainland cities along the eastern coast of the continent be obliterated too.

Such an act did not sit well with many of the scientists and quite a few of the original crew. In the end, it was decided that even though the outer perimeter fence might fall, the minefields inside it and outside the inner perimeter fence would dissuade the raptors. Then there were the ATVs and choppers along with the emplacements on top of the Marine Complex.

Shiran boarded the gunship with Sergeant Tadashi Adachi. She took the chopper east, intending to start her sweep of the fence line where it met the lake just beyond the rice paddies. The forest beyond looked quiet as she banked west to follow the perimeter fence as it curved north. A herd of apatosauruses could be seen in the distance moving away toward the distant river. The forest turned to plains as the curve continued until she came up on the northern forest as she continued on her northern heading.

"Do you see anything? Over," asked Conor over the headset.

"Nothing. All's quiet. Over," replied Shiran.

The forest and ridges outside the fence west of the Marine Complex approached as Shiran took the gunship slowly forward. Shiran banked toward the forest, flying parallel to the outer perimeter fence and a few meters above the treetops. Out of the corner of her eye, the forest moved. Shiran glanced to her left to see a huge weighted net approaching rapidly along with several large boulders. The barrage slammed into the side of the gunship, knocking it sideways. A rotor was lost as a lucky boulder smashed into it, then the weighted net engulfed the cockpit.

The forest in front of her moved as she attempted to bank to the right, and another weighted net with a multitude of boulders were flung at the passenger section of the chopper. The second net engulfed the passenger compartment, clinging to the chopper, and a boulder cracked the armor-reinforced Plexiglas in front of her.

"Damn!" exclaimed Shiran as she banked right toward the cleared area between the perimeter fence and forest.

"Going down, ma'am," declared Tadashi as the chopper's nose lowered and it lost altitude.

"Marine Complex. Chopper 1. Mayday!" shouted Shiran into her headset mic as she fought the controls, trying to steady the chopper's erratic wobble.

They were just outside the perimeter fence at the base of the ridge where Conor and Shiran had shared a kiss. The chopper was still a meter off the ground when another boulder hit the chopper broadside. The chopper went sideways, and the remaining rotors bit into the ground as the chopper fell spinning. They dropped the remaining meter as the rotors shattered into deadly shards. The armored Plexiglas was dotted with fragments of the rotors, and there was the sound of something cracking. Sergeant Adachi screamed in pain as a length of jagged rotor impaled his left shoulder and pinned him to the copilot seat. The front of the chopper rolled, and the passenger side door came to rest on the ground facing upward. The tail rotor was pointing in the direction the chopper had been heading prior to being attacked.

Shiran shook her head to clear it and saw double images for a moment. She tried the comms and didn't even receive static. Turning her head, she looked at Tadashi below her. Blood covered his face, which was a mask of pain as he groaned. She reached up and grabbed a handhold as she released her safety harness. Shiran slowly lowered herself to stand on the inside surface of the passenger door. Squatting, she looked into Tadashi's face for a moment as he grimaced in pain.

"I think we landed, ma'am," said Tadashi.

"Save it, Marine," said Shiran as she grabbed the first aid kit. Opening it, she took out the large gauze pads and ripped them open, placing them around the shard piercing his shoulder. "Can you hold that in place?"

"I think so," replied Tadashi as Shiran grabbed the painkillers and opened the bottle. She took out two pills and put them in Tadashi's mouth.

"Swallow, Marine," ordered Shiran. She watched as he closed his eyes and swallowed. There was less pain in his face when he reopened his eyes a moment later.

"Ma'am, you need to grab your M-71," stated Tadashi.

Shiran turned to look out the compromised armored Plexiglas. Past the shards imbedded in the Plexiglas, scarlet figures ran toward them. She stood up and grabbed her Navarro M-71, then crouched down and shoved the business end out of the hole where the shard broke through to embed itself in Tadashi's shoulder and the seat behind.

Firing in short bursts, two of the nearer raptors collapsed to the ground as javelins thudded against the cockpit. A loud thud occurred on the door above her as a raptor stabbed downward with its javelin. The weapon rebounded off the armored Plexiglas. Another raptor threw its javelin as she sent a three-round burst in its direction. She watched as the raptor kicked back and fell to the ground, jerking for a moment, then lay still.

The sound of the door opening above her made her look up. The raptor had determined how to open the latch. She saw Sergeant Adachi point his Gerst S-7 with his right hand and fire next to the left side of her helmet. The shot resounded through her headset, and her left ear rang as a hole appeared in the raptor's face. A mass of brains and bone formed a volcanic eruption at the back of its head. The door slammed shut as the raptor collapsed on top of the pilot door.

"Might want to lock that door, ma'am." Tadashi winced as he lowered his Gerst.

Shiran stood up, pushing the door to ensure it was shut, and worked the lock. She knelt down again and sent a three-round burst toward an approaching raptor, which fell to the ground as it threw a javelin in her direction. The tip broke off when it struck, and the two parts of the javelin fell to the ground outside the cockpit of the chopper. Another raptor appeared around the edge of the cockpit close to the gunship, and Shiran loosed a three-round burst into its chest as it stabbed downward, missing her gun barrel and sinking the point of the javelin into the ground. The first raptor got to its feet and started limping back toward the forest's edge, and Shiran allowed it to leave.

No other raptors were visible outside her range of view, and Shiran took the opportunity to switch magazines in her M-71. Looking outside, she still saw no movement, so she reached into the first aid kit and removed the microfilament saw. Opening it, she carefully sawed off the end of the rotor a few centimeters from Sergeant Adachi's chest while he watched outside. Finished, she threw the end of the rotor out the hole she had been firing through. Shiran checked outside again and looked into Tadashi's eyes.

"Can you move forward so I can saw the other side off?" asked Shiran.

"I can try," groaned Tadashi as he leaned forward against his seat restraints holding him in place.

Shiran glanced outside again, then stood up and reached behind the corporal with the microfilament, quickly sawing through the other end of the impaling rotor. The forest exploded into a fiery hell as she looked up. Trees became raging torches of flames, and fiery raptor bodies flew through the air as others were torn apart by a wall of metal rounds sweeping through their ranks. Nowhere in her field of vision was a raptor standing, and Shiran knew that the cavalry had arrived. She looked up to see Chopper 2 outfitted as a gunship, hovering above the mutilated ruin of its sister ship, protecting the wreckage from further harm.

A few minutes later, what was left of Chopper 1 was surrounded by a vanguard of ATVs there to protect and rescue Chopper 1's occupants. Four camouflage-clad, heavily armed people exited the ATVs and approached Chopper 1 as Shiran reached up and unlocked the pilot's door, smiling grimly as she recognized the individual in the lead as her husband.

CHAPTER 79

Conor was in the operations suite of the Marine Complex monitoring Shiran as she flew reconnaissance just outside the outer perimeter fence. The red raptors were out there and had been for the last two weeks, but they had not attacked. The *New Horizon* visuals and long-range radar indicated that they were building what looked like battering rams and catapults. They had also gathered some of the great beasts and held them captive. It was only a matter of time before the outer fence would be attacked.

He stood watching the video feed of Chopper 1 as it flew slowly near the forest's edge just outside the outer perimeter fence. A cloud of green smoke had risen into the air two days prior, and the raptors at the eastern end of the lake had vanished. The movements of the raptors indicated they planned to do something soon. Hopefully, the fences and minefields would dissuade them, but there were a lot of raptors out there.

"Do you see anything? Over," asked Conor over the comm mic he wore.

"Nothing. All's quiet. Over," came Shiran's reply.

A moment passed, then suddenly, the static was broken as Conor watched a huge weighted net and boulders fly at Chopper 1 toward the pilot's side.

"Damn!" came Shiran's voice over the comms as Chopper 1's cockpit was engulfed by another weighted net and pounded by boulders that appeared in front of them.

A moment passed, and Sergeant Adachi's voice said, "Going down, ma'am."

"Marine Complex. Chopper 1. Mayday!" Shiran's voice declared as Conor watched the chopper lose altitude. The chopper was nearly down when a boulder came out of nowhere and hit the door on the pilot's side, pushing the chopper sideways and making it drop faster. The rotors bit into the ground and shattered as the chopper rolled. The tail of the chopper angled upward as the chopper rolled and impacted the ground, pointing in the direction the chopper had been going. Then there was static.

Conor stood there for a moment, staring at the video display of the severely damaged chopper. Master Sergeant Zander cleared his throat, and Conor looked in his direction.

"Rescue op, sir," stated Evan Zander as Conor stared in the master sergeant's eyes.

Conor nodded. "Chopper 2. Chopper 2. We have a down bird that requires rescuing. Over."

"Roger that. Over," came the voice of Brad Guillete.

Conor looked back at the video feed and saw red raptors leave the forest from the south of Chopper 1, running toward the damaged bird.

"Master Sergeant, take over here," ordered Conor.

"Where are you going, sir?" demanded Evan.

"Out with the ATVs," replied Conor.

"Your place is here, sir," stated Evan.

"Damn it all, Master Sergeant. Take over. I'm going. We have the perimeter fences and minefields. Activate the mines if we're attacked!" shouted Conor as he hit the stairway, running.

"Roger that, sir," replied Evan as Conor ran down the stairs.

Conor was at the base of the stairs and with the group the master sergeant ordered to the ATVs as they headed out the door. ATV 2 had its rear end jacked up, awaiting the new axle being manufactured on the *New Horizon*. Sergeant Nikolai Ivankov tossed Conor a body armor as they jumped inside the first ATV and closed the door. The three usable ATVs at the Marine Complex were just starting out as they watched Chopper 2 demolish the forest beyond Chopper 1 with rockets that set it ablaze. Conor pulled on his body armor and fastened the straps as the ATV pressed him into his seat. Finished, he looked up to see they were already halfway to the gate leading to the copper mines along the base of the cliff face.

Nikolai looked at Conor and said, "Their plan is to draw us out."

"I know that," replied Conor as he finished strapping his body armor in place.

"Good. It is best to know when it's a trap," replied Nikolai.

"Let's hope we're up to it," responded Conor grimly.

The gates opened as the ATVs approached, and nothing appeared out of the forest. Passing through the gates, the parade turned south toward the grounded Chopper 1 as the gates closed behind them. A minute later, they were near the damaged chopper with red raptor bodies littering the ground nearby. Chopper 2 remained hovering overhead like a hawk, ready to unleash death on those who had dared to attack its mate.

The ATV Conor was in rounded Chopper 1 as the other two ATVs took up position facing the raging inferno that had once been a forest at the base of the nearby ridge. Conor and Nikolai left the ATV and ran to the downed chopper. Conor could see movement in the cockpit and knew a moment of relief as he recognized Shiran through the ruined Plexiglas. Staff Sergeant Amanda Hall and Lance Corporal Dwayne Abrams rounded the chopper from the rear, joining Conor and Nikolai, carrying a heavy Kevlar blanket.

"Are you all right in there?" shouted Conor.

"I'm fine. Adachi has a length of rotor through his left shoulder!" shouted Shiran through the crack in the Plexiglas on the passenger side.

"Give us a moment," returned Conor.

"You shouldn't be here," said Shiran as he neared the cockpit.

"Like hell! Now shut up and let us rescue you!" exclaimed Conor loudly.

There was a dead red lying on the pilot's door that they had to drag off. The body kept catching on the broken shards of rotor that was embedded in the Plexiglas. Conor felt a shiver run up his spine at how close those shards had come to penetrating the whole of the cockpit. The body of the red raptor finally slid to the ground at

Conor's feet, its body torn in multiple places by the knifelike pieces of rotor. Amanda threw the blanket over the cockpit, then Nikolai and Dwayne boosted Amanda to what was currently the top of the cockpit. Standing there, Amanda reached down and opened the pilot's door.

"What's the plan, ma'am?" asked Amanda as she looked down at Shiran.

"I'm going to release him from the safety harness, then I'm going to slap emergency bandages on the wounds. Hopefully, it won't kill him. Have Chopper 2 land for emergency evac," replied Shiran.

Conor nodded and activated his comm. "Marine Complex. Rescue Op. Over," said Conor.

"Rescue Op. Marine Complex. We read you. Over," came the master sergeant's voice.

"Marine Complex. Rescue Op. Have Chopper 2 land for emergency evac. Over," replied Conor.

"Rescue Op. Marine Complex. Roger that. Who? Over," replied the master sergeant.

"Marine Complex. Rescue Op. Sergeant Adachi is wounded. Shard through the left shoulder. Over," said Conor.

"Rescue Op. Marine Complex. Roger. Chopper 2 landing. How's the second? Over," said the master sergeant.

"Marine Complex. Rescue Op. Roger Chopper 2. The second says she's fine. Over," said Conor as Chopper 2 created a whirlwind around Conor and the others.

There was a scream from Chopper 1 and quick, barely seen movements as Shiran slapped emergency bandages to the back of Tadashi's left shoulder. Conor watched as Shiran helped him out of his seat and to his feet. Sergeant Adachi reached up with his right arm, which Amanda grabbed as Shiran shoved her head between Tadashi's legs and rose to her feet. Together, Shiran and Amanda were able to get Tadashi on top of the cockpit as Nikolai and Conor reached up to help him down. His face was a deathly pale as he reached the ground and collapsed.

Dwayne Abrams gently picked Tadashi up and carried him to Chopper 2 as Amanda assisted Shiran out of Chopper 1's cockpit.

Reaching Chopper 2, Dwayne carefully placed Tadashi in the copilot seat and strapped him in.

"Good luck, Sergeant," said Conor as he backed up with the lance corporal. He signaled to Chief Warrant Officer Brad Guillete to take off as he cleared the rotors.

"I'm going to reload when I'm on the cleft, sir!" shouted Brad.

"Roger that. Now go!" Conor shouted back.

Shiran came up from behind and embraced him as she said, "You still shouldn't be here, but it's nice to know how much you care."

Conor bent down and kissed her deeply as the Marines formed a guard around them, grinning. When they pulled apart, the Marines were still grinning, and the two grinned back. Conor looked to see that Chopper 2 was already landing beside the new hospital on the cleft while several people waited for its rotors to slow. Out of the corner of his eye, Conor saw movement to the south and turned his head to see red shapes racing toward the perimeter fence with beasts dragging wooden constructions behind them.

"Red smoke!" shouted Sergeant Ivankov, pointing to the south.

"Over there too!" shouted Lance Corporal Abrams, pointing to the east near the lake.

"Rescue Op. Marine Complex. We have a problem. Over," said Master Sergeant Zander's voice calmly.

"Marine Complex. Rescue Op. I see that. Over," replied Conor.

Conor and the Marines with the ATVs watched as boulders were launched from the forest, striking the fence and poles that held the fence. One pole bent, and more boulders were launched from the forest and now from the nearer catapults the beasts were dragging. The pole bent nearly to the ground as yet another pole supporting the perimeter fence was attacked.

"Marine Complex. Rescue Op. Activate the minefield. Over," said Conor.

"Rescue Op. Marine Complex. Activating now. Over," came the reply.

Suddenly, the world around the rescue party appeared to explode. Conor and the Marines outside the ATVs were blown off their feet to land roughly on the ground. Dazed, Conor rose to his elbows and looked toward the perimeter fence. What fence? Most of the fence near him lay on the ground, and looking east, he saw the fence was down for nearly half its length. Additionally, the first fifty meters inside the perimeter fence was a ravished wasteland of freshly tilled dirt where the minefield had once been. Conor looked toward the inner Compound where the newly built inner perimeter fence had once stood. The new fence built for the added protection of the industries, Marine Complex, and piers contained within lay on the ground also.

"What happened?" whispered Shiran as she looked in horror at the devastation.

Conor rose unsteadily to his feet. Hiran's last words about ensuring their demise resonated in his mind as Conor groaned, "Hiran."

CHAPTER 80

Qu'Loo'Oh' had been on the cleft for many months and was amazed at these humans and all they accomplished in the year they had been here. Their culture was a mixture of the simple and the wondrous. Qu'Loo'Oh' crouched to smell the marvelous roses her friend Hiroka raised in her garden. The fragrance was like nothing she had smelled before. She lay down near the roses on the flat stone that had been crafted for her by the humans.

She felt younger because of the doctors' continued ministrations. The doctors had her take three pills every day and said they were working as expected. They also performed what they called minor surgery on her hips and had her do something called physical therapy for nearly three months. After that, her hips now felt at least a decade younger.

She found her time among the humans almost magical as she watched them perform seeming miracles. The ships that could sail on air to the star in the sky and the city they were building displayed a power beyond her people's capabilities. Even the two small ships that sailed through the air on wings like a dragonfly and conveyances that ran on wheels were fantastic. Yet they utilized the simple and had simple pleasures, such as their restaurant where they ate and the sugary creation that Qu'Loo'Oh' tasted at the place they called the Flour Mill. Then there were the festivities they had every seventh evening, when they gathered to dance, dine, and play games.

Then there was the Bookworm, where Francesca had introduced her to the many books of fictional tales about magical places. The books were familiar and yet astounding to her that her people had not thought of such a method to keep records. Francesca had shown her pictures of ancient techniques of producing the same page for as many copies as one desired before resetting the print for the next page, then binding them altogether with a separate machine. Amazing. Even more amazing was the amount of information on the tablets and laptops the humans had at their fingertips. Qu'Loo'Oh' had asked Francesca why print books if the information was available on those marvels, and her response had been that some people enjoyed and often preferred a printed book.

The days passed in Elysian contentment for Qu'Loo'Oh' as she lay in the sun outside the garden. She also spent many hours conversing about her language and the history of her people with others at the Bookworm. They were probing into the old texts that even she had been afraid to touch because of the fragility of the parchment they were written on. With the assistance of the one they called Hattie and machines they had taken to the sacred cave, they could read a text without even opening it or moving it.

Much had been revealed to her about her people's history by these humans, and she had learned much about them. If there could be a way for the two people to coexist, she believed they could accomplish much together. True, there were humans whom she knew would wish no part of her kind, such as the one who had attempted to kill her and had injured her friends in the attempt, but then there were her human friends who appeared more interested in the pursuit of knowledge and not making an issue of differences.

One day the humans approached her and asked how to make peace with her people. They knew her people were preparing for war, and they had shown her pictures of a great fleet being built. She discovered that there were many colonists who wanted to destroy the fleet outright. This gave Qu'Loo'Oh' pause. If these humans could destroy a whole fleet of a thousand ships, could they not destroy the cities they came from? Reflecting on the achievements that the humans had accomplished in the last year, she believed they could.

Qu'Loo'Oh' knew that among her people, the act of surrendering, for either side, would turn the loser into a vassal state in which the leaders of the winning side would do with the population as they wished. She suspected from what she had learned about the humans that the same held true. In both instances though, there were good leaders and bad leaders, and the vassal state would prosper or suffer at the whims of either.

A different resolution to this conflict was required, but what it was, Qu'Loo'Oh' could not say. It would require both Ques'Coat'L' and humans to learn to live side by side in harmony. She knew that the one named Conor might come up with such a solution. Conor reminded Qu'Loo'Oh' of her eggling Qu'Fal'Ral' in many ways when it came to resolving a conflict.

Hopefully, the issue would not end like the argument between Martinez and Hiran. Qu'Loo'Oh' did not understand all the specifics about that incident, but it had left Conor worried. Why he was worried, he would not say, but she suspected that it was more than just the amassing army of the Qua'Tol'Ec' nation. Conor told her that the one named Hiran was the reason the humans had been stranded here and that some of Hiran's last words were that he ensured their demise. A shiver went down Qu'Loo'Oh's spine as she stood looking out over the edge of the cleft.

The army of the Qua'Tol'Ec' nation was out there. The humans knew it and were watching for the moment the attack would come. Qu'Loo'Oh' knew it would come soon because of the green smoke that was sighted two days prior. The human's flying beast was skimming over the trees to the southwest when it happened. Nets and boulders brought the flying beast to the ground just outside the fence. The mechanical beasts were rolling toward the fence shortly thereafter as those inside the damaged flying thing fought on. The metal beasts arrived, along with the other flying beast, and drove off the attacking Ques'Coat'L'. Red smoke appeared above the tree line to the east. Suddenly, the fence and ground just within its boundary were lifted in an upheaval, and a long continuous loud explosion could be heard. The war had begun.

*****

The ships arrived as planned with only one lost at sea when it ran afoul on a reef near one of the southern islands. They spent a week ensuring the ships were securely beached before starting inland. Qu'Fal'Ral' organized the hunters, and within a few short hours of the last ship's beaching, the party of nearly two hundred were heading inland. They vanished into the forest, hoping to reach their destination within a week. When they were a day's walk past the lake, they turned inland and went past the ancient city. As they passed through its edge, two hunters were lost, attacked by a great snake.

A five-day search revealed the entrance upon reaching the cliff's base at the far side of the lake, giving the hunters over a week to hunt and prepare. On sunrise of the ninth day, the hunter stationed above the tree line signaled that there was green smoke. The war party moved forward into the cave and, as they moved deeper into the dark, lit the torches. The map said it would take two days to traverse the cave system. Qu'Fal'Ral' left three at the entrance as he studied the map—one stationed above the tree line on the cliff and the other two at the cave entrance with a horn.

The horn was to be sounded at sunrise, midday, and sunset of each day. Hunters with horns were stationed every time the horn sounded inside the cave system to relay the sound of the entrance horn. Qu'Fal'Ral' and the war party reached the splitting point right after the morning horn of the next day and divided into three equal groups, taking different routes. The group with Qu'Fal'Ral' reached what they were looking for at noon. There were wooden barrels stored in the cave ahead filled with fluid that smelled like alcohol.

The hunters settled down to await the sounding of three horn bursts, which would signal the beginning of the war. While they waited, Qu'Fal'Ral' thought back to a time seven years ago when his mother, Qu'Loo'Oh', who laid his egg and raised him, was lost during a sacred hunt here in this land. She had been highborn, and her body had never been recovered after much searching.

Three horn bursts sounded, reverberating through the cavern system. The Qua'Tol'Ec' warriors moved forward through the last part of the cave toward the cleft, weapons ready.

CHAPTER 81

Master Sergeant Evan Zander watched the security view screens in horror after he pressed the switch that activated the minefield. He heard the muffled explosion of the mines, and a slight tremble could be felt even in the Marine Complex. When he had depressed the switch, all the mines exploded just inside the outer perimeter fence, and much of the fence toppled to the ground. The view screen showed the ATVs, damaged chopper, and five people lying on the ground beyond the downed fence. He looked at another view screen to see that the inner fence was down and that the minefield they had laid just outside of it had exploded also, creating a wasteland of fresh dirt pocked with craters.

"What happened?" whispered Corporal Natalie Green as she looked at Evan Zander from her security console station.

"Hiran," muttered the master sergeant as his gaze shifted to other view screens in the room.

Over half of the outer perimeter fence lay on the bare, desolate ground in every screen where the minefield had been installed. The primary line of defense the colony had been relying on for protection from the imminent raptor attack was gone. The only thing standing between the raptor horde and the cleft were the Marines, three ATVs, and now only one gunship chopper. True, there were rockets and miniguns mounted on the roof of the Marine Complex, but they would soon be depleted against the raptor army.

Evan looked around the operations suite at the frightened faces that looked back at him. They all knew the Marines had been relying on those perimeter fences and minefields to dissuade the raptors if they attacked. Evan switched modes with these thoughts. All these people he had talked into assisting the Marines were in danger. The Marine Complex would fall without the outer defenses, and the people here should not be here, and it was his fault they were. His arrogance had brought them here, offering them a light job, while their maternal conditions prohibited heavier labor.

"Corporal Green, these people shouldn't be here," said Evan evenly.

"They'd never make it back to the cleft without the ATVs," said Natalie as she pointed to a view screen where red raptors and the machines pulled by the great beasts were already past where the outer fence had been.

Looking at the view screen again, it was obvious the ATVs would not be returning soon. There was a firefight going on out there past the perimeter fence, and one ATV had been overturned with bursts coming from its gunports as the crew fought on. The other two ATVs were valiantly protecting the overturned ATV.

"Corporal, take these people to the pier and board the shuttle now," ordered Evan.

"Master Sergeant?" questioned Natalie.

"Do it!" snapped Evan sharply.

"What about you?" asked Natalie, getting up slowly, pulling at her maternity top to straighten it.

"I'll be right behind you. Now go!" ordered Evan.

Leaving her seat, Corporal Green started helping the people to the elevator and stairs to get them down to the piers. She checked the bathroom and bunk room they had installed for the operations personnel. When they were all gone, the master sergeant looked at all the view screens again and noticed *Longboat 4* sitting beside the complex with the starboard wing lying on the ground. A figure was at the door of the longboat looking out. The light of inspiration suddenly flared in Evan's eyes. The master sergeant switched the comm channel to three and hoped that Lieutenant JG Sobolov answered.

"Longboat 4. Marine Complex. Over," said Evan. He waited for fifteen seconds and tried again. "Longboat 4. Marine Complex. Over," repeated Evan.

"Marine Complex. Longboat 4. Dah! What's going on out there? Over," asked Dominic Sobolov.

"Longboat 4. Marine Complex. A big hairy fur ball. We're going to be up to our necks in raptors within minutes. Over," said Evan.

"Marine Complex. Longboat 4. I can see that. Over," returned Dominic.

"Longboat 4. Marine Complex. Does the Benson drive work, and can you move the longboat? Over," asked Evan.

"Marine Complex. Longboat 4. It will move, and the Benson drive works fine, but it will not fly. Why? Over," returned Dominic.

"Longboat 4. Marine Complex. Send anyone you don't need to the shuttle, then move the longboat to the base of the elevators with its ass end pointed down the street between the foundry and lumber mill. You'll figure it out from there. Good luck, sir. Out," said Evan.

Looking at the view screens again, the master sergeant saw that the fight around the ATVs had turned into more of a retreat, with raptors avoiding the ATVs when possible. Two ATVs had towlines attached to the overturned ATV and turning it upright. People near the longboat were already moving toward the pier, and *Longboat 4* jerked and slowly started moving forward. Evan Zander switched channels back to the ATVs and spoke.

"Rescue Op. Marine Complex. Over," said Evan.

"We're a little busy right now," came Lieutenant Commander Conor Raybourn's voice.

"Roger that. When you get that ATV back on its feet, head to the elevators," said Evan.

"That was the plan," returned Conor's voice.

"Avoid the main street between the lumber mill and foundry. Attempt to persuade the raptors to use that route," said Evan.

"Why?" asked Conor's disembodied voice.

"There's going to be a nasty surprise waiting for them," replied Evan.

"What surprise? Wait! I see it. What about the people at the complex?" asked Conor.

"We'll be on the *New Horizon*," returned Evan.

"Roger that," returned Conor.

"Roger. Out," said Evan.

The master sergeant placed all the miniguns and rocket launchers on the roof facing the south and west on automatic. Evan ran downstairs and did a quick check of the rooms and was just finishing when he heard the first explosion. Running outside, he looked to his left and saw that *Longboat 4* was already moving down the street between the lumber mill and foundry. To his right, he saw Dr. Raisa Romanov run out of the munitions prefab and toward the piers. They met at the head of the pier as the first raptors appeared around the southeast corner of the Marine Complex. The miniguns on that side of the complex must already be depleted of ammunition.

"Little late, Doctor," said Evan.

"I was busy," said the doctor as she looked back, raising her hand, which held a remote. Raisa pressed the button, and the prefab exploded, knocking her and Evan off their feet. A huge mushroom cloud formed above where the prefab had stood. Part of the southeast corner of the Marine Complex was gone, revealing the ravished interior.

"Glad you're on our side," said Evan Zander, looking at the havoc and charred remains of raptors it had left behind.

The prefab was a raging inferno, acting as a barrier to anything wishing to pass between the Marine Complex and the lake. Any antagonist would have to pass along the west side of the Marine Complex to reach the pier until those fires died down. Depending on the raptors' resolve, they would have a few minutes because of the miniguns and rocket emplacements on the west side of the complex. Until the munitions ran out, it would prevent such a move. He helped Raisa to her feet, and they ran down the pier where his wife, Chief Tami Zander, stood working on the docking clamp control panel. Dr. Romanov walked up the gangplank and boarded the shuttle as Evan Zander went to his wife. The rattle of miniguns and rocket explosions made a background noise as he came to a stop beside her.

"Is everyone aboard?" asked Evan.

"They're aboard. But most of the people from the Marine Complex are pregnant," replied Tami.

"It can't be helped. Are your fuel tanks full?" asked Evan.

"They're full," replied Tami tensely.

"If you take it up slow, they should be all right. All you have to do is achieve orbit. The *New Horizon* can have a longboat tow the shuttle the rest of the way," returned Evan.

"I know that," replied Tami tautly.

"What's wrong?" asked Evan.

"The docking clamp isn't working. It will disengage manually, but only if someone is on the pier and pushes that button," stated Tami Zander, pointing to the cover plate protecting the release button for the clamps.

"What happened?" demanded Evan.

"I don't know," stated Tami, pointing at the ruin under the cover plate she had removed from the docking clamp controls.

"Hiran," muttered Evan vehemently.

"He did this?" whispered Tami in disbelief.

Making a decision, Evan growled, "Get aboard."

"Evan, no!" cried Tami seeing his choice.

"These people need to be saved. Those raptors get here, and they'll sink the shuttle. Now get aboard before the colony loses any more," growled Evan.

Tami fell into Evan's arms as he escorted her up the gangplank to the shuttle. Evan grabbed the Navarro M-71 and the Vinter sniper rifle she kept near the hatch. He kissed Tami for the last time, tasting tears, as she looked up into his eyes.

He turned and said, "Channel 7. Now close the hatch and get these people out of here. Goodbye, my love."

Evan had one last call to make before setting the comm to channel 7. He set the personal comm to channel 7 secure mode 5, which was rarely used, and clicked the call button. He waited nearly fifteen seconds before a response came.

"Evan?" came Ezekiel's voice.

"Yah! Ezekiel, take care of Tami and the kids," said Evan.

There was a slight pause.

"I will. I'm sorry, Evan. I will miss you," replied Ezekiel.

"I'll miss you too. Goodbye," said Evan.

"Goodbye, Evan," whispered Ezekiel.

Walking down the gangplank, Master Sergeant Evan Zander came to a stop beside the control panel. Two raptors were coming around the northwest side of the Marine Complex as he watched. Sighting down the Vinter 10 mm, he sent them to raptor heaven, then looked at the cockpit of the shuttle. Tami was sitting in the pilot seat and doing preflights as he lifted the cover and hit the release button of the docking clamps. The shuttle floated free and moved into the open waters of the lake. Evan watched as the shuttle completed its turn, and after a moment, it started moving forward.

He set his comm to channel 7 and hit the button for continuous open communications. The rattle of the miniguns and rocket bursts lasted for nearly four minutes since the prefab had exploded. Evan shot any unfortunate enough to make it around completely. It took nearly two more minutes before more raptors appeared around the north side of the Marine Complex. Evan shot off five rounds while he began to sing a song older than the United Systems.

> From the Halls of Montezuma
> To the Shores of Tripoli,
> We will fight our country's battles
> In the air, on land, and sea.
> First to fight for right and freedom
> And to keep our honor clean.
> We are proud to claim the title
> Of United Systems Marine.

The master sergeant fired the Vinter once more before dropping it to the ground. Then taking up the M-71 from where it hung at his hip, he started firing three-round bursts into the oncoming raptors as he started singing again.

> Our flag's unfurled to every breeze
> From dawn to setting sun.
> We have fought in ev'ry clime and place
> Where we could take a gun.

NEW HORIZON

> In the snow of far-off northern lands
> And in sunny tropic scenes,
> You will find us always on the job—
> The United Systems Marines.

A javelin pierced his left thigh, making him cry in pain, as he stopped for a second to change magazines in the Navarro M-71. Finished, he started singing and firing at the horde of raptors approaching him. Javelins fell around him like rain, and the old scarred crocodile submerged behind him.

> Here's health to you and to our corps,
> Which we are proud to serve.
> In many a strife, we've fought for life
> And never lost our nerve.
> If the Army and the Navy
> Ever look on heaven's scenes,
> They will find the streets are guarded
> By United Systems Marines.

Master Sergeant Evan Zander depleted the magazine and started changing magazines again as three more javelins found their marks. He was able to fire off another half of the magazine in three-round bursts before simply pulling the trigger back, unloading the rest of the magazine into the oncoming raptors. Finished, Evan collapsed to the ground, blood streaming from his wounds, as he turned his head to watch the shuttle ascending into the clear blue sky. His sight dimmed, and he smiled as he thought he heard a voice whisper, "Goodbye, my love."

*****

Chief Petty Officer Tami Zander closed the hatch to the shuttle as tears streamed down her dark cheeks. She stumbled between the passenger seats toward the bow of the shuttle as the passengers watched silently, afraid to say anything. Reaching the cockpit, Tami sat down and strapped herself in resorting to routine to get her through the next few minutes. She started her preflights, not daring to look outside, as she felt the docking clamp release. Petty Officer First Class Ramirez used the thrusters to push them away from the clamps and back into the lake while slowly turning. Finishing the turn, Ramirez brought the shuttle to a dead stop with the bow of *Shuttle 1* pointing out into the lake's long choppy blue surface.

"Chief?" queried Ramirez.

"Channel 7," ordered Tami Zander.

A moment passed in silence as Tami wiped her face with her sleeve, then looked up with bloodshot eyes at her runway as Ramirez set the comm to channel 7. Tami started the Benson drive, slowly building up speed as she went. The shuttle's bow parted the waters of the lake like a knife as it sprayed up to each side. Master Sergeant Evan Zander's voice singing came over the comm as they gained speed. They were almost to the other side of the lake's ten-kilometer surface before she brought the nose up and started gaining altitude. Banking slowly, she took the shuttle back a kilometer south from the pier, gaining altitude. The song ended, and the sound of a Navarro M-71 on full auto came over the comm as Tami looked toward the pier where red shapes seemed to flow like a river of blood.

"Goodbye, my love," whispered Tami Zander.

CHAPTER 82

The sound of an explosion was heard as another group left the Overlook toward the elevator. Ezekiel stepped out and looked to the south toward the Marine Complex where a fireball rose into the sky. A short time later, the radio attached to Ezekiel's belt clicked, then vibrated. Walking into the back room, he opened the radio channel he and Evan used. A tear ran down Ezekiel's cheek as Evan Zander said goodbye, and the comm circuit went dead. Brushing the tear away, Ezekiel stepped out of the back room of the Overlook and stood behind the counter. Over twenty people were in the Overlook. All of them carried weapons that the Marine Complex had sent to the cleft over the last two months. Commander Blankenship had already taken over a hundred people down to guard the elevator's base, which had been fortified with reinforced concrete barriers.

"Ezekiel?" asked Tom Tollifer, worry in his eyes.

"It is nothing," said Ezekiel quietly.

"Ready to go down?" asked Tom.

Ezekiel nodded and took up the Navarro M-71 sitting on the granite counter. Ezekiel put the strap around his shoulder and checked the Gerst S-7 at his waist belt. He walked around the counter to stand beside Tom Tollifer, and Ezekiel placed a hand on his shoulder.

"Yes, it is time," replied Ezekiel shakily.

Tom looked at Ezekiel again and saw pain in his eyes but did not ask what had caused the pain in the brief time he had been in the back room. They walked to the front door of the Overlook together and exited with the others following behind. Ezekiel heard shouts coming from the bridge as they walked toward the elevators. Running across the bridge were three of the five outcasts still living on the east end of the cleft. Out of breath, they stopped near Ezekiel and Tom.

"What is it?" demanded Tom.

"Bill and Wesley are dead," wheezed Palesa Theron between gasps, referring to Bill Pratt and Wesley August, who had been two of the early outcasts.

"What happened?" demanded Ezekiel.

"There's raptors coming through the caves," replied Palesa, referring to the cave the outcasts had been using to live in on the east end of the cleft.

Ezekiel peered toward the east end of the ledge and saw red shapes gathering there. He looked toward the west end of the ledge and didn't see any red shapes. Hopefully, that situation would remain the same.

"Tom, put four of these people on guard at the bridge, then take another eight and grab anything heavy from the equipment over there and build a barricade on this side of the bridge," ordered Ezekiel, pointing at the equipment waiting for distribution beside the elevators.

"What's the plan?" asked Tom.

"We need to keep them on that side of the river," said Ezekiel.

"What are you going to do?" asked Tom.

"We need more equipment," returned Ezekiel as he watched the shuttle rise into the air and circle back over the lake. Tom tapped four people on the shoulder and pointed to the bridge, then tapped eight to follow him to the elevators. Ezekiel looked at the others and told them to follow him as he went into the Overlook. Going to the back room, he pushed over the wooden barrels stored there. Then those with him started pushing them out of the Overlook to the bridge to add to the growing barricade.

"We stay behind the barricades and hold," ordered Ezekiel.

"Think we can hold them?" asked Tom as he stood behind the barricade.

"It depends on how many are coming this way. We may need more people," said Ezekiel.

Tom tapped Janice Svensson on the shoulder and muttered something to her. She took off running down the street at a sprint. Ezekiel knew from conversations with her that she had been a track star for her nation and had competed internationally.

"I told her to bring twenty if possible," said Tom.

"There may not be enough arms," replied Ezekiel.

Tom showed him the case of six Gerst S-7 sidearms with ammunition and magazines found near the elevator and said loudly, "Let's get these magazines loaded."

A few minutes later, Janice came leading another nine people who had gathered in the clinic. All the children and others who were incapable of fighting were gathering there. They were still coming up short on firearms and gave those without brush machetes to defend themselves, but if it came down to that, they knew the battle was lost.

"Those we can't arm with firearms reload magazines!" shouted Ezekiel.

"I agree," replied Tom. Then he ordered loudly, "If someone falls and you're not armed, take their weapon."

"Let's hope they can't cross the river further up," muttered Ezekiel as the red raptors that had gathered at the end of the cleft started advancing.

"Are we sure everyone is out of those buildings?" asked Tom, pointing to the buildings on the other side of the river.

"If they aren't, it's too late now," stated Ezekiel.

"Up there!" shouted one of the people guarding the bridge, pointing upriver toward the back of the cleft.

More raptors could be seen pouring around the end of the building on the other side of the river. Muzzle flashes came out of two of the apartment windows on the third floor above the clinic. Three raptors fell as the others pulled back. A raptor attempted to jump the river with a running start and almost made it, except another unseen marksman took it at the apex of its jump. The raptor fell back into the river kicking as it floated down to the bridge and went over the edge.

"That group must be coming through the distillery cave!" shouted Jacob Valdez.

"Let's hope the people in those apartments can hold them!" yelled Tom Tollifer.

"What about the comm suite?" shouted Jacob back at Tom.

"Janice! Through the Overlook and the back entrance. The comm suite," ordered Ezekiel.

"Roger that!" yelled Janice, running.

"I don't know if we'll be able to hold them off," said Tom.

"We don't have much choice," said Ezekiel grimly.

Suddenly, javelins fell on their position as raptors stepped out of the entrances of the nearer shops that were under construction across the river. There were raptors on the roof of the new hospital throwing javelins too. The defenders returned fire, but three had already fallen, and Tom had a javelin through his right shoulder. Tom staggered backward, and Ezekiel grabbed him as he saw Jacob Valdez fall and lay still with a javelin through his chest. Ezekiel pulled Tom into the Overlook as more javelins fell like rain on the bricks of the boardwalk.

An arm holding a Gerst S-7 appeared from a window of one of the apartments above and started firing at the raptors on the roof of the hospital as Tom and Ezekiel entered the Overlook. Two of the raptors fell from the roof to the street below and lay with their brethren that the bridge defenders had killed. Ezekiel set Tom against the wall and looked at the wound. The javelin went through the shoulder, and Ezekiel was afraid it would kill Tom if removed.

"I need the first aid kit, Tom," stated Ezekiel.

"Give me your Gerst," said Tom, holding out his left hand.

Removing his Gerst S-7 sidearm, he put it in Tom's hand, and then he placed the two magazines on the floor beside him. Tom nodded as Ezekiel ran behind the counter and grabbed the first aid kit while Tom watched for a chance to assist the defenders. Returning, Ezekiel gave Tom two pain pills, then sawed through both ends of the javelin slightly above the entrance and exit wounds. Finished, he placed bandages above the ends of the javelin still in Tom and taped around his chest.

"Better?" asked Ezekiel.

"If you want to call it that," said Tom through gritted teeth.

Looking out the doorway, Ezekiel counted at least six raptors lying on the street across the river, and seven defenders lay unmoving between him and the bridge barricade. Ezekiel shook his head, for all their superior firepower, they were not doing well. There was already too many losses for the number of raptors that Ezekiel had seen coming from the far end of the cliff. It was also apparent that there were raptors coming through the distillery cave, which meant that there were more than he had seen. The barricade at the bridge would most likely fall because they would be overwhelmed. He felt a momentary loss of hope, then thought of his friend Evan and steeled himself for what was to come.

The attack came shortly with Tom and Ezekiel adding to the return fire. Five more of the defenders fell, though this time, they accounted for themselves better as the raptors fell back. Ezekiel knew that it was only a matter of time, but the raptors weren't going to give them any because more javelins started falling from the top of the hospital and more raptors stepped out of the empty shops across the river to add to the barrage. Another three defenders fell before the raptors retreated, and the people at the barricade were ready to break. The street was littered with javelins and bodies. The raptors had to be running out of javelins, but the defenders should still have ammunition. They were too close, making it too easy for the raptors.

"Fall back!" yelled Ezekiel.

The defenders looked back at Ezekiel as he pointed to the crates by the elevator.

"We have to hold!" someone shouted back.

"Half of you behind those crates! The other half in here! Cross fire. They have to be running low on javelins!" Ezekiel shouted.

The raptors appeared again as the defenders were organizing to fall back, and two more defenders fell in the brief firefight before the raptors again fell back. The defenders ran, half to the Overlook and the other half to the crates, as raptors again appeared, throwing javelins that hit two of the people running toward the Overlook. One fell to lay facedown with a javelin through his back, while Palesa staggered in with a javelin through her thigh. Ezekiel grabbed her out of the way of the next barrage of javelins and set her beside the window.

Ezekiel ejected his magazine and looked. There were three rounds left and one in the chamber. He had another full magazine in his pocket, then he'd be out. He shook his head. Not good. Glancing outside, he saw raptors coming down the bridge and fired the four rounds. Some fell as the defenders shot at them, but too many were not falling. He was rewarded by seeing the one he had aimed at fall over the bridge railing as he slammed his last magazine into his Navarro M-71. The raptors that made it across veered toward the crates near the elevators as Ezekiel added his fire to that of the rest of the defenders.

One raptor jumped on top of the crates and then to the guard wall at the edge of the cliff. It took three rounds to the chest at point-blank range, and it vanished over the edge. A moment later, another raptor attempted the same maneuver to be treated in the same manner. Ezekiel saw one of the defenders by the elevator peek over the crate to jerk back with a javelin in his mouth. A defender by the crates fired her M-71 at a raptor, taking it in the chest and head, then fell back clutching her shoulder as it was pierced by a javelin. Three more javelins pierced her chest before Stefanie Lanier fell backward over the edge.

Five more raptors ran toward the crates as Tom and Ezekiel fired at them. One broke off and came toward the entrance of the Overlook as Ezekiel fired at it until it fell just outside the door. Ezekiel saw Palesa fall with a javelin through her neck from where she was firing her Gerst S-7 sidearm through the shattered window of the Overlook. She dropped, pulsing her lifeblood out on the polished floor. Suddenly, there was an explosion upriver that rocked loose items in the Overlook for a moment.

"What the hell was that?" whispered Tom.

"Distillery," stated Ezekiel.

There were at least two dozen raptors swarming across the bridge when Ezekiel looked again. He dropped his empty M-71 and picked up Palesa's sidearm. Ezekiel slid it over to Tom, whose Gerst had its slide locked back as Roberta reloaded from Palesa's spare magazine.

"What about you?" asked Tom, catching the Gerst.

Ezekiel went to the wall and took down a spear and shield. Tom shrugged and started firing at the oncoming raptors as Ezekiel ran over to the door near Tom. Suddenly, the lead raptors started falling as the sounds of multiple Navarro M-71s came from the elevators. A raptor made it through to the Overlook door, and Tom threw the empty Gerst at it as he rolled away. Ezekiel stepped forward, raising his spear as he crouched behind the shield.

The raptor impaled itself on the spear as its head came over the top of the shield, snapping. Ezekiel raised his arm, embedding the edge of the shield in its neck as he pushed it forward to keep it away. A Kinley-Grant combat knife pierced its right eye as Ezekiel fought to keep it back with the shield up, and suddenly, the raptor was deadweight. Letting go of the shield, Ezekiel grabbed the spear with both hands and yanked it from the raptor's body, raising it just in time to jam it into the jaws of another raptor.

The raptor fell, jerking, and raked the talons of its foot along Ezekiel's right thigh. Ezekiel fell back in pain, then raised his head to look out the Overlook door. There were no more raptors coming, and people holding M-71s were firing at those across the bridge in retreat. Roberta was at his side with a bloody KG-3 combat knife, cutting the leg of his trousers off. Another person appeared and took over for Tom. Tom helped Roberta finish cutting the trouser material from his leg and started wrapping it around the wound.

Ezekiel watched as the new defenders moved forward and out of sight. Tom handed Ezekiel a Gerst S-7 with a fresh magazine as one of the defenders, Evangeline Dalisay, removed the javelin from Palesa's neck and gently moved her to the side. Then Evangeline took up position with her Navarro M-71, watching the buildings across the street through the window.

"We're supposed to stay here and pick off strays if we see any," said Evangeline.

Ezekiel nodded. "I could use a drink."

Tom winced and slowly rose to his feet, then walked across the room to the counter. Tom returned holding a bottle as Ezekiel sat back against the doorframe, watching out the front door. Sitting back down on the other side of the door, Tom opened the bottle, then took a swig before he passed it to Ezekiel. Taking a long swig, Ezekiel wiped his face with his shirt sleeve and returned the bottle to Tom.

"You look like crap," said Ezekiel.

"You're no prize either right now." Tom grinned.

Both men started chuckling as they took another swig to ease the pain of their wounds.

CHAPTER 83

It was a beautiful day as Lieutenant Commander Michael Anderson walked into the comm suite and headed to the microminiature repair room where two technicians were working on part of the new mainframe for the AI they were building. They nearly had 80 percent of the motherboard completed, and the *New Horizon* had about 70 percent of the circuit boards required for the interactive functions of the AI completed. The *New Horizon*'s factory would start producing memory storage cards after the interactive functions were completely finished and tested. With luck, the colony would have a working AI in the back of the comm suite within the next planet year.

Chief Heather Tate was on watch with Seaman Lachowski in the comm suite and looked up when Michael entered.

"Good morning, sir," said Heather.

"Good morning, Chief. How's everything going?" replied Michael.

"Same as yesterday, sir. The raptors are outside the fence, and the *New Horizon* says there's no change since they arrived a week ago," replied Heather.

"The green smoke the other day and the raptors to the north vanishing means they're up to something," said Michael.

"I agree, sir. Somehow, I think we'll find out soon," said the Heather.

Michael nodded. "I'm going to work on the drones for the second lieutenant. Perhaps if I can get one or two of them working, it might help."

Michael walked back to the workroom he had set up beside the AI room. Corporal Barbara Gabrielson was just laying down a screwdriver as she pushed on the cover plate to test its seating. Nodding, Barbara reached for the remote before she noticed Michael was watching her.

"Good morning, sir," said Barbara brightly.

"Good morning. Is everything going all right? I thought you had training with the Marines," asked Michael.

"Everything's fine, sir. The master sergeant said I'm ahead of schedule on my training and asked if I'd mind trying to get one or two of the drones operational. The door was unlocked, so I came in and started working," replied Barbara.

"So how's that going?" asked Michael, remembering that he had forgotten to lock the door yesterday.

"Fine, sir. I was just going to check to see if the engines start," replied Barbara.

"Let's try them then," said Michael.

Barbara worked the controls, and the drone came to life. She then did something that caused the drone to lift about twenty centimeters off the table. Leaving it to hover for about thirty seconds, she then worked the control to lower the drone back to the table.

"Looks good, sir," said Corporal Gabrielson.

There was a long low sound that continued for a moment, and Michael looked around in surprise. The sound came again, and he looked outside the door of the investigation room but saw nothing. It sounded a third time while he was in the hallway, and it seemed to emanate from further back in the cave where the plastic barrier they had erected as a temporary wall stood. Something moved back there. Michael's neck hairs stood up, and he froze. Was that a flash of red on the other side of the plastic further back just where the light stopped?

"Corporal, let's get out of here," Michael said lowly.

"What's up, sir?" whispered Barbara as she came up beside Michael.

"I think we have raptors," said Michael quietly.

Barbara froze for a second, then drew her Gerst S-7 sidearm and worked the slide, chambering a round, then whispered, "Think we can make it?"

"I don't know. Now run," muttered Michael as he slid the belt with the Gerst S-7 sidearm holstered to it from beside the door.

They both exited the door running for their lives toward the comm suite. A javelin missed Michael and bounced down the hallway, but another javelin hit Barbara in the lower calf, leaving a deep bleeding gash as she ran ahead of Michael. She stumbled, and Michael grabbed her by the waist, pulling her onto the open door of the comm suite where Chief Tate stood with a Gerst S-7 aimed down the passageway toward them.

"Hurry up!" Heather shouted as she fired past the two runners.

They passed through the door, then Heather fired two shots down the hall before the door slammed shut behind them, and the chief worked the lock.

"That should hold them for a bit," said Heather.

Michael grabbed the first aid kit and slapped a bandage on Barbara's leg. Heather Tate looked at Petty Officer Timothy Powell, who was staring at them from the microminiature lab.

"What the hell's going on, Chief?" asked Timothy.

"Raptors. We need to get out of here," stated the chief.

"Sure they're not out front too?" asked Michael.

"Haven't checked," said the chief, walking to the front door, peeking out.

"Powell, bring that ethanol jug," ordered Michael.

"Looks clear, sir. What's the plan?" said Heather as Powell brought the ten liters of ethanol used for cleaning from the microminiature lab.

"Put the ethanol in front of the passageway door. We have anything else that'll explode or catch fire?" asked Michael.

Heather grinned. "There's ammonia and chlorine in the cleaning gear locker."

"Get them and put them by the ethanol," said Michael as he finished wrapping Barbara's leg.

"More tape, sir," said Barbara as Powell ran to the locker and got the ammonia and chlorine. Banging started at the passageway door. The banging grew more persistent and then a scraping sound as something with a metallic sound started, testing the door's edges.

"You sure?" asked Michael.

"I need to be able to walk," said Barbara.

"All right," said Michael as he started applying more tape.

"No, use duct tape," stated Barbara. "I don't want it to come off."

Chief Tate took some duct tape out of a drawer and handed it to Michael, who started wrapping it around Barbara's leg.

"We don't have much time. Is there anything we can use to start that on fire when they break through?" asked Michael as he finished wrapping and handed the tape to Heather.

Heather walked over to the front door and opened a box on the wall beside it. She withdrew a flare gun and held it up as she stated, "I'll take care of that. Let's get out of here."

Going out the front entrance of the comm suite, they saw Chopper 2 vanish over the edge of the cliff. Michael looked east and saw raptors swarming out of the distillery storage cave entrance on the other side of the river. Someone was shooting at them from this side of the river as they rounded the corner. A few dead raptors lay on the new boardwalk on the other side of the river.

Janice Svensson arrived to find out that her message from Ezekiel was too late. Michael had her assist Timothy Powell and Freda Lachowski to take Barbara to the back door of the clinic. Heather Tate and Michael took up positions on each side of the comm suite's front entrance, Michael with his Gerst sidearm while the chief aimed the flare gun at the pile of solvents near the back passageway door.

"Seems we're constantly rebuilding this suite," said Michael.

"Hopefully, after this, it will be the last time, sir," grunted Heather.

The door opened a couple of moments later, and Michael shot the first raptor, causing a roadblock to those behind as the chief fired the flare at the containers. The flare sped across the room and hit the floor in front of the containers, ricocheting into them. The containers burst into flames and sprayed the raptors with flaming liquid. The feathers of the raptors in the first ranks burst into flames as those behind fell back. The chief closed the door as flaming liquid and smoke came their way.

They could hear the crackle of gunfire all around as the sounds reverberated off the back walls of the cleft. Michael saw a raptor jump the river to land and collapse at the river's edge, then slide back into the river.

"Not going to be healthy in there for a bit," stated Heather.

"Is there a way to lock this?" asked Michael.

"Not to keep them in. The air-conditioning will take the toxins out in a few minutes," replied Heather.

"Then we'd best get out of here," said Michael, getting to his feet.

"Clinic?" asked Heather.

"I might have a better idea," said Michael.

"You have a plan?" asked Heather.

"The distillery has a back entrance," said Michael.

Heather's eyes lit up. "That would make a big fire."

"Yes, it would. Have any more flares?" said Michael.

"Two in my pocket. Hope we don't burn everything down. There might be people in the apartments above," replied Heather.

"Most of the structure is concrete and rebar. I'm more worried about the explosion, but it can't be helped," replied Michael.

"Let's do it," said Heather.

The two ran to the distillery's back entrance and found the door unlocked. There were quite a few barrels in the back that were kept there for Ezekiel to use to refill bottles as they emptied and a wall with filled bottles of wine and other spirits all bottled.

"Looks like there's enough here to make a fairly big fire. It'll be a shame to set it off though," stated Heather.

"Can't be helped. Chief, go up front and check to see if we can get out the front. I'll stay here and draw the attention of the raptors when they come out of the comm suite," Michael said.

Heather nodded and went to the front and checked the door. When she tried the handle, it opened and called back saying so. Michael heard her moving things around in the front of the shop as he watched the comm suite door. A couple of minutes later, the chief returned, handing Michael a Navarro M-71 as she opened a musette bag.

"Where did you find those?" asked Michael as he watched Heather heft another M-71 off her shoulder.

"This place is pretty much owned and run by Marines, sir," replied Heather.

Michael shook his head. It figures that the master sergeant and his Marines would have firearms stashed in a place they controlled. Heather reached into the bag and gave Michael two spare magazines for the Navarro, three magazines for his Gerst, and four grenades.

"Were they planning on starting a war?" asked Michael.

Heather shrugged. "It sounds like there's a battle going on out front. Let's hope we're not trapped."

Michael watched the comm suite door for a moment, then looked at the chief. "Do you know how to rig a grenade?"

"For a trap? I might." Heather chuckled.

"Show me," said Michael.

The chief set the trap up for Michael, and when she was nearly finished, Michael stopped her. "The back door to the clinic is probably open."

Heather thought about it for a second. "You're probably right."

"Give me the flare gun, then take the musette bag and check. If it's not locked, stay there. I'll take care of this," said Michael.

"If you distract them here, you may not get out the front door," stated Heather uncomfortably.

"I'll have to take that chance. Someone needs to make sure they come here, and someone needs to watch the back door of the clinic," replied Michael.

Heather nodded. Michael made sure she reached the back door of the clinic and went inside, then he waited for the comm suite door to open. It didn't take long. Raptors started swarming out of the comm suite, and Michael started firing. Five of them fell, but two got back up as the rest of the raptors moved toward Michael. He closed the door and locked it, then finished the connection for the trap.

Walking to the front of the distillery, he opened the front door a crack.

A javelin thudded into the wooden frame. Michael closed the door again and looked around. He had a bad feeling that the back room of the distillery had a stash of munitions also and that once the trap was sprung, it wouldn't be too healthy to be inside the distillery. Since going out the front door didn't seem possible, he needed a plan, and there didn't seem to be many options. There were some casks along one wall, bottles lined the back wall and the counter, and stills lined the other wall.

Michael went over to the casks. Most were too small, and the large ones were full. He went over to the far wall where there were four small stills and two larger ones. Lifting the lid of one of the large stills, he looked inside to discover it empty and clean, and the interior looked large enough. He set the Navarro M-71 inside first, then started climbing in. He had just squeezed inside and pulled the lid back on when the whole world went to hell.

The explosion and fireball swept through the front of the distillery, setting fire to the wooden casks. Bottles shattered and added to the flames as the front door was blown out of its frame and into the river. Michael almost lost his tenuous hold of the lid as flames scorched his fingers and the hair on his head when the lid shifted slightly for a moment. Something banged against the side of the still and set his ears to ringing.

Michael stayed in the still for several minutes, and it started to get warm. When he heard the sound of M-71s, he raised the lid and looked out. The back wall of the room was aflame, along with the casks across the room. The counter, too, had flames on it, and there was a river of flame coming from the back room to cross the floor to the drain in the middle.

He crawled into the heat quickly and reached inside the still, grabbing the M-71. Then he ran outside where he collided with Maria DiAngelo as she stood eyeing the two red raptors prone to the ground at the door of the clinic.

CHAPTER 84

Hiroka Tamura watched Chopper 2 land near the two remaining cleft prefabs. She had been practicing with her katana when she had heard the explosion of the minefields and ran to the edge of the cleft. She had watched as Chopper 2 had been loaded with someone and return. Dr. Bess Hollinger with several other colonists were already running toward the landing area with a stretcher as Chopper 2 rose and headed toward the cleft.

When the chopper arrived, Hiroka, Rachel, and Qu'Loo'Oh' approached and helped Sergeant Tadashi Adachi from the copilot side and into the stretcher, taking him to the clinic. He had lost consciousness on the way back to the cleft and had fortunately remained that way through the whole experience. Hiroka was sure the pain of the embedded rotor through his shoulder was excruciating. The bandages around the wound were soaked with blood, but the doctor assured them he still lived.

The pilot, Chief Warrant Officer Brad Guillete, jumped out of the chopper and grabbed the ammunition cases from Staff Sergeant Amanda Hall, who went back to the storage area beside the MILDET prefab to grab more. Hiroka leaned her katana against the gunship and followed Amanda, taking a case containing rockets. She went back to the gunship where Brad had placed his load by his wife, Rachel. Rachel assisted him in removing the minigun ammo case in the port side, then started handing him rockets after Hiroka set them down and went back for another load. When she returned, she assisted Amanda with loading the miniguns and rocket launchers on the starboard side of the gunship.

"What happened?" asked Hiroka fearfully.

"When the minefields were activated, they blew up, and the fence was also rigged with explosives and is mostly gone. Chopper 1 is scrap, which is how Tadashi was hurt. The ATVs are bringing the second lieutenant who was piloting back," said Amanda grimly.

A silence fell between the two of them as Hiroka assimilated what Amanda had relayed. The defenses were gone. The only thing standing between the cleft and the army of raptors were the three ATVs, Chopper 2, and the Marine Complex. Then she saw the shuttle rising in the distance and knew that the colony was without power except in essential areas on an emergency generator.

"Can we hold out?" asked Hiroka.

"There aren't enough rounds or rockets in the cleft to take out that army," stated Amanda. "We need a miracle."

There was a problem with the port rocket launcher, and Brad Guillete crawled under the gunship. Rachel took the tool kit from the back of the gunship and handed him the tools he requested as he lay on his back. They were still working when Amanda and Hiroka finished loading the miniguns and starboard rocket launcher. Chief Warrant Officer Rachel Guillete looked at Staff Sergeant Hall as she placed a screwdriver into the hand that appeared from under the gunship.

"Amanda, Brad needs a gunner," said Rachel.

Staff Sergeant Hall looked at Rachel in her maternity outfit and said, "I can do that, ma'am."

"Take over here. I'm going to take Qu'Loo'Oh' and Hiroka to the clinic and see if we can help there," said Rachel.

"Roger that, ma'am," affirmed Amanda.

"Brad," said Rachel loudly.

A hand appeared from underneath the gunship, giving a thumbs-up. Amanda helped Rachel to her feet. Rachel and Hiroka then went to the side of the gunship where Qu'Loo'Oh' stood. Hiroka picked up her katana that she had been practicing with prior to the gunship's arrival. They went in through the clinic's back entrance and walked up to the reception area through the recovery ward. Qu'Loo'Oh' took the padded nest that had been installed for her in a corner of the reception area. The two women went over to the day-care and nursery entrance.

"Will you be all right, Qu'Loo'Oh'?" asked Rachel.

"Nap time," stated Qu'Loo'Oh' in reply.

"You go help with the day care, Rachel. I will stay with Qu'Loo'Oh'," said Hiroka.

"She should be all right," replied Rachel.

"With what's going on, I think someone should be with her," said Hiroka, glancing at the front door where a frightened woman entered with a child and shrank back in fear from the raptor.

Hiroka waved her through and attempted to reassure her, but the woman shied back, hugging her child to her breast. She hurriedly entered the day-care and nursery area, moving to its far side as Hiroka watched. Rachel Guillete moved over to her and said something, but she shook her head and hugged her child closer. The cries of the children were loud, which made matters difficult for the caregivers since it tended to cause a chain reaction of the same among the other children.

There was the crack of a Navarro M-71 outside the clinic's entrance, and Hiroka went to the door. It happened again somewhere above her, but her attention was drawn to the other side of the river near the back of the cleft. Hiroka's eyes grew wide as she saw red raptors withdraw behind the edge of the building on the east side of the river. A raptor appeared running and jumped. The raptor would have made it if the shooter above Hiroka had not taken it at the apex of its jump. The raptor collapsed when it came down on the west bank's edge and fell back into the river to float downstream toward the waterfall.

The sounds of gunfire came from downstream, and she glanced briefly in that direction to see raptors attacking a hastily made barricade at the end of the bridge. There were javelins flying through the air and people lying on the boardwalk. The defenders were firing on the raptors, but it seemed as if most of the fire missed. She saw Ezekiel pull Tom Tollifer out of sight as another flight of javelins seemed to fill the air. She saw no one coming down the street toward the clinic, and it appeared that such a move would be decidedly unhealthy to do so at this time.

A javelin appeared in the door before her, and Hiroka pulled back. Hiroka closed the door until there was only a crack left to peer through as another javelin sank into the door. There were flashes of red on the rooftop across the river, and Hiroka closed the door the rest of the way. She then walked back to Qu'Loo'Oh' and picked up her katana. The dozing raptor opened an eye and watched her.

"Not good," said Qu'Loo'Oh'.

Hiroka was confused momentarily before she understood.

"Not good," she agreed.

Four people appeared through the doors of the recovery ward. Two of them were helping the third who had a reddening bandage wrapped around her leg.

"What happened?" asked Hiroka as Rachel appeared at the day-care door.

"They're coming through the comm suite," responded Barbara Gabrielson.

"Did you lock the back door of the clinic?" asked Rachel.

"No. Lieutenant Commander Anderson and Chief Tate were setting a trap in the comm suite and said they'd be right behind us," said Timothy Powell.

"Someone needs to watch the back door," stated Rachel as she went to the door leading back down the hallway.

"I'll do it," declared Barbara as she pulled her Gerst S-7 from her holster.

"I'll go with her," said Timothy Powell.

"Are you armed?" asked Rachel.

"Chief Tate gave me her Gerst," said Timothy Powell, showing her the sidearm as he turned to follow Barbara.

"Good luck," said Rachel.

There was the muffled sound of an explosion as the two went down the hall. A couple of minutes later, a much-larger one sounded outside the clinic, seeming to shake its walls. A short time later, an explosion sounded down the hallway then the crackle of gunfire.

Jacqueline Vinet came out of the emergency ward looking confused, wearing an apron covered with blood. "What's going on?" asked Jacqueline as Rachel walked over to the recovery ward door and peeked down the hall.

"Firefight," said Rachel.

There was a sound at the front door of the clinic, and Rachel turned and raised her Gerst S-7. When the door opened, a red raptor ran into the clinic toward Jacqueline as Rachel fired three times. Jacqueline fell as the raptor collided and collapsed on top of her. Another raptor appeared and ran toward the day care to be met by Qu'Loo'Oh' as she tore out its neck. Rachel started firing at the doorway until her Gerst locked back.

Hiroka watched in horror for those first few seconds, then something came over her. A warmth seemed to grow and radiate in her forehead. Then a calm pervaded her thoughts as though something had taken control. She unsheathed her katana and struck at the next raptor through the door as it came toward her, decapitating it. Leaping over the body as it fell, she struck at the next raptor, removing its right forelimb and its left foot with the return stroke, causing it to collapse on the floor as she jumped back to avoid its jaws.

Two more raptors entered the door and went around each side of their injured comrade to approach Hiroka. The one on her left jabbed at her with a javelin, which she cut in half, along with taking the beast's right hand. The stoke carried through to slice through the neck of the raptor on her right as she turned. Finishing her turn, she drove the point of her katana between the teeth of the raptor to her left and deep into its brain as the one on her right dropped, its lifeblood pulsing out onto the floor.

With a quick jerk, she withdrew the sword and jumped over the snapping jaws of the raptor still struggling on the floor. Twisting, she drove the katana deep into its chest, ceasing its struggles. She withdrew her sword and sliced through the neck of the raptor, moving on her right after coming through the door. The raptors moving to her left backed against the wall as Hiroka came to a stance with the katana above her head parallel to the floor. The two to the left of the door were against the wall and hissed at her, while the remaining one on her right stood looking at Qu'Loo'Oh', who stood before it. Francesca stood behind Qu'Loo'Oh' in the doorway of the day care with a chair raised in her hands. The raptor looked at Qu'Loo'Oh' and spoke in the Ques'Coat'L' language.

"Qu'Loo'Oh', what do here?" asked the raptor.

"I learn. I will not let you hurt these intruders or their younglings, Qu'Fal'Ral'," stated Qu'Loo'Oh'.

"You are outcast. Your life is forfeit," stated Qu'Fal'Ral'.

"My eggling, your life is forfeit if you do not submit," stated Qu'Loo'Oh', indicating Hiroka.

The raptor, who was obviously a male from the bright-scarlet plumage, raised its crest and lowered it as he looked at Hiroka. There was a look of fear in his eyes as they slid from Hiroka to the two raptors against the wall who remained motionless, hissing at the demon standing there with a bright metal weapon dripping with raptor blood. Two other raptors stood hissing in the doorway, refusing to come in. The small one with hair as dark as night had driven a fear into their hearts. Defeated, Qu'Fal'Ral' lowered his body to the floor and submitted to Hiroka Tamura as his followers did the same.

CHAPTER 85

Commander Hadden Blankenship stood on the edge of the cleft. He watched as the ATVs arrived at the downed chopper and forced the retreat of the raptors. One of the downed choppers' crew was brought out of Chopper 1 and loaded into Chopper 2, which almost immediately took off, heading toward the cleft. The other member of Chopper 1's crew embraced one of the rescuers, and Hadden knew that the member coming his way was Sergeant Adachi. Suddenly, the ground inside the perimeter fence seemed to lift into the air all along the fence line. Most of the fence line fell, and those gathered around the ATVs fell to the ground. Hadden heard an explosion and looked down knowing it was too early to hear the explosions from the outer perimeter fence. The inner fence and its minefield were experiencing the same fate as the outer fence.

"What happened?" whispered Staff Sergeant Amanda Hall standing beside the commander.

"Hiran," ventured Hadden lowly.

"What do we do?" asked Amanda.

He felt a dread build within him. The raptors were organized, and there wasn't enough weapons or ammunition to stop the oncoming horde. He stood there overwhelmed for a second, then shook off the feeling. They were still alive, and he wasn't ready to admit defeat yet!

"You help Chief Warrant Officer Guillete. He will need help with the injured and reloading the weapons on the gunship," ordered Commander Blankenship as he lowered the electronic binoculars.

Looking out over the forest to the southwest, he saw red smoke rising above the tree line. The commander ran to the prefab to don his body armor and grab his Navarro M-71. He ran to the elevators where people were gathering and took control of the situation, ordering people to arm themselves and meet him at the base of the elevators as he started down.

A cloud appeared behind the Marine Complex with the sound of its explosion, following slightly behind as the elevator started down. The commander saw two figures at the head of the pier fall to the ground, and the shuttle at the end of the pier rocked. Then the commander lost sight as the foundry blocked his view. *Longboat 4* rounded the foundry as he was reaching the base and started down the street between the foundry and lumber mill as Commander Hadden Blankenship watched in astonishment. The commander switched to channel 3 as the longboat approached.

"Longboat 4. New Horizon Actual. Over," said the commander.

"New Horizon Actual. Longboat 4. I read you. Over," came Lieutenant JG Dominic Sobolov's voice.

"Mr. Sobolov, exactly what the hell are you doing?" said the commander, breaking protocol.

"The master sergeant suggested placing the longboat near the elevator with its tail pointing down the street," replied Dominic's voice.

The commander saw the plan immediately and said, "You need to anchor down when you're here."

"I will use the anchor cables, but I do not think it will be enough if I engage the Benson drive," returned Dominic's voice.

The commander agreed with that assessment and looked around. His gaze fell on the two loaders and noted that they were still full of ore. An idea formed as he reached the base of the elevator, and he shouted, "Ms. Felter!"

Agnes Felter came up and looked at the commander.

"I need those two ore haulers over here on each side of the longboat once it's anchored down," ordered Commander Blankenship.

"Those ore haulers belong to the foundry, not the Navy," replied Felter.

"I don't care! Do you want to live through this or argue about property rights? Now get some people in those trucks and get them over here!" retorted Hadden.

"I'm the president of the colony, Commander," shouted Felter.

"With all due respect, Ms. President, you're only acting president, and I don't give a damn," replied Hadden.

"You need to do as I say!" Agnes Felter shouted.

"No, I don't, because I'm declaring martial law, and everyone here now works for me. We will remain under martial law until this emergency is over. Now shut up and soldier," stated Hadden heatedly.

"But we need to evacuate to the cleft!" shouted Agnes.

Hadden Blankenship looked with disgust at her and said slowly, "Almost every Marine we have are in those ATVs. We need to hold the base of the elevators until they return. Now get those haulers over here and get them strapped to the longboat as Lieutenant Sobolov tells you to do, then man the wall, or I'll give you to the raptors myself."

In the distance, he could hear the rattle of miniguns and the bursts of rockets from the direction of the Marine Complex. He ran to the east side of the foundry near the lake and watched as the shuttle started its takeoff and the sounds of the defense armaments died down from the Marine Complex. Hopefully, the generator they had installed to power the comm suite, clinic, and other essentials could handle the load until this was over and a longboat or shuttle could be brought back to supply power.

Something moved at the end of the pier, and Blankenship raised his electronic binoculars to peer at the lone figure holding a Vinter HR-19 sniper rifle. The sounds of the Vinter resounded off the cliffs as he watched, and someone nearby told him to turn to channel 7. The commander watched grimly and said nothing as he listened and bore witness to the last stand of one of his oldest friends, Master Sergeant Evan Zander, as the shuttle rose into the heavens in the distance.

Hadden returned to the base of the elevator where Dominic Sobolov was shouting orders to the haulers as cables were attached and anchor lines sunk into the ground from the cleats around the tires. Finished, the men around the haulers ducked inside the vehicles and closed the doors. Dominic closed the hatch to *Longboat 4* as the miniguns on the haulers came to life, pointing down the street. Blankenship saw Dominic at the pilot seat of the longboat and turned his personal communicator to channel 3.

"Mr. Sobolov, wait till I give the signal," said Blankenship as he walked the west side of the walled enclosure, looking for the ATVs to round the far end of the lumber mill near the concrete and stone works.

"Dah, Commander, that is the plan," returned Dominic.

A raptor appeared around the edge of the foundry, and the miniguns on the haulers tore it to pieces.

"What's the channel the haulers are on?" asked Hadden.

"Channel 6," came a voice from behind.

Changing channels, Blankenship called, "Haulers, this is Commander Blankenship."

"Hauler 1. What do you need?" came the reply.

"I need you and Hauler 2 to save those miniguns until I tell you. Let the people on the wall handle this until then," ordered Hadden.

"You sure?" came the voice from Hauler 1.

"Do you think you have enough rounds to take out the whole war party?" asked Hadden.

There was an extended pause, then "No."

"Then save your rounds until I tell you," ordered Hadden.

"Yes, sir," came the voice from Hauler 1.

"Hauler 2?" queried Hadden.

"Hauler 2. Yes, sir," came the response.

Raptors started appearing around the end of the foundry and were picked off by those holding Vinter HR-19s. Another group came around the edge of the lumber mill and were dealt with likewise. The horde could be seen advancing slowly with great beasts towing trebuchets, catapults, and other heavy equipment. Some had stopped and were firing on the Marine Complex, whose armaments had grown silent. Hadden looked around and saw Lieutenant JG Vanda Kisimba.

"Lieutenant Kisimba!" shouted Commander Blankenship.

"Yes, sir," called Vanda.

"You're my second. If something happens to me, take over. We hold this position. Do you understand?" said Hadden.

"Yes, sir," snapped Vanda.

Haddden Blankenship looked back to the east and at the roof of the foundry behind the longboat. He saw movement up there, and suddenly, a rain of javelins was descending on the defenders on the far side of the elevators. Several defenders fell, while others took cover or attempted to help the fallen. There were more than a dozen people lying on the pavement and several more who had javelins piercing their bodies as they lay against the wall.

Three of the defenders with grenade launchers on their Navarro M-71s started dropping grenades on the roof of the foundry. There were explosions, and Blankenship saw raptors tossed in the air as the grenadiers sent another volley to the roof. There were more explosions, and red feathers flew. Suddenly, the bottom of the north wall of the foundry pushed forward from a force inside, and the whole wall collapsed, taking the roof with it. Flames shot up with the coal dust that filled the air. The defenders along the wall near the foundry hit the deck as flames passed over them. A seeming wave of flame mixed with dust washed over the longboat toward them and down the street, obscuring everyone's vision.

"What the hell happened?" shouted Diego Quintana.

"Coal dust," replied Hadden.

"You've damaged the foundry!" screamed Agnes Felter.

"Ms. Felter, what do you think is going to happen to the sides of the foundry and lumber mill when Mr. Sobolov lights up the Benson drive?" asked Hadden.

The commander received a blank look in response and wondered how the woman standing in front of him ever made lieutenant. He was beginning to see why Brad Guillete had requested a transfer to the Marines when Hadden offered him a commission to chief warrant officer.

"Man the wall and soldier," growled Hadden at the still befuddled look on Agnes's face.

The sound of miniguns came from the west, and Hadden looked to see the ATVs at the end of the lumber mill near the concrete and stone works. Some raptors appeared on the roof of the lumber mill, but after the foundry, the riflemen were prepared for that move, and only two javelins found their marks as the M-71s swept the roof. Suddenly, Gunship 2 appeared above. The roof of the lumber mill only contained the bodies of dead raptors as the miniguns swept it of opposition. The gunship moved to take position above the ATVs as they appeared to the west. The gunship started lowering boxes to the ATVs as it stood guard over them.

Hadden switched to channel 5. "Mr. and Mrs. Raybourn, are you still with us?"

"We are, sir," came Second Lieutenant Shiran Raybourn's response.

"How's it look?" asked Hadden.

"There's still a lot of raptors out there, sir. I don't know if we can stop them all," said Shiran.

The raptors were congregating at the end of the street near the Marine Complex. Some of the raptors' heavy equipment were already battering away at the walls and roof of the structure, while other equipment were being brought forward to attack the defenders at the elevators. Some of that equipment were already pounding away at the foundry and lumber mill.

Blankenship touched his personal comm. "Mr. Sobolov."

"Dah, sir," replied Dominic.

"Do you have an uplink to the *New Horizon*?" asked Hadden.

"Yes, sir," returned Dominic.

"Relay to the *New Horizon* that *New Horizon Actual* requires the longboats down here yesterday. Firestorm on my confirmation," said Blankenship.

There were two longboats still on the *New Horizon*, and they had been equipped to perform a napalm bombing run. Hadden still hoped to avoid utilizing that option, but he suspected that the raptors would leave him no choice. What would determine that was whether the master sergeant's audacious plan of using the Benson drive worked and convinced the raptors that this conflict was not worth the losses. As Hadden thought about the situation, there was a commotion on the other side of the elevators as someone yelled, "What the hell!"

A dead raptor's body was being pushed off one of the defenders. Private Vivian Caylor was still alive as Corporal Anya Kaur dragged her over to the cover of the wall. Her leg was definitely broken, and there was a nasty cut in her scalp that was bleeding profusely. Hadden could hear the crackle of gunfire above him. Looking up, Hadden watched as another raptor fell from the cleft to make a long descent down to an abrupt end. Then a person came over the edge, making the long fall skewered by three javelins to come to rest just as fast. Hadden recognized Stefanie Lanier as someone turned her over. The feeling of dread and helplessness reappeared as Hadden realized what the disappearance of the vanished raptors implied. They vanished into the caves!

"Kisimba, I need twenty people up that elevator now!" yelled Blankenship.

"Aye, aye, sir," Vanda confirmed.

She grabbed nineteen of the nearest people not carrying Vinter HR-19s and pushed them toward the elevators. Then looking around, she yelled at Ensign Edward Black and told him to take charge of the party going up. Looking back over her shoulder, a calm look settled on Vanda's face as she pointed down the street, directing Hadden's attention to the now advancing horde. Hadden gave orders to target those well in advance of the oncoming army. A firefight broke out on the east end of the wall, and Hadden ordered the hauler on that side to assist as raptors came around the east side of the foundry. The crackle of M-71s could be heard overhead as the elevator of reinforcements reached the top.

Hadden watched as the raptors started entering the far end of the passage between the foundry and lumber mill. He ordered his riflemen to start firing to keep them back. Bodies piled up as the raptors continued their advance, some hurling javelins at the tail end of the longboat. Hadden ordered the haulers to fire on large groups when opportunity arose. The sound of gunfire filled the air, and raptors fell like wheat to a scythe to be replaced by more. An explosion sounded above Hadden's head as the elevator reached the top, and he feared the elevator would come back with all its passengers. The cart and its passengers swayed briefly, then the defenders got off. Hadden returned his attention to the street where the trebuchets had stopped and were being set up as the raptors started loading the slings.

Hadden touched his comm and yelled, "Now, Mr. Sobolov!"

If there was a response on the communicator from Lieutenant JG Sobolov, it was drowned out by the gunfire around Hadden. Then hellfire slowly erupted from the nozzles of *Longboat 4* as Dominic Sobolov brought the drive online, testing the anchoring lines as he gently increased power. The longboat's stern skittered slightly to port, and the whole wall of the lumber mill went up in flames. An anchor line to the starboard side hauler gave way, and Dominic touched the dorsal thrusters to bring that side down. Then the longboat's tail moved to starboard, and the foundry wall vanished along the street. The wall melted away or was turned to smoke in the blue flame coming from the longboat's engines. During that brief time, the raptors and heavy equipment that had been visible had disappeared in the maelstrom that had swept over them.

Hadden informed Dominic to cut power as the smell of burnt feathers and tantalizing aroma of cooked chicken wafted in the air. The ground further down along the street was a molten pool and, beyond, a blackened wasteland. What was left of the lumber mill and foundry was a smoking ruin. Even the distant Marine Complex looked scorched. At least a quarter of the raptor army had been obliterated in those few seconds the Benson drive had been engaged to unleash the flame of stars upon the land.

Hadden's jaw set grimly as he looked upon the destruction he had wrought. The dead out on the field must number in the thousands, but he had been given no choice. His eyes swept the ranks of the colonists. There were over two dozen bodies that had been dragged back out of the way and others who leaned against the shielding wall. How many of the injured would survive was unknown. The fight between raptor and human needed to end.

Near him, someone yelled, "Look!"

Hadden directed his attention to where the individual was pointing. Far above where the waterfall started was in flames. He knew a moment's confusion, then realized what the explosion from the cleft had been. The river between the distillery and waterfall must be on fire as the alcohol draining into the river flowed downstream.

Hadden's radio called for his attention. "*New Horizon Actual. Longboat 2.* We're three minutes away. Over."

"*Longboat 2. New Horizon Actual.* I want you to create a wall of fire between the Marine Complex and the ATVs. Attempt to avoid casualties on either side. Over," replied Hadden.

"*New Horizon Actual. Longboat 2.* You want a wall of flame between the Marine Complex and the ATVs with no casualties on either side. Over," repeated the voice from *Longboat 2.*

"*Longboat 2. New Horizon Actual.* Roger that. Over," said Hadden.

"*New Horizon Actual. Longboat 2.* Two minutes. Over," replied the voice from *Longboat 2.*

"*Longboat 2. New Horizon Actual.* Roger. Out," returned Hadden.

The wait seemed to last forever, then suddenly, two longboats streaked in from the west. Just before they reached the ATVs, dark objects left the under chassis and came to life, streaking to their target, the blackened ground. A wall of flame erupted between the ATVs and the Marine Complex as the napalm formed a flickering barrier between the elevators and the raptor army beyond. The two longboats were lost in the distance as they went to make their turn on the other side of the lake and return.

CHAPTER 86

The overturned ATV bounced up and down on its suspension system as it landed upright. It took a minute for the people inside to resume contact with a comment about milkshakes causing the delay. Conor shot a three-round burst out of his viewport as he watched the now upright ATV finally start moving. When the raptors had pulled back, Shiran had ordered a check of the miniguns and ordered ATV 2 to deplete on targets of opportunity, then switch boxes while the other two ATVs provided support through their ports. She wanted them to save the miniguns for the fight back to the elevators.

Not wanting to chance becoming entangled in the downed fence lines, they headed to the gate, which still stood and was open. Raptors and their heavy equipment were entering the Compound through the gate, which still had fencing upright on both sides. The fight was short, and the raptors retreated as the ATVs rammed through their ranks while spitting death and destruction around them. The miniguns targeted groupings of raptors as the crew fired bursts from their own weapons out the gunports.

Javelins rained down on the ATVs, and a few entered the armored interiors through the gunports. Private Darcy died instantly with a javelin entering his right eye, piercing his brain. Another took Corporal Cuevas in the neck, covering much of the interior of the ATV in blood before he died. Corporal Green received a javelin through his thigh, which he bound in a tourniquet to stop the blood before returning to his gunport to fight on. There were other injuries not as severe, like the gash that ran over ten centimeters down Conor Raybourn's left arm. Shiran Raybourn bound it quickly in a bandage and tape before both returned to their gunports. By the time they reached the west side of the lumber mill, the bandage was soaked in blood, which dripped as he closed the gunport and changed magazines.

It seemed like he had been firing his Navarro M-71 for hours, but in actuality, it could not have been longer than fifteen to twenty minutes. They forced the raptors back from the west end of the lumber mill and away from the concrete and stone works. There was a lull as the raptors congregated in a wide arc around the ATVs, starting near the outer fence and ending near the inner fence by the lumber mill. They appeared to pull back slightly as Chopper 2 arrived overhead.

The chopper unleashed rockets against the raptors' heavy equipment and destroyed five pieces as it moved forward, then cut loose with miniguns at another piece. The chopper shifted its attention to what appeared to be a large battering ram being pulled by a triceratops. The raptors fled back from the ATVs as Brad shot it with another rocket. The gunship came back and hovered above the ATVs, lowering a line that had an ammo case attached. Marines jumped out of the backs of the ATVs to grab the case as it touched the grass. Overhead, Staff Sergeant Hall hit the release and reeled the cable back up to the gunship so she could attach it to the other one sitting in the back seat. The second case was lowered, and the ammo was distributed to the ATVs posthaste as the raptors started moving toward the ATVs again.

"Gunship 2. ATV 1. Over," called Shiran.

"ATV 1. Gunship 2. I read you. Over," came Brad's reply.

"Gunship 2. ATV 1. Thanks for the resupply. What's going on out there? Over," said Shiran.

"ATV 1. Gunship 2. The commander is holding them back from the elevators, but they will be moving forward soon. There's a lot of raptors out there," came the reply.

"Gunship 2. ATV 1. Keep your eyes open for targets of opportunity. Out," said Shiran.

"ATV 1. Gunship 2. Roger that. Out."

Conor saw a raptor fall from the edge by the elevators, and after another moment, another fell. A couple of minutes later, an elevator containing over a dozen armed people rose to the top. When it reached the top, it rocked slightly as though pushed by a strong breeze. Conor frowned. It would take a hurricane to make the elevator rock like that. A couple of minutes later, he saw smoke creeping along the roof of the cleft and rising to the heights as it reached the edge. Something had exploded on the cleft.

Suddenly, the fires of hell poured out of the street between the foundry and lumber mill. The east end of the lumber mill vanished as clouds of white smoke rose into the air. A moment later, the flame shifted to the east, and the west side of the foundry collapsed. The blue flame reached out, laying waste to a large portion of where the raptor army had once stood. The flame didn't reach the Marine Complex, but in the brief time, it blackened the whole north side of the complex. The blue flame vanished after only a few seconds, but the devastation it had caused made all the Marines in ATV 1 gasp in shock.

Beyond the collapsed buildings, the ground was scorched black for nearly two hundred meters, with smoking corpses lying on top of brown and wilted vegetation beyond the black zone. There were flaming figures running then finally collapsing to the ground while the raptors' wooden machines blazed like funeral torches. The raptor army was drawing back from the carnage that had happened in a few brief seconds. Further out where the army had only felt the heat but still stood, some of the great beasts had broken loose of their bonds and were rampaging through the horde away from the devastated inner Compound. Others struggled against their bonds and were brought down by their captors.

Conor's face grew grim. There were a lot of dead out there. Would the raptors capitulate or continue their attack? The remaining horde still represented a significant threat, and it was doubtful that the longboat maneuver that had worked once would work again. Conor looked over at Shiran and could tell her thoughts must be similar to his. Conor was monitoring channel 3 when he heard Commander Blankenship order firestorm.

"Second Lieutenant, the commander just ordered firestorm. Two minutes," said Conor.

Shiran nodded acknowledgment to Conor, who relayed the confirmation back as she called Gunship 2. "Gunship 2. ATV 1. Firestorm in two minutes. Land now. Over."

"ATV 1. Gunship 2. Roger that. Out," came CWO Guillete's reply.

The gunship landed in the middle of the ATVs, and after a short wait, *Longboats 2* and *3* streaked through the air low and headed east. A wall of flame erupted between the raptor army and where the flattened inner Compound fence was. The flames lashed about wildly, and dust obscured their vision as the turbulence of the longboats' passage swept through the area. The dust settled slowly, and as it did, Conor could see that the raptor army had withdrawn another half a kilometer. The wind shifted, and the smell of napalm entered the gunports of the ATV. The ports were closed as the ATV crew went into a fit of coughing until the air filtration system cleared the interior.

A few moments later, Conor saw the two longboats coming back across the lake in formation low. They swept directly over the top of the raptor army, causing items to rise into the air and more dust to obscure Conor's view of the army. The sound of a sonic boom filled the air as the longboats went ballistic over the plain beyond. They rose skyward on blue pillars of flame to disappear somewhere above the clouds. When Conor looked out, most of the raptor army had their snouts pointed skyward, their jaws agape.

"Gunship 2. ATV 1. Give us overhead vantage. Over," ordered Shiran.

"ATV 1. Gunship 2. Roger that. Out," came the reply as Shiran and Conor turned on the built-in screens in front of them.

Most of the horde was still looking skyward, but some were stealing glances at the wall of flames and ATVs. Something had changed. The army did not retreat, but neither did they advance. The Marines in the ATVs remained watchful and anxious as the wall of flames burned lower from a lack of material to burn. Time passed, and the raptor army remained motionless. Gunship 2 reported that there was some movement inside the horde, but it was negligible.

The commander contacted ATV 1 and requested Shiran to send one ATV to the elevators. Shiran looked at Conor.

"Tell him it will be a couple of minutes. I want to send ATV 3 with wounded and dead," said Shiran

Conor nodded and relayed that information as Shiran had the two dead placed in ATV 3 with Steven Green, who had taken the javelin through the leg. The other Marines, with the exception of the driver, were redistributed in the other ATVs as ATV 3 departed. It took nearly an hour for the ATV to return with a refrigerated trailer in tow. Commander Blankenship stepped out of the vehicle with Jacqueline Vinet. They both wore body armor and even Jacqueline carried a Navarro M-71. Conor left ATV 1 and approached the group, eyeing the trailer.

"Good afternoon, sir," greeted Conor as he saluted.

"Good afternoon, Mr. Raybourn. Give me a hand with the trailer," said Commander Blankenship.

"What's the plan, sir?" asked Conor.

"Hopefully, peace negotiations," said Hadden.

Conor was puzzled but walked to the back of the trailer and assisted Hadden with opening its doors. Francesca and Jacqueline came over as the two men worked the locking bars, and Conor wondered what was going on. The doors opened, and inside stood two raptors, causing Conor to go for his sidearm. He felt the commander's hand on his arm before he pulled, then he recognized Qu'Loo'Oh' standing beside a bright-red raptor inside.

"What's going on, sir?" asked Conor apprehensively.

"Prisoner. Highborn and son of Qu'Loo'Oh'. The cleft was attacked through the caves," stated Blankenship grimly.

Conor thought about that for a moment. "Bad?"

"There are quite a few who are severely injured or dead. The remaining raptors are at the base of the elevator with Hiroka under guard," said Hadden.

"Where's Rachel Guillete?" asked Conor.

"In labor." Hadden smiled.

Conor nodded. The smoke that had poured out and rose upward along with the flames at the top of the waterfall had indicated that something was happening on the cleft, but he hadn't known exactly what. He looked at Hadden and the grim look on his face again and asked, "Hiroka?"

"She's fine. The raptors either respect or fear Hiroka. I'm not sure which. She will be bringing the raptors with Francesca when we're ready," replied Hadden distractedly, but Conor could tell something was wrong.

"Something's wrong. Who died?" said Conor.

"Master Sergeant Evan Zander was the first casualty of this war," said Commander Blankenship grimly, glancing at Conor then ATV 1.

Conor stood stunned. He respected Evan Zander and all he had done for him. He looked at ATV 1. Zander had been mentor to Shiran and most of the Marines, and his death would not go well with them. A moment of rage filled him as he looked at the raptor army, wishing to call back the longboats and lay waste to as much of the army as he could. He pushed the thoughts away knowing that would not bring the master sergeant back.

Conor had one more question. "How are we going to do this?"

"Let's hope Qu'Loo'Oh' and her son, with our interpreter's assistance, can end this," said Hadden as he motioned Qu'Loo'Oh' out of the trailer.

The raptor limped out of the trailer, and Conor noticed a line of fresh stitches lining the outside of her upper-left thigh. She stepped up to Conor and grasped his arm as she looked into his eyes. Her crest rose and fell on her head. "Hope," said Qu'Loo'Oh'.

Conor understood and nodded as the other raptor came out of the trailer slowly and stopped beside Qu'Loo'Oh'. The raptor said something that Conor did not understand, and Qu'Loo'Oh' replied. Conor gave Qu'Loo'Oh' a questioning look, and she explained that she had translated for her son what she had said to Conor.

The small group walked out into the field between the raptor army and the ATVs. Hadden and Conor assisted Qu'Loo'Oh' as her limp became more pronounced. When they reached a midpoint between the army and the ATVs, they stopped. Jacqueline Vinet held the three-meter rod with a white flag that displayed a black hieroglyph sketched on it and sank the end into the earth so it fluttered in the breeze as they waited. Francesca told Conor that the symbol translated as hope in the raptor language.

CHAPTER 87

They were there for nearly two hours before the ranks of the army nearest them parted, and a party of six bright-red raptors emerged. The six raptors approached the party of humans and raptors slowly. When they were still a hundred meters away, the commander looked at Qu'Loo'Oh' and said, "Now."

Qu'Loo'Oh' said something to her son, who started walking toward the raptors. The raptors stopped and waited for Qu'Fal'Ral' to meet them. He stopped near them, and they started to converse. It took nearly an hour. There was a lot of hissing, raised crests, lowered heads, snapping teeth, and other raptor gestures that indicated a variety of emotions.

Finally, one of the raptors who appeared more resplendent in its adornments than the others moved up beside Qu'Fal'Ral'. The raptor appeared older than most of the small group. There were patches of white feathers on its body, and individual white feathers sprinkled the red that covered the rest of its body. The raptor moved stiffly but proudly held itself erect. The two started walking toward the human party with Qu'Fal'Ral' slightly behind the leader, while the others followed about five meters behind.

When the lead two were within ten meters, the leader indicated for the party to stop. The leader looked over the humans for several minutes, then its attention centered on Qu'Loo'Oh'. Its crest lowered and raised, and it said something to Qu'Fal'Ral'.

"That one said it recognizes Qu'Loo'Oh' and that she is the mother of Qu'Fal'Ral' and that she is an outcast," said Francesca.

The leader swiveled its head to look at Francesca and chirped something. Francesca chirped something back, and its head lowered.

Then Jacqueline Vinet chirped something, and the leader looked at her also with its head still lowered. Conor began to wish he had been able to dedicate more time to learning the raptor language. The raptors behind the leader and Qu'Fal'Ral' were talking to each other quietly as all this was going on. They were obviously agitated that the humans before them could speak their language. He looked at Qu'Loo'Oh', who was standing still but holding her head high and in defiance. Conor decided to say a phrase he had been able to learn of the raptor language because Qu'Loo'Oh' said it to him often.

"Hope and peace," said Conor to the lead raptor in its language.

The lead raptor centered its attention on him. It raised its head and its crest high as it cocked its head to look at him from each eye. The raptors to the rear were silent as their leader studied Conor. The leader chirruped something at Conor, and he looked at the women questioningly.

"He asked if you are the leader," said Francesca.

Conor looked at the raptor leader and said no in the raptor language. He then indicated Commander Blankenship, who stepped forward to look the leader in the eye. They studied each other for nearly five minutes before the leader looked at Qu'Loo'Oh' and said something to her. She replied to the leader and said nothing more.

The leader raised itself up and recited what appeared to be a speech.

"He says his name is Qu'Ran'Tau' and the ruler of the Qua'Tol'Ec' nation, a nation that controls most of the eastern coast of the continent to the west of this sacred island," translated Francesca.

The ruler of the Qua'Tol'Ec nation lowered its head and body to the ground, placing its javelins and knife on the ground in front of itself as the other raptors of the party followed suit. Commander Blankenship looked at Qu'Loo'Oh' and the women questioningly.

"They submit," said Qu'Loo'Oh'.

"What does that mean?" asked Hadden.

"It means that they will do as you command the way I understand it," interjected Francesca.

"Lieutenant Commander, please tell the second lieutenant to send an ATV to bring my wife and the prisoners here for release," ordered Hadden, looking at Conor.

They waited for nearly an hour for the ATV to bring Hiroka and the raptor prisoners forward. Three of the raptors were in the trailer because of injuries while the other thirteen followed. Of over two-hundred-plus raptors that went through the caves and attacked the cleft, only seventeen survived the assault, with Qu'Fal'Ral' included in those remaining. Another three were inside the caverns and were told to retreat to the entrance they came through. The raptors stopped when the ATV came to a halt. Hiroka opened the door and walked back to the end of the trailer with her husband and Conor.

The prisoners crouched on the ground with lowered heads when Hiroka stopped and looked at them. Hadden and Conor looked at each other, wondering what Hiroka had done to make the raptors react in that manner. They opened the trailer doors, and the three raptors limped out and, upon seeing Hiroka, followed the example of their comrades.

Hiroka pointed at the army in the distance and said a single word in the raptor language, "Go."

The prisoners rose from the ground and moved slowly toward the waiting army, assisting their three injured companions. The three humans went back to the waiting party of humans and raptors. They saw the one named Qu'Fal'Ral' crouch to the ground and lower its head when Hiroka looked at him. The leader chirruped a question, and Qu'Fal'Ral' responded. Conor gave Francesca a questioning look.

"He says that the small one has a long metal knife and that he and his remaining warriors now know her as the Silvery Flower of Death," said Francesca.

"What happened?" asked Conor.

"She slayed five raptors in about as many seconds," replied Francesca. "The remaining raptors surrendered to her."

"How's Michael?" asked Conor as he wondered what happened on the cleft.

"A little scorched but alive," said Francesca. "He's directing the work of putting bodies in cold storage and assessing the damage."

"Scorched?" asked Conor.

"He was in the distillery when it caught fire and exploded," replied Francesca.

Conor blinked and said, "It's a wonder he's still alive."

"Michael and the people from the comm suite stopped a third of the raptors on the cleft," said Francesca. "Ezekiel and Tom rallied people to keep the other raptors back. They were both wounded, and there were a lot of good people lost defending the bridge until help arrived."

"It's a wonder any of us are still alive," said Conor.

The Marines set up a canopy, with a table and chairs underneath, for the leaders to negotiate. When they were finished, the six raptor leaders were motioned forward to stand in front of the table under the shade. The raptor called Qu'Fal'Ral' had been told by the leader Qu'Ran'Tau' to stay, and the young raptor stood off to the side under Marine guard. Qu'Loo'Oh' joined the colonists on the opposite side of the negotiating table as a translator with Francesca.

Introductions were made, and Commander Hadden Blankenship ordered the raptor leaders to have their army depart the island. Francesca and Jacqueline interceded by talking Hadden into allowing the raptors to have retainers and a crew for one ship during the negotiations. They also suggested that one of the raptor pavilions be erected south of the Marine Complex since the negotiations might take some time. The commander was not happy with the prospect of extended negotiations but agreed to the arrangement.

Using Qu'Fal'Ral' as a messenger, the bulk of the remaining army was soon moving south to depart the island. The negotiations took several weeks. At times, the translators needed time to discuss and determine what a word meant for both sides. Other times, it would take days for the colonists to make a decision on a point to be concluded. The acting president, Agnes Felter, refused to participate in any of the negotiations, though she demanded that all things discussed and to be resolved must be brought before the council for approval. This made both parties at the negotiating table irritated, and at times, it appeared the negotiations would break down.

One of the first things the Ques'Coat'L' or red raptors had asked was to be allowed to collect the dead to bury. The commander had agreed and assigned the Marines to assist using ATVs with trailers without consulting the president or the rest of the colonists. Hadden had taken the heat, but Bess Hollinger backed him in the matter, citing that the dead bodies represented a biological hazard with the diseases they might carry. The matter of assigning a raptor ambassador to the island was put forward. It took three days for them to agree to allow any red raptors to remain on the island after negotiations.

The colonists learned that Qu'Loo'Oh' was Qu'Ran'Tau's mate in disgrace, which meant that Qu'Fal'Ral' was highborn. The leader of the Qua'Tol'Ec' nation was not a hereditary position, and another from the Ta' clan was being groomed for that position. Qu'Fal'Ral' was being trained to be an ambassador for the various clans to represent the leader in his absence. It was proposed by a minor leader named Ta'Cav'Mir' that a new ambassador be chosen for the clans and that Qu'Fal'Ral' be chosen to build a pyramid mound here on the island for the fallen warriors and be trained by his mother in the human language, then take her position someday in the future. Conor felt that the proposal was meant as a slight to the current leader, but after a short pause, Qu'Ran'Tau' agreed.

The monument to the Ques'Coat'L' dead and the number of raptors to be allowed was a point of contention and took the rest of the week for all to agree. The colonists would only allow two hundred Ques'Coat'L' on the island at any time. Severe limits were imposed on the numbers of green raptors and great beasts they could utilize. It had taken the rest of the first week and most of Jacqueline Vinet's diplomatic skills to convince the colonists and Hadden Blankenship to agree to this arrangement.

After the first week, the Ques'Coat'L' nobles brought up the subject of what the humans desired in compensation of the vanquished Qua'Tol'Ec' nation. When clarification was requested, Qu'Loo'Oh' informed them that the whole of the Qua'Tol'Ec' nation were theirs to control. If they so choose, they could enslave the nation or simply demand tribute, either of which were the norm among the Ques'Coat'L'. Qu'Loo'Oh' explained this to the human negotiators and that they needed to make a decision on how they desired to proceed. The commander decided that he needed to talk to the acting president and her cabinet before continuing.

"We should seize the power over them!" stated Agnes Felter.

"Ma'am, that's not how the United Systems does business," said Hadden Blankenship.

"It most certainly is. We occupy territories all the time," replied Agnes.

"So you want to send an occupation force into a country encompassing the size of the eastern seaboard of North America?" asked Conor. "Where do you plan to find the troops to do that?"

"They submitted. They are ours to do with as we please," returned Agnes.

"I've talked to Qu'Loo'Oh' on this matter. Enslaving them works for a generation or two, then they rise up in revolt. Demanding tribute lasts longer but ends the same way as the later generations demand more of those paying the tribute and the payee becomes disgruntled," interjected Francesca.

"Then what do you propose?" demanded Agnes.

"Peace and hope," said Conor.

"What?" screamed Agnes. "People died!"

"On both sides," added Hadden quietly.

"We could kill them all," growled Wayne Wheaton.

"Yes, we could and continue the war," said Conor. "And next time, they might overrun us."

"We need peace between both our people," stated Jacqueline Vinet. "We can't occupy them, and this war needs to come to an end. Peace is our best chance."

"I'm the president! You have to do what I tell you!" shouted Agnes, glaring at Hadden.

"I have to obey legal orders. I will not bomb a people who have surrendered, and I will not enslave them," replied Hadden. "We do not have the manpower to occupy them. The only option is a peace treaty."

"I agree," said Conor.

"You're disobeying my orders?" demanded Agnes.

"I'm merely pointing out your options, Madam President," said Hadden.

"You agreed to bring these decisions up to the colony to vote on," added Jacqueline.

"This is my decision!" screamed Agnes.

"Then make it a good one," said Conor dispassionately.

"You don't tell me what to do!" shouted Agnes.

"Then what are your orders?" asked Hadden quietly.

"Fine! We'll put it up to the colony," snarled Agnes.

A meeting of the colony was held on the eighth night of the negotiations between humans and the Qua'Tol'Ec' leaders. Options on how to proceed were placed before the colonists. It took nearly three days before a vote was taken, and the consensus was for peace between the colonists and Qua'Tol'Ec' nation. A colonist then asked about an alliance between the colonists and Qua'Tol'Ec', but many didn't want to commit to an alliance that might result in the colony being dragged into a war. The offer of neutrality between Qua'Tol'Ec' and the various warring Ques'Coat'L' nations was the most any of the colonists would consider.

A colonist, who was soon joined by others, questioned whether trade between the Qua'Tol'Ec' would be possible or even considered. There were many colonists who opposed this idea until it was made clear that any trade would be conducted on the continental mainland where the Qua'Tol'Ec' lived. It was decided that those who wished trade with the Qua'Tol'Ec' nation would be allowed to join in the negotiations. There were people who vehemently opposed the idea—Agnes Felter among them—who did not wish any dealings with the Ques'Coat'L' but were outvoted by the rest of the colony. Jacqueline Vinet endorsed the move wholeheartedly, believing that it would give the humans and Ques'Coat'L' a common meeting ground to base future relations on.

When the humans told the Qua'Tol'Ec' nobles their decision, the leaders could barely believe it. Their leader graciously accepted the outcome and recognized the humans' claims to the main island and its chain of seventeen islands to the south. Three of the nobles were not happy with the decision—Ta'Cav'Mir' leading them—but accepted the ruling of their leader.

The negotiations were going into the third week, and now several more colonists were attending the arbitration, which reached a new level. The leaders were more than willing to discuss trade. The time spent determining the limits of the trade deals grew sluggish, and Hadden placed Conor in charge of the proceedings while he attended to other duties. Sometimes the proceedings took a full day over a minor point as Conor and the colonists debated terms.

The Marines, with the assistance of many of the colonists, were building a new perimeter fence nearly three kilometers south of the old one. A couple of the colonists had expressed interest in starting farms now that the contents of Cargo Bay 7 were made available. Grain, fruit, and vegetable produce they were familiar with was something the colonists had only vague memories of. Now those very products could be made available with time and hard work.

When the Qua'Tol'Ec' nation's nobles finally departed at the end of the seventh week, they assigned twenty of their retainers to Qu'Fal'Ral' to begin construction of the monument. A detachment of four Marines was assigned under the newly promoted Sergeant Cherry to provide protection and security to the remaining raptors. The colonists already had over half the new perimeter fence constructed and expected to complete the project in another two weeks. Qu'Fal'Ral' offered to have his assigned attendants work with the Marines in providing security to the open area of the fence until it was completed. Conor brought the offer to Hadden and Shiran, and they agreed with reservations.

Two months later, the fence was completed, and ships arrived carrying the 180 remaining attendants for ambassador Qu'Fal'Ral'. They presented the colony with gifts for their new deal, and Qu'Loo'Oh' assured them that the gifts were highly prized among her people, and it would be considered an insult to reject them. There were bolts of fine cloth, leather goods, rare aged lumber, household items made of various precious stone, and other items. A chest contained ingots of gold, silver, copper, tin, pearls, and precious gems.

The colonists, in turn, spent nearly a month deciding and putting together a return gift of different items to present to the nobles on their first visit to the mainland. A variety of books were created in the Ques'Coat'L' language—some chosen by Qu'Loo'Oh' from the sacred cave, and others, translations of human books Qu'Loo'Oh' had enjoyed. More practical items were also created, such as bowls made of copper, stainless steel needles, fishhooks, saws, knives, swords, spears, compasses, crafted tinderboxes, and many other things. Hadden had Hattie create fine jewelry out of a portion of the chest contents using the ship's factory.

A few months later, Conor stood beside Shiran watching the artisan Ques'Coat'L' cut large blocks of limestone for the construction of their monument. The trip to the mainland went well, and the return gift was well received by the Qua'Tol'Ec' nobles. The shuttle returned, loaded with various items that four of the colonists had traded for at the vast market in the raptors' capitol city. The future looked bright, and Conor looked at Shiran, who stood beside him as their hands were entwined in unity.

CHAPTER 88

It was nearly nine months since the brief war had engulfed the colony. With the new inner and outer perimeter fences installed, along with minefields, Conor had finally felt comfortable enough to visit the moon installation for a month. He had been quite enthusiastic over the discoveries made by the moon base crews and felt his time there had been too short. But he was looking forward to his return planetside and reunion with his family.

The shuttle moved gently forward into the docking bay of the *New Horizon* until the light jar of the docking clamps was felt. Conor sat back in the pilot seat and sighed as the first part of his journey home was completed. His brief stay on the moon went off without a hitch. He had been intrigued by the devices of the raptors from ages ago. Working with Petty Officer Barbara Gabrielson, he had learned a lot about the technology the raptors had left behind and was somewhat envious of Michael with his position as the moon base commander.

Even after all the losses they had suffered, Conor was still hopeful for a brighter future. He reviewed the losses and additions to the colony. True, there were many things they had lost that would have to be rebuilt. On the other hand, they had also gained access to the mines and equipment on the moon and now a tenuous peace with the major species inhabiting this planet. Hattie estimated that the last two points added significantly to the colony's viability. What the colony needed right now was a period of peace and some hard work to build up their strength to go forward.

When the docking maneuver was complete, Conor released his harness and floated aft. Passing through the hatch, he requested permission to come aboard and headed down the passageway leading to the bridge. Conor floated into the bridge of the *New Horizon* and was greeted by Commander Blankenship, who put down the tablet he had been reviewing. Hadden cocked an eyebrow at Conor.

"How was the tour?" asked Hadden.

"That's quite a setup they had up there," said Conor.

"Hopefully, the scientists can figure out the gadgets. It would be handy not having to produce equipment to do the job," said Hadden.

"Well, they have five of the vehicles working again, and they think they've figured out a part of the foundry," returned Conor.

"I was reading that in your report just now," replied Hadden.

"Most of the foundry is automated, but it looks like it takes at least fifteen to twenty operators. It also looks like they ran in shifts and operated twenty-four seven and processed around ten tons of refined material a day," said Conor.

"I like the quality of the lunar material, but we don't require that much at this time, and I don't want to haul that many people to the moon and back. The longboats and shuttles will only last so long before they require an overhaul or replacement," replied Blankenship.

"Michael suggests we gather ore for two months and then run the foundry for one month at eight hours a day. If we do that, we might produce fifty to sixty tons of refined material every three months," said Conor.

"I like that plan," said Hadden Blankenship.

"I thought you would. He's suggesting that the ore collection shifts be limited to eight people a month. That gives him four more people on the processing and refining shift, bringing it up to fourteen. He'd like two more volunteers for that month to start with and see how it works out," said Conor.

"Let's do that. I have three volunteers already. So he'll have seventeen on the processing and refinement month to man the foundry and operations suite," said Hadden.

"How is the raptor spacecraft project coming?" asked Conor.

"They've been able dismantle part of the craft to trace some of the functions and circuits. It would help if the people on the moon could find a blueprint and schematics for the craft. They think the propulsion is very similar to our Benson drive. Right now, they want to take it to the surface to examine, but I'm not letting that happen until Mr. Sobolov has his hangar bay built," replied Hadden.

"Perhaps we'll find another raptor base on the moon. It's strange that there were no spacecraft at the mining operation," said Conor.

"The craft may have been destroyed when they were attacked by the ancient enemy the Ques'Coat'L' refer to," said Hadden.

"Yet the mining operation wasn't attacked," said Conor.

"The entrance to the mine is somewhat hidden. If there were no craft there at the time, it would explain it," said Hadden.

Conor nodded. "When's the next longboat to the surface?"

"You'll be going down with me at eighteen hundred. Supper at the Overlook has already been arranged, so five hours from now. I have something to do first, and I'd like you present," said Hadden.

Conor cocked an eyebrow. "Secrets?"

"I'm not sure. I'll be relieved in one hour. Why don't you find something to do until then and then meet me at Cargo Bay 7?" said Hadden mysteriously.

Conor floated and looked at Hadden for a minute, but he had picked up his tablet and started reading reports. Obviously, Conor was not going to receive any hint about Cargo Bay 7. He shrugged and kicked off to float toward the hatch leading aft. He stopped by his cabin to splash some water on his face and brush his teeth, then sat down and made a call to the Marine Complex. Second Lieutenant Raybourn's face lit up when she saw who was on the other end of the line.

"Conor! Where are you?" said Shiran.

"The *New Horizon* in my cabin. How's Conrad?" asked Conor.

"Missing his daddy. You'll be back this evening?" returned Shiran.

"Commander Blankenship says we have reservations at the Overlook for supper," said Conor.

"We do. Rachel is planning to be there with their baby. It's too bad Brad had to go to the moon to relieve you," said Shiran.

"He seemed pretty interested in being able to tear into some of the equipment we found blueprints and schematics for, but he told me to relay that he loved her when I got back," said Conor.

"I have to go, Conor. Gunny Rusu is at the door and looks impatient." Shiran grinned.

"I'll see you this evening," replied Conor as the circuit cut out.

Conor pushed back from his chair gently and looked at the clock. Forty minutes to kill. He kicked off and left his cabin heading aft. He decided to use the time to make a tour of the *New Horizon*, so his first stop was the engineering section. Conor worked his way forward from engineering, poking his head into different spaces as he went. He found the commander was waiting at the entrance to Cargo Bay 7 as he floated forward. The hatch was still sealed as he grabbed a handhold and stopped himself. He gave Hadden an inquisitive look as the commander shrugged.

Commander Blankenship then placed his hand on the screen and his eyes to the retinal scanner and said, "Your guess is as good as mine, Lieutenant Commander. This bay was only to be opened by the captain if, for some reason, the *New Horizon* could not make it back to Sol system."

"Why haven't we opened it prior to this?" asked Conor.

"I'm not really the captain, and to tell the truth, I've never really thought much about it until now. I talked to Hiroka and Hattie. The system will allow me to open the door," said Hadden.

"So why wait for me?" asked Conor.

"I just want someone to witness me opening it. That and I'm a little nervous as to what could be inside. Why have orders to only open it if we couldn't get back?" said Hadden.

"You think it's a weapon?" asked Conor.

"I don't know," replied Hadden, frowning, as he opened the hatch.

The two men floated into the bay as the automatic lighting came on when it sensed movement. Inside the bay was significantly cooler than the rest of the ship, but most of the cargo bays were kept cooler for storage purposes. Really cold. Conor floated over to a unit against the wall as Hadden floated to another beside it. It looked like some sort of refrigeration unit. The rest of the wall looked like it contained medical equipment of some sort, but Conor had no idea what purpose the equipment served.

Along the back wall were racks with at least four dozen standardized battery packs that the ATVs and helicopters used. Those batteries were also used for backup power systems on the longboats and shuttles. There were other crates and boxes on those shelves, and the far wall was lined with crates and boxes too. The lights dimmed as they floated and searched questioningly around the cargo bay. A hologram of a man whom Conor recognized materialized in the center of the bay. The holographic figure looked at the two men floating in the cargo bay and commenced speaking.

"Commander Blankenship, I assume you recognize me, but if you don't, I am Jonas Sage. I can only assume that since it is you who opened the cargo bay that something has happened to Captain Hiroka Tamura. This hologram of myself has been programmed to identify all members of the crew dependent on who is acting commander. It is not interactive in any other way. I also assume that you are here because something has happened to prevent the *New Horizon* from returning to Sol system. The contents of this cargo bay were carefully selected for such an event, assuming that the *New Horizon* is partially functional and you can find a place to start a colony. Whether that is on a habitable planet or you have to build a habitat for yourselves, we hope that the materials here will help. Before you are refrigeration units containing samples of most flora and fauna species on Earth. Equipment along the wall is capable of incubating any fauna you select to maturity. You will also find military rations to feed the existing crew for a full year, and most of the other equipment provided is self-explanatory. I regret that this first voyage of exploration has ended for you and can only hope that the materials contained here will ease your efforts in establishing yourselves until help can find you. Commander, I wish you and all those who have survived well and mourn any losses you have experienced."

When the message finished, the hologram blinked out of existence. The two men floated for nearly a minute, contemplating the message. There was no way for Jonas Sage to know how unlikely it would be for any rescue mission to find them. It would take centuries to reach them with what they understood about the FTL capabilities. Whatever had happened during the explosion that had caused the FTL drive to send them nearly ten thousand light-years from Sol system still wasn't understood by Conor or Michael, and they had spent many hours discussing the chance occurrence.

"That was unexpected," said Commander Blankenship.

Conor nodded. "It appears a guardian angel might be watching over us. First, the discovery of a habitable world, then the discovery of the raptor mines on the moon. Now this."

"But we've paid a high price to arrive where we're at today," said the commander.

Conor agreed with that sentiment. Of the original crew of 787, only 641 remained. There were friends and antagonists who had passed on, but many would be sorely missed because of the contributions they had made. However, the colony had grown too. There were now 719 living humans that made up the colony, and that number would grow significantly in the coming years.

CHAPTER 89

The tree fell as Conor made the last cut and stood back. The cabin he was building stood atop the ridge where he and Shiran had shared a kiss on what seemed ages ago. The new perimeter fence ran through the area only a kilometer to the west with the new gate along the road that ran to the copper mines just north of the ridge. The cabin as planned was to have three bedrooms, with a large area combined to be a dining and living area. The foundation was already laid out, and the stone walls were mostly completed. Hopefully, the roof would be on prior to the rainy season the area experienced during its winter months.

With the discovery of what Cargo Bay 7 had contained, the foundation for a stable had been added to the cabin and a tunnel to a future barn was being planned too. Kers Joshi had told them that the two Morgan horse foals were developing well and would be ready when Conrad was three Earth years old. The cabin and stables should be finished by then, so his son could bottle-feed them. Nikolai and Barbara Ivankov were building a cabin lower down on the southwest side of the ridge and were willing to look after the cabin and livestock when the Raybourns had duties elsewhere.

With the discovery of what lay in Cargo Bay 7 and the new peace treaty between human and raptor, three of the colonists had decided to try their hand at farming. Three of the cabins were already finished with diesel power generators authorized by the commander and built by the ship's factory. They were given one ATV to rotate between them so they could plant and harvest crops until the new machine shop could produce more equipment. A tractor, along with attachments, was already on the assembly line. The whole colony was looking forward having produce not normally seen on board the ship now that the seeds for such were available. Then there was the long-term goal of having the fruits that would come from the orchards each farm had planted from Cargo Bay 7's seeds.

Conor directed his gaze south toward the new foundry Tom Tollifer was constructing. Its top could be seen in the far distance close to where the coal seam ran well beyond the new outer perimeter fence boundaries. The foundry had its own perimeter fence and would have its own working generator run by the coal it mined. A power cable was being buried nearly ten meters underground from the foundry to the cleft, so there was an alternate source of power available to the cleft or power could be sent to the foundry from the longboat or shuttle supplying power.

Once Chopper 1 was repaired, two more haulers were planned as soon as the foundry was operational, which should increase production of refined metals for the colony. The commander wanted four ATVs and two choppers all powered by internal combustion. The colonists had also voted to allow the limited construction of internal combustion engines for the construction of more heavy equipment. The commander wanted to reserve the new battery packs to keep the equipment they had started with operational until a class B factory could be built because of their reliability and versatility in harsh environments such as the moon.

A new lumber mill had been erected just inside the south perimeter gate. A new Marine Complex was being constructed south of the ruins of the old. Where the foundry had once stood, a hangar was under construction from the blueprints Dominic Sobolov had submitted for the refitting of the longboats and shuttles. Five kilometers beyond the south gate stood the beginnings of the memorial pyramid the raptors were constructing. They were guarded and supervised by the Marines, and only a limited number of raptors were allowed inside the Compound.

A machine shop was under construction where the lumber mill had stood so parts could be constructed for the longboats and shuttles. The shop was also promising to put into production ATVs and choppers. They would be powered by internal combustion engines until such a time that a class B factory could be built since a type A factory like the *New Horizon* had could not produce the batteries used by their current vehicles, while the batteries from Cargo Bay 7 would be reserved for longboats, shuttles, and other vital purposes.

Things were looking up as Conor watched Shiran caring for Conrad near the soon-to-be doorway of their future home. Conor and Shiran were planning on keeping the small room above the Overlook as a place to stay if there was an emergency. Conor sighed and set down the chain saw and looked at where Hadden and Michael were moving the finished log from the lumber mill they had been working on in place. With luck, the walls and roof would be completed in another month, and they could start working on the interior, but it was time to call it a day and head back to the cleft.

Conor wiped his forehead with his shirt sleeve. "Everyone ready to go?"

"I've had about enough fun for today." Hadden grinned.

Michael nodded and added, "Time for a shower and a beer."

Shiran and Francesca came over carrying the infants in their arms with Hiroka between them.

"We're ready," said Shiran.

They all climbed into the ATV and headed to the cleft elevators. The group split up going to their various residences on the cleft to freshen up and meet later at the Overlook. They arrived to discover the Overlook with most of the Marines and others who supported them since they established this small enclave of humanity. Roberta took their orders, which were quickly prepared. After the meal, everyone sat talking and drinking various beverages.

The conversation drifted finally to the scientific argument Samuel Rusu had started between Steven Yates and Joseph Green. Steven had finally conceded that perhaps the outer moon had been intentionally moved into orbit many millions of years ago. However, Steven was not willing to believe that such a planet killer had been intended to strike the planet or why any rational creature would do such a thing. But there were Joseph's findings indicating that the planet had suffered a major catastrophe some fifty million years ago and that the evidence suggested terraforming had occurred shortly thereafter.

Hadden had stayed quiet during the discussion, and as it was winding down, he said, "Something interesting was discovered by the astrophysics section aboard the *New Horizon*."

"Interesting? Who found it?" asked Conor.

"Maria DiAngelo. It appears to be an artifact. They suspect it's a ship. It's inbound," replied Hadden.

"Is it under power?" asked Michael.

"No. She says it reads cold. No radiation or infrared readings," said Hadden.

"Why does she think it's an artifact or ship?" asked Shiran.

"Because it looks like one. A very big one. Approximately thirty or more kilometers in length and at least five kilometers in diameter. We suspect from its orbit that it's the world ship that brought Qu'Loo'Oh's people here," said Hadden.

He laid a photograph of the artifact on the table. The artifact looked like a cigar. There were three noticeable holes in the hull of the ship that looked like meteor strikes or battle damage. The reported size of the artifact was astounding. Even the United Systems had no craft as large as the one pictured. The largest ships they had built were only six kilometers long at most with storage areas to keep many of the passengers in cold storage.

"What are these holes?" asked Michael.

Hadden laid down two more photographs. They were enlargements of the damaged areas, and it was quite apparent that it was caused by a massive explosion of some sort. The metal was twisted and warped, and several levels of decks of the craft's interior were visible.

"I'd say that's battle damage. I've seen missile strikes, and those look a lot like them," said Shiran.

"I agree," said Hadden.

"Who attacked them?" asked Conor.

"The ancient enemy that Qu'Loo'Oh' warned us about and the records we've translated have told us about," suggested Francesca.

"Then why didn't this ancient enemy attack the planet?" asked Shiran.

"The records say that the raptors, or the Ques'Coat'L', as they are known, defeated the ancient enemy, but their world ship was badly damaged," stated Francesca.

"I would say that part of the record is true," said Hadden.

Then Hadden laid another photograph down. Large hieroglyphs were visible. They were the same style as many of the hieroglyphs etched into the raptor equipment on the moon. Everyone examined the writing for a moment before the silence was broken.

"That has to be the world ship," said Francesca.

"Most likely," said Hadden.

"So what happened to the ship of their ancient enemy?" asked Conor.

"The records aren't clear on that point. It may have been totally destroyed, or it may be floating around out there like the Ques'Coat'L' world ship," replied Francesca.

"So what's the orbit?" asked Michael.

"Maria DiAngelo and Hattie are still working on the specifics, but it should be in range to investigate in twenty to thirty years with a shuttle," said Hadden.

"Unless we take the *New Horizon*," said Michael.

"I'd rather not do that. It would take too many people to man the *New Horizon* for such a mission, and the colony requires the *New Horizon* here to provide support," replied Hadden.

"In twenty years, we might be able to build a ship for the purpose of exploring," stated Conor.

"You should talk to Mr. Sobolov. When he returned from his last mission, he submitted a plan for a ship. It would have a crew of thirty or more with a fairly large science package. It would also carry two longboats along the sides for the extra boost their engines would provide and for further exploration." Hadden smiled.

"Really?" asked Michael.

"I just gave the plans to Ishaan Khatri to review," said Hadden, referring to the engineer from the old science division.

"Sounds like a plan if it can be done," said Conor.

"I agree. We have plenty of time, and it'll take a few years to get into range, and by then, our children will be able to help," responded Hadden as he put his arm around Hiroka, who had a noticeable bulge to her waistline. Hiroka blushed but gave Hadden a tender kiss to his cheek.

Hadden Blankenship stood and raised his glass, tapping it with a spoon. The Overlook grew silent as people turned their attention to the commander as he held his glass high.

"My friends, we've been through many trials since we've arrived here. We've lost many friends and acquaintances during that time. But we've accomplished much and have built for ourselves a home." Hadden paused for a second, then said, "To the future."

"To the future," repeated Conor loudly as he raised his glass, and those around the table did so also.

"To the future." The toast was repeated by Ezekiel and Gunny Rusu, who sat at their corner table. They raised their glasses, and all who gathered in the Overlook raised their glasses in turn.

Later that evening, Conor was having trouble sleeping and went to the balcony of their small apartment above the Overlook. For some reason, he had an uneasy feeling this world was not finished testing their fledgling colony. The full moon illuminated the river valley below. Lake Martinez reflected like a mirror with the moon and a field of stars glimmering on its surface. In the distance, he could see the Zander River that cut through the river valley of Foreman Island down to the sea. A breeze carried the scent of a vibrant, living world, and somewhere in the distance, the cry of a beast from a time before man roared in challenge.

CHAPTER 90

The battle had been fierce, and her people had fought well, but the humans had held them off. The humans had shown restraint even after the betrayal of one of their own. There had been losses on both sides, and the fierce warrior Master Sergeant Evan Zander, whom Qu'Loo'Oh' had grown to respect, would be mourned by all. She had learned that he was the first to fall in the great battle and had done so with honor. Many had fallen during the battle, and legends would be told and written down of all the great warriors who stood and fought in the battle.

Qu'Loo'Oh's people had not known what to expect after their devastating defeat. The Qua'Tol'Ec' nobles were prepared to capitulate and offer complete submission of their nation to human rule. They were confused and confounded when the humans offered peace. However, the humans made it clear that they would not be so lenient if they were ever attacked again. This was something never heard of in raptor culture. In exchange, the island and the chain of islands to the south were to become the domain of the humans.

She told her son, Qu'Fal'Ral', that if provoked, the humans could lay waste to all raptors on the planet. She told him that even though the humans had the power to do so before the great battle that they restrained from unleashing such destruction. After looking at the field where over half the raptor army had perished in just a few heartbeats, Qu'Fal'Ral' believed her.

Her son had consulted with the nobles who survived, and many things not normally done were enacted. The weapons of Master Sergeant Evan Zander, which were normally kept as prizes, were returned. The raptor army withdrew, and only a boatload of nobles and their retainers remained to negotiate for a new peace that existed between the humans and raptors.

It took several weeks to negotiate that peace. The raptors requested assistance from the humans to collect their dead and received help from the Marines who utilized the ATVs with cold storage trails. A site far to the south of the perimeter fence was selected by both sides of the conflict as a location to bury the raptor dead. On the third day, nobles and their retainers attended the mass funeral of the humans who had died. They commented on the individual monuments that the humans placed above the burial mounds and were told it was an ancient custom of the humans.

The raptors, in turn, requested permission to build a pyramid monument on the site of their dead, which would take many years to build. After several days of discussion and arguing, the surviving colonists granted their leaders that privilege with conditions. Only two hundred Ques'Coat'L' raptors would be allowed on the island at any time with only two green raptors per Ques'Coat'L' raptor to assist in the endeavor. The great beasts they could utilize in the project would be limited to ten or less.

The matter of trade was approached. There were individuals on both sides who wanted trade, while others wished nothing to do with it. The colonists unanimously agreed though that no technology higher than the Ques'Coat'L's current level would be traded or taught to the Ques'Coat'L', and even though the Ques'Coat'L' might want such, they would have to discover how it was done on their own. The Ques'Coat'L' nobles and retainers did not like this, but Rachel and Qu'Ran'Tau' admitted to Qu'Loo'Oh' that it was for the best.

Conor, Rachel, and Qu'Ran'Tau' admitted to her in individual conversations conducted in private that the advancement of the Ques'Coat'L' needed to happen gradually, or warfare would break out and consume the various Ques'Coat'L' nations of the world. Qu'Loo'Oh' reflected on this wisdom and knew that there was truth in it. The Qua'Tol'Ec' waged war on the other Ques'Coat'L' nations on the continent and sometimes even with nations over the great oceans over many things—offenses given, land, treasure, fishing stretches being just a few. A leader less wise than Qu'Ran'Tau', given the weapons the humans possessed, would wage a campaign of domination and possibly erase not only the other nations but also all their people, along with the knowledge they possessed.

Qu'Loo'Oh' hissed and thought of the sacred cave she had lived in for so long and how the knowledge was stored there to prevent such a loss. She felt she had chosen well when trusting these new people called humans who had a thirst for knowledge, and her people had chosen well when Qu'Ran'Tau' was elevated to Qua'Tol'Ec' leader. Qua'Ran'Tau' told her that peace with the humans represented a chance for the Ques'Coat'L' to achieve the past glory that their people had once known and sail among the stars. Perhaps not for many generations, but he believed it would be sooner than what the Ques'Coat'L' might accomplish without the humans to show them that it could be done.

Qu'Loo'Oh's banishment was repealed, and she was appointed special ambassador of the Qua'Tol'Ec' nation to the humans. Her eggling, Qu'Fal'Ral', was assigned by the Qua'Tol'Ec' nobles to direct the construction of the pyramid monument and ambassador in training. The nobles promised her an egg from each of the six noble families to hatch and raise in hopes the egglings would learn new ways. She withheld from the nobles information of the sacred caves and the information stored there, intending to share that secret only with her eggling, Qu'Fal'Ral', and when the time came, the egglings she would raise.

Qu'Loo'Oh' watched as the humans rebuilt their home on the cleft, expanding and building with an eye to the future. The humans built a new fence a thousand body lengths to the south of the previous one, enclosing the ridge she had once used to spy on the humans. The one named Conor and his mate, Shiran, who had once locked mouths there, were building a home on top of the ridge. They told her they were going to start a thing called a ranch where they would raise some animals called Herefords and Morgans. They also told her that there would be a grove of fruit trees along the south side of the ridge that this world had never seen.

There were new shops starting on the east side of the river that bisected the cleft the humans lived upon, while some on the west were still under repair or renovation. She was amazed and intrigued by the different items humans bought and traded. Some of the items were familiar, and others were something specifically human. There was a new barbershop that did both men's and women's hair, something her people did not have to worry about. But on further consideration, there were shops that groomed the feathers among her people. Another shop specialized in what the humans called appliances, such as toasters, coffeepots, blenders, microwaves, and many other items. It seemed as though the humans had a myriad variety of items they could create. Qu'Loo'Oh' couldn't imagine what it would be like to live with such marvelous items to assist her in life.

The humans on the cleft completed the new healing facilities, and she had been amazed at all the things it had contained. There were various machines to look inside the body, other devices for monitoring the heart, and many other things that monitored other things about the body. The humans told her that with the machines, they saved many lives and even extended life.

Then they took her to the place they would teach their young and continue learning themselves, which they called a university. While being shown all the rooms and equipment for learning, they had taken her to an area called a museum. The room contained items that the humans displayed in cases to learn more of Qu'Loo'Oh's people. Her human friends told her that as the colony grew, so would the hospital and the university, which was why there was room set aside east of the building to expand.

During her time in the human settlement, Qu'Loo'Oh' noted that there were humans who radiated fear of her or even hate. She knew that it would take a long time, perhaps generations, to alleviate such feelings if ever. There were always those who would fear the unknown and strike out against it in distrust and rejection.

Qu'Loo'Oh' knew there would be problems on both sides of this issue with the humans and Ques'Coat'L'. There were individuals from both species who were aggressive or even violent about their hate of the other. Some of her human friends had almost died because of those differences by one named Norman Pool. There were Ques'Coat'L' in power who believed others were inferior and used their position to take advantage of others and take credit for what those beneath them had done. She knew there were humans who did it from her talks with her human friends and that Ques'Coat'L' did it too. Qu'Loo'Oh' hissed knowing that such thinking was what destroyed a civilization. Even a green raptor would turn on a red raptor if not treated with respect.

Qu'Loo'Oh' didn't know how these humans would change her world in the future, but they had already moved the Qua'Tol'Ec' people in new directions. Perhaps with time, the Qua'Tol'Ec' nation would find a way to make peace with the other Ques'Coat'L' nations in the world. If peace could be maintained between humans and raptors, she believed much could be accomplished. Then perhaps someday, the Ques'Coat'L' people could even journey out among the stars as the ancients had in the past.

EPILOGUE

Bahri Hiran awoke as something splashed nearby over the sound of the waterfall colliding with the lake surface. Martinez's body lay faceup beside him with his legs awash just out of reach of the whirlpool created by the waterfall's entry. Martinez's body and his own were covered in mud. Somehow, he had lost his left shoe, and his shirt was torn across the front. Hiran reached and grabbed the haft of his knife, removing it from Martinez's chest. When he did, his eyes widened as he saw the nose and eyes of a huge crocodile just a few meters away. He slid backward through the mud slowly so the beast would not quicken its pace toward Martinez in fear of losing its prey.

His back came up against the rock face of the cliff as he faced the body of Martinez and the crocodile beyond. He turned his head slightly both left and right, looking for escape. A crack was in the cliff face to his right that looked barely wide enough to squeeze through, and he started edging toward it and almost screamed as pain shot through his left forearm. He returned his attention back to the crocodile slowly moving toward its meal as he placed the elbow of his broken forearm against the mud and pushed himself slowly centimeter by centimeter toward the crack, hoping fervently that it was wide and deep enough for him to enter once he reached his goal.

Finally, his head felt nothing behind it, and he pushed back with his legs, attempting to enter the crack. Something sharp pierced his side, and in surprise, he let out a cry, drawing the crocodile's attention. He turned and squirmed into the crack vigorously, ignoring the razor-sharp rocks that bit into his flesh as he fled the death raging toward him from behind as it roared of unrelenting hunger.

He felt something cold and wet touch the sock of his left foot as the beast's snout pushed him further into the crevice. There was an angry roar of rage as the thwarted beast beat its snout against the crack and snapped it razor-sharp teeth together in annoyance. Hiran curled up in his refuge as the infuriated beast finally relented and turned to take Martinez's body up in its mouth. Bones crunched as the monster ate its gristly meal.

A helicopter appeared low in the sky, hovering nearby. The beast looked up at it with the leg of Martinez stuck between its teeth as Bahri huddled as far back into the darkness of the crevice as he could. The chopper hovered, watching as the crocodile snapped again, removing the morsel embedded between its teeth. The beast then slowly entered the water, apparently forgetting the meal curled behind it, and vanished. The helicopter remained for another minute, then moved off in an obvious search pattern along the shoreline.

Hiran waited. Somehow, he fell asleep. Nightfall had arrived with his only light being the crescent moon in the clouded sky. The sound of the waterfall filled the air as he looked out of the opening of his narrow slit of safety. Huge green eyes stared at him from the water just a few meters away, and a ripple of movement agitated the surface of the tidal pool as the beast moved forward. Its bulk left the water as the monstrosity moved toward his crevice. The stench of reptile filled the air as it came up to the opening, looking in patiently at Hiran, waiting for its meal.

Hiran withdrew as far back as his meager shelter would let him while the beast nudged the opening hopefully. They sat there staring at each other until Hiran's eyelids grew heavy, and he finally lost the battle against the exhaustion. He awoke, and through the slits of his heavy eyelids, he saw blue skies prior to finally forcing them open. The monster lay in the muddy shoreline facing him mere meters away, sleeping. Its enormous sides heaved as it lay there breathing noisily.

Bahri looked up and saw that the crack he was in went up quite a ways. There was no way out except up so long as the monster outside remained, hoping for him to come out. He started to climb. His left arm was useless for the task, and he had to rely on his right to keep him in place by bracing on the wall of the crack as he pushed his body upward with his legs. It took well over an hour, and he was exhausted by the time he reached a narrow ledge that led behind the waterfall. He edged slowly and carefully along the precarious perch, nearly falling to the patiently waiting crocodile below.

It was beginning to get slippery, but the ledge widened as he slipped through the drizzle of water that obscured his view. There was a cave back there, he was sure of it, and a few minutes later, he fell face-first into a small pool of water at its entrance. He crawled forward through the water and out onto a dry area. He was cold, but exhaustion overcame his discomfort as his eyes closed, and he lost consciousness. He had no idea how long he was out, but he was ravenous. He pulled his stiletto from the sheath where he had placed it and turned the handle. A narrow beam of light sprang forward, giving him some illumination to see what was around him. He got to his feet and started walking further into the cave. It was fairly large, and the sides were smooth from the passage of water. He walked further into the cave, and it widened out even further with what must have been banks where the water rarely reached because the rocks there did not have the smooth look. He climbed out of the dry riverbed to shine his light around. Something moved, and he took a fist-sized stone and killed a lizard that was half a meter long. He ate it raw and curled up to fall asleep again.

He had been in the cave moving steadily further into its depths for what seemed like days when he heard noises. He turned off his light and hid as many red raptors armed with torches and their weapons passed by on the opposite bank of the dry riverbed. When they were gone, he followed until he saw a split in the cave system. He decided to take the opposite route the raptors went down. They were obviously working their way up to the colony, and he had no desire to return there. The route he chose kept climbing, and it took many days. He had no idea how long he remained in the caves. There were times he nearly starved to death before finding something to kill and eat. He was delirious, and there was a constant ache in his left arm from the break that he had not set and the fact that he kept bumping it hard against the cave sides and floor when he fell. Then one day, he saw a light ahead of him, and he scrambled toward it.

The exit to the cavern system was high up on the cliff. Bahri had to climb slowly using his fingertips and toes, clinging to the cliff for nearly fifty meters going upward. The cliff started sloping, making climbing easier, with grass and trees appearing around him to offer purchases for him to use in his climb. He reached a ledge and slept curled against the bole of a huge tree.

He continued upward for several days, eating what he could find. It grew cold as the trees started thinning out, and he killed an animal that had fur, which he skinned and donned the skin of for warmth. He was cold but felt he could not risk a fire because of the people in the cleft below. He had seen the shuttle return and other equipment moving below him and knew he had failed. Bahri felt ill; he broke out in a sweat as he dug a shallow hole in the side of a dirt bank to crawl in.

He awoke to a noise early in the morning. It sounded like footsteps, and he feared that someone from the crew had found him. Remaining still, he opened his eyes as the rank smell of something unwashed assaulted his nose. His hand sought his knife, which he had stuck in the ground in front of where he lay, and a large leathery foot pinned it to the ground as his fingers touched the hilt. The leg attached to the foot was covered in coarse brown hair, and the large metal end of a rifle muzzle was pressed against his face. Bahri grew still, allowing only his eyes to shift and look at the figure standing over him. It was a large creature that was manlike but covered in the same coarse hair as its legs. A belt with a pouch and a huge knife was around its waist, while a necklace of bones and teeth adorned its neck and chest. The creature stood at least two and a half meters tall and weighed nearly 150 kilos, but Bahri recognized the creature. He had seen one before, only then the creature had been well-groomed and adorned itself in precious metals, and that creature had not realized Bahri had discovered its true nature. He knew because Bahri Hiran always wanted to know exactly who was giving him orders.

GLOSSARY

Character Index

Aabir Issawi	Petty officer second class, personnel
Agnes Felter	Lieutenant, electronics material officer or EMO
Akio Sakuta	Petty officer third class, electronics repair
Amanda Hall	Sergeant, US Marines
Anarzej Gataki	Lieutenant, supply officer or SUPPO
Anthony Finley	Petty officer second class, gunnery
Anya Kaur	Petty officer second class, supply
Bahri Hiran	Ensign, assistant supply officer
Barbara Gabrielson	Petty officer third class, electronics repair
Bess Hollinger	Lieutenant commander, chief medical officer
Brad Guillete	Petty officer first class, electronics repair
Carol Moore	Petty officer first class, engineering
Caroline deLang	Chief petty officer, medic
Catalina Ramirez	Petty officer second class, boatswain
Charles Fooks	Petty officer third class, electronics repair
Conor Raybourn	Lieutenant commander, operations officer or OPS boss, FTL specialist
Diego Quintana	Chief warrant officer, science division, astrophysicist
David Smith	Petty officer first class, damage control
Dwayne Abrams	Lance corporal, US Marines
Dominic Sobolov	Ensign, deck officer
Edward Black	Ensign, damage control

Ekavir Hatwal	Lieutenant commander, first officer or first lieutenant
Eshimo Kataoka	Petty officer third class, engineering
Ethan Sanders	Petty officer third class, engineering
Evangeline Dalisay	Petty officer third class, boatswain
Evan Zander	Gunnery sergeant, US Marines
Ezekiel Yap	Petty officer first class, mess specialist
Felipe Martinez	Lieutenant commander, chief engineer or CHENG
Francesca Chandra	Chief warrant officer, science division, cultural anthropologist
Fred Foreman	Seaman, boatswain
Freda Lachowski	Seaman, boatswain
Georgia Cambi	Chief warrant officer, science division, botanist
Hadden Blankenship	Executive officer or XO
Heath Stiles	Petty officer second class, engineering
Heather Tate	Chief petty officer, radioman
Hector Lopez	Petty officer first class, engineering
Hiroka Tamura	Captain
Ishaan Khatri	Chief warrant officer, science division, aerospace and industrial engineer
Jacob Valdez	Petty officer third class, engineering
Jacqueline Vinet	Lieutenant, science division, FTL specialist
James Upton	Chief petty officer, chief master-at-arms
Janice Svensson	Petty officer third class, radioman
John Martins	Petty officer first class, boatswain
Jon Lavie	Chief warrant officer, science division, archeologist
Jonas Sage	Inventor, financier, and sponsor of the *New Horizon* expedition
Jose Flores	Corporal, US Marines
Joseph Green	Seaman, boatswain
Karimah Mirza	Petty officer second class, radioman
Kers Joshi	Lieutenant, medical doctor
Lenard Barrett	Lance corporal, US Marines

Leonard Barstein	Petty officer third class, missiles
Maria DiAngelo	Chief warrant officer, science division, astrophysicist
Maria Ortiz	Chief petty officer, engineering, FTL specialist
Matthew Cherry	Corporal, US Marines
Michael Anderson	Lieutenant, engineering, FTL specialist
Nattalie Hoffman	Lance corporal, US Marines
Nikolai Ivankov	Sergeant, US Marines
Norman Pool	Chief petty officer, engineering
Palesa Theron	Petty officer second class, engineering
Paul Rand	Lance corporal, US Marines
Philip Roe	Petty officer third class, engineering
Rachel Krupich	Sergeant, US Marines
Raisa Romanov	Chief warrant officer, science division, chemist
Richard Hunt	Petty officer first class, damage control
Richard James	Petty officer third class, machine shop
Roberta MacIntrye	Petty officer third class, personnel
Samuel Rusu	Staff sergeant, US Marines
Shiran Rosenstein	Staff sergeant, US Marines
Silas Cheptoo	Chief warrant officer, science division, biologist
Stefanie Lanier	Petty officer second class, quartermaster
Steven Yates	Chief warrant officer, science division, exogeologist
Tadashi Adachi	Sergeant, US Marines
Tami Pennington	Chief petty officer, Boatswain
Thomas Tollifer	Lieutenant, machine shop
Timothy Powell	Petty officer second class, electronics repair
Tregan Johnson	Corporal, US Marines
Vanda Kisimba	Lieutenant junior grade, personnel officer
Vivian Caylor	Private, US Marines
Wayne Wheaton	Chief petty officer, electronics repair
Wilma Nolan	Chief petty officer, engineering

Ques'Coat'L' Names

Qu'Fal'Ral'
Qu'Loo'Oh'
Qu'Ran'Tau'
Ta'Cav'Mir'

Equipment

Quinn drive	FTL jump drive
Benson drive	In-system drive, fusion
LRL-73	Long-range lidar
MSDR-17	Marine radar
NAPACS	Satellite communications system
SAC-23	UHF transceiver (portable)
SPI	Spatial positioning indicator system
Gerst S-7	9 mm sidearm
Kinley-Grant KG-3	Combat knife
Navarro M-71	6 mm machine gun
Vinter HR-19	High-powered 10 mm sniper rifle
EMP grenade	Electromagnetic pulse grenade
Q-5	Plastic explosive

ABOUT THE AUTHOR

Brian F. Gehling was born in 1958 in Carroll County, Iowa, where he was raised and worked on the family farm. In 1977, he joined the United States Navy, where he served until 1997. After his service career, he studied various subjects at Des Moines Area Community College (DMACC) and Iowa State University. Since the service, he has worked in security, construction, agriculture, special needs, and as a business owner.

Brian discovered a love of science fiction at an early age, and that appreciation has continued to this day. A friend one day suggested that if he never started writing this story and its sequels, he'd never get around to accomplishing that goal.